The of Rainbows

By
Mark A. Cropper

Pen Press Publishers Ltd

© Mark A. Cropper 2007

All rights reserved

No part of this publication may be reproduced, stored in a retrieval system, or transmitted in any form or by any means, without the prior permission in writing of the publisher, nor be otherwise circulated in any form of binding or cover other than that in which it is published and without a similar condition including this condition being imposed on the subsequent purchaser.

First published in Great Britain by
Pen Press Publishers Ltd
25 Eastern PLace
Brighton
BN2 1GJ

ISBN13: 978-1-905621-74-3

Printed and bound in the UK

A catalogue record of this book is available from the British Library

Cover design by Jacqueline Abromeit
Illustrations by Mark Cropper
Typeset by Kathryn Harrison

A CHILL GREY MIST clung to the warrior's cloak with vengeful fingers of moisture. The decaying sweetness of the battlefield stench choked his senses and confused his mind with images of purgatory as he tried to find meaning within the dismay assailing his soul.

Nearby a thing, once of mortal flesh, cried out its final, friendless, lonesome moan. Another, harsher voice mocked that same demise with a crude burst of brittle laughter. Further off they were stripping the dead. The last thoughtless desecration of life ere the corpses were cast into the hastily dug charnel-pit. Nothing was sacred in this field of death, not even the grasping claws of the gods of war. Nothing!

He began to retch…

…A sudden unreal act, remote and impersonal. He saw himself, as from a distance or in a dream, crawling on all fours, struggling like an injured insect to escape the horror of these grotesque heaps of once living flesh, recoiling in revulsion from the icy touch of hands that even in death reached out to grasp a handful of life.

His mind could stand no more and slipped with grateful ease back into the dusty, numbing paths of memory. To another time, another place, peace, innocence.

Childhood.

> **Time Turns
> and feelings change.
> Once more I stand
> to view in mind,
> hesitating at the lip,
> least that first tremulous step,
> awakens pains long past behind.**
>
> - (Past thoughts)

Chapter One - A Beginning (of sorts)

AMONGST HIS MOTHER'S bright flowers he played his childhood games. Down sloping meadows rolling head-over-heels until the long grass was flattened into a glistening sheen of wetted stems and his spinning head caused his legs to wobble as he tried to stand. He leapt over the silver singing waters of the rill which formed the southern boundary of his home or balanced precariously upon a fallen tree to peer down into the deeper pools where fishes might be seen darting from shadow to shadow. Through the woodland his laughter would ring, carefree and innocent, during those languid days of childhood summer.

His magic was a sparkling gift of love which sang in his soul and erupted in brilliant splendour to turn the colours of life into visions of fairyland, the wonders of existence into mysteries of incomparable beauty.

It matters little what the name of this young Wizard-of-Colour might be. One might even see, as did his own kin, that names are far too important a matter to burden one so young as he. *'Tis better to take time to discover a person from the truth of their nature than to fall into the trap of assuming knowledge and in so doing know nothing at all.* Indeed those who knew him best recognised the brightness of his spirit and realised in wonder there might be no limitations on what was possible for him.

His mother, The Lady-of-Flowers, in response to any questions regarding his name would, with the wisest of smiles wrinkling her face and with a soft chuckle of indulgence over those who knew no better, have answered, 'Almost any name could serve at this time, for he is young and free and his nature is yet to develop. I suppose I generally think of him in terms of colour, for when all is said and done it's his colours which fill his days with wonder and those he loves the best. Yes, pick for him a colour and he'll waken a thousand in return and bind them in a form of beauty to fill your essence with glory.'

She'd have smiled again at their lack of understanding and offered a sugar-coated bun to appease their bewilderment. Then, wanting no more of their foolishness, she'd turn, with a gentle sigh, to look out of the kitchen window where she might catch a glimpse of her children at play among the flower beds or in the shade of the fruit trees on the slopes of the downs overlooking the house, perhaps waving should their eyes meet across the distance.

In all probability they'd have been further afield wandering in the woodlands which bounded the oaken halls of the Dragon-Church. They might be gathering the sweet, wild blackberries which grew in abundance there allowing them to feast with childish gluttony and purple-stained fingers. Perhaps they might have gone to the Dingle-Dell, where the wild white waters roared, to catch frogs in the pools left from the summer squalls or, yet again, ventured out into the salt marshes gathering gulls' eggs from the pebble flats beyond the tall rushes. Or they might just have been wandering, roaming aimlessly wherever their mood might take them, without purpose unless the exercise of freedom be reason enough on its own.

The Warding of Hereth, as this gentle land was called, rested in the far northern reaches of Santolin. Its farms and orchards, nestling in the narrow belt of land between the sea and the Mountains-of-the-Divide, were overlooked by the downs of Hereth, where the Stone-Circle stood.

In truth there is little to say about Hereth. Its three villages, Rossbridge, Saddleford and Crowswood were not much more than hamlets. Although the Rossbridge fayre was renowned, it was in reality just a local affair, an autumn event, and for the rest of the time little happened of note.

For the main part the locals were but a simple folk who farmed the land and kept to their own affairs. They felt safe and protected for, as everyone knew, they were close to the Dwarven-Holm and who would dare to threaten their peace? Besides, theirs was a fertile land watched over by the Lady-of-Flowers and what could be better than that?

In the Hall the Lady-of-Flowers, awaiting her children's return, would have no worry. She'd have known they would stay together and look after each other and besides her eldest, the Maiden-of-Calm-Watching, would tend to them using her own gentle wisdom to curb the excesses of their childish impetuousness and extravagant play.

When evening fell and darkness called their footsteps home they'd oft' sit at their mother's feet before the hearth and listen in wonder as she recited the poems of the Ancient-Ones. Her tranquil voice would invoke anew the bardic magic, words of wonder left hanging in the air as curtains of expectation, dreams of yesteryear renewed. Of the Cycles of time she told, of the Ryngold, of the saga of the Eloveen-Kings and of the dreadful Stone-of-Power, when the Lords-of-the-Void contended with the Lords-of-Light ere the turnings of the seasons had begun. These were Legends from a time before the great Cataclysm and the parting-of-the-peoples, when the Well-Springs-of-the-Earth had yet to rise in power.

They sat in silence, entranced by the tales she spread before them. From her lips they heard of the coming of the Eloveen-Kings from beyond the Ryngold into the land of Ancient-Maddon. They'd listen, trembling with fear at the very thought of Elovsenal turned evil by the Stone-of-Gwarle, and then knew the full horror of the terrible War-of-Kings and the years of darkness following the Dark-Lord's banishment on the Isle-of-Death.

Their hearts would swell at the naming of Gentil, the First-Wizard who led the armies of men into battle. And they'd sigh in wonder over Hymforth-the-Seer journeying alone through the Ryngold into the Lands-of-Light seeking aid from the Lords-of-Light and of his return with the Army of the Neleven-Fey.

They heard also of the three heroes – Elot, Antol and Harvan – and their part in The War-of-the-Stone. Oh such wonder was the epic tale of Alan-of-Colon's journey into the darkness to confront the evil. In their hearts they stood with him, eyes sparkling, upon the barren shores of N'Tsarette to face the dread power of Elovsenal, the dark Eloveen-Lord. Tears of relief would dampen their cheeks and cloud their sight when the beautiful Avondale was returned to him from the chill emptiness of Elexan, The Isle-of-Death.

They would tell their own tales too, simple stories of childhood truths. In so doing, if any wished to see, they'd reveal of themselves and their natures also.

When the wildest of winds played loudly on the window shutters with angry goblin fingers, when dragons breathed menace into the gloom of the gathering storm clouds, the Calm-Watcher would rekindle the wonders of spring and recall the gentleness that flowed with the waking of life. Thus they would know she was with them, would look after them and calm their troubled thoughts in the peace of her vision. Then the moon would wake from its slumber to climb the night skies and dust motes would dance as fairies where the silver beams filtered into the hall, lighting their way to bed.

When the night was still and their minds troubled by the thousand unanswered questions of childhood the Lord-of-Numbers, the second eldest, would explain the wonders of the world to them, making sense of their bewilderment. Some times, very special times, he would bring out one of his prised manuscripts and from the hidden words cast forth a mandala of order to reveal the secrets at the heart of the universe and thus answer their misunderstandings with explanations from the beginnings of time. Oh how he gloried in his love of existence and ever strove to understand more.

On other nights, when rain imprisoned them and cold dampness awoke the bitter taste of boredom in their breasts then the third child, the Lightning-Bringer would laugh at the gloom and shout into the dank air. She'd set the heavens afire with her flames until the rains fled from her fury leaving nothing behind save the forgiving freshness, which lingers in the wake of a storm.

This Young-Wizard had his part too. He would waken the soul of an idea, colour it in the hues of life and, through the simplicity of his nature, would clothe them in the attire of his vision to show them the beauty of their own being. Then they would marvel at him seeing something strange, fey and wonderful and they'd sit in awe to marvel at the kindling of his power.

Best of all though were those special evenings when the Lady-of-Flowers would gather them close to her side and speak to them of their father The Baron. They would sit in silent rapture as she described his exploits in the Lands-of-Men. Wondrous tales were these, of distant lands and far off cities where the Baron served The High-King of Santolin, standing against the powers of the world. A mighty knight was he, a captain of men, a warrior of high renown and valiant deed, a lord of substance amidst the leaders of men.

She would tell of their meeting in the Lands-of-Mist, of his rescuing her from a life of cruel, joyless servitude, recounting their flight to safety through the dark colourless Kingdom of the Goblin-Lord.

They fell still with silent dread as she spoke of the monstrous being, the Lord-of-Mists and of his evil minions, the terrible grey creatures known as the Warriors-of-Mist. They shivered to hear of their cold cruel anger, their hatred of all the arts and their despite for all things of magic and wizardry. Their hearts filled with dread as she spoke of the creatures' efforts to enslave the world and subdue all the bright lights of existence, leaving nothing save the drab grey emptiness of their colourless void.

Then she would banish their fears and cause their hearts to swell with pride as she spoke of their father's part in that terrible war. They heard of his exploits and of his valour as he rose to eminence among the hosts of men. Oh how they longed for him to be with them and each prayed in the depths of their soul for his return to their side.

Later, in the dark of the night the Young-Wizard would dream of him, tall and proud, the protector of their world and of all they loved. Thus he would sleep in peace, safe in the knowledge of his father's being.

On one of these evenings, when the Young-Wizard was beginning to reach out towards his time although still too young to be called more than a child, their mother brought her four children the first word of change.

It was late-year when the golden leaves had given way to a sombre decaying brown and the evenings were drawing in with mists and the foreboding of winter.

'Come,' she said, her tone revealing the expectation of something new. 'I have word for you, news of your father.'

They gathered close, thrilled even at the mention of him. 'What is it?' the Lightning-Bringer asked excitedly, as ever impatient and eager to know. 'What news?'

'Wait,' the Lady sighed as she banked up the fire and set the supper upon the hearth table. She slowly warmed the poker and, with a glimmer of a tease, lingered over the ritual of mulling the wine. 'Here, take wine and sit yourselves down,' pausing until they complied.

'I have received a letter from The Lake-Lands, from the city of Latal, from your father. He says that he feels at last that his tasks are almost done and that it is to hand over the mantle of his responsibilities to others.'

'Show us,' they cried as one.

'Yes please, Mother,' the Calm Watcher offered her own gentle plea, 'Read his words to us.'

Thus she turned to the cabinet where her papers lay and drew out a parchment. She spent a moment looking over this, lingering at several passages as if in secret self-indulgence.

> 'Dear Flor,' she read, 'For thus he always calls me,
> and greetings to you all. May these my words find you in health and in good spirit.
> Long are the days since I have last looked upon you and I grow weary from our parting. Perhaps the time has come for me to hand over the responsibilities of my post to other, younger shoulders. The long years have indeed taken their toll on me. I feel that I deserve a time of rest.
> As the first chills of winter cut over the plain, I realise that I no longer relish the thought of campaigning. Therefore I have decided that the time has come for me to hand the mantle of power to another and to give up my soldiering ways and return to my hearth and home...'

'He's coming home!' they cried out in a furore of excitement.

'Yes my children,' she softly sighed, 'He's coming home.'

The time of preparing was frantic and filled with expectation. Each moment stretched endlessly and yet still proved to be too short to complete all the necessary jobs. Done they were though and so the time passed until, some three weeks after the midwinter feast, the day arrived.

The Young-Wizard can recall, even to this very day, that moment when he first faced his father over the threshold of their home. He can still see in his mind's eye the tall figure of the Baron framed in the doorway of the hall, clad in the armour of his calling, a broadsword at his side, a silver helm tucked beneath his arm. A hard, angular, life worn face crowned with a crop of bristling snow-white hair. Eyes, sharp, piercing, ice-grey eyes silenced the youngster's shout of joyous welcome and froze his thrill of expectant love in the diamond hard grip of their uncompromising gaze. His silence was echoed in the stillness of the Lord-of-Numbers and the Young-Wizard's two sisters. It seemed the only love that shone was in the eyes of their mother as she proudly proclaimed him to them. 'Children, this is your father. He has come home.' As ever her words stilled the fear that rose in their breasts and denied the trembling touch of their first doubts.

Yet there was no denying the warning inherent in that first moment, an indication of how things were to prove. Their smiles of welcome were met with a wall of ice, as if he sought to expose them, to uncover their weakness and the secrets of their natures. The children's eyes met in silent bewilderment over the strange severity of his demeanour and they stepped aside, cowed by his steely gaze and watched on, as were they no more than vassals, as he strode past them through the portals of their home.

There he stood in the Great Hall, lord and master of all he surveyed. His oh so critical glance missing nothing as he unbuckled his baldric and hung the great broadsword above the hearth.

The Baron had returned!

The atmosphere grew strained and subdued during those first few days. The Baron for his part, which is when all is said and done only proper for a knight returned from the wars, commenced to set his house in order. He paid his family little heed as he turned his mind to the task of assessing, logging, counting, checking and cataloguing the assets of the estate.

After several days he called them to him, to 'Speak with you all.' They gathered, as commanded, in the great hall and he came to stand before them.

His eyes flicked to the broadsword and the cloth-covered shield which hung beside it over the hearth as if regretting the loss of his campaigning life. His fingers were locked behind his back, his toe tapping with impatient irritation as he waited for them to be still. Finally he spoke.

'Good wife,' his words were formal and strained, grating upon the ears of those listening who knew only gentleness and love. 'I see that you have managed my estates well during the years of my absence. The Halls are in good order, the granaries full, the lawns and orchards tended, the gardens rich with provender, I am well pleased.' But his eyes were as stone, giving lie to his words. It seemed that in truth he despised her gifts of life and scorned the works of her nature.

The youth heard the sharp intake of breath and watched in trepidation as those steel eyes turned to the Lord-of-Numbers probing as were he some enemy rather than of the Baron's own flesh.

'However,' he continued at last, his attention returning to The Lady, 'For many years, as you well know,' his tone was harder now, colder, 'I have been far from home. I have done my duty and done it well, serving the commands of my Lord and contending with the enemies of truth that are abroad in the world.' Those piercing orbs bore down on them as if searching for evidence they might understand some secret in his words.

'In this time I have learned to mistrust the SO CALLED mysteries, the tricks and deceits of magic. For they are but illusions set to trap the unwary and to drive us from the paths of duty which are the lot of men. It is my desire that we learn to work together for the good of us all, following in the paths of truth. That we grow strong in heart and have no dealings with the vagaries and mendacities of the Arts.'

The Hall was still. Eyes wide with fear and expectation focused upon their mother. For once, perhaps blinded by her love and knowing in her heart little but the memory of what he had been, she hid from her own disquiet and the fear in her breast. Thus accepting his words as right and fair, she bowed her head and smiled her agreement.

What? The Young-Wizard felt his heart still and his flesh grow chill. *What? It shouldn't be like this. This was not as he had expected. Who is this man? This Baron? For surely he's not the hero I've awaited so long, not the loving father returning to the bosom of the family to protect and provide for us.* He gazed in fear at the stranger before them. *Baron? Father?* Searching in vain for the awakening of his dreams, the fulfilment of his childhood. All he saw were the ice-grey eyes, the dull grey cloak in which the Baron habitually wrapped himself, the cold, empty brittleness of this stern lord's world and felt his spirit tremble in the wake of this terrible vision.

Now, slowly, purposefully the Baron turned his attention to his sons and daughters. There was no warmth in his face, no tenderness in the words he spoke. 'I have been away from this house for a long time, away from your mother and away from yourselves, doing the bidding of My Liege and Master, perhaps too long. Would that I had been here during this time, that you might have learnt wisdom from my lips.' A scowl furrowed his brow, shaded his eyes. 'I see you have grown in years and that your ways and natures are well formed and that soon the time shall come for you to go forth to take your place in the world. Tell me. What are your plans and aspirations?'

The first to respond was the Calm-Watcher, she being the eldest. Her words were spoken slowly and chosen with great care. She had heard his words to her mother and was wise to the hidden nature of what was occurring. With her natural understanding of truth she answered him, 'Father, it is indeed many years since I have looked upon you. Yet I have followed your adventures with interest and pride. For Mother has not shirked in her duty to tell us of you and of the nature of your deeds. I have heard of your many victories and learnt of your position of greatness in the domain of men. It seems that I can do no better than to follow in your ways, to seek the path of truth and to follow the lead that this will give me.'

He smiled, hearing her words and being pleased with that which he understood.

The second, being the next to eldest, was the Lord-of-Numbers. He, knowing well the true nature of things and recognising with instinctive insight what his father had become during his time away from home and being blessed with no small measure of guile, answered in his turn. 'I have begun to see of late that the truth of all things can only be found by knowing the fullness of their nature. Therefore my path leads me towards the study of things. I know when I see clearly that I can accept the truth of what I find in the rulings of my own life. Yes, I shall hunt to discover the truth and shall turn against that which I find to be false.'

The Baron frowned anew. He'd heard the hidden message in the words but was, as yet, unable to contend with it.

Then spoke the Lightning-Bringer, bright and sharp as always. She knew the nature of the clouds that hid the sun and the ways of the winds in the heavens. 'Dear Father, you have indeed been away from home for such a long time that I don't really know you. As have my sister and my brothers, I have listened eagerly to the tales of your ventures. Now I long to hear your understandings from your own lips, thus from you shall I discover the path that I must follow.'

Again the chill, humourless smile crossed his face. He thought that here indeed was one that he might bend to his own will. Though verily, he knew neither the subtlety of her nature nor the power of her tempests.

'And you?' the Baron asked the youngest. 'What shall you become?'

'I am to be…' He lifted his eyes to meet the stern, chill visage, which now transfixed him. Fear dried his words on his tongue and sat as stone in his heart as he struggled to find an answer. At first there were no words. Then within his mind came an image, a vision of the brightest of all the wonders of the world. 'I am to be…

'The Wizard of Rainbows.'

The Baron grew deathly silent, his face blanching at the sound of the words and the anger they awoke in his being. Eventually he spoke. His words escalating from a gruff whisper to a roar of thunder, every word dripping with the bitterest ridicule. 'The WIZARD OF RAINBOWS? Chasing after dreams like some demented half-wit, serving no man and no purpose, a waster of time and of reason. What foolishness is this?'

The Young-Wizard trembled in the violence of his father's wrath. He didn't, couldn't understand the anger or the cause of its awakening. He saw only that it was he who had brought about this terrible reaction and knew in the depth of his soul the enormity of his crime. Guilt sprang like a serpent to throttle the thoughts in his mind. He must make amends, undo the damage he had wrought.

'No!' he tried again. 'I shall be a warrior, a knight, just like you.'

The Baron laughed his cruellest laugh, hearing only the babbling of a child's wild dreams. 'Aye indeed, The Rainbow-Warrior, Sir Prism, tilting at illusions to gain a secret pot of gold. Huh! Some warrior you'll be.' Still laughing, he turned away.

Behind him, broken and ashamed, the child fought alone. 'I shall... I shall be a warrior... I shall.'

In his hurt he turned away from his true nature into the gloom wrought of his own words. *I'll play no more with colour. I'll reject the call of the Rainbow. I'll learn to fight, to take up arms and live the soldier's way. I shall become a warrior and win renown. Then I'll win back the respect of my father.* The tears of shame burned bitter in his eyes but he paid then no mind welcoming the discomfort in the belief that his suffering would harden him and help him in his endeavour.

It might be seen that the world itself turned to grey as the Young-Warrior, for he scorned the name Wizard now, grew in the cold shadow of his father's roof. He strove, beyond hope, to meet the supposed demands of the Baron's harsh world.

When the joy and light of his home departed, he knew it not. Neither was he aware as the cruel lines of sorrow were etched upon the wilting bloom of his mother's face. His eyes were directed towards warlike things now and left little space in his heart for the truth to settle.

He had, as he swore, forsaken his bright apparel and turned his face away from his former delight in the thousand wonders of the spectrum. He imitated his father's dress, black, grey and unadorned. He filled his waking thoughts with tales of warriors and fighting.

He turned his back upon the friends of his childhood also and his secret playmates of the wilds. The little-folk too were filled with heartache at the loss of his bright wondrous smile and the sound of his laughter ringing through the forest glades. The woodland creatures knew a darker life now, his lights no longer dancing in the evening skies. The sweet singing linnet piped a new, mournful, lonesome song over the meadows of Hereth.

'He is gone',
The wind whispers.
Gone as the wild geese go.
Flying south to the sun.
We hear their sad farewell across the forests of autumn
their echo from afar.

*'Will he ever return to us
as they,
Coming with the spring rains
to freshen our lives?'*

*'He is gone',
The trees sigh.
Gone as the once golden leaves.
They are fallen
leaving us alone to face the winter cold.
Oh! but they were so fine, rain-glistening in the evening sun,
as was the glory of his shining.
Will we see him once more
with the new buds of spring,
with the promise of summer?'*

*In the forest is a shadow,
on the meadows a cloud.
Upon the High-Downs
the watching stones brace themselves against the winter winds
We who have waited through the cold countless years for today
shall wait again,
to guard for his coming.
We shall watch over him until his own spring'.*

He would play at war, slashing the heads from his mother's blooms as were they goblin raiders and he'd laugh with a cold, humourless mockery at their demise.

His brother and sisters were ill at ease with him also. They could see his hurt, knew of his torment, for they felt the depths of his unhappiness in the silence of his being. Yet they couldn't understand the nature of the changes in him and didn't know how to reach out to him. His eyes were set upon things the like of which they had no knowledge. They saw his anger and his determination and watched, helpless, as he turned his back towards them. At length they left him alone to do as he would.

Thus the seasons turned. *Winter is best. It bares none of the lies hid in spring's promises of life. More real by far are the bitter snows, whiter than death's bland claws. What use is the bright, light-gift of the sun?* The years turned again. Too soon his wooden sword became a blade of steel. His colours were little more than a vague echo of childhood, neither wanted nor needed.

Eventually came the day when, with an awful inevitability, these matters could be contained no longer. It was harvest time when they gathered together, as custom demanded, at the table in the Great Hall. They were all there, the Baron, the Lady-of-Flowers, the Calm-Watcher, the Lord-of-Numbers, the Lightning-Bringer and the Young-Warrior. Food was laid before them, spiced ham, wildfowl, vegetables rolled in butter, steaming and hot, a joy as always for those with a mind for such things. The room however, despite the roaring fire, was chill and the diners sat in silence.

'What ails?' the Lady asked from within her own ill ease. 'What is so wrong that we sit here night after night our eyes downcast and our tongues bound in silence?'

There was no reply. The dread of waking the serpent of their fears forbade any.

'Will no one answer me?'

The silence stretched into infinity.

'I shall answer.' The Calm-Watcher broke the spell of waiting. Her usually soft voice cracked like brittle glass, talking not to the Lady but to the Baron seated at her side. 'I shall speak my words although I doubt that YOU will want to hear me.'

'What words do you think to speak to me, daughter?' His voice little more than a breath, yet as ever his tongue was barbed with scorn.

'I shall speak to you of my thoughts,' she still spoke quietly, though not for long. 'And I shall tell of my vision. I shall speak of my understandings and my truths. You ask "What ails?" Mother. Well, I shall give you an answer.' And to her mother alone. 'Will you hear me?'

'Yes, my dear, I'll hear,' she answered her daughter in a whisper. 'Whatever you have to say. This time I'll hear.'

'You'll say what I allow you to say!' The cold threat was implicit.

'I shall say as I must!' the Calm-Watcher snapped back. 'You demand too much of us. We have listened to your words and your directives too often. It is time to speak! Look at us. Just look and consider what you see. We sit here cowed and afraid, least our words awaken some terrible fate. What fate? Tell me that. What fate could be worse than this? We used to be a family. We used to be happy, to know our place and the truth of our own natures. What have we now?'

'We have order. We have rules. That's what we have.'

'No we don't!' She sobbed the words. 'We have blindness. We have thoughtlessness. We have NOTHING!'

'SILENCE!' She stilled him before he could interrupt. 'It's time to talk of truth and my truth will not be denied. Look about you.' She spoke, harsh and demanding, into the Baron's face. 'What do you see? Do you know? Truly I doubt it! Well I shall tell you. You see those who grew together, who were bonded by the ties of their own nature and the love that held us. Do you know who we are? DO YOU KNOW?

'See The Lady – your wife – our mother. Do you know her? Have you retained any idea just who she really is, what she is? Once you did. Once you held her in high esteem but no longer. It seems you have forgotten so I shall tell you, remind you of what you once knew. She is the Lady-of-Flowers. Do you recall anything of what that means? It means she has at her fingertips the forces that are the essence of creation. Her very nature is the very thing you would have her reject. You call the centre of her being a delusion, a deceit! I call it a wonder beyond the grasp of your sterile imagination. She IS the Lady-of-Flowers.

'See also your son,' she continued without pause. 'Do you know him? Do you know his nature? He IS the Lord-of-Numbers. In his hands he has held the secrets of existence. In his mind he has reached into the heart of the universe and wrought a mandala of wonder from its foundations.

'See your daughter the Lightning-Bringer! Can you see her? Or are you blind?

Do you not see the waking of her lightning? Can one jot of the things you hold dear match a single spark of her existence?

'And your youngest son. What of him? What have you done? You have taken one of the wonders of the world and turned it into a thing of hate and meaninglessness. In your spite all you have done is create a sick parody of yourself, without feeling or even hope. How dare you?

'And now look at yourself, Oh great Lord. What are you become?' It was her turn to burnish her words with scorn. 'What do you see there? Anything? Anything at all? For I shall tell you what I see. I see one who has become no more than the thing he professes to hate. I see a creature wallowing in a mire of hate and anger, of lies and ugliness. You claim to seek the truth. RUBBISH! You strive to deny it at every turn!' She grew still, watching, calm, as was her nature.

He spoke. 'What of you?' derision.

'I AM the Calm-Watcher. Didn't you know? It is my name and my nature. I watch. I see what is and in the calmness of my own being I come to an understanding. Here is my understanding! Here is my Truth. These are my words! Hear me!' she commanded, rising to her feet.

'You came back to us, to be with us, but it seems you know us not. You say, "Live for order and duty" as if these words were realities with meanings of their own. You profess to the truth but you deny the very reality lying at the centre of everything. You say magic is a lie and an illusion set to trap the unwary. Well I say you are wrong! You have lost sight of truth. You have turned your love into bitterness, your wisdom into cynicism. You deride the ways of magic as tricks and deceits, but lose sight that the truth of life lies in harmony not order.'

Drawing herself tall she stood before them, fell and mysterious, cloaked in her silver robe, ready to speak her judgement of him. 'Your cold truth is a false truth!' she accused, pointing her finger at his breast. 'Your science wreaks with the foetid odour and corrosive deceits of the Lord-of-Mists. It seems you follow with pride the ways of those you once counted sworn enemies.' She paused, holding him in her scornful gaze. 'This path of yours is nothing but a mire set out by the creatures of the void, a pointless, empty, meaningless lie. Without love to provide a meaning, without beauty to waken the spirit, without magic to quicken the soul, life is no more than a cold, empty shell, futile, without hope and without reason. I reject this vision. I reject this empty path. I reject your drab lies, your ice eyed anger, your cold iron will. I reject it all!'

He was on his feet. The clarion shout ripping through the peace as a war-horn's brazen blast. They fell back trembling in awe as the tumult of his anger wrenched apart the foundations of their lives. They recoiled from his power too, wanting to run, to hide.

Wrenching the sword from where it hung over the hearth, he raised its razor tipped point to her breast.

She stood still as stone, knowing now he paid no head to the truth of her words or to the tears of sorrow coursing over her cheeks.

His anger was livid, powerful as an avalanche, uncontrollable, unstoppable and horrible to behold. 'How dare you?' His voice was more deadly than the sharpest of blades. 'How dare you defy me? You are nothing! NOTHING! No one at all. By my grace alone you live here. By my word you live or die.

I am your Lord and your Master! You will do as I say. I demand it so.'

Yet her resolve did not crumble, neither did she tremble in fear. But her words, when she spoke, were filled with the sadness of her heart. 'No. I shall not do as you say. Your demands are wrong! Your words are wrong! Your path is wrong! You are wrong!'

With eyes turned to stone and a voice crueller then breaking ice, 'Then Be Gone! ... GO! ... Leave this place, you belong here no more!' saying the words of banishing, cold and terrible. 'This place is no longer your home. These people are no more of your flesh and blood. You are no longer my kin. Take your name and go. Not I, nor your mother, nor your brothers or sister shall know you. You are outcast! BE GONE!'

'No,' the Calm-Watcher whispered from the depths of her sadness. 'You still don't see the truth. It isn't I who must leave.'

'No!' declared the Lord-of-Numbers drawing unto himself from the powers of the Universe and steeling himself against the immanent affray. 'She is our Sister.'

'No,' cried the Lightning-Bringer, her energies burning as fire in her breast.

'No,' whispered the Young-Warrior, gripping the hilt of his sword.

'NO!' exclaimed The Lady-of-Flowers. 'This shall not be. I shall not permit this senseless cruelty to continue. It is enough!'

'You'll not permit it? You fools,' the blade of his broadsword blackening before their eyes.'**Do you presume to think that I can be denied?'**

He wrenched his shield from where it hung above the mantle and they in turn recoiled in horror as the cloth fell away to reveal the dread emblem of The Void. Turning now, his eyes burning with hatred and as he crouched before them they saw what he had become, A Warrior-of-The-Mists.

'I defy you,' The Lady declared, 'I defy you and all who tread this dull path that you would have had us follow,' at last perceiving the way things were. Despite her love for him, despite the longing carried throughout the long years, she drew herself up in power and brought forth her wand of growth. 'It is not she but you who must go. Now hear my banishment!

'I reject you! You are not he whom I married, not he whom I loved, not he for whom I have waited through the long years. It is you who do not belong here! It is you who shall leave! Be Gone!'

One final, dreadful time he cried out his terrible battle cry and loosed his loathing upon them. His hand darted out to snatch the wand from her hand but it flared with a light no darkness could bide and the veil was ripped from their eyes and they saw at last what stood before them.

With gasps of growing horror they watched the image begin to waver. An awful transformation as his very nature changed, corrupted, metamorphosing from man to beast, a terrible creature of scale and fang, drawling with caustic slime.

The truth became crystal clear as the icy lust of its greed turned upon them, burning with frozen fire. Now, with the veil stripped from their eyes they witnessed the full terribleness of its deceit and knew the awful danger confronting them.

Thus the Lightning-Bringer rose in fury, awakening in a cry of realisation the fullness of her storm. Her fury took flight raging on tempest wings until the heavens burned bright with her anger.

The Calm-Watcher cast aside her silver cloak of tranquillity, letting loose the five elements from the bindings of the world.

The Lord-of-Numbers' voice grew stronger, chanting out the Canticle of existence and conjuring energies from the very fires of creation.

Even the Young-Warrior drew out his shining, new sword.

The creature recoiled from the fierceness of their anger spitting venom and bile in the face of their wrath. He held high that dread shield to hide from the brilliance of the magic now grown palpable about the Lady. He cried out in defiance of her, calling out to the dark powers of the Void for aid, lashing out with his blade to carve a path of darkness through the plasm of magic.

The conflagration exploded into a maelstrom of energy, shattering the blackened blade into a million tiny cinders. The creature screamed anew.

Now the Light of the Lady grew with her power. Now the Calm-Watcher brought order to the raging energies of creation. Now the Lord-of-Numbers formed them into a weapon of light and the Lightning-Bringer drove then at the beast, fire from the heavens and the hurricanes of the four winds. He fell back unable to contend with their might. Unable to stand in the face of their wrath, he turned and fled, leaving them and the house forever.

They wept.

'It is gone,' the Lady-of-Flowers sobbed, 'He is gone,' as she gathered her children together hoping to find comfort for the grief that so tore their hearts. 'It is over.' But her words belied her own pain. It would never be over, not for her, not ever. Life is seldom simple. There was a price to be paid for these terrible things. From every conflict there are casualties.

'I remember him, Mother,' the Calm-Watcher spoke softly in her sorrow. 'I remember the brightness of his smile, the warmth of his love, the light of his wisdom.' She wrapped her silver cloak tight and turned her face to the fire, losing herself in the paths of her memories. Better the peace of the past to the pain of the present.

The Young-Warrior trembled at his mother's side. He'd seen the terribleness of all which occurred, been wounded by the poison of that bitter tongue. Not just his words either. Other words spun through his mind, words not meant for his ears it's true but he'd heard them all the same, in the angry retort of his sister.

'...*and turned it into a thing of hate and meaninglessness. In your spite all you have done is create a sick parody of yourself, without feeling or even hope. How dare you?*'

Shame and humiliation rose as a fever in his breast, choking his thoughts. *Is that truly how they see me?* He stood in silence, turned and went back to his room, the remnant of his shattered sword still clutched in his hand. They watched him go, unable to find the words to reach out, to comfort him.

In his room there was no rest, no sleep either. He paced the floor, blaming himself for all that had come to pass. The magic of his childhood was gone forever. All that was left was his resolve to persevere. Yet he too had seen the creature of darkness and felt the dreadful power of its hatred. He accused himself of doing nothing but quaking in the face of its might and trembling in fear before its evil. Within his breast the resolve grew hard. 'I shall become a warrior true. I shall prove myself. I shall be worthy.' From that time on he denied his sadness and thus he began to plan.

Was he isolated before? Then it was so much more now. His brother and sisters watched his inner struggle unable to reach him, unable to find the way into his pain. Day by day his countenance hardened with resolve. Day by day he grew away from them. Still he planned.

Six long months passed by. At least by this time a little of the former peace and happiness had returned to the Hall and as was their way they gathered each evening for their dinner and to share the day's events.

It was a fine meal that evening, cold meats and spiced mushrooms, ever a favourite. The wine was red and gleamed as sunset in the crystal goblets. They laughed freely, jesting over the Lord-of-Number's great appetite and his lack of girth despite it. For once the Young-Warrior was with them and actually joined in with their mood.

However, his family well knew things could never be the same as before and they quietened with an anticipated expectation when he stood before the fire to speak. 'Midsummer is near,' he began.

'You're going to leave us.' The Lightning-Bringer, ever quick to see, spoke for them all. 'It comes as no surprise. Your disquiet has been well evident to us for a long time.'

'I have things to do.' He spoke simply.

'Things to do?' the Lady asked. 'Is it really as simple as that?' Cold words, which hid the turmoil in her heart. Full well she knew that the signs portended changes and an awaking of powers. She feared also for what must surely be. She knew well the nature of what lay ahead of him in the vibrations at the centre of her being. Oh how she feared for her son at this time. 'You have things to do? What things? Where do you go? Shall you ever return?' Questions all without answers save for the dread certainty of the danger that awaited.

He'd expected the same and so sealed his heart and spoke his planned reply. 'I intend to go to see the Dwarves at Carrow. I can say little more at this time.'

'The Dwarves?' the Lady gasped. His words were unexpected. This was one path she had not foreseen, or even considered. Growing still, her thoughts whirled through the webs of probability, down the trails of the unknown. Finally she smiled. 'Yes,' she commended, 'This is good. The Dwarves are wise.'

Thus on Midsummer's eve, after they had set blaze to the Oak-fire and broken their fast with corn and mead, he took his satchel and went from them, climbing the face of the downs overshadowing his home.

They watched him go, waving their farewells standing at the doorway to the hall, catching sight of his form in the fading light as the sun began to sink over the far-off salt marsh and the western sea. Even when it was dark and he could be seen no more, they waited.

He climbed long into the night following a well-trod path to the summit where the standing-stones waited. Far below the red embers of the Oak-fire set themselves as a beacon. *Return, one day, return.*

At midnight, when the moon was full, he stood in the centre of the great circle of seven rectangular stones of power. Here, in a ritual as old as the earth itself he spoke the words of a vow, a mystery as ancient and sacred as the stones about him, spun in words of power, terrible and binding.

> 'Hear me you Powers.
> Hear me You who pen the lines of Fate!
> Hear me You Governors of the Turns of Time!
> Hear me, Weavers of the World Web.
> Hear me Stones of the World-Spring.
> For I shall make my oath unto you!
>
> Know you The Beast
> The Dark Fiend,
> The Creature of Evil,
> The Lord of Mists,
> The Keeper of the Void?
> Then Know you my Enemy.
>
> For thus do I swear,
> By Sun and by Moon
> By Ocean and by Sky
> By Air and by Earth
> By water and by Fire
> By the Powers of Day
> And by the Forces of the Night
> I shall not rest.
> Not for fear,
> Not for wealth,
> Not for sorrow,
> Not for Love,
> Not for Fate.
> Not even for death,
> Until I have faced my enemy.

Perhaps then, when all is done, I might find peace from the pain that so torments my soul.

In these words was the path into the future set. Such utterances spoken in the fell hours of night have their own consequences. One should well beware nor such vows be rashly made. Many ears might hear the words and none might know or choose who might be the listener. Yet, even knowing this, he spoke his terrible oath and his voice rang clear upon the air. The creatures-of-the-night were stilled and heard him in silence, as did others less easy to name. Each listened and with their own understandings took from his words whatever they desired.

When the sun climbed over the mountains to cast its golden glow upon the dew-glistening meadows and pastures of Hereth, it found the Young-Warrior once more abroad. He'd spent the long hours of night among the stones and only when the first touch of dawn dimmed the stars had he risen to make his way down again. Turning away from the Halls he had known so long, he followed the Dingle stream seawards. Before long, the light of morning had yet to touch him, he passed into the lands of the fen and the salt marsh, following the trails of shepherd and the withy gatherer, winding his way through the long reed beds.

At noon he paused beside the still waters of the pool of R'sorve. He didn't notice the bright plumed birds darting over the waters gathering flies. He didn't see the swan gliding serenely beside the tall bull-rushes, but sat with eyes downcast to eat his meagre meal of bread and cheese. When ready to leave he stood, gazed onwards towards the rising heights of the Iron-Hills of Ghilsmun where he must go, and continued on his way.

The passage through those perilous wastes was long and torturous. It was near to evening when he dragged his weary feet up the final stone pathway towards the great arched entrance of the caverns of the Carrow of Dwarvenholm.

In the shelter of the arch he waited. Fear touched his breast as his eyes cast over the runes and carvings upon the portal, upon the fluted columns of onyx, which framed the entrance and beckoned towards the darkness within. Yet this was no time to flinch from this path so newly taken. With a deep breath he held himself tall and stepped forward into the future that lay within.

Cunning polished-stone mirrors caught the rays of the fading day and cast the entrance into a pall of sunset blush. His footsteps echoed in the silence much louder than was real, urging him to tiptoe. He moved downwards between more columns and yet more. The light, somehow moving with him, gave the impression that he passed through time rather than space. Eyes, unseen, watched him. He could feel their questing touch.

He continued walking slowly onward. The way was long with no side passages or doors leading to other chambers. Eventually though it widened into a hall, a giant cavern carved into the heart of the mountain. The scene was lit by the flickering of the forge-fires and dominated by a massive silvered anvil. This was the famed Carrow-of-the-Dwarvenholm.

Beyond were the shadows and shapes of the waiting smiths, the Dwarf-Lords, silent and still as the stone about them. Their piercing eyes burnt on his cheeks. Their immense strength and patience bore down on him, humbling him so that he felt small and of little import. Their stockiness and power gave the appearance of size, though in reality it was the Young-Warrior who was the larger. There were, he later learnt, forty-nine Forge-Masters. The fiftieth, The Master-Smith, High-Lord-of-the-Carrow was the one who stepped slowly forward and who broke the silence.

'We heard your words on the night air,' the rough voice rasped without preamble. 'We have awaited your coming. Tell us, Child-of-Hereth, what is your need?' Being of the earth the dwarven peoples have little use of subterfuge and guile. They speak as they see and hide not from what is.

'I need a sword,' he answered with his own simplicity.

'And shall we, The Dwarf-Smiths-of-the-Carrow, part so easily with the gleanings of our labours? The prised arts of dwarven craftsmen are not things to be purchased with gold nor given casually as gifts into anyone's hand. Do you think that we would spend a thousand years of knowledge in each hammer blow, carve our runes to tell the histories of the Dwarven craftsmen from their beginnings in the Well-Springs-of-the-Earth, but to give them away? What have you to be worth such a thing?'

'I have nothing, not even myself. You heard my words on the night air. You know the meanings in my soul. Yet I have not asked you to give me a sword, nor any of the wonders of your craftsmanship. I said that I need a sword. What I ask is that you teach me to make my own.'

The great hall grew as silent as a tomb. Eyes burning with the light of a thousand years at the forge grew shadowed as they fixed upon this strange, bold, youth.

'You ask that we teach you to make a sword?' came the incredulous reply at last. 'Teach you, some Child-of-man, a beardless youth who's not yet even grown in the ways of your own kind and who does not even know his own nature, to make a sword? You ask that we hand to you the deepest secrets of the dwarven-folk were they but a trifle? Why, by all the value of the treasures of the famed Mines-of-Ashiblae, should we do such a thing?'

For a moment his heart quaked. *Do I ask too much?* He took a deep breath, stilled his worries. 'I ask for no secret. I want no gift. I need a sword, a sword I can trust, in which there is no trace of betrayal. It seems to me that only a sword crafted by my own hand, with the sweat of my own flesh, perhaps even my own blood, should that be the need, only such a sword can serve me. It is said that the truest of all blades are those of the dwarf-smiths. It is also said that the finest of all the dwarven craftsmen are those who serve before the Carrow. This is why I have come to you.

'I know that my years are few and that my youth stands against me. I know that my flesh is feeble and not fit to the task. I know too that my vow has set me upon a path through the years ahead of me. I must grow strong. I must become as hard as steel. This is why I have come to you.

'I need a sword which is of my own nature. I ask again. Teach me to make my sword?'

They did not answer, rather one by one they gathered about the Carrow forming a circle where they stood, still clothed in the silence of their thoughts and as still as the stone about them, waiting. Seconds past, then minutes, which stretched into quarter of an hour. Nothing happened, no movement, no reaction, no sound, nothing. Time turned slowly towards the half-hour. Still there was nothing.

Suddenly the Master-Smith reached out and placed his hand upon the anvil. Then one by one the others followed suit, dark hands, strong hands sinewed and hard as iron, resting upon the burnished silver. Without sign or warning each, in the self-same instant began to hum. This was no tune, nor song. Each simply hummed a single note and each note was different from all of the others. The sounds jarred and clashed merging into an awful tumult of noise, growing louder and louder, crashing about the hall as a solid wave of sound. The Young-Warrior stood in the midst as the thrumming, booming vibrations beat upon him, washed him in almost visible sound until he feared that his skull would break under the pressure of the noise.

Though he knew not why or how he did so, he too walked forward and placed his hand upon the vibrating silver.

The sound was tuneless, formless, rhythm-less, yet even so within the tumult harmonies formed and broke, merged again and tore asunder. Tones fought as it were for dominance, prevailing or fading. There was meaning, a strange and incomprehensible sense of purpose. When one sound vanished, another would replace it. Gradually the themes began to draw together, closer and closer until there remained but one single ringing tone, pure and clear as true in its beauty as the chiming of a bell in the belfry of some unearthly cathedral.

The sound stopped. Only now, deep within his being, the tone continued as a vibration that would forever resonate in his soul.

'We have chosen. You shall craft your sword.'

Of that crafting neither he nor I shall speak. There are secrets so sacred and fell that they must remain unspoken until the ends of time. All that may be recounted is that the seasons had turned fully three times over before the task was done. When he did finally come forth from the Carrow to stand again in daylight The Young-Warrior was no longer a child. The crafting had tempered him, hardened his sinew and put strength into his flesh. Now he, as much he as the steel, was formed into a weapon of might.

The sword itself, 'the Dwarf-Sword' as he thought of it, well that's another matter entirely. Seldom has such a weapon been seen in the halls of men. Its fine honed blade was some three feet in length, shining as silver shot with cobalt. The sworls and patina of its tempering were a wonder, ever dazzling the eye. Runes were engraved upon its faces, the sun and moon, the circle stones, for Hereth. The words of his oath were written there also, terrible and final. The hilt was bound in dragon scale, the pommel formed of silver as bright as the Carrow itself. Unspoken still is the nature of the sword for therein lay its true glory. Perhaps if told that when struck the blade would chime as a bell in the belfry of some unearthly cathedral you may begin to understand.

Come shine my bloody armour bright
Give strength my arm
and clear my sight
Come wake the dreadful warring cry
That I in triumph
Now Can Die!

(From: The song of the setting sun)

Chapter Two - The Young Warrior

IT WAS INDEED a much-changed young man who returned from the Halls-of-Ghilsmun and the forges of the Carrow. The Lady-of-Flowers, tending the herb-garden by the rill edge, saw him whilst still afar striding up the Dingle path.

At first she saw a stranger, a young warrior approaching. She noted the sword

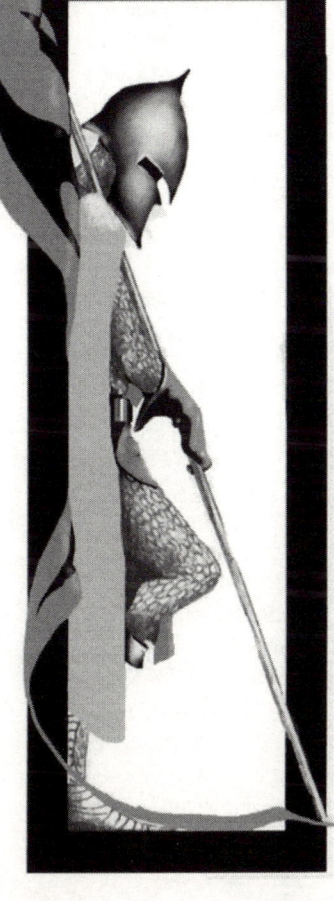

strapped over his back and the glistening of dwarven mail beneath the grey cloak draped about his broad shoulders. She saw too, with shocked surprise, the device of the Earth stones upon the face of his round shield, *Who would dare bare such a sign?* but recognised the proud set of his head and the easy confidence with which he walked towards her. *Who is this?* Then she saw his eyes.

'You are grown, my son.' Her welcome was wide as the universe, bright as the sun. As she took him in her arms he felt as a child again, although he now towered over her. Stepping back she filled her soul with the sight of him until the tears of joy in her eyes blurred her vision and she laughed. 'Come, come, now see what you've done? If you've caused me to burn the baking then you'll see you're not too big to put over my knee.' Not that she'd ever done so even when he was a child.

He held out his arms and kissed her cheek. 'It has been too long, far too long. You must tell me everything that's happened, of my brother, my sisters. How fare they? How are you? How is everything?' He too lapsed into laughter and took her arm as they turned towards the hall.

The Lord-of-Numbers stood in the archway watching them approach. His face lit with a smile as he too looked the young man up and down, sharp eyes missing nothing. 'You've grown, Brother,' laughing the truth. For indeed the Young-Warrior did look down into the face of his slighter, though older kin. 'I see you've a tale for us.'

'Where are our sisters?'

'They too have grown,' the Lady's voice was tinged with just a hint of sadness. 'The Lady-of-Calm has found a partner among the Eddar and has gone there to live. Your Sister-of-Lightning went with her as her companion.' She paused, once again her face was touched with sorrow. 'It seemed best.' More was left unsaid. 'Just your brother and I dwell here now awaiting the time of choosing. But enough of this.' Suddenly businesslike, 'Come take a glass of wine. We shall talk of all this over dinner.' And as they supped from the crystal goblets, 'Take off your travel-stained robes, my son. Wash the dust from yourself. I must away to prepare.'

The Lord accompanied him to his chamber though, for the most part, both remained silent. When he realised his brother's eyes were fixed upon The Dwarf-Sword the Young-Warrior offered it to him for inspection.

'Is this what it was about?' There was real interest.

'Not only this, but yes it was. I needed a sword to match my nature, one I that might trust.'

The Lord-of-Numbers cast his eyes over the blade, seeing in its form much others might not have seen and knowing things others might not have known. 'It's a thing of wonder, that's for sure.' He sat on the bed as the Warrior changed. 'I'm unwise. I unknowing about warlike things. It's not my way.' He paused looking at the younger man. 'I find these "warrior-ways" as incomprehensible, alien to my nature. Though, when I look at you, I can see even more that I don't understand.'

'But,' after a pause, 'I see no harm, not in you or this sword.'

The Warrior stopped his ablutions and turned a quizzeled eye at his older brother. 'Surely you'd realise I'd bring no harm to this house. I know I've changed in many ways since I left. Years have passed and I've grown. Aye grown and learnt many strange things and ways. I have, as the Dwarves say, "Stood before the Flame" but you're right. I bring no harm and the sword is of me and my essence. It bares my name in its forging.'

Dinner that evening was as a feast and their conversation covered may matters. The Warrior spoke of his life among the Dwarves, of their base humour and their long thoughtful silences. He spoke of their 'Harmonising' and of the sound of their laughter ringing through the Caverns-of-Light.

'What will you do?' the Lord-of-Numbers wanted to know. 'Now you have your sword, I mean.'

'What will I do?' He turned the matter over in his mind. 'It's probably too soon to know. I'm only at the start of my life's journey,' he answered carefully. 'I don't know where or how I'll go from here. The dwarves say, "Wait, for the time will tell its own beginnings," but they live for hundreds of years and time is of little consequence to their thinking. I suppose my hope is to meet with one of the Guides of Elswood or some other man-at-arms who'll teach me the skills of weapon mastery. I want to become a warrior true.' He spoke no word of his father. 'Some time I hope to join with the King's Armies. But that time's yet to come.' Again there was far more unspoken than said.

The Lord-of-Numbers spoke of his own life too and above all of Valandrii who he now walked with. He invited the Warrior meet her when at the next Rossbridge market. Valandrii, it seemed was daughter to one of the herbalists of Crowswood, who he'd chanced to meet during the autumn-fayre last year.

The Lady told of the Eddar, the Dragon-Riders of Amarkhaan and of how the two sisters had chosen to spend their lives beyond the clouds. Awareness that he'd probably never see them again brought a sadness to his breast but he could well understand the call of freedom that was the heart of the Eddar's nature. Perhaps, had fate dealt him different cards to play, he also might have known their desire to rise beyond the confines of the world.

They filled the evening with talk of Hereth and of the goings and comings of its folk. They'd built a new guildhall in Crowswood and finally repaired the bridge at Rossbridge. Farmer Loomas had bought a new breed of milk-cow from one of the Steadings down in the lake lands. It had come to naught though for his prise bull Summer-Kand refused to do his duty and the claim of higher milk yield was never proved.

Other matters too were spread between them but they said nothing of the time before the Warrior's departure nor of their father, or Creature-of-Darkness, who had dwelt amongst them. The silence of those unspoken thoughts drained the evening of any real pleasure and left a sour taste to their thoughts as they made their ways to bed.

During the following days the Warrior felt restless and out of place. Memories of his childhood lurked about every corner to remind him of another time. He hunted in the woodlands beyond the Dingle but found little there but more reminders of things he'd sooner forget.

He did go to Rossbridge, though not with his brother, and found a degree of peace and contentment at the bar of The Swan, and more indeed in the dark ale served therein. He purchased a horse, a large creature of muscle and power. Trone he called it, after the steed of Alan-of-Colon in the tales of old. But he was never really at ease with horses and at best merely competent in the arts of riding.

As time passed he began journeying abroad, restless of spirit and thought. Sometimes Trone would take him to the high passes of the Mountains-of-the-Divide. There he'd look down on the forest of The Elswood where the White-beam and golden-beech trees formed places of secret wonder. Somewhere among the trees lay the Elves' Crystal City, Al-Sinnian and he often lingered hoping to see sign of the woodland folk. His hope was unfulfilled though and he did no more than watch. Eventually he'd turn away to other matters and other trails.

More often his trek went northward into the barren lands. He found something mysterious about the mist-shrouded peat bogs and the dark pools, never the same twice. The solitude of these wild places offered him peace and he soon learnt to cherish the call of the heron and stork that resided there. Little could compare to the joy of watching the will-o'-the-wisps sparkling over the waters in the dark of the night.

There was a hostelry he came to know quite well. 'The Shambles' they called it, although the owner, in better times, had named it 'THE-GOLD-DRAGON'. It was a dour place where the marsh-men who tended the flocks of swan and duck came.

It was a dirty place too, for the innkeeper felt little need to do more than wipe the slops from of the tables.

He was called Inskip Candle, though his customers preferred 'Tallow', meaning he was more grease than wick, and he called them 'slobs' and served them with a surly ill grace and foul tongue.

Our Young-Warrior found a kind of companionship here in the sullen rectitude of the weather beaten marsh-men. The brevity of their conversation and their highly prised privacy were well suited to his need for a place to think. For their part they found no threat or awkwardness in his long silences. 'No one in their right mind would come to such a god-forsaken spot in search of company,' one of them declared with unlooked for frankness. 'So 'e fits in here right enough, for no one in their right mind would try eking out a living in this bloody wilderness as we, let alone claim to enjoy it?'

Winter came, the mists rolling down from the barren wastes and snow blasting over the rush beds on bitter winds, but he could often be found there, though there were seldom any other customers at all. He'd have to bang loudly at the door and shout out his presence before Tallow would venture down to unbar the door. During that hard winter he came to know Tallow and he, him. The inn-keeper wondered, only half-believing, when he heard the Young-Warrior's talk of his home in Hereth and of his childhood in the Great-Hall. But in the end, it might be true to say that a strange unspoken friendship grew up between the two. Indeed, whatever else there did grow an unspoken trust each for the other. *No questions means no answers. No answers means no lies.*

Spring came early next year. The snows rolling back northward left the land even more mired than usual. The geese returned early too, carousing over the reed-beds before splashing into the dark pools of the fens. The Young-Warrior was there to see them, to welcome them as it were although perhaps not to their liking. He'd taken to carrying a hunting bow and the arrows that, if his aim were true, might allow him to bring a gift with him to the dilapidated inn.

Looking back, it was probably as much his fault as anything else, that he was injured. It was on one of these hunts through the fens chasing a flock of the crimson legged grey-duck, *Gellend*, the marsh-men called them. He'd seen them swoop low over the reed beds and heard their squawking arrival somewhere to his right. His concentration was on the birds and none on any danger that might lie there.

It leapt at him, unexpected and unseen, a creature of slime and claw which had lain hidden in the marsh. A horrendous thing it was, scaled and filled with the lust for blood. It lashed at him intent on taking his life in a single instant. He'd seen but the briefest glimpse of movement and rolled sideways in the saddle. Trone reared and fled in panic, both saving him and spilling him to the ground. None-the-less the talons, missing their hold, raked a great furrow along his thigh. He rolled over in the mud, aware of nothing but the pain filling his body and the creature roaring over him.

He saw its eyes, terrible orbs of lust and hate, flame over him and felt his own anger rising inside, seeing in some dark recess of his mind an image of the creature in the Hall-of-Hereth. He rolled again as it lashed out at him once more. This time the claws went wide.

In growing panic he scrambled to his knees, *Oh God my leg doesn't work*, drawing the Dwarf-Sword to hold before him. The creature tried to attack again but he held it at bay with the point. It wasn't as big as he'd first thought or as terrifying. It was but a thing of the wild. *Attack! You have to attack.* Somehow, without conscious plan, he was on his feet, panting and sweating with effort, pain and fear. It lunged towards him again, claws reaching for his life. This time he blocked the swiping blow with the flat of the blade and suddenly, with the ringing sound of the clash chiming brightly over the marsh, the moment was over. With a scream of frustration and failure, the creature vanished back into the mire and mists.

The Young-Warrior sank back to the ground, lay there on the rough marsh grass, his blood mingling with the foul sludge of the bog. *I can't stay here. What if it comes back? I've got to move! I must!* Somehow he found the strength to struggle to his knees and then to climb back to his feet. *My leg won't work. I can't walk!* He tried using the sword as a walking stick staggering, fighting to stay on his feet, to continue.

It is unclear if one of the marsh-men found him and brought him to the inn or if he managed to hobble there himself. He did get there though, weak and almost incoherent through loss of blood and pain. There were neither doctors nor healers to tend his wounds though.

Tallow laid him out on a table. He was almost unconscious now, delirious and weak through loss of blood. The inn-keeper, for once having washed the beer dregs from his hands, sewed up his wounds with sacking thread and then, having some vague idea that it might help, poured spirit over the whole. The Young-Warrior half rose from where he lay, screamed in agony and fell back, still.

Time passed. Eventually someone sent for Setti, a strange, half-wild medicine-woman, who eked out a hermit's existence at the edge of the wilderness with her fey daughter Ra.

'Light 'N' flowers,' Setti had said, waving various bones and roots about the still unconscious form. 'Light of the rainbow, 'N' flowers of the mind.' She laughed a strange, probably demented, cackle and left, not even taking a drink with the group of concerned marsh-men gathered there.

However the girl Ra remained, sitting silently by the youth's side, watching. She called for water and cooled his fevered brow but did no more.

The talk of Flowers reminded Tallow of the lad's tales of his mother the Lady-of-Flowers. He sent Dawson, one of the poorer of the marsh men, southwards to find her. No one knows how but find her he did and after several worrisome, waiting days he returned with her to the inn.

By this time the Warrior had slipped into coma. It was probably just as well. His mother tended him. She'd inspected Tallow's work and brought her own unctions to dress the wound.

Later, having received the Lady's calling, Rix, one of the carters from Rossbridge, came bringing his daughter Sandre with him. Together Tallow, the Lady, Ra, Rix and Sandre carried The Young-Warrior to the wagon and Rix drove them homeward.

The mists were gathered in the hollows by now and tainted the trail with fog and ill humour. The later spring rains brought little joy either as they brought him forth from the moors and back to the Hall. There at last they laid him in his own bed and waited for what would be.

Fever's trembling grasp clung to him for many days as his Mother put forth her skill. Sandre, the carter's daughter, stayed to help the Lady. Ra, who for her own unspoken reason had come south from the wastes, insisted on remaining also. His wound was indeed grievous. In other hands he might well have been crippled for life.

During one of the early days of pain and fever he heard his mother talking. '…what happened and therefore can only hazard a guess as to just what we might do to remedy the harm.'

'But, you've redressed the wound,' an unknown voice, later recognised as Ra, queried. 'We've managed to clear the poison and driven the corruption away. Even now his fever lessens.'

'Were only things as simple. He's been through an ordeal which none of us know and faced perils from within as well as without. Even should his flesh knit, there's no way of knowing about his heart, his spirit also. Wounds of the flesh are not my main concern.'

'What can we do?'

'Be strong and lend him our strength…' But the voices drifted beyond his grasp. He could not regain them. *I'm not broken, Not defeated. I'll fight. I'll fight.*

He awoke another time, hands were washing him, a face smiling, a strange distant echo of friendliness. She spoke but the words were lost again.

In the dark he awoke once more. His mind was clear now, with no confusion over what had happened. He recalled the fight and the wound. He wriggled his toes. *Well I'm still alive.* He started to cough.

'It's all right. It's all right now.' A soft gentle voice. 'Here try some water.' A hand lifted his head, cool water, just a sip to ease his parched throat. He slept again.

Time passed and he began to wake more frequently. Usually either the dark haired Ra or the slim, curly-blonde Sandre was there, to tend him, although sometimes his mother came too. Her calm, knowing eyes examined him closely and then she'd prepare strange potions for him to drink. He knew better than to argue, no matter how foul they tasted. He grew stronger, strong enough to tell his mother of what had happened in the mist shrouded marshes and to drink still worse of her medicinal concoctions.

The girls found their own different ways to look after him. Sandre was kind, caring, gentle of voice and hand, ever ready and eager to do his bidding. Ra tended towards silence. She expected more of him, made him look after himself. He preferred Ra's approach and all three of them knew it.

'What will you do?' Ra asked one evening when he'd finished supper.

'What do you mean?' He felt his face redden.

'Well, you're well on the mend now and you can't stay here forever, even if Sandre might wish you could. By next week you should be up on your feet again. Least ways, you will if I've anything to do with it. It's time you started to think about your future.'

In truth he'd done little else for the past few weeks and all to no avail. His thoughts constantly ruminated over the fight with the creature in the marshes. He saw again the nearness of his defeat at that beast's hands. Was he truly made of the stuff of warriors?

'I intend to become a Warrior, Ra,' he tried to explain. 'To learn to fight. At my very first encounter I was nearly slain. That wasn't good enough. I've got to learn weapon skill and war-craft.'

'I can't really see you as a Warrior,' she mused. 'Oh I can see that you're strong enough and know from your wounds you've already faced an enemy, but your voice is gentle and your eyes are too kind. I can't really imagine you fighting in a battle and killing your enemies with your mighty sword.'

He laughed with her. 'I'm not really sure that's how it is, Ra. Warriors do have to fight, that's true enough but it's more than that. Being a warrior is about standing up for what you believe in, about doing what's right, about helping others.' But her words seemed very true and echoed the fear that rode in his heart. *Can I do it? Could I really Kill?*

'And killing...' Somehow she knew.

'Yes, and killing.' *I must learn to kill, I must. What if at the end of things I'm unable to take the life of my enemy? What if, as in the marsh, my hand turns aside from the task? No I MUST learn to revel in the taking of life. I must find the blood lust to drive my hand. I MUST learn to become a killer. I'll not let the failings of my nature betray me.*

'You asked what I'm going to do. Well I'll tell you. When I'm fit enough I'll go to the King-of-Santolin. I intend to become a Warrior of the King as was my father in his youth. Yes I intend to follow his footsteps and take up arms. *Surely they'll teach me battle skill and, in the heat of the fighting, I'll learn to overcome my reluctance. I'll learn how to fight, to kill, and to feast upon the lives of my enemies.*

'I chose this path long ago now, Ra, and my way is set. I already have the Dwarf-Sword as my arm. Yes I shall go to join the King.'

Her look was far away and fey. 'Any path leading to where we have to go will suffice. Although it seems to me that you have chosen the harder way.'

He had a similar talk with his mother several days later. 'You have skill in your hands, my son, can you not put that to use rather than follow a path towards destruction?'

'I've already chosen my path.' Not wishing to make the Lady unhappy, 'I know you don't like my choice and this troubles me greatly but it's the path I've set myself and the way I must follow.'

'When?'

'I think after the harvest feast.'

'But that will take you into the winter months and it will be hard travelling abroad when the snows come.'

'Of course I know, Mother.' He checked himself, 'I mean; I know you're right, but in the winter the King's army returns to its encampment. If winter is no time for travelling then it's also no time for campaigning either. I'll go to Sarum. That's where I'll find them.' He'd rehearsed argument many times.

'I see you're decided in this.' The argument was done. 'Have you chosen a name to use in the lands of men, a name so we might know of you among the warriors of the King?' She was not cold, just resigned to what would be.

'I thought to call myself Droven, after the hero of old. For I too see myself cast adrift within a sea of Fate's strange tides.'

She smiled secretly to herself. It was also true that Droven was known as The-Holder-of-Light. Perhaps in this matter truth would have its say after all. She felt relieved, although without clear reason.

The weeks passed and soon he was up and about. He began to train, to harden himself for what might lay ahead. He ran about the grounds of the hall and climbed the steep slopes of The High-Downs to build his stamina. Gradually the chill light of his quest began to flare in his eyes once again.

In Rossbridge he purchased another horse, a grey with white mane and tail. He didn't named it. The beast was not really to his liking, being strangely still and distant in its manner. However it was a noble creature which matched well his cloak and armour.

With ever quickening pace the weeks sped past. Summer turned and as the mists of autumn began to close in, the leaves over the Dingle turned to gold and the geese began to fly in from the northern wastes. The day of his leaving approached all too soon.

They sat in the Great-Hall, the log fire blazing and filling the silence with its own crackling conversation. The servants had cleared the table save for the jug of mulled wine and now only the three of them remained.

The Lady coughed, clearing herself for the difficult words she wished to say. 'My son,' she began, 'the year has turned and your time is upon us. You've spoken of your path and taken the name Droven, as of old. I for my part see no clear thing. I fear that you face little but a fell and perilous future in the direction you've chosen. It was not always your way nor your nature.' She'd try one last time.

'You don't have to take this path. You do not have to follow in your father's way. There are other paths no less noble no less true. Your brother is wise to the skill in your hands and the making of your dwarven sword. Can you not find a way from his wisdom and learn a different path from within the knowledge he holds?'

'No,' the Lord-of-Numbers spoke quietly though his words echoed in the hall. 'No, Mother, we should not try to govern his steps. We mustn't try to hinder either him or his going. He, as I and all people, must and will find his own way. Well you know it, Mother. If you bind a tree with wire it can be bent to the form of your desire but it's ever a poorer thing to what it might have been. Should we try to hold him what would we achieve? At best, if best it be, we should chain him to ourselves and in so doing prevent him from growing, forever. At worst, if worst it be, we should drive him from us and turn him from all that he has known.

'No, not that. Rather let's find it in our hearts to trust him, that's our way. It always has been. Let us trust the love we bear for him and which he bears for us. Let us trust the love we nurtured throughout the years of our childhood and hold to what we know is true.'

'We'll not gainsay him, nor hinder his passing. We'll aid him, giving whatever we can to strengthen him. We'll send him forth with our blessings and then, when or if he returns, we'll welcome him with joy. Should he never come back? Well, then at least our memories will be pure and untainted by rancour and will brighten the years that part us.'

The Lady grew still. She'd heard the words of the Lord in the depths of her being. Then standing slowly she gathered her strength, for she was indeed the Lady-of-Flowers and wise in the truths of life.

'My Son, Child, Warrior, Pilgrim, Wizard or whatever you choose to be, I see truth and beauty in your brother's words. Perhaps I see clearly now. You have chosen your path and although it seems a terrible doom and saddens my heart, I'll not speak against it again. If I'm fearful for you, it's only right and proper. I'm your mother and after all it's only natural that I should worry as you go out into the world.' She smiled and patted his hand affectionately.

'Your brother said we should send you with our blessing and our love and that we should aid you as we might.'

She stood, slowly, tall, formal. 'These are my words, Young Warrior. They may seem strange, perhaps hard to understand or confusing in meaning, but these are the greatest of all my gifts.'

She grew still, her eyes clouding in thought and when she spoke it was as if from a far away place.

'The seeds of the Future are but newly sown. Who can know how they shall grow or what fruit they shall bare?' She paused testing the strands of probability. *'Even so, comes a vibration on the World-Web, the dark hymn of Fate's fell choosing.*

A Soldier's sword
and a Pilgrim's robe,
A Wizard's staff
and a Magi's Power
and ever the Rainbow's light.

Your journey leads you into danger. That is sure. I see warring and battles, though tis not in battle where the danger lies, least it be the battle within. The greater journey though remains within yourself. It is the longest path of all which leads to understanding.

There is a road of darkness and awful peril, a path which shall take you to places beyond the knowledge of men. I see light too, a light to awaken the universe. Aye, I see both darkness and light, For where the dark is deepest there shines light the brighter.

When all is dark, when everything seems lost, when life itself seems turned to nothing then remember this; In the beginning the light that burned fairest was your love of colour and this love was a brightness that set the world aflame. It is here that your truth shall lie.'

After a moment she took a single ruby strung on a silver chain and hung it about his neck, kissed him softly once on each cheek. 'Take this and with it my blessing. *In the darkest places of your mind this shall bring light and with it the knowledge of the love that I bear you.'* She took also a simple brown worsted cloak and draped it about his shoulders. 'To keep you warm on cold nights and to protect you when arms and armour no longer serve.'

The Lord-of-Numbers came to stand beside her. He handed the Warrior a simple hawthorn staff. 'My Brother, our paths part here, perhaps for a time, perhaps for ever. You follow a path strange and fell to me, a way beyond the depths of my knowledge. I see but little of your trail and don't know how I can aid you. Take this. It's the simplest of things, cut from an ordinary tree and save for the strength of its own nature it's without power or magical virtue. Even so it is my gift to you. There may come a time when, as you venture down roads I cannot foresee, you may need a staff to lean on.'

*

𝐁oldly he rode, his mind aflame with the promise of the adventure before him. Proud was he also, his head held high, his face set towards a future of his own choosing. He scarce looked back as he moved away from the hall into the mists of autumn. A grey warrior upon a grey steed, setting out into a grey morning.

On his saddle hung a satchel with several days' journey-fare. Tied to his belt, the bag of jewels which his mother had given him and a second pouch of jingling coins. The gems were not magical things, but non-the-less of considerable value in the minds of men. 'You must take care with these. Keep them hidden from sight and only use them one at a time,' his mother had told him. 'You'll be among strangers and there are many who'd not hesitate to slit your throat for just one of these.'

On his back, as always these days, hung The Dwarf-Sword, its hilt bound in soft leather to protect it from the constant light drizzle.

The day lived up to all its promise of being damp and dour. Puddles were forming on the packed earth of the Coast Road. The North Western wind drove a chill salt spray to dampen him even more. By noon his spirits were beginning to flag.

That first night he managed to find a resting place, how-be-it one with little hope of comfort, in the rooms of a sailors' tavern, The sign, swinging above the paint black door read, THE BEACHED WHALE. PROPRIETOR; JOCCAM LUSTRIL. He'd espied this ramshackle building of salt-whitened clinker perched on high on a cliff-edge overlooking a small weather beaten bay where two crude fisher boats sat at anchor. Inside five sea-fishermen sat about a table playing some kind of game involving small stones and coloured circles of shell. They didn't appear to be enjoying the game. It was just habit. They didn't look up either when he entered.

The landlord, grotesquely fat and sweat shiny, draped in an ale and grease-stained apron turned a wry eye towards him. 'Yeth?' his lisp seeming cruel rather than comic.

'A meal and a room for the night?'

'Three copperth.'

He rummaged in the bag and found several of the small round coins, although he had little idea of their value. 'Here.' He placed the charge on the slop damp bar. 'Some ale too?' He placed a fourth coin down.

The inn-keep actually managed to smile. 'Right, young Thir. Thit youth here and I'll get the girl to fetch the food.'

'I've my horse to see to first.' He was beginning to actively dislike the man.

'There'th thtabling in the yard round the thide,' he was informed. There was no offer of help. He found his own way to the yard and tended to the horse in the crude, lean-to stable.

Once back inside, he settled at a table near the fire. The innkeeper had drawn a jug of dark ale, which he brought over with a rough metal mug. 'Food won't be long,' he informed the youth. 'Room'th through the door under the thtairth. It ain't much but it'll do you f'r one night.'

'Thanks.' He wasn't sure whether he meant it or not. The ale was heavy, almost sweet with an unfortunate aftertaste of fish. He'd not want too much more of that. Then the girl came with the food, a pale faced, skinny, black haired lass of some fourteen or fifteen years. She placed a tray before him and skittered back to the kitchen.

He ate, not really an appetising meal though there was enough to satisfy his hunger. Salted fish, green leaves and carrots swimming in gravy and hard black bread to mop up.

There seemed no reason to stay there long, sitting at his table supping ale in silence, ignored by and ignoring the fishermen still at their game. The day had been long and bed called.

With the grey light of dawn barely lighting the room he arose. The innkeeper served him a breakfast of goat's cheese and more of the black bread. Then he was out and on his way again.

This hard, stone gravelled road to Barril was an unwelcoming trail, cut for the most part through the face of bleak grey cliffs and washed almost constantly with salt spray. The second night offered even less welcome fare than the first. A cave, well hardly that really, provided a minimum of shelter. He had no fire and supper was but cold cheese and way-bread. He shivered away the hours of darkness. Dawn offered little more cheer nor did the next few days. Even when the rain died the wind seemed intent on keeping him cold. He didn't complain though, even in his thoughts. Such fare was to be endured as part of his new life but no one said that he had to enjoy it.

Barril, when he arrived there some five dreary days later, appeared a much more hospitable sight. The town lay in a deep cove where the river Bruun cut through to the ocean. Some fifty whitewashed and slate-roofed houses were gathered together about a narrow harbour. There was a market place and several bustling quayside hostelries.

He lingered for two days, hoping the weather might break. However, rather than clearing, the skies took on a sour, amber hue and offered a few flurries of snow to whiten the rooftops for an hour or two before being chased away by the sea breezes.

The carters having crossed the Santolin-Heights reported that the way was clear for now, although they could not say if it would remain so for long. With this information, he quickly gathered his belongings together and took to the trail once more. His fear that he might be caught, mid journey, by an early winter fall gave added haste to his departure. He took the coast road for another ten miles or so before turning south to follow the carters'-trail up through the tree lined foothills of the Santolin-Heights and beyond towards the distant wastes of Dollin.

Winter did little more than threaten. Even so, the Young-Warrior was left to his own companionship as he climbed up the winding road. The high winds sang to him here, a wordless song of the wilderness. The tree tops too danced their waltz of hours and seasons. When night fell over the narrow mountain valley he camped by the waters of a turbulent stream, slumbering to the chatter of its passage over the rocks.

A further two days found him high in the mountains. Nearer the snow line now, he wrapped his cloak about himself as protection from the bitter winds and rode bowed low over the grey's back.

Mid-afternoon the trail led out from the pinewoods onto a narrow, cultivated plateau. A man tending a line of sprout plants stood, stretched his back and waved when he heard the sound of the Young-Warrior's horse. He called out also but his words were lost in the thin mountain air. The Warrior returned the wave and smile. He saw too, with a thrill over the prospect of spending a dry night, the farmhouse waiting further down the trail. Nearness revealed this as something more than just a farmhouse though. The walls were thick and defended with battlements. The door was bound with riveted iron bands. The windows scarce more than arrow slits. This place was more like a small fortified castle.

As he approached the door opened and a young woman stepped beyond the threshold raising her hand in greeting. 'Good afternoon to you, Sir,' she bade him in a strangely accented voice, reaching forward to take the horse's bridle. 'Do be coming in and resting a while.' She peered at him from below the fringe of her long copper hair. ''Tis few be the travellers who do be abroad at this late time of the year I can tell 'e.' The hint of suspicion coloured her tone.

'Why thank you, Miss,' he responded with a smile. 'I'm not surprised there's few. It's a cold wind that's accompanied me these last few days. I'll be glad enough when I get to Sarum.'

The sound of the farmer's approaching footsteps turned him. His gaze met a hard, weather worn face, firm of feature, with eyes like coals. The smile of welcome drove away any thought of hostility. 'Welcome, welcome, young man. Be at peace.' He gestured to the door, 'Step inside. The day's turning chill and the night will like as not see a heavy frost. Come in and rest the night with us?'

'I thank you kindly, Sir,' he answered formally. 'I'm called Droven and am on my way from North Lands to join the Kings army at Sarum.' They needed an explanation and he felt that the name he'd chosen might serve.

'Then twice be you welcome, lad.' The farmer's eyebrow lifted a shade but his smile broadened. 'I'm Coll. Once I did serve as a sergeant in that same army.' He paused for an instant, and then laughed at himself. 'Though t'were long years ago now since I hefted my shield in the battle line.'

He moved towards the door. 'Come inside, lad. Mandelle, my only daughter and the light of my life,' he chuckled to himself, 'shall take your steed to the stables and assure that the stable lads do tend him well.'

'Go, girl,' he laughed playfully. 'Make sure that that Fallow gives 'n a good rub down and that the fire is stoked up. 's going to be a cold'n tonight.'

'Come then, lad, Come join my hearth and be welcome. There's bitter airs abroad and I dare say that you'll find a warm bed and a belly full of good home food better by far than the cold ground and journey fare.'

They entered the doorway and passed through the waiting hallway into a great chamber. The offered warmth was immediately apparent from the roaring hearth whose sudden heat brought a flush of redness to the Warrior's face. His eyes, quickly growing accustomed to the gloom of this great oak-beamed hall, lighted upon the array of weaponry, adorning the walls, pole arms, spears, and battle-axes. Hanging in pride of place over the massive hearth was a great sword and an emblazoned shield, The Anvil and Crown of Santolin and, above the crown, three golden rings. *Kings Guard!* He bowed his head, an instinctive gesture of respect.

'Come, warm yourself,' the farmer/sergeant continued. Clapping to summons a servant, 'Wine, mulled wine for our guest.'

The Warrior unfastened the Dwarf-Sword from his back and rested it against the hearthstone. He pulled one of the leather stools closer to the fire and sat himself as directed. Then he turned to thank the farmer, but his words were stilled by the troubled look upon the man's face and the hint of an unspoken question. The moment was broken in an instant as a serving girl entered carrying a jug of wine. For a few minutes nothing was said as the man set about warming the wine with a red-hot poker and then pouring the goblets to the brim.

'Be welcome again, Young Droven. That was the name? Be at home with us.'

He stood again raising his goblet to the farmer. 'Thank you, Sergeant Col. It is an honour to rest under your roof. I thank you for your welcome.' The words lapsed into an awkward silence as they both took seat before the fire, the Warrior reaching out towards the flames to warm his still chilled hands.

The girl Mandelle returned, bustling in with a laugh. 'Well, I do see that he's given you wine, Sir? That do be a wonder. He 'tain't be the most sociable of beings our Farmer Coll, warrior of the plough.' Her easy way dispelled the awkwardness as she teased her father. 'You has t' go and get 'n to bring the tools in from the fields, Father. If you don' tell 'n they'll not think on it, 'n' then'll be leave'n' them there. They'll just be set t' rustin' and then you'll be gettin' in a temper and we'll all have to suffer.'

He stood and followed to obey his daughter's words. 'No man is ruler of his own home. I don't care what they say.' He laughed playfully slapping her bottom. 'Forgive me a while.' Then he was gone.

'I do have my duties too, Sir. They shall not delay me long.' She paused, 'Don't mind him,' a second pause, 'and don't you be bothered by his tough and surly ways neither. He do know little of gentleness and gentle ways. He do keep himself apart now, least ways he has for the past few years since Mother died.' She brushed aside his look of sympathy. 'I do look after him now. We do well enough. The drovers on the trail and the folk who travel with the Pinexae caravans, which do pass through in the summer time, be companionship enough. We do have a good life here.'

She moved unexpectedly to his side and ducked to kiss him fleetingly on the cheek, a brief touch of warmth and waft of womanly scent. 'I do thank you for coming and for your concern. Tonight at least we do have your company to warm our home and our hearts an' to take his mind off other things,' and she moved off again, disappearing into the house.

He sat, nursing the wine before the crackling fire. The sounds of life, of movement elsewhere in the house, a laugh, voices, the clash of pottery and iron pots and bustling activity, seemed wonderfully normal, homely and safe. The fire blazed, driving away the chills of the last few days. In truth this was the first he'd felt warm since leaving Barril.

The crackling of the wood-borne flames, the light flickering on the rows arms, reminded him of the forge fires of Carrow and sent his mind drifting back to his time with the dwarves. After a while he took up the Dwarf-Sword, drawing it to lay the blade upon his lap where he could watch the flames dance over the runes engraved on the shining metal. He took an oilcloth from his satchel and began to burnish the strange blue surface, losing himself in the whorls and scrolls of light.

''Tis a noble blade, this sword of yours.' Coll had returned and now stood close behind him looking down at the youth's work. 'Aye noble indeed. Not a thing of man-craft either if my eyes be true and I doubt them not.' The suspicion of earlier had returned. 'Whence came you of such a thing?'

'Your eyes do not fail you or are partly true leastways, Coll. I forged it in the Halls-of-the-Carrow.'

'YOU FORGED IT!' Coll's cry of surprise echoed in the room, shaking the spears that hung there.

'Yes, it is so, I was taught the art for this sword alone,' he replied defensively and then as if to justify his claim he continued, 'The Dwarves-of-the-Carrow taught me how to craft the steel. Under the Master-Smith's hard, demanding eye and judgement I was helped to fashion the blade. Upon the silver anvil of the Carrow itself I forged the cutting edge. Nonetheless, though I cannot claim this to be of dwarven-craft, it does have their knowledge and wisdom in its power.'

'Who are you?' The words were no more than a whisper.

'What?'

'Who are you, Young-Warrior, that you come to my home as one unbidden with the first breath of winter in your hair? Who are you, with the name of a hero beyond the gates of history on your lips and a cloak of grey about your shoulders? Who are you, who bears a sword crafted against the traditions of a thousand dwarven years and who carries a shield on which the Earth-Stones themselves are pictured? Who are you, who can command the dwarves to teach you their secrets? Who are you to come into my home with a face from my own past, to awaken memories which I have so long hidden?'

The Warrior, dumbstruck by the passion of the other's voice, couldn't understand the cause of this reaction and didn't know how to answer or explain. 'I named myself Droven,' he started, 'Though that's not a given name. I am from The Hall-of-Hereth where names are not given. I am as you see me, a young warrior not yet tried nor tested.'

'Of Hereth I know some, although I've never been there.' It was as if a realisation was growing in him. 'Tell me, Young-Warrior. Who are your kin and how named are they?'

'If you have word of Hereth then perhaps you may have heard of us. My father was of noble blood and once served in the army of the King, The Baron-of-Hereth was he, a warrior and captain of renown among the Armies-of-the-West.'

Coll interrupted him with a shout of joy. 'Well upon my soul! Well indeed! I should have known it. I should have seen. For well I knew your father. Was he not my lord and my captain? Was he not my friend?' The old sergeant's voice cracked with emotion. 'Welcome, oh yes welcome indeed. Son of my friend? I should have recognised you from the start. You bear your father's face, or that of his youth leastways.'

He prattled on, scarce able to contain himself. 'Be at home here. No. My home is yours. The son of The Baron? Well I'll… I should have known you, if not by your looks then by your manner. Your mother speaks clearly through you.'

'My mother? You knew her also?'

'Knew her? Aye. Well I knew her indeed. Who, I ask you, who that has been smiled upon by The Lady-of-Flowers would be likely to forget? Besides was it not I myself who waited in the Deserts-of-Aran when My Lord your father went forth into the Lands-of-Mist to bring her back from the grasp of the Goblin Lord? Do I know her? Indeed I do. I was a companion of your father and his friend. I thought myself The Lady's friend also and treasure in my heart the memory of that which was her gift. Even now I hold most dear the rose that was ever her sign.' He shook his head from side to side trying to free his thoughts from the surprise that assailed him.

'Mandelle, Mandelle! Come! Come quick! This is no stranger, no not indeed. He's none other than the son of my Lord, my Captain of old.' He hesitated catching his breath. 'Come on, Mandelle!' he yelled even as she came through the door. 'Mandelle, this is The Warrior-of-Hereth! The son of the Baron-of-Hereth my lord and friend. Mandelle, meet the son of my friend.' He gestured with his hand presenting the youth with what almost amounted to being a bow.

Her smile was warmer than the fire, reaching into his heart and touching his very soul. 'Welcome, Warrior. Welcome, friend.' Without warning she threw her arms about his neck hugged herself tight against him so that he had to struggle to stop from falling from the stool. Coll laughed loudly beside them, aware of the Young-Warrior's quickly reddening face and the obvious cause for it.

'Mandelle, leave him be or you'll have him off the stool onto the floor.' Her father chuckled. 'That's if he don't pull you down there with him.' He guffawed again.

'Father!' the young woman gasped, startled with the sudden realisation of what she was doing. She leapt up covering her own embarrassment with an earthy laugh, 'I've got chores to finish, if you want to eat before midnight.' Then winking at the youth she scampered away again.

'Forgive her impetuousness, my friend,' Coll returned, 'She has often heard me talk of my time with your father and mother. I do tend to ramble on a bit about times gone by. And as we have no kin since… Since…' He paused as a cloud of greyness crossed his brow. 'Well, anyway, to her you are almost kin. Aye, to me too. You shall be as a son to me, well, if that's not too bold of me.'

'You are too kind,' the youth replied, 'You and your daughter both. You call me friend and Son, even more, and at our first meeting…' He paused steadying himself for what he knew he must say. 'I am honoured by your welcome, most honoured to meet one who was once a friend to my father.' The words tasted like bile on his tongue, yet what else could he say to this ancient warrior who had know the Baron during the time of his greatness.

Coll looked at him hearing the change in his tone. 'What ails, lad? What is it that troubles you?'

'I don't know how to tell it. I have sad news for you. The Baron, your friend is no more.' *Oh how easily the half-truth slips from my lips,* 'It's now some years that my mother has been alone.'

The Sergeant's face fell. 'Oh no. Oh no indeed. I hadn't heard. I didn't know. I haven't heard of him for several years, perhaps longer than that.' He tried to reach an understanding, to find an answer to the news. He failed. 'It seems that the world is ever turned dull with pain and suffering. Is there no one free of its touch? We thought back then, when the Goblin-Lord was defeated, that the world would turn to light. Yet it is not so.' Then he lapsed into the silence of his own thoughts and memories. He sat without awareness on a second stool beside the young warrior.

The youth for his part could find no words. *How could I tell him the truth of what happened? How could I face him with that? His memories are too precious for me to destroy them.* Although in truth it was more he who could not bear to face the memory. Instead he sat and gazed at the fire, losing himself in the hidden kingdom at its heart.

'Here, more wine.' Mandelle had returned to find them so. She refilled their goblets but did nothing to dispel the mood that was on them. She sensed the nature of what had transpired and, being well aware of her father's blacker moods, had the wisdom to know when best to leave things be.

Later as they sat at the great table, Coll with Mandelle and the Young-Warrior, Transin the farmer's foreman and some sixteen others joined them.

'It's the way of my hall,' Coll explained proudly. 'We're like one big family. Not master and servant. It's my wish that we come together at such times as this, even those who serve on us.' Though the two maids bustled back and forth to the kitchen bringing forth the food, when all was set on the table they too took their seats alongside the others.

Coll stood at the head of the table, a great jug of mead at his side. 'We have a guest with us this day.' He bowed and gestured to the Warrior. 'He has come unexpectedly out of the North and will rest with us this night. I name him My friend, The Warrior.' Several eyebrows lifted. 'He is the son of my lord, he who was my captain and my friend, The Baron-of-Hereth. Be welcome with us, my friend,' not giving the youth chance to reply, 'Right that's the formal bit over. Now let's get eating.' He lifted the heavy silver lid from a great platter and set to carving meat from a huge side of pork. Mandelle took the jug of mead and poured the goblets, which were passed about. In keeping with the farmer's wishes the meal was set to with gusto.

There was an easy banter about the table, friends and companions of long years who had learnt to live together in harmony. It was natural that Coll and Mandelle would monopolise the youth, wanting to know of Hereth, of his brother and sisters and of The Lady-of-Flowers herself.

Later still, when the company moved back to the hall, they sat about the great fire and Julie, a young servant girl, sang to them in a voice of silver and gold. Some of the others spoke with the youth wanting to know of his home and of his adventures.

At Coll's request he brought out the dwarf sword and showed it to the company. 'Look close, my friends,' Coll bade them, 'It's likely you'll never see its like again.' His voice grew heavy with awe, 'Dwarven or not there's mystery bound in its fabric and wonder in its nature.'

The company clamoured to hear him tell of the dwarves. 'We do see them,' one of the stable lads told him, trying to prove that they were not really so rustic. 'They do come through during the summertime on their way to the Cities. But even if they do stop they do be a quiet, queer and secret people and tell us little of themselves.'

'No, not secret,' the Young-Warrior explained. 'You misunderstand them. It's just that their nature is very different to that of men. The dwarves are of iron and stone. Their dwellings are carved of the earth and their forges are indeed their pride. Some, they say, have burned true for over three thousand years. You see it is in truth a terrible thing for a dwarf to travel abroad, for in doing so they leave their forges to grow cold and silent. It's like breaking a trust, a solemn duty. The same as you leaving the land un-tilled, letting your pastures becoming wild, giving up your duties and abandoning that which you hold most dear. They are silent because they are sad.

'In their halls the dwarves have a love of beauty which sings in their very beings. They have a sense of rightness and of order. I called them friends, and they me, even though in truth I was never more than a child to them.'

'Do tell us of the Dwarven-Holm,' Mandelle asked quietly from where she sat close to his side. 'Please?'

He nodded to them and smiled his agreement, and they grew silent, waiting for his words. 'The Dwarven-Holm-of-The-Carrow,' he began, 'Carved from the heart of the mountain in a past so distant that even the dwarves themselves have no knowledge of the time. It's a place of such wonder to defy description, of a beauty that stills your heart and takes your breath away. There are thousands of halls, each with its own nature... There is one formed from living crystal that sets the soul afire with its glory...'

'But don't it be dark there, dark and cold, deep in the heart of the mountain?'

'Dark? Why no,' he laughed, 'No, not dark at all. The Halls are filled with light. There are shafts of silver to trap the sun and bring its rays into the heart of their kingdom. There are the Singing-Halls where the dwarven bards live in a place of constant harmony.'

'Singing?' the songstress of earlier asked. 'I didn't know dwarves have song...'

He looked at her and saw the wonder in her eyes. 'Not singing as you might know, not as you sing. Yet they would cherish the beauty in your voice. No. Dwarven music is like no other.'

'Can you tell us? Show us?'

'Perhaps,' he offered after a moment's thought and took up the Dwarf-Sword once more, drawing it slowly from the scabbard as not to scare them. Then with the rim of his once again empty silver goblet he struck the side of the blade.

The room was suddenly filled with its chiming, the weapons on the walls reverberating in harmony with the purity of the sound. They sat in silence as the sound slowly died away.

'Ah,' the girl sighed as she wiped away the tears that welled unbidden to her eyes. 'I see.'

Much later when all but Julie, the Young-Warrior, Coll, Mandelle and two of the farm hands had taken themselves off to their beds, the girl sang again. It was a sad song this time, a tale from the Age-of-the-Stone, of Eloveen-Kings and their fall from light. She sang of the ride of the Neleven-fey, who came forth thorough the portal of the Ryngold in a time of terrible need and stood among the ranks of men in their struggle to defeat the Dark Lord, Elovsenal. She told also of their terrible sadness when, once the war was done, men turned from them and treated them as nothing.

Did I not come when first you called me?
Was I not true with ill before me?
Did we not fall, My kindred all?
My blood was spilt, did you not see?

Now shall I turn my face from living?
Shall I too, turn my mind from light?
Shall I turn my truths from Maddon's roots
To join forever the Ever-night?

Sad are my eyes, and dark from crying,
Sad is my soul and still from dying.
Too sad is my mind, bereft of trying.
I'll silence my tongue, lest I start lying.

I'll seek me to hide where the gulls go highest,
In Faerae-Nith where my heart is lightest.
I'll dwell there alone and remain in hiding
And tell no more of the love that is brightest

For a time the Young-Warrior found himself drawn back to his childhood and the Halls-of-Hereth where he sat again at his mother's knee to hear the telling of such tales.

'Well, Coll, I must thank you for your kindness and your fine hospitality for I fear the path to bed calls me. I must be abroad early in the morning, the journey lies still long before me. I hope to join the King's army before the snows fall to whiten the plains and make such a journey impossible.'

'Well spoken, young sir,' Coll congratulated him. 'It's yet a fair distance to the plain. Though I do tell you true, it shall be a fine welcome you'll find. Our king has need of willing warriors at this troubled time.'

'Troubled? I have had no word of this.'

'Aye, lad. Well a bit troubled anyway. There are dark clouds forming over the Lake-lands and if I'm not in error there shall be the sounds of battle ringing over the grasslands ere the seasons have full turned again.'

'Battle? War? What – have the goblins risen again?'

'Goblins? No not goblins or their like, for there's more than their kind of evil that walks abroad through the lands under sun and moon. No this is just as like the greed of men. Tales tell of a new lord among the Lake people and it be he who do threaten the peace and calls men to arms anew. 'Tis probably no great thing, yet evil must be cut off at its root or who knows what might fester and grow in its shade?'

Battle? War? And what then? Is the time of my testing come so soon?

He retired with the Sergeant's words still sounding through his thoughts. His sleep too was troubled by visions of what might be.

At dawn the Warrior was early abroad.

'Bye then, young sir.' Mandelle kissed him farewell. 'If you do be coming this way again then you must be sure that you do call in and see us.'

'Aye, lad,' Coll agreed. 'You'll ever find a welcome at these doors. So when your captain gives you leave, you come hot foot to us and treat these halls as your very own. And should you see your mother,' he continued almost bashfully, 'then tell her I do send my regards…'

Coll's people gathered about the doorway with the farmer and Mandelle to bid him their farewells also waving from the side of the road as they packed him off with a second satchel stuffed full of bread and cheese.

His mood was lighter now, all the brighter for the night's comfort and his thoughts grew cheerful and ready for the challenges ahead. He mused the miles with daydreams of becoming a great warrior, a hero amidst the armies of men, and filled his mind with thoughts of the adventures that might lay in store about the next bend in the trail. By nightfall the mountains closed in around him again and the hard earth had to serve as his bed once more.

Some two days after leaving Coll's gentle valley the winding trail climbed down from the final high ridge and the Young-Warrior found himself emerging from the wooded mountain passes onto a vast rolling plain. The snow still held off and, although the wind was chill, the riding was easy. Sarum, he reckoned, must still be some five or six days away however kind the road.

Thus it was with considerable surprise that, as dusk fell on the eve of his third day out on the plain, he noticed the night ahead lit with the fires of a vast encampment.

The Army! He told himself realising it could be none other than the King's Army, his destination and his future. All at once he felt an unwelcome twinge of doubt about the life that lay in wait such a little way ahead. He rode into the night hoping to cover the distance. However when tiredness began to weigh down his eyes the fires ahead seemed little closer than when he had first seen them. He camped on the grass, wrapping himself in his cloak having to be content for yet another night with the dreams of what might yet be.

*

Morning reached out with an icy grasp of silence to wrench him from slumber. Frozen fingers of fear clawed at his heart. He leapt to his feet drawing the dwarf sword, ready to face whatever danger threatened. There was none. Yet still he was filled with the certain knowledge that everything was wrong. His heart pounded in his breast. His senses reeled. Muscle and sinew were strung into bands of iron as he crouched in the grass ready to face whatever might come. There was still nothing, nothing save the awesome silence that had dragged him into wakefulness. No sound touched his ears, not a single trill of birdsong, not the whisper of wind through an outstretched wing, nothing. To his ears the silence was louder than the clarion call of Hell and bore down on him in a wave of terrible emptiness.

What's wrong? What's happening? Realisation. *It's the Army! The King's Army! Something is happening! Something terrible is going to happen! I must go! I must…*

With trembling hands he saddled and bridled the horse, slung his bedroll over the pommel and strapped the sheathed sword across his back. He mounted. Then, with a kick of heels, the world erupted into a maelstrom of rushing wind and pounding hooves. In an ever growing, roaring, crashing fury he drove the horse towards where the terrible doom loomed up in his mind.

He saw, without comprehension, the ranks of men drawn up on the plain, spearmen at the centre, bowmen in a single line behind them, a few mounted knights to the right. Standards hung limp from their staves. Everything was motionless, waiting. Here and there a spearman coughed to clear the night-time dryness from his throat. A horse stirred with nervous impatience. A sergeant's gruff voice. 'Steady, lads. Steady!' The sound was lost somewhere in the stillness of the morning.

They're waiting! Waiting... Why?... Why don't they do something? Still the rattle of hoof beats rushed him in headlong panic towards them. Heads turned, faces in the drawn ranks of men. He heard the shout, the barked order, but it meant nothing to him. He spurred himself ever onwards every instant closing the gap. Two riders wheeled from their company. They came towards him, to intercept his headlong charge.

'Hold there!' Words without meaning, 'What's the haste?' A gruff campaign hardened voice. 'HOLD!'

He slowed his horse as he neared them. His mind was a tar-pit, thoughts clogged and refused to form. He looked at them, armour, shields, spears but saw nothing, understood nothing. 'What's happening?' Words, his words but his mind had even to grapple with these.

'Don't worry, lad,' the trooper responded to the youth of this strange newcomer. 'I think it's going to be all right.'

'All right?' *All Right?... All right... All right?* It's not all right. It's all wrong! His head pounded. Pain grasped at his mind like a claw behind his eyes.

'No battle.' *A half-wit*, the soldier surmised. 'The Captains are in parley, lad, talking. They think there might be a way to avoid fighting. It's going to be all right, peace!'

Battle, Peace? 'NO!' he shouted in mounting fear over the wrongness of it all. 'It's wrong! It's all wrong!' He lashed his spurs into the horse driving it once more into the crashing headlong flight, unaware even that the others had turned and were chasing after him.

The passion of his voice shook them to the core. As they drew closer their eyes met. The two drew apart one to either side of the rushing horse. 'Wrong? What do you mean wrong? Do you want a bloody battle? Do you want people to die? Be bloody grateful that's what I say.'

He could see clearly now. The two armies were drawn up some fifty paces apart. In the space between, a small group of men were gathered together. His head was a cauldron of pain. He pressed a hand to his temple trying to fight it, to force his mind to work. The ranks seemed to part as he thundered through their midst allowing him passage, spearmen in bright tunics and steel helmets, long shields resting on the ground.

There was a sudden cry of joy, a cheer welling up from the ranks. A bright golden standard was raised. Swords and spears were beaten on the shields. Men clapped each other on their shoulders. There was to be no letting of blood, no carnage would rule this day.

He drew the horse to a standstill looking frantically about. The terrible sense of wrong bore down on him. 'It's wrong!' he shouted amidst the clamour. 'NO! It's all wrong!'

'Look, you crazy bloody sod. That's the royal standard. They've agreed a peace. Look, you stupid bastard! Can't you see? Don't you understand? It's all over. There ain't going to be a battle! The bloody war is over! OVER!'

Cold fingers of dread grappled with his heart and denied the words and the sights that filled his eyes. He gazed about in confusion seeking something, anything of substance on which to hang this sense of doom. There was nothing, nothing at all.

He turned to face the King's army. Red, red and silver, and the other, black and grey. *Red and silver, The Crown and Anvil, The King and those beside him must be his captains. Grey? Who are these?* Their faces were turned from him yet still the sense of wrong grew.

'WAIT!' Time slowed. Heads turned, turned to face him, to see who came so suddenly to disturb their meeting. Eyes fixed upon him. Cold eyes, grey eyes, eyes like ice that reached out to pierce his soul. Then came the recognition, the terrible awful truth, bursting in his mind, quickening his being, driving away the confusion in an unstoppable wave of fear.

'NO!' His terrible cry of anguish rang out over the field stilling the shouts and laughter. The moment was silent.

'Oh Yes, My Boy! OH Yes indeed!' The Ice-eyed Lord turned to him. A cold venomous laugh dripping from his tongue. 'Come to play with the soldiers have we?' The grey eyes turned back to the King. 'Well, well, just look who's come to join us? Why if it's not Sir Prism, The Rainbow-Warrior?' The splinters of his ridicule cut through the Young-Warrior's mind as broken glass.

'NO!' he cried out again wrenching the Dwarf-Sword from where it hung at his back.

The Grey-Baron moved quick as a striking snake, his blackened blade stabbing for the youth's heart with a cry of hate. Blade met on blade. The lesser blackness shattered in an explosion of cinders. The chiming of the dwarven steel sounded over the armies, ringing on sword and shield, breastplate and helm. Ringing. As a bell in the belfry of some unearthly cathedral.

The illusion shattered.

Now all at once the full truth of the deception was revealed. 'GOBLINS!' came the hated cry of the suddenly maddened ranks of men.

'Kill!' echoed the drooling jeers of the foul grey creatures facing them.

Order was lost, command no more. No shield wall formed. No sergeant stood to rally his men. No orders were shouted over the ranks of soldiers. There was just a terrible charge of screaming, shouting, cursing, hate-driven foes. Faces dissolved into nightmare masks as they ran to the slaughter. Blades cut the air, crashed on blade, on shield, on helm, on flesh, an awful, horrid symphony of slaughter. In the midst of all the clamour Death won the day.

Barely two yards before him man and goblin grappled in a struggle of death. The creature's axe rose high in the air descended almost slowly. A shield was raised, just in time, the flat crack of metal on wood lost amongst all the other sounds of war. Then came the counter thrust, a slicing blade ripping into the creature's bowels. Another spear, already dark with blood impaled the man from behind sending him sprawling upon his victim. They lay there, both of them. Their death cries merged into a single discordant scream.

All about the warrior the battle flowed, a melee of struggling, swearing and screaming figures. Bodies were falling, blood spilling bright and dreadful in the clear morning air. The grass became a quagmire of blood and gore, the remnants of life soaking into the earth. In this domain of horror the Lords of Carnage ruled. All planning was lost, all order obsolete, all meaning gone. Here only the call of death was heard, the lust for blood sated.

A creature rose before him spitting hatred, lunging with a trident-spear to impale his body. He parried the attack, shattering the weapon into nothingness, sending the screaming creature grovelling to its knees. He withheld the blow. Another pounced on him from behind, sending him sprawling from the saddle into the mud, the blood and the gore. He was on his feet in a bound, turning as it attacked anew. He shattered its scimitar, but rather than slide the sword into the soft grey flesh he thrust his shield into its grotesque face driving it away. *I WILL NOT KILL!*

He met another, turned them aside also, passing through the madness, as one possessed. He was invincible. The Dwarf-Sword became a whirling halo of light about him, shattering any weapon that came close. They tried to face him, to bring him down by weight of numbers but they could not contend with the fury of his wrath. In the end he stood alone in the mist of the conflagration.

The disturbance of this perplexing, bloodless struggle seemed to draw all eyes. For a moment the battlefield grew still, but only for a moment. Nonetheless, it was enough to give the King a chance to gather a band of men about himself in a tight shielded circle. Others joined them, men at arms, veterans of other battles. Oh how dreadful well did they know their trade of slaughter. For now at last the shield wall began to form, opening out the circle into a living barrier of steel. Once formed it began to move. Onwards they came, step by bloody step, slowly, grimly, soulless in their determination. The wide silver blades of their spears thrust, turning black with goblin blood, then thrust and thrust again. The wall moved forwards another step, over the carnage of their work. More men gathered to the line, more spears, more thrusts, more deaths.

It was then, to make everything a thousand times worse, that the Young-Warrior heard it. Through the din of the battle, over the cries of the dying, the screams of the wounded, the curses of the living, came the sound of laughter, brittle, cold and bitter.

It laughs at me! It laughs! Am I nothing more than a plaything for its own amusement? It brought me here, to this, drew me here like a toy dangling on a piece of string. It shaped me with its vileness, Robbed me of what I was to create me in its own image Twisted me to its own design, little more than a broken part in its own twisted plan! NO! NO! 'NO!' His voice cried out into the heart of the battle.

His eyes were opened at last, opened to all the terrible, mind-shattering sights that surrounded him. He watched, helpless and motionless, as the wall of shields smashed through the heart of the goblin horde cutting a swathe of death amongst the now panic stricken creatures.

Far from the carnage the terrible, grey Warrior-of-the-Mists gathered to itself a cadre of huge goblin warriors and made his way from the field. Everywhere else the senseless killing continued until not a single one of the creatures remained alive. Even then the men continued to hack at their twisted remains.

What was war anyway, but a maelstrom of turning, burning, churning hate? Hate and horror, glory laid low, choking on its own filth, a mud-stained terror, bankrupt pride, pointless valour, just a hate-driven lust of destruction, desolation and death. And everywhere was the fear, hopeless, mindless, reason-less, endless fear. There was no honour, no chivalry, no mercy, just slaughter and always the hate.

A chill grey mist clung to the Warrior's cloak with vengeful fingers of moisture. The decaying sweetness of the battlefield stench choked his senses and confused his mind with images of purgatory as he tried to find meaning within the dismay which assailed his soul.

Nearby a thing, once of mortal flesh, cried out its final, friendless, lonesome moan. Another, harsher voice mocked that same demise with a crude burst of brittle laughter. Further off they were stripping the dead, a last thoughtless desecration of life ere the corpses were cast into the hastily dug charnel-pit. Nothing was sacred in this field of death, not even the grasping claws of the gods of war. Nothing!

He began to retch, a sudden unreal act, remote and impersonal. He saw himself, as from a distance or in a dream, crawling on all fours, struggling like an injured insect, to escape the horror of these grotesque heaps of once living flesh. His body recoiled in revulsion from the icy touch of hands that even in death reached out to grasp a handful of life.

His mind recoiled too, snapped back from the paths of memory, back to the stench and the horror that surrounded him. This was never how it was supposed to be, not this confusion, this empty confusion, this meaningless storm of confusion. Where was the reason? Where was the sense? Where was the glory, the splendour, and the pride? This was never right! It was all so UGLY!

He struggled to his feet once again, resting upon the Dwarf-Sword as were it no more than a staff. Now the Young-Warrior's eyes moved over the scene surrounding him and his spirit grew cold as he saw what had become.

THIS IS NEVER RIGHT! Anger began to grow within him. *This path was never meant for me!* The anger grew into a fury, welled up inside his breast threatening to engulf him, anger from the stupidity of this senseless carnage, anger at the pointless waste of life, anger of a thousand different hurts, anger over the words of the Baron (The Warrior-of-the Mists), anger at the evil that dripped from its terrible venomous tongue, anger from his sense of failure, anger at the cold emptiness of his existence. Anger! a terrible, unstoppable anger, driven by the thoughtlessness by which so much life and hope, so much beauty and promise could be casually desecrated and cast into ugliness.

Deep within his centre a single spark ignited. His anger fanned this into a flame, his fury into a roaring furnace, his rage into a terrible conflagration of power. His hands were raised before him, reaching out to ward off the terrible sights about him. The power welled within him, filling him, boiling, burning, bursting from him as a tumult of energy.

RED
Blood red...
RED

Overwhelming red...
RED
Bursting red...
RED
Turning grass and earth...
RED
Arms and armour...
RED
Living and dead...
RED
Victor and vanquished...
RED
The burning sky...
RED
Bloody Red!

He looked down at himself, at the shield still hanging on its strap with its emblem of the Earth-stones he'd once borne with pride now stained with dirt and gore. He lifted it breaking the cord with a sudden wrench before casting it high over the mounds of lifeless flesh. He walked slowly over to where his horse stood, reins dangling in the mud. There had never been a bond between him and the creature. He took his pack and the hawthorn staff from its back. Then unloosened the saddle, removed the bridle and bit, freeing the creature to do as it may. He stripped off his cloak of grey, his steel helm, his coat of dwarven-mail and he left them discarded in the mud. He looked to the Dwarf-Sword, still in his hand... *It was ever true, true to its nature and to what I might have been. This at least has not betrayed me.* He sheathed the blade and strung it over his back. From his pack he took the brown worsted cloak and threw it about his shoulders. Finally he picked up the hawthorn staff in his trembling fingers, turned his back on the red nightmare that his life had become and walked mindlessly away into the wilderness.

> If we live in fear of open air
> of freedom in the skies,
> fear the light
> the burning light,
> fear of an Iccarus fall,
> How then the dragonfly
> who climbs to dance on the wind?
>
> (From: The song of the Sunset-Sands)

Chapter Three – The Pilgrim

THERE CAME A time of emptiness, of blankness without awareness or thought, existence with neither meaning nor memory. Days wound into nights, nights into days, circles of light and dark turning endlessly without triggering thought of passing time. Snow slowed his passage but he was not cold or troubled by its white silence. He walked through a forest – tall, majestic, sheltering trees reaching far above him. He was lost without knowledge of being so. His only reality was the terrible confusion filling his mind.

The Keepers-of-the-Forest found him wandering through their domain. Silent were they and secret in their ways. They knew him for what he was. The bright colours of his childhood were a truth to them, cherished in their memories. They watched over his wandering, tended to his needs, unseen. He would eat when hungry, unaware from whence the food had come. He would sleep when tired and wake beneath a blanket of leaves. He travelled far through the woodlands but never knew. In truth his mind made its own journey and existed in its own tormented space.

When the other things, the dark malevolent things hunting him through the land hoping to ensnare him and to turn his ways into a future of their design, found his trail the Keepers-of-the-Forests knew of it. Thus when these grey and soulless beings began to track him their footsteps led them into traps, their trails to dead-ends, for them permanently. For the 'Little-ones' hold such creatures as abhorrent and will not bide them to exist in their keepage. The Young-Man had no knowledge of these matters though.

A wild running river fled beside him, mountain born, its touch shocking him back into awareness for an instant with an icy reminder of snow-capped peeks. There was a time of heat too, when the trees no longer shaded him. He lay to sleep hidden in a land of tall wind-blown grasses, followed a path, a trail of some kind, where his feet found easier passage through this rolling land of waving stems. *Lodor.* It was awareness devoid of interest, simply the recognition of a fact, *Lodor, where the wild horses run.*

Sometime, days, weeks or even longer had passed. The path began to lead him up a steep sided down. Without intention he followed the trail's stark white slash up the grassy slope. *Chalk, as are the downs over Hereth.*

He grew tired, for the climb through the heat of a late spring afternoon seemed interminable. Soon the climb became a struggle of wills, a grim war against the earth, which ever tried to thwart him in his attempt to reach the skies.

So it was, as the sun began to dip its head beyond the far-off horizon, he finally breasted the brow to face the seven giant standing-stones thereon. It was an ancient circle, glistening fuchsia in the sunset's final rays, placed there beyond the mists of time or memory by the same craftsmen who had set the stones over Hereth. He felt an inner familiarity, a kinship, a sense of timeless peace and eternal waiting and walked slowly, as if passing from dream to reality, between two of the giant megaliths. He brushed his hand against their surface in an unconscious gesture of familiarity as he moved to stand at the centre of the circle, *Circles as of time,* where he was caught in the light of the setting sun. The rays sparkled on the mica hidden in the rock, danced from stone to stone, from pillar to portal, from rock to eye, awakening a mystical half-life of whirling spinning light. He felt the touch of mystery within his spirit and his mind slipped into that timeless place the ancient builders knew so well.

In the forest is a shadow,
on the meadows, a cloud.
On the high downs we wait for the coming of chaos.
We who have waited ten thousand years
Now guard over his awakening

He sits on the lawn of fine grass, resting his back against the greatest of the stones.

From the earth he shall take his beginning.
From the waters he shall take his power.
From the fires he shall take his strength.
From the air he shall take his love of life.
From the silence he shall take his words.
From the light he shall take his vision.
From the mystery he shall take his knowledge.

But how can he know?	It is his nature.
But he knows not his nature.	He can feel himself.
But he knows not what he feels.	He can find himself.
But he knows not where he is.	His acts will show himself
But he knows not what he is	He shall love himself.
But he knows not how to love.	He shall speak of himself.
But he knows not the words.	He shall see himself.

> But he knows not what he seeks.
> Ah, the pilgrim shall surely know.
>
> For he is The Pilgrim.

They name me Pilgrim, Pilgrim of what? A seeker, Seeking what? Doing what? He knows not what he seeks. What must I seek? He struggles to find an answer in the words but their mystery eludes him, memory drifting like the tendrils of a dream. *Pilgrim? I'm no longer a warrior, that's for sure, but Pilgrim?* Thoughts tumble through his mind, random questions, images, ideas and memories. *Who am I anyway? What am I?* Somewhere, deep within the centre of his being he finds the echo of a name. A resonance formed of his own beginning awakens as, without conscious intent, he speaks the thought aloud.

'I shall be the *Wizard of Rainbows*.'

*W*ords and meanings come spinning through time. In one instant he recalls the brilliant colours of his childhood and his soul cries out into the void of their passing. *They are gone! Lost. I threw them away. For what? Nothing. I have nothing left.* His spirit hovers at the brink of despair. *Rainbows? Colour? What do I know of these? Nothing! I cast aside any echo of such things. Now I have nothing! But I did know. Once I did! I really did!* Gradually a realisation trickles through his thoughts, the awakening of an idea. He begins to see a possibility, a path reaching out as it were into the future.

In the stillness of his emptiness he chooses and, by so choosing, this path becomes his own. Now, having chosen, he voices the words like a challenge to fate.

'I will be the *Wizard of Rainbows*!'

*W*ords form and tumble once again through the tunnels of time. 'Now I see it. I'll do as they say. Yes, this will be my way. I will become a pilgrim, a pilgrim of truth, a seeker of knowledge. I'll take the Pilgrim's Road to seek the Rainbow. I'll discover the truths of its beauty, the realities of its wonder, the secret meanings of its nature. I'll seek myself in the glory of its colours.'

Then he slept, watched over by the stones, a sleep untroubled by dream or vision.

> There's a new beginning
> and a new ending,
> A new singing
> O'er the plain.

The darkened sky lightened, passing through a period of grey to a brighter, lighter blue. Seven tall stones stood shimmering with the sun's light touch, long before the grasslands far below knew of the day's awakening. The young man who lay in the shelter of one massive monolith stretched and yawned. Rubbing the sleep from his eyes he sat up and began to look about. His mind was alert, bright as the morning, for the first time since... *since?* The question didn't trouble the calmness that awoke with him. The stones as always watched in stillness. He knew their truth as well as he remembered the mystery of the previous evening. The wonder remained with him as real and free as the resolve he'd reached in the heart of the night.

Yes indeed, I shall be a pilgrim and take the pilgrim's path and I'll follow that way wherever leads me. As they named me, so shall I be, the Pilgrim, a seeker of truth. I'll search for the mystery of the rainbow. I'll ask my questions of its nature. Perhaps I'll find myself in its colours.

For a short while he struggled to draw aside the veil hiding the past days, weeks or even months from his thoughts, to regain the memories of his journey to this place. He wondered just how long he'd wandered, mindless and thoughtless, since that terrible battle upon the Plain-of-Sarum. However the knowledge of that time was but a fog slipping beyond his grasp before he even reached for it. He let it lie.

There seemed little need for haste. The clear morning was fresh and alive. The song of the sand marten trilled through the air to match the Young-Man's mood and the gentlest of breezes ruffled the grass and his hair as he searched for wild mushrooms amongst the rippling stems.

It took little to satisfy him So he sat, leaning against one of the stones, and opened his satchel for the extras. In the realisation of the journey ahead he began to wonder what provisions he had for whatever lay ahead and so took stock.

He wore leather pants, held up with a stout belt on which hung a skinning knife. On his back, a once white cotton shirt. He wore hard, warrior's sandals, robust and showing little sign of wear. Of course he still had his brown worsted cloak and the hawthorn staff that lay close to his side.

On the grass was a canteen of water, half full. He found a tinderbox in one of his pockets, nothing fancy, just a tool fit for its task. In addition to the mushrooms he'd just put there, the satchel contained a small iron cooling pot and a pack of way-bread wrapped in oil-cloth. *Where has that come from?* He had no idea.

There was a small bag of coins too, silver and bronze he noted, as they tumbled into his hand. He didn't know their value at all. In a second bag were several jewels, glistening, sparkling gems that reminded him of his mother and home. Instinctively he reached for the ruby hanging about his neck, drawing comfort from its familiarity. *It's not much*, he told himself, *not much but it will do for a start.*

Then there was the Dwarf-Sword. He drew the blade once more awakening the memory of its making, the wonder of its blade and the events that had led to its crafting. He traced the runes with a fingertip, read again the words of his oath. *It alters nothing. Be I Warrior or Pilgrim, or even Wizard, My word remains. It is my enemy, forever.* But what to do with such a weapon? Swords, however true, are hardly the accoutrement of a pilgrim. *A pilgrim with a sword, whatever for? Shall I seek to cut the knowledge from the heart of the rainbow? I think not.*

> **We shall take care of it.**
> **We shall hold it until your need returns.**
> **We shall be the guardians of the blade.**

Thus, in trust, and he laid the sword upon the stone at the centre of the circle. *It shall be safe?*

It shall.
Until you come again
We shall guard it for you.

He stepped away to stand outside of the circle of stones. Light caught upon mica, shimmering sparkles of light, brilliant specks of burning colour, ever brighter, turning brighter, whirling brighter and brighter until it became so dazzling that he could look no more and covered his eyes with his hand.

The sword was gone, taken into safety though he knew not how or whence. Peace filled his heart though and he knew he was free to go. He bowed to the stones, each in turn. He understood neither their wonder nor the touch of their hand upon his life. Yet he thanked them and deep in his heart he knew they were good.

Unencumbered by either his past or, as yet, his future, he stood alone on the high down. The strengthening wind set his cloak billowing about him. At that moment, had there been anyone to see, he would have appeared the very essence of mystery, but no one saw. Well, none but the eagle soaring the high thermals. And, what do eagles know anyway?

Perhaps the Pilgrim, if that's who he now was, felt a moment's disquiet about where his feet had brought him during his time of mindless travelling. The grasslands far below, he realised, were without doubt those of the savannah of Lodor but that told him little. Lodor's vast grass plain formed a belt across half the Lands of the West.

He looked about hoping to see a sign which might give him a better idea. He stood at the eastern extent of a great crescent of down-land. In every other direction was the endless grass. Far, far to the east, at the very edge of his vision, lay a dark line of forest. Ah but which forest? To the north, nothing but grass. To the south, a bank of cloud crowning what could only be the jagged peeks of mountains, Bronden, Elscri? So that appeared to be his choice, to go eastwards, towards the forest, or south towards the mountains?

It mattered little. In the end he went south. There was no real reason for the choice save that the slope was gentler that way and his passage the easier for it.

There followed a strange, almost restful, period for the Pilgrim. He felt no need for haste as yet. Nor for that matter did he feel any real sense of purpose. He simply moved onwards. There was scant sign of any real path to follow. Trails wandered here and there, leading his feet this way and that. He tended to turn south or east had he the choice but it was of little importance to him.

He hungered now also, for food was scarce and he was reluctant to use up the few supplies he carried. Wild strawberries grew in abundance here, but they were small and although sweet did little to ease the pangs in his stomach. He found other berries too, white and sharp to the tongue. Those he chose to leave.

He heard the neighing of the wild horses, the sound of their passing too, but he did no more than glimpse their shadows and find the traces of their passing.

One afternoon he was lucky enough to find a pheasant's nest with six eggs. He cleared an area of grass and built a fire that he might feast upon his find. Another time he chanced upon a hive of bees but lacked either the skill or the bravery to avail himself of their treasures.

Gradually he moved further southwards and found himself in a land where the grass grew tall, at times even higher than he. His path became confused midst the waving stems, his sense of direction also. However, he quickly realised that there was benefit in being so hid. If he took enough care and trod with stealth he would chance upon the creatures of the grassland too, catching them by surprise. Once or twice he had a stone in hand. He dined on rabbit most days.

It was during one of these creeping hunts that he met the auric. He'd heard of them of course. What young boy hadn't dreamed of seeking his fortune among the Auric-Hunters. But the auric herds run on the Great Plains, far east, beyond the Mountains-of-the-Divide. The last thing he might have expected was the find one here.

Yet here it was, standing on the path before him. Its head was lowered and its great crescent horns pointing at his heart. He stopped too, stood completely motionless as their eyes locked. It was stunning, huge, weighing more than any farmstead bull. Its fore-shoulder was higher than he, yet it possessed all the grace of a deer or antelope. Its coat was a shining wonder of short golden hair, so smooth it might have been groomed. He wasn't afraid, even though the beast could kill him without a thought. He didn't even consider the danger. He felt safe, as if he knew that it would not charge. What he really wanted to do was to walk up and stroke its coat. He didn't move.

After four or five minutes it stirred, swung its head from side to side as if disbelieving what it saw, then turned and strolled slowly off into the grass.

It was gone and he was left wondering if it had been there at all. *I wonder what the great herds must be like?* The thought of thousands of these magnificent creatures moving in a great swath over the plain was beyond his imagination. Perhaps one day he would see them. Then came the thought of the Auric-hunters. *How could anyone hunt such beautiful creatures, let alone profit from their slaughter?*

Day merged into day with little to separate one from another. When the rain fell he wrapped himself in the brown worsted cloak. When his feet tired he lent on his hawthorn staff. From both he found the welcome memory of home.

The land was gradually changing, becoming more rugged and somehow wilder. Breasting a hill he realised he was finally drawing closer to the mountains. Their deep blue-green pine-covered slopes and stark craggy peeks clawing at the skies. There were wooded copses, set amongst the grasslands and soon he carried a bow of hazel-wood and arrows tipped with rabbit-bone heads.

The freedom of the wilds, the plentiful wildlife and the gentleness of the climate suggested an idyllic passage through this unknown land. However, instead of ease, the Pilgrim felt a growing disquiet, an inner feeling that all was not as it should be. Then he found the slaughtered horse, one of the Sevre, the wild breed that roam the Lodor plains. It had been hacked to pieces, the remnant left to rot in the open. Someone had built a fire, careless and thoughtless against the bowl of a giant oak tree, the scars of the burning a savage insult to nature's wonder. A closer look uncovered a scattering of bones, gnawed and split.

Goblins! The thought was unbidden and unwelcome. With it came the sudden realisation of just where his feet had brought him, *Naril*, the goblin kingdom of old. Fear touched his heart then and lent a caution to his movements.

That night he slept hidden beneath a thicket, knowing that come morning he must plan what to do.

*

First light drew him aching and un-rested from the land of dreams. He'd not slept well at all, jumping at the slightest sound. Although in truth there'd been little to hear but the natural rumours of the wilderness. The canyons of his imagination managed to turn these into more troublesome omens.

Looking upward into the dawn sky from where he lay he noted the pinprick light of the last fading star. The moon had long since gone to find its rest. That first hint of morning spoke the promise of a nice day ahead, the clear blue sky set with one or two small white clouds. The sun would be warm and welcome. He began to think of food; perhaps he might find a use for his newly made bow and arrows.

A sudden, single, jingling laugh rang out through the clear morning air snapping his nerves in shock and causing a wild flurry of panicking songbird wings about the grove. He pushed himself to a sitting position and peered out from his hiding place wondering what the disturbance might mean.

Then he saw her. Standing alone, bathed by the first touch of sunlight at the edge of the clearing, was a girl of the woodland kin, an elfling, fairy kind. She stepped into the open, her deep green cloak flowing in the wake of her movement, her elfin face framed in the halo of cascading, sun burnished hair.

Apparently unaware of her hidden watcher, she turned slowly where she stood. Her face lifted skywards and once again the peel of her laughter thrilled through the grove. Then she moved, a simple turn of wrist, a single controlled step. Each gesture lived with a gentle flowing grace, both strange and magical. A dance she wove, a mysterious elfin-ballet, which transfixed him as if by a spell, an enchanted reel of woodland, a tale of wildness and freedom. Her steps were slow at first, moving to the rhythm of some unheard beat. Then, gradually, they grew faster and wilder, free, vivid and alive, her feet danced with effortless skill upon the dew sparkled grass, waking the day in sprays of silver glistening mist.

Her motions spoke of excitement and the forces of existence, of the whisperings of the forests and the secrets of the winds, of the Well-Springs-of-the-Earth and the Circles-of-Time. Faster and faster she whirled in the bright early sunlight until her form became a dazzling blur of light and shadow, an image of the very fires of life and she shone brightly with the essence of freedom.

Come dance with me,
through the enchanted forests of The Elswood.
'neath the light,
the silven light of Chelimbrelle,
the Elven star.
I shall dance you a dance of passion
a reel of awakening.
Of the green-wood
of the delight of freedom

Come dance with me,
through the shaded avenues.
Be not concerned,
though your ways are not my ways
we shall come to no harm
from the life within us.

Come dance with me,
am I not lovely?
I shall dance you a dance you will remember
even to the endings of your being

Come dance with me
Let me feel your life,
let me touch your living,
Let me see the freedom awaken in your heart.

She was still, suddenly so, her crystal green elfin gaze fastened on his own. A bright smile of greeting brought a new light to her face. 'Welcome, Pilgrim.' Her voice chimed with strangely accented sounds and the deep pools of her emerald fairy eyes glimmered with gentle, inoffensive amusement. She bowed low before him.

She knows me. She knew I watched. She's here for me, danced for me. He felt exposed, uncovered as if caught spying on some secret, sacred and half-forbidden thing, guilty as were his every thought revealed to her. 'Who are you?' Almost choking his clumsy enquiry, he clambered to his feet and stood before her. His every awareness was quite lost in the wonder of her delicate beauty and the mystery of the moment. She was tiny, her head barely reaching his shoulder.

'There are many paths, many journeys in this world, Young-Pilgrim, many trails stealing their secret ways through this land of wonder,' laughing chimes of happiness. 'Perhaps we might take such ways, my Pilgrim, you and I. Perhaps we shall go together, perhaps apart. Who knows? We meet, mayhap by design or maybe by chance. Who can tell? Once met, what then? Might we travel together through these perilous lands for a while? Will you walk with me? Will you follow my footsteps through this oh so troubled domain? Will you share your own road and your own awakening with me? Shall we wander through the mysteries of our dreams together? Will you dance with me, my Pilgrim? Will you dance with me in the clear daylight?'

'I don't understand!' And oh how he wanted to understand her. Instead confusion filled him, burned almost as a pain in his breast. 'What do you mean my own way? Who are you? What do you want of me? I don't know.'

She smiled again, like the sun breaking free of a cloud and his confusion vanished in the wonder of her. 'Of course you know.' She laughed again, magical, free. 'As I said, my Pilgrim-of-the-Wilderness, there are many paths and many journeys, many destinations planned and unplanned both within your mind and without. You may fly on the winds of change to the ends of the earth and not find that which you seek, though it were before your eyes every instant of the way. You may sit, still as the stones, take root as they in the centre of the Earth-spring for the rest of your existence and yet never once touch upon the meanings of your own reality.'

'You know what I seek?' *She does, I know she does!*

'You may pass through the wonders of the universe and never even see the simple beauty at your feet. You may venture unknowing through this forest of lies and not even know you touch the pillars of the Gates-of-Hell.' She laughed, seemingly at herself and the brightness of her beauty gave lie to the chill warnings in her words.

'Come dance with me,' stepping towards him she reached out her hand. 'through the woodlands of daylight. Come dance my dance through the mysteries of the forests. For there are indeed mysteries 'neath the bows, lessons in the tree tops.' She took his hand urging him onward.

'Wait. Oh please wait,' He was all but lost to her now. 'You might at least tell me where we are going, what it is that we are to see.'

'Haven't you seen enough of me already, my Young-hidden-Pilgrim?' She dropped her eyelids demurely for an instant before shimmering anew in the promise of her laughter. 'Did you not see my dew-spun dance of morning 'neath the day's new sun? Did you not know me then, see me as I am? Do you REALLY not know me, my Pilgrim? I am after all no more than myself.' She spun about in a swirl of wonder. 'My own people like to name me "Ouray", the Untamed-Dancer. They have looked into my nature and seen what I am. Being fairy kind they accept what they see. I, on the other hand, like to think of myself as Annquiie, like the fire-flies who dance through the mists of Eshenmoor on warm summers evenings.'

'Then I shall call you Luminae, The Fire-Dancer, for your brightness shines into my soul.' The words sprung unbidden from his lips and flew from him free as butterflies gliding through the rays of a sun-kissed morning.

Glowing with delight, she turned and, quick as a flash, reached up to touch her gentle lips upon his own leaving a lingering, tantalising taste of her sweetness to ensnare him even further. 'Such beautiful words, my Pilgrim, such a silken, silver tongue. Lo, and as you name me so I am.' And, with a sigh: 'So must I beware, sweet wordsmith? Least you take my heart from me in this our journey through these dour forests.' Then spinning away from him she pirouetted on the grass, her hair fanning out once again in its glorious whirlpool of glistening copper silk. Even before he could react she was back by his side, her tiny hand once more enclosed in his.

He was lost to her, bewitched by the enchantment of her beauty and the mystery of her dance. Clearing the final cobwebs of doubt from his thoughts he laughed with the joy of being with her. Throwing caution, restraint and inhibition to the wind. 'You win, my little Magic-Sprite; I can resist no more. I shall join you where-so-ever you might lead me.'

She joined his laughter, harmonising with the happiness that burst in his soul. 'Hark! The forest calls to us, Pilgrim. Can you hear its wind-song weaving through the treetops? Come dance with me, Young-Pilgrim, come dance with me through the hidden halls of the greenwood.'

Stopping only to pick up his satchel and staff and to throw his worsted cloak about his shoulders he joined her. 'Lead on, my fair, fey, Fairy-Fire-Dancer, lead on. Where you so step, so I shall follow.'

She curtsied to him, her smile brighter than the morning. 'Ah but you are gallant, my Young-Lost-Pilgrim, gallant and trusting. What if I should lead you unto your doom?'

'I shall come laughing and still follow your way.'

'What if my way is the path of danger?'

'I shall trust that if so then such is the need.'

'But what, Pilgrim, what if I lead you to the Gates-of-Hell?'

'Then you will lead me to safety again.' He paused, his gaze seeking meanings in the pools of her eyes, 'Will you not?'

She stopped and looked up at him. Her eyebrow arched in a moment of questioning. 'Aye, my Pilgrim, from the Gates-of-Hell, from the clawed, grasping fingers of the Lord-of-Mists itself should that be the need.' The echo of the fear hidden in her words spun in the air as she paused again silent and still. She looked up into his eyes.

Seeing what? He wondered.

'*Questaalari vosta el castnorrelle mesnillamnii sorthamafiirini a' basarrii na silimnae a vistarsae a' gasatii na Samnallae valandri a' shivimnae na savonphille?*' She whispered a question to the air.

'What do you say? I cannot speak in the Elven tongue.'

Her eyes seemed to draw his own, to fill his existence with her being. 'Do you probe my own nature? Would you have me tell of the rising at the centre of my being, Pilgrim? Would you know even the echoes of my troubled thinking.'

He nodded. 'Aye, my beautiful Elf-maid, these I would know.'

She smiled, hesitant, unsure. 'These were my words. "Who are you to taste the nature of my springing, the essence of my summer blooming, the glory of my autumn burnishing, the silence of my winter?" Must I also ask, who are you?'

'Who am I? That's my question too. I am but a traveller, cast adrift by my own uncertainty. Most of the time I am as unclear as is my troubled past. Of late I'm beginning to see myself as a seeker of truth. Once I was no more than a Child, once a Dwarves'-Apprentice and once a Warrior, but no more. Now I am simply a Pilgrim seeking my own truths. I see you as my eyes see, as my heart sees, as my spirit sees, as my being sees.' He was still. 'I see a wonder, beyond beauty, an awakening that will warm my soul forever.'

She laughed again, pure as the tingling trickles of water in the bubbling songs of a springtime rill, the music of her happiness ringing through his mind. 'This I did not expect.' Her eyes sparkled as the stars. 'Well do I know that these fell lands and dark woods are full of danger, yet the greatest danger I did not see.' She laughed again and spun to tiptoe before him to place another darting, honeysuckle kiss upon his lips.

'Come dance with me? Come tread the woodland way.'

Then she was gone; only the trail of her laughter drawing a path for him to follow through the leafy wilderness. He spied her darting through the trees ahead but when he thought he had caught her she was nowhere to be seen. He looked about himself, confused, fearful lest he had lost her. Then from nowhere she appeared before him, stealing a kiss before he even knew she was there.

'Come, Pilgrim,' her laughter's chime resonating within him in tune to another vibration, causing a harmony of peace to still the heavens, 'Daylight has awoken, the forest calls.'

Through tree-shaded valleys she led him in a wild game of hide-and-seek, speeding down sun-cut avenues where crimson moths danced their own minuets in the golden dust-born rays of brightness. Again she lost him only to surprise him when she sprang from a thicket to place another gentle kiss on his cheek.

He laughed with joy, unsure if he should catch her or wait just to wonder over her delightful catching of him. Over lush meadows they burst, startling the red deer to break their feeding and leap high and free before vanishing in the undergrowth.

Finally he caught her in a narrow tree-lined vale where a troubled stream bubbled from the rocky crags into pool of crystal water. Here he drew her to his breast, stilled her laughter with a tender, gentle kiss, held her enfolded in his arms. He breathed her nearness, wondered at her beauty, the awakening of her form, the fire in her being, the yearning of her nature. She lifted her face to meet his ardour, wrapped her arms about his neck, drew him with her to the leafy forest floor.

She giggled, mischievous, almost childlike, her eyes sparkling, her smile out shining any sun, 'Well, my Pilgrim, well, well, well,' and laughed again at the surprise on his face. Then she spoke with not much more than a whisper of breath. 'Ah, and what now? I trust my heart, my eyes, my ears, my hands my spirit, my soul. Must I deny their truths?' It seemed that the centre of her wonder awoke to a new understanding. The glorious peal of her laughter sung in his heart. 'Will you dance with me?' she sighed.

'I don't know how.' He almost sobbed with his need to be able to join her in her wonder.

She laughed again gently, almost as if to a child. 'Oh, My Pilgrim, but you don't even know how NOT to dance.' She lifted her arms about his neck and turned her face to him.

He bowed to meet her, slowly, almost afraid, and touched his lips to hers.

They linger, the sweet taste of her filling him until she drowns him in the warm caress of her loveliness. She meets him as an equal, parting his kiss with the tip of her burning tongue, tasting the fires of his passion, held in his arms, the wonder of her form tight against him.

Kisses linger more and more as the passion grows within him. She moves against him, sighing with expectation, awakening his senses until every moment stretches into eternity. *She is mine. She gives herself, her wonder, her being, her everything to me.* He accepts her gift, tastes as she tastes, touches, as she touches. Hands discover their own adventures of exploration.

She grows wild in his arms, free as the wind in the tree tops. He is an eagle, soaring through the wonder of her freedom. She is like a faun, untamed, unbound and his own wildness awakens to frolic with her in their wilderness. She is deep as the midnight and he filled with the mystery of her. She opens herself to him, her secrets, her living where he discovers the warm delight of her being. She touches him unafraid of his passion, of the fires awakened within him. She gives of herself, freely, wondrously, totally, filling herself with him. Their bodies are one, their awareness one, their existence one.

If their day passes without further note it is no wonder. This was their time, their beginning.

However, when evening painted the skies crimson, the newly risen moon found them laying together in the shade of an ancient yew tree, quieter now. For the thousandth time he looked down at her marvelling at her elfin beauty, of the gift, of the wonder of the moment. He kissed her softly.

'Come then, my Pilgrim.' She broke the spell with a sigh of contentment. 'There are tasks to do whilst the light remains. If you build a fire, I'll catch us a trout or two for our supper.'

She took a willow wand rod, tackled it with twine and a single filament of her hair. A tiny thing of feather and wool set on the smallest hook he had ever seen, she tied to the tip. Forgetting the fire he watched her nimble, silent passage over the rocks to the pool where waters fell in a singing glissade. There she crouched, still as the bolder beneath her, watching the water. The faintest of splashes, a ripple of water and she cast, a graceful dance to the gods of nature. Her fly hovered momentarily and drifted to settle light as gossamer on the surface. The water bubbled, a slight pause and? She flicked the wand high with a peal of delight at her success. The ringing chime of happiness filled him as she drew the fish to her hand. So easy, so fairy.

She cast again and again brought forth another fish. A third time also before making her way back to him her trophies held aloft.

'What?' She laughed, though she'd known the feel of his eyes throughout, 'No fire. Must we eat this raw?'

'I've never seen the like of that. Not even the fishermen of the northlands can dance with the fishes till they fly to hand,' he told her as he brought the sticks together and sparked the tinder into life. 'It seemed so simple and right, so lovely.'

'It is but an art, and one easily learnt,' she replied as she tended to the trout. 'Perhaps if there's time I shall teach you.' The cavities she filled with pine nuts and wild herbs, garlic and sage. Then set them upon stakes over the flames. Soon they sat, side-by-side and picked at the flesh with blow-cooled fingers whilst a bowl of leaf tea brewed in the embers.

They sat 'neath the bows of the tree drinking tea as night spread out over them, lighting the heavens with a million tiny fires. **'Alath, Alath, Torah fanliithil, Chelimbrelle.** Chelimbrelle, watch all those who wander through the forests of your night.'

'Which?'

She pointed it out, a bright spark of silver high in the eastern sky. 'Chelimbrelle, The Lady-of-the-Night, we bow to you.' Her whispered prayer. 'They say that she shines forever in the very heart of Elven-Holm.'

The tea finished, she lay back against him resting her head upon his chest. He felt content, happy, at peace with himself, his fingers toying thought-free with the silken tresses of her hair. 'How did you find me?' He asked the question that had troubled his mind throughout the day. 'Did you know that I would come? Did you come? Were you sent here for me?'

'I knew of your coming as were it already written on Fate's endless pages. It's spoken on the winds of morning. I was sent, but not sent. It was I who chose to come. Oh Pilgrim, your path is but at its beginning and I have so little time. I shall take you through these lands of dark memory. But…' For a moment her voice sounded troubled. 'No it isn't as easy as that. The bards felt your beginning long, long before your birth. The Well-Springs-of-the-Earth awakened our thoughts. I came, because you would be here, to guide you through these darkling mountains lest harm befalls you.'

'But who sent you?'

She stilled further questions with a finger placed on his lips. 'No one sent me, my Pilgrim of so many questions, although many told me to go. I came of my own choosing. It is my way. I wanted to dance for you.'

'I still don't understand anything you say.' Frustration filled him. 'Who is it that you think I am?'

'I try not to think of such things or of meanings and portents. The future is but a silken web, made but of gossamer possibilities and the paths therein change as they may, far, far beyond my simple understandings. You are here and I am with you and our paths lead us together as long as may be. But…'

'But?'

'But I cannot answer your questions, my Pilgrim-of-Dreams. Only you can do that. I can but see your way safely through these mountains and canyons, and…' Her voice trailed into a whisper.

'And?'

She didn't answer, rather took his hands in hers and lifted her face to kiss and still his questions with her beauty. In the darkness, when only the faintest embers remained, she drew him close to her again. 'And questions are for other times and other places,' she whispered, against his ear. 'The day ahead will have questions enough of its own, my Pilgrim.'

He lay back. All his doubts and queries lost in the magic of her closeness. She turned to him, touched his face, his eyes, his lips with an elfin finger. 'I shall tell you a story,' she whispered to him.

There once was a young carpenter who lived in a small cottage at the edge of a great forest. One day when he was at his work the King's daughter came riding by. The carpenter, hearing the hoof beats, went outside to see who was there and so looked upon her. He was stricken by her great beauty and his heart was filled with love for her.

For many weeks he dreamed of her. He couldn't eat, nor sleep for his longing to see her again. Even his work became little more than a chore to pass the time. Eventually, in the fear that his heart would break, he decided he must go to her and declare his love. And thus did he do.

However when he stood before her and expressed his love she saw nothing but a carpenter, coarse and crude, knowing nothing of the ways of princesses and palaces. She listened to his words, his protestations of love but then she said. 'If you truly love me then you will bring me the biggest, finest cut diamond in all the world. Then shall I know the truth of your love.' She thought that her words would drive him away so he would trouble her no more.

The young man went home in great sadness, his spirit all but broken and his soul despairing. Indeed he was but a carpenter and even a single diamond was more that he could ever hope to see let alone own or give as a gift to his love. The thought of the finest diamond on earth was beyond his imagination. However, he was strong of heart and he devised a plan.

For one whole year he went forth seeking out the finest piece of wood in the whole forest. He took it to his workshop where he sat many a long hour until he knew the very essence of its nature.

For another year he set to carving the wood. Having carved the shape he polished each facet of his carving until at the end he had crafted a thing so fine that the wood itself shone as a diamond and like a diamond reflected the lights of the rainbow in its faces.

Eventually he took the wondrous gift to the palace and set it before the Princess. She picked it up and held it to the light. 'I wanted a diamond,' she said as she tossed it from hand to hand. Then looking him in the eye she cast it into the fire. It was, after all, only wood and not a diamond at all.

Then the carpenter went out, his love turned to anger. He used his skill to make other jewels of wood and found those who would not cast them aside.'

'Well I think that the treasure she threw into the fire was the greatest gift anyone could give.'

'No, only the second greatest. She never even saw the first.'

Then the Pilgrim understood her and held her tightly, lovingly in his arms. 'Shall you be my princess, my little Firefly? Shall I bring to you the treasure of my creation? Will you burn it in the heat of your fire?'

She giggled again, snuggling against him. 'Oh, my Pilgrim, the very least of your treasures is far too precious for some wild elfin dancer. But, nonetheless, I shall take any you offer and I shall hold it as the greatest treasure of all. For so it is, so shall it be.'

Drawing her to his breast he stilled her words with a tender, gentle kiss, held her enfolded in his embrace once more.

She slept in his arms but he, shunning sleep, lay awake in the darkness marvelling over the wonder of the moment. Eventually sleep took him down its misty path, peaceful, contented, at ease with everything. When they awoke in the first half-light of morning they made love again, gently and tenderly and the world itself sighed at the beauty that was theirs.

*

Breakfast was but a portion of the rough way-bread from his satchel, nuts, grain and wild mushroom, which they toasted over the rekindled fire. Then they quenched their thirst from the crystal waters of the brook.

The Fire-Dancer broke the moment with a wistful return to reality. 'The morning is well on us and with it the time to move on, my Pilgrim. Daylight calls us and the trail lies ahead.' She laughed aloud at the expression on his face, the chimes of her happiness ringing through the valley. 'Oh, my Pilgrim-of-the-Night,' she sighed. 'But would you keep me here forever? A private toy for your pleasing?'

'I can think of nothing more delightful, my fey, Fiery-Dancer.' He smiled down at her, basking in her glow. 'Will not eternity wait for us a while?'

'Not for even a single moment I'm afraid,' came her sad reply, 'The road awaits us and will accept no delay. Come.' Picking up his cloak she draped it about his shoulders and handed him the staff. 'Come then, Pilgrim-of-the-forest.' She took his hand and led him back to the trail. 'Let us see what offerings this day has to bring us.'

Thus they recommenced their journey, taking the rocky path out of the wooded valley and following its winding way into the folds of the mountain foothills beyond. Wherever the path allowed they walked side by side, hand in hand, as children, light of heart and free of spirit. When the way narrowed she would take the lead.

The trail grew torturous indeed, winding its serpentine way amongst rough craggy boulders of grey granite cast aside by the mountains. The day began to pall, and the sense of doom returned as he followed her. 'There is no other way, my Pilgrim-of-the-trail,' she whispered to him in the encroaching gloom feeling his reluctance slowing his feet. 'This is a fell and loathsome road where our journey must lead us.'

'Is there danger?'

'There is always danger, here as much as anywhere...' Her words were left hanging in the air as some awful omen. Her bright light dimmed as the spirit of the land bore down on them.

At one place they chanced upon a clearing in the midst of a wood, a place of ill humour and darker mood, fire blackened and wreaking of decay. 'Goblins!' She gasped a sigh of sadness into the gloom as she surveyed the senseless desecration of life. 'Only they would so wantonly leave their mark. Their spirits grow brave again. They sense that the Time-of-the-Vortex is at hand.'

'The Time-of-the-Vortex? What's that? I don't know, I mean, I haven't heard of this. Tell me.'

She turned to him, her eyes shining with tears but her words when she finally spoke were for herself rather than him and coloured with the weight of her duty. 'Shall I speak of this? Shall my words give life to what I fear?' and to him. 'My knowledge is small. Those who do know of these things tell both in hope and fear of the Coming-of-the-Vortex. It is a magical thing beyond my own knowledge. The whisperings through the reaches of time are of little help. They speak in riddles and confuse more than they make clear. They tell of beginnings and endings of the breaking of bonds and the freeing of powers. The tenets of power are obscure. I know not how to explain.'

'Try, please try.'

She began to walk on again as if the movement might clarify her mind. Then she tried again. 'I can only tell as I have been told. Not about the vortex, it is but a name to me an omen of the future that might be, but what I do know I shall try to explain.'

'Please.' He needed to know, to have at least some sort of understanding. 'Please tell me.'

'The order of things is often seen as a web, an invisible net of bindings and controls by which each thing is linked to every other. It was not always so. Once, in a past that lies beyond even the memories of the elven wordsmiths, there was a freedom and a wonder beyond imagination. We speak of magic as something rare and mysterious but then it was a glory. Magic and magical power were then, as they truly should be, things of love and life.

'However; there were those who sought to bend such things to their own wills and to turn that power into hate and cruelty but true magic has its own nature and has ever denied them that which they would own.

'Thus denied, they lusted all the more and in their hate drew to themselves other powers, dark and evil. Energies that would deny the forces of light and life and would turn the joys of love and growth into grey despair. And still they craved more.

'There was a conflict, long, long ago, in the time we know as the "Cataclysm", when the powers rose up one against the other. It was a terrible time of war and destruction when light contented with dark and the very fabric of existence was like to be torn asunder. Then the Well-Springs-of-the-Earth and the Keeper-of-the-Cycles awakened to the fullness of their powers and brought order to the chaos and bound the forces in the webs of their making.'

She paused, as if afraid to say more. 'The Elf-lords are afraid now, afraid of the return of chaos. They tell that these bindings are loosening. The skies cry of it. The seas awaken to it. Even the Well-Springs-of-the-Earth tremble now, for the Earth-Stones cannot contain it.' Her voice grew stronger, wilder. 'The magic shall be set free again, Free to any, free even to them, the grey-ones. They lust after the power, for they hate the powerlessness that binds them. They believe they shall awaken into their magic, they and their Dark-Lord. Even now they grow stronger.'

'And me?' he barely whispered the words. 'What is it that you see in me? What do you expect of me?'

'I, we, expect nothing. You are beyond our expectations. You are unbound; your mysteries are beyond expectation. You are the hope, our hope, my hope also. Yours IS the Vortex!' She knew with a certainty that could not be questioned. 'You are their hope too.' The warning filled the silence. 'They shall seek to turn your hand, your mind, your heart, your spirit.'

The words echoed in his mind like a death knell: *Yours is the Vortex*, and in the centre of his being with the resonance of truth.

So they walked on saying no more, following the trail deeper and deeper into this dark land of mountain and rock, forest and hard wilderness. The signs of the goblins grew ever more evident, crude scribbling on rocks, blackened trees, bones, always the scattered bones.

That night they camped on a small hill set in the forest, finding a clearing and a stone hearth set there by a more careful people. She lit a fire, small and smokeless and brewed a pot of herbal tea to slake their thirst. She carried way-bread, which they nibbled together. People tell of the elven-way-bread but the stories go too far. It is nourishing and pleasant to eat but no miracle, nor magical food. They still hungered when they'd finished that which she allowed them.

'This is truly a sad and downcast land, my Elfin-Lady,' he said, looking out into the growing gloom. Then, trying to brighten her mood, he went to her and held her in his arms, shocked to find her trembling. 'What ails? What is amiss?'

'This place, this land, this time and, though I know there's little choice, I would rather it were otherwise and that our feet could take us on other journeys, to other lands and down fairer paths. If only. This terrible place is not welcoming to those of my kind. My nature and my soul cry out against the things I see and feel. No this is no land for an elfin-dancer. There are things abroad here that would freeze my very soul had they the power. Do you not see them?'

He turned his eyes from her, stared out into the gloom. There were shapes perhaps imaginings of the mind but no, there was movement too and, and eyes, cold grey eyes, seeing eyes that wanted, needed yet echoed with emptiness. Figures, forms moved in the darkness creeping about them.'

'Agh! Bitch.' A guttural bark of loathing cut through the night. 'Back again eh? Bringing him. Agh! Bringing him to the Waking? Agh! Bringing him to us are you? Agh!'

The elfling stirred, rising to her feet and peered out into the gloom. Her laughter rang as an incongruent thrill of life against the coldness that surrounded them, 'Well met, my cold, grey friends. Well met indeed. Yes we are coming, as well you know we would, but it's not to kindle your hope that we take this road. So think not to hinder us nor to offend. I warn you – beware, my putrid friends of emptiness, lest I wake the night with a dance of living and turn your blood to fire. Will you dance with me, silent ones of the night?'

'Agh! Bitch, We'll dance with you alright. Agh! A dance of death, Bitch! Agh.' The cruel laughter that followed sounded as lifeless as the words. 'Dare you come to us, Bitch? Agh! Dare you risk your blood for the pleasure of destroying us? Agh!'

'Destroy you? I've no wish to destroy you, though your sadness cries out for healing? I only desire to show you the wonders of the world and the beauty of the greenwood. To help you to discover the gentleness of the spring flowers on the shores of the Eshenmere, the sun-cut avenues of the Elswood, the sweetness of the songbirds in the clear mornings, the joy of spring awakening into bloom. Do you not hunger for the passion of life, the wonders of life, the joys of life? These are, after all, no more than the meanings of life. Will you not dance with me for the glory of your own hearts?'

The scream of brittle anger echoed about them… 'Agh! Bitch, would you face the taste of my cold steel in the heat of your belly? Agh!'

'Oh be gone, I tire of your prattle. The night is the time for sleep not talk. Be gone!' She began to turn slowly spreading her arms wide. 'Go now or my dance shall flame in your soul forever.'

'Agh! We go but don't worry when the time is come we'll see you dance. Agh! You can dance your dance of pain and madness for us Agh! Then!'

The movement ceased as they departed and the fire-dancer sat, or rather slumped to the ground again. Her shaking hand reached for that of the Pilgrim. She clung to him in the darkness.

'Goblins?' he asked.

'So some might call them but they're not those who truly bear that name, not those in the service of the Lord-of-Mists. No these are poorer things of cold and emptiness.'

'But are they not dangerous nonetheless? I mean, will they not return and set upon us in our sleep?'

'No, my Pilgrim, have no fear of that. They dare not, for all their brave words. They cannot harm you. To do so would destroy all of their hopes, all of their plans. They want to be able to gloat, to see the promise of the Wakening.'

'But you tremble.'

'Not because of fear but of their nature. They are winter to my summer. The very touch of their spirits freezes my soul. I cannot bide them, nor they me. Their danger to me is their nature, not their actions.' He felt her sadness touch him and held her closer. 'Their existence is so lifeless, so empty, so…'

So he held her in his arms, cradled her there throughout the hours of night. It was a dark, star-less night where the land seemed to moan of its fate and cry of its sadness. In the morning they continued.

Slowly the way climbed higher. The ash and oak woods gave way to pine and larch and in the clearings gorse and tough bracken grew. They stopped eventually beneath the towering peeks of the jagged mountains. A narrow passage lay before them, a harrowing slash cut through the sheer wall of grey rock. In this place the Fire-dancer's mood turned even more sombre under the weight of her dour thoughts.

She bade them wait before entering the gorge and sat a while on one of the fallen stones gathering her willpower for the task ahead. The Young-Pilgrim responded to her demeanour with his own patient silence.

'We are near a perilous place and our feet will soon draw us into the heart of what was the goblin realm. Beyond this passage we enter the Galghathag, The Darken-Forest.' She looked to him, her brow furrowed in concern. 'It should take about three days to pass through, days of danger and fear. Are you ready for such?'

'How can I know? I've never even heard the name Galghathag before, let alone what waits there for me. I but follow your footsteps and trust your knowledge. Should you lead me to my doom, then what care I? I go willingly. Yet you shall not do so of your own judgement and I trust your heart. I guess I'm as ready as I can be.' He paused for a time, taking a drink from his canteen.

'You must know one thing though, for it is something of which I have not spoken.' He looked down into her deep emerald eyes. 'I was a Warrior who would not kill. I shall not, as a Pilgrim do other. I will not take a life.'

She smiled, slowly mysteriously, 'Therein lies our hope. Could I love you were it otherwise? The elven kin are of life and magic. Our nature is to shun the ways of death.' She reached up and kissed him again. 'Fear not, my Pilgrim, that's one thing I shall never ask of you, not ever.'

'What lies beyond that vale? Where do we go then?'

Again her eyes were sad as if she wished he'd never asked. 'Beyond? Beyond is the future and the mysteries it holds. Beyond also, lay the lands of Bronden, They are distant as yet but nonetheless they await us beyond the vale. Aye, Bronden and the Lands-of-Men, where nature is tamed and the soil brought to the plough. From there your way reaches out before you like a ribbon of stone, to Varista and the road to the far-famed cities of the Eastern-lands, even further, to the desert lands; and yet beyond.' Her voice was sad and empty. 'No way for a fiery elfin-dancer, no way for a child-of-the-forest. Not yet.'

He looked at her, breathed in her sadness. But he had no reply.

*

The sun had passed noon before she stood again and took his hand to turn and face the narrow pass through the mountains. 'The time has come.' A few paces found them entering the dark, sunless crevasse. It seemed, by entering that passage, they passed through into another existence, a place of cold and lifeless desolation. In the very depths of the pass was a stone arch looming high over the path.

'The gate of Galghathag,' she whispered, fearful of awakening any sentinels or such which might lay hidden to guard the way, even though she knew none existed. 'That some even call the Gates-of-Hell.' She pointed to where the rock face was carved into two mighty pillars of stone, burnt and cracked now by some strange conflagration. Figures were carved on the faces of the stone, grotesque forms of misshapen beings, crude, explicit carvings of death and desecration that recoiled in the mind and filled the soul with revulsion. 'Do you still trust me, my Pilgrim?'

He looked at the horror of the forms, felt his heart shrink, chilled and cast down. 'I do,' he whispered in reply. 'Though my heart quakes, my spirit trembles and my eyes are filled with all these terrible images of doom. Yes, still I shall trust you. For I have heard your laughter in my being and seen the wonder of your dance. Yes I shall trust you whatever.'

Her smile shone an instant, unexpected glimmer of brightness in the gloom. 'Come then, my gently trusting Pilgrim, let us face the nightmare of the Hidden-Vale and discover what meanings are held for us within?' She reached out to take his hand and they stepped together into the darkness of the crevice.

Even as they took their first tremulous steps inward they felt the fell touch of the place's ill humour. A chill mist seemed to gather about them reaching out with grey, moist fingers to grope at their hearts and wrench away their will.

There came a time, when the walls became lost in the gloom, that the passage opened out about them. Still they moved onward. The path was rock strewn. The very land burnt and cracked as by the fires of some long forgotten battle. Boulders lay split asunder as if smitten by some Giant's mighty hammer. Silence brooded over all, mirrored by the covering of sad, grey dust.

'Does anything, can anything live here still?' Shuddering as his words, which should have echoed, vanished into nothing. Who might hear those words? Who here might hear anything at all?

'Live?' Her voice sounded strange, out of place. It seemed her life was something alien, unwanted in this domain of decay. 'No not live, at least not as we know of it. There's no joy here, no happiness. Whatever life there is here remains unwillingly. They were trapped here, the creatures of the wilds, the unbound ones, waiting, always waiting and plotting. Yet these are not the creatures of evil that rule. They, the servants of the Lord-of-Mists, were driven into deeper, darker, hidden places and are not yet ready to face the truth.

'There are things here, cold and deadly, things of darkness and of the night, fell, foul and evil of nature. The tribes of the Goblin-Horde might be found, if one wished to seek them out, but, no matter how foul they might seem, it was not even for these the veil was cast. There is no call to rest easy here.'

He shivered at the tone of her voice and asked no more.

Ahead, waiting as an ominous dark shadow, lay what appeared to be a vast, leafless forest. The path led them to its edge and then into the darkness itself, They stopped, peering into the gloom. Eventually they walked slowly onward. There was no other choice.

The trees, as everything else in this terrible place, were grey, dark grey and moss laden. Bare branches reached high overhead closing out the dark forbidding sky. The sun was but a memory here, had it ever been known. There were creatures too. Moths, great moths of more than a hand's breadth, grey and black, glided on secret wings from tree to tree. Webs straddled the path and brushed at their faces with cloying strands as they walked. Despite their fear that they might, they saw nothing of the spinners. Slithering things were heard but not seen, moving through the gloom. In one dark place a channel told of where an ancient stream once had ran. What water remained was still, a still, dark pool, foul and stagnant, where they dared not tread. They walked on.

'Did you come this way before?' His voice lost in the gloom. The weight of the decay of the place had begun to seep into his very soul, started to quench his spirit. 'For, now I've seen what lies here, I fear I'd never knowingly come back this way, well, lest my need was very great indeed. Is our need that great?' He said no more.

'It is all so ill.' She spoke to herself, voice choked. He turned to look at her, saw the glimmering wetness of tears on her cheeks. 'They took all the beauty of the wilderness, all the promises of the great forest and turned it to a lie. There is no life here, no joy in the trees; they sing of death and killing of torment and pain. Where are the flowers of morning? Where will set the silver mists of spring, the golden echoes of autumn? They are no more, those who once tended the trees. Gone, gone.'

He put his arm about her shoulder, his only answer to her pain and walked close beside her. Their footsteps too were lost, muffled into nothingness by the endless covering of damp grey moss rolling away under the trees, treacherous and deceitful and never, ever dry.

Some time, they knew not when for the passage of time had long lost all meaning, the darkness seemed to draw in about them. 'In the Forests-of-Dressan,' she broke their silence, 'And in the High-woods of the Elswood night comes gliding on star-spangled wings. Yet here it creeps on us as a cloud of misery, dark and secret. We must make camp while we can still see.'

There was no comfort here, no place to build a fire, not that any would light in the sad dampness of this dour forest. Nor was there anywhere dry or sheltered for them to set up a camp. In the end they just stopped and he lent his back against a massive tree trunk and held her in his arms with the cloak wrapped about them. Strange enough sleep did come…

In the darkness he awoke to find her clinging, shivering in his arms, trembling in horror at the evil of their surroundings. In the distance came the thrumming boom as of a mighty drumbeat counting out the hours of night… Something screamed, a long drawn out cry of fear and pain, but the drum was the louder. Somewhere else a creature howled into the night, challenging the drummer with its own terror but even that was stilled by the might of the drum. Silence fell again, a silence worse than any sound. They clung to each other all the tighter. If they slept again it was at best a fitful sleep full of ill omen and fear.

The eventual return of light showed as little more than a grey tinge to the darkness. In its gloom they ate of the way bread, and drank from their canteens, making haste the sooner to have done with this place. A thousand questions filled the Pilgrim's mind but could not be spoken. So they walked hand-in-hand in silence. Each lost in the paths of their own thoughts.

At one place the path climbed, leading them out onto a hill or mound that forced a clearing midst the trees. Broken stones, fallen walls, told of building, of habitation. 'Khalag.' She spoke the name as were it an obscenity. 'Thus they call it now. Khalag: the Goblin Citadel. It's all gone now, long gone. Although once it was named "Tanalain" and they spoke in awe of its glory and of its many wonders. But that was long, oh so long ago. They say then, in the far depths of history, that Tanalain was known for its greatness and famed for the healing of its wise ones. Long ago now though, aye, far too long, perhaps too long for any spark to remain. Who knows?'

For a moment as they stood there the sun almost broke through the dark covering of cloud and brightened the place with the memory of its golden light and for that moment their hearts lifted. 'We are mid way through the realm now. We have journeyed well.'

Each knew a cold dread at the very thought of returning to the darkness of the trees so they lingered here in the vague sunlight. They ate another meagre meal sitting on the stones of a fallen wall. Too soon the clouds closed in again. Ahead and behind the mists seemed to gather. Stealthily weaving through the lifeless forest as if driven by some pseudo life of its own. It felt that they were watched and was little wonder that the Pilgrim began to imagine vague shapes and creatures moving in its chill secret heart.

'They call it Galomist.' She too was drawn as he. 'It is a chill, foreboding thing that saps at the will and dampens the soul, but it's only a poor reflection of what was before, perhaps which is to come again.' She said no more. The day returned to grey, and they to the misted trail and their loathsome journey into the gloom filled forest.

There were other ruins deep in the heart of the forest, moss covered heaps of stone, dwellings perhaps, citadels and keeps or maybe meaner, humbler places. Nonetheless they gave some vague echo of hope, a reminder that someone once lived here

When night once again closed in over the land they found themselves at the foot of a small hill. They climbed the slope seeking to distance themselves from the forest and the mists. At the summit they entered a lowly stone circle. Not one of the Earth stones but something newer. They even found a measure of comfort. There was wood gathered by others, on other journeys. They brought the kindling together and lit a fire to warm and dry themselves. Once again they lay in each others' arms for warmth and comfort, wrapped in the worsted cloak.

The Pilgrim couldn't sleep at first. 'This seems so far from the fair lands of Hereth. So very far, I wonder if I'll ever return to the halls of home?'

'Tell me.'

He did so, recounting his life as a child. He told her of the Lady-of-Flowers, of his brother the Lord-of-Numbers and his sisters the Calm-Watcher and the Lightning-Bringer, of the hours of playing in the Marches-of-Hereth. He spoke too of wandering besides the ringing waters of The Dingle stream and of the vast wildness of the Salt marshes, of the High-Downs. Eventually sleep stole upon him, led him half-unknowing down its own misty trail.

He sits beside her upon a rock where a small spring bubbles into the sunlight, listening to its light, tingling ringing song. They follow the trickle of glistening, bouncing, dancing water, stepping over the rocks to see where it is joined by other springs, other trickles. Soon it becomes a narrow brook, singing, laughing in the sunlight. He walks hand in hand with her along the path running beside the growing stream, through green willow-woods, over lush meadows, which open before them into a vast river valley.

They move on, following the path at the edge of the shimmering waters. Further on a crystal bridge spans the river, slender, fine as glass. Beyond the bridge rising up from far bank, lying dark and brooding, stands a castle.

'Shhhh.' She touches a slender finger to his lips, stilling the questions as they form, wakened by the mystery of the moment. 'You must choose your way.'

'My way?' I'm being tested. 'I can see different ways. There's the bridge and the water. There's also the way back, though to take that path is to turn away from the path of learning and is not open to me. What is my choice?'

'The bridge is high and crosses the water. From its span you may see a vision of the whole world should you so wish. The river is deep and dangerous but therein is a lesson to be learnt.'

'Oh yes, I should like to see the whole world and to look upon its wonder. And, Oh how I fear the challenges of the river. But I am a Pilgrim and I seek understandings not visions. I choose the water and whatever it means to me.'

She smiles and takes his hand in her own. 'Come then, Pilgrim, we shall go together you and I. We shall learn together, you from me and I from you.' Drawing him with her she steps into the swirling water at their feet.

At first he is fearful of the troubled water. He feels it tugging at his feet drawing him deeper into its currents. The bottom slides away and he struggles to swim. His confidence begins to grow as he feels her beside him. He sees her swimming strongly. Again fear grips him as the currents draw them apart. He cries out, mouth filling with water. He is sucked under, floundering, drowning, but her hand reaches for him, catches his own and pulls him back to the surface. Again the waters take him and panic rules. Again she reaches out to him. One final time he is drawn from her, driven under the water. He reaches out his hand, trusting and she is there. Now he sees that she too is in distress, struggling, gasping as the waters close over her. He dives into the gloom of the tide and there he finds her, catches her and draws her back to the surface. Finally their feet touch the bottom once more and they struggle, exhausted onto the bank where they collapse on the lawn at the river's edge.

For a time he can do nothing but lay beside her, catching his breath and resting from his exertions. Eventually he sits up and looks about himself and, with sudden realisation, sees they are both quite dry.

'I don't understand. What?'

She turns and points to where the crystal bridge spans the water. 'Look.' Following her direction he sees two figures have left the greyness of the castle and now hurriedly approach the bridge. The first is a huge man, of such girth that he seems to almost sink into the ground as he walks. The second seems to be little more than a child, a waif, emaciated and frail. They reach the bridge and stand before it looking up over its arched span of crystal. They talk and although the Pilgrim cannot hear their words he understands the child is afraid to cross the bridge, fearing the crystal might break. Eventually the man steps out alone as if to show the other that the way is safe. Slowly he climbs the arch.

'It will never hold him! He's too heavy!' But, once more, she stills his words with the touch of her tiny finger.

The bridge creaks and moans at the task asked of it but it stands the strain and slowly he climbs to the top. Now the huge climber turns and beckons to the other, calling out that the way is safe, although the words remain lost in the distance between him and the Pilgrim. The child now climbs towards him, reaching out to take the man's offered hand.

However, as they touch and their fingers entwine, the strain becomes too much. The crystal cracks, shatters and casts both man and child into the foaming waters.

'I must save them!' The Pilgrim leaps to his feet. Yet even as he does so the image begins to shimmer and waver, the water glistens with golden light and the scene fades and is gone, river, bridge, man and child are no more. Just the green lawn reaching up to the grey gates of the castle, and whatever might lie within, remains.

'Who broke the bridge?' she asks. 'Man or child?'

'What happened? I don't understand. What does it mean?'

But now her eyes are fastened on the dour, bleak walls of the foreboding castle and the fell pathway climbing up to the blackness of the looming archway where the twisted gates hang ever ajar. 'The time has come, my Pilgrim-of-Dreams. It is for this we have come, why we are here.' She speaks softly, as much to herself as to him, her voice chilled by her own thoughts of what is to be. 'I can feel the darkness growing.'

He follows her towards the shadows of the arched entrance. 'What is this place?' But his question remains unanswered. She reaches out a dainty hand to push against the cold iron door. It swings inward, silent as death, and they step together into the gloom beyond. Movement seems strangely difficult here. It is as if they are passing through a strange domain of cloying fog, a palpable thing, which slows their steps and draws the warmth from their hearts. All at once their senses are assailed by an awful stench of decay, of rotting flesh, which surrounds them. This is a place of utter desolation. Everywhere a cold, damp, grey, foul smelling moss hangs from the stones deadening any sound.

'Is it real?' he asks her.

'Real?' To him, even her soft voice seems unreal. 'I'm not sure reality has any meanings here, Pilgrim-of-Questions. This is but a place of mists and in the truth of this time perhaps made of mists itself. Is a dream real? And if we dream then are we real to them?' she points.

There are creatures here, cold creatures of malice and decay. They gather on the balconies, on the battlements. Eyes of ice seeking to fasten upon the two newcomers, with silent accusation. Yet there is a distance also, a vagueness about their existence, as were they in another place, another reality. All that passes between is the bitterness of their hate-filled jealousy.

From somewhere unseen, unknown, comes a single drumbeat, the same which wakened them the previous night… Time itself stands still. Then, as a secret stolen awareness, comes a new sound, an empty moaning permeating the atmosphere of the place, a continual groan of torment. The air seems to thicken with fear, tension growing, moment-by-moment, almost unbearable.

The drum sounds again and from the gloom they come, other beings, haunted, colourless figures, shrouded by the cloying mists, They move, dragging their wearied feet with thoughtless, purposeless, shuffling steps through a carpet of dust. Beings that have been robbed of their beauty by the emptiness of their despair. Their pallid, hopeless faces are wracked with anguish. Their empty eyes see nothing but the gloom of their own hopelessness.

His eyes are drawn after them, mesmerised by the emptiness of this terrible parade of the damned, the slow relentless, shuffling procession through the gloom. 'Who are they? Who are these misbegotten beings? What it this? What is happening here?' He doesn't even know that he has spoken. His questions vanish into nothingness.

'No!' Realisation is as a dagger of truth piercing his heart with ice. For their steps are not as purposeless as he'd thought. Oh no indeed, not pointless at all. For their parade leads them, step by step towards a place of utmost horror. Surely this is no more than a temple of slaughter, a citadel of obscenity, where they step, one by one, in a slow relentless, shuffling procession, led to stand upon an altar of blackened stone to face a fate of pure evil. This was indeed nothing more than a march of the damned.

He is frozen now unable to move, even his thoughts refuse to form, refuse to accept the reality of the place or the horror that transpires before them. First one, then another bows to kneel upon the altar before a terrible black cauldron. Each in turn picks a blackened blade from the stone and in a soul bursting silence, slides it over their own throat. Each in turn bows over the glistening black-bowl, letting their blood flow down into the sticky darkness, and each slumps lifeless and always silently, into the endless, dark maw of the pit. And to each death the drum booms out its awful knell of victory.

One falls sideways, hangs over the lip of the hole, arm dangling above the void. But a thing of terror steps out from the shadows to push the corpse down into the darkness. It turns, face up towards the two watchers. The sneer of hatred freezes their minds. Then it steps back into the shadows and another steps forward to kneel upon the blood-soaked stone.

'What is this?' he screams into the gloom, his voice echoing among the cold grey stones. Anger wells up in his breast filling his soul with fire. 'Who dares to create such evil?' Who or what would allow this abomination? He begins to know. Oh yes he knows!

'Beware!' She gasps beside him, her fear a sudden palpable force in the air about them. 'Beware for this we are come. The Sleeper awakens. He knows of you already and his hatred grows. His evil mind has been reaching out to find you. Beware! He is aware of you! Beware!'

He looks again at the altar, at the pit and the cauldron of blood, his own fear rising in his breast, trembling at the horror in her voice. There is movement, something stirs, awakened by this terrible sacrifice of life: a being, drawn of the mist, straining to break into existence from the gloom. A form, a horrible, grotesque creature, grows as it were from the foul-shadowed depths of that accursed pot of blood. It appears as a dread thing of fang and claw, of evil greed and hating lust, feeding on the death and desecration of the place.

The drumbeat quickens, rolling into a thunderous roar, a crescendo of sound that welcomes the obscenity's beginning.

As it awakens the thing draws power from the awesome fear bred in that castle, a fear that grows also in the Pilgrim's heart. On the dark grey walls the creatures begin to chant, tuneless and meaningless, unless evil has its own meaning. The drumbeat is suddenly silent, the castle silent, the creatures silent. The creature begins to rise. Its form is of mist of mist and horror. Terrible strands of mist reach out from the Creature-of-Madness, and in touching, feed upon their lives, their weakness, their hopelessness and those beings not yet slain begin to fall to the ground, lifeless, meaningless.

His own scream of terror freezes in his breast as the creature rises before him. Here it has waited, drooling and brooding over its fell domain. Waiting for him to be drawn into *its awful, ghastly web. It leers at him, laughs with savage, delightful malice over the words of his vow. It draws itself high over him, smothering him into the shadow of its evil mists. He is transfixed, helpless, lost.*

Something moves. A tiny spark gleaming in the heart of the nightmare, a burning, twirling whirling flame. A fire spirals and flashes with brilliance, spinning a web of her magic about him. She dances a new dance now. A dance of terrible burning anger, of wild, untamed power, a wonderful ballet of incandescent fury that bewilders the creature's eyes with dazzling energy and sets the pilgrim free.

'Run!' she screams.

'Run!' he echoes and he flies from the place knowing he is no match for that terrible thing of hate and madness. The foul laughter shrieks and rebound about this terrible domain of despair.

'Run!' he screamed aloud into the darkness, sobbing in fear lest that terrible thing of madness and death might follow. He was on his feet, crouching defensively midst the circle of stones. The cold dampness of the place seemed almost welcome.

She stood beside him, panting, her eyes shining, wild with the fury of her magic 'Be still,' she commanded him. 'Be still, my Pilgrim-of-such-fearful-dreams! Be still. It has awakened and seeks you; even now it tries to reach out of its foul demesne. It cannot reach you yet. Its time is not yet come. Not yet, it hasn't the strength to break the bindings.'

He sank to his knees before her. She stood close, resting a hand on his head as if in blessing. 'It was so terrible. So...' About them the darkness crackled with cruel laughter sending shivers of panic through his breast.

'This isn't the time or the place to speak of this. Be still.' She put her arms about him, held him to her and cradled him as a child. But her eyes were as a hawk and her body was tense with readiness.

Beyond the circle the mist closed in, evil, cold, waiting for them. Within its formless embrace creatures gathered, unseen, unformed, lurking in the darkness to brood upon their endless hate. A terrible sense of foreboding descended upon the two figures crouched amidst that circle of stones. A doom that cast their spirits into a well of dread, a sense of wrongness, a feeling of awfulness seemed to claw at their hearts. The grey mist wound through the forest touching the trees with the frost of its chill passing. There seemed to be a design to its movement, as if it possessed the intent to reach them, to freeze them, body-and-soul, forever.

Another dance was trod in that death-reeked place. A terrible ballet of life, of fury and of fire, until even the fell creatures of the forest fled before her and the mists of desolation stole back to hide in the forest.

There was no more sleep to be had that night, nor any wanted. So they packed their bags and left the mound, the sooner to be free of the place. She led him by the hand as the Darkling-forest closed in about them. The sense of evil was all about them, hating them and their lives, envying their gift of living, calling out to them with meaningless oaths and threats, though none dared to face the fury of her magic. However they knew in their hearts what it was that followed close behind them whispering curses into the nothingness.

They knew too that some malevolent force now set the tendrils of the Galomist to seek out a way to entrap them. But her eyes would shine in anger and her dance of burning, binding life would set the forest aflame with beauty and the mist to recoil in screaming steam. At one point they stopped to rest and the mists again enclosed them but now the coldness no longer dared approach...

'What happens if it touches us?' he asked of her.

'It's the Galomist,' she whispered. 'Its touch is as ice. It freezes the blood, drains the soul. But do not fear, Pilgrim-of-terrors, my dance is more than a match for this thing at least.' She paused yet again, thinking. When she spoke her voice was as hard as iron. 'Before we leave this place I shall show you its real horror.'

It was turning towards noon when the path began to climb and the trees thinned. 'We're through,' the Fire-dancer breathed as they emerged from the forest to stand once more before a grey rock face and the fissure through which they must pass.

Beside the last tree she drew to a halt. 'Look, Pilgrim, now, as I said I would, I'll show you in truth that lies in this sad domain. I spoke of the Galomist in reply to your question. Now you'll see the true horror about us.'

She reached out a hand and touched lightly against the trunk of the tree. 'Its heart is frozen, its life is **gone**!' Then, with the last word, slapped her hand hard against the wood. There was no sound, not a thud or crunch. It seemed that her hand broke through some sort of binding and the very form of the tree turned to dust. Slowly the corruption spread up the tree. He watched, eyes wide with horror as the whole thing became dust. Worse came than this though, far worse for as the branches lost their form they fell against other branches, other trees and the desolation spread. Faster now, spreading away from them in a great swathe of destruction until there was nothing but a vast rolling plain of dust. In the distance the far, far distance he saw the ugly grey tower rising out of this sea of silent horror.

There was more. About the walls of the tower, as a cancer grown of its foulness, were pits of corruption. Fumes belched skyward turning the clouds to a sour amber hue. Figures moved there. Not tens, not just hundreds of them, not even thousands, but tens of thousands; a crawling, writhing encampment whose fires burnt like the flames-of-hell.

'The Goblin-Horde,' she whispered into the gloom. 'They wait for war. Soon they'll march.'

They turned away in horror, not wishing to see the path they had followed or the sights they knew waited there. They simply followed the trail into the cliff face before them. When they entered the narrow defile into the grey fissure of rock they didn't linger but passed quickly through the arch to emerge into the bright sunlight of the new vale beyond, glad only to be free.

That night they camped by the bank of a small river, lit a campfire on the pebbled beach and ate freshly caught trout on newly cut twigs. The heavens spread out as a sea of stars. The moon too gave welcome to their being. In the peace of the moment they forgave the days of gloom.

She sat opposite him, her face and form lit by the flickering firelight. She was the same as before but he saw her differently now, no longer a fragile thing of woodland, song and laughter. He'd seen her wonder, her life. He'd felt the depths of her pain and watched the awakening of her power. He'd seen her as an elfin queen at the peek of her magic. Her force and light filled his being with awe.

'What was that thing?' he asked of the night. 'Who are you? What are you?' A thousand tumbling questions fled through his mind.

'Be still, my brave Pilgrim, be still,' she whispered into the darkness. He heard the pain in her voice and his heart opened once more to the warmth of her tenderness. 'You know what it was, what it is. There is no need to ask.'

'Yes. I do know.' The grief welled up inside him once more, awoke the memories of what might have been and turning his thoughts and being to anger. 'Oh yes, I know only too well what it was. There will come a time when I shall be strong enough to face its evil. I shall confront it and prevail, not run from its terror like a whipped dog.'

She reached out towards him, laid a gentle hand upon his arm. 'Be still, my Young-lost-Pilgrim, be still. Indeed there'll come a time when your own power shall waken anew, when my own shall appear as little more than a child's toy. But for now, be at peace. For that time is not yet come. Be at peace for this moment at least.'

However, when the night had fallen, she set wards about their campsite and spun a dance of concealment over their trail. 'The time of The Awakening has come,' she explained perhaps to herself as much as to him. 'Its evil shall not rest nor sleep until the matter is done.' Whispering: 'The time of waiting is past, the whirlwind is unbound. When comes the Vortex?'

'Is that what I've done?' The terrible thought awakened in his soul. 'Have I awakened that thing of evil?'

She laughed, softly, gently, 'Oh no, my Pilgrim, not that.' She reached over and touched his cheek with her finger. 'You could no more awaken that thing than you could keep it asleep. No, it planned to draw you to its evil but there were other forces at work also. We were but there at its wakening, witness to the terribleness of that truth, as was right, that but nothing more.'

The Pilgrim watched her in the light of the early moon. He saw the gentleness of her form, the almost fragile daintiness of her movements. He recognised the wisdom of her knowledge and intuitively understood the importance of her quest. 'Who are you, Little-Fairy? Forest guide? Fire-Dancer? Elf-Queen? Who are you? I have seen your mystery and known your passion. I have bathed in your laughter and trembled in the face of your wrath. Who are you that we should so meet in this troubled land?'

'And who are you, Pilgrim-of wonder? Have I not heard the cry of your grieving in the night air, seen the tears shed for the magic you fear lost forever?'

'But it is lost!' He almost shouted his pain at her. 'Left behind in the years of my childhood, lost to me at least. For I cast it aside as a thing of little worth, denied with my very being the gift it was to me. How can I ever find it again?'

She laughed once more, gently marvelling at his innocence, stroking his hand with the feather touch of her fingers. 'Can we ever truly lose our own nature? Can a tree lose its tree-ness or a mountain, its mountain-form? Oh no, my Young-Pilgrim, it's not the magic that's lost but you yourself. Magic is not a thing of study and learning, nor a thing to be cast aside, nor taken up again. It is as love or fire, a thing of mystery and excitement; an excitement that lies at the very centre of our being. We do not DO magic, we ARE magic! When you find yourself once more, then you'll find that your magic is there waiting for you, waiting as it always has been.

And then,' she barely whispered the words, 'then the heavens shall wake with the wonder of the glory which is yours.'

She laughed again, leaping to her feet to dance for him. No dance of magic this time but rather just of happiness, a dance for him alone in that wilderness glade by the river's edge. He joined her laughter then, in his own clumsy way, he gambolled beside her driving away the fey humour that had sat with him. When he spread his cloak upon the grass she joined him with a beauty that was hers alone and lay with him until the morning.

Day burst fresh and bright, to awaken them with the sound of songbirds and life. Not far away a fawn lingered to sip from the water's edge. A rabbit scampered off into the shelter of a brier thicket. Their hearts filled with wonder and laughter. They were together, carefree and unhurried. Whilst he rekindled the fire, the elf-maid foraged for mushrooms. She cried out in delight at finding a nest of pigeon eggs and milked the sap of a maple tree. Then, as she cooked their breakfast of omelette and mushrooms, he fashioned arrows from the hazel stems, fletched them with duck feathers found on the grass. It was not that time no longer mattered, for both knew in their hearts it did indeed move them onward, rather they chose to hide from the meanings of such and lived in the joy of the now.

They travelled easily, stopping when and where their mood might take them. Sometimes it was to look at the beauty of the land about them, at others just to be together. More often though, they halted to look back wondering. Behind them the sky was changing. Dark clouds were forming over the Darkling-Vale, clouds of ill omen, of fear and woe. The Pilgrim half expected to see the Goblin-horde following on their heels. Instead, came a wind from the north-east, a wind tasting of the forest and, on its breath, the dark clouds drew back behind the mountains.

'What?' he asked of her.

'The wakening of the whirlwind, the turning of the world,' was all she would answer. 'There is a new song, a new singing, a new sound over the hills of Naril. It is a discordant song of darkness and hate.'

Still, they were at peace together, calm and light of mood. For a time she tried to teach him words of the elven tongue, giggling with uncontrolled mirth at his inability to master the sounds. He, in return, told her of the Dwarven-Kingdom, of the wonder of the Carrow.

'I'd like to see the Dwarves in their carven halls,' she confided. 'For, as you say, away from their forges they are ever a sullen people.'

When the river turned away north they left its bank and climbed up to cross into another vale. At the brow they looked down a long valley to see the sun sparkling, far distant, on the water of a small lake. A new river, silver banded, wound away to the north-east. Here and there white-coated sheep grazed the day lazily away.

She seemed quieter, somehow sadder now as they followed the path towards the water's edge, taking his hand in hers and staying close to him. The sun was still high when they reached the shore. Nonetheless she led him to a small tree-lined peninsular and set about making camp beside the rippling water. He saw the boat pulled up on the shore, knew it to be hers without the words being spoken. He knew the twinge of pain in his heart for what soon must be.

He cooked a meal of cony, shot earlier in the day, which they ate with their fingers in the light of the fading sun. When the moon arose she danced for him. No magic dance this, lest love be magic of its own. She came to him warm, tender and hungry with time's sad need.

Later, when the moon was full, he asked her again… 'Why?'

She leant over, kissed him softly. 'I had a hope, a dream, my own sweet Pilgrim, a promise of the future and I have awaited its awakening. I came to see, to marvel and to know the truth of what was to be. I came to love also, though I knew it not.' She kissed him again, slowly lest the moment be lost. When he wound his arms about her she snuggled into his breast as if he might hold her forever.

'I waited for you, for surely I knew that you would come and I fulfilled my hope in leading through that place of dark despair and in seeing the things we saw, the Awakening, and in bringing you safely to this place. Yet now the task is done I find that I grieve.'

'You are going?' It was the truth and he knew it. 'You have shown me many things yet I understand little. You have wakened my heart and filled it with your light. You have saved me from my terror with the wild beauty of your dance. You have healed my wounds with your silence. Now you are going to leave.' He wanted to be angry, to deny the truth, but his heart would not so betray her. He would not rebuke her. Rather he touched his lips to her head and kissed her brow with feather lightness.

She knew his heart, shared in his sorrow and sank back into the comfort of his cradling arms. 'Were it possible, I should stay,' she whispered, 'but it is not so. For in staying you would not grow and I should but diminish. Our lives would become little more than a sad memory of today and, as the darkness enclosed us, we should learn to despise each other. No, I cannot stay. To do so would be the betrayal of all that is good. No, however much we might wish otherwise… Your way lies on the road, mine on the river. I must return unto the Elswood and the Halls-of-Al-Sinnian. They wait for me, those who sent me. My master waits for the news I shall bring to him and the understanding he requires.'

'Your Master?'

'Yes, gentle Pilgrim, my Master. And, in truth he has waited long for my return and his impatience is not a thing to hold lightly. It is long now since I set out from his halls, long since we shared in the Dance-of-the-Morning. It was he who woke the fire in my dance and he who spoke to me in riddles of mystery. It was he too, who set my feet upon this journey of wonder, who showed me what might be. Yes, sweet Pilgrim, The High-Dancer-of-Al-Sinnian is my master and only he can set me free.'

'If he is your master, then who am I? You have wakened my heart and filled it with a flame that shall burn forever. Are you my mistress?'

'Oh yes, Pilgrim-of-my-Being, your very own mistress.' She giggled with innocent duplicity and kissed him again. 'I am other things beside. Now I shall set you free also, for as I must follow my own path, then you too shall follow yours. Should we meet again within the pale mists of the future then I shall dance for you again. I am at the end of my journey. My quest indeed nears its conclusion. Yours is but at its beginning.'

'Tell me? What was your quest?'
'I sought to find the meaning of the Fire-dance.'
'What is The Fire-Dance?'
'I am.'

Then she laughed again, wild and free as the wind. The ringing of her voice thrilled through the woodland as a call of life. She stood shaking her head until her silken hair fanned out about her in a splendid halo of glory and she danced for him alone. Then she danced the true dance of the Elfin-kind turning the universe aflame with the full, glorious blaze of her magic.

He knew her surer than he could ever have believed. He heard the truth of her being in the wonder of her dance and deep within his soul the knowledge of her love burnt as bright as the fire-flies over the mists of Eshenmoor.

Come dance with me,
among the wild flowers
of the Elswood,
among the tall pines,
the sun-cut avenues.
Come fill my ears with the music of your being,
the bright images of innocence,
with the elfin pipes
softly falling reels.
Come dance once more
before the winds of change
claim us forever.

She was gone, paddling the small craft out over the lake's glimmering waters. Gone into the brightness as the morning enfolded her in its embrace and hid her from his eyes. Gone before he had even begun to understand the wonder of her. Gone leaving but the echo of her glory resounding as fire in his heart. Gone, and he had not even told her that he loved her. Gone.

He lingered there on the shoreline of the lake where the winds sang of her in the rushes. He camped beneath the trees that rang with the memory of his wild elfin queen. He listened for her laughter ringing on the high breezes, for her song over the meadows, for the soft sigh of her breathing over the shimmering water but she was not there. She did not return.

> If all my problems were solved
> If all my worries proved to be naught
> If all my fears were groundless
> If all my torments were but dreams
> How would I find the mountain?
>
> (Past Thoughts)

Chapter Four – The Road of the Pilgrim

It was the rain that eventually brought him back to the trail, a storm, driven in on the north wind's cold wings. Squalls rushing over the lake drenched his campsite left him little choice but to seek shelter elsewhere. Once he'd started to move there seemed little point in stopping. He just continued towards the East and whatever future awaited him.

Now the time for lingering was done, the Pilgrim made good speed. He felt driven by a sense of vulnerability. When not full of images of a small, wild elfin-dancer his thoughts would return to the events of the Darken-Vale and the terrible Creature-of-Mists now awakened in its darkness. His eyes too often strayed backward to scan the mountains for the darkness arisen there. His imagination more inclined now to see the hill top mists with ominous disquiet.

The signs of goblin passage were less evident here, save for the occasional blackened tree stump and almost obligatory scattering of gnawed bones. Once or twice he believed he'd glimpsed a hint of gloom in the skies behind him and on other occasions he was sure he'd felt the touch of cold grey eyes. Yet these might have been no more than the fancies of his imagination. Nonetheless, he moved with cautious steps and wary eyes. In the evenings he broke off his travels early to hunt for dinner. Then, having made his camp and cooked his catch, he'd while away the night in thoughts of his fire-haired dancer.

The road here was generally well kept and walking was easy. Even so, there was little sign of any others who might pass this way nor, for that matter, was there any sign of those who tended to its upkeep. However, even prior to his first sighting of habitation, some seven days after leaving his lakeside camp, the indications of humankind had become gradually more evident.

Sheep, grazing lazily as sheep are want to do, dotted the vast landscape of hill and moor. Grey-stone byres and sheepfolds stood out stark on the hillsides.

The sun once again prepared to take its leave of the day and as it lowered its face towards the western hills he began to look for the night's resting-place. The unease born of goblin eyes had not touched him for some time now and he was beginning to relax. A well-placed arrow had won him a small buck earlier in the day and now he even hummed softly to himself in prospect of the feast ahead. Then, breasting yet another rolling hill, he found himself looking down upon a small farmstead nestling in the narrow valley below.

He paused, stepping out of view amongst the cover of a stand of aspen, to examine the scene below. Three white-painted, thatched cottages and a large barn huddled together inside a stout wooden stockade. In the yard stood an old wagon and in the enclosure behind the centre house a wearied looking horse munched dolefully from a manger. The drift of smoke rising from the chimneys announced that the settlement was inhabited and that those inhabitants were preparing for their evening meal.

The Pilgrim didn't actually move for quite a time. He felt somehow unsure, almost afraid to find out how these people might receive him. Nonetheless he did eventually find the nerve and, having brushed the dust from his cloak and rinsed both hands and face with water from his canteen, he began the descent into the valley. Several of the sheep looked up nervously and sidled off from the pathway as he walked towards them. Sheep realise you can never be too sure with humans.

From somewhere among the cottages a dog began to bark. A door opened and a man stepped out to look at what had stirred the dog. He stood watching as the still distant stranger descended towards him from out of the sunset. The man called out something, though the Pilgrim couldn't understand the words at that distance. A second figure appeared from another of the cottages and a short discussion took place. There was another call, sharper, commanding and the dog was quiet.

By the time the Pilgrim neared the stockade several people were gathered there. The men who had first appeared walked out of the gateway to face him. They were clad in leather and wool with wide-brimmed hats. One rested a curved shepherd's crook on his arm, the symbol of his trade. There were two gangling youths, legs longer than trousers, and three flaxen-haired children gathered close to the gateway. Two women and another older girl, dressed alike in woollen shawls and bright chequered skirts, stood slightly behind. Simple, country-folk were these, with weather-hard eyes and land-strong sinews. The smell of baking soda-bread greeted his senses as some kind of welcome. He stopped to face the shepherds.

'Good evening, Sir,' he addressed the man holding the staff, noting with relief that his words turned the initial worried frown to a smile. 'I am travelling eastwards to Varista. I saw your dwellings as I crossed over the hill and I hoped I might find a night's rest here?'

Quick glances passed between the two shepherds. 'Be you welcome, young man.' He spoke with a strange singsong lilt to his voice. His welcoming smile grew broader. 'I am named Elim, as was my father and his father before him, see? This is Llewyn my neighbour and friend.' He gestured to the other man who bowed his head. They looked for his reply.

'Thank you for your welcome, Elim.' He puzzled over the question of his name. 'I am a pilgrim come over the mountains in the west on my journey. Those that know me just call me Pilgrim.' The two shepherds eyed each other, troubled by the strangeness of the young man's words.

'Pilgrim is it?' he sang. 'There's strange, not a name really, see. Over the mountains you say? Your feet will be tired then, tired from such a journey. So you best come inside and be welcome.' The young man followed their advice and soon stood in the midst of the small company.

Elim continued to direct proceedings. 'This is Morgid my good wife and this Llewyn's wife Gethyll and this her sister Cyline.' The three curtsied with smiles lighting their russet-cheeked faces. Cyline, a girl of some thirteen perhaps fourteen summers blushed and absentmindedly brushed a wisp of golden hair back under her bonnet in return for his smile.

'This is Elim my eldest son, this Drufus, Llewyn's eldest.' They bowed solemnly to the Pilgrim and he to them. 'This is my younger son Gormal and these are Brewlyn and Salwyn.' They curtsied in turn as had their mothers. The shepherd then addressed them all. 'This is Pilgrim.' He stumbled slightly over the name, 'He is welcome among us. He has come over the mountains; see, on his way to Varista. There's a long way.'

'I thank you all for your welcome.' A formal speech befitting the occasion. 'I have indeed come very far and seek little more than a night's company and rest. Please call me Pilgrim for that is what I am of late.' Again the eyes asked their unvoiced questions.

'If it be to your liking you may use the store house.' Elim pointed to the third cottage. 'It was my own father's house, see, and you shall find it comfortable. It would be proper if you join us in our diner this evening. Mind you our fare is poor and not for lords and the like.'

The Pilgrim bowed back to him. 'Well I'll thank you again, Elim, although I'm no lord nor would I want to be treated like one. Whatever you offer is more than enough.' He paused unsure. 'I do not know of your ways or your customs. If it gives no offence I should like to offer of my own to share with you.' In his satchel, wrapped in burdock leaves was the sizeable haunch of the venison from the buck he'd shot earlier. He offered it to them. Their instant smiles attested to its acceptability.

'We thank you most kindly, Pilgrim, Of late we have had little chance to hunt up in the wilder-lands see. Your gift is most pleasing to us.' He laughed. 'Perhaps we'll dine like lords after all.' He passed the gift to his wife. 'Come let me show you to your resting place and let the women get on with the feast, for such shall this seem to us.'

He paused at the door to the house and looked back at the pilgrim. 'If my first frowning was less than welcome, Pilgrim, then I must ask your understanding, see. The truth is that we have been much troubled of late by the creatures of the hills.'

'What, the goblins?' He'd wondered just how these folk might manage against them, or with that which had awoken. Unfortunately he knew the dreadfulness of the answer in his heart.

'That name is theirs, though I think it just as well that it was not spoken here.' He dropped his voice to a whisper. 'Bad luck see. Might draw them to us.' He opened the door still speaking. 'They become bold these days see, sneaking among the flocks and take for themselves the lambs and ewes. Steal them they do.'

Then his voice grew hushed yet again, full with emotion. 'There's worse than that though, far worse, see. The steading of Thymmle, always north it is, was attacked by a band of the things. Terrible it was. Yethyl, Thymmle's wife was killed you know. Their farmhouse was burnt to the ground. Sad it was, her with three young children, no mother now to look after them, see? He took his people back to town. Said that it wasn't safe to stay here. Advised us to go with them they did.' Elim coughed, suddenly aware and embarrassed by his words. 'Anyway that's my problem. So come you inside and make yourself welcome. It's a bit plain see but the bed's fine and it's both warm and dry.'

He opened the door into a simple room. Fleeces were piled against one wall awaiting transport to market. There was a bed of sorts in a small alcove and a hearth on another wall. It was crude and rustic, for sure, but to the Pilgrim it looked wonderful. Right then the halls of Hereth and the comforts of home seemed oh so very far away.

'Let me thank you again, Elim, this is splendid. I'll have one good night's sleep here at least.'

The shepherd smiled, pleased by the words. He stood and watched the Pilgrim hang his satchel over the bed head and rest his hawthorn staff against the wall. Just then the girl Cyline arrived carrying a large jug of water and a woollen towel. She kept her face lowered shyly as she put the jug on the floor and placed the towel on the foot of the bed. 'Thank you, Cyline. That is very thoughtful of you.'

The fact that he had remembered her name brought a sudden smile. Then covering her mouth to hide her nervous giggle, she hurried away.

Elim left shortly after, saying that he would send for the Pilgrim when the meal was ready, leaving him to himself and his thoughts.

Goblins, The Awakening, What is happening? He could not make sense or even clarify his thoughts about the matter. *Time will tell as the Dwarves say.* However in his mind there grew a terrible picture of the Goblin-horde and the smoking remnant of this little farmstead. With the vision came the thought that Thymmle's advice had been sound. It would take more than unspoken names to keep these people from harm. This was no longer a safe place for the shepherds and their families to stay.

The evening was warm and pleasant, a gentle breeze taking the edge off what might have been too humid. They'd placed a table in the courtyard between the houses and set lanterns about the eves of the cottages to light the scene.

'You are our guest, Pilgrim,' Morgid said as she ushered him to one end of the table. 'It is right that you sit at the head.' Elim sat at the other end in what must have been his own chair. The others were spaced, on benches, about the table, leaving a place for Morgid and Gethyll beside their respective husbands. The children sat beside their mothers, Elim-junior and Drufus sat side by side. Opposite were Gormal and Cyline. The Pilgrim found himself seated between Cyline and Drufus.

Elim stilled their tongues as the two wives took their seats. Then he stood, took a jug of mead in his hand and walked about the table filling the goblets at each place. 'We wish to welcome our guest and our new friend, Pilgrim, to our table. It is our hope that he takes as much as he gives and when he leaves, that he does so more the richer for being here with us.' He then laughed out-loud. 'Right my hungry ones. Time to eat.'

Dishes were passed around the table and the clatter of finger eager cutlery filled the air. At first no one said much at all so engrossed were they in the process of the meal. What might have been no more than a meagre supper of mutton stew and salt bread had been transformed into a veritable feast with venison and a whole array of vegetables. Their platters were filled and the air sounded to their happy repast.

'So then, Pilgrim,' Elim said leaning back into his chair with a smile of contented fullness. He sipped the sweet mead and fed titbits to Tam his black and tan haired sheep dog. 'Tell us then about yourself and your journey, pray? It's not often that we meet with one of distant parts see, lonely here, you might say. How come it is that you are abroad in these wild lands?'

'I hardly know where to start,' he began, responding to the man's open curiosity with an equal good humour. 'I come from, that is I spent my childhood, far to the north of here in the Bounds-of-Hereth. That's a small, fertile plain that lies in the shelter of the Long-Downs in the land of Santolin. Hereth is a gentle country of woodland and pasture, fine orchards and fields of wheat and barley. It lies close to the sea where the wild gulls fly, hard by the great salt marshes.'

He paused wondering what or how much to tell. 'I left there hoping to become a warrior and to join the King's army at Sarum. But even before I joined there was a battle, a horrible struggle with the goblins, who came under the cover of cold deception, to set upon the King. It was a terrible thing of chaos and slaughter. Anyway...

'After that I wandered for a long time until I finally resolved to become a pilgrim as you now see me. I travelled down through Lodor and entered the fell lands of Naril where I met with an elfling. We were together crossing the mountains. She is gone now, gone back to her people and I have come eastward and found your haven of happiness and comfort waiting me here.'

'An elf?' The wonder of his words awoke Cyline from her usual shyness. Now her eyes grew wide with excitement. 'Oh how I wish I knew an elf. I dream about living in the Elswood and... Was she very beautiful?'

'Oh yes, Cyline, as beautiful as all the wonders of the wilderness and then more. She danced of the forest and of the sun and of...' He stopped suddenly embarrassed, 'She took my heart and bound it in cords of pure joy.' He could say no more.

Husbands and wives looked at each other and knew and they smiled their secret smiles.

'You say you were at the battle at Sarum?' Llewyn asked after a time. 'The battle when the goblins first returned?' His doubt spoke through his eyes.

'Sarum?' The question awoke the hidden memories and a sense of dread passed over him. 'Yes. I was there alright. It was a terrible thing, a terrible, ugly, senseless thing of death and destruction.' The horror in his voice spoke louder than his words. 'Aye I was there.'

'But see you, that battle was four, nay five years ago, and you seem scarce more than a lad now.'

The words made no sense. 'Four or five years? It can't be. It can't.' He was shocked into a state of numb disbelief. 'I wandered for a time, just after the battle, perhaps a year but no more than that, since then. No never five years.'

They saw his confusion and recognised the truth in his eyes. 'Well, lad, I don't doubt your words,' Elim had declared for them all. 'Though, see, there is a mystery here and that's no mistake. No wonder either if there be elves involved. Strange and wilful creatures are the elves.' He paused once more, suddenly aware of his words. 'Meaning no offence that is, for I have never had dealings with any of the woodland folk see. So who am I to say? But…' Then another thought crossed the shepherd's mind. 'Elves is it? What indeed were elves doing in Naril? It's a mighty long way from their forest homes of the Elswood isn't it? Oh, I think that it must be something very special to bring them so far.'

'There was only one,' he whispered. 'She said came because of me. I don't understand how or why. I don't even understand how one such as she could be drawn to me but that is as it was. Now she has gone back to the Elswood.'

'Did she have magic?' Cyline asked again from her wonder.

'Magic? Oh yes, she had magic. She was magic, a dancer of fire and light of life and excitement. Yes, she was magic.'

'What did she do?'

'She danced to my soul at first. She danced to the fishes too and they leapt to her hand. Then when there was need she danced a wild magic of life and drove away the grey creatures of the wilderness that were set against us. In the darkness she danced a terrible dance of fury and fire that freed me from… From…' He stumbled on the words, the memories. 'I cannot speak of that. She danced for me.'

They sat in silence, seeing things of which they had no understanding or knowledge, yet each knew the touch of mystery in his words and questioned themselves. *Who was this strange young man who sits here with us? He said that he had been at the battle where, were that true, he would have been not much more than a child? He speaks of an elf with the purity of love in his eyes. He has known a fear too, something so terrible that he cannot even tell of it.*

'And now you go to Varista? There's far.'

'Yes, Varista,' he replied to Elim, grateful for the escape.

'We've never been on a journey that far, look you,' Elim confided, 'But they do tell of the wonders of that place even here you know. The Silver-City they call it. Say that it is a great wonder. What will you do there?'

'Oh I don't know yet. I'll see what there is to see and learn whatever I can learn before I move onwards again. It is but a destination, part of a greater journey to… to… I'm just a pilgrim of the road. Where it leads, so I follow.'

Again they looked on him in awe. 'Well, Pilgrim, there's a thing I can tell you. We do not know of these things ourselves see. We are but shepherds of the flocks and scarce go further than Genvre with our fleeces. Further than Varista you say? There's a thing and no mistake. But we are honoured to have you with us this night and I dare say we'll remember this for many a year and tell it to our grandchildren when we're old.'

'Wife,' he turned his gaze to her with a gentle smile and a laugh. 'Go you, fetch your fiddle, I think we shall give our friend here another memory for the road ahead.'

Soon she sat on the doorstep of the cottage drawing her bow over the strings to bring forth a merry tune, filling the night with brightness and calling the children to their feet to dance out their happiness in wild polkas and reels.

Cyline danced too, wistful and slightly strange. She'd loosened her long golden hair and turned round and around with her flowing locks fanning out about her. It was somehow sad. The others seemed to ignore her most of the time. Although the children liked to go to her and have her swing them about as she danced.

When the youngsters had eventually and reluctantly retired to their beds, those remaining sat in the moonlight with a final goblet of mead. Cyline rested on the grass nearby gazing dreamily into the star filled night.

Elim had been quiet for some time, lost in his own thoughts. Finally he spoke, revealing the truth of his concerns. 'The creatures I spoke of, goblins, though that name fills me with dread, the goblins are abroad again are they not? And growing stronger?'

The Pilgrim looked up into his troubled eyes and nodded gravely. 'Yes, Elim, there can be no denying it. The goblins are indeed abroad again. The sign of their passing is everywhere in the wilderness and up in the mountains too. I fear, as I can hear in your words do you, that this is no longer a safe place to be raising your family and your flocks. I sensed also that you heard more in my words than I said. That is the truth also. A darkness has awakened in the hidden places. The world changes and not always for the better. Who can know what these changes may mean and for whom?'

'I think I was already resolved see,' Elim said sadly. 'Now I am sure. We shall gather our flocks and move back to the towns within the borders of the Varista Marches. There are armies there to protect us. Even though the taxes are high.' His lips turned in a rueful smile.

'Yes,' was all he could say. *It is awoken and reaches out for power.*

They retired to bed late, the moon having already sunk towards her rest left the night to sing them to sleep with the light of the stars. However, the Pilgrim lay restless on the bed unable to find the sleep he sought. Somewhere in the darkness however sleep did come and he drifted with it through the long forgotten pathways of dreams.

The Shepherds were already up and about when the Pilgrim eventually arose. They'd looked in on him and found him asleep and, seeing his tiredness, saw no need to disturb him. When he came stretching into the daylight they greeted him with many a smile and offered him bread, sheep's cheese and fresh ewes' milk to drink. He lingered over breakfast watching as the folk hurried about their business.

'Well then, Pilgrim, You'll be wanting to be on your way then?'

'Elim…?' the Pilgrim asked, unsure of how to broach the matter on his mind.

'Speak your mind, my friend,' came the shepherd's reply, he being aware of the hesitation in the young man's voice.

'There are things I need, that I wish to purchase.' He took the bag of coins from his satchel and dropped a few onto the table. 'I do not want to offend,' anticipating the other's protest. 'If I tell you of my need then you shall name me a fair price.'

Elim looked uncomfortable with the idea but nonetheless nodded his consent. Thus the Pilgrim purchased a new pair of woollen trousers, homespun, hard-wearing and strong, a soft shirt of lamb's wool and a supple sheep's leather jerkin. Despite his feeling of awkwardness Elim was grateful for the coin. He, like the Pilgrim, knew the days ahead might well prove the need for hard money.

Suddenly businesslike, now the trade was done, Elim called out for his family to gather at the gate, to bid farewell to their guest.

'Thank you for your kindness, Elim, and all of you. Your company has lightened my journey and the memory of your friendship shall warm my thoughts on the road ahead.' He bowed to them and hitched his satchel over his shoulder. Each of them bowed or curtsied their farewells and even Tam, Elim's dog, gave a soft bark and wagged his tail.

Pausing as he crossed over the brow of the hill, the Pilgrim looked back to the stockade, waving farewell in reply to those of the group still watching by the gate. His eyes flicked upwards to the now far-off mountains but there was no sign of darkness to trouble his thoughts. *Nonetheless,* he thought to himself, *Elim had best make haste.* Then he turned and left the little oasis of friendliness behind.

The well-kept road helped the Pilgrim to make good speed once again. At first he continued to scan the sky over the now distant mountains but there was nothing. There were no more signs of goblin passage either. By the second day the final view of the mountains' white peeks were left behind.

The road led him onwards through a rock-strewn land of rolling sheep-moor. Even here though the Pilgrim found his mind beset with a sense of unease. Perhaps it was the absence of people, for he had thought to come across other shepherds and their flocks. He did see the occasional sheep grazing here and there but not in the quantities he might have expected. In the end he concluded that the return of the goblins had already caused the country folk to return to the towns for safety.

By nightfall nothing had shown itself and he began to relax. It was probably no more than his imagination.

His caution was gone by the end of the second day and he'd wakened on the third morning with the sounds of birdsong to warm his heart. Humming the soft songs of Hereth, he strode down the roadway. It was a little disappointing that he'd not seen other shepherds or found other habitation but the day was fresh and clear and the countryside far too pleasing to dampen his spirits.

Evening found him near a small wood that reached out into the moor, from a greater forest in the higher land to the north. With the promise of shelter and firewood and a sigh of relief, he turned aside to seek a campsite. He'd shot a jack hare earlier and now, with high spirits and expectation of his evening meal, he hunted the undergrowth collecting firewood.

It came from behind, unexpected and unseen, dropping from one of the trees where it had lain in wait.

Perhaps the rustle of leaves gave warning, an in-drawn breath or maybe just an instinct born of the wilderness, but he was turning even as it attacked, avoiding the iced burn of the slashing blade.

His attacker, having missed in the first frantic onslaught, rolled over on the ground, sprung to its feet, spun and lunged again. He kicked out in near panic, felt the jar as his foot connected. There was a grunt of pain, a glimmer of flickering light and he heard the sound of something clattering on the ground.

With a cry of thwarted rage ringing through the darkening glade it sprang again. Clawing fingers reached for his face, his eyes. He spun quickly sideways blocking the attack on his arm then twisted away again, crouching to meet the next attack. It backed away also, eyes almost closed by its grimace of hate.

The surprise of that first sight was more shocking than a blow. This was no warrior or some creature of the wilderness. No, this was a goblin maid, vibrant, wild and livid with danger! The brilliant burst of her vivid, scarlet hair outshone the sunset.

'What! What the hell are you doing?' he screamed at her.

She didn't wait to answer but leapt at him again, turning at the last moment to lash out with her foot. The blow caught him midriff, doubling him over in a rush of breathlessness but it was not enough to incapacitate him.

'Agh! Got Y' Bastard!' her voice croaked in an exalted shout. Crouching before him she tensed for her next move. Only he was ready again so they circled warily, watching each other like hawks.

She was thin, almost painfully so, clad in a short-sleeved leather tunic which fastened down the front with thongs and was held tight about her waist with a wide belt. Her willow, slender legs were bound by the straps of sandal-like shoes. Her face, despite the glistening ivory buds of extended canines, was unexpectedly neat and well proportioned with high cheekbones and pointed nose and chin, somehow delicate, marred only by the hatred burning in the deep grey pools of her elongated eyes. Her glorious incarnadine hair was wild as her nature. She crouched, waiting, gasping for breath, watching.

Suddenly she leapt again, hoping to catch him by surprise once more but he was ready. He grabbed her wrist as she struck out and found himself grappling frantically with the screaming, kicking creature. She tried to claw his face again but he caught that wrist too. They stood face-to-face, struggling, each trying to gain an advantage. Then he tripped her and they crashed to the ground in a heap of wrestling limbs.

He was heavier, stronger and, although her suppleness made her hard to hold, she was really no match for him. His confidence grew with the realisation. 'STOP!' Not wanting to hurt her. 'Stop fighting me!' He rolled over her, trying to pin her to the ground.

'Agh! Let go then you fuckin' great bastard.' Screaming in fury, she bucked beneath him, rolling sideways to throw him off balance. He grabbed for her, fingers catching her leather tunic, jerked her roughly backwards and wrapped his arms about her waist.

He clung to her, pulling her struggling form tight against him and his awareness was suddenly full of her, the smell of her, the sense of her femaleness and the surprising softness of her hair brushing against his cheek.

'Agh! Let go, shit-head!' Words somehow more shocking than her attack grated with loathing as she wriggled to escape him. 'Agh! Get off of me!'

He held on to her tightly, struggling to subdue her wildly kicking, bucking body. 'Then stop fighting me, Goblin!'

'Agh! NO! Get your crap-stained paws off me you fuckin' arse 'ole!' She bucked and twisted free, knocking him backwards and rolled over to straddle him with her slender legs. He managed to catch her wrists before she could claw his face. She opened her mouth, bared her fang-like teeth, stooping to bite.

He met her with the thrust of a shoulder, knocking her backward with a cry of pain and grabbed her. 'Look, Goblin, I really don't want to hurt you.' He pinned her to the ground. 'I don't want to fight you at all.' With a heave he rolled her over.

Her reply was a bitter snarl of anger. 'Agh! Get off you fuckin' great lump of slime! Agh! Get off me!' She twisted, arching her body, threw him off and, rolling free, scrambling on all fours to get away. The woods rang with her screaming fury as he caught her ankle and dragged her back.

'Won't you just stop fighting for a… SHIT!' She'd kicked him in the face. The shock and pain filled him and grabbing her belt he flung her sideways into a tree, knocking the breath from her. She was still stunned when he rolled her over, face down, and sat astride her legs, pinning her by the shoulders. 'Look, I said I don't want to hurt you or anything. Just stop fighting me!'

'Agh! Let go of me! You fucking bastard!' Still she wriggled to escape him.

He held her tight, struggling to subdue her wildly kicking, bucking body. 'Then stop fighting me, Goblin! Look I really don't want to hurt you. I don't mean you any harm at all. If you'll just lie still I'll let go. But you must stay still.'

Her reply was a bitter snarl of anger. 'Agh! Get off! Get your shit-stained hide off of me! Agh! Get off me or fucking kill me!'

'Look, Goblin!' Still managing to hold her. 'I don't want to kill you. I don't want to kill anyone. I don't want to hurt you or anything. Look it wasn't me who attacked you! You started it.' The words seemed lame, stupid.

'Agh! For fuck-sake you stupid, fuckin' pillock!' She growled though clenched teeth as she fought for breath. 'If I'd been quicker. Agh! You'd be dead now and I'd be suckin' on your fuckin' bones. Agh!' But she lay still beneath him now, no longer struggling save to control her laboured breathing. She probably hoped he'd continue talking until she'd regained enough strength to take him by surprise.

Looking about he noticed his bow where it had fallen in the attack. He made his plan. 'If I thought you could be trusted I'd let go, but I don't.' He grabbed her arms and forced them close to her sides, held them as he shifted his weight onto the small of her back. Then, trapping her arms with his knees, he reached for the bow and freed the cord. 'Lay still!' He pulled one arm up behind her back and bound the wrist.

'I said, Lay still!' She'd begun to fight again as he pulled her other arm. Then he was off and, gripping her arms, dragged her kicking screaming form to the nearest tree. He held her there, binding her wrists over her head, to the tree.

She just slumped, her head hanging in capitulation, her hair forming a tangled flaming curtain over her face. She'd lost and knew it and now awaited her fate and the burning knife that would end her existence.

He sat on the ground beside her, trying to catch his breath. 'Look, I don't know what this is all about. I was just going about my business and then…'

'Agh! Cut the fucking crap, you stupid bastard!' She seemed to be pulling herself together quickly enough. 'Agh, so I attacked you. What do you fuckin' expect? I'm a fuckin' goblin! You're fuckin' human! It's what goblins do. Agh! I wanted you for my grub! Well now you've got me for yours! Agh! So why don't you get on with it. Agh! I hope you fuckin' choke!'

'Oh for goodness sake!' His instant of amusement ended. He was appalled, 'I'm not going to kill you, or eat you. What on earth do you take me for?'

That was her turn for surprise. She lifted her head and looked at him with a quizzed, half fearful expression. 'Agh! What are you goin' t'do then?'

'I don't know.' He didn't either. 'I'm not going to do anything. Look, it was you who started this. You tell me what I'm supposed to do with you! You tell me!'

'Agh! Go fuck yourself! Arsehole!' She spat at him.

Somehow, for the first time really since she'd attacked, that angered him. He stepped near and grabbed the front of her leather tunic, pulling her roughly towards him. 'Look, Goblin, I've had just about enough of your foul tongue.' He almost hit her then but instead put his hand under her chin and lifted her face close to his own. 'So SHUT UP!' He shouted the words at her and dropped her back to the ground.

She was deadly still as he looked at her, waiting for him to act. Only he didn't know what to do. For the lack of any other idea he began to gather the twigs and dry-wood together from where they'd fallen in the attack, at least it gave him the time to gain control over his anger.

Soon he knelt to strike the tinder and fan the flames into blaze. When he pulled the hare from his satchel he heard her move and turned. Seeing the sudden intensity in her stare, 'Are you hungry, Goblin?' holding the hare for her to see. She grunted. The truth of her hunger set in the fire of her eyes. 'When did you last eat, Goblin?'

'Two full fuckin' days, Man. Agh! Then only a fuckin' mole!' The suspicion of a trick lay heavily in her voice.

Mole? She's been eating moles? 'You can have some of this if you want,' he gestured at the hare.

Her eyes opened wide in shock. 'Some of it? To eat? You want a food truce?' Her surprise cut the air between them. 'Agh! You want to make a food truce with me? When you didn't snuff me I thought it was that you just wanted to root me first. Agh! Then you'd fuckin' do for me. Food Truce?'

Food Truce? 'I don't know what a food truce is. Tell me.'

'A truce, you know, Man? Time, terms and gain. For one day, Agh! You will not try to kill me; I will not try to kill you. We share the camp. The food is the price of the truce. Agh! Your food and my food.'

At least it seemed to be some sort of answer. 'Yes, Goblin. We can have a Food Truce.'

'Agh! Shit! I have no fuckin' food, Man.'

No food, no truce. 'Is there a way?'

'Agh! Fuck! I shall owe you. My truce shall last until I have paid. Agh! Will that do?' She didn't like the terms. It gave him power over her but somehow he knew that she spoke the truth. 'Agh! Man. You are not so bound.' It matched the balance of the situation.

'OK. I accept the truce on these terms.'

'And I,' she replied. 'Agh! We are in Truce.' *Formal words.*

'We are in Truce,' he echoed her words.

'So tell me, Goblin,' he tried after a moment, 'If I untie you will you want to fight again?'

Again her face showed the shock of hearing the unthinkable. 'We have Truce.'

'Right. Just making sure.' It seemed to be all that was needed so he went to her and unfastened the bowstring from her wrists.

She didn't move at first, just sat there, rubbing where the cord had bitten into her flesh. Then she rose to walk over to the fire. She was even thinner than he'd first thought. Her arms and legs seemed somehow spider-like, little more than sticks really. Her movements were precise and darting-quick but she lacked the grace, the naturalness of an elf, My Elf. The Pilgrim watched, curious of what she might do. She squatted down before the flames and seemed to examine the way the fire was built.

'Agh! A good fire, Man!' For some reason she seemed to be impressed.

Not knowing how to respond he tried, 'Do you want to start the meat? I'll look for some herbs and roots.' She turned to look at him clearly not understanding what he was saying to her. 'The meat needs cooking.'

'Agh! Cookin'? Man stuff, burning! Oh bollix! You'll ruin the fuckin' blood.' She spat her disgust into the fire.

'Have it your own way, Goblin,' laughing at the expression on her face. 'Go and get your knife and cut it in two. I'm cooking mine. You can do as you want with yours.'

She chuckled, a strange, unexpected sound like the crushing of autumn-dry leaves. 'Agh! You have it YOUR way then, Man.' She scrambled into the undergrowth, reappearing after some five or six minutes clutching the knife. Then crouching down beside the fire she began to cut the meat in two.

There was a patch of kale-leaf growing at the wood edge and having picked enough of these, as well as a few cloves of wild garlic, he returned to the camp. She hadn't started to eat yet, but sat waiting for him with the two pieces of meat before her.

She felt his questioning eye. 'Your catch, your choice. Agh!'

He took one piece, not really thinking. It didn't matter. Both were more than enough for a single meal. His real interest was her. There was something surprisingly formal about the way she saw things. It was as if her world was totally ordered and governed by rules.

He took his half and continued to cut it into pieces for the pot with the garlic and kale. She sat there watching intently, still not starting to eat.

'Go on, you're hungry, Goblin, start.'

Again she looked at him in surprise. 'Agh! You don't mind?'

'Of course not. Go on eat.'

She shrugged her shoulders, 'If you say so.' Needing no more prompting she buried her face into the meat, biting off a huge mouthful. She ate noisily, obviously savouring the moment. The Pilgrim did not think to interrupt her despite his near revulsion over her behaviour.

His own meal was as yet half cooked when she wriggled back to lean against the tree and belched with a loud contented freedom. 'Agh! Bollix Man! That was fuckin' great.' She cracked a shinbone in her teeth and began to suck on the marrow.

He winced again at the crudeness of her tongue. 'I'm glad you enjoyed it.' And returned to his cooking.

'Agh! You fight fuckin' good, Man,' she declared. 'Too strong for me! Agh! So why didn't you kill me? Agh! Or fuck me silly? How come you don't want to hurt me nor nothin'?'

'I don't want to fight.' His answer was soft and full of meaning. 'I don't want to fight, or hurt, or kill or harm anyone, there's been far too much of that already. If you had asked, I'd have shared my food with you without that, made you welcome in my camp.' She was looking at him with total incomprehension. 'Look I'm just a pilgrim travelling my road, seeking my, seeking... Now what's up?' Her face had turned ashen white with fear, eyes suddenly wide, transfixed. 'What's up? Whatever's the matter? Tell me.'

'Pilgrim?' Her voice rang with total despair. 'Oh fuck! I've just fuckin' ambushed the Fuckin' Pilgrim.' Her eyes flicked about waiting for the oncoming doom. 'They'll fuckin' kill me, skin me alive, if ever they find out. Oh shit! The fuckin' Pilgrim!' She lifted her eyes to him. 'What have I fuckin' done? I nearly killed you!'

He laughed, a cold humourless laugh, feeling shocked to the core by the intensity of her reaction. 'I don't know, Goblin, but it seems it's you who was in danger not me.' *She might have answers.*

It was too much, far too much for her mind to grasp. She laughed aloud, almost crazily. 'Too fuckin' right! I didn't even know the danger and now you'll fuckin' do for me good.' She seemed resigned.

'I'm not going to kill you, Goblin.'

'Not kill me?' His words didn't seem to make sense. Of course he was going to kill her.

'Of course not. We're in truce. Aren't we?'

She paused, long and hard, grappling with the strangeness of his words. 'Agh! Truce, We are in truce? Yes we are in truce. You honour the truce? Shit, why? My *Kla*?'

'Of course I do! I gave my word, Time, Terms and gain! Do you think I would break it?'

'Yes! I mean No. I. Agh!' Confusion robbed her of any sense. 'I do not, cannot understand. Forgive me, My *Kla*!'

'*Kla*? What's that?'

Bowing in supplication she touched her forehead to the ground. 'I choose. You are The Pilgrim, Agh! Power-Lord and, My *Kla*, my Truce-Lord.' She was silent for a moment, biting her lip as she thought. She smiled again. 'Agh! I will serve you well.'

'Serve me? What do you mean serve me?' This was all becoming too much for him as well now. 'Look I don't want you to serve me. I don't want anyone to serve me. I don't need any servants! I couldn't ask that of anyone. All that I ask, all I want is that we don't actually kill each other. There's been too much killing and death already. I don't think I could stand it if I brought about your death.' But it was clear that his words shook her to the core.

'Look,' he continued, *Perhaps there is an answer.* 'I'm just trying to survive, I don't want anyone serve me.' Another thought crossed his mind. 'I'll tell you what I do want though.'

'What, My Kla?' She waited to hear of her terrible doom.

'I want us to be friends.' She looked blank as well she might. There's no such notion as friendship in goblin relationships. He tried again, 'We shall have, Friend-Truce!'

'What is Friend-Truce, My Kla?'

'The hardest truce of all, Goblin.' He was thinking on his feet, as they say. 'It means that we will NEVER seek to harm each other. It means that if we want we can help each other. It does not tie us to each other save if we want it to, it does not bind us in any way. It just means that we are friends.'

The confusion filled her eyes, but she struggled to understand 'Friends' and failed completely. The ways of this quiet being were too strange for her to grasp.

'So do you accept my Friend-Truce?'

'I don't really understand, My Kla. Agh! What are the terms?'

'Terms?'

'The Law of the truce, for time, for term, for gain.'

'I'm not sure that there are…' He thought. 'The time is ALWAYS. I shall NEVER try to harm you. You will NEVER try to harm me. That is it.'

'But… But what is the gain?' Bewilderment spun in her eyes.

'The gain is ours alone. You live and I don't have to kill. It is so because we wish it to be so. We might even help each other.'

'Agh! I do not understand you, My Kla, but I will accept the Friend-Truce and shall try to learn of it. We are in Friend-Truce.'

'We are in Friend-Truce. You are my Friend, I am yours.'

'You are my friend, I am yours.' She repeated the words without understanding. Perhaps that would follow. 'Agh! You will have to show me what this means, My Kla.'

'To begin,' he smiled again, 'I'm not anyone's Kla, I'm just a pilgrim travelling alone in the wilds. Now I'm your friend. You can call me anything you want. Others have named me Pilgrim, so that's as good a name as any at this time. You can call me that or maybe just "Friend" or even "Arsehole" if it takes your fancy.' Shock creased her face for a moment before she grinned back at him. Returning the smile he asked, 'What should I call you?'

She was silent for a long time. Some kind of battle was troubling her thoughts. In the end a decision was reached. 'Most other goblins call me Shit-head, 'cause of my hair. You see it is not the way of goblins to give of their names. Agh! There is power in naming. But, I am Icicle.' She lowered her head almost shy.

'Icicle? It's such a pretty name. My friend Icicle.'

She smiled then, a smile of true happiness. Those steel grey eyes shone like the purest sapphire. There was something truly resilient about this being.

By this time his meal was cooked and it was his turn to eat. She watched in silence a soft look of wonder on her face. At the end there was still some left. 'Would you like to try this?' He offered the pot towards her.

She shook her head quickly, but then. 'To taste,' and moved over to take it from him. Sitting cross-legged on the ground, she'd watched how he'd eaten from his knife, and did likewise. His eyes caught the black of her knife. 'Agh! This is OK. Not too fuckin' burnt. Tastes good.'

He laughed as she cleaned the pot. 'See, I thought that you might like it.' He waited for a moment. 'Icicle…?'

'Yes, Friend?' She lingered over the sound of the word.

'The knife, may I see it?'

She wiped the blade against her leg and tossed it over without a thought. It was made of stone, something like onyx or perhaps jet, honed to a razor sharp edge. He started to turn it in his fingers, feeling the balance, the strength. But its coldness was almost painful, as was the sense of doom laid upon it. There was something secret about it, some unfinished task. He really didn't want to know what. He hurriedly tossed it back. She caught it in mid air and tucked it back under her belt.

'I don't think I've ever seen a knife like that. Where did you get it?'

'Agh!' She smiled at that. 'I made it myself, Friend, when I was just a smog.' *Child?* She didn't seem that much older now. 'Just as fuckin' well though. Agh! It's saved my fuckin' hide a time or two. And kept me from feeling the twigs of more than one fuckin' goblin buck.' She looked at him and smiled again. 'It's the way of goblins. We make our own weapons. Well that's how it was… It is the only way to trust them.' She looked up at him staring into his eyes. 'It scares them too.'

'Scares them?'

'Too fuckin' right! The stupid sods think that black is too strong, they think that if I cut them that they will belong to me! That makes them scared of me! That and my hair.'

'Your hair? But it's beautiful…'

'Yeh!' She dismissed his praise. 'But NOT fuckin' goblin! Agh! They think I'm touched by the Powers.' Her voice drifted away as if just realising what she was saying.

'Is that why you're alone? I wondered why you were here. I mean, we're a long way from the lands of your people. Is this why you're here alone like this?'

'That and other things too. Agh!' She didn't expand. 'I can ask the same, Pilgrim. Why are you here? Why didn't you kill me? Or fuck me? Or even want me as your slave? You had enough fuckin' cause. I attacked you. Agh! A goblin would have wanted something. You gave me food. I don't understand.'

'Me? I said it before; I'm just a pilgrim on my journey. I don't kill, save for food and that gives me no pleasure, only meat. Why should I pave my way with the corpses of the dead, those I've slain? I value life, and the living. Why should I want the death of a little goblin called Icicle? No. How could I ever get to know you? I seek…'

Her eyes grew somehow softer. 'What? What do you seek, Pilgrim?'

'Oh, I don't know that I can say, explain. It's too much. I seek many things, Icicle. It probably sounds silly but I suppose that most of all I seek to find out just who I am.'

'You are… you are The Pilgrim.' That sounded almost too final.

'Yes,' he had to agree. 'I am The Pilgrim, whatever the name means. You've named me, and you're not the first. But what's meant by it? I really don't know. Each, I fear, sees their own meaning and their own promise. Yes I'm a pilgrim and as a pilgrim I seek. That's what pilgrims do, travel to the ends of the earth if so needed to seek their answers. What of you, Icicle, what do you seek? Yes, tell me about yourself; what do you really want?'

'What do I want? Agh!' She seemed surprised that he might even be interested. 'I want many things too, Pilgrim. Agh! I am *Hhaag*, alone, well I was. I don't really know what I am now, *Klahagh?* I'm not sure. Your words seem to fuck-up my head! Agh! You don't want to rule me even if I wanted it, so. I always thought that I wanted to be *Ghaal*, to belong to my own group. One day I wanted to be part of a *Ghalg* perhaps even to become *Gha*, a leader of a band.' She sounded wistful. 'I want power, Pilgrim. Agh! Every bit of my fuckin' body screams out for it. I need it like you need air. I crave it with my very being. It's the only thing that gives life meaning. I am not as You, I do not shun killing. Agh! Not if it gets me what I fuckin' want, not if it fills my belly. Agh! It's the goblin way. Power is everything.' She looked at him, seeking sign of rejection in his eyes.

'I don't judge you, Icicle. You are what you are, and now you're my friend.'

She rose to her feet, unexpectedly, and walked over to stand before him. Then she knelt, but inches from him and took both his hands in hers. 'Yes. Agh! I am your friend now. Agh!' She smiled at him again and, once again, that unexpected warmth shone in her eyes. 'You are The Pilgrim…' There was a meaning here, waiting to be spoken. 'I want what all the Goblin people want, Pilgrim. I want what was taken from us. I want what was ours. What was promised.' The intensity of her need burnt in her eyes. 'Will you return it? Will you give it back?'

'Will I return it? I don't know what you're talking about. Tell me.'

'When The Vortex is yours, Will you return the fire to our souls? To my soul?'

'The Vortex?' *Even she knows of it.* 'I don't even know what this Vortex is. It's just a name to me. Tell me.'

'Tell you? You're The Pilgrim and you want me to fuckin' tell you? You're supposed to be a fuckin' Power, *Klagash*. You're supposed to have the fuckin' answers. You want me to explain?'

He held her eyes for a moment, then nodded his assent.

'There is change in the wind, Pilgrim,' she continued. 'The skies scream of it. The earth moans of it. The seas roar of it. The bindings are loosened, the constraints lifted. Things long asleep are awakened. Things hidden in the dark begin to stir, things that were better undisturbed.

'We, the People, the Goblin People, even the Thirteen Tribes are free to come from the gloom. I am come into daylight. I came to see, to try to know. I came looking for you also. I came looking for an answer! I want it back! WILL YOU GIVE IT TO ME?'

She rose to her feet again, turned her back to him awaiting his words.

'I don't know, Icicle, I can't tell you of things I don't understand. I don't even know what the words mean. *The Vortex*. This I will say. This I will promise. When I do know, when I do understand, if when as you tell The Vortex is mine, whatever that means, I will tell you the truth.'

'Agh! Truth!' He heard her spit into the fire. She was silent for a long time then, still as stone. Eventually she turned again and squatted on the ground before him. 'Agh! It is not as I asked, Pilgrim, but it is an answer. Yes, your truth is enough for now.'

There was another period of thought. 'You want to go your own way, find your own answers, Pilgrim. There are those who have other ideas, other plans. Your truth will not be enough for them, not for those of the Tribes.'

He heard the warning in her voice. 'The Tribes? What of them?'

'Agh! They are not as me. They have their power and their place Agh! They will not wait, Pilgrim. They will seek you out, track you down and try to bend you to their ways. They will want to rule over you and possess the power that shall be yours.' Moving even closer, she knelt on the grass before him and stared into his eyes. 'They want your Magic, Pilgrim. They want to control you. They want to take your spirit, take its colour for themselves. They want to turn your rainbow grey!'

He had no answer.

They sat in silence as the stars climbed the night sky to look down on them. If stars have minds they might have wondered about the strangeness of the scene below, but they don't, well at least not as we might understand. The Pilgrim spread out his cloak on the ground and sat cross-legged looking into the fire. The strange red-haired goblin returned to her tree and stayed leaning against the trunk.

Sometime, when the fire had died to little more than embers, sleep took the Pilgrim and he curled up, wrapped himself in his cloak. Even later, in the very heart of the night he awoke. She was still there. Their eyes touched and she smiled mysteriously but there were no words. In the first, half-light of dawn he awoke again. She was gone.

The small wood seemed somehow quiet and empty in the first, misted light of morning. The overcast sky threatened of rain and dawn showed as little more than a vague orange blush in the lower sky. The songbirds for their part were still too.

The Pilgrim felt totally alone as, with little more than disinterested habit, he knelt to stir the fire back to life. The breakfast of re-boiled tea, dry bread and sheep's cheese did nothing to brighten his mood. Unsure whether the goblin lass had actually gone he was reluctant to take to the road until sure. Eventually, having cleared away the signs of the fire, he shrugged, took up his staff and returned to the road once more.

Daylight turned to a darker grey. Drizzle rather than rain drifted mist-like over the moorland, dampening his spirit as much as his clothes. The cloak offered a degree of protection but the air was warm and before long the damp worsted became stifling. In the end he threw back the hood and let the water drip through his long, dark hair, *I really must get it cut sometime*. The stubble of beard was uncomfortable, irritating.

His thoughts, no less annoying, turned round and around, unfocused and confused, not finding answers to any of the questions that formed. *Who is Icicle any way? What's she got to do with me anyway? ...It's probably just as well she went on her own way. I can hardly imagine taking her into the lands of men*, he concluded. *I wonder what people would make of my being friendly with a goblin? Somehow I don't really want to know.* He almost smiled at the thought, recalling the shepherd's reaction to the barest mention of the goblin peoples. He remembered also, with an unwelcome taste of bitterness, the anger that had turned the warriors of the King's army on the Plains-of-Sarum into creatures of death and destruction, hate and loathing.

At least I'm not like that. Should I be? For sure I don't think like them? I actually quite liked Icicle. They'd probably see me as a traitor, a traitor to my own kind. And what kind is that? For certain I'm not like those at Sarum. I hate killing and do anything to avoid it. Why's that? I've never really got to the bottom of that matter either. Other people seem to be able to kill. It's like they just don't see things in the same way as me. They seem to want to hate, anything will do, anything or anyone different to themselves, Man, Elf or Goblin. Not that they're really that different, the colour of their skins, their tongues for sure but they're not really so unlike each other. They wouldn't like that thought either, he realised, recalling Elim's reaction to his talk of elves and the Fire-Dancer. However, that took his mind into another realm completely; one that woke the joy in his heart and made him careless of whatever the day might decide to offer.

As if in response to his lightening of mood, midday saw the misty rain ease off. The sun strained to shine through the cloud and the puddles began to dry again. Although he was aware that there were still no people, shepherds or whatever, the signs of their presence were growing more frequent. He passed another small farmstead sometime about mid-afternoon and stopped to draw water from its well.

Several miles further on, was another empty house, left tidy as if the shepherds might return at any moment. He forewent the chance to overnight there and continued on for another hour finding rest by a small pool where a spring rose up from the moor-land It was a quiet night and he woke early keen to be on his way.

The new morning had barely woken, the sun just lifting its face over the rolling hills before him. The ever-present birds sang out their customary greeting in high-pitched chorus. Then came another sound, sharp and crystal clear, resounding through the dawn air. At first he stopped, struggling to understand, to recognise. *Bugle. It's a bugle.*

Reveille echoed over the land, rang through the morning air, calling men to arms and birds to panic, a jarring, unnatural message that woke in his breast the awareness that his journey alone was probably at an end. Ahead lay the Lands-of-Men and whatever might await him. His sense of haste suddenly departed and the remaining reluctance caused him to linger over tasks that would usually take but moments. He not was afraid of what lay ahead or even shy to the idea of meeting others. Rather it was a yearning for the wilderness with its untamed beauty and strange folk he must leave behind. *She'll not come seeking me, dancing or sparkling in her bright life-laughter, not in the dowdy halls of men. Shall I ever see her again? Will we meet beyond, on the hidden paths of the future?*

He washed the sleep from his eyes in the clear water of the trickling spring and finger-combed his long hair before tying it back with a leather thong. *Well then,* he told himself, throwing the cloak about his shoulders and picking up his satchel and hawthorn staff, *there's no point in waiting. As Icicle might say: 'Fuck it! Here goes.'* With the thought bringing a gentle smile to his lips and lightening his tread, he did indeed step out towards whatever fate awaited him.

It didn't take long to find out. Less than a mile down the road a vast encampment spread out over the plain. Tents, white, sharp and tight – there must have been over five hundred of them – were set out with military precision into four great squares, two on each side of the road. In the centre, just to the right of the road, stood a large pavilion over which a standard hung limp in the still morning air. A wall of stakes, gated to allow the road's passage, surrounded the camp and in the guard-post at the gate two sentries, armoured with shield and spear, patrolled to-and-fro. The smoke, drifting leisurely upwards from the countless breakfast-fires, gave the whole scene a hint of unreality.

The two guards at the gateway drew themselves to attention. A third, who had been hidden from sight by the wall, hurried off towards the pavilion. The Pilgrim waved a hand to them, and strolled down the road.

By the time he'd reached the guard-post several others had arrived and a murmuring buzz stirring through the camp gave recognition to his presence.

'Halt!' the guard shouted, formal, ordered and military, and the Pilgrim complied, resting lightly on his staff.

Another soldier, an officer, clad splendid in silver and black, stepped beside the guardsman who barked again. 'State your business.'

'I'm a Pilgrim travelling from Santolin. I seek passage through the lands ahead to the City of Varista.'

If the officer felt any surprise, or anything else for that matter, his face gave no sign. 'This is the road to Varista,' ignoring the soldier who had first spoken. 'Although the City is still some sixteen days' march away. I am General The Lord Asheld, Guardian-of-Western-Bronden. Enter the Camp, Pilgrim. I would have words with you.'

Without further ado, and with the unquestioned knowledge that he would be obeyed, the General turned, leaving the Pilgrim little option but to tag on behind, following towards the great pavilion. Two other guards fell in beside him. They too showed no sign of friendship or hostility.

In the shelter of the pavilion's awning, a table and several chairs were drawn together. 'Sit there.' The General pointed to one of the chairs, having sat himself down first, of course. 'Tea shall be brought.' The helmet was removed, uncovering a chiselled face set with eyes of stone.

In the silence of the moment the Pilgrim cast his eyes about. The camp was busy with its daily business. Cooking fires were being doused, steam and hissing coals. Squads of black-armoured spearmen began to parade between the tent lines. The sound of barked orders punctuated the noise of the morning.

The thought came unbidden, *Elves dance and Dwarves forge, Goblins swear and Soldiers shout. And Pilgrims only watch.* Overhead the huge standard rippled slightly in a breath of early breeze, a silver boat sailing on a black sea.

'What do you see?' the General snapped the Pilgrim's attention back to the present.

'Everything is very ordered, Sir,' the Pilgrim offered, wondering how, or if, he might break the reserve of formality surrounding the general.

'Order is everything,' the General snapped again. 'Without order is chaos and in chaos lies disaster.'

The Pilgrim could think of no reply, though did it occur to him that Icicle might well have said the same thing. *I doubt he'd want to know it though.*

They waited without further exchange as several officers, five in all, joined them. Each stiffly saluted before being instructed to 'Sit there.' Only one was introduced. 'Kaville, my Executive Officer.'

The Pilgrim surmised them to be the general's lieutenants. They were dressed much as he, save that the horsehair crests of their helms differed – red, green, yellow and blue. Both the General and Kaville had crests of white.

Eventually, with all seats filled, an orderly arrived carrying a tray of cups and a huge flask of tea. He placed these upon the table and saluted. 'Permission to pour the tea, Sir!' the orderly's voice like a whip.

Once the General had nodded his approval the tea was summarily poured and cups handed around, the General first, of course.

'Well then, Pilgrim, pray tell us, why do you journey to Varista?' The General brought the proceedings back into order.

'Simply that, Sir, I am a pilgrim on my road. I quest for knowledge and Varista is the next destination on my journey.' They sat waiting as the tension built, *Am I supposed to feel pressured or intimidated?* but he'd spent too long alone in the wilderness to mind silence.

The General turned to his lieutenants, 'Well?'

'No mention of duty, Sir,' said one.

'Who sent him, Sir?' tried another.

Kaville, the Executive Officer, said nothing. He sat there stroking his extravagant moustache as if trying to acquire an air of superiority.

'No,' the General corrected, managing to sound somehow school-masterly. 'Look for order or its lack! He says he is a pilgrim questing for knowledge. Pilgrims seek knowledge. He comes on foot as is usual with pilgrims. His cloak shows the dust of the road and his walking staff is strong and fit to the task. This road is the road to Varista and someone seeking knowledge would indeed desire to go unto the Silver City. There is order in the words.'

'So tell us, Pilgrim, from where do you travel?' Soft words in a voice of iron as the General turned back to face him.

'I am from The Land-of-Hereth in the Kingdom-of-Santolin, Sir.' He wanted to laugh, to break the spell of ridiculousness this strange formal inquisition had planted in his breast.

'What say you?' He spoke again to the Lieutenants.

'His voice is of the North, Sir.'

'Sir!' One spoke importantly, thinking to impress. 'The sergeant of the second maniple of the first cohort is from Santolin. I even think I have heard him speak the name Hereth.'

'Good man, Rannan, send for him.'

Rannan shot to his feet and saluted. 'Sir!' And spoke to one of the guards standing close by. The man hurried off across the road to one of the camps, disappearing among the tents. The Lieutenant returned to his seat.

'By what route have you come then?' the General continued.

'I came by way of Barril on the northern coast. From there I turned southwards, crossed over the Heights of Santolin and over the Sarum plane. My journey took me down through the grasslands of Lodor. I skirted the high peeks of Naril turning eastwards.' He hesitated, unsure how to proceed. 'I passed through other, darker places too on that fell road, and now, eventually I have come here.'

'A long road, young man.' The General did seem impressed by that. 'Goblins?'

'Yes, Sir, there are signs of goblins everywhere in the wilder lands. They're growing bolder and are reaching out from their hidden places. The scars of their campfires lie, as a blight, throughout the Land-of-Naril. There are signs too among the pastures of the shepherds to the west of here. I stayed at a farm but a few days west of here and was told of goblin raiding parties troubling the herders.'

'So the goblins are coming are they?'

'I don't know that, Sir. I had thought, believed that they were banished, no more. I did not think that they would come once again to threaten the Lands-of-Men. But now for sure it cannot be denied, they are abroad again.'

He looked up as the messenger returned with another. *From Santolin? Hereth? Do I know him?* There was something familiar, but...

The sergeant came to a halt before the band of officers. In an instant his whole form was as ridged as iron. Salute. 'Sah! Reporting as ordered, Sah!' his voice barked, almost unintelligible.

'At ease, Sergeant,' the General barely whispered. 'From Santolin, Sergeant?'

'Sah! Yes, Sah!'

'Good, good,' the General continued. 'Do you know of Hereth, Sergeant?'

'Sah! Yes, Sah!' the voice barked again. 'Home of my kindred, Sah, north of Santolin, Sah, near the sea, Sah!'

'Good, oh yes very good indeed, Sergeant. Look at this man.'

The Pilgrim felt the touch of the sergeant's eyes on him and lifted his own to meet the inspection. For a moment they gazed at each other. Then recognition came. He saw the sergeant's face whiten. *Fear? Why fear?*

'Do you know him?'

'I do. Yes.' The military formality caught up, 'Sah! From Hereth, Sah! Son of the Lady, Sah!'

'The Lady, Sergeant?'

'Sah! Yes, Sah! The Lady-of-Hereth, Sah! From the Hall…' the voice trailed away.

'Sergeant!'

'Sah?'

'Tell us what you know.'

'Yes, Sah! This is the youngest son of the Lady, Sah. They live in the great Hall-of-Hereth, Sah. Their Father is The Baron-of-Hereth, once High-Captain of The Kings Army, Sah, Well, so he was, Sah. Fought in the Goblin Wars of Old, Sah!'

'Seek the Order of things,' the General instructed his lieutenants once more. He turned again to the sergeant. 'His father is The Baron but you name him "The Lady's son", Sergeant?'

'Sah! Yes, Sah! They are said to be magical folk, Sah! The Lady is the Lady-of-Flowers, Sah! She is wise, Sah! A healer, Sah! Powerful.'

The General's gaze returned to the Pilgrim. His voice softened somewhat as if feeling some sort of kinship now. 'This seems strange, Pilgrim. I do not know of magic. Tell me.'

'I don't know what to tell really. It is as… as…' The name came to him suddenly. *Douglas Staffbinder, one of the sons of Hewel Staffbinder the smith of Saddleford. Only, he's too old. Should only be my own age.* 'Douglas. Yes Douglas Staffbinder, Sergeant Staffbinder? Yes?' He saw the nodded confirmation, 'Yes it is as the Sergeant says. My mother is the Lady-of-Flowers. One might call her magical, my brother and sisters also. But they are not here and my being here isn't magical.' Doubt began to creep into his own mind. *So just why am I here? Why here and why now?*

The General looked at him, almost kindly were it possible in such an eagle-like visage. 'I see many things young man, some of them not seen too, if you take my meaning. Perhaps it is better not to speak of them at this time and in this place. Tell us what you can though.'

Before the Pilgrim could answer, the General turned back to his Lieutenants. 'There is something new here. Higher orders are at work. I see their signs. Note! Not just a pilgrim, but a Lord's Son. Not just a Lord's son either, but that of a commander of armies. We seek word of the goblins, and he comes from the Mountains of Naril with tale of them.' He had made his point.

The questioning eyes returned to the Pilgrim.

'Sir, of the goblins I can tell some. Although my news is not good.' He paused wanting to make the awfulness of his words alive for them. 'As I said before, my journey has taken me into dark and terrible places, Sir. Although it wasn't my intent, I have learnt something of the goblins and their Grey-Masters. I've been into the Galghathag…' He waited for a reaction to the terrible name. None came. 'I ventured into the heart of the goblin kingdom of old. I have seen a terrible thing there, the rising of dark powers and the Awakening of Their Foul Lord. The Goblin Tribes are rising again. They even raid the sheepfolds not many days away, already. They see their time coming, but I am unsure of much more.'

'Numbers, do you know their numbers?'

'No, Sir, for I don't, I mean I didn't, see things in terms of numbers. But I know of their evil and their hatred. The Tribes ARE gathering that's for sure. Their Lord has awakened and his power grows. They've sulked long in their dark demesne, biding their time. Their waiting nears its end.'

'Well, young sir, we are ready for them, Ready.' His voice rang with sudden life. 'My order will meet their chaos, my truths, their lies and illusions.' He stopped, thought driven into silence. 'You shall need to make haste unto Varista, Young Sir, to meet with the Magicians of Varista in their Halls-of-Learning. Perhaps they shall be able to unravel the mysteries of this.'

Suddenly he was The General again.

'Sergeant!'

'Sah!' Snapping to attention.

'Take six men from the ranks. Draw horses and thirty-five days' rations, provisions for your patrol and one other. Escort the Young Pilgrim Lord to the Magi in Varista. I'll give you a message for the High Command also. When you've done so return here.'

'Sah! Yes, Sah! Six Men, Sah! Escort him to the Magi in Varista! Message for the High Command! Return here! Sah! Right now, Sah?'

'Collect your men, Sergeant, and return here ready to travel, one hour from now.'

'Sah! Yes, Sah!' A final salute and he was gone.

'There, drink up your tea, young man.' The General smiled at the Pilgrim's grimace over the strong, sickly-sweet brew. 'Soldiers' tea,' he explained. 'It'll put fire into your belly.

'Right!' He turned to his Lieutenants. 'The first Cohort will form a screen four hours out. Set pickets and a communication line back to here.' He seemed almost excited. 'If they come, avoid contact if you can but whatever happens keep me informed.'

He turned to another. 'Take a patrol, two maniples should do, and go into the sheep lands bring back any of the shepherds you find and try to discover where the goblins are lurking. Ten days should suffice. You can send runners with news.

'If you please, Pilgrim, I'm asking you to pass word of these matters to the Magi in Varista, I'll give the sergeant a message to the King's High Commander. That should suffice.

'Right I want the other Cohorts to parade at midday, armed and armoured. Keep them informed. If men know what they're about they'll do their duty all the more the readily. Right! About your duties!'

As one they snapped to their feet, crashed a salute and turned to leave,

'Right, young man, you've not eaten this morning. I shall send for food.' He smiled at the Pilgrim's questioning look. 'It's a question of order. You arrived just twenty minutes after the reveille call. That means the call disturbed you and brought you here. No time for breakfast fires.' He then spoke to the orderly. 'Breakfast!'

'Sah!' And the man was gone with a clash of boot heels.

The Pilgrim sipped at the sickly tea once more and tried to make the best of the situation. 'Sir,' he tried, 'you were right about the goblins and my journey. There are indeed forces at work in the world, although I don't seem to understand much of the things I see.' He paused, waiting.

The General nodded for him to continue.

'I was not alone in the wilderness, Sir. I travelled with an elf. She had waited for me and led me through the mountains. Her magical powers kept us free of the goblins, and of the grasp of the Creature-of-Mists. This is no small uprising, General. The evil of the Galomist creeps abroad. Too soon the grey Warriors-of-the-Mist will walk again in the lands of men. I fear that sometime soon the whole world will quake with their rising.' The fear burning in his heart stilled his words.

'A new Goblin War!' The General's excitement rang like a gong. 'It's for this I'm here, lad, the first defence of the Lands-of-Men. I'll not be found wanting, no not indeed. If the Elves rise too and the Dwarven peoples join us then surely there's no need for fear?' He paused again almost swelling at the thought of what might be.

Oh NO! He actually wants a war! Is this the way of all men? The Pilgrim's heart quailed, froze in his breast. *Killing, that's all they seem to understand, just killing and more killing, God, how they revel in their thoughts of fighting. They're no different to the goblins from whom they claim to defend the Land. Hate and... And...* There was nothing more to be said. He sat there unmoving, repulsed and revolted by the eager expectation that burned in the soldier's eyes.

The orderly arrived with food, bacon and eggs, hard brown bread and more of the undrinkable tea. At least it gave the Pilgrim a reason for silence, not that the General seemed to notice.

'Look, lad,' he offered as the Pilgrim finished the meal, 'I've many a task to do and must be about them. The Sergeant will be here soon. You go with him. Make haste to Varista and tell the Magi what you know. Yes that's right. I'll be about my business, you wait here for the Sergeant.'

The Pilgrim stood with the Commander and nodded his farewell. He couldn't bring himself to reply to the others' 'Good-day' and sat gratefully once he was alone again.

To the very minute the Sergeant returned. He was accompanied by six other troopers, all mounted on black horses. One led an eighth horse, obviously intended for the Pilgrim. Another led a string of four laden packhorses.

'If you're ready, Sir?' the sergeant tried.

Ready? I doubt that I ever shall be. There seemed little choice. He stood, hitched his satchel over the saddlebow and pushed his staff into the roll behind. Then he mounted the horse. 'Yes, let's be on our way,' he agreed as the Sergeant pulled alongside.

'As you say, Sir.' The soldier sounded cold, formal. His eyes still held the tinge of fear.

The Pilgrim nudged the horse forward. 'I'm uneasy with the "Sir" bit, Sergeant, Douglas. Please just call me Pilgrim.'

'If that's how you want it, Pilgrim?'

'It's what I am now, just a pilgrim of the road seeking knowledge. Can't we just leave it at that?'

The Sergeant's eyes turned on him with an intensity that was almost overwhelming. After almost two minutes he spoke, 'Aye, I'll call you Pilgrim.' His words seemed to belie the agreement. 'And aye, Pilgrim you might well be. Now that is, but I was at the battle on Sarum Plain. I saw. I know what I saw.' There was no answer. Perhaps time and the trail ahead would heal things.

But it didn't. The troopers had their own ways and their own views of those 'Not-of-the-shield'. It wasn't that they were unsociable but rather that he just didn't count in their reckoning of things. They'd talk amongst themselves, sharing their own jokes, familiar and comfortable with their own way of life. The stranger in their midst was of little consequence.

The miles rolled by quickly now and gradually the Pilgrim did come to know a little more of them. The sergeant, Douglas Staffbinder, he had known of at home. He'd won the log-lift at the Saddleford fayre, the year that the Pilgrim had returned from the Carrow. He was well liked by the farm-kids and had spoken more than once with the Pilgrim, although they'd never been friends or playmates. It seemed unlikely they ever would be now.

Beside him, there was a Corporal, Lostock, a man of Bronden with a raucous laugh and a tongue every bit as foul as Icicle's. There was Josie, almost a giant, who said little and cared for the horses. Art' was little more than a youth. The others teased and perhaps even bullied him but he seemed to accept this with good grace and a cheery smile. Two were brothers Dinin and Farle. The last was an older man, Tarlin, who said little and kept himself apart, even from the other troopers.

By nightfall, that first day, they'd passed through several villages and halted at a roadside inn. Here, as the troopers set to drinking with a will, the Pilgrim sought his bed leaving them to their enjoyment. Their morning-thick tongues did little to break the growing awkwardness. However the Pilgrim didn't really mind. He kept his thoughts to himself and grew to cherish the peace and the freedom their distance afforded him and in that space found a place to relive his memories. He filled his mind with thoughts of The Fire-Dancer, wherever she might now be, and longed again for the solitude of the wilder places.

The days passed quickly on the road. There were small towns and other inns. They didn't really need the provisions they'd packed. After a time the road led them away from the sheep-pasture and into a land of wheat, oats and barley. Here the sea glistened in the distance and gull-cries replaced the sweeter birdsong of the moorlands. Villages and towns were plentiful here at the ocean's edge and the road led through many of them. However, the Pilgrim was uncomfortable with the bustling noisome streets and it was with very mixed feelings that he marked their final approached towards the great walled city of Varista, perched as it was at the edge of the sparkling blue ocean.

> **Now see the muse a new fate weave,**
> **upon some silken, silver skein,**
> **a web cast close, drawn taught,**
> **as by some weird arachnid kin.**
> **To know, unkowing,**
> **unseeing whence it came.**
> **To feel, unfeeling,**
> **Yet fearing to return again.**
>
> (past thoughts)

Chapter Five – Varista

TALL, PROUD AND no less than a mountain of man-hewn stone stood Varista, the Silver City. Tier upon tier of wall and roof, tower and turret rose ever skywards to touch the heavens with the palace dome's silver-spire. In the shadow of the immense outer wall, the pilgrim felt cowed and defenceless as if the whole might topple and crush out his existence forever.

Their small party was no longer alone on the road, nor had it been for many days. Now they were merely part of an endless tide of people and a very minor part at that, which flowed in and out of the city's immense portal.

Through this great archway they passed, under the disinterested City-Guards' eyes, and with the staccato tattoo of hooves ringing in the passage's confines entered the cobbled barbican beyond. It seemed a grey, stark, and soulless place, dark and unwelcoming chill despite the warmth of the day outside.

The Pilgrim looked about in what amounted to panic, trying to take in the bewildering confusion of sight and sound assailing him. It was too much, far too much, too new, too strange, a tremendous cacophony beating against his senses like a mighty hammer and the stench of ten thousand confined lives turned his thoughts to mush.

There were other soldiers here who greeted the sergeant and his men with military gesture and comrade familiarity. They dismounted and Josie stepped forward to take the horses in hand while the Pilgrim unpacked his satchel and staff.

Here he stood, totally bewildered, at the centre of this chaotic maelstrom of shouting people, calling for stabling, portage, directions or just for others to make way for their passage. One group appeared to have returned from a long journey and were being met and hugged by a throng of wail-

ing family. Others were calling out their farewells or receiving instructions as to their various destinations.

The Sergeant, having approached unobserved, took the Pilgrim's arm. 'Come, Sir.' He saw the soldier's words rather than heard them, and found himself led through a second archway. In the momentary quiet the Sergeant's voice regained its usual command, 'Lostock, I'll take the Pilgrim up to the Tower. You and the men see to the horses. We'll meet at the Sword-and-Bucket at nightfall.' The corporal nodded his understanding and, shouting for the others to follow, disappeared from view.

The Pilgrim was alone save for the Sergeant. 'It's all a bit too much at first ain't it?' the soldier empathised with his young charge. 'You do sort of get used to it eventually though. Anyway there's little point in hanging about, so let's be getting on. It's a fair walk from here I can tell you but, as they don't let horses into the city proper, we ain't got much choice anyway.'

Leading the way through the arch, the Sergeant moved on to the bustling thoroughfare beyond. Shops and houses stood crammed together and even straddled the way overhead with extravagant arches of stone. Laden barrows and stalls lined the street displaying their wares. Hawkers, peddlers and every sort of being called out their cries and offered the services of their trades. The smell of food cooking and the familiar noise of an alehouse caught his attention and reminded him they'd not breakfasted that morning.

The soldier pushed the way forwards through the throng, affecting an air of controlled aggression that made many a folk pause and step aside. There were steps upward and other arches through which they passed. There were other buildings too, workshops, warehouses and the like. The bite of ammonia from a tanner's yard caused their eyes to water. An armourer's hammer tolled out the seconds of the day.

At one point came a shout of anger and the sound of a struggle. A figure, an urchin, rushed into the street. He froze at the sight of the Sergeant but then darted sideways and disappeared into a side alley.

Eventually their long climb brought them to another high wall and another arched gateway. There was no air of indifference about the City Guardsmen here though. They stood tall, their weapons ready at hand, the flash of eyes from beneath their crested helms even sharper than their spear points.

'Sergeant?' one snapped.

'I'm ordered to take this one to the Tower of the Magi.' He handed the man a rolled-up scroll. The parchment was unfolded and scrutinised.

'Who is he?'

'My charge, Guardsman,' the Sergeant snapped back in what could only be taken as a rebuke. There was a moment of tension whilst the guardsman weighed up the other.

'Pass then, Sergeant.'

They did so quickly, entering a very different part of the City. 'I never did like the City Guard,' the sergeant confided once out of earshot. 'They think they're better than the rest of us, Lords of the bloody City. But they're no more than peacekeepers if you ask me, keeping the rabble of the lower city away from the Lordie ones. You wouldn't see them making a forced march over the wilder-lands, oh no, they be far too high and bloody mighty for that.'

Hardly hearing the words, the Pilgrim took in the sudden splendour now surrounding them. The roadway was much wider here, paved with white and grey paving slabs, clean and shining in the sunlight. There were houses, mansions and villas, set back behind high-walled gardens, even trees and shrubs to lend a little green among the stone. The way often opened into courtyards where fountains bubbled and marble statues stood watch. Here the people promenaded in their finery or sat at leisure taking in the late morning sunshine.

They climbed more steps, marble now, lined with the statues of fabulous creatures. Then even more, reaching higher and higher. There was another high defensive wall, and more of the resplendent guardsmen to check their passage. They passed ever upwards, drawing closer and closer to the silver-domed palace and the slightly lesser marble tower at its side. It didn't take too much guesswork to realise it was to this lesser tower they were heading.

Soon enough they climbed the stairway onto the highest terrace and stopped before the arched doorway of the white marble tower. At this point it appeared to rise to the very heavens. High above the doorway, the tower's face was set with windows and balconies although the lower reaches were smooth and featureless. Its great oak door was carved with runes and inlaid with silver. Above the carving of a great war-dragon stood sentinel.

'Well, Pilgrim, here we are. I guess our journey is about at its end. This, in case you haven't realised it, is the Tower of the Magi,' the Sergeant needlessly informed. The Pilgrim, hearing a tremor of fear in the soldier's voice, turned to see him unexpectedly drawn and pale. 'Aye I am afraid. Who wouldn't be so near to the magic within these Halls?'

They stood there for several minutes doing nothing. Eventually the Pilgrim took matters in hand, stepping forward and pushing the huge door open. It was almost dark inside, just enough light to see. He stepped into the hallway not afraid, more curious, with the soldier following close behind. The door closed silently behind them and, deep within the building, a gong boomed sombre and foreboding.

'Magic,' the Sergeant whispered in fright.

'No, not magic, just a trip stone at the doorway,' the Pilgrim informed him, wondering to himself why they'd go to such trouble.

A scarlet-robed figure appeared in the passage, as if forming from the thin air. 'You have entered the Tower of The Magi of Varista. Beware lest you raise their wrath.' His deep imperious voice echoed through the hallway. 'State your business?'

For some unknown reason the Pilgrim began to feel irritated. *Why the need for all this drama and trickery? If these Magi are so powerful, then surely they don't require such childish devices.*

'I was sent to escort this pilgrim to see the Magi, Sir,' the Sergeant answered in a voice that fairly rang with awe. 'My Lord Asheld, General of the Army of Bronden, Guardian of the Western Border-lands felt his news would be of great importance and value to them.'

'He felt it, did he?' the man continued. 'Well I shall be the judge of that. State your news,' the imperious voice commanded.

The Pilgrim was silent. His fingers drummed on the hawthorn staff as he looked into the speaker's eyes. Where one might expect to see power and danger, he saw nothing but bluster. 'I think,' speaking slowly, 'I think I would rather talk to the Master than his man. I am here to see the Magi.'

Hearing the soldier's in-drawn breath he turned. 'Sergeant Staffbinder, Douglass, you've done your duty, there's no need to remain,' seeing at once the look of relief on the man' face. 'Should you return to Hereth, say that you have seen me here.'

The Sergeant bowed. 'Yes, Sir, If I return.' There was more left unsaid, but no words or time with which to speak. He saluted sharply and turned on his heel. The door opened for his passage and closed behind with an almost silent sigh. *Everything is just show.*

'Come.' The sentinel turned leading the way. Several flights of granite stairs turned about the inner tower in a great spiral. Doors lined the way, closed and secret. At one point he heard chanting but the sound soon disappeared behind them. They climbed higher and higher until the Pilgrim's breath burnt in his chest and his heart pounded with the effort. At the top of the stairs was a grand hallway with seven passages leading away in a star. They followed one, turning right into a small anti-chamber and finally halted before a large closed door. 'The Council-of-the-Magi,' he announced pushing the door open.

The light in the room was dazzling, all the more so for the gloom of the stairs and passages leading there. The Pilgrim walked slowly forwards and stopped, several paces into the room. He stood there blinking to allow his eyes to adjust. The floor was white. The walls were white. The table before him was white. Even the six men sat behind the table were dressed in white. There was a single empty chair at the left end of the table.

'Go, Drosstid.' The man in the centre chair raised his hand in a gesture of dismissal. Came the sound of shuffling feet behind him and the hushed click of the door closing... *For crying out loud! Why all the drama?*

He didn't speak for some time, nor did they. It felt like a game of will power, as children play when they stare into each other's eyes and try not to blink. This was getting just too silly. 'I am a pilgrim of the road, Sirs,' he began. 'I have–'

'Enlightened Ones!' the voice cracked. 'You shall address us as such. We are The Lords Enlightened.' The one in the centre spoke. His crystal-blue eyes peered out from beneath a wild bush of silver hair... 'We are the Magi-of-Varista.'

Magi? Lords enlightened? Magic? There's no magic here! No wisdom, nor searching for truth. Just the games of fools.

'If you want,' he answered lightly, hiding the trace of anger growing steadily in his breast. 'I've travelled through the lands of Naril and ventured into the Goblin Realm of the Galghathag. The General said I should tell you of what I saw there.'

'You still haven't named us as "Enlightened Ones".' The man sounded petulant, childish, causing the Pilgrim's feeling of annoyance to rise even more.

'Nor have you introduced yourselves!' he snapped back. *This is all getting too silly. What on earth is going on?*

The spokesman rose slowly to his feet, leant forwards on hands that gripped the table edge as talons. His eyes burnt with only just contained fury. 'Introduce ourselves? We are the Council of The Magi-of-Varista. You think we should introduce ourselves?' His voice dripped with malice and bitter venom. 'I am Starbinder, The Lord-High-Alchemist-of-Varista.' He turned to the man seated to his right, almost a carbon copy save for the thinness of hair. 'This is Magisar, The Lord-Principal of the Magi,' and to the bearded one at his left, 'This is Cornell, The Lord High-Chancellor of Magi. This is The Lord of the Household, Lord Hastiir. This The Lord of the Rolls, Lord Cassander and this is the Lord of the Artefacts, Lord Faranti!' He pointed his finger at the Pilgrim menacing, threatening. 'Quake then, and tremble in the face of our power. And who are you?' The last words were little more than an insult, a hiss of rudeness.

But the Pilgrim didn't quake, nor tremble, lest it was with annoyance. He spoke softly, calmly. 'I am but a pilgrim. The Pilgrim-of-Hereth. I suppose you might name me thus...' he paused. 'My Lords I have grave news of the Goblin–'

'Enlightened Ones!' he almost screamed.

'Enlightened ones.' *Oh what's the point!* 'I've been to the Galghathag.'

There was no recognition in their eyes, no reaction to the dread word. 'Do you bring anything of magic?' the Lord of Artefacts demanded.

What? They're not even interested. 'No, not magic, only news of what I've seen.'

'Why should we be interested in the travels of a young man? Do you know something of Magic, is your news about magic?' asked the Principal.

'Something, I suppose.' *What the hell is going on?*

'Tell us what you know and be sure you leave nothing out,' the Principal continued.

'I've been travelling through the lands of Santolin and Lodor, taking the Pilgrims' road in search of understanding. I entered the Land of Naril and there began to see the signs of the Goblins. They have broken the bindings confining them and even now begin to spread out into the Western lands. In Naril also I met and travelled with an Elf.' *Perhaps they'll respond to this.* 'She was magic.'

'What magic? What did she have?'

'She danced, danced the fires of nature, the light of life...'

'Danced?' The Lord of Artefacts' voice rose to an angry scream. 'DANCED? You call dancing magic? Magic is of Power, POWER and KNOWLEDGE. Don't you know even that? Don't you see? Magic must have power, must have energy, a focus and a route. Any who use magic must have knowledge of–'

'Be still!'

A quiet, almost gentle voice somehow filled the room with peace and the Pilgrim turned to see that an old man had entered the chamber. He seemed ancient, stooped with both the weight of the years and the pile of manuscripts held in his frail arms. His white robe was stained with ink and crease-lined with dust. Yet for all his frailty this one at least was filled with a vibrant energy that almost burnt.

'What do you want?' the High Alchemist snapped in irritation, apparently holding this newcomer in scant regard.

Ignoring the Magi completely, he walked to the table, placed his pile of manuscripts on its top and straightening with a groan of relief. The pile slued sideways in front of the Magi. Now he turned about in a slow shuffling circle, examining what was happening. Eventually he stopped and lifted his head to look into the Pilgrim's eyes. 'Welcome, Pilgrim.' He bowed his head slightly, 'I'm Rustle,' choked a self-deprecatory laugh. 'They call me that because of the papers. I tend to the records you see. It's not a bad life. Well the food isn't bad and living here is fine enough, if you don't mind the company that is. I get to read all sorts of things and the time to try to understand them. It's been a long journey, Young-Pilgrim, pray take a seat.'

The Pilgrim noted a chair close by the door where he had entered. He shook his head. 'Thank you but no. I've no need.' His annoyance at the Magi was still burning in his breast, although lesser now for the strangeness of the old man's behaviour.

'Silence!' the High Alchemist demanded again.

'Ignore them, Pilgrim. They're all fools,' Rustle continued without pause. 'They think they're something special, that they know something of Magic.'

'Think! THINK!' The Alchemist was almost incandescent with indignation. 'We THINK we know about magic? WE ARE THE MAGI! The knowledge is OURS, Ours.'

'Yours?' Rustle's voice was suddenly deadly, like a burning sword of fire cutting through ice. 'The knowledge is yours is it? What knowledge would that be then? What do you know? You're all sham and tricks. Your knowledge is nothing but the babbling of children. You think you've a right to Power? Then you're even more stupid than you appear. NO ONE has a right to power! NO ONE! And you don't even realise that! Your hunger's like a vile greed. You know nothing. All you do is lust after whatever you cannot have!'

The Principal's face was grey with fury. 'How dare you? How dare you, WE are the Magi-of-Varista, YOU are NOTHING! NOTHING.' He stood leaning over the table as if his eyes would burn a hole in the old man's breast. 'What are you? Nothing but a book-man and a keeper of records, Rustle, the paper-folder, Hah! Where's your power then?'

The old man just smiled. 'Just this once, Starbinder, God what a stupid name, just this once I'll do as you ask. Just this once I'll answer your question. Although, and I tell you true, you'll soon rather I hadn't.'

'Where is my power, you ask? Why, you ignorant fools, it lies in every word I read, in every paper, every scroll, every scrap of information I can glean. There is my power, not in the grasping lust for things denied but in the love of knowledge. Oh yes that's my power, the knowledge gained over a 157 years of study.'

'What knowledge?' the Principal spat.

'Knowledge of You for a start.' He stopped curling his lips in derision, 'Magi? Magi you call yourself? Pah! Today at last is a day of naming. I will begin it by naming you! Shall tell you what you are? You're little but grey, empty vessels, the unknowing tools of the Lords-of-the-Void. Here you sit like Lords, stretching out your webs of hate, reaching out for what you crave.'

His voice was like iron, hard and uncompromising, giving judgement to their failings. 'The Power you crave is not yours to have. It never shall be. It was denied to them and it shall be denied to you. Long, long ago, they saw the greed, those who guard such things, and so stripped their power, from them or any like them, before they could destroy everything.'

'You think anger, hate and greed can draw it to you? Well it can't. You don't have the knowledge or the power! Even now, when faced by what holds balance on everything you crave, what will bring about your demise, even now you see nothing. Don't you know who you face? Don't you know who stands before you? Does the name "Pilgrim" mean nothing?'

'Pilgrim? Why? Should it? Who do you think this is?' They'd never seen the old man in such a mood. Even as he spoke, fear touched their breasts and blanched their faces.

Rustle stood up straight. His voice, when he did speak, no longer croaked as an old man but rang with authority and energy. Every word was filled with meaning and reverence. The words he spoke were of ritual and omen drawn from the knowledge of things lain down in the mists of antiquity.

'As it is written so it shall be. It was so written and thus it is come into being.

> The Child shall be the Oath-taker.
> The Oath-taker shall be the Sword-maker.
> The Sword-maker shall be the Warrior.
> The Warrior shall be the Wanderer.
> The Wanderer shall be the Pilgrim
> and the Pilgrim shall be the Wizard.
> The Wizard shall loose the bindings of the world.
> The Wizard shall free the Vortex.'

He turned to look into the faces of the Magi. 'He shall deny you everything you crave. I name him now, though this naming shall be my last. He shall be:

'The Wizard of Rainbows.'

The old man staggered as he turned to face the young man who stood so transfixed by his words. 'I'm sorry, lad.' His shoulders drooped as the years descended. 'I wish I could be here to help you more. I wish I could answer your questions. I wish that...' He gasped a sudden in-drawn breath. 'At least I've been here to greet you. Ignore these fools they are nothing.'

'Here,' he offered the chair. 'What's happening?'

'Thank you.' Rustle sat, his head slumped in exhaustion. 'What's happening is just nature, lad. My time is at its end and it's about time too. I've lasted far too long as it is. I guess I never should have but I wanted to know.' He paused as if the very effort of speaking was too much. 'Don't fear, young man, It's not your doing, not your being here that brings this, not because of you but because of me. I waited, refused to move on until, until...'

He was still for several minutes.

Eventually he lifted his head once again and looked a final time to where the Magi sat in stunned silence. 'You won't understand, but see, here's the secret. He offered help rather than demanded answers. That's the reason you'll never gain what you seek.' He lifted his hand and rested it upon the Pilgrim's arm. 'Here, I've a gift for you also.' Chuckling to himself, he took a brooch from his tunic and placed it in the Pilgrim's hand. 'Here, I make you Magi! I have the right to and they can't stop me. Not that it'll do you any good. But at least it'll serve as a pass through the city.'

'I don't understand. What's happening?'

'My waiting is over. I pass the future on to you.' He was quiet, but the Pilgrim had no reply.

Eventually the old man spoke again. 'Tell me, Pilgrim, was she, the Elf-maid, the Dancer-of-the-Flames, was she really as beautiful as the omens tell?'

'Oh yes, Wise One,' the Pilgrim smiled. 'As beautiful as the sunrise over the mountains of dreams, as beautiful as the moonlight on the silver waters of the sea of tranquillity. She danced the dance of life and living, of love and loving. She danced her fires in the coldness of the Galghathag and turned aside the darkness that craved our souls. She danced a wonder to waken my heart, a new dance that shall endure forever.

Come dance with me,
I shall dance you a dance of the greenwood
of the delight of freedom
through the enchanted forests.
'neath the light,
the silven light
of Chelimbrelle, the Elven star.

Come dance with me,
among the wild flowers of the Ever-wood,
among the tall pines,
the sun-cut avenues.
Come fill my ears with the music of your being,
the bright images of innocence,
with the elfin pipes'
softly falling reels.
Come dance once more
before the winds of change
claim us forever.'

The old man was still now and still would he forever remain.

The Pilgrim turned to face the Magi who sat stunned to silence by what had transpired. They no longer glowed white, for now their gowns were grey, grey and lifeless. 'I came with news. I came with information. I came with hope that the knowledge of the things I witnessed might be of importance.' He looked down again at the still figure of the old man through the moisture that clouded his eyes. 'It seems there was only one of you with the ability to understand and now he's gone, gone on his own secret journey.'

'Of what did he speak?' It was the Chancellor who found the question.

But the Pilgrim could do nothing, say nothing, could feel nothing but the cry of his own soul. 'I don't know. I don't understand anything about what's happening.' The sense of endless frustration began to well up inside. The confusion once again filled his thoughts with a million un-grasped meanings. 'I don't know anything at all. I came with my words hoping to gain understanding, hoping that someone might be able to explain. He waited for me to come. They all wait. They all have their secrets in which I'm bound. I don't know why! The most important thing to him was The Dancer.'

He felt the tears begin to sting in his eyes. 'Why couldn't you wait, old man?' He knelt on the floor before him and took the cold hand in his own. 'You knew more of me than I. You even named me the Wizard of Rainbows as were it a truth. I don't even know who you were.' The tear formed and trickled over his cheek, dripped silently upon the ruby hanging at his breast before dropping in a single bead to dampen the old man's lifeless fingers.

The Pilgrim stood and faced them. 'Can you answer?' he accused them. 'Do you know anything of the waking of the whirlwind, of the power of the Vortex?'

But did they hear him? Did they listen? No! Their eyes were not on him, nor their attention. Slowly he followed their incredulous stares to where, in the hand of Rustle's corpse, lay a single rose, a bloom of blood-red perfection.

'Magic!' He heard the voice with his ears, but the depth of the greed, the lust for power that drove the words ripped through his soul worse than any blade. He turned. The Lord of Artefacts towered over him, eyes aflame as he pointed towards the jewel. 'That's MAGIC!' he screamed. 'A jewel of transformation, Rubelous Hortelanious. Give it to me!' He grabbed at it.

The world was suddenly still, slowed as if time itself waited. The clawing hand closed about the gem, and caught at it. Those terrible fingers began to redden, to glow as if a fire burnt within. The Magus' scream filled eternity. His body crumpled to the floor where he knelt sobbing. 'What have you done? My hand! What have you done?' He sobbed through the tears of pain.

Even in this he denies the truth. 'I have done nothing.'

'But my hand!' He held up his hand to show the damage. There was nothing, not even a blemish. The man's eyes opened even wider when he saw what was. 'It's unharmed.' It was too much. His mind failed to grasp reality.

The Pilgrim took hold of the ruby and held it in his palm so they all might see. 'It's a gift from my mother,' he said simply, 'The gifts of the Lady-of-Flowers do not harm.' His heart was filled with disgust and all at once he wanted no more of this place. He turned and walked to the door.

'Wait,' the Principal called, pleaded.

He looked back at the six men, saw the urgent, half demented need burning in their faces. 'No,' as if considering the matter, 'No I've nothing I want to say to you,' and stepped through the doorway. As he turned towards the stairs he could hear their voices raised in argument.

*

The brightness, as the Pilgrim emerged from the gloom of the tower, was almost painful. The midday heat reflected on the marble and granite sparkling and confusing the eye. He blinked several times trying to adjust to the glare, and sat on a step.

Below, in the lower reaches of the city, the atmosphere would prove oppressive and smothering but here on the higher terraces was a cleanliness borne of sea breezes.

What was that all about? he wondered, *I was only there moments. What did it mean?* There were no answers to the questions, no understanding at all. His moment of doubt turned bleak, as if a pit of emptiness had opened within him. What was the point? He'd come expecting answers, although… Why did he have to die? And like that? Just. Who was he? What did he know? He seemed to know something.

There came an instant of anger. A thought even flicked across his mind, to go back and shake the answers from him. In the end he shut the memories and the doubts away in his mind to examine later. More and more things seemed hidden in that little mental box.

Turning the silver talisman over in his hand he began to wonder what to do with it. He was half-tempted to throw it away but the old man had said that it would serve as a pass through the city. He fastened it to the left shoulder of his robe. *Magi? He said he'd made me a Magi.*

Eventually, as much through the boredom of inactivity as anything else, he began to look about. Towering above him the Silver-Palace shone in the noonday sun filling his whole gaze with the glory of its wonder. He pondered. Should he go there with his news, his story? *No I won't. There's no point.* Instead, turning his back to the beautiful edifice, he chose to walk slowly down towards the city again.

The guards at the first gate snapped to attention, spears lowered as he approached, but they saw the brooch on his shoulder and, with blanched faces, bowed low allowing him passage. He didn't speak, just moved quickly past, grateful to be away from their gaze.

He wandered then, wherever his feet led him, eyes filled with the marvels of the city, the people no less than the buildings. A dame wafted past him dressed as a peacock, her great, feathered fan whispering in the breeze as she walked. He espied another dressed as a pheasant, the long tail sighing as it brushed the flagstones. The swordsman on whose arm she paraded was little more than a strutting dandy resplendent in scarlet leather and draped in a silken cloak. The Pilgrim noted their instant look of distaste and felt vulnerable and rustic in his dusty, travelled plainness. Then, as with the guards, their expressions turned to fear and they turned hurriedly away.

Once past, he unclasped and hid the brooch beneath his robe. *Is magic such a terrible thing that people are so afraid? Where is the wonder, where the joy? They have much to answer do these so called Magi.*

He moved lower, leaving behind the grand walled mansions. Although there were still enough of the gaudy citizens to trouble him, his eyes were soon filled with other sights. Varista truly was the silver city and silver was evident everywhere, gleaming in the sunlight upon a thousand different surfaces, fittings, finials, engravings, mouldings everywhere the eye fell.

Shops lined the thoroughfare, wonderful emporiums displaying their finery behind crystal windows. In the courtyards marble and onyx fountains cast sprays of cooling, scented mist into the midday air.

However, the Pilgrim saw little sign of happiness or joy. The people, despite all their wealth and opulence, seldom smiled and the only laughter heard was bitter and jarring, born of spite and derision not mirth.

He passed through a market place. It had none of the noisome chaos of those in the lower reaches but formed an ordered cultured place. The stalls were laden with the finest produce of the world, scented and lush. He purchased an apple with a bronze coin dug from his pouch but he ate only half. It had little taste. Its flesh lacked the crispness of those from the orchards of Hereth.

Stopping beside an ornate fountain he sipped water with cupped hands to quench his thirst. Their eyes followed him as were he a thief robbing them of what was theirs. Then a twinge of pointless guilt brushed his thoughts and reddened his cheeks. He hurried on and away.

What is this place, all this finery and splendour, this wealth? What's the value of it all anyway, if the sight of me taking a simple drink can trouble them so? What am I to them? Me with my travel-stained cloak and my inner disquiet. What are they to me? Do they fear they'll lose it all so easily or that I or another might take it from them? How? Is their wealth really so insubstantial?

Leaving that plaza, he moved gradually downwards towards the sea and the harbour. Here the people were less haughty and seemed able to accept his passage without trouble. The smell of the fresh, salty air went some way to clearing away the other City scents and for once, the first time since entering Varista, he actually felt at ease.

He wandered along a quayside of gently bobbing boats. Having purchased a cup of minted tea he sat at a pavement table to while away the afternoon, content at least for a short time. A massive craft, set with huge azure sails, broached the harbour gates. He watched as the crew went through their frantic paces, rolling sails about the spars as the craft hove to.

Eventually his feet led him to a wide square overlooking the water where on the steps of a grand fountain surrounded by a host of entranced children sat an armoured knight. The Pilgrim moved closer wondering what kept the children so spellbound.

The warrior saw the Pilgrim approach and smiled a welcome and winked in hidden, somehow secret, complicity then returned to his tale.

Speaking in a deep baritone voice, rich and full of wonder, he told of far-off, wonderful lands where dragons guarded their hordes of gold and jewels. Tales he wove, of heroes bold and the terrible adventures of their quests, of beautiful princesses waiting in their lonesome, towering castles and of callow youths, still wet behind the ears, setting out to effect their rescue. Strange tales were these, quite unlike those the Pilgrim had learnt at his mother's knee. As time passed by the Pilgrim too fell under their fanciful spell and sat on the fountain's rim to hear the magical sagas unfold.

Much later, when the sun withdrew its bright mantle from the sky and clothed the sea in a gown of scarlet and gold, the knight brought his oration to a close. With his booming laughter ringing over the plaza, he began shooing the children away. They scuttled off to their homes and families with minds filled with wonders to brighten their lives and colour their dreams. Soon the warrior and the Pilgrim found themselves alone at the fountain side.

'I was listening. I hope you didn't mind,' the Pilgrim began, breaking the silence before it formed a wall to prevent companionship. 'To tell the truth, Sir Knight, these were wonderful stories. I've never heard the like of them before.'

The other looked over at him in surprise. 'Lands rot, lad!' he exclaimed with a loud guffaw, 'I'm no bleedin' knight.'

'Not a knight?' The Pilgrim's eyes fell in confusion upon the broadsword and the Lion emblazoned shield resting against the fountain wall. 'But...?'

The warrior threw back his head and laughed. No cruel laugh of derision this, but a warmer, healing sound that drew the Pilgrim into its embrace. 'No, lad, I'm no knight, though I guess I've seen more than my fair share of fighting and killing sure enough.' He laughed again, perhaps at himself and his own frailty. 'Yes, I've seen more than enough of that. No I'm not a knight, a fighter perhaps or warrior or… or…? Who cares anyway? For sure not the children or these people.' He waved his hand to imply that he spoke of the people of Varista. 'No, they're far too busy with their meaningless little lives…'

The warrior grew quiet again before bursting into yet another explosion of mirth. 'What care I? I tell my tales and pass away my time. And, when all is said and done, I know where the ale is good, Pilgrim, and I know more than that too.'

'What more do you know?' Intrigued. 'Tell me.'

'I know the truth and the lies of this place. I know that,' he gestured with an elegant wave towards the higher city reaches. 'I know the realities of that place too. I saw the glint of that silver thing 'neath your robe, Pilgrim. But you ain't one of them, that's for sure. You ain't of this place either. No.' The hint of a half-remembered thought crossed his mind. 'I'll tell you what. You come with me and I'll show you another city to cloud your mind, one not so fine or wealthy.' He stood and led the Pilgrim through the crowded streets once more.

They passed another of the many gateways, not guarded this one save perhaps by the stench beyond, to enter what indeed was a very different city, one forever shaded by the great outer wall.

Down dark streets they passed, through passages where the light of day was ever a stranger. Bright-eyed children catcalled them. Sallow-cheeked women with hungry, haunted faces smiled their suggestive invites then mocked their rejection with loud, crude insults. Men, drunken, stumbling wretches, bowed low by their hopeless poverty paid them no heed as they passed by. They hung their heads and avoided any eye contact as if ashamed by the lowliness of their condition, fixed in the belief they were less than other men, not fit to walk the same ground.

There were places of decay too, the home of urchins and orphans, the outcast and the beggar. 'Just a copper mister, 'n' y' can do what y' wants wiv me. Y'know, mister, any fink.' The Pilgrim's attention was caught by a lovely, if grubby, young girl standing before them with her hands on her hips. 'Go on, mister, what d'you say? Fancy a little bit then?' She tossed her head of silky golden hair provocatively and pulled her beauteous face into a pout more at home in a thirty-year-old. Her eyes of steel, cold as stone and empty as a moonless night, told of her cruel-taught wisdom, the lesson of the gutters.

She's just a child. A child with eyes that hold the pain of a thousand years. He took a coin from his pouch and tossed it to her. 'I want nothing of you, child. Be on your way.'

'Fanks, mister.' She laughed and turning with a suggestive wiggle of her hips left them alone once more.

'What the hell is this place?' The anger burnt within like a dagger of ice. 'The squalor, the despair, it's horrible. How can it be like this?' He looked towards where he knew the other city rested. 'This place in the very shadow of all their wealth and finery. How can they let this go on, the dirt, the suffering, the pain and the awfulness of it all? These people are starving, dying before their very eyes. Don't they know? Can't they see?'

'How could they?' the storyteller confided sadly. 'They've no choice at all and no knowledge of it either. They're divided by Fate's wall, a wall so mighty that in all probability no one could cross it. This is how things are, how they've always been. Varista, the Silver City? It's just how Fate shaped it. I tell you, were they to see, just for one instant the truth of the situation, were they to accept the awfulness of that reality, why, then everything would crumble to dust, rich and poor alike. For whether they like it or not, this is the consequence of their wealth. As Fate gave, so Fate took away. They have, so the others have not, that's the truth of it. How could they face that? No, they turn their backs on what is and fill their minds with lies so to hide from reality. They blame each other for the way things are. The rich blame the poor for their poverty. The poor blame the rich for their wealth. In the end they are alike, crippled by their need not to see. And why? Because in the end they actually believe that the way things are is right. They've invented their own reality simply in order to continue.'

But the frozen-eyed stare of the street-girl still burned in the Pilgrim's mind. 'There must be another way, surely.'

'Aye, lad, of course there is. Come.' He took the Pilgrim by the arm leading him to yet another part of the city closer to the docks where the boatmen, fishermen and merchants plied their trade.

Here the bright lights of a quayside tavern called to them with the sounds of merriment within and the Pilgrim found himself hustled through the door into the bustling, smoke laden atmosphere of a crowded barroom, beat on by sight, sound, smell and confusion. The thoughts of other things evaporated in the chaos.

'Come on, lad,' the warrior cheerfully yelled through the din as he dragged him into the tumult. 'Ale!' he yelled to the barkeep, laughing again as his words were met with a torrent of abuse. As two brimming tankards were slid down the bar towards them. The warrior's laugh boomed and with a flick of his wrist a handful of coins were tossed through the air, only to be snatched mid-flight and vanish into the copious pockets of the barman's beer-stained apron. As he turned to deal with others of his boisterous charges, the two newcomers were left to raise their tankards and wash away the taste and grime of the city streets with the strong, dark ale.

The throng parted to allow them passage as they moved further into the room to a table near to the hearth. There was no real need for a fire on this balmy eve.

It became quickly evident that the storytelling-warrior was well known here and just as clear that his company was as welcome as the gold he'd so casually cast at the innkeeper. Many of the revellers spoke to him, toasted him with a raised glass as they passed. Some who approached patted his shoulder, or mock fought him, ducking and diving, with a laugh and smile. They called him 'Shimmian' and most seemed to know him.

The Pilgrim too found himself welcomed, patted and shaken almost as much as the warrior, as if simply being in the company of the man were acceptance enough.

More of the heady ale arrived and shortly after a huge-limbed-barmaid performed a miracle of balance as she carried three giant trays of food to their table. She set before them the platters of meats and cheeses, rough fresh-baked bread still hot from the oven. There were vegetables too, stuffed-leaves and peppers and other things the Pilgrim could not name. Soon after, even more ale arrived.

Thus the evening became a haze, a thousand images of sound, taste, odour and colour. Someone began to sing, a coarse song of the sea, sung with more gusto than tune. Even the Pilgrim found himself joining in with the others, confused, bemused, yet for once almost at peace, even happy as he gave way to the moment and let the evening flow over him. Only the echo of an angel, with thousand-year-old eyes, stayed to trouble his soul.

Later, when the rowdiness had subsided into a quieter mood they rested, sipping their ale as another of the serving girls sat on the bar to play a guitar and sing a sad song of the oceans.

> *On the dark shore margins ask not of motion*
> *The oceans who dance with the moon.*
> *But list' to the waters,*
> *The seven seas daughters,*
> *the song of the sirens*
> *who chime o'er the surf.*
> *Ask not of motion.*
> *They cannot answer.*
> *Ask not of motion.*
> *They do not know.*

'I was thinking,' tongue loosened by the ale and words freed by the friendliness about him, 'I came here looking for knowledge. I don't know anything of cities and of city people. You know I went to see the Magi. I thought I had information they might need. I thought, hoped, I hoped they might have answers. They had nothing, knew nothing. They were nothing, just tricksters and liars. I saw the grand people of Varista too, fine and noble they seemed. Yet they live in splendour whilst in the shadows of their halls other people are living in squalor. I see tradesman and craftsmen, sailors and merchants, soldiers and guardsmen and I understand nothing at all. You know I'm supposed to be a pilgrim seeking knowledge. Well all I've managed to find so far is confusion.'

'And what exactly do you think you should understand, my friend?' Shimmian seemed surprised at the tenor of the young man's words. 'Most folks would have these images shut away in the closed regions of their minds never to look at again.' He peered intently into the Pilgrim's eyes. 'There's a way with you, lad, and that's no mistake, more to you than meets the eye if I'm any judge.'

'And are you, Shimmian? For it seems to me that there's a paradox here too and, at its centre, is you. If it's strange that I should see this and speak of it, then how much stranger to find you here to open my eyes? What drives you, my friend the Storytelling-Warrior? What drives you into such places as this? I'm a pilgrim, as you noted, in search of my understandings, my meanings in my journey. What about you? If the quest for knowledge is my calling, well surely, telling stories to children can hardly be yours.'

Again the Pilgrim felt the piercing touch of Shimmian's eyes. 'You see too much, Pilgrim.' He laughed again as if to break the mood. 'And there you have me. In the past I've been many things and followed many different trails and shall probably tread many more before my time is done.'

'Tell me then,' the Pilgrim laughed in reply. 'Tell me what brought you to this place and what you seek. Yes, you tell me your tale and I'll tell you mine.'

'Yes,' several of the others clamoured. 'Tell us your tale, Shimmian, come on.'

'Landlord, bring our erstwhile companion some of your finest ale,' another called in mockery of finer places. 'Ale to wet his tongue and to make his words the sweeter.'

The storyteller laughed and bowed his capitulation. Then standing he looked about himself with a veteran performer's eye, sat upon the table edge, that they might see him the better, and rested his booted foot upon the wooden bench.

'Hush then, my friends, hush.' He lifted the ale, slowly to his lips. The room about grew still as the tension mounted. He drained the whole in a single drawn-out draught. The room was silent, waiting.

My beginnings, dear friends, for 'tis to there I must return to start my tale, my beginnings were in the Land of Rael that lies in the South-lands beyond the Bay of Tears. They say of Rael, 'The land is a land of constant change and therefore as such is always new.' It's an ancient land with tales that go back to the beginnings of time. My people are well proud of their history too but they choose not to dwell in the past. No, those of Rael would sooner face the lands of the future and whatever awaits them there.

Rael is a beautiful country of rugged hills and mountains, barren places, wild and lonely where a man may learn to be himself. A vast pastured plain sweeps down from the mountains to the great river on which the City of Hallkah sits.

The halls and walls of Hallkah were my home. It was there where as a youth I was apprenticed to a captain of the Guard and schooled in the ways of war and the passage of arms. At an early age, even among my own people who are ever quick to learn, yes at an early age I spoke the words of the Warrior's vow and took up arms in the service of the city.

Aye, right proud and noble was I, strutting like a peacock, young and free and full of all the joys of living. Aye, and many a young maid fell to my plumage.

He paused, as much for effect as to take a breath. When he spoke again his voice was cold and bitter, hard with the taste of the past.

Then they came… riding like fiends of hell, sword in hand. Namani, our enemies of old were they, riding from out of the deep south, full of hatred for a thousand years' slights and wrongs, cruel of heart and intent on rekindling the enmity between our peoples. They crossed our borders and put our people to the sword, our pastures and villages to the torch until the skies were dark with the burning.

Then we rose up in anger donning our armour and riding out to do battle. It was a terrible thing, that battle on the High plains of Golgan. For they were a mighty foe and in their own way as great a warrior people as were we.

There was no giving or taking of quarter in that awful strife, no calling for mercy, nor giving of clemency. My splendid new armour ran red with the blood of my enemies; my sword arm ached as were it made of lead ere that day was done.

Before nightfall it was over. Many had fallen, good men, proud men, aye, on either side. Although they were mighty, skilled in the use of arms and the stratagems of battle, in the end, we did prevail over them. We struck them down into the blood-soaked turf and sent the remnant fleeing back to their own lands.

Then our Lords called to us, gathered us together amidst the carnage of the battlefield. There surrounded by all the stench and slaughter they spoke to us.

'Oh my proud warriors, you have done great deeds today. You have proved yourselves true men of Rael… But… Do not be too heartened by your great victory. Do not be overjoyed that you have sent them scampering back to their dung-filled hovels like the beaten dogs they are. Just look about you.

'Look at our dead. These men, our friends, our brothers, brave men, noble men, worthy men who shall no longer walk with us through our green pastures nor ride with us through the hunt of the mountains. Look at our fields and the dead of our villages. What harm did these gentle folk do?

'They have done us a great wrong. They have burned our homes and slaughtered our cattle. They have ravaged our women and young girls. They have taken the pride of our land and struck it into the dust.

Now they sulk in their hovels and hide in their foul holes. Is this as it should be?'

'NO!' we cried. 'NO!'

'Let there be an ending to it forever. They are weak now and defenceless against us. What say you that we seek recompense for their destruction? What say you that we make repair for our losses? What say you that we return their evil upon their own heads?

'What say you that we avenge these brave fallen sons and brothers, heroes, comrades in arms? How say you?'

Then we beat our swords upon our shields and cried out in one voice.

'REVENGE! REVENGE!'

Into their land we rode and great and terrible was our coming and the destruction we wrought. Once again came the terrible moment of slaughter, the cry of battle. Once again our swords ran red with blood and gore. Terrible and invincible were we.

At least those of us that were left.

The warrior paused, his face wracked in the pain of those terrible memories. It seemed he'd forgotten the inn and the audience who sat spellbound about him. Only the pain of the past remained.

I tell you now. Awful indeed was that ride of terror.

We heeded no cry for mercy, no plea of submission. Righteous, were we, right and filled with the fire of our retribution. Their dead we left in the fields where they fell, left them there to rot.

Our own dead too.

Aye, our dead. For I tell you true, how many of their men fell at our hand? Well how many of ours fell to theirs also? Friends, companions at arms, one-by-one they fell. My own brother, Dathin, too, though he was but a youth, he died in my arms, spilled his last blood upon my lap and turned my mind to fire.

In the shattered ruin of Pece, their once great city, I found myself captain of a band of men. War hardened warriors were we, a band of killers who had ridden through the fires-of-hell and paved every inch of our way with the corpses of our enemies. I doubt that one spark of humanity could be found between the lot of us.

In the heart of the burning city he came to us, our commander, the Lord-High-Marshal. He commanded one final effort. That we take their holy place and throw down the symbols of their Gods. For that was their last refuge, the place of their last stand.

Thus we did, willingly, one last bloody time, running with glee into the carnage with me at the head, screaming out our terrible war cries.

One by one they fell at my side. My own men giving their blood as an offering of the damned to slake the thirst of this oh so greedy land. I too, in that last battle, fell sore wounded to the ground, the great rent in my side spilling my own offering of blood over the white marble floor.

For what?

For, as I lay there bleeding he, our oh-so noble lord, stepped through the carnage like a Lord-of-the-Earth. His eyes glowed as fire fixed upon one thing.

GOLD.

I watched in awful realisation as he set about ransacking the temple, its gold, silver jewels. Right then I knew as if a cloth had been torn from over my eyes. This was no striving for retribution, no honourable ride for vengeance, no great crusade. We were no more than beasts of the gutter, serving until no longer of use, then cast aside and trodden under foot, that he might fill his purse.

Then, although I was hurt sore, it wasn't so bad that I couldn't feel my own anger, not so bad that I didn't roar out in my fury, not so bad that my sword didn't feed on his flesh and leave him to his own screaming death in that ruin.

So I took his purse and dragged myself away. I would no longer be a part of this lie.

After I was healed, and that at the hand of a druid of their people, I travelled, wandering from land to land. I sold my sword to the highest bidder and took companionship from the gold in my purse. I was loyal to nothing but myself. The more I travelled the more I understood. There is no glory in war, no honour behind the shield. I cannot believe in good and noble causes that call men to arms. There are none. The only cause that drives men is greed, greed and hatred. I want no part of them.

In the end, sickened by all I saw and seeing nothing but the vaguest promise of hope, I came here, to Varista. And here I sit in the square and tell my tales for children. And when the night comes? Well, when the night come, then I come here.

The tavern was still, each of the listeners struck by their own thoughts of the tale and of the cruelty and awfulness they had heard. Then Shimmian laughed, loud and brazen, shattering the mood with the clamour as of a broken bell.

'Come, my friends,' he laughed. ''Tis but a tale, naught but a dark tale. Dark tales are for dark nights and dark ale is for alehouses. Landlord! Fill up the glasses. 'Tis time to hear our Young Pilgrim's tale.'

So the ale was poured and drunk and the mood changed once more as the attention moved to the brown-clad pilgrim. The room grew quiet while they waited for him to begin.

He spoke quietly, though none there needed to strain in order to hear. Beginning with Hereth, he told his life and childhood in the shade of the downs. Soft were the words that wove the tale of his mother The Lady-of-Flowers and of his brother and sisters. Then harder, colder words spoke of the return of the Baron their father. Those listening grew hushed with awe as they heard of the terrible conflict in the Halls-of-Hereth and of the things that followed. It is hard to know if they believed his tale of the dwarves and his sword, but his tale was there for the telling and required not their belief or understanding. He left nothing out.

He told of his brief time as a warrior and of that terrible battle on the plains of Sarum. Those there lived with him the time of confusion when he wandered through the forests of Dressan and the grasslands of Lodor. They climbed through the day and stood beside him on the high downs in the shelter of the great standing stones.

He spoke with gentle wonder of the flame-haired dancer of the woodlands and their journey together through the perilous lands of Naril. Their faces blanched with fear when he told of the Galghathag and the terrible awakening of the Creature of Chaos in the castle of despair, of the Galomist and the rising of the Goblin-horde. Though they knew nothing of such things they saw the truth in his eyes as he told of her dance of fury in the darkness and of the trail through the Darkling forest.

His were not the only eyes to sparkle when he recalled the wonder of her magic and the glory of her dance and told of their parting beside the lake. The room grew as still as a moon lit night when he spoke of the Elfling's farewell.

*Come dance with me
among the wild flowers
of the Elswood,
among the tall pines,
the sun-cut avenues.*

*Fill my mind with music
the bright songs of innocence,
with the elfin pipes'
softly falling reels.*

*Come dance once more
ere the winds of change
claim us forever.*

*Come dance with me
beside the crystal fountains
of Al-Sinnian
where the slender towers of Elfdom
are mirrored in the singing waters,
where the chimes of evening
greet the fairy star
Chelimbrelle.*

*Come dance once more
before the gentle light of morning
draws us apart.*

*Come dance with me
one last time.
The winter of our time approaches.*

*Come dance with me
not in sorrow
for that which ends
but in joy for the dream
which shall continue forever.*

Come dance once more
before the echoes of time
part us, you and I.

Come dance with me
now and forever.
Our dance is not of substance
and shall not decay.
I shall dance for you in my thoughts.
Shall you, for me?

Come dance with me
in the halls of your mind,
in the stillness of your being,
in the silences of your moments.

Come dance once more
ere the winds of change
claim us forever.

The silence hung still in the alehouse air as if something sacred and secret had passed by, as if something precious and mysterious had reached out to touch the souls of these rough folk. Although after a time men began to talk again and returned to their entertainment before heading homeward, each of them retained the memory of that special moment, treasured it as something of value.

Later, much later, when the inn was grown quiet and only the Pilgrim and warrior remained, the storyteller spoke his own troubled thoughts.

"Tis as I said, there's a strangeness about you, lad, and no mistake. You see what others do not see, try to understand what others do not even recognise. You've spoken of things that live only in the dreams of men, dark dreams at that.

'It seems to me that the land in which you walk abroad is itself the stuff of legends and omens. For you and for those you travel with. The world turns, Pilgrim. I on feel it on the wind. And somehow, ah, but who am I to know? Who am I to seek understanding?'

'Who else, my friend the Storytelling-warrior? If you don't know, then who else? For I tell you I understand nothing. Oh I try, I struggle to understand, to know what is happening, to see the meanings before me, but in truth I'm lost.'

'No not lost, my friend, if friend you are. You're here and your path stretches out behind and before you. Who can know of your passing? But you are named and have named yourself also. The Earth-Stones named you. The Elf-maid named you. The creatures of darkness named you.'

'Icicle named me,' he whispered to himself unheard.

'The wise man Rustle named you. So must I also name you? And shall my naming draw me into the web that surrounds you?' He laughed to himself, wryly as if to some secret of his own. 'Yes I suppose I must. And in doing so? What then?'

'Well... we, or should I say I? Yes, I shall just have to see. You are The Pilgrim, whatever that portends. Somehow your coming changes everything forever. I don't understand this either.'

'What do you understand then?'

'That the world turns, Pilgrim. The world turns and a new beginning has come. Perhaps there's a cause I can follow after all.'

'I don't understand!'

Shimmian laughed, suddenly breaking the mood. 'Well, lad, I think what I'm saying is that I should join you. That is… If you'll have me, I'll travel this road a ways with you and see what there is to see. I've never been able to resist a challenge I can tell you, whatever that challenge might be. I could never be one to just sit and watch the world turning about me.' He laughed again. 'And if it is true, what the sages say; "That for every act of man there is a consequential reaction in the web of the world." Well then, hells-rot! Let Fate's coin fall as it may, because I tell you true, my Pilgrim friend, I haven't a clue what I'm doing.'

The Landlord found them still there mid-morning when the drayman came to replenish the inn's supplies. The rattle of barrels being rolled into the cellar brought them from their slumber on the hard wooden benches. The sweet, boiling tar that the landlord called tea thrust them crashing into awareness. The worthy's noisome jocularity drove them from the shelter of the inn into the turmoil of the city streets. Having stayed awake long into the night planning what they should do in preparation for their journey, there now seemed little to stop them getting on with the tasks before them.

Shimmian led the way to a hostelry, in a street not far from the inn, where he stabled his horses, a pack pony and a proud war-horse. The latter was a fine noble creature though the years had taken their toll. Having reached an agreement with the shrew-like proprietor to exchange the stallion for other ponies they went to the paddock to look over those on offer. There was little to choose between them. The bargaining wasn't too hard or acrimonious. Even so, Shimmian wore a sullen face as they led their string away.

'It was too hurried,' he sulked, declaring the horse-trader to have had the better of the deal and that at any other time he'd have obtained far more creditable bargain than just four ponies and the panniers for carrying provisions.

It did little to help matters when, much to Shimmian's dismay, the Pilgrim refused resolutely to ride, 'I never did like riding and now I don't have to I'm not going to.' Thus it was with an awkward silence they led their string through the narrow streets to market to buy what provisions.

In the mad tumult of the city's trading place, the warrior's mood lifted quickly enough as if enlivened by the bustling chaos of the midday-city.

To the Pilgrim the whole place seemed even worse than on the yesterday, noisome and oppressive. He seemed almost incapable of maintaining his concentration on anything for more than an instant. Oh how he longed for the silence of the wilderness. The humid intensity of the noonday heat turned the air stale in their mouths. Even the quayside provided only a measure of relief. By mid afternoon they'd been driven back to the inn, stabling their string in the shelter of the courtyard behind.

Despite all their plans to retire early in order to make an early start, things didn't turn out that way. The news of Shimmian's departure had spread through the dockland community and all who knew him, there were quite a few, came to say their farewell. Thus, for a second time, the evening turned into an orgy of food and drink and drew them into the early hours in a haze.

They did rise early though, mainly with the prompting of the Landlord who had the clutter of the evening's revelling to contend with. He helped them with the final loading of the ponies too and stood in the courtyard to wave them farewell.

For every Lover and every friend,
Every colleague and every acquaintance,
Every chance meeting and every stranger
But saw me with their own eyes.

Chapter Six - The Road East

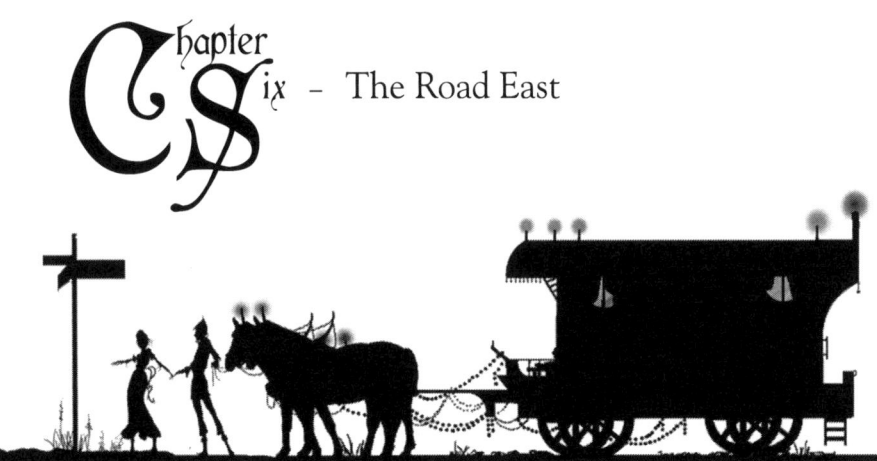

WITH THE GREY light of morning spreading over the rooftops, whilst Varista's denizens were still abed or, at best, just rising for the day, they moved through the still silent streets. The taste of the previous night's indulgences added to their regret as they nodded to the guards of the eastern gate and passed through the high arch to the road beyond.

Others were abroad even at this early hour: merchants, carters, an occasional warrior. Each kept to their own affairs, too busy to pay their surroundings much mind. In the shelter of the city wall young herd-boys led their laconic charges down to the river, their cries and laughter denying the possibility of rain. Everything was normal.

Some six miles from the city a drinking-shrine, built about a wayside spring, afforded a chance to rest and wash some of the crud from their mouths. Ale-born apathy left them sitting on the fine carved stone sipping the cool water from Shimmian's steel goblets. As morning flowed over them and their thoughts gradually cleared, the day began to brighten, offering a welcome gift of warmth, although the sun still had to fight to show itself through the remaining clouds.

Now their spirits began to lift and the time came to start thinking about moving on. The distance ahead seemed somewhat daunting when they considered the matter in the clear light of day but the road would get no shorter for their waiting.

Then, as Shimmian begun to repack his satchel, two other travellers approached the spring. One, a dark clad warrior-maid, led a small black donkey on which the other, a woman also, rode.

The warrior was dressed strangely indeed, at least to the Pilgrim's unsophisticated eye, in a coat of minute discs, or scales, sleeved to just below the elbow and hanging loose to mid thigh. It was hard to distinguish the material or even the colour of the coat, for it shimmered and changed constantly with every movement.

The overall impression was of a metallic substance, or perhaps some kind of lacquer. Under the coat she wore black leather trousers, loose fitting too and short; barely knee length. On her feet were sandals, bound with thongs. She carried no sword or shield but in her right hand held a staff of sorts. The lady on the donkey was draped head to toe in a dark green, hooded cloak, hiding her from view.

'Oh bloody hell,' muttering under his breath, 'Sanain.' Shimmian stood and stepped forward to greet them, bowing low in extravagant welcome.

That his gesture met little but a cold wall of silence seemed to be expected and caused no offence. The warrior-maid's eyes were still as stone, somehow hawk-like watching, waiting.

'It's a nice day, Mistress,' Shimmian tried again, never, as he often claimed, one to turn aside from a challenge.

'Yes.' Her iron hard voice echoed the glint of steel in the eye that locked on the man before her. She stood taller than Shimmian by at least half a head. The lady on the donkey reached forward to rest her hand upon the warrior's shoulder causing her to relax. Well, her tense-sprung rigidity eased a little although her eyes lost nothing of their alertness. 'The day is fine.' Words to soften an insult, had one been taken.

The Pilgrim drew a goblet of water from the flow and offered it to the lady on the donkey, as his own gesture of welcome. 'We thank you, Pilgrim,' the warrior-maid answered as the goblet was taken by a finely manicured hand: long, sensitive fingers, no rings. Having sipped but a drop of the water the green-robed lady passed the goblet to the maiden and dismounted. She was but a hand's breadth shorter than her solemn guard.

'You are welcome, Mistress,' Shimmian continued brightly, still talking to the lady. 'I see that we travel in the same direction. Perhaps we might share the road.'

'No, that will not be...' Again the lady touched her lightly on the arm. 'We can share the road.' It was an agreement of sorts. Now, whilst the lady sat upon the stone wall of the spring, the maiden watered her donkey.

'I am Shimmian, once of Rael, Mistress,' Shimmian began the introduction, continuing to address the lady in green. 'This is my friend, the Pilgrim.'

'Once of Hereth,' the Pilgrim added, not quite at ease with Shimmian's want to speak on his behalf.

'I am Calin-Sanain of Asain. This is My Lady.' There was a finality about the words. No other name would be offered.

What is Sanain? Shimmian had spoken the word almost as an oath. Asain, he knew vaguely, was a country of the North, somewhere beyond the sacred forests of The Elswood. Save for the name he knew little more. *And just who is 'My Lady?' Have these people meanings for me?* But silence ruled his tongue for the moment.

Having reached some sort of uneasy, silent agreement it wasn't long before they moved on together. The sun finally broke through the clouds bringing both warmth and a lightening of mood for the travellers. Shimmian had chosen to walk at the left side of the lady's donkey, Calin-Sanain to the right.

The Pilgrim following on behind, leading the string of laden ponies, took advantage of his isolation and began to look about. He saw the light shining bright on the white painted fascias of farmhouses and mansions far out over the plain. Noted too the lush fields and the orchards. A skylark hovered over a buttercup-spotted meadow and a gentle zephyr brushed through the grass and corn, stirring the leaves of the poplars lining the way.

Behind, the city's indistinct shadow slid from view in the afternoon haze. Ahead, still far, far away, a ridge of blue mountains reached high into a now cloudless sky with white-tipped fingers and the Pilgrim felt the gentle cloak of peace settle on his spirit.

There were many others on the road by this time, going about their various affairs, mainly local folk, farmers, tradesmen and such like. A nobleman passed by in a splendid carriage of black and gold. A caravan of seven mule-drawn wagons, laden with sacks of corn meal, approached from the other direction. Shimmian, as was his way, greeted those they passed with a smile and cheery word.

Some time around mid-afternoon they caught up with a brightly painted Pinexae travelling wagon. Much to their surprise they found that the dark-haired lass who led the horses walked hand in hand with a blue-clad Elf. The Elf bowed low to them and smiled a greeting of open friendliness. The Pinexae girl turned her large amethyst eyes upon them to greet their hearts with the warmth of her being. Without really intending to do so they slowed to join with the couple and walked on to the accompaniment of a hundred jingling bells.

A little further on, a carter rolled laboriously along with his train of ox-drawn wagons, slowing the pace of those behind even more. He was loaded high with precious fabrics and lace that he hoped to trade in the Northlands, he'd explained to Shimmian with many an apology. Before too long however he waved farewell and turned aside at one of the many crossroads, trundling his wearisome way from their sight.

Shimmian-the-Warrior, (or was it Story-Teller?) never one to give silence too much of a chance, began to talk to others on the road. He spoke of his journeys on this and other roads and of adventures in far-off lands. His tales, as at Varista's marble fountain, grew increasingly fanciful and preposterous in their telling. Although they brought many a smile to those with whom they shared the road, the warrior-maid and her green-clad charge retained their shield of aloofness throughout.

When night fell they took lodging in one of the many wayside inns. The six of them, the Lady and Calin, the Elf and Pinexae, Shimmian and the Pilgrim, shared both table and meal, although neither the lady nor her warrior guard took of the wine or beer on offer.

Introductions were made again, the sky-blue clad Elf speaking on behalf of the Pinexae lass, 'This are Pina *Altheka Pinexae*.' He told them in his strange broken tongue. The wide eyes smiled their amethyst magic at the sound of her name and, resting her hand lightly upon the elf's arm, those watching felt the thrill of her spirit. 'She are not knowing of your mouth words, only the tunes in your hearts. She are my soul's song. I am Niivalsta *Avistalaii iralinelle*. We go of need to the wise ones of Al-Sinnian in the Fair Elswood.' There was no need for more explanation. They shone with the love binding them.

'I take it your aim is to journey over the High Pass to Finestre, and from there you'll take the road north to the Elswood?' Shimmian, having shaken off the mystery of her gaze, seemed once again intent on being centre stage.

The elf and his love exchanged the most fleeting of glances. 'The road are unknown to us, Shimmian. It are our need and our intent to go unto the Elswood.

More I know not. The road we follow is but of today,' the Elf confessed. 'Do you have good knowing of the way we should travel from here?'

'It's many a long year since I've climbed the passes of the Great-Divide,' Shimmian commenced to explain, 'but yes, I guess I do have some knowledge. There are several ways to cross over. The quickest way from here is by the great bridge at N'Crion and then over the High-Pass, as that way is known. It isn't an easy road, that's for sure. The way is narrow and torturous. It climbs high through one of the bleakest places in the mountains of the Great-Divide but it's the quickest way by far, from here anyway. It's the way I suggest we take.'

'Is there no easier way?' the Pilgrim asked, as much to widen his knowledge as from any desire to avoid that way. 'I know as little of the mountains as any here, or of what lies beyond for that matter. Are there many passes through to the East?'

'Not many, my friend. The mountains of the Great-Divide have always been a problem to those travelling between west and east,' Shimmian continued, taking on the role as Fount of all knowledge. 'At one time the only way you could approach the east was by journeying far into the south and cross by the Low-Pass at Harithan. It was either that or an even longer trek north and then to go by way of the great Marshlands. That was a perilous journey indeed, for there are wild and dangerous creatures in those fell lands.'

'About two hundred years ago Hazrelled, the High-King-of-Varista, ordered the building of the great bridge and the cutting of the High-Pass, as this way is known. There's another way now though. It's called The-Latal-Pass and crosses over from the Lake-Cities. That's even newer. It's easier too and chosen by most of the traders and such, but it's well out of our way now.'

'Why this High-Pass then?' As the Pilgrim, Calin was curious rather than questioning.

'Well it's simpler and straighter, although in truth the going is considerably harder. The trouble is that, by the Latal way, it would take some four weeks before we reached the Lake-lands and two more before we even entered the foot hills of the mountains, another two weeks to cross over and then yet another three travelling southwards back to this same trail. You can cross into the Elswood from The-Latal-Pass though. So it's possible for Niivalsta to try that way. I still reckon this is quicker. Even at worst estimate it shouldn't take more than four weeks. It'll probably be more like three. My friend the Pilgrim and I are on route to Finestre, and beyond. This is the way we intend to take.'

The Pilgrim nodded his agreement.

'We too travel eastwards to Finestre and beyond. Our journey is to Tabour of the famed Tower. We shall join you over the pass,' Calin informed them.

'The Pilgrim travels to Tabour also. I intend to stay with him till Finestre at least, if not further,' Shimmian rejoined. 'Perhaps we'll travel together for longer than just the pass.' A broad smile creased his face.

'If it be to your liking Pina and Niivalsta shall join with you also,' the Elf added after another intensive, silent exchange.

'Good. Then that's settled,' Shimmian declared with a grin. 'We'll share the road. It's been a long time since I crossed over the Great Divide. It was difficult journey then but, for all its hardship, the going should be easier with a group of us.'

Calin finished the matter, 'The road over the mountains is reported to be wild and there might be dangers. I am Sanain. I shall guard the way.' She seemed to be speaking to Shimmian although throughout her eyes remained on the Pilgrim, sapphire eyes, pure as limestone spring water.

Having spoken her piece, the Sanain said no more but sat polishing her strange staff with a well-used oilcloth. It came as an incredible surprise when, having oiled the whole, she suddenly pulled it apart at the silver ring revealing that this was in truth no staff at all but some strange kind of sword and scabbard. The blade was slender and long, shining blue as does the finest steel, the haft almost one quarter of the sword's length.

However, the Pilgrim saw more, much more than he had expected to see. Oh how well he knew the tempering blush of that blade and the hours of sweat and labour spent in the melding of the steel sinews forming the heart of its creation. *It's Dwarven!*

She felt the sudden intensity burn in the Pilgrim's eyes and lifted her head slightly to catch his gaze. Her own widened in surprise as he touched his fist to his heart, which is the dwarven way.

He said nothing but his wonder increased, as did the questions that rove his thoughts and troubled his dreams that night. *Who are they, this strange warrior with her Dwarven-sword and even stranger, silent companion? Why all this silence anyway? And, why doesn't the Pinexae lass speak? What are they to me?* He found no answers but that was nothing new.

Early next morning, having breakfasted at the inn, they continued eastwards. Niivalsta suggested tying the ponies to the back of the wagon, giving the Pilgrim far more freedom to travel as he might. Not that it really changed things that much. Shimmian tended to walk beside him, perhaps not always talking but somehow constantly protective of him. The man seemed almost childishly eager to point out each new or unusual thing they passed and the Pilgrim began to recognise a strange sort of hunger in his new-found companion, a loneliness, perhaps a need to be accepted. It wasn't hard to comply for Shimmian was a companionable and friendly fellow and his chatter did much to help the miles speed by.

Some four or five hours after leaving the inn they reached a parting of the road. The main, wider, more travelled route turned away northwards. The other trail continued eastward towards the mountains. A Way-Stone sign set by the side of the road told, in bold black print and signed with arrows, that the road Northward led to Latal-shire and that to the East was the way to Finestre, strangely spelt as *Fin-astari*.

'Well this is our road.' Shimmian pointed to the lesser way and they turned eastwards towards the mountains. This, they soon discovered, was a rougher trail winding its way through a country of rolling hills and forests. It seemed, despite all the signs that this was a main thoroughfare created with much labour and considerable thought, it was far less travelled than in past times. The surface was still in good repair though and the passage of miles proved easy enough.

Before long they found themselves travelling through a wilder, emptier land. The mountains, still some way ahead, reared up before them, a grey, impenetrable wall of stone that threatened to block their way, somehow daunting to the spirit as they reached upwards to grasp the heavens with their white-capped peeks.

Niivalsta seemed to thrive in this wilderness as if the lands of men had dampened his spirit and only now could he breathe freely enough to be himself. He began to play his flute as they travelled, dancing and skipping beside his love's wagon. At times he lingered, picking posies of wild flowers from the roadside verges, which, at his insistence, she set in her hair until crowned in the swathe of their splendid glory.

They were indeed a strange pair these two, light and bright as the morning. The elf chattered away almost constantly, even though she seemed quite unable to respond save for the glory of her wonderful smile-lit eyes. It was enough.

The sun was already lowering towards the horizon far behind them when they breasted yet another of the rolling hills and found the Warrior Calin waiting. Here they looked down into a deep wood sided valley where the silver waters of a great river flowed. A long, white, arched bridge spanned the flow.

'The River Cri,' Shimmian informed them as they halted to look at the scene before them. 'That's the bridge of N'Crion, the last vestige of the Lands-of-Bronden. We'll camp this side of the bridge. See, there's a site beneath those trees.'

They made camp, as Shimmian had suggested, in the trees' shelter. Wind fallen branches and kindling were gathered and soon a small fire burned to keep away the night's chill. As Niivalsta set a picket line between the wagon and a nearby tree for the ponies, Pina set a pot to boil. She appeared quite adamant that this was to be her role and as Niivalsta laughingly put it, 'Her cooking is a delight as you are knowing not. Soon you shall happy to be.'

Taking his bow, Shimmian vanished for a time before returning with a broad smile on his face and two brace of cony thrown carelessly over a shoulder. In moments he'd taken control of the situation again, laughing loudly at his own jests as he organised the camp and those within it.

Pina accepted the food with her glorious smile and soon the smell of cooking rabbit filled their noses and the fire spat and hissed with dripping fat. Niivalsta had not lied, unless it was by understatement. They'd never known the like of such a meal, the subtle flavouring and skilled blend of spices. Her role was indeed set.

'We must guard the camp tonight,' Calin said simply whilst they ate. 'There are signs of the grey folk. If you, The Pilgrim, take first watch, Shimmian the next, then I and Niivalsta shall see us through to the morning.' It seemed fair enough, even Shimmian did not demure. The next task was to prepare their sleeping places for the night.

It was still early as they gathered by the fire. The awkwardness bred of their unfamiliarity dispelled when Niivalsta took out his flute and began to blow a soft lullaby into the night air. Pina sat at his feet, her bright Pinexae eyes shining with love.

'Where do your people live, Niivalsta?' the Pilgrim asked from where he rested. 'For you do not seem to be an Elf of the Elswood.'

'You are seeing as are the truth, Pilgrim, I are as my people say, of the *Sylk*, a Sea-elf. We travel the oceans and with the dolphins dance,' he laughed brightly. 'Yet I are, as all elves are, drawn to the sacred forest, though never I have walked beneath those leaves.' He took Pina's hand and raised it to his lips. 'It is with great longing that my feet tread me with my beloved to that place.'

'I know an elf of The Elswood...' he spoke into the night.

'It's good to speak of ourselves,' Shimmian broke the stillness. 'You know, we're going to spend many days together. We should get to know each other.'

'Yes,' Calin responded. 'This is good. Who knows what trials we shall face on the trail? It is right to know who will stand at our side should trouble arise. I shall speak openly of myself.' She hesitated for a moment, clearly uncomfortable with what she would say next. 'However, of the Lady I can say little, save that she is under my protection and that we travel together to the famed Tower of Tabour.'

With a sudden flash of compassion the Pilgrim intervened. 'We've no wish to pry nor to hear what isn't meant for our ears, Calin. Surely we all have our own secrets and unspoken thoughts. It's best we agree that if we wish to speak we may do so and if not there is no blame. As for myself? I'm on my journey, following my quest.' *How much do I tell?* 'I am as you see me, a pilgrim. My road reaches out before me, although I don't know to where, as yet. To Finestre at least. Then to Tabour and then to... to who knows where, to the lands beyond tomorrow perhaps.'

'You have chosen a strange, lonesome road, Pilgrim,' Calin replied, a wonder softening her voice. 'It would seem too hard for me not to know where I am to travel, to be so...' her voice trailed away as if her mind, set to the service of others, couldn't really grasp the reality of such freedom.

'It's not such a hard or lonesome road, Calin,' the memory of a beautiful elf dancing through his mind. 'There are many who touch my life.' He paused. 'To tell the truth, I can't really say I chose it anyway. It seems more that I just follow a way laid out long ago. I don't mind really, well not too much, but I do feel a burning need to understand and that appears to be denied to me.'

He stopped. *Do I say too much?* 'Others seem to know more about me and my journey than I do myself. I just wish that they'd tell me.'

'You have the road travelled a long time?' Niivalsta enquired.

'Yes. A long time indeed, or so it seems. This road and other, darker, passages.'

'But you carry no weapon,' Calin again.

'I don't need a weapon, Calin, I'm not a warrior, although once I thought to be one. Now I'm just a pilgrim. I don't fight, nor even kill if I can help it, save for food that is. Even then I don't enjoy it. I'll not knowingly take another's life.'

'I do.' Her voice was little more than a sad, soft breath, cold and heavy with meaning, 'I am Sanain.' The word sounded like a sentence rather than a description. 'I kill. It is my nature.' And that sounded as nothing but fate's doom.

'Sanain?' She seemed more approachable now, ready for the question. 'It's a word I don't know. What is Sanain?'

She stood, slowly, silently. The sword was drawn before they even saw her move, its blade singing a deep song of stillness as it sliced the air. She spun, turned, twisted, faster and faster until the sword and bearer were no more than a blur, the silver, whirling blade creating a wall of living steel about her. She was still, the sword once more enclosed in its scabbard. 'I am Sanain.' Drawing the sword anew, slowly, she held it out, resting upon the palm of each hand as if for inspection. 'This too is Sanain,' she added, sounding cold. 'With this I kill, take of life. It is what I am.'

'Who do you kill, Calin Sanain?'

'Any I choose, Pilgrim.' The truth was evident. 'Any I must.' The sadness seemed louder than the voice. 'I pay the price.'

What price would the Dwarves require for a sword that would take a life? he wondered to himself. But he said no more of the matter. Eventually he tried again. 'I have another question, Calin.'

'Ask your question, Pilgrim, you have the right.'

I have the right? What right? Does she know me also? 'I don't mean to pry, nor to ask of things forbidden, only to answer the things I don't know.' He explained softly. 'It might seem simple, yet I have wondered since first we met. Your tunic of scales, what is it made of? I don't think I've ever seen anything like it before.'

She laughed, a soft, warming laugh that turned the tension to mist. 'So you do not challenge me with the hunger of your mind, Pilgrim? Why? Why not?'

'I have no need, Calin. Once I made my own dwarven-sword.'

Her eyes lifted. 'Ah, I thought...' She never said what it was she'd considered. For just an instant though, he found what might have been companionship in the expression of this death-hardened Sanain. 'Then I shall answer your curiosity, Pilgrim, for 'tis no great mystery. The scales are those of one of the Fire-drakes-of-Nith. It was my challenge, set by the Golden-Witch, during my time of proving. The sword-stave was carved from the wing-bone of the same creature. There is nothing stronger, or lighter.'

For some reason Shimmian had been quiet throughout the exchange. 'That was no mean task for a lass, Calin.'

'I'm no lass, Lord-of-Stories.' Her laugh was cold and humourless. 'I am Sanain.' Words that drove him back into his former silence. 'No, Shimmian,' she offered quickly. 'I meant no offence. I'm no one to question the ways of a Lord-of-Rael.' For some unknown reason this sent him even deeper into his quiet.

'It's time for me to take watch.' The Pilgrim took up his staff and went to find a place away from the fire's glare. In the darkness he sought a rock where he might rest as his eyes adjusted to the night.

Once more I find strangeness all about me. It seems clear that the Lady and Calin have not joined with us by chance, any more than Shimmian. Maybe Niivalsta and Pina too seek meanings from my journey. But what, I wonder, does it all mean for me?

It seemed again that Fate had written its own tale for this brown-clad pilgrim. *Where does my choice come into play? I'll not be the plaything of Fate. That's something I'm sure about anyway. Perhaps chance too might lend a hand before all is done.*

He was still lost in thought when Shimmian came to relieve him and send him to his bed-roll. Sleep came easy that night; the rush of the river and sound of the wind sang a soft lullaby to soothe its passage.

Morning had scarce broken when the wagon rolled out over the bridge followed by the string of ponies. The Pilgrim, coming last, stopped to gaze down into the fast flowing waters but there was nothing to see in their depths. The spanned arches though were a wonder to behold and filled him with admiration of the craftsmen who had set the stones so well.

Once clear of the bridge they began the long climb back out of the valley and in less than two hours they breasted the ridge and passed beyond sight.

Now this was true wilderness once more and all of the party found themselves alert and watchful. Although they saw no further sign of the grey folk, Calin began to scout ahead of the party. She'd disappear and then reappear without sound or sign. There was something wonderfully cat-like about all her movements now, as were she a creature of the wilds herself.

The Lady, at Niivalsta's insistence, rode with Pina on the wagon. The Elf walked to the right and the Pilgrim to the left. Shimmian came behind, bow in hand with a sword slung over his back. They hoped they were ready should any danger come. None did though. Anyway, to the Pilgrim's eye, the greatest danger appeared to lie in the stark mountain slope that reared up before them.

Through the following days the road led them deeper and deeper into the wilderness and ever nearer to where the towering and somehow threatening ridge of mountains waited. In their secret thoughts they began to grow concerned about just how they were going to cross over that barrier.

'Does this road carry us right through the mountains? They seem so high and…'

'Aye.' Shimmian tried to smile away their concern. 'It cuts right through to the other side. It's high there, and bleak and cold. I was there before. There isn't much of comfort, but it will do.' Perhaps he was in part grateful that the matter had been finally raised. 'Look, I know it looks a bit daunting from down here but the road has been here for many years and the way remains passable. Like I said, I've been this way before. It's high there, sure, and a bit scary but don't worry, we'll be OK.' Somehow his words did little to ease their minds. Nonetheless, they made good progress as the road carried them up into the foothills.

Game was plentiful, so there was little need for the provisions carried on the pack train. Sometimes they'd wait whilst Shimmian, Calin or Niivalsta hunted.

Each evening they'd camp at the roadside. As dusk fell, they'd light their fire and Pina would tend to their meal in the growing night. She loved to cook, bubbling with enjoyment over the expressions on their faces with every new delight she produced. And produce she did. Was it magic? Who can tell? What did they care anyway with such wonders to please them?

In the darkness as they awaited sleep Niivalsta would take up his flute to play haunting melodies of the sea. Sometimes Pina would dance too, strange gypsy polkas, in the firelight.

The road became steeper, the way more torturous and the two ponies strained at the caravan harness to meet the challenge. At times it became necessary for the men to actually manhandle their way upward. Their pace slowed as they climbed higher and higher towards the mountain pass.

As Shimmian had said, the road was there but one would hardly call it safe. It clung to the rock face over chasms falling thousands of feet into dark, secret canyons. Here the eagles ruled. Their cries sounded shrill through the thin mountain air. At night the heavens were spread out above them and they could peer into the very depths of eternity.

The hours merged together into an interminable struggle to keep the wagon moving up the steep incline of the rock-strewn, rutted road even though Shimmian and Niivalsta had managed to rig a harness so that the other ponies could help with the pulling.

As things turned out, and despite Shimmian's promise otherwise, the way was but barely passable. The slopes and hairpin bends proved a nightmare of straining muscles and nerves. If that were not enough, when they did eventually reach the end of the climb, they emerged onto a terrifying stretch of road where the way had been cut out of a sheer cliff face. It was like travelling through a tunnel where one side was nothingness. A single foolhardy venture to see what lay below left the Pilgrim's head spinning with the mind-numbing impression that the drop went on forever.

This trial led but to another. Cliffs closed in about them threatening to block their way entirely. Vast walls of grey rock enclosing them tightly so the wheels of the wagon scraped the sides, swaying alarmingly as they jarred and jolted their way over boulders and fallen rocks. At one point it seemed the pass really was too narrow and the wagon would be stuck there forever, but they passed through.

Night found them on a high ledge overlooking a vast mountain valley. Somewhere above, water dashed from rock to rock before cascading out into the void turning the view below into a vast misty cloud. They built their fire close to the mountain face and, having fed the ponies their oats and eaten their own hurried meal, they huddled in their blankets fighting off the cold.

Sometime in the night the Pilgrim awoke. Dreams, omens, perhaps just visions drawn from his own fears weighed heavy on his soul and he felt reluctant to return to their domain. Instead he slid from his blanket and went to sit on a rock looking into the dark shrouded valley far below.

'Ah, you couldn't sleep either.'

He jumped, spinning about. At first almost guilty to be so caught, then stunned speechless to find it was the Lady who'd spoken. He hadn't known that she could or even would speak.

'The turning of the world troubles my soul, Young-Pilgrim.' Her voice was soft and gentle, with the same hint of healing kindness as his mother's. 'There's something amiss, tonight. Let's find what is to be seen on this dark night. Here,' she reached out to take his hand, 'Come see,' and led him from where the others lay sleeping.

Eventually she stopped where a large boulder provided both a resting place and somewhere they might look backward over their trail.

Far away, oh so very far away, the moon danced silver upon the Varista's slumbering bay, unreal or at least seeming so in the ghost of this night-time hour. The silence screamed aloud and stillness echoed with the anguish of nothing. Further still, even beyond the horizons of their thoughts, something dark stirred. One by one, slowly as if of little consequence, the stars went out. It was neither cloud, nor the coming of dawn or storm, but rather as if a grasping claw of hatred ripped away their light forever. The Pilgrim's thoughts froze in his mind.

'The chains are breaking asunder,' she whispered into the darkness.

He turned, seeking an answer in her eyes but saw nothing but the glimmer of moonlight on her tear damp cheeks.

'I don't know,' she answered his unspoken question. 'I see only as you see. I don't know what meets my eyes. Nor can I tell of what it might portend. However, I do know I'm troubled to the core of my being.' She grew still then, still as the stones of the Earth-Spring. Her voice, when she did eventually speak was but a whisper on the night air, yet the words seemed to fill his mind.

> *'There is a wakening,*
> *There is a trembling*
> *There is a reaching out for power.*
> *Undone are the bindings,*
> *Untied are the knots,*
> *Unfettered are the chains*
> *Of Fate.*
> *Where now the Stones of Morning?'*

Once more her eyes turned to him, holding him and stilling the turmoil in his mind.

> *'It is almost your time, my YoungPilgrim.*
> *You should not dally on the road.'*

Who are you? What are you to me? What do you know of me? What do you want? But he said nothing. There was nothing to say.

Thus they passed into another world, a place of extremes, of towering peeks and plummeting chasms, a land where waterfalls fled from glacial flows, rushing, gushing, leaping out into the thin alpine air to spill upon the mountainside far below. This was no place for mortals with their petty fears and meaningless plans but one where the spirit might touch eternity and fly with angels. How men had even dared to enter this domain, where the eagles ruled and where the homes of the Gods might rest, was beyond understanding. It was little wonder their passage was so despised. By day they travelled uneasily along this tortured trail, clinging to mountain slopes and crawling as bugs through the wonder of this awesome splendour. At night? Oh yes, at night they dwelt with the stars.

Day by day their struggle continued. There was one place where a gentle meadow, spread out across a plateau deep in the heart of the mountains, afforded a place to rest awhile. A narrow vale where they eased their aching bodies and Pina laughingly danced about their campfire full of joy at the chance of being able to prepare a full meal for once. And, with the help of Shimmian, who'd felled a mountain goat, a feast indeed did she set before them that evening. The ponies were left to wander free and to feed off the rich grass that grew there.

Only Calin remained ill at ease, vanishing to search through the vale for whatever it might be that troubled her

The following morning they returned to the struggle.

*

For a third time that day the trail narrowed to little more than a gash between two rock faces. They looked uneasily at each other wondering if the wagon would pass through this time. The oppressive repetitiveness of the whole situation bore down on them. Just how long would this go on for? However, they need not have worried too much, though it was a tight squeeze.

'And that,' Shimmian tried to reassure them as they emerged into the opening beyond, 'that is the last of these passages. Trust me, I've been this way before. The worst is over now. From here the trail is all downhill, winding its way out of the mountains and down into the hills of the Finnestava. I'd think another four or five days should see us right through.' Somehow his words failed to cheer.

The early evening mist seemed to mirror their mood, slowing their movements and dampening their spirits. Niivalsta could hardly find a smile as he helped Pina back onto the wagon seat.

Calin moved away on her constant vigil, keeping to the edge of the narrow valley before them. It was more like a ravine really. The sheer walls of grey mountain rock as ever reached up over them, denying the sunset. Only in the centre, where the trail cut a white scar through the rough mountain grass, were a few trees clumped together. Slowly they forced themselves to move towards these.

The fall came without warning, a crashing, crushing, smashing, roaring rush of rocks and boulders, splintering into dust and flying debris to block the path behind them. Niivalsta screamed a loud cry of warning and, catching Pina about the waist, pulled her into the shelter of the wagon. Ponies cried out in fright wanting to run but Shimmian caught their bridles and manhandled them to a standstill. The Pilgrim crouched together with the Lady close by the others, stunned by the shock of the sudden arrival of chaos.

'Ambush!' Shimmian's voice was little more than a spit of hatred, crackling sharp after the din. 'Goblins!' followed by the hiss of his sword. Niivalsta reached beneath the wagon awning and pulled his long bow free.

Where is Calin?

Then came a laugh, bitter, humourless and cruel, echoing in the silence that followed the tumult of the avalanche. 'Agh! Got Y'.' A burst of exaltation. From the trees a group of beings emerged, ten, twelve perhaps fifteen of them. Armed and armoured were they, scimitars, and axes, several spears. The leader, from his size he could be none other, stepped forward ahead of the others. He half stooped, crouching behind his shield, letting the tip of his giant cleaver-like blade rest on the ground.

'Agh! Bastard, shit-arsed, muck grovellers. Drop y're fuckin' weapons or we'll eat you alive.' The goblin's power-filled laughter rolled down the valley again.

They didn't move. The Pilgrim heard the strain as the Elf's bowstring tightened.

'Wait,' Shimmian cautioned. 'I'll give the word.'

The goblin seemed in no hurry, He leant on his shield and picked his teeth with an extended claw. 'Agh! So you're gonna fuckin' fight are y'? Even better.'

'Wait!' The Pilgrim rose slowly to his feet and stepped out into the open. 'There's no need for fighting or killing, Grey One.'

Eyes, cold eyes, turned to pierce the Pilgrim, slit eyes, icy, grey, lifeless eyes and the huge goblin grew still. A minute passed, tense, biting seconds grinding like heartbeats. 'You...' A raised finger pointed straight at him. 'You can go. Agh! This time!'

It knows me! It recognises... The Pilgrim felt the shiver of horror over the things confronting them. 'I stay!'

'Agh! Your blood is not wanted!' The goblin waited for him to move. 'I said, you can go!'

'My blood is mine, Goblin, and not for you to want or not!' He stepped forwards to stand on the open roadway. 'I go or stay as I please and now I choose to stay with my friends. Why not just let us pass? There's no need for this.'

'Agh! For fuck sake! Do y' think we're gonna give up the killin'?'

'Why not, Goblin? What are you to me that I should crave to see your death? What are we to you that you should desire us harm? I want no killing, Goblin, no death or slaughter, not mine not yours. Go. Leave us in peace. I'm on my journey and I mean you no harm. I don't fight nor kill, Goblin, and these are my friends. We don't wish to fight. Let us pass, we want none of your death or warring.'

'Tough shit! Agh! Stupid fuckin' bastard! Agh! You won't get another fuckin' choice.' He shrugged and turned to look over the others in the party. 'Agh! Fuck me! What a bunch of arse 'oles. A man. Agh! Fighter too and an Elf. Fuck me, it's years since I tasted Elf meat.' The eyes moved further, 'Agh! Bitches too! That's even fuckin' better.' He turned his head to look back at his band. 'Agh! D' you fuckin' hear that? There's bitches, Agh we're gonna have us some fanny! Agh!' He turned back to face the Pilgrim, 'Agh! Like I said, you can pass. The others die!' A cruel smile contorted his face into an even more evil expression. 'Agh! Well, those two die! The bitches might live if they please us enough.' He looked back to the Pilgrim. 'Agh! So make y're fuckin' mind up. Agh! You goin' t' live or die?'

'Look, Goblin, I've already made my choice. I do not take life. I shall not kill.'

The Lady spoke. 'That's the choice for you too, Goblin!' Her voice was as a knife cutting through the cords of fate. 'To choose life, and go. Or to choose death and fight!' There could be no other choice now.

The goblin laughed. 'I like it, Bitch. It's a good choice, life or death.' He laughed again, somehow driven by madness rather than humour. 'Agh! I choose death!' He laughed again. 'Agh! Are you gonna stand and fight with those two?'

'Not two, just one.'

Calin's voice came from the shelter of the trees behind them, cold and hard as granite. As one the creatures turned about. She came, silent as always, from the tree line still resting upon her sword-stick as were it a staff. She stopped amidst the band of still stunned creatures, looked over them and shook her head oh so very slowly, sadly. 'I'm sorry,' she seemed to speak to the air.

Then they died, all of them. The leader didn't know from where the blade came that stole his existence, but he was the only one. For Calin danced her dreadful dance of death among them, a blurring ballet of black and silver slaughter and they fell, all of them, none making a sound nor meeting her with even a suggestion of resistance. Only a few, those who were furthest from her at the beginning, even thought to run. By the time the thought had formed it was too late. They could think no more.

The valley was silent again, silent as the graveyard it had become. 'It was their choice,' the Lady spoke her judgement. She sounded as sad as the Pilgrim felt. *Their choice? True, but what a waste.*

In the midst of the field of blood Calin stood still as a tombstone. Her face had turned white as if all the life had been taken from her. Then slowly she sank to her knees and bowed her head. Her cry of anguish turned their souls to ice for it sounded as if her heart had been rent in two.

The Price! He knew that he was right.

No one spoke, nor thought to look at the bodies to see if any still lived. It would have been pointless and they all knew it.

Eventually Shimmian took a spade from the wagon and began to dig a pit. He worked in silence too, shaking his head when Niivalsta approached to help. When all was done he dragged the bodies, one by one and threw them in, then covered the whole. It was fully dark by the time he'd finished but no one had built a fire or thought about setting up camp. They stayed much as they had throughout.

Calin still knelt in the field of blood somehow shielded from the others by her own wall of pain. To approach her would seem an act of sacrilege, unwelcome and profane.

It was the Pilgrim who eventually broke the spell of his own thoughts and found the will to go. He stood close, looking down at where she knelt. It came as no surprise to find, when he lay his hand upon her shoulder, that she shook.

'You are Sanain. You paid the Price.'

She lifted her head to look at him her eyes burning with the fires of her torment. 'Yes, I am Sanain.' They were cold words without comfort. 'They chose to die, Pilgrim.' Words that did not explain. 'They longed for death. The pain of their empty souls was too much to bear.' Her eyes held his, burning even brighter. 'They want… They look to you for an answer. They even thought they would die at your hand and that at least would have some kind of meaning.' Then she stood and turned towards the others with the Pilgrim following close behind her. At the last minute she stopped again and turned to face him. 'Thank you. You did not condemn me.'

'You are Sanain!' Perhaps he understood. *Surely you can't condemn someone for being themselves.*

They moved on again. There was no way they'd remain in that place. Shimmian led with a burning brand held high to light the way, willing to face even the treachery of the road and the dark of the night to get away.

They finally stopped as the hour neared midnight. Pina lit a hastily built fire and cooked a thick broth. They ate in silence and went to their beds the same. For once they set no guard. There seemed no need.

Morning came. The bright sun, calling the mountains to life, belied the horror they knew they'd left behind and failed to lighten their spirits. It was Pina again who took charge of things brewing her tea and serving griddle scones and cured bacon. Eventually she went to stand before Calin.

She stood there, those wide amethyst eyes glistening with tears and took Calin's hands in her own, turned them and kissed each palm. She stooped too, and kissed the Sanain's brow. Then she picked up the sword, drew the blade, held it before her and kissed that too. Then, having sheathed it once more, placed it back into Calin's hands.

The warrior turned to face her, tears welling in her own eyes. 'Yes, Pina, I know you're my friend.' Then they hugged and Calin firstly smiled then laughed. 'You're completely impossible, Pina!'

Somehow, even though the Pilgrim wasn't sure how, the spell was broken. Breakfast was eaten with a new enjoyment and before long they'd packed the wagon and were once again under way. As Shimmian had promised the road was indeed much easier now, although in fairness it might well have been their eagerness to get away from the place that led them to think so. By noon Calin's return to her normal self was complete and, once again, she scouted ahead to find a campsite.

Much later as the Pilgrim sat beside the glowing embers of the fire Calin came to sit by his side. She was quiet, staring, as did he, into the flames. 'You did not go?' she asked.

'No. I chose not to.'

'You are strong, Pilgrim.' It was not praise.

'And you are, Sanain.'

'I am.'

'Do you judge me, Sanain?'

'You are judged.' He didn't miss the wording of her reply.

'Do I live, Sanain?'

She'd not lie. 'You live...' she paused. When she continued he had the impression she was entering an area into which she had never ventured before. 'I thought that the choice would be between good and ill, between light and dark or even between love and hate. You chose not to kill. Having thus chosen, then I shall do as I can to protect you. But your road is yours alone.'

The Lady who sat near laughed lightly. 'Yes, Calin, but we'll share it until Tabour at least,' and Calin smiled.

Thus, some twenty-seven days after leaving Varista, they passed out of the mountains into a region of forest and hill. Once again game was plentiful and they feasted on venison. Five days after the events of that terrible valley Calin returned from her scouting to say that Finestre was within a few hours' march. Soon after she pointed out the minarets gleaming over the treetops.

*

As Varista had stood overlooking the great bay like a proud monument to the power of man so Finestre, resting in the heart of the wilderness, was a symbol of his integration with the beauty of creation. Set in a wonderland of mountain, lake and forest, the unadorned, alabaster walls caught and mirrored every hue of nature's wonder until the entire city seemed to be but a part of the landscape, belonging to rather than dominating over the whole. The high minarets of the temples were but images of the tree-lined slopes, the sharp pointed roofs of the buildings seemed like echoes of the peeks high above.

In such scenery it was little wonder men's minds turned to higher things. First had been the simplest of shrines, little more really than a mound of stones and a flat rock on which a fallen rabbit might be burnt in offering to Fin, the ancient god of the mountains. The huntsmen who trapped through this land had set it on the summit of a small rounded hill, overlooking a long lake valley.

Others who came to worship there were moved to build a small temple about the shrine. Still more came bringing their own gods, for this was a place to believe in such things. Thus year-by-year, generation-by-generation, new temples were added. Now other gods beamed or scowled down upon other worshipers. There were not just temples to the gods though, there were temples to other things also: learning, soldiering, merchants, travellers. There was the temple of silence, the temple of water. There were in fact more temples than one might ever guess, even temples within temples. For it seems the way of men to vie with each other in their works and none wished to be left aside.

About the hill were the homes of the priests and priestesses, the bishops, monks and nuns, palaces, manses, monasteries and convents, the almshouses and hospitals. Each attested, with their own simple or ornate splendour to the glory of their faith. Even beyond the city limits men had left their worshipful mark; the cave homes of the hermit and the mystic pock-marking the mountainsides. Yes, one might say 'Finestre was indeed the City of temples'.

Not just temples and priest halls either, for with these came people to service the needs of the worshiper and holy man. Inns, shops and markets had sprung up around the outside of the temple mound, even so keeping somehow apart. Craftsmen set up their stalls and workshops, and Finestre grew until the whole became a thriving metropolis.

Thus the party trundled down the long road from the mountains and passed between the first two Shrines-of-the-Gate and in through the unguarded portal. They looked in wonder at the magnificence and strangeness of the sights that met their gaze.

From ahead the sound of bells and chanting drew their attention. A band of monks, some twenty or thirty with shaven heads and bare feet, clad in saffron robes, appeared from somewhere within the city. They came slowly, walking in single file, past the wagon and the dust-stained travellers, on their procession from the city, to? To wherever... In less than a minute the sound of their passing had diminished to nothing.

The travellers exchanged bemused glances. 'Finestre,' Shimmian needlessly declared, although his rum smile attested more to amusement than information.

As they passed between the towers of City's shrine-gate, it soon became apparent that the temples had spread well beyond the temple mound. They stopped beside one such holy place, in the courtyard outside a travellers' inn. It was in truth little more than a small, white, stone shrine.

'May the goings and the comings of Aestae be with you,' a young priestess declared as they drew alongside. 'There is room and comfort within, travellers.'

Shimmian bowed low to her. 'We thank you, sister. It has been a long road.'

'Then shall you be all the more welcome as are all the weary whom Aestae blesses.' She in turn bowed back and gestured that they go to the inn. 'There is lodging a plenty and a yard for the wagon and stabling for the ponies behind,' she told them sounding more like a vendor than holy-woman.

From somewhere deeper in the city a bell tolled out the hour. The young priestess knelt and touched her head three times upon the ground before standing to face them again, smiling serenely.

They thanked her and, taking her advice, approached the inn. To the Pilgrim, accustomed to open skies and the sounds and sights of nature, this inn was opulence incarnate. Although the others seemed to accept the grandeur as expected, he felt a twinge of guilty indulgence as he viewed the room allocated him.

In many respects it was rather a sad meal that evening. For resting heavily on each of their minds was the thought of the parting soon to come. Niivalsta and Pina were to travel north from here in search of help from the Elf-Lords in Al-Sinnian. Even though but companions of the road, they had travelled far together and had grown used to each other's company.

'I hope you find what you seek in the Elswood,' the Pilgrim offered as a parting blessing the following morning after they had breakfasted. 'They say that many are the wonders to be found 'neath those hallowed bows.'

'I have fearing no need, Pilgrim. But a little thing it is we seek.'

Then Pina came to them, smiling her secret smile. To each she offered a small gift. None had seen her crafting these things, yet they knew with surety that each was from her own hand. To Shimmian she gave a neckerchief of silk embroidered with the symbol of a broken crown. The Pilgrim saw the storyteller's eyes widen in sudden surprise but she just continued to smile and touched a finger to his lips to still any words.

For the Pilgrim she'd fashioned a sash of many colours woven with her own hands. It was bright and when tied, it formed a rainbow about his waist. Her amethyst orbs met and stilled the questioning of his eyes and held him in silence with the sweetest, most innocent of looks. Then she winked at him.

Who is she? What is she? It came as a sudden, shocking revelation that he had never, not even once, questioned who Pina was or what the Pinexae are. It seemed too late for such matters now. He returned her smile and kissed her cheek in farewell.

What gifts she bore for the Lady or Calin the Pilgrim never knew.

Following Shimmian's advice they went together to the Travellers' Temple, that of Astiira, the God-of-Journeys. As was the custom, travellers gathered there to tell their tales or plan their journeys. Often companies formed here for the road ahead.

Over the years Astiira's Temple had grown into one of the grander, larger buildings on the hill. At its centre was a huge domed hall, The Hall-of-Meetings, watched over by the statue of Astiira, cloaked and ready for the trail, his right hand reaching out as ever to show the way onward. About the statue were set the standards of the Cities. The Silver-ship of Varista, the White swan of The Lake cities, The Golden crown of High-Caravail, The Sacred-Tree of Al-Sinnian and the White Tower of Tabour.

So it was that Niivalsta and Pina, bowing their final goodbyes, turned toward the Sacred-Tree and the journey before them. The others, having offered their own farewells, made their way to the sign of The White Tower.

A tall life-hardened warrior, with sword at hip and a longbow strapped over his back, stepped out to greet them as they approached. 'You travel to Tabour?' His voice was deep and mellow. 'I am Cog.'

Calin meet him eye to eye. 'I am Calin, Sanain-of-Asain. This is my Lady.' She bowed her head the slightest amount. 'We do indeed travel to Tabour.' Shimmian for once seemed willing to let her take the lead. 'These are our companions also. This is Shimmian The Storyteller-of-Rael,' Shimmian bowed with his customary extravagance and smiled broadly, 'and this is The Pilgrim.'

'Once of Hereth,' the Pilgrim added.

'We have travelled over the mountains from the famed Silver City of Varista and plan to travel on together. We would welcome any who wish to join with us.'

Cog said nothing for a time; his questioning eyes were fixed on Shimmian. 'I too am from Rael.' *They are known to each other! What truth lies here I wonder?* 'and kinsman to this *Story Teller* of yours.' There were a hundred meanings in his tone and a moment of tension as their eyes locked in some strange struggle of recognition and secret understanding. Finally it was Cog who bowed his head in unspoken acknowledgement of an agreement between them.

'I am Plie.' There was no mistaking the gentle elfin voice. They turned to face a tall, strikingly beautiful, green-clad elf, an elf but more. Hanging from a cord across his back was a golden harp proclaiming him to be one of the famed Bards of Al-Sinnian. No other could own such an instrument. 'If it is fitting, I too would join with your party and follow your road.'

He looks at me. Seeing what? I wonder.

Calin replied for them all once again. 'We welcome you, Plie, Tune-smith of Al-Sinnian. Your company shall honour us.'

The last to speak was a girl of the desert people, dressed, as her ways demanded, in the sand-coloured desert-robe of her kind. Lowering her eyes demurely, she spoke from behind her gauze veil. 'I am Daughter-heir to Guesta merchant of Istar. I return now to my home and would join also with your party on the road east.'

'Be welcome, Daughter-of-Guesta,' Calin accepted her, only once again it was to the Pilgrim the shaded eyes turned.

He smiled, 'Yes you're more than welcome. My path leads beyond Tabour and even beyond Istar itself in all probability. We'll be able to travel all the way together, if you'll allow,' he added with a hint of caution, but the warmth of her veil-hidden smile drove away his doubt.

With business-like order Calin, Cog and Shimmian began to discuss their plans for the journey ahead. The Tune-smith and Lady stood off to one side, content with their own silences, leaving the details to others. The Pilgrim, also happy enough to accept the other's choices, found himself a quiet bench, on which to rest and watch the scene about him.

There was much to see and perhaps to think about. Far over the other side of the hall he espied the Sword and Anvil of Santolin and was half tempted to seek news of home. Near by hung the Running Horse of Pashad and a little further off the coiled serpent of Niss. People of every nature milled about here in a chaotic melee. Many were warriors, knights and soldiers of fortune. There were merchants aplenty too who seemed intent on outdoing each other with the fineness of the garb. He saw several elves and his eyes scanned about urgently. *No she is not here.*

Then, to his surprise, he noticed a band of the Dwarven Kin, grouped together in lonely isolation as they looked about. Though a hardy folk they do not travel easily, nor willingly let their home forges grow cold. He was even more surprised to see them approach the Sacred Tree of Al-Sinnian. *What's that about? There are many mysteries in this place.*

'My name is Hkainae.' He'd not heard the desert girl approach and leapt up with shock at the nearness of her voice. Her laugh was rich and smooth as honey. 'I'm sorry, I startled you. My name is Hkainae.' She flicked aside the veil and smiled. No slender elf-maid was this desert girl. Her bronze-skinned face had strength, her eyes, when he rose unbidden to his feet, were level with his own, dark brown almost jet, set in bands of kohl. His gaze was met by hers, captivated by a warmth and mystery that all but robbed him of wit.

'Hkainae?' *I sound like a fool.*

'Yes,' she paused, 'Hkainae.'

She expects something, something of me. 'Oh.' Realisation struck. 'They call me Pilgrim.' Her eyes filled with questions. 'It's my nature at this time.' Her eyes blinked with confusion freeing him from their sorcery. *She doesn't understand.* 'It's the way of my kin, Hkainae,' he offered. 'We see that names can be such terrible things and say that we should not bind ourselves to one nature. Rather we name ourselves for what we are. Which is why I name myself Pilgrim now.'

He felt his tongue loosening and an eagerness to say more, to explain himself. 'I've been several things in my time, Hkainae. Once I was a warrior, before that an apprentice of the Dwarf-smiths-of-the-Carrow. In my childhood they...' Her eyes stilled him.

'These are strange things you say to me, Pilgrim, but no matter.' She smiled once more and again warmed him with her eyes. 'The way ahead is long and we shall spend many days together. Yes we shall walk together and share our stories with each other. There is more than enough time to grow to know and understand who and what we are. We shall become friends, you and I.' She reached out and took his hand drawing it to her face where she brushed his fingertips with but the lightest touch of her dark lips.

After a strange, but not uncomfortable, silence she sat on the bench beside him, their eyes feasting over the assembled sights and wonders that surrounded them. 'Where is Hereth?' The desert girl's eyes wandered over the many standards on display.

'Far away to the west and the north, Hkainae, close unto the borders of Santolin. You see the sign of the Sword-and-Anvil?' He pointed. 'That's the sign of Santolin. The sword is for the might of the army. They say that the Kings of Santolin are the protectors of the West. The Anvil is for the Dwarves. Hereth lies close to Santolin's northern border.

'Some say that we are of Santolin, those of my kin, but my mother says not. Hereth is my home though, where I was born and raised. It's a gentle land set beside the sea on the edge of the Great Salt marsh.'

'This is good, Pilgrim.' The name was still strange to her tongue. 'I can see there are many things to know of you. This is true of me also. We shall be able to fill the hours on the road discovering all there is to know of each other. You shall tell me of your country. I shall tell you of the Desert, **Hkamoot.**'

Suddenly she became practical. 'Right, we have sat here long enough. You shall come with me and show me to your lodgings. It is best if I move my things to where your party is based so to be ready when the time comes for us to move.'

The Pilgrim found himself complying with her command without minding.

Having appraised Shimmian and the others of what they were about, he followed to her lodgings in one of the merchant guildhalls near to the Temple of Merchants.

It was like a palace, this hall, a place of richness and opulence, of gold and jewels, the floors formed of the finest polished marble. The room to which she led him was light and cool, the windows hung with silk.

She was packed ready, in panniers for ponies. On the bed were laid out her travelling robes. 'The ponies are in the stables out at the back of the hall,' she explained. 'If you would help me with these?'

'Of course.' He hefted a pack on each shoulder and followed her. She had a train of four ponies, and it took another three trips before they were laden. Just a final valise was left.

He stood at the window looking out over the city while she settled her fare with the innkeeper. On her return he closed the door behind them and led the way back to the party's lodging.

By then the brightly painted Pinexae wagon was gone.

I wonder what she'll make of our humble abode, he mused. He needn't have worried. She seemed not to mind the change at all, or at least she had the grace to hide it if she did so. The manager found her a room next to the Pilgrim's, which seemed to please her too. Although in comparison to that which she'd left it was poor indeed. Once again he helped her with her luggage and settled the ponies with his and Shimmian's.

*

They left Finestre some five days later, having restocked their ponies in the city's markets. Shimmian was much happier this time. He declared that he had had the best of the dealings throughout, although in truth the Pilgrim couldn't really see what gave him right to the claim. To the train of their four ponies and the Lady's donkey, Hkainae added her four. The Warrior Cog rode a grand War-horse, Navone. A proud, noble creature was Navone, far to dignified to serve as a beast of burden.

The first few days were pleasant indeed. The road, trailing through the lush forests of cedar and mountain ash, was ever full of new and wonderful sights. Mindful of the dangers of the mountains and with thoughts of the goblins' rising, Calin, Cog and Shimmian took to scouting ahead. The Lady and Plie seemed drawn to each other, travelling side-by-side much of the time, although few were the words that passed between them.

This left Hkainae and the Pilgrim to lead the pony train. It was no real burden and afforded them the chance to walk together. Hkainae for her part showed little hurry to talk, content for the moment with the sights about them. She'd often laugh and point out in wonder the marvels that the forest had to show. Bright birds of scarlet and azure darted between the high branches. Sharp-eyed bucks leapt through the undergrowth. There were other creatures too, although they never saw them, the wild cat and the lynx and wolves that sang to the moon through the midnight hours.

By the end of the first week the road had carried them down from the foothills and out onto a vast plane of sun-browned grass and shrub.

'It is like this for most of the way now,' Hkainae explained to the Pilgrim in dismay. 'I can tell you that by the time we reach Tabour we will be sick of the sight of nothing but grass.'

At least the walking was easy and, although the sun burned hot in the mid hours of day, a constant cooling wind brushed their faces to temper the heat and cause the grasses to sing at its passing.

It was here, out on the plain, that the Pilgrim finally saw the great herds of auric. They were to the north of the road, too far really to make out the detail of the individual beasts. Instead they seemed just a vast, living wall moving over the land. Just how many of the creatures there were was hard to guess, many thousands at least. The herd stretched from horizon to horizon, and still there were more.

Later they saw the great caravans of the auric hunters, following the herds and moving as endlessly as their prey. Often at night the huntsmen's fires glowed out in the dark.

'So tell me then, Pilgrim,' Hkainae asked one morning as they strolled side by side down the highway through this now empty grassland. 'What led you to take the pilgrim's path? You said in Finestre that you had been other things beside.' The day was mild, the sun clouded for the most part by a thin covering of mist making walking a pleasure indeed.

'It's a long story, Hkainae.' He moistened his mouth with a sip from one of the water bags on the pony. 'For there are many things for you to know and understand in order to reach an answer.' He took another swallow. 'I was born in the far-western land of Hereth. As I said before, Hereth is a gentle, loving land, rich in game and pasture. There, the wild fowl over-winter and the rivers run wild and free as the wind. My home lay in a small vale in the shelter of the High Downs of Hereth where the Earth-stones stand. My mother lives there still, my brother too, yet they alone now my sisters… Ah but I go too fast.' Thus he began to tell her his tale.

Oh how she loved to hear the strange names he used even though much of what he said in those first days was far beyond her understanding or knowledge. She'd sighed with such wonder when first he spoke his mother's name. 'The Lady-of-Flowers, oh what a glorious delight.' Then she'd hushed again to let him continue. She was a good audience, her dark-eyed gaze filled with wonder as he spoke.

She shared her tale too, telling of her life as the daughter of one of the Merchant-Lords of Istar, and he tasted for the first time her love for the barren places of her homeland, the mystery of the desert, **Hkamoot**.

From time to time others of the party came to share their company and their tales. It was for her though that he so carefully spread his words, for he bathed in the glory of her attention and savoured the joy of her wonder.

She gasped in horror when he spoke of the creature that his father had become and all but shook in fear over the telling of that terrible conflagration when they had cast it from their midst. She grew still as the stones when he spoke of his oath and laughed with unexpected delight at his tales of the dwarves. For The Dwarven people were but a distant legend among her people. 'Had I not seen the Iron-folk in the temple in Finestre,' she'd declared, 'I doubt I would have believed such tales as more than children's stories.' She did seem to understand the forces that drove him though, perhaps, even the need, which stayed his hand from taking life.

Plie was with them when he spoke first of the Fire-dancer in the woodlands of Naril. Perhaps the elf's closeness awoke the true beauty that he had shared with her and the love flamed in his heart once more.

'Ah was she so beautiful that she stole your heart forever, my pilgrim friend?' Hkainae had asked, her voice as soft and gentle as a summer breeze.

'She didn't steal it, Hkainae. I gave it freely and she took it and cared for it as were it the most precious thing in the world. I've no fear for my heart. She'll tend it well.'

The desert maid squealed in delight, for she saw truly the love in his eyes. Who would not be filled with happiness over such a sight?

So he told of her dance of magic in the forests and the mountains. 'We came to a terrible place.' Even now his voice shook at the memory. 'A place of decay and horror where the cold grey of the Galomist...' He stopped, the touch of Plie's hand resting on his arm.

'There are things of which words should not be spoken, Pilgrim. It is enough that your Fire-dancer brought you through in safety.'

'She did, Plie, her dance was a thing of burning brightness that drove away the creatures of evil which assailed us.'

'Then better leave them so driven,' the elf advised.

'We had short enough time together,' he continued the tale, taking the elve's unspoken command. The Galghathag remained a secret, unnamed. She laughed, as did Plie, when he spoke about trying to learn the Elven tongue. And later, much later, he saw the glimmer of tears in her eyes when he spoke of their parting by the lakeside in the Marches-of-Bronden. She walked in silence beside him, sneaking her hand into his as a gesture of comfort, knowing well the pain of that parting.

'Do you know her?' he asked of Plie, both eager and afraid of what the answer might be. 'She's of your kindred and spent her childhood by the crystal fountains of Al-Sinnian. Did you ever see the wonder of her dance?' The memory of her wonder was fresh and alive in his mind.

Will you dance with me?
Aye, I'll dance with you my lovely dancer of the mists
In my mind,
in my sleep,
in the halls of my memory,
forever.

'There are many who sit in the halls of the High-Dancer and many who weave the wonder of the Dance-spell. Yet perhaps, there was one whose burning dance stays in my mind. Yes, perhaps.' It was enough. The Pilgrim took solace from the possibility and was somehow gladdened.

'Oh, Plie, tell us of Al-Sinnian,' Hkainae begged. 'Tell us of the wonders of the Crystal-City and the Sacred Tree.'

The Elf-Smith simply smiled, a secret hidden thing, and shook his head. 'We can only know that which we know.' He answered mysteriously. 'For only the eye can see, Hkainae, and only the ear can hear. The mouth can but taste and the nose but smell. The skin can feel and the hand can touch. But my words cannot give you these things. If perchance you ever come to walk beneath the bows of the Elswood or to hear the chiming of the Crystal fountains, then you shall understand. If not? Well then it were better that your imagination keeps its own picture. Tell me, Hkainae. Could you tell of the wonder of the desert that flows in the sand?'

'I cannot.'

But when the night came and they sat about the campfire, she sang to them the strange songs of the desert people. Then although they did not understand her words their minds were filled with a vision of the sands.

Day by day the miles passed by. Calin and Cog and at times Shimmian and Plie also ranged ahead. The thought of the goblins ever alive in their thinking although there was no sign of any danger, or at least none that they informed the Pilgrim about.

The road, as Hkainae had prophesied, became a monotonous toil through a land of waving grass, featureless and boring. Even a lone tree, standing far out on the plane became a thing of excitement.

There was one day though when the skies darkened and the wind-driven rain squalled over the grasslands. They wrapped their cloaks about themselves and bowed their heads to the road. However, despite the greyness of the day, Hkainae laughed with delight and threw off her shoes to dance barefoot through the puddles that formed, splashing with childlike glee until the others could restrain their laughter no more and let their mirth warm their spirits.

When the sun returned, it brought a fresh sparkle to the day and awakened ten thousand flowers to bloom in a song of life. They walked through a cloud of tiny blue butterflies then, a mist of minute azure wings that danced to a chorus of joy piped on high by the sun-larks that nested out on the plain.

There was another time when, having seen another of the auric-hunter's caravans far out on the plain, the Pilgrim was reminded of Pina's highly painted Pinexae-wagon. He mused aloud, 'I wonder how Niivalsta and Pina fare? They must be near to the Elswood by now.' The thought of the Pinexae lass had been a troubling thought to the Pilgrim ever since leaving Finestre. 'Do you know something?' He tried to form his thoughts, 'It occurred to me that I don't even know what, who, Pinexae… What?' But his thoughts ever sought to elude him.

Plie laughed softly as he walked beside the youth, seeing the struggle. 'No, my friend, be not troubled. It's a marvel that you can even frame the thought.'

'Do you know?' It seemed easier if he kept his thoughts free of the question.

Plie stayed quiet for some time. 'Yes I know,' he said at last, 'And so do you, my Pilgrim-friend. Your mother would not have failed in teaching you that tale. Now of that I am sure.'

My mother? What does he know of her?

Then, as if to fill the time as they walked, Plie began.

The tale of the Pinexae reaches far, far back into the mists of the past, before the Cataclysm, before even time itself was counted. To Ancient Maddon where all things which now are, saw their beginnings. For their story is part of The Lay-of-Ages, of The Tale of the Stone, the dark Stone of Gwarle that was set by the Lords of the Void to enslave the Land.

In that dark time there came from the Ryngold, The Eloveen, three Kings of Light, Elovhath, Elovneth and Elovsenal. They came to save the Land and to protect the men who lived therein. Yet as the story goes, Elovsenal sought ever to gain power that he might contend with the forces of Chaos and thus was himself turned from the path of Light and became a Lord of Chaos, a servant to the Lords of the Void. In his evil he rose up against his brother kings and the people of the land and terrible was his coming.

Thus was the War of Kings brought into being, when the terrible forces of the Void did battle with the powers of light. It was from hence that the years of The Age of Stone were counted, when the lands of the West were cast into the darkness of the Gwarle. It was a terrible time of hardship and cruelty when men fought against men. A time that ended eventually with The Second War of Powers when the Evil in Gwarle awoke once more and the powers of the land were drawn into deadly conflict. It was then that The Three heroes, Antol, Elot, Harvan were drawn together and went into Elexan itself and slew the dark lord there and broke the Stone of Darkness forever.

'Are you telling us that The Pinexae are descendants of The Eloveen?'
'No not The Eloveen… If you remember the tales it was not only they who came through from the Lands-of-Light.'
'Neleven-Fey.' He felt the elf's smile.
'Who was Neleven-Fey?' Hkainae felt the touch of wonder once more. 'I have never heard such tales as these.'

Thus, driven by her fascination the Pilgrim too began to recite that tale once more.

The Neleven-Fey, it is said, were Lords of Light also, although not as the Eloveen. They came in a time of need did the Neleven-Fey. A time when the Dark Evil of the Stone had turned its face against the lands of men and when the evil of Elovsenal, the Eloveen Lord reached out to destroy the Ryngold and to bring chaos into the three Universes which were the Lands-of-Light.

It is a sad tale, Hkainae. For they were gentle people of goodness who knew not the evil they faced.

Hymforth-the-seer, went through the Ryngold at that time. It was because of him that, when the warriors of the dark came forth in power and made war among the groves of the Halls-of-Tallosind, the Neleven-Fey came out from the mountains. They stood with the armies of men and shed their blood alongside them. It was only by their hand that the Two Kings prevailed against their foe.

However, at the end when Elovsenal was eventually vanquished and banished unto Elexan, The Isle-of-the-Dead, there was a time of terrible darkness. In that time men turned their faces away from The Neleven-Fey and rose up against them. It is said that they went back to the Ryngold seeking to return to their homes but they could not pass through. For they had tasted of war and killing and had not stayed their hand. This was the price that they paid. They were banished from their own homes, condemned to stay in the lands of men forever.

Thus, both rejected by the Lands-of-Light and by mankind, they called themselves the Banished-Ones, and took themselves to an Isle to live alone from the world. They named their Isle Faerae-Nith, after their own kind and they shunned the lands of men for which they had given up so much.

It is told, In the legends of the Rising-of-the-Three, that Alan of Colon, The Antol, went to them and was healed of the torment of his mind. That Ellen Eloveen, Elot, went *also and received the Elmest, the weapons of light, from their hands. But little more is told for the Name of the Neleven-Fey passes from the tales of men.*

'I knew the tale, Plie,' the Pilgrim admitted to the Elf, sheepishly. 'But not that The Pinexae were they.' There seemed no more to say.

'Few are those who do, my friend,' Plie answered with a smile. 'Among the elves, though, the tale is known. It was with the Neleven-Fey that the Elven-Kindred hid during the dark years following the Cataclysm. We consider ourselves their friends through time.'

One other evening, when the skies were so clear that it seemed they camped in the midst of the heavens, they let the campfire grow cold and sat late in the night letting the wonder of the universe speak to their souls.

Shimmian turned to Hkainae, seeing her gaze reaching out over the star-spangled plain. 'Tell us, Hkainae, What calls you? What do you see as you gaze so intently over these flat grasslands?'

'Oh I see so many things, Shimmian. I see a land in conflict with itself, half pasture and half desert yet neither. I can taste the world on the wind, the ice fields of the frozen north, the bitter salt spray of the distant seas. I smell the dryness of the sands. Yes the sands. And, I know that this land, as all lands, will one day know the touch of the desert **Hkamoot**.'

'I see a land of meetings, where all the peoples of the earth might gather, might cross each other's paths.' She paused looking up into infinity. 'The heavens give me most though. For in the skies I can see a singleness that I can love. These are the same stars that shine over my home, that light my father's halls, that light the dunes of my people. **Hkamoot**.'

'And you, Calin, what do you see?' Hkainae asked.

The Sanain did not reply for a long time but sat still as stone. Her eyes reached out into infinity. 'I see a plain of grass lit by a sea of silver stars. I see a battlefield where the armies of the world might contend for no reason but the love of the passage of arms, where the air might ring with the clamour of war and men might cry out into the night and know at least this once the reality of their own mortality.' She broke off with a gasp.

'I see a blackened sky lit by a million tiny fires, each one offering a welcome and an answer to a thousand questions. There is a promise here, of choices and freedom and possibilities, the fulfilment of dreams, every instant here is but a moment awaiting its place in the flow of time.'

No one broke her silence. They sat, still, listening. At length she spoke for a third time. 'I see an empty plain where a child stands alone, lost amidst the carnage that was once her family. I see that same child choosing to stifle her hurt, to mask her pain so as not to crumble to dust and blow away on the breath of the world's wind. I see her taking a ring and placing it upon her finger as a token of her choice. I see a beginning being taken, but no ending, just loneliness.'

'And you, Pilgrim. What do you see?' Calin asked.

His voice was hushed and his gaze rested upon her face. 'I see that which I didn't understand made clear, Calin-Sanain. This is more than I ever hoped to see. You honour us.'

'And you, Shimmian? You asked the question. What do you see?'

'I too see a million stars, each one a choice, each one a path, each one a way ahead. I see this vast plain as a place of choices. I know too that I'll not pass by without having made my own.'

'What of you, My Lady?' the elf's soft tones sounded.

'I see, as I always see, the Earth turning and the powers at play. And you Harp-smith, what do you see?'

The elf sighed, '**Chelimbrelle**.'

There was another, darker incident to face on that journey across the plain. Day was drawing towards its close and Calin and Cog were ahead of the party seeking a resting-place for the night. The Pilgrim, Hkainae and Shimmian had been walking together discussing the differences between the lands of Hereth and Rael. Shimmian's talk was as usual growing more fanciful by the hour.

When their talk began to lag the Pilgrim suddenly noted that Hkainae's attention had been drawn elsewhere, to something far out across the plain. Her steady gaze drew his eyes. Birds were circling, vultures, carrion, hovering over something on the ground. Ahead, Calin and Cog had seen the same and now turned aside to investigate.

'What is it?' Hkainae sounded worried.

'Something fallen,' Shimmian replied. 'It's probably still alive or the birds would already be feasting. They await its end, whatever it might be.' He nodded towards where the two warriors were moving. 'Anyway, we should find out soon enough.'

They watched as the two stopped and bent over to examine something that lay hidden among the long golden grass. There was a sudden animated exchange between them and Cog wrenched out his broad sword, crouched to scan the horizon with his hawk-like eyes.

'What have they found?' Hkainae sounded nervous. The Pilgrim and Shimmian exchanged glances, the same thought on their minds. Their pace quickened.

Cog called out something, urgent, insistent, but the wind singing in the grass robbed the words of meaning. Calin stooped to examine whatever it might be. They saw her reach out, straighten, turning, oh so slowly, clutching the front of her tunic and still twisting she crumpled onto the grass. Her cry of pained anguish rang out over the plain.

'Calin!' the Lady's cry startled them, even more so when she barged past, to run wildly across the grass towards her fallen Sanain. The others followed behind an unspoken fear giving haste to their steps also.

Cog was cursing. '... to the bastard fires of Hell and damnation. I'd round up every last one of them, the filthy, loathsome creatures.'

The sight that met the Pilgrim's eyes though drove out all awareness of what might or might not have been said. There was a creature here, a sick grey thing of horror and evil, of darkness and decay, sprawled on the grass, lifeless, if ever it had a life. No wonder the carrion had spurned such fare. Even the grass seemed to recoil from its unwholesome touch.

The Beast! My Foe! Do they reach out for me even here? They're after me even now! His thoughts tumbled, confused, unformed, without sense.

'What is it?' Hkainae spoke for all.

'A bloody Goblin!' Cog answered, his voice thick with loathing. 'That's what it is!'

'Oh no, Cog, this is no goblin.' The lady was speaking from where she knelt beside the fallen Calin. 'This is something far worse that that. It's a thing of darkness for sure, of darkness and evil, a Gnoll or even worse, a Shape-Changer or one of the Necromancers' creatures.'

Shape Changers?

'What is happening?' Hkainae's voice was little more than a shrill scream of panic. 'What is happening to Calin?'

Their eyes as one turned back to the fallen Sanain, recoiling with horror over what met their gaze. Her face was withered and white, her skin appeared to be erupting, boils and corruption blistering as some terrible, decaying putrescence scoured through her body. Even as they stared her whole form seemed to shrivel.

'She touched it! Contaminated her own flesh with blight of Necromancer evil.' The Lady's voice grew stronger, angrier, filled with power. 'See, even the grass cannot bide its closeness.'

'The Necromancers?' The Harp-smith's voice was strained and full of fear. 'Then there is nothing that can be done,' he explained in a voice wracked in sorrow. 'Any who touch her will be contaminated also. I thought such evil was a thing of the past, gone forever from the land.'

'No not gone, Elf. Only sleeping, waiting for the time to awakened anew. And that time grows near.' Her eyes flicked to the Pilgrim for but the barest instant. She turned back to attend to Calin. 'Hush now,' she informed them all. 'Be still, my friends, I have work to do.'

'Beware!' Plie gasped seeing her reach out towards her warrior.

But she paid no heed to the warning. Rather she began to chant a strange wordless song. Sounds hung in the air, breathed their own meanings to the wind, to the air to those watching. They felt their worries flee, their thoughts still, their troubled spirits grow calm.

Magic! She weaves a spell on us, on Calin. In the back of his awareness the Pilgrim heard the elf sigh.

The chant continued, growing stronger, purer. From within her robe the lady brought a small, silvered mirror and a phial of clear liquid. The latter she poured into her palm and using her index finger she drew a strange sigil upon her Sanain's brow.

What followed was almost indescribable. Even to those watching it seemed to defy the eye. From where the sign was drawn a dark shadow appeared. It was as if some entity of darkness gathered to reach out towards the Lady. She took her mirror and still chanting her strange, wordless song she caught the sun's light upon its sliver face and reflected it into the centre of the shadow. The darkness seemed to grasp at the light, to grapple in some impossible conflict, dark against light. At times the darkness seemed to almost touch the mirror. At others it coalesced into a tiny ball of blackness. The end was inevitable, for what darkness can stand against the light of the sun? There came a sound, as of the ripping of the veil-of-night and the terrible sphere of midnight fled the light, going back to the creature from whence it had been spawned. There was a crash like thunder and a scream as of a soul burning in the fires of hell. The body burst into flame and was totally consumed.

In the moments that followed nothing moved or spoke. The Elf, the Pilgrim noted in some sort of vague disinterest, was kneeling before the Lady, his head bared. Time itself stood still until, somewhere, in the far, far distance a single nightingale trilled. The spell was broken.

'Ah what a wonder,' the Elf harpist's voice rang heavy with awe. 'A Druid. Praise the day that we crossed your path, My Lady. None other than a High-Druid could have turned aside that ill. Unless...' His eyes turned towards the Pilgrim.

She stilled the harpist's words with a single glance. 'Do not say so.'

Do not say so? Don't say what? What do they know?

'Look at Calin!' Cog exclaimed no less smitten by all that had happened. 'She's whole once more.' Indeed she was, and as they looked at her she began to stir, as if waking from slumber.

The Elf spoke again, urgent and earnest speaking not to the Lady but to the others. 'What you have seen is a marvel beyond marvels, a wonder seldom seen on this earth. Yet, because you have witnessed these things a burden falls to you. You must not speak of these things, you must not...'

Again the Lady stilled him with the lightest touch of her hand. 'The time for silence is past Harp-smith,' she whispered sadly. 'It will serve us no longer.' She shook her head and the hood fell free revealing that her long black hair, with its shock of white over her brow, was bound with a single band of silver.

Cog, still kneeling by Calin noted the moment that her eyes opened. 'Calin, I was afraid. When you touched it you fell. Praise be that you're all right now.' He took her hand. To comfort her?

She looked back at him. For a moment confusion spoke through her eyes, then she smiled. 'Yes, I'm all right. Well I think so.' She didn't push his hand away. 'It seemed that the daylight had turned into black ice and I was lost in the darkness. Then the sun shone and the Lady called me back.' She sat up, leaning on Cog's arm, shook her head to clear her thoughts. 'Where is the creature?'

'Gone!' Shimmian declared in a fear trembled voice. 'It burnt, shrivelled to dust and to nothing.' He offered her his hand but she held on to Cog and stood.

'Right!' Plie suggested. 'Let us be gone from this unwholesome place too. Surely we can find a camp nearby where we can discuss these things.'

Thus they did, turning back to the trail eager to be away from there. Only the Pilgrim lingered, and that for but the barest moment. His eyes flicked over the place where the creature had lain. *What goes on?* he asked himself. He had not missed the exchange between Elf and Lady. *What do they know?* It seems that always others knew more of him than he knew of himself and the truth of that tasted sour indeed.

A campsite was, as expected, easily found. It was set in a sheltered hollow by the roadside where countless others had camped before. There was a well there, a circle of fire-stones already in place and even a picket line for the ponies. In seemingly no time at all camp was set and the fire blazed away for their evening meal. Hkainae, even though it was not her turn, unpacked the cooking pots and began to fashion the meal.

Nothing was said for some time, even after the eating was done. They sat about the campfire waiting. For once, even Cog had joined them, sitting close beside

Calin. Every once in a while his eyes would rest on her face as if seeking reassurance that she was indeed all right.

'I don't understand this at all,' Shimmian, perhaps to the others' relief brought them back to the reality of what they had seen. 'What Calin and Cog found should not have been. Such creatures as that were banished long past and sent beyond the veil.'

'What was it?' Calin rejoined. 'Goblins I've seen before but never, no never of that thing's kind. I couldn't see any sign of wound or of how it died. It felt like death itself. I think it tried to steal my spirit.' She turned to look at the Lady who sat on the other side to Cog. Her gaze was met with a gentle smile.

'Who cares what it was!' Cog demanded. 'It was evil. A foul, evil thing that had no right to walk under the sun!' His voice was thick with loathing and a half-concealed anger. 'It is enough that it has been destroyed and that none came to any permanent harm from its evil.' His gaze returned to Calin. 'Are you fully recovered?'

'I am, Cog. Thank you for your concern.' She felt once more the touch of his eyes and, for this time at least, she appeared not adverse to the attention. She continued to talk to the warrior. 'I too had heard that the goblin tribes were no more, or at worse were left sulking in the darker reaches where men seldom go. Yet this is not the first time I have tasted of their evil on this journey, Cog. We were beset amongst the mountains on our way to Finestre.'

'That thing was no goblin!' the Elf spat as if the word itself was bitter to his taste. 'It was a creature from who knows where. What it means, or what it portends I do not know…'

'Ah, my dear friend Plie,' the Lady softly chided. 'The time for secrets has passed us by. It is time to speak.'

'It is as you say, Druid, that time is past. There are many strange things abroad,' the Elf confessed. 'My heart is troubled indeed. As Calin said, these things should not be walking abroad under the light of the sun. When the Lords-of-the-West defeated the Goblin-Lord, his minions and all the other vanquished creatures that lay under his thrall, retreated into the secret, darker places of their hidden domain where they were bound to remain. Yet all is not well for it is true indeed, of late they are begun to walk abroad again. Yet also I fear for other reasons.'

'What do you know, Plie?' Shimmian asked.

'I know that The Goblin-Lord was but a creature of another, far more loathsome thing. I know too that despite all our efforts this thing lies hidden from all our scrying.' Plie stood then, his form lit by the firelight. He lifted his harp and turned to face them.

'There is trouble from many sources. There are rumours and mutterings. There are words on the wind.'

He played a single crystal note.

'I hear of beginnings and of endings'.
Another note.
'I hear of a breaking of bonds and the freeing of power'.

For a moment he lowered the harp. 'My friends, I do not know how to explain.' He seemed saddened by his lack. 'The tenets of magic are vague. The weave of Fate's threads is ever unclear. There are forces that bind and limit. There are forces that constrain and protect. My heart trembles with fear. My spirit is shriven. I think that the bonds are loosened.

> *The four Winds cry of it.*
> *The earth trembles because of it.*
> *The waters of the earth are bound in a whirlpool of awakening.*
> *They tell of a wildness,*
> *of an Awakening,*
> *of powers reaching out to grasp that for which they lust,*
> *scheming, plotting, grovelling for that they desire!*

He played another note. 'Thus speak The Word-Smiths of Al-Sinnian.'

> *'In the forest there is a shadow.*
> *Over the meadows is a cloud.*
> *Upon the High-Downs the stones awaken,*
> *Their waiting is done.*
> *O'er the Hills is a calling, words on a midnight wind.*
> *Waking the whirlpool to glory, forever unbound.*
>
> *We have guarded for his coming.*
> *We have watched for his time.*
> *We have seen his springing, his own beginning*
> *Now there is a new ending,*
> *For whom the new song?*
>
> *For the blade is sharp indeed,*
> *which cuts the knots of Fate,*
> *Too sharp for unknowing hands?*
>
> *From the skies we have taken the future.*
> *From the Earth we have taken the past.*
> *Now we have nothing but hope.*
> *It is enough.*

The Tune-smith and his harp were once more silent.

'Your words are strange, Elf,' Cog broke the silence. 'I can't claim to understand. Which is probably just as well. My path in life is not one of understanding but of doing. I leave understanding to others. You say that there are those who know more of these matters. Perhaps they're even among us and yet keep their secrets.' He sounded angry. 'If they want hold their tongues from us, then so be it. I'll trust their reasons.' He lowered his eyes and looked down into the fire.

'I don't know if you speak of me or not, Cog.' The Pilgrim felt driven to say something. Although from the look of surprise on the warrior's face it seemed clear that this had not been so. 'But now I think it's time to tell what we know.' He looked at the Lady. *Will she stop me?* 'The words were mine, Cog. Words of an oath; which ever drives me. The Evil has indeed awoken. I know its foul touch on the weave of my life. I've even seen its face.' Eyes burned as they peered through the evening gloom. 'I walked through the…'

'NO!' Plie almost screamed at him. 'Don't say the words.'

'It's too late for silence, Plie,' the Pilgrim sounded sad. 'Do you think that thing can be hid simply by keeping silent? The shepherds thought so. Will their silence protect them when the Horde marches?' He shook his head in sad reply. Again he looked to The Lady.

'I've walked through the world too long, Pilgrim,' she answered mysteriously. Then smiled, 'Say what you have to say.'

'Yes,' Calin agreed. 'Tell us of that for which even the goblins hope.'

'I don't know anything!' His words were like a cry of anguish. 'I don't understand anything. I simply follow my road.' He paused again, clearing his mind of his confusion. 'If it even is my road that is! I think others see matters clearer than I; know more than I do. But I'll tell what I have seen.'

'I walked through the darkness of The Galghathag,' Plie gasped. 'I was drawn there, taken, led by hands, both light and dark, but there I went. In the darkness I saw things that I couldn't face. I saw a horror beyond belief. It has awakened. Now this I shall not name. It needs none. Its evil is beyond understanding. It's awakened in the darkness and even now reaches out for power. Its power is a terror, which feeds on the lives of others, that glories in their pain and grows strong on the stench of decay.

'The Goblin Tribes are arisen once more. The forces of darkness gather. I have seen the Galomist reaching out.' He could hardly speak now.

'Calin, you wanted me to tell of what the goblins hope for? Well, I don't know. I don't know what it is that they want. I don't know what the elves want. I don't know what you want either.' He looked at the Lady and waited.

'I want nothing now.' She reached out and rested her hand gently upon his arm. 'I came to see. There was a balance. I had to know. There was a chance that you would choose another path. I had to know. That was my charge.'

'Would I have died?'

She bowed her head. 'You might have chosen to go. You might have chosen to fight alongside of us. You chose not to take a life. It was the best choice of all. I don't know what shall be. I don't know if you'll find what you seek or not. Should that be so, and should it be that you become what we all hope, I have no fear. Now all I want is for you find happiness somewhere when all is done. I have my own path now.' She smiled and was silent.

Shimmian spoke, his voice strong and commanding. This was a new Shimmian, one who had made his choice and knew the way he must travel. 'So, the terrible words have been spoken, the truth has been revealed. Evil is arising again, reaching out, goblins and dark forces? Well this comes as little surprise to me. In Finestre the Dwarves spoke of it, the troubled murmuring of the earth. My friends, I fear the time of this pleasant journey is at its end. I see a new and darker path ahead of us all now.

'Cog,' he turned to the warrior who raised his head, and looked back with a steady gaze, 'Go unto the King's Hall at High-Caravail and give witness to what you now know. The armies of the King must be drawn to arms. For my part, I must return to Rael.'

'I shall join Cog in this.' Calin's voice came as a surprise to all. 'My Lady?'

'Yes, Calin, that time has come. Your path is yours to choose. I can no longer hold you to mine. I have my own destiny to face. I shall go with Plie unto the Elswood. Long have I wished to see the Crystal-Fountains and the Sacred-Tree, although not in this manner. Not with this news. I fear that it is my task to call the Elves to war.'

Cog stood and bowed his head to Shimmian. 'As you command, My Lord. We shall go to High-Caravail and speak there of what we know.'

It seemed that the discussion ended there, however for one of the party the matter could not be so easily put to rest. He sat out on the side of the road, far from the campfire, long into the night. A thousand thoughts and images from the past set to trouble his mind. The old wound in his thigh ached, troubling him with reminders of other creatures. There were memories too of The Baron his father, for still the pain and guilt burnt in his breast. He saw again the terrible thing arisen from the pit in that grey despairing castle. There was an aching fear also, fear of a future that was not of his making, of a road not chosen by himself. *What do they know of me? What do they expect of me? They watch, their eyes waiting. But they don't tell what they see or for what they wait. It feels, as if in their secrets, they do know of me and what will be.*

'I feel a sadness in you tonight, my friend.' Hkainae sat herself on the grass verge beside him, reaching out to touch his hand. Perhaps, at that moment, she understood his pain and loneliness, if not its cause and drew herself close. 'At least for now we do not have to be alone.' Then taking his hand sat beside him in silence. In the stillness of that star-lit night they drew what comfort they could from each other's friendship, and they watched the morning break together.

With the dawn came a new purposefulness and a new sense of urgency among the party. Their movements were driven by a sudden need for haste. Gone now was the time for leisurely strolling.

Two wearisome days later, the great city of Tabour rose out of the plain before them and, ere the noonday sun looked down upon the road, they'd entered through the high gateway into the city.

The Lady with sudden businesslike urgency, the band of her calling set firm on her brow for all to see, purchased a pair of horses from a hosteler's stable just inside the city gate. White they were, proud and fine, deep chested; horses that would run forever.

Shimmian and The Pilgrim sold their ponies also. The Pilgrim felt no need to possess more than he might carry now. The Warrior, all pretence otherwise now gone, bought himself a war-horse, a huge chestnut stallion. Cog purchased its twin as a steed for Calin.

Thus Hkainae and the Pilgrim found themselves at the point of parting with the others before they'd even found themselves lodging.

The Lady came first, standing before the Pilgrim in a silence as deep as the ocean, holding him with her eyes. She took each of his hands in turn and kissed each palm. Tears sparkled in her eyes.

'Farewell my...' But she silenced him with a look. *She is right. There are no words for this time.*

She turned to Hkainae. 'You are one who was not foreseen, my child.' She took her hands also and brushed them with her kiss of parting. 'Be strong, Hkainae. His way is not for the weak. I hope that you are without suffering in this. I give you my blessing, for what it is worth. So fare you well, Hkainae, my duty calls me.'

Even before Hkainae could answer, the Druid had turned away leaving only the confusion of her words.

Plie smiled as he faced them. 'There are many paths through time Young-Wizard; perchance we shall meet again on some distant road. Would that we might have travelled further together but it could not be. Alas, the messages in your words and the memory of Al-Sinnian call me home.'

'Should you see her,' the Pilgrim replied, 'tell her of my–'

'No.' His smile broadened. 'Those words are for you alone. If I see her I shall say that you spoke of her dance.'

'Yes, thank you, Plie.' It was enough. 'Farewell, Elf Lord, until that future time.'

The Harpist bowed to the Desert Girl. 'Fare-you-well, maiden and friend of the road. May all go well with you and your family.' Formal words, desert words.

'The sands of the desert are hot, Plie, yet shall your memory be as spring-water to my soul.' The elf bowed once more. Then he too turned away.

'This is indeed a day of partings.' Shimmian-of-Rael stood before them dressed in armour and ready for the road. 'We have travelled a good road Pilgrim-of-Hereth.'

'Yes, it was a good road.' But the Pilgrim's eyes asked a thousand questions.

'There are many things which have been left unsaid, my friend. Perhaps it is best that they remain so. My time of wandering is done. I must give up the freedom of the road and return to the call of my duties. I too have seen meanings in your journey, Young-Pilgrim, meanings both for you and for those you touch. Be strong, my friend. Be clear in your vision. See the truth of what is there, not just what you wish there to be.' He laughed wryly, perhaps for that moment it was the other Shimmian speaking. 'Ah, just listen to me, you'll do as you must. Goodbye.'

The Pilgrim felt his eyes sting as the tears blurred his sight. There were no words.

> *You shall be with me always.*
> *In the halls of my mind,*
> *In the silence of my moments,*
> *In the stillness of my being.*
> *There you shall dwell.*

Then he held the warrior in his arms, a final embrace.

Cog and Calin came together. A closeness seemed to be growing between them. 'We have come to say our goodbyes friends of the road.' Calin spoke for the two of them. 'Fare-you-well, Hkainae-of-the-desert. Fare-you-well also, Pilgrim-of-Hereth. I hope with all my heart that you find that which you seek.' Her eyes lowered for but an instant, a strange almost childlike smile crossed her face. 'I have a request of you.'

'A request?'

She smiled again. 'I don't know what others see of your journey, Pilgrim. I don't understand their hopes or their fears. I don't see the promise that the elves and goblins see alike. I see only that you do not kill and even so you did not judge me, because I do. I ask that you kiss my brow as a blessing.' She suddenly knelt before him. He could do no other.

She stood before him again, once more Sanain. 'I have a gift for you also.' She took a small, white-stoned ring from her finger and held it for him to take. 'It is but a trifling thing, my friend, but it held a meaning.' Her eyes flicked to her companion for an instant. 'It is the sign that I was alone. I need it no more.' He took it and set it upon his little finger. 'It is of little importance,' she continued. 'and holds no power or lineage for it is nothing but a simple moonstone set in silver. There may come a time when you will pass it to another. Do so freely, that is its nature. If any ask it is called the Ring of Lue.'

He bowed to her. 'If we meet again through the passage of time, Calin-Sanain, I'll tell you what befell it. For now I thank you for the gift and more so for your friendship. Be happy, Calin.'

She smiled and looked once more to the warrior at her side and the Pilgrim suspected that his wish was already granted.

Now they too turned to go. 'Cog?' the Pilgrim called him back. He gestured towards the departing Shimmian. 'Who is he?'

The warrior followed the young man's eyes. 'He is my Lord, Shimmian-Lord-of-Rael, once known as the Elder son of Sandor-High-Marshal-of-Rael.'

'…It is said that he slew his own father.'

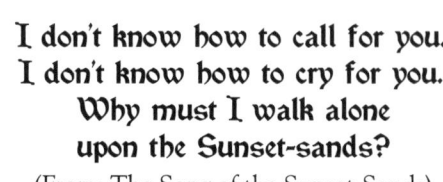

> I don't know how to call for you.
> I don't know how to cry for you.
> Why must I walk alone
> upon the Sunset-sands?
>
> (From: The Song of the Sunset-Sands)

Chapter Seven – Of Towers and Deserts

Side-by-side at the city gate they watched their friends depart upon their various journeys. The sadness of the moment stood with them lending heaviness to their thoughts and stilling their tongues. The city paid them no heed though. Why should it?

Eventually the Pilgrim turned to Hkainae. 'I hope they fare well, each of them, wherever their paths may take them. I wonder if we, I, will ever meet them again?' His spirit retained the pensive stillness bred of his sadness. 'You know Hkainae, sometimes it seems that everyone I meet must eventually turn aside and that in the end I'll be left alone on my path. Perhaps that's the way of all life, of the road and the world. Maybe the truth is that we are all alone anyway and that, at the end, alone is what we'll be.forever to be left alone.'

The silent truth of his thoughts filled the air between them. 'What of me?' Whispered words, bitter to her taste. 'Am I also but a part of your passing? To travel with you, beside you, to be left aside as you move on your way?' She answered herself, 'I know that is not how things are, but I know too that there will come a time when our paths shall part, when the passing of time shall draw us down the different roads of our futures. But for now…' She took his hand and turned him round to face the city streets. 'Now we are together and now we have this fair city to explore. Come let us see what delights it has to offer.'

Into the city markets and thoroughfares they wandered, immersing themselves in the countless wonders of sight and sound on display. They drank minted tea on the wooden veranda of a small cafe, served to them by an ebullient Tabourian. They laughed at the antics of a street clown who juggled ripe melons with such consummate skill that each fumble and fall looked to be but an accident and his recovery but a moment of luck. They purchased sugar pastries from a street vendor and ate the dainties in open delight as they strolled through the pleasant warmth of the late afternoon.

The people of Tabour were of a friendly, open kind. They smiled their greetings as the two passed by. It seemed that they recognised the Pilgrim by his robe and accepted him and his calling as something valuable, a part of their world to be cherished. Perhaps they wished that they too knew the freedom of the road.

The evening meal was shared back at the small café, a simple repast of cold meats and cheeses and tender raw vegetables all washed down with sparkling red wine.

The following morning, at the insistence of the café owner, to whom they had returned yet again to break their fast, they directed their feet towards the famed Tower.

Hkainae turned aside the offer of an escort through the streets declaring that she had been there before, and that she knew the way. Nonetheless her feet lost the road shortly after they'd left. It mattered little. Simple questioning soon brought the help they needed and had them moving in the right direction once more.

The streets grew narrow here, for this was the oldest part of the city. The passageway was overhung with dwellings and shops. Each building draped with brightly coloured cloth, brocades of red and gold, sapphire, and turquoise, struggling to outdo its neighbours in splendour and ostentation. The sudden change to stark white marble was compounded by the shops' brilliance.

A huge white wall seemed to block their passage. It was high, perhaps forty or fifty feet or so and quite featureless. A simple archway opened into a dark passage that led downward and through to whatever lay beyond. For some unknown reason the Pilgrim felt a twinge of an unexpected and undesired hesitation.

'Come on!' Hkainae called in exuberant excitement as she took his hand to pull him forwards. 'It is the Tower, The Tower of Tabour. You must see.' She laughed joyfully. She'd seen the wonder for herself and longed to see the reaction of her companion.

Although still tempted to resist, he allowed himself to be drawn into the arch. That strange sense of reluctance stayed with him as an unwelcome companion, slowing his feet.

They emerged into daylight.

And there the Pilgrim stopped, shocked into silence by the enormity of the sight before him. The Tower reaching up towards infinity, unadorned and unblemished, a white Tower of glistening crystal, was everything, everything in the universe. It filled the eye, the mind, the spirit, the soul, standing as a needle thrust upwards into the heavens outshining even the sun with its perfection, a challenge and a promise, a vision of wholeness that made life itself obsolete. Beside this gleaming spectacle, the white marble constraining wall seemed dull and empty.

The Pilgrim stood, filled with the silence of the moment. His whole being was stunned, shocked by the vision before him. *I am come.* His soul cried into that silence, *I am here.* The yearning in his being reached out drawn from him, called, called...

You are come indeed, Wizard. Reveal your magic!

The silence of his screaming soul filled the universe. He knew no magic. He'd thrown it all away and thus in his failure was he denied! Denied its perfection, excluded from its promise and its wonder. He stood there looking, fearing that his heart might break with the sadness that welled in his breast.

It's mine! It should be mine. But I am rejected. I should belong here, but I am refused. He knew the terrible totality of his loss. MAGIC! *I have no magic! I cast it aside for nothing but a lie. I threw away everything. I am unworthy!* He brushed away the tears that stung his eyes and dribbled over his cheek. Somewhere in the back of his awareness he realised that Hkainae was talking.

'...They will expect you to tell them.'

'I'm sorry. What did you say?'

She smiled, 'Stunning is it not?' and smiled again, misunderstanding completely the nature of his mood or the cause of his confusion. 'We have to go to the Keepers.'

'The Keepers?' Even more confusion. *Who keeps whom?*

'Yes, the Keepers.' She tried to break through the cloying webs of his vagueness, but failed. 'We have to go to see the Keepers, The-Keepers-of-the-Library. Oh, you didn't know. The whole outer wall is one huge library.'

It made no sense at all. 'Library?' *What is she talking about?*

'Yes.' She spoke like a parent to an aberrant child. 'It is a giant library, where the Keepers keep their ledgers, the records, the words that they have scribed.'

They hide the tower behind a wall of books? This makes no sense at all. Do they think that words will contain its power? Or keep out that which desires it? Even his inner words made no sense.

'We have to see them.' She almost pleaded now. 'It is the custom. We go to them and they ask us what we think about the Tower. They then write down our answers, write down our words in their books. It is what they do.' She finished.

'It all seems so strange, so, so...' he couldn't find the words. 'I don't understand anything at all!'

'Come then, my friend,' she suggested kindly, 'Perhaps they will have answers for you,' and resting her hand on his arm led him towards a door, the only door to be seen.

It opened silently and they stepped into the coolness of the simple white chamber, spotlessly clean. 'We must take off our shoes and wash our feet.' She gestured to the stone bath provided. 'It is the custom. It cannot be permitted to allow dust to be trod into the library halls.'

He looked at her, watched her do as she'd asked of him and he copied her. *What is this about?* He had no words, even for his questions. He followed her through another door.

The old man sat crouched behind a desk. His head was bowed over a huge ledger squinting at the writing with ancient myopic eyes. He looked up at their entrance and stretched to ease away the cramps of too much motionless study.

'I am Hkainae, Daughter-heir of Guesta Merchant Lord-of-Istar,' she declared, stepping forward to stand before him.

The keeper nodded his head in greeting and attempted a rheumy smile. He turned to the picture of the Tower that dominated the room. 'We are the Keepers-of-the-Tower,' he explained. 'We are charged with the duty of trying to understand its nature and its meaning. I have questions that I must ask of those who come to stand before the Tower.' He picked up a quill, dipped it in the pot of ink on the desk and crouched back over the ledger. 'How shall I name you?'

Names! Always names!

'I am Hkainae, Daughter-heir of Guesta Merchant-Lord of Istar.' The quill squealed on the parchment as he wrote, repeating the words aloud to himself.

'Why have you made this journey to the Tower of Tabour?'

'I am on my way home to Istar from Finestre. I travel with another, we came together to see the marvel.' Once again he bowed to his scribblings.

'You have looked upon the Tower?'

'I have, Keeper.'

'I ask you then. Tell me what did you see?'

She was still for a moment, deep in thought. 'I saw a tower that has stood here since the very beginnings of time. I see a wonder, I see a sign, perhaps a message for man. It seems to me that the Tower is a symbol of man's own futility.'

The pen scribed out the words once more. 'I thank you, Hkainae of Istar. There are many who have seen this. Some feel that this can be the only real explanation.'

The old man's eyes turned to the Pilgrim now. He dipped the pen once more and asked his question. 'How shall I name you?'

What's the point? Do they wish to compound my failure? 'I have no name!' His voice was hard, tinged with the bitterness that burnt in his breast. He heard the sudden gasp as Hkainae recoiled at the impropriety of his reply. It didn't matter.

Confusion clouded the old man's face. 'But, but you must give a name. You must! It is the custom, the way of the Tower. Tell me your father's name. I shall name you as his Son.'

FATHER! *He dares to demand me to name my father?* Anger flared in his mind like a bolt of lightning filling his being with fire. *So they challenge the very essence of my failure, the cause of my ruination. I WILL NOT BE ITS PLAYTHING!* 'NO!' His voice cracked out like a whip. 'I'll have no part of my father and I'll give him no part of me!' The fire burning in this strange young man's eyes stopped the Keeper's shocked reply before it could form on his lips.

'You seek names? Well, I'll give you names! My mother is the Lady-of-Flowers! My elder sister is the Calm-Watcher! My brother is the Lord-of-Numbers and my second sister is the Lightning-Bringer. Scribe that in your ledger and see if the paper doesn't burst into flame. I am a pilgrim. Once a child, once the Dwarves' apprentice, once a warrior, once lost without thought or reason. I am only a pilgrim. I came from Hereth in the Marches of Santolin.'

The Keeper recoiled from the vehemence of his anger. 'Forgive my presumption, my Lord.'

'**I am no Lord!**' He spoke slowly as if to a child, each word measured and filled with ice. I'm simply a pilgrim.'

'Then I shall describe you as The Pilgrim-of-Hereth,' seeing an answer, a way of escape. 'If you will so permit me.'

'It will serve.'

The Keeper's hand shook as he penned the words. Having finished he looked up again, half afraid to continue. 'Why have you made this journey to the Tower of Tabour?'

'Why do you think? It drew me here.' The Pilgrim could feel Hkainae's eyes burning. The scribe continued to write.

'You have looked upon the Tower?'

The Pilgrim nodded.

'I ask you then. Tell me, what did you see?'

Once more the terrible empty sadness overcame him... 'I saw the centre of everything.' In his mind the words of the Elf-harpist returned once more. *There are forces that Bind and limit. There are forces that constrain and protect. The bonds are loosened. The winds cry of it. The earth trembles because of it. The waters of the earth are bound in a whirlpool of awakening.*

> *O'er the Hills is a calling, words on a midnight wind.*
> *Waking the whirlwind to glory, forever unbound.*

'It's the centre of the Whirlwind.'

The Keeper's face reflected the confusion, as well it might. He'd never heard of such a reply. Nonetheless his head bowed over the book and the pen began to write.

'Keeper?' The old man lifted his face half fearfully at the sound of the Pilgrim's voice, but the look of anger was replaced by a calmer, questioning expression. 'What is all this?'

'Ah.' This was much safer, more familiar ground. 'You stand in the midst of the Great-Library-of-Tabour. Here are the records of the ages. Ten thousand times ten thousand are the volumes stored within. Among them, some say the greater part, are the ledgers of the Tower. In these are the answers to the very questions that I have put to you. Some call this The University of the Tower for such is the power of the knowledge stored within these precious tomes.

'There are over five hundred Keepers-of-the-Words, of which I am but one. Some ask of the tower. Others scribe the passing of time. Others tend to the books. Theirs perhaps is the hardest of tasks, for the paper decays rapidly and the words must be copied anew least they are lost forever.'

'But, why?'

'It is our duty, our life. None know the reason or purpose of the Tower. No one even knows who built it or the meaning that it has for the world, save that it has indeed stood here since the very beginnings of time. We, The Keepers, are charged with recording the thoughts of those who look upon its wonder. We are charged with asking each who comes, young and old, to share their wisdom concerning what they see. We keep the ledgers of their replies that we might know the answers to fill our ignorance.'

'How will you know? How will you know when you hear the right answer?'

The man's eyes clouded with confusion. 'My task is to hear the answers and to record them in the ledgers.'

'Oh. I see.' The Pilgrim turned to face the desert girl. 'It's time to leave, Hkainae. There's nothing here save an eternity of wasted time.'

He didn't speak again, or even check she followed. The pain that wrenched at his soul when they passed under the arch seemed to scream that he was deserting his very nature. *I shall be back.*

Hkainae walked in silence beside him. She'd not seen his anger before and didn't know how to contend with the feelings of hopelessness it engendered in her heart.

At length she tried. 'What was wrong, Pilgrim? What was it that so enflamed your mind? You frightened that old man with your anger, offended him with your words. He did you no wrong.'

'Not him.'

'If not, then what, Pilgrim?'

How can I say? There's no way she can understand any more than I do. Memories? Lost hopes? Pain? 'It's the whole thing. The Tower, the Library, it was the total pointless futility of everything.' There were no words. 'I can't explain.'

'Take care, Pilgrim. You are not as others and perhaps see the world through your own strange eyes.' She too could find no words.

She came to him late that night. The moon that had barely risen when he took to his bed was bright and full in the heavens. 'Hkainae?'

'It is I.' But this was no Hkainae that he had seen before. Clothed in black was she, the black of the desert people. Her head was wrapped in a silk turban that swathed her face also that only her sparkling eyes showed. Across her back hung a sabre; at her side a dagger. She placed her candle beside his bed and stood over him, shadows and light. Her face, when she drew the veil aside was painted, eyes black with kohl, lips red as blood. 'What do you see now, Pilgrim?'

There were a thousand different replies but only a single answer. 'I see my friend.'

She tilted her head to one side considering his words. Her silence was as deep and full as the still breath of the desert. 'You see clearly then.' She relaxed and sat at the foot of his bed. 'There were many words you might have said, my friend.' She sighed, almost wistful. 'Some of fear, some of love, some of beauty, some of danger or parting. I suppose that, in some token, I wished for another reply, that our paths might follow another way. But friend is best of all.' She stood and walked round to sit on the edge of the bed beside him, took his hand in hers for a moment. 'We are indeed friends, Pilgrim, and so shall we be forever. What more do you see?'

'I see a mystery. I see things that I do not understand. I see messages. I see questions.'

'And shall you ask your questions?'

'You're my friend. I don't need to ask.'

Nonetheless she began to answer. 'You see me now as my own people see me, Pilgrim. Yes, I am the same, the Daughter-Heir of Guesta, but I am **Shabraht** desert-kind. I have trod the paths of sand and slaked my thirst in the bitter pools of the wastes, **Hkamoot**.' Drawing a dagger from her belt, she held it pointed at her own throat. The steel shone bright and keen in the moonlight. 'As this blade am I. Two-edged and biting sharp. Yet I shall do no harm.' The blade was returned to its sheath. 'I am strong, Pilgrim. I am as strong as the wind that blows o'er the sands, **Hkamoot**; strong as the sun that burns the winds, strong as the night that cools the sun, strong as the truth that binds the world. And, I am strong enough to be your friend, Pilgrim.' Once again she reached out to take hold of his hand. 'What so troubles you, my friend? Do not fear, you shall not harm me with your words.'

He smiled at her. *Perhaps.* 'I'll try to explain, to answer, but I doubt I have the words or even know where to begin.'

'You feel that there is something wrong, here, here in the city?' she offered.

It was as good a place to start as any. 'No, it's not really like that, Hkainae. The wrongness isn't in the City. It's in me. My words to the Keeper were true. The Tower did indeed call me; draw me. I was meant to be here, to...' *To what?* 'It was too pure, too perfect... I'm not whole, Hkainae, not as I should be. That's why I was brought here: to be tested. It judged me, rejected me, even ridiculed my coming! There lay the cause of my anger, at fate, at life, at myself. Yes, that most of all I'm angry at myself.'

She didn't reply right away but sat digesting his words. That she did not understand caused her no trouble. She was his friend. She trusted him and that trust was more than enough.

'I heard the words of the Druid and the Elf. I saw the expression in their eyes when they looked at you, both hope and fear... Is it this of which you speak also?'

'It's my lack of knowledge!' He could feel the tears wet on his cheeks. 'I don't know anything, nothing at all! I'm like a blade of grass, plucked at will by some unseen hand and then cast, carelessly into the wind of Fate. I've no say, no understanding of what I'm supposed to do, no choices before me.'

'Calin said that you chose not to take a life.'

'But I choose for me and not for them. And it's to me they look, Hkainae.' His voice told of the anguish in his heart. 'They all have expectations, need answers to calm their fears, to provide the fulfilment of their hopes, to wake the promises of their dreams. I saw their faces too. My fear is that I'll fail them.'

They stayed in silence, bathed in the stillness of the night. There seemed no need for words between them. Later the Pilgrim realised that during that moment of peace he'd found a jewel as precious as the love that burned in his heart for his beautiful Fire-Dancer.

At length the desert girl stirred and broke the silence. 'Ah, the skies lighten.'

With that gift of sunrise his mood lifted and with it came the desire to return to the road once more. 'Morning? Then it's time to say goodbye to this City and farewell to the Tower. For now.'

'Indeed, Pilgrim, I was busy in the early hours of the night before I came here. As you slumbered my feet took me to the merchants' halls. I heard more grave news there also. It is clear that the thing on the plain was not alone. The merchants are troubled indeed.

'Several caravans have been attacked as they crossed the plains. The roads are no longer safe for the lone traveller. A trader out of Salmah, to the north of Dormon, was set upon by dark creatures of the night. He fought them off with fire and sent them fleeing back from where they came, but he says he will go no more on his journeys across the grasslands. The Rangers talk of burning farmsteads and of creatures raiding through the lands. The Merchant Lords are troubled indeed. There is war on the wind, and war brings an end to profit.'

'Remember the words of Plie,' the Pilgrim advised her. '*The bonds are loosened. The Winds cry of it, the earth trembles because of it. The waters of the earth are bound in a whirlpool of awakening. They tell of a wildness, of an Awakening, of powers reaching out to grasp that for which they lust, scheming, plotting, grovelling for that they desire.* The words fill my mind, Hkainae. I'm driven by a sense of urgency, a need to...' His eyes showed the truth of his words. 'The whirlwind awakens.'

Thus it was that early the same day their feet once again knew the feel of the road. They travelled southwards into a barren, rock-strewn land where, where channels and canyons had formed by erosion of the occasional rainstorms. Their steps were longer now, eating the miles. Hkainae's ponies were kept on tight rein and the pair's eyes were ever vigilant. They trod the road in darker mood, only too aware of the danger that might lay hidden in the rugged land all about them.

However the day proved uneventful, the day after also. Yet they kept their eyes alert and took turns guarding their camp through the hours of night. The land gradually gave way to a gentler terrain. The road, skirting the Mountains of Dormon, carried them along a winding trail through beautiful rolling foothills. Here crystal streams fed an untamed land of magnolia and mountain oak. The glissades of water gave harmony to the rustle of the wind through the treetops with a whistling song of other trees, other far away forests.

*

'There's something out there!' Hkainae's whispered warning dragged him from sleep, a sleep of troubled roads, where every path seemed to lead into danger. 'I heard movement in the woods.' She pointed. 'I think it might be goblins!' The first tremor of fear gave pitch to her voice.

He sat up, perhaps even grateful to be free of his dreams. She was close and, in sudden empathy with her fear, he slipped his arm about her shoulder. 'Don't worry, Hkainae,' he said, as he peered into the darkness.

In return came the familiar, if unwelcome, touch of cold grey eyes on the Pilgrim's awareness. This was followed shortly by the slithering, creeping, rustling of movement, sneaking through the woodland undergrowth and over the rocks, gathering about their camp.

In the darkness Hkainae, without a word of explanation, opened her pack and dressed herself in her black desert garb slinging her sabre over her back.

They waited wondering what was to happen and if or when the attack might come. The Pilgrim added more wood to the fire. Then still more, until the clearing was bright with it's flickering light.

'Why not show yourselves?' the Pilgrim spoke into the night. He didn't shout or even raise his voice. 'The night is dark and cold, my grey friends, and our fire warm. Why not come and join us? We mean you no harm.'

The reply was a brittle burst of laughter splitting the darkness. 'Agh! Man. We'll warm ourselves on your fire all right, and feast of your flesh soon enough man. Agh! Are you so eager to die?'

'There's no need of killing, goblin. Must death always rule? Come into the light that we might talk and know each other on this dark night.'

The sigh of steel-on-leather as Hkainae's blade was drawn sounded loud in the night. But the Pilgrim did nothing, just stood before fire and waited. They came slowly from the trees, one by one, crouching, almost crawling. Each of them was revolting in their naked hatred and lust.

There were seven of them gathered in a ring about the campsite, leering at the two travellers within, snarling, threatening, but they did not approach. They were for the most part pathetic creatures, thin and dirty, half-naked. Some carried wooden clubs, one a short-sword. Another bore an axe.

'Welcome, grey ones, what is it that you want of us?' he asked, his voice almost wearisome. 'Don't be troubled. We come in peace.'

'Fuck off, Bastard! And Bollix to your welcome and your peace!' one spat, perhaps the leader, but even then the words were tinged with uncertainty. 'Agh! Peace!' It spat again. 'It's you who should be fucking troubled! You come in peace. Agh! We come in hate!' It laughed again, a cruel, bitter, humourless burst of sound.

'Why hate, goblin? There's no need for this,' he answered once more, resigned to the probable futility of his words. 'I want nothing of hate or of the killing that oh too easily becomes its voice.'

'Agh! Tough fuckin' shit!' It spat once more.

'Don't you know who I am, goblin?' He spoke slowly.

'Agh! Yes!' Again the cruel laugh. 'Agh! You're my fuckin' grub an' the bitch's gonna give us a day or two's humpin' Agh! If she lasts that long.' The goblin rubbed his groin with obvious crude meaning. 'She any good?'

The Pilgrim could almost feel the redness of Hkainae's burning anger. 'I am **Shabraht**, Desert Kind, goblin. Do not presume too much.'

'You goin' to fight, bitch?' He laughed once again in derision. 'Agh! All the more fun, you die and he dies. We eat!'

The Pilgrim suddenly laughed, almost shockingly bright. 'So when you have killed us and supped on our flesh? What then?' He'd seen his answer and now let his voice grow heavy with meaning. 'What then of the dreams of the night, goblin?' Perhaps now he knew something of his meaning to these folk. 'What then of the emptiness of your soul? What of the promises to return that which was taken? What of the future? Who then shall own the VORTEX? Do you really not know whom it is you face? Shall I name myself to you?'

He heard their screaming spirits recoil from his words. The speaker became still as ice. 'Agh! No! Speak no names!' he shouted in anger. 'Agh! You we will let go! Agh! For the promise of your words, you go! Agh! The bitch stays. Agh! She is for us!'

'There's no promise, goblin. Just words. I travel on my journey. She's Hkainae, Daughter-heir of Guesta, **Shabraht**, desert kind, my friend.' He turned to her suddenly sure of what he must do. 'There's no need to fear now, Hkainae. Put up your sword. They cannot, dare not harm us, not you or me.'

'Agh! Cannot?'

'No, goblin. Listen carefully to my words for now I'll tell you and you know well that I tell the truth. If you even try to harm or hinder her then I'll turn away from the Pilgrim's road. I'll wander alone in the desert and lose myself forever in the terrors of the sand. I'll not wake the vortex! What then of the whirlwind? What then of the breaking of bonds? What then of your most secret of hopes? What then of the promise, goblin? What then?'

The creature screamed again in frustrated anger and crashed his axe into the trunk of a nearby tree.

Another of the creatures spoke. 'Agh! It's too much! Let them go! Fuck it! Agh! It just ain't worth the fucking risk.' And that one stood, turned and walked away his wooden club on his shoulder. Another followed the first and then another.

Soon only the single goblin stood before them. He stood straight, lifted his battered axe and advanced. Time stopped. The Pilgrim heard Hkainae's gasp and saw her sabre tip raise ready to meet the attack.

'NO!' he spoke to her. 'Put down your sword. I'll have no killing. I'd sooner it was me who died than even this miserable retch.' He turned to look at her. The soft sadness in his eyes stilled her protest. 'Don't take its life. I beg of you.'

'You would let a goblin live? After what you know, after what it said, after its threats and hatred, you would still let it live?' she asked, not understanding any of what seemed to be transpiring.

He chuckled then, unexpectedly struck by the completely absurd unreality of this whole situation. 'Oh, Hkainae. My dear, dear friend Hkainae. Don't you yet understand who I am? I'd let anything live. I'm just a pilgrim seeking answers. Somehow I don't think I'll find them in the blood of those I meet upon the road, whoever or whatever they might be. But see, morning breaks. Come let's pack up our camp and be on our way.'

He didn't forget the goblin still crouching by the fire watching them. He just chose not to consider him at that time. However when all was ready he did turn to face him. 'Well, goblin, you're still here then?' There was no rebuke or insult. 'If you hunger, there's meat in the bag there. Not much I'm afraid but enough.' He pointed the sack he'd purposely left beside the fire. 'It's dried but not cooked. I expect that you'll prefer it that way. The blood won't be ruined.' He laughed again and taking the lead pony's halter in one hand and Hkainae's hand in the other he led the way from the clearing. It was hard to say who was the most dumbfounded, Hkainae or the goblin.

*

After seven more days they left the mountains behind and ventured into a far harsher land than any he'd known before. This was, as Hkainae explained, the leading edge of the desert itself. She began to talk to him of the land, to explain about survival in this wilderness of sand and desolation. She showed him how to milk the moisture from the tough skinned cacti and how to dig for the roots of the sweet potato when they found sign of its growth.

Hkainae talked more now, filling most every moment with her chatter as if to drive away the thoughts that troubled her mind. Thoughts of what might lay ahead and of things left behind. It seemed that she tried to delay with words the truth that each step led them closer to Istar and the day of parting. She wished to fill his thoughts with memories for that time when he might no longer hear her, when they walked their different paths through the world. She wove him a picture of wild desert ways and lit his heart with her visions of the beauty that lay in the sands.

By this time they were passing through a place of true desert, where life struggled for existence and only the hardy survived. In the night, the dark moon-less night, they sat and watched the stars turn through the skies and she sang to him.

I am the sand.
I am the sun.
I am the heat.
I am the scorched earth.
I am the wild place.
I am the burning wind.
I am the silent land.

I am as secret as darkness,
As mysterious as silence.
As hot as Hades
As hard as iron.
As wild as life.
As free as time.
As deep as eternity.
As beautiful as love.

I am Desert.
Hkamoot!

'This is my land, Pilgrim my friend. May you ever be welcome here.'

He bowed to her, smiling but sincere. 'Your dry desert land has a beauty that I never expected. It's engraved in my thoughts now and forever. Should any now ask me from whence comes my silence, I'll answer that once I was touched by the sands. But they still won't understand.'

She laughed. 'And shall you bring your little Elf Dancer here, when you are joined once more?'

'I don't know, Hkainae. Her wildness has its own mystery, her dance its own heat and her nature its own beauty. I fear that her sap would dry and that she'd burn to nothing midst the sands of this wilderness.'

'Shall I ever meet her then?'

'Again I've no answer. I know only that should this be, you'll see the light of the forest in her eyes and know of another beauty to stand beside the stillness of your desert.'

She sighed and answered sadly. 'Desert and forest. No we shall never meet.'

When the morning came and the sun awoke to burn the mists from the hollows they espied before them Istar's glimmering-white minarets hanging as a mirage over the horizon before them.

Despite the fact that they had first seen the city in the early hours of the morning it was well past midday when they finally approached the Gates of Istar. Unlike the other cities of his journey the Pilgrim was surprised to find the gated closed, guarded by a sentry dressed in a white turban and the long, black, draped coat worn by the desert people. The soldier waited until they stopped before the gate before he addressed them. Strange words he spoke, in a tongue confusing to the Pilgrim's ear.

Hkainae answered in this strange unknown language. She called her name. He heard the name Tabour also but understood no more. Nonetheless the gate swung open and they led their pony train forward. The guard bowed low to each in turn. 'Welcome you to Istar, friend of Hkainae, Daughter-heir of Guesta, Merchant Lord of Istar. May the blessings of the day ride with you and may the City of the Sands be a blessing to your soul.' Knowing not how to answer, the Pilgrim bowed low also.

There was a quiet, pensive order to this city; a sense of timeless waiting which took the bustle away from the markets lining the thoroughfares. The air was thick with the pungent taste of the exotic spices and perfumes on sale. A piper sat, cross-legged upon a woven mat under the bows of an acacia tree. His haunting melody hung in the gentle afternoon breeze. Here and there groups of severe faced men-of-the-desert lounged in the shade playing some strange game on the chequered flagstones. They sipped red, minted tea and passed the pipe of a hookah between them. Some greeted Hkainae with a salaam or a bow of a head and she acknowledged them in like fashion. Hawk bright eyes fixed the Pilgrim with a questioning intensity.

'My Father's Hall,' she informed simply as they approached what was no less than a palace of glory, polished white marble inset with blue mosaics. The portal, no lesser word would serve, led them into a courtyard planted with orange trees and date palms. Peacocks paced the tended lawns with measured pride, their soulful cries accenting the peace. At the centre a huge fountain threw a spray of scented water to cool the burning dryness of the air.

On cue seven white-clad servants hurried to take their ponies and, as they retired, a desert warrior approached, crimson and jet. Knives were tucked into the sash about his waist and twin scimitars showed over his shoulders. He stopped, still some ten or twelve paces from them and bowed low, his head nearly touching the ground 'Welcome home, Daughter-heir of the illustrious and most magnificent Guesta, Lord-of-Merchants, Trader of the World, long may the visions of his wisdom serve and guide–'

'Liam, oh Liam,' Hkainae interrupted the flow of words with a burst of bright laughter. 'Do you really need to be so formal?'

But he bowed his head even lower apparently intent on continuing the eulogy.

'No, Liam,' she stopped him before he had chance to begin anew. 'I have a guest with me this day. The sun has been hot, the sands dry and the road has indeed been very long.' She turned to the Pilgrim with a bright smile. 'This is Liam, Chief of My Father's household. He is all things to me, teacher, guardian, protector, confessor and friend.' And then back to the desert-warrior, 'Liam, this is my friend of the road. He comes from the far distant Land of Hereth where people do not use names in the same way as ourselves. He is known as Pilgrim for that is his nature at this time.'

Now Liam bowed low to the newcomer. 'If you are a friend to my cherished mistress then shall you be as a Lord unto me. May you find rest and comfort here. You are far from your home-fires and amongst a strange people, yet here you can rest in safety. Pray, how should I address your Lordship?'

'Thank you for your welcome, Liam,' the Pilgrim returned. 'Your words warm my heart. They call me Pilgrim, for at this time that's my nature. I'm but one person, following my trail and living my life among other men each with their own journey. I'm no Lord, nor am I anyone to give service to. I am as Hkainae said simply a pilgrim. Please just name me as such for that would please me. Perhaps in time there might be other names. Even friend. I saw Hkainae's eyes light when she looked upon you. It makes my heart glad.'

Were it possible in such a sun scoured face Liam would have blushed red. Instead his face cracked with a smile. It was true that he lacked any real understanding of the Young-Pilgrim's words. But he had trod the sands, **Hkamoot** and he knew how to tell the truth with his eyes. He turned back to Hkainae. 'Come then, Guesta-Daughter-Heir. You have indeed been long away from your father's side. I would be most tardy in my duties if I keep you here talking as he waits eagerly for your return, and any news that you might bring.' He added the last with a mischievous chuckle.

They entered through an ebony doorway, into a sumptuous hall and through this into a cool, quiet waiting room. 'Please wait here, my friend,' Hkainae bade him before leaving quickly through a curtained door.

He found himself standing alone amidst the grandeur of the chamber. The walls and ceiling were hung with ivory silk. The mosaic floor was inlaid with silver and gold. There were cushions and fine upholstered couches. Upon a silver table sat a crystal pitcher of water and a bowl of exotic fruit.

Eat no morsel nor drink a drop that has not been given. To do so would be seen as the act of a thief. Do not ask for salt for salt is beyond price and who would deny that to another? Wait for such things to be offered. Such an offering is the act of a friend and the gift given, friendship, is more precious than any other. He remembered Hkainae's words. These were the ways of her people, desert ways to be honoured. So he relaxed and waited.

Time passed, ten minutes perhaps fifteen. It did not matter and impatience was not a part of his waiting. From one side came the sound of muffled footsteps the silk curtain was drawn aside and the Pilgrim turned to meet with Guesta, Hkainae's father. She was with him, two paces behind.

He was a corpulent man, appearing somehow taller than his real height. Hkainae was considerably the taller. His whole form was draped in the all-embracing folds of precious brocades, his head bound in a turban of white silk set with a single turquoise gemstone. His neck was hung with chains of gold. Yet richer by far than all the finery was the smile of welcome lighting his well-rounded face.

Hkainae stepped forwards and taking the Pilgrim's hand she offered him to her father. 'Father, this is my companion of the road of whom I have told you. He is The Pilgrim-of-Hereth, my friend.'

'Welcome, welcome indeed,' the deep baritone voice boomed. 'Welcome to our humble home. My daughter, light of my life and the desert sands, names you Friend and friend unto me shall you be also, to me and to all my household.'

He turned to the table and in a ritual as ancient as the desert sands he spoke. 'The day is hot, the sands are dry.' Picking up the pitcher he poured a glass of water. 'Although the sun and the sand are beyond my control, water I have in plenty.' He offered the glass. 'Here, drink, quench you thirst and wash the sand from you throat.'

The Pilgrim accepted the glass with a bow, mindful of what he had been taught. 'Water is life and the gift of water is the gift of life. What greater thing could one man give unto another? I thank you for your water. I thank you for your gift,' and he sipped the iced water, which was indeed a boon to his parched throat.

'My tent is humble; my possessions are of little account. Yet such that I have I offer.' He extended a silver platter on which bread and fruits were arrayed.

Taking the smallest morsel of bread, the Pilgrim bowed once more. 'Yet your welcome is more precious than all the gold in the mountains of Khadil. I thank you.'

'I too have trod the desert sands. I too have trod the hard road. I too have been in the wilderness, **Hkamoot**. In token of this, I have salt. It is the meanest of all things yet it is beyond worth to those in need.' He held out a small rough stone bowl, chipped and worn.

The Pilgrim took a pinch of the salt and placed it on his tongue. 'Your salt I take, though at this time I need it not, I too know its value and its worth. When I set my tent in the desert I too shall have salt for others of the sands. Then they and I shall know we are not alone in so doing.'

The merchant laughed, breaking the spell of the ritual. 'Strange ways, eh, Pilgrim? Strange indeed for one not of the sands.'

'Strange? Yes I suppose so, but the words are beautiful and reach back to a past so distant that the world itself knows their truth. I thank you with all my heart for the friendship you've offered.' The sincerity of his words rang clear in the air.

The merchant's smile grew even warmer. 'I begin to see that of which my beloved daughter has told me,' he mused. 'You have travelled far and long, Pilgrim. May you find rest and comfort and recovery within my home. That which I have is yours, take freely as your heart desires. A room is prepared for you. When you have rested and refreshed we shall meet again.'

The sun as ever trod its road through the heavens, turning from white through yellow and gold to the richest crimson in farewell to the day. In the coolness of the evening they sat upon a veranda overlooking a pool where golden carp circled in pampered ease sipping titbits from the merchant's jewelled fingertips. Food was served, delicately spiced meats and cheeses, strange scented rice cakes, by servants dressed as their master in the richest of clothes.

The Pilgrim sat on the golden threaded cushions beside Hkainae and her father. His thoughts, it is true, were troubled by the opulence and the disquiet of having others wait upon him, yet he hid such feelings and accepted the sumptuous hospitality and the delights of their table. Later, as the sky spread out a canopy of stars they lay at ease sipping scented sherbet from crystal goblets. A minstrel picked out a soft echoing melody from his balalaika somewhere out in the darkness.

'The road from far off Santolin is long indeed, Young-Pilgrim,' the merchant began. 'Prey tell us of your journey and of the wonders that you have seen.'

'Oh yes! Go on,' Hkainae encouraged. 'You must tell my father of your home in Hereth and of your family so very far away. Oh, Daddy, it sounds so strange and wonderful.'

With a smile of hopeless resignation, for he knew there was no way that he could deny her request, he began to spin his tale once again. He conjured his pictures to warm their hearts and souls and led them with him through the paths of his childhood, led them to play in the green woodlands and meadows of Hereth. The night was near spent when they at last made their separate ways to bed.

The next day was indeed a day for rest and recovery. He arose after the midday hour and spent the afternoon lounging in the shade of the fig trees. Hkainae waited on him, pampered him worse than any pet, tended to his every desire. The sadness of his inevitable departure lay as an unspoken cloud upon her heart. Perhaps her attentiveness was but a secret wish to restrain him.

In the evening they again sat on the veranda by the carp pool. Guesta, who had been absent for most of the day, began to muse over his own life. Creating a new perspective for the Young-Pilgrim. In this proud merchant was a man unbowed by the enormous worries of his estates. For Guesta life was but a wonderful game, a balance of pieces on some vast checkerboard. He saw the world in terms of opportunities and risk, measured his progress in ledger books and stock tallies. He saw the cities of the world as possibilities, potentials and chances to trade. He saw himself as the mover of powers, an influence over the forces of the world. His delight was not simply gain-for-gains-sake, but a far more complex business of bargain and counter bargain where the smallest victory, for the sake of the cleverness of the barter, might be seen as being of far greater worth than all the massive profit of inter-city trade.

The third day was much as the second although the evening from the very start took on a far more sombre mood.

'What ails, Guesta?' the Pilgrim asked his host, sensing that only by bringing the cause into the light could the matter be resolved. 'I see a sadness on your face and a trouble in your heart.'

'Oh, then forgive me.' The man looked abashed. 'It is not fitting that I trouble you with my thoughts. Rather, we should fill your time here with enjoyment and mirth.'

'If every day were filled with sunshine wouldn't we tire of the sun?' the Pilgrim asked gently. 'If all was rain, wouldn't we learn to despise it?'

The merchant looked at him, silence ruled to moment. 'I am afraid that my troubled thoughts might weigh heavily on you my guest.'

'As with the sun and the rain so too with friendship, Guesta. If all you show me is the smile on your face then all I can return is the smile on my own. Don't hold on to your sadness. It might be that I could offer something of worth in return.'

Again the merchant was lost in silent thought. 'I have a fear, Pilgrim,' he said simply at length.

'What is your fear?'

'My fear is that soon you shall depart and with you my daughter also.'

'No, Fath–' But the Pilgrim stilled her protest with the tip of his finger on her lips.

'I am not blind. I see the closeness that lies between you. I see too that the path that you tread is one that would hold many prizes for one such as she. It may be that she will wish to leave this place and venture out into the lands beyond. My way is that of freedom, Pilgrim. I would not attempt to dissuade her from this path, even were it in my power to do so. She must make her own choices. She must live her own life. She must follow her own path. Nonetheless I fear. I fear that should she so go then I shall lose her forever, that, never again will I hear the soft fall of her feet, the ring of her laughter, the warmth of her smile and that never again will she walk through the halls of Istar. Few indeed are those who return from the sands. **Hkamoot!**'

He speaks not of the desert. There is another matter here. The Pilgrim looked into the merchant's face and saw the reality of the fear that lay there. He saw his own fear too. He knew that for Hkainae the pull of the desert was very strong and that she might well wish to join him. He did not know if he could gainsay her.

'I am an old man, Pilgrim,' Guesta tried to laugh away the mood. 'You should not heed my senseless fears. I have seen the warmth of your heart and I know that should she join you that you would treat her with a care as would I.'

The Pilgrim turned to his friend. 'What do you say, Hkainae?'

She didn't answer for a long time but sat with her face turned from them, her thoughts hidden. 'You ask much of me, friend,' she replied. 'The Druid spoke truly. You do follow a hard road, hard for you and for those you touch in passing.' She was still once more, looking into the reaches of her own heart. 'It is true that there is a promise in this road of yours. My heart yearns to know that way indeed.' She saw that her pain was but an expression of her fear of the parting to come. And she knew that such pain can never be denied. 'I know too that this is your road, not mine. No, my friend, companion of the road, my way is to face the truth of what is real and to accept that reality. I shall stay in Istar when you leave. I shall stay until my own way becomes clear.'

She knelt before Guesta, taking his hands in hers and looking deep into his eyes. 'You have no need to fear as yet, my dearest Father. I shall not heed the call-of-the-sands, as did my mother. This path is not my way. Be at peace.'

In the time that followed many thoughts were almost spoken but then denied as unfitting for the moment. Eventually it was Hkainae who found the words to express her pain.

There is a mist over Dormon,
a moon over Istar.
There is a wind in the east,
a hot, wild wind of the sand.
This is the way of the desert.
I shall not fight it.
Our parting shall be as our meeting.
I shall cherish the both.

There are storm clouds over the dunes,
Whirlwinds tumbling,
a wind from the east,
a burning, wild wind of sand,
Singing of the desert.
Will you sing to me?
Tell me of your journey once again,
of where you go,
when we part.

There is a stillness beyond the horizon,
a peace of tempest passed.
Now there is no wind from the east,
no wind, no wind from the sands.

Help me to find my own silence.
If you see me cry,
accept my tears.
They are my gift of parting.

That time was soon on them. Of their secret words, I shall say nothing.

She went with him to the city gate, stood there to see him walking slowly away down the roadway towards the desert. She climbed the steps to stand on the city wall to watch him all the longer.

Even when he had vanished into the mist of the distance she remained there. 'Be at peace, Pilgrim. I know in my heart that you shall find what you seek. Accept its truth. As I accept the truth of our friendship. Accept its reality as I accept the truth of our parting. Be at peace.'

*

The minarets of Istar wavered in the heat-haze behind him, becoming ever more indistinct with each onwards step. Shortly after the noonday hour the last hint was gone. He was alone. Just him and the road, alone after oh so long. With an unfamiliar heaviness dragging his feet and a heart that echoed with an empty loneliness, he trod the road into the wilderness, towards the desert proper, towards whatever awaited him beyond the blistering sands.

He missed those companions of the road, their chatter helping to fill the hours and to distract from any discomfort from the walking. Now his body ached. Pebbles became increasingly adept at finding their way into his shoes causing him to break off his progress in order to sit on the roadside to remove them. The strap of his two satchels chaffed his shoulders no matter how he positioned them. The water skin's cord was even worse. He stopped several times to relocate his positions about his person hoping without success to find comfort.

That first night he found a way-well, a rocky depression by the roadside built to provide a traveller a place to rest and replenish their water supply. The deep dug well, provided with bucket and rope, afforded him the chance to quench his growing thirst and to wash the dust from his face. His supper was a thankless meal, dried meat, biscuit and water, even the latter brackish. He slept but fitfully rolled in his cloak and was almost relieved when the sky lightened and he could be on his way again.

This was indeed a desolate, barren land, devoid of trees or any but the toughest vegetation. A rock strewn plain, sun blasted where the hours passed as slowly as the miles underfoot. Yet he saw the desert buzzard hovering on brazen pinions in the thermals. He watched the dance of the jerboa over the burning rocks and saw the signs of the creatures that eked out their hard lives here. At night when he lay to rest he looked through the star speckled heavens into the heart of eternity. Somewhere, he found an answer to the pain that stung in his heart and the memory of Hkainae found its place amidst the treasures of his thoughts to remain with him always.

It seems to be part of the way of life for people to fall into routines of living and thus it was with the Pilgrim. Before long the days became the same. He would rise with first light, not waiting to break his fast. He'd walk through the gentle hours, then stop during the midday, taking a meagre meal and sheltering best as he might through the afternoon heat. Towards evening he would move on again, walking long into the night. Whenever possible he'd take of nature's gifts and even grew to accept, if not actually enjoy, the tough cactus root. He even took to carrying a parcel of their spiny flesh to suck when the sun dried his mouth.

When night fell, if he could, and this was usually the case, he would camp at one of the way-wells. There he'd eat a final meagre meal and lay to rest with thoughts of wooded slopes and lush green valleys, clear forest glades and tumbling bubbling streams. She would dance for him, laughing in her bright elfin joy. He'd call out to her across the distance, made little by his dreams, and he'd tell her of the singing in his heart.

Day passed to day. One week drifted into the second. The land plunged ever deeper into a heat-tormented place where even the tough scrub grass gave up on its battle to survive. All was barren, blistering rock. Hot winds stirred the sand into dust storms that drove against him, cracking his lips, scouring his face raw. The sun bore down, endless merciless, bleaching rock and sand until all colour was gone, just the awful, unremitting glare of light on white. He bowed his head and trudged on, a tiny insect-like speck passing through the bowl of the depression, longing for the cooling breezes of night to brush his face and ease his discomfort. Then night would fall, almost without warning, and the desert turning suddenly chill would find him wrapped in his cloak, shivering and hoping for the coming of dawn.

He travelled on.

Eventually he entered a most terrible place, nothing but sun-baked sand. Here, just as the sun approached its terrible zenith he came upon a marker beside the road. It was a rock, roughly hewn, crude and unformed, yet upon its face words had been chiselled. He bent low to read them, brushing away the sand that half obliterated the lettering.

>
> HERE LIES A PILGRIM
> WITHOUT NAME
> WITHOUT A REASON
> FALLEN BY THE WAY
> *Think on this, Reader,*
> *They came from afar, these pilgrim travellers*
> *They trod this trail as you have trod*
> *they suffered as you have suffered*
> *They died, as you might die.*
> *It is no light matter to take the Pilgrim's way.*

Kneeling in the sand before the stone he traced the lettering with his finger in order to pick out the meaning from the words. *What do they mean? Why is this here?*

Of course he knew others had trod this path before him but he'd not really given much thought to them. He knew his own need, his own cause, but *what could have* driven them to take this perilous road? What did they seek that led them to these terrible wastes?

With some strange insight a picture grew in his mind, a picture of these lone travellers, of those who had trod this path before. A vision, of countless souls whose worn, wearied, blistered feet had packed the earth of this sun-baked road, passed before his eyes. He saw them, one, two, ten, a hundred, a thousand people reaching as if in an endless line back into the misty canyons of time. They came, men and women, old and young, Man and Elf and others. Heads bowed they trudged onwards. He felt their pain. He felt their struggle. He felt their endless all encompassing need driving them onward. Although all seemed pointless it drove them on. Although they knew that they would never reach their destination it drove them on. Although they faced their death in the task it drove them on. He saw them walking, heads bowed against the heat of the day. He saw them shuffling on feet scarce able to step. He saw them, some stumbled, some fell, some struggled back to their feet, some continued only to fall again, some who would never rise. He saw their sun-bleached bones white in the desert sands.

A tear trickled from the corner of his eye. A tear for all those who had gone before traced a glistening line through the dust on his sun-browned cheek. A tear for those who had suffered so much in the search for their truths dripped from his chin to fall on the ruby at his breast. A tear for those who despite their need and determination had failed; for those who would never return to their homes and loved ones. A tear that dripped silently, unseen to sand.

Is this how it ends then? There's no end to this path but a lonesome death amongst the dunes? Is this my fate? I never even considered the possibility. Just who do I think I am, some hero from a story, a character out of a legend, a joke?

Here, for the first time since leaving the stones in Lodor, he knew a doubt. *Should I turn back? Should I?* His eyes fastened onto the stone and the words carved thereon once again. To the stone and to the earth that was this unknown pilgrim's lonesome grave.

There was a change. For from the spot where the tear had fallen there was a stirring. A tiny shoot pushed its way skywards, stretching upwards, budding, blooming even as he watched. A single bloom, a blood red rose formed as if one of his mother's prized blooms had been brought here, planted in these harsh desert sands.

He looked at the rose and remembered his mother's smile. Looked at the ruby and remembered his mother's gift. He remembered her kindness, her smile, her gentleness. He felt the beauty of her memory in the beating of his breast. 'In the darkest of places of your mind this shall bring you light,' she'd said, 'and with it the knowledge of the love that I bare you.' Ah! So did she know of this also?

I shall not turn back.

'I SHALL NOT TURN BACK!' he called to the desert. 'I'll not turn back!' he called to all those who had gone before. 'I shall not turn back!' he called to those who waited with hope. 'I shall not turn back!' for the dark-eyed girl of the desert, who showed him how to face the truth. 'I shall not turn back,' for a green-clad Druid and an Elf with a golden harp who had walked beside him waiting for the turning of fate. 'I shall not turn back!' for Shimmian with his terrible secrets. 'I shall not turn back,' for Calin-Sanain with her gift of death, and for Cog the man, with his gift of love, 'I shall not turn back.' For a street urchin of Varista, with one-thousand-year-old eyes, 'I'll not turn back.' For a Magi called Rustle, who waited to die, 'I shall not turn back.' For a red-haired Goblin called Icicle, 'I shall not turn back.' For a wild elfin Fire-Dancer who had opened his heart, 'I will continue.'

He stood, picked up his satchel and water bag and hung them about his neck. He stooped and picked up the hawthorn staff that he had rested on so long. *There may come a time when you might need a staff to rest upon as you venture on your way...* his brother had said.

'I'll go on,' he said to The Lord-of-Numbers and to The Lady-of-Flowers. 'I'll find my answers. I'll find my rainbow. I'll find my meanings in the wonder of its lights,' he said to himself and he returned to the road, supported by the staff in his hands and strengthened by the ruby that hung about his neck.

*

'ASKALA!' A harsh yell wrenched him from sleep.

'ASKALA!' Faces, wild angry, shouting, cloth veiled faces. They were all about him, gesturing, pointing. Hands tugged at him, grasping his arms, dragging him to his feet.

'ASKALA!'

Askala?

'You! Travilleen persin.' The accent was thick, demanding total concentration before understanding came. An angry, bright eyed, bearded face was thrust into his own. The owner of that strange spiked beard continued to shout as if attempting to force understanding through the volume of sound. 'WHA YOU HEER FER?'

'I'm a pilgrim,' he answered simply, keeping his voice level despite the panic, which welled up in his breast.

'PEELGREEM? WHA EES PEELGREEM?' The grip lessened and he stepped back.

'I am a pilgrim, a searcher, a seeker of truth.'

'WHA EES THEES TRUTH, SEEKER?' The words were truly unknown to the man.

'I seek to find myself, to find the truth of who I am.'

For a time the desert man said nothing. His brow furrowed as he struggled to decipher the meaning from the words. Suddenly his face cracked into a smile. Then an almost physical wall of laughter struck the Pilgrim. The man called to his fellows in an almost unintelligible, unpronounceable string of words. They too joined in with the joke. 'AH! PEELGREEM! You ees a loosin you silf? You is loosin you way an no' noin where you silf ees? No? You ees loss?' His eyes suddenly turned hard, his tone threatening. 'Ees alrigh, I findid you.' Again the others guffawed in response to the man's incontestable interpretation. 'WHA YOU GIFT ME F FINDID YOU?'

The Pilgrim stared back into the other's coal black eyes. 'The day is hot and the sands are dry. The sun and the sands are beyond my control but I have water to quench your thirst.' He stooped and picked up his water bag and handed this to the man.

'Water ees life,' the desert man answered, hesitant, unsure of what was happening. 'Theese ees the gift of life.' He took the canteen but did not drink.

'My camp is humble,' the Pilgrim continued. 'My possessions few. That which I have I gladly share.' He offered the other a piece of the broken way-bread.

'Welcome ees good,' he muttered accepting the bread; but he did not eat.

'I too have trod the desert sands. I too have known the heat of the road. I too have known the wilderness. In token of this I offer you salt even though it is the meanest of things.' Continuing the ritual he handed over the small bag. The man took it, pinched a few grains and returned the bag.

'Salt ees good. I ave salt also for ovvers.' He waited, just enough to end the matter. 'Well, Peelgreem. You ees know thee desert way, ees good. But why I dreenk you water? Why I eat wiv you? You ees not of my peepul. Wha you know of thee sand?'

The Pilgrim waited, not knowing how to answer, not understanding what it was that the other wanted. Then, unbidden came the memory of Hkainae, Desert-Kind, he recalled her love of the land.

He stooped and picked up a handful of sand.

'*I am the sand.*' He showed the sand to the desert man.

'*I am the sun.*' He held his hand upwards towards the still rising globe.

'*I am the heat.*' He opened his hand to the warmth of the rays.

'*I am the scorched earth.*' He let the grains begin to trickle through his fingers.

'*I am the wild place.*' He turned slowly letting the grains spread out about him.

'*I am the burning wind.*' He flattened his palm as the breeze took away the last few grains.

'*I am the silent land.*' His eyes were on the horizon.

'*I am as secret as darkness.*' He closed his eyes.

'*I am as mysterious as silence.*' He reached to his chest and took hold of the ruby.

'*I am as hot as Hades.*' The bright sunlight caught upon the glory of the jewel.

'*I am as hard as iron.*' The jewel burned brighter and brighter.

'*I am as wild as life.*' It seemed that the light within the jewel grew brighter than the sun.

'*I am as free as time.*' He closed his hand about the stone.

'*I am deep as eternity.*' All at once a sadness began to grow in his soul. A sadness for all who had gone before, or all that was lost, for all that would fail.

'*I am as beautiful as love.*' His eyes stung with the salt of his tears.

'*I am Desert.*'

As an echo of what had happened at the pilgrim's grave, he caught the tear on the face of the ruby and let it fall, dripping slowly to the earth.

Time stopped.

The silence of the watchers shouted like a siren of fear. Eyes swivelled; glances were exchanged. Within the band there grew a tremble of terror. They watched, open mouthed, as the ground stirred, the tiny shoot appeared, the stem grew, the leaves spread, the bud formed.

Even within the grasp of his fear the desert-warrior fought off the terror. He was no coward and knew he must take the initiative lest all be lost. He had to do something to gain control of the situation that was so rapidly slipping from his grasp. He stooped, quickly reached out to snatch at the stem, to pluck the rose even as it opened into flower.

'AI!' he screamed aloud. The rose was as fire, a burning, blinding force that filled his being with pain and sent him sprawling to the ground in terror. 'Wha ees thees?' he cried. It said much for his bravery that he stifled his sobs of pain and turned his hand over slowly to inspect the blistering burn that he knew must find on his palm.

There was nothing, no burn, no blackening, no discoloration, not even a blemish. It was too much for him to comprehend. His eyes lifted to the youth knowing not what he looked for. Then he bowed his head again awaiting the thunderbolt that would pound him to dust.

'There's no need to be afraid,' the Pilgrim's voice was soft, gentle and understanding. 'The rose is simply a gift from my mother The Lady-of-Flowers,' he explained. 'Her gifts don't harm. That which you felt was but a warning for you not to destroy something that is beautiful. Even roses have thorns. We are a people of life not destruction.'

The desert man could stand no more. He wrenched off his headdress and bowed his forehead to the ground in supplication. 'Forgeev me, Mastah,' he pleaded. 'I am notheen. Wondroos Weezared, forgeev your servant.'

The Pilgrim reached out and touched the man's head. 'Don't fear, Warrior-of-the-Sands. I'm no wizard and I bring no harm to you or your people.' He beckoned the man to stand. 'I am as I said, no more than a pilgrim, a seeker of truth. Drink the water I offered. It was done in honesty not as a device. Eat of the food. It was given as a token of friendship. Take the salt, for no one should withhold that from another. Be at peace, my friend, and be welcome at my camp.'

The warrior gathered his strength and smiled. He was not to be burnt to a cinder by some terrible magical blast. He regained his feet and mustering the still dignity of his kind he sipped of the water and ate of the biscuit.

Now the others began to edge nearer. They'd watched the pageant unfold and pointed to both the Pilgrim and the rose, marvelling at what they had witnessed. He smiled and stepping to the well he cast the bucket down, heard the splash and the gurgle of water and drew the bucket back to the rim. They watched as he filled his battered cup and offered it to the nearest. They understood his gesture well enough and gathered excitedly before him to accept the water.

All at once the scene began to change. Others came, camels laden, women and children, herds of goats. Tents were erected, fires lit. The sounds of life and activity filled the early morning. There was one last tent that when all else was done the people came together to set. Then they came to him and with many a bow and salaam invited him to join them.

The floor was carpeted in thick woven rugs, the walls hung with embroidered silk. The head-warrior dressed now in a gown of white silk met him in the centre of the tent. Here the ritual of hospitality performed once more. The whole camp was there, the warriors and the old men, the wives and the children. It was a huge excited throng who bustled about him lavishing on him the gifts of their friendship.

There was one youth who came to stand beside him in silence waiting for him to take notice. 'Pilgrim?' the boy asked in a voice free of the harsh desert accent. 'They have asked me to speak with you. I know your tongue and perhaps that shall ease your stay with us.'

The Pilgrim smiled his welcome and invited the boy to sit beside him. 'I'd not expected to find one who could speak so clearly here,' he confided. 'Where are you from?'

The youth smiled. 'I'm called Harold. My mother came from the people of the Lake-cities.' His words of explanation seemed to be all that he would offer of himself. 'I'll be an interpreter. What should we call you?'

He gave the well-rehearsed answer, 'Those who know me name me Pilgrim, for that is my nature at this time.'

The headman came and sat beside them. He bowed and spoke to Harold. There followed an exchange. 'This is Khalif MoiRanaita, Desert Kin **Hkamoot** He is called Khalif. He asks for a boon, Pilgrim.'

The Pilgrim nodded that he would hear the request. 'The rose is a wonder the like of which his people have never seen. He asks, that it be permitted that, taking the greatest care, and treating the creation as precious beyond gold, that the rose is taken and planted in a casket to become a sign of your coming?'

'Of course, Khalif.' Although the boy interpreted, he spoke to the man. 'In the heat of the sun the rose would quickly shrivel and die.'

The words were met with the broadest of smiles. Orders were given and there came a rush of activity. 'It wouldn't have burnt,' through Harold, the Khalif informed him with a laugh. 'We set a tent over it and would've tended it with the greatest of care.'

In what seemed little time at all one of the desert wives appeared carrying a golden bowl in her hands. Within the bowl set in what appeared to be the best loam was the rose. The Pilgrim felt a sudden warmth and memory of home fill his heart.

Realising that there could be no thought of travelling on this day, the Pilgrim settled back to enjoy the company. Many came and, through the boy Harold, told their tales and asked their questions. He told them of his journey, of the places he had seen and the people he had met. They laughed, if not in disbelief, then at least in childlike wonder when he spoke of the dwarves and smiled in their hearts when he spoke of his beautiful Elf and her magical Fire-Dance.

He learnt of them also. They were on an urgent journey across the sands. Their trail had brought them from the southern plains some eighty days from here. There was a calling of all the tribes of the desert people. The Sultan of Dormon had sent word that The Desert-Tribes must gather. They knew no more than that. *The powers are loosened. The winds cry of it. The lands tremble of it.*

He also learnt some, although only a little, regarding the way ahead. They knew little of distance for the ways of the desert are subtle and deceitful **Hkamoot.** It was true also that this part of the desert was generally shunned by their kind. They said that the old men's stories spoke of such paths across the cruel sands **Hkamoot** and that far, far away to the east lay the Mountains-of-The-Sun. There was no word or knowledge of what might lay beyond.

In the cool of the evening they feasted on spiced meats and sweetbreads and drank of the liqueur of the sands, a drink of liquid fire. Dark eyed dancing girls entertained them to the clash of cymbals and tambourines, wild and exotic. Jugglers and acrobats performed their acts of skill and dexterity. Late in the evening the warriors gathered together and danced together in a blur of spinning sabres.

Come morning, they were gone. Were it not for the gifts that they had left him – a fresh skin of water, parcels of goat's cheese and bread and a small silk bag of rock salt – it would have been hard to tell that they had passed that way at all. It almost seemed that the memories of all which had transpired the previous day was no more than a dream of the desert.

He rested one further day at the oasis recovering his strength. But he knew the journey awaited him and, in the first clear light of the following morning, he picked up his satchels and his bags and, resting on his staff, he took to the road once more.

Thus the desert closed around him and the veil of heat bore down, driving away all thought. There were distant hills, wavering purple mountains that walked beside him, amber devils of dancing dust spinning their pirouettes across the desert face. There was the road, always the road, stretching out as an endless ribbon of white.

Days merged into each other until time became a meaningless circle of light and dark. There was a place of wind when he tried to hide behind the rocks to avoid the scouring blast, only, in the end to fight, step by step, onwards, ever onwards. The journey had lost its meaning. Everything had lost its sense. Still he walked on, step after step, mile after mile, on and on and on.

He began to hate this road and its endless white defiance of him, to hate the dust that caked his mouth and dried his throat. The sky, cloudless, blemishless became a battleground, the sun an enemy. Yet within his mind he found companions to fight beside him Hkainae with her knowledge of the sand, **Hkamoot**! Calin, with her terrible calm strength, The Lady for her silence, Shimmian for his laughter, even Icicle for her naked anger. And always, dancing before him as a sprite of the living was Luminae, the Fire-Dancer.

> *Come dance with me.*
> *I shall dance you a dance of passion,*
> *a reel of awakening.*
> *Come dance with me.*
> *I shall dance you a dance you shall ever remember,*
> *even to the endings of your being.*
> *Come dance with me.*
> *Let me feel your life?*
> *Let me touch your living?*
> *Let me see the freedom in your heart?*
> *Come dance with me…*

Onwards, ever on.

There came a time when the road began to climb, taking him higher and higher relieving him from that terrible, endless, blistering heat and the choking wall of dust. There were mountains, red like sandstone, where the endless white path led him skywards. Clouds surrounded him, chilled him, cloaked him in cold white mist, took him from the world, hid the world from him.

The clouds thinned.

Far, far below was a valley, painfully green to eyes grown used to naught but sun and sand. Even from here he could see the tiny red rooftops of habitation. His journey was nearing its end.

> Ask not the rainbow of colour,
> least her light-crafty smile bemuse you.
> Rather watch for her laughter
> at the heart of the tempest.
> Remember the grail
> Dream hidden, of gold.
> For the promise of peace
> in the cold eye of darkness
>
> Ask not of colour, she cannot answer
> Ask not of colour, she cannot know.
>
> (From: The Song of the Sunset Sands)

Chapter Eight - Beyond the Mountains of The Sun

THE MORNING SUN burnt away the early mist. Now no longer an enemy it turned a friendly face to greet the Pilgrim as he stood in the high pass, looking down into the wide river valley. He welcomed that warming blush, and stretched to ease the night's aches. Then, having rolled his blanket and packed his meagre possessions, he set off down the trail towards whatever it was that awaited him below. High above the Pilgrim a tiny speck circled in the blue. The eagle noted with disinterest the movement of the man on the roadway below. Then discounting the sight as inconsequential, it wheeled away over the mountains. Eagles have far more important things to occupy their minds than the casual passages of men.

It took him more than three hours to reach the first tree at the roadside. Further on others would form a pleasant leafy avenue through which he could stroll. The mountain rock soon relinquished its brittle starkness to a gentler land and more than once he'd given way to the temptation to linger and revel in the feel of the lush grass verges.

He felt no need to hurry, the red-roofed buildings below were going nowhere and he would find out soon enough who dwelt there. Lazy trickles of smoke drifting skywards offered their welcome. Cattle could just about be discerned in the checkerboard of fields and pastures surrounding the cottages. There was a normality that appeared almost peculiar to his too often troubled eyes.

Distances can be somewhat deceptive in clear mountain air and it was in fact well past noon when his feet carried him down to the first of the dwellings. Long before then however someone had spotted the traveller descending from the pass and word spread through the villages. A host of laughing, bubbling clamouring children ran up to meet him only to hide their faces in sudden shyness from his smile. They followed on behind dancing and skipping with the joy that only children seem to know, or ran before him announcing his coming with incoherent screams of excitement to those who waited ahead.

The mountain stream that had accompanied the road for much of its way from the peeks turned tumbling under a wooden bridge and through the village that lay in a small hollow beside the road. At the water edge a group of women were washing clothes. He could hear their giggling laughter as he approached and felt a shiver of dismay when his nearness stilled their tongues. There were some twenty cottages in all, lime white with red-tiled roofs. Some had roses, clematis or other climbing plants adorning their faces.

He turned, crossed over the bridge and was met by the twelve men of the village who had stood waiting, quietly watching his approach down the road. Their eyes were quiet, their faces calm. A thirteenth walked forwards. He was dressed in a sky blue robe, his head shaved and his eyes spoke of eternity. He too stopped awaiting the Pilgrim, still, as still as the mountains above. It was as if peace radiated from him. In his hand he held a simple, earthenware goblet.

'Welcome.' The voice echoed the serenity of the eyes. It said everything that there was to say. The goblet was offered.

'Thank you.' He heard his own voice, coarse, grating, uncultured in comparison. The water, for it was such that the goblet held was as a drink of light. He felt it washing away the dust from his travels, the aches from his limbs, the very troubles from his thoughts in its cool, tingling touch. 'Where am I?' he asked, knowing no other question.

The man smiled. 'You are here, Pilgrim. You are where your feet have carried you. Where else would you be?'

'Oh.' *Such a simple answer.* 'Thank you for your welcome and the drink. My journey has been long, hard and of late often lonely. It's long indeed since I knew the company of others. Pray tell me. What is your name?'

'Oh, Pilgrim.' The man smiled again. 'Your road has indeed been long. It seems that you have forgotten that which you learnt as a child. I am He-who-Welcomes those who travel this road.' There was no hint of rebuke, just a gentle reminder of who the Pilgrim was. 'Come,' the Welcomer continued. 'A place is prepared for you. After such a journey you will be tired.'

Having handed back the goblet, still full to the brim despite the water that he had drunk, the Pilgrim followed on behind the blue-robed figure. They walked slowly amongst the cottages, watched by the villagers, to a small bungalow at the far end of the buildings. Entering through a glistening bead curtain, they stepped into the simple room within. There was a small round, stone-topped table on which were set a pitcher and bowl of water, beside these a neatly folded towel. Behind the table was a woven cane backed chair and beside one wall, a strung bed.

'Be at peace, Pilgrim,' the smooth voice bade him. 'Rest awhile and regain your strength. When you awaken I shall return and take you to those who wait.'

Those who wait? 'Yes, thank you. I am tired. Yes…' But the other was gone. The Pilgrim crossed the room and rested his staff against the bed head. He hung his satchels and water skin on the back of the chair. Yawning with tiredness he washed his face in the gently warmed water. Then still drying himself he sat on the side of the bed. Despite the strangeness of this place, despite the mystery of his welcome, despite the thousand unasked and unanswered questions, he lay back. He was so very tired indeed. He closed his eyes. *Those who wait.* The words circled in his thoughts. *Those who wait.* They seemed like a mantra. *Those who wait.*

Silencing all concern, any troubled thoughts.

Those who wait.
    Those who wait.
        Who wait.
            Wait.
                Wait.
                    Wait.

Sleep came, enfolding him in its embrace leaving his thoughts to ramble on their own paths through the mists of nothingness into the hidden realms of dreams.

He is in a cool blue room, sitting quietly, crossed legged upon a small mat. He's waiting, patient but poised, waiting for something to happen. There's a sense of non-involvement, of un-pressured acceptance. Before him sits an old man dressed in a long brown cloak. There's something familiar about the man. It seems he has always known him, but…

Even as he tries to gather his thoughts, to remember he becomes aware the other is speaking.

'What is the purpose of your journey?'

'I seek the purple butterfly.'

'What do you want of this butterfly?'

'To understand you must realise that it's not the butterfly, nor the finding of the butterfly that's important. It's the seeking that is the purpose.'

'Ah yes, so it was…'

Then the dream began to fade.

'Wait! Who are you?'

But it's too late and as is the way with dreams, the more he tries to hold on to the image the faster it fades. It was only on awakening that he remembered. On a silver chain about the old man's neck hung a single rose red ruby and in his hand had been a simple hawthorn staff.

He was unsure of how long he had slept, minutes or hours, perhaps even days. However he was totally refreshed now and felt ready to face whatever mysteries the day might have in wait. Scarce moments after he'd opened his eyes and sat up, the bead curtain jingled and the Welcomer appeared in the doorway.

'You have rested well.' It was a statement of fact. 'It is morning.' An answer to the unspoken question. 'Take some breakfast. Then I shall return.' He was gone again.

On the table were set a loaf of bread, cheese and a pitcher of cool milk. With sudden realisation of his own hunger he readily complied. *It's like a dream, everything prepared, planned, known before. They, he, knew I would come, waited for me, made ready for me. What am I to them? What are they to me? I wonder what follows next?*

'It is time now, Pilgrim. Follow me.'

He caught up his staff and satchel, threw his cloak about his shoulders and hurried to catch up with the other. He followed him over the bridge only too aware of the villagers who stood watching. He smiled but they turned their faces from him and lowered their heads in a gesture of respect. *They stay away from me. What do they know? What do they see?* They turned back to their homes, lives, tasks.

The hour was still early, mists still hung in the hollows and dew still glistened on the grass stems. The new morning tasted fresh and bright as he walked. He followed the man in blue, adopting, with unconscious mimicry his quiet poise and unhurried step, resting his staff lightly in the crook of his arm.

There were few people abroad at this early hour, a man leading a horse-drawn cart, a youth charged with mustering the cattle for milking, a shepherd leaning upon a stone built wall whistling to the dog that moved unseen among the sheep. The children of the previous day did not show themselves. The Pilgrim did see their wonder filled faces peering out from behind hedgerows but they avoided his eyes and stayed hidden. *Even the Children, what do they know?*

They passed another village similar to the first. The people there had gathered beside the road to see them pass. They bowed their heads in quiet respect. Throughout, not a word nor sign passed between the Pilgrim and his guide.

Several hours of steady walking brought them past some four more villages and eventually to the banks of the river that the Pilgrim had seen from the high mountain pass. It was wide, the far shore almost unseen. The little that was visible was ill defined in haze of distance. However, these cool waters danced their own sparkling dance and sang their own secret songs of bullrushes and water lilies. At the road's end a small boat, tied to a wooden jetty, bobbed gently in the swell of the river.

Still un-speaking the Pilgrim followed the man into the boat, stepping warily for the craft swayed alarmingly threatening to tip them into the water. The guide took up the single paddle and pushed them out into the river. Further off upstream a crane took to the air with a cry of alarm and a whoosh of grey wings. In the shallows a small green frog stared, goggled eyed at their passage from a half-submerged lotus leaf before departing in belated panic with a splash and a spreading circle of ripples. All else was quiet.

Several times the Pilgrim was drawn to break the silence. A question about a building on the shore, an observation about the river but the other's stillness stopped the words before they formed. He watched the motion of the paddle as the boat was propelled forwards. *It's the flick at the end of each stroke*, he decided, *that's the crucial part.*

The island rose from the river, cliff edged, stark and the Pilgrim knew without asking that this was their destination and, with a measure of relief, watched the dock approaching. The man offered him an arm to help him alight from the craft and he soon stood on the jetty stretching away the stiffness from his limbs.

'I shall go no further, Pilgrim.'

He turned to see the man paddling the boat backwards into the stream. 'Thank you…' The expression on the man's face froze his offer of thanks on his tongue. *He's afraid. Afraid of me! What does he know? What does he see?*

The little craft slid out into the water and vanished around the island shore. Finding himself suddenly alone was quite a surprise. It took time for him to gather his thoughts before he began to look about.

The jetty led out from a carved dock, of sorts. It was more like a narrow step really. From this rose a flight of stairs, white, worn, cut into the grey rock of the cliff face. *I guess I'm expected to climb.*

His eyes flicked a final time back to the now empty river. *Why was he so afraid? The villagers too, were they afraid like him? Is that what held their curiosity in check? I don't think they were aloof, nor were disinterested. They were afraid! Afraid of me! Of what I am, of what I seek, of why I am here, of what I might become?* A thousand unanswerable questions raved through his mind.

Eventually he turned to the stairway and began to climb. At first, without any conscious thought he began to count the steps, twenty, forty, fifty, one hundred, still he climbed and still he could see no sign of the top. He had to stop several times, lost the thread of his count, and continued upwards. At one place he found a small spring flowing from the rock. Beside this was a silver chalice. He slaked his thirst, then continued. The day was drawing to its close when he finally climbed the last steps and emerged onto the island proper. This was in fact little more than a roughly circular rock, set as a stone within the river. The top was a flat, grassy plateau on which he stopped, frozen by the sight that met his first look.

The late sunlight caught on crystal, spun a web of rays to bind his spirit in wonder. A thrill of welcome filled his whole being. *Earth-Stones! Power-Stones! Here?*

A Stone Circle, it was as those of Hereth or Lodor, but not as he knew them to be. These were not of stone but crystal, seven pillars, a temple of light, of wonder, of mystery. He walked forward towards the dome of light a new song suddenly singing in his soul.

He is come.

Slowly, as if time had lost all meaning, where he himself was but a dream, the Pilgrim walked into the centre of the circle.

A single ray of crimson light danced upon the face of one of the stones, a shimmering, glimmering dance of beginning. He sees a being formed in the essence of the light.

Come sit with me and hear my words.

They sit together on a red carpet, bathed in a wonderful, warming red light. This being of light says nothing. Nonetheless the Pilgrim finds himself growing more and more aware of the earth below him. He feels the soil, the rock, the depth, the hugeness, the age of the world. It seems he knows the earth in every part of his being. He is the earth, its strength, its endurance. His body is rooted, drawing into himself its own essence. He accepts the offered gift, becomes one with the earth.

Do you know my words?
'I have them.'

Now an orange aura of living light takes his being, shows him the form in the second of the stones. She stands with him, lovely, ripe, a being of passion and desire. She draws him to her side, sumptuous and seductive. He does not want to resist as she leads him to sit beside a fountain of light, marigolds and gardenia all about them. She bends over the pool, scoops up the liquid in her cupped hands and offers it to him to drink. He lowers his face, half-afraid, lest by touching her with his lips he might dissolve into her being. The liquid is cool to his tongue. It wakens him, excites him; it fills him to the very extremities of his being. He is alive, wholly so, filled with life, restored.

Do you now my words?
'I feel them.'

For a third time the stone's shimmering golden light enfolds him, a fire of purity and energy. The being within is of fire also. It reaches to him, a hand of flame. He is afraid, hesitant. *I'm here to learn.* Gathering his willpower and courage he steels himself and takes the hand. There is no pain, nor any burning. Rather he is drawn into a place of fire, an inferno that bathes him, purifies him with tongues of living flame He fears to breathe, dares not breathe, cannot breathe. Eventually he can hold his breath no more and he draws the inferno inside and he breathes the fire, is filled with fire. He is fire! His whole being is of power and energy.

Do you know my words?
'I know I can.'

He turns to the fourth stone. She sits upon a jade stone before him, naked, bathed in her forest of light as pure as emerald, stars are shining on her brow. He sits before her, wondering.
She lifts her hands, places them over his eyes, and draws him into a realm of nothingness.
What do you feel?
'I feel nothing!' His heart cries out. 'There is nothing.'
For what does your heart cry?
'For all that is, for myself, for the world, for everything.'
Know the centre of your cry. Reach for it!
His soul takes flight with wings of thought, his spirit soaring as a snow-white dove into a realm of peace and joy.
Take.
Fingers touch him with a gentleness, which opens his heart and, as in the spring following the deprivations of winter, he takes what he needs.

Do you know my words?
'I love them.'

The fifth draws him into a shroud of azure light where they sit in silence. Again everything turns dark, empty, meaningless.

There is a sound, primordial, formless, little more than a vibration of matter. He opens his being and breathes in the essence of all sound, holds it within. He matches it with his own nature, echoing the vibrations with his own nature until he is the sound, the sound is him. He takes the sound and makes it his own, until it speaks his name, ringing out as the chiming of a bell in some heavenly cathedral.

Do you know my words?
'I speak them.'

The sixth comes wrapped in an indigo cloak of mystery and leads him once again into darkness.
Look into yourself, it bids him, taking his hands.
In the very depth of his soul he finds a speck. He focuses upon this, feeds it. It grows brighter and brighter. Brighter until is vision is filled with light, blinded by the brilliance. Gradually he begins to understand. He takes the shadows too, defining, clarifying, until he sees the being of light before him once more, smiling.

Do you know my words?
'I see them.'

The Seventh stands before him holding single violet rose.

In the darkness was I,
afraid and alone.
I felt the ground under my feet, so I stood.
In standing I saw the world
My heart hungered.
My body thirsted.
and I desired to live.
My desire became a fire in my breast.
Burning, consuming,
Until I flew from the flames on wings of air.
Yet in the heavens was a beauty so rare
that I could only soar on wings of love.
I called to the heavens, spoke my love.
I called to the world
I called to myself.
The Universe answered me.
It came to me, showed me its being.
It surrounded me,
enfolded me,
nurtured me
and returned me to myself.

The Pilgrim reaches out to take the offered rose, but even as he does so he realises it is no more than an illusion. He took it all the same, and smiled his thanks.

Do you know my words?
'I know.'

The circle of stones began to shimmer once more, light whirling, turning, spinning, lifting. Shapes began to lose their meaning, the crystal stones, the grass at his feet, the island, the river.

*

The river – not the same in which the island had stood but another, of lesser flow – the river sang to the Pilgrim of freedom and of morning. The road, a familiar band of white trod earth, led away into the distance. *The final road? If ever there is a final road.*

Slowly, revelling in the moment but hesitant too lest time itself stole the instant from his memory, he raised his eyes to see what lay ahead. The road reached out its narrow ribbon into a gentle land of hill and moor, forest and pasture. It pointed as a wavering finger towards the mountain that crowned the horizon, climbing up, ever upwards to the snow-capped peek, to a place where the earth and the heavens met.

He didn't look back as the past was beyond him for now but, taking a determined grip of the hawthorn staff, stepped out once more. His heart told him that there was no danger, the time for that was past him, for now. For some reason one of the childhood songs of Hereth rose in his mind and he hummed the tune as he walked on. There was indeed something Hereth-like about this place, a gentle greenness, a sense of life and growth.

The day passed slowly, pleasantly, carrying him though the rolling land. He was able to stop at noon, to drink from the clear waters of a stream before crossing the moss-green stepping-stones and onward. On several occasions he found blackberries growing in the hedgerows, reminding him of his childhood and home. By evening, although the road was already beginning to climb, the mountain remained a distant peek on the horizon.

Night fell quickly here, shadows racing ahead, heralds of the darkness to come. It was with considerable relief that he saw the light shining brightly ahead. Eager footsteps sped him towards the promise of habitation and shelter and perhaps company.

Soon he stood before the door of a small thatched cottage. The light within awoke a thrill of expectation and in hope of what might await inside he knocked at the door.

A tall, pale faced, bespectacled fellow answered the knock in moments and the Pilgrim felt himself bathed in the warmth of his welcoming smile. 'Welcome, oh welcome, Young traveller. Come in, be welcome. Make yourself at home. Sit, please. Be at ease.' And a thousand other gestures of friendliness flowed over the Pilgrim as he was bustled inside. He sank, limb weary into the comfy armchair that was presented. A cup of mulled wine was thrust into his hand and his tired feet were lifted to rest upon a cushioned stool.

'Ah, you are a traveller of the road I see,' the man's voice tumbled on, giving the Pilgrim little chance to thank him for his kindness, or to make any other reply for that matter. 'A pilgrim no doubt, you have come far too on your quest for answers I see from the dust on your cloak and the tan of the sun on your skin. Many come here, travellers of the road, pilgrims such as yourself, others too on their various ways. They chance upon my little roadside dwelling and often spend the night under my roof, helping me to pass the time. I hope too, that I, in my own humble way am of help to them also.'

Thus he burbled on and on as the Pilgrim, bathing in the warmth of his generosity, gave way to the gentle geniality. Later they ate a simple meal of bread and cheese and sipped a little of the mulled wine, after which they sat in armchairs to rest. All the while the man spoke.

At times the guest may have hovered on the edge of sleep, but the host seemed not to mind. He spoke of his own travels, of a journey he had taken through the lands of men. He told of his own quest too, of passing through stranger lands than any the Pilgrim had known. He spoke also of a time when he became lost, of turning aside from his road, of losing himself and almost his own nature in the turmoil… He spoke too, in a soft loving voice, of his God. He did not name himself priest nor holy man but said that he was but a simple being just trying to do the best he could.

'…I was lost and he found me. I was fallen, and he picked me up.' He told of his God-of-Love who had helped him to find his way again, when he had lost all hope that this could ever be. He talked of how His Love was in truth the very answer to his quest. He spoke of the reason for living, the purpose of life that he had discovered in following that path and of the Love that now filled his days.

The Pilgrim too felt the warming touch of that God also and he understood the truth of the love that was its nature. There was even that within him which called out to be a part of that love, to be enfolded in its wonder.

But this was not to be.

When daylight once again greeted the world he arose and, as they breakfasted on the balcony in the warmth of the early sun, he at last found the chance to thank his host for his kindness and his words. Then with a sad farewell he bade him goodbye and returned to the road and the mountain.

*

Thus his journey continued upward. At this time the road was not arduous and the day pleasantly warm. He found himself humming once again as he thought over the words of his host from last night.

It might be said in truth that of all the things he knew upon that trail of understanding this was one he almost regretted leaving behind.

That evening he stopped beside a tree standing by the trail. Mighty and ancient beyond understanding it was. Its huge branches provided refuge for countless birds and other creatures of the wilds. In the hollows formed by the arches of the massive roots lay a warren of rabbit burrows, where its bright-eyed denizens could frolic with impunity in its shelter.

He sheltered there too that night, dreaming dreams of growth and passing time, of seasons and the laws of the earth…

*I am a seed, knowing the first taste of life.
I see the long grasses. I see the tall trees.
I am afraid…
I'll never survive.*

*I am the young plant, awakening to life.
The sun shines, it is too bright.
The rain falls, I will drown.
But the sun and the rain they nurture me…
I grow.*

*I am the young tree, facing life.
The wind blows. The storm rages.
I'll break. I'll fall.
But I am not broken,
The wind and the storm… They make me strong.*

*I am a tree, amongst other trees.
I am unique, I am different.
I am alone.
But we share the same sun. We share the same rain. We share the same storm.
I am a tree, amongst other trees.*

*I am a tree. I have no fear of living.
A bird nests in my bows.
A rabbit burrows beneath my roots*

*

By the third day the roadway had carried him higher up the vast slope of the mountain. The day was cooler here; the deciduous woodlands of the lower lands had given way to stands of tall pines. The Pilgrim was grateful for the warmth of his cloak again as he made his way gradually higher.

It was close to noon when, on turning yet another twist in the trail, he came upon a small wooden shelter built beside the path. It was a rickety structure with a turf roof through which the smoke trickled without a chimney. He stopped, and peered inside through the simple opening that served for a door. An old man sat cross-legged on an ornate carpet. The smoke from an ancient iron stove lent an iron-blue tinge to the air and brought tears to his eyes at the first touch. Set atop of the stove was a gently boiling kettle.

The old man looked up and, on seeing the Pilgrim, smiled a wide gap-toothed grin. He half bowed and with an extravagant wave of his hand, invited the young man inside. Seeing no reason to decline, the Pilgrim bowed his head and stepped through the low doorway. The roof was low, forcing him to stoop. However the man gestured for him to sit and once he had done so offered a cup of tea, refreshing and welcoming warm.

They drank in silence, although their eyes touched. Eventually the man put down his cup and reached out to take the Pilgrim's now empty vessel too. He refilled them both but, rather than offering anew, he removed from his wrist a silver band and still un-speaking handed this to the Pilgrim.

The youth was taken quite aback, not knowing how to respond. Then a thought came to him. *'There may come a time when you will pass it to another.'* Calin had said. *'Do so freely for that is its nature.'* In deference to those words he took her gift, the moonstone ring, from his own finger and gave this to the man.

'Ah,' he said, placing the ring upon his finger. 'For this I have waited long indeed.' The man stood then and without another word he ducked out of the hut, turned and walked off down the trail leaving the Pilgrim alone with little more than his confused thoughts, the tea and the silver band.

The Pilgrim stayed there a while, for it was near noon and he welcomed the rest that the hut afforded him. He finished the tea and set the silver band upon his wrist. There was no sign that the old chap would return again.

After about an hour he decided to be on his way. So having washed the cups and left them neatly beside the stove, he too left the hut and took to the road once more.

*

Then on the fourth day as he climbed ever upwards he espied an ancient mystic sitting cross-legged upon a rock beside the wayside.

'Tell me,' he asked of the Pilgrim, when talking distance was reached. 'What is it that you seek on this oh so wonderful mountain?'

'I seek the Rainbow, Sir,' he answered politely. 'It is my hope that within the light of the rainbow's colours that I shall find the answers that I seek regarding my own nature.'

'Ah I see,' came the reply. 'And when you have found your Rainbow, and when you have asked your questions, and when you have received your answers, and when you realise that which you are, will you then be able to answer the riddle?'

'The Riddle?'

'A dreamer had a dream in which a pilgrim stood talking to a mystic sat upon a rock.'

'I don't understand.'

'Who is the dreamer?'

*

Day followed day, the road growing steeper with each passing hour, steeper, rougher and harder. There came a time when it could no longer be called a road but a trail and then a track, one long climb carrying him up the face of the mountain. Behind him the land spread out in a vast panorama, breathtaking in its wonder. Still he climbed. He grew weary, struggling to continue in the rarer air but still he climbed. His breathing grew laboured, painful. Each movement became an effort, a contest of willpower. Still he climbed.

There was a fissure, a cleft in the rock which, when he passed through, led to a stone bowl cut in the hard mountain rock by the roaring force of the highest waterfall that he had ever seen. It was a raging torrent falling from the very heavens with a cry of thunder, pounding, smashing; crashing from rock to rock, a shimmering, violent cascade of water, plunging endlessly into a giant pool.

Here, arching over that pool, framed by the ageless rock, formed by the far-flung mist into a crescent of wonder, he found his rainbow.

Rainbow? Such a simple word for such a sight. Nothing had prepared him for this: an awesome arc, fusing the colours of the universe into an eternal bridge of blinding light. It overwhelmed his senses, stilled his thoughts, stole his soul with the terrible wonder of its beauty.

He gazed and gazed and gazed, and, and what?

There was no sudden instant of enlightenment, no bright wakening of some inner being. It was indeed a rainbow, grand, beautiful beyond measure, perhaps the most splendid thing in all creation, but just a rainbow.

Why? He sank to his knees at the edge of the pool. *So far! Exhaustion overcame him. Why? What has it all been for?* He lay on the ground beaten beyond endurance, unable to comprehend. Thoughts came to him, memories, random, uninvited pictures of the past, rising up to taunt him. Again the terrible emptiness welled up inside him.

I am alone!

Yet in the depths of his heart he knew that he was not alone, nor would he ever be. She danced there her magical, elfin dance of fire and love.

> *Come dance with me,*
> *let me feel your life,*
> *let me touch your living.*
> *I shall dance you a dance of awakening,*
> *a burning reel of passion.*
> *I shall dance you a dance to remember*
> *until the endings of your being.*
> *Come dance with me.*
>
> *Come dance with me?*
> *Now and forever.*
> *I shall dance in all your thoughts,*
> *In the halls of your mind,*
> *In the silence of your moments.*
> *In the wonder of your being.*
> *Come dance with me?*

No! I'm not alone. Not whilst you remain as the slightest speck within me. You knew me. You believed in me. You saw my future through the wonder of your being. Thus he grew in strength once again. *Who else then? So many have touched me, called to me, believed in whatever it was that they saw in me... What of them?*

Icicle, my fair foul-mouthed friend, what would you see here that could give you hope? Rustle, who I never knew yet who waited denying even death, what would you see? Shimmian, where are you with your stories and secrets so terrible? Would you know? What truths would you show me that which I cannot see? Calin-Sanain, with your price of death? My Lady what of your hopes spoken only with your eyes? Hkainae, Desert Kind, How shall I tell you of this?

Accept the truth.
Accept its reality.
Be at peace.
Yes my friends of the road. I shall accept the reality. Whatever it may be.

He sat by the pool, the thunder of the waters ringing in his ears. The spray soaked him, wetting his hair, streaming over his face to mask the tears, which fell so freely from his eyes. He cast his mind back along the path of his travels, back to its beginning, deep into the memory of that night upon the Downs of Hereth. *Stones, so often the Stones. What of them? Are they the movers of my fate, any fate? Do they have another meaning? Or was it some other power?* The image of the creature his father had become grew in his mind. *So much to think about. So much to bring to mind. Why? What for?* Unbidden, came another memory. *'I shall be the Wizard of Rainbows.'* At that moment he laughed at himself a bitter laugh of self-derision. *Is it then all of my own choosing?*

He began to think at last, to piece together the fabric of his own journey. The process was slow indeed and many hours did he struggle. Gradually a realisation began to grow within him. *Why should I expect any different? Why should I think the answer will be given so freely? After all this, as all journeys, is a path of learning from start to end. There never was a right way for me to travel. There never was a safe way for me to follow, where all would be well. There was no hand to steer my path, whatever they may have wished. The road was mine and for me alone. It is the same as with the dream brought to me that night in the Galghathag. The bridge was but an illusion of safety. The fat man was an illusion of danger. 'Who broke the bridge Man or child?' Neither! What broke the bridge was the belief that there could be a safe way.*

…No! There was no bridge, no man, no child. They were but illusions brought to teach me. Then came the full realisation. *The Rainbow is an illusion also, a creation of light and mist, a trick that nature plays upon the eye.*

'Well then, my lovely Fire-Dancer,' he spoke his thoughts aloud, shouting over the crashing rush of water. 'So I must choose again. At first, as a child I chose as a child, then, perhaps unknowingly, to turn against myself and that which I was. As a youth I chose to make my own vow, to choose my own path. The Dwarves knew me as I was, I chose too, to take the warrior's way, as a warrior I chose not to kill. Upon that lone down in Lodor I chose again to take this road. In the Greenwood I chose to trust my heart. In the mountains I chose once more not to kill. I chose to continue. And now I shall choose again. I shall choose as I told Icicle. I shall choose the truth and not the illusion. I choose to accept the truth as it is. If the rainbow is but illusion, then I shall see it as that and nothing more.'

He turned again, casting his eyes over the vision before him. This time he actually saw what was; the water that cascaded over the rocks, the spray flung out into an airy mist, the mist, which hung in the air to split the light into a thousand sparkling droplets, a million specks, each had its own nature, its own beauty. It was so utterly beautiful, so splendidly wonderful. A ruby glow reached out into the heart of his beginnings. An orange flush awoke anew the passion of his life. A golden gift of the sun flamed in his heart. Life's eternal green now filled him with its love. The crystal blueness vibrated in the core of his being. The indigo opened his eyes to the mysteries of the universe and the violet was so pure it reached into infinity.

That which he was awoke, for he loved the wonder and the beauty before him. He saw himself reflected in the moment also and knew the glory of his nature and the love, yes, even love, for that which he was. His being awoke. His spirit sang aloud. He knew. 'In the beginning the light that burned brightest was your love of colour.' And ever it was so.

In knowing he reached out to take what was his by right. Colours wove about him dancing in glory. Red shone the earth that is the beginning of all things and now welcomed his beginning also. Orange danced the water of life, a tribute to his passion. Yellow burned the sun in eternal answer to his power. Green flowed the mists bathing him in love. Blue were the Heavens as they called out his name. Indigo fell the shadows that showed him his truth and violet was the mystery revealed. He took them all, worshipped them all and he drew from them their very essence and made of himself the vessel of their splendour.

He cried out into the heart of creation. He spoke into the face of infinity. He whispered into the depths of eternity, 'I am

The Wizard of Rainbows.'

As a newborn star, his light burned bright upon the face of the mountain. The heavens sighed.

> Alone!
> As some mystic,
> Sage and knowing,
> some dread dream-time image growing,
> My self-reflected being
> Showing,
> Alone.
> Upon the Sunset-Sands.
>
> (From: The Song of The Sunset Sands.)

Chapter Nine - Wizard?

IT WAS COLD in the thin air where a high pass cut through the snow bright slopes of the Mountains of the Sun. Wind-whipped flakes flecked the brown worsted robe with white. He looked back, down into the shadows. The events of the past few days, weeks, felt somehow unreal. It was hard to even remember all that had transpired since he stood here before.

The hint of a self-indulgent smile lifted the corners of his mouth as he resisted the urge to make some gesture to show his passage.

At his feet the two satchels lay heavy with the provisions they'd given, but the memory of the fear-filled eyes of the valley-folk was enough to stop the smile before it formed. *Why were they so fearful of me? Who do they think I am that their eyes always turn aside from my gaze? Am I really something to be so afraid of now?* But he'd known that expression on the faces of Varista's people when they'd seen Rustle's Magi crest. He still wore that broach pinned to the underside of his cloak. *Surely they don't see me as being something like that? True magic is nothing to fear, don't they know that?* He laughed wryly to himself. *I don't even know it myself and I'm supposed to be a wizard now.*

Seeking distraction, the newly reborn Wizard looked up into the clear blue expecting perhaps to see the speck of the eagle that so often circled there. The skies were empty now, lifeless, as was the hare on which the bird currently feasted.

Wizard? He chewed his lip nervously, still not truly believing that which he knew to be real. A frown crossed his brow with the awareness of the enormity of what he now possessed. Then he spoke his thoughts aloud to the morning, 'I am the Wizard of Rainbows.' Sometimes it's difficult to state such a truth, although it might also be the case that simply saying the words could strengthen the reality. On this occasion it seemed little more than self-indulgence and were there any to see they'd have noticed his cheeks flush in embarrassment. Before long though, the smile returned as his eyes bathed in the gentle blue sheen of glacial ice on the mountain slopes above, the golden glow of morning on the bare rocks about him. 'Yes I am.' In mounting glee he took of the essence of the colours and bound them to himself that his being was one with the wonder all about him.

Far below, the sleep-silent valley lay wrapped in night. The tiny villages, the thread of river and the crystal circle were left unseen. It was only here in the higher reaches that the sun as yet shone. *Perhaps a welcome; perhaps a warning.* He still recalled his Pilgrim journey through the crucible of sand and the memory left him with an inevitable feeling of trepidation, knowing only too well what awaited somewhere far below. *Still,* he told himself, *I have to do it and there's little to be gained from waiting.* So he strapped both satchels and his water skin about his shoulders, took the hawthorn staff in his grasp, flicked up the hood of his worsted cloak against the chill wind and stepped out once again towards the future.

Some six hours later he emerged from the damp blanket of the all-encompassing cloud and knew again the weird sensation of moving from reality into unreality, perhaps the reverse. From here, still high on the mountainside, the great hazed expanse of the desert was spread before him, daunting for all its familiarity. By the time he had climbed down that seldom-trod path to the lower slopes all appreciation of distance was lost. The very air he breathed was a dry, burning torment to his throat.

I can't go on like this, he told himself and sat, with heat aware carefulness, on a rock to think things through. There he sipped from his water bag whilst wondering what to do. The very thought of the journey ahead filled his mind with dismay. He had survived on the path here but he knew only too well the price to be paid for passage through the sands, **Hkamoot**.

An arid plain of sun-blasted rock lay baking all around him. Grains of windborne sand had already begun to settle in the folds of his cloak. Perhaps, he mused, were he to stay here then he too would be firstly covered by sand, then turned to stone himself before finally being worn to dust and blown away on the desert wind. At this time his whole existence seemed filled by the redness of the desert as were its very heart reaching out to him. He saw the beauty of every shade and set them in his soul as treasures forever. The sun glared at him, stinging his eyes with its brilliance, warning him of its power over this harsh domain, of the fragility of his own mortality. But he had known the touch of this same light glistening on the snows of the mountains, the freshness of its morning glow glimmering on dew wet stems of a morning meadow.

Was it any wonder that, within the rainbow of his nature, the truth was revealed to him? And within this truth came the understanding of the possibilities that might be. *Vibrations of light, vibrations of life.* As the mists of the waterfall had split the light into the million shards to form the rainbow, so within the magic of his gift he chose from the vibrations of light. He matched the snow set blue of the high peek glaciers and cast in his own mists a shield of its coolness as protection from the sun's terrible onslaught. His smile was not of victory but of wonder. Each moment, each discovery a thrill that sang in his heart.

He began to walk.

That journey, through the last few hours of the day was strangely restful. Shielded now by his magic he was able to take the time to look about and see the true beauty of the sands. This was no lifeless place; rather it fairly teamed with creatures. He recognised the trail of the side-winding snake, caught the skipping motion of the gecko in the corner of his eye. He had time to notice the scorpion and the sand-frog; he saw the nests of the jerboa and the mighty palaces of the red ants.

He began to recognise too the thousand shades of the sands, the purple of the distant hills, the raw red harshness of the wilderness. He took of their wonder and bound the essence of their nature within himself and he was glad for the beauty that was his.

When night fell he set aside his shield of light and marvelled over the wonder that the universe spread over him. He fed the midnight to the ever-growing rainbow of his soul, the silver glistening moon to the light-song of his heart. The night owls called to him. Creatures of the darkness sang him to sleep.

The life that was his grew strong and the magic of his being revelled in the glory of all that was revealed to him. He even thanked fate for what had been granted to him. He didn't consider the cost. Can such gifts be without a price? He forgot also, at least for a time, how they'd hung their heads, averted their eyes and turned their fear-filled faces from his gaze.

It took a full sixteen days to pass through that terrible cauldron of sand. Long before then he'd realised just how awful that former journey had been. On one occasion he gave way to the urge to drop his protection and spent an hour of torment trying to move on. There was a day when there was no well at dusk when he walked on into the night. He feet ached, tired from the journey, but that was nothing.

There was a place of stones, a plain of pebbles where even the largest was no larger than his fist. More often there was just the sun-parched earth, the drifting sands and the endless expanse of amber. He walked on. Eventually the dunes gave way to a rock-strewn wilderness where cacti and the tough scrub-grass managed to eke out an existence.

The dance of the hours continued, sunrise to sunset, noon to midnight and the Wizard knew the rhythm of their turning as he trod the road back towards the West. Again as the scarlet band of sunset began to spread out over the sands he sought a place to rest. He watched, absentmindedly, the hawk that hunted over the desert. It circled round and around on outstretched pinions, bright eyes, bright thoughts, stilled, a twist of feather, a turn of head, a sudden intensity. The wings fold. It drops, like a stone, down, down, down. The cry and startled panic of wing beats as it turned from its prey broke through to the Wizard's consciousness but not enough to make him ask the question. The desert rat, unknowing the events above had its own fears to contend with. It might be hard to believe but there are worse deaths than the sudden grasping shock of claws.

Barely a mile further lay the circle of rocks of a way-well. There was a moment of familiarity. His mind filled with images of the desert people and his last time here. *What happened to them? What were the meanings of their journey?* He wondered as he drew the water. *Will they come again? Will they set their tents about me and fill my time with their songs and laughter? Shall I meet them again before I finally leave this desert land?* He knew that familiar sense of loneliness and looked out over the sands, pausing for a short while before setting his camp by the side of the well. The horizon stayed empty, the Wizard alone. The desert as always held its own council. As night stole the colour from the sands he kept hold of the crimson glow of sunset, bound it into a stone to warm away the night chill.

And in the blanket of descended darkness he sought a now familiar solace to his isolation and he filled his thoughts with images of a fire-haired elfin dancer. *I shall go to The Elswood, to Al-Sinnian. Will she welcome me? Will she dance once more for me in the cool shaded groves of the elfin wood?* He teased himself with the questions for he knew she would and thus slumbered contentedly, rolled in his cloak, until morning.

The following day, not long after noon he stopped again beside that lonely pilgrim's grave. The rose of his sorrow was long gone, nonetheless he lingered there. The memory of his mother and home were a gift to his heart. *What will they make of me now?* he wondered. *What would they make of this strange gift of light? Not fear that is for sure.* There seemed little need for haste at this time. So he set his camp close by the grave, ate a light meal seated upon a rock near to the road's edge, and took the time to seek out the fruit of the sharp spiked cacti to supplement his rapidly diminishing rations.

The night seemed chill as dusk drew in, surprisingly so after the heat of the passing day. A trickle of mist crept amongst the stones and boulders. It was little more than a hint of moisture at first, like a memory of damper places, stealing through the shadows. He watched, mindless as those first insubstantial tendrils thickened to a soft smothering grey.

Then he was on his feet, backing away from the threatening talons. GALOMIST! The scream of recognition resounded in his soul. *Galomist! Here?*

> **There is a wakening.**
> **There is a trembling.**
> **There is a reaching**
> **Out for power.**

He felt the enmity, the cold grey hatred at its heart, felt also the touch of its evil reaching out towards him and the terrible grey cruelty of the creature who had brought this into being. He knew, only too well, the cost of its foul creation. Once more he recalled the horror of the dreaded grey castle and its oh so awful denizens. With that memory came another vision – of these bright burning sands cowered and broken, cast forever into the greyness of that other place.

A sudden burning anger welled up in the centre of his being. *What right has this abomination to trouble this wild, wonderful land?* **Hkamoot!** Without conscious thought he drew the memory of the burning desert sun from his inner rainbow and cast its brilliance into the mist. The screaming, horror recoiled from his lights in a spluttering turmoil of hissing steam as were it in truth a living entity.

He followed after, chasing any sign of the stuff over the rock-strewn sand. Once again his lights burned vivid and the mist evaporated, then again, and again, and again. He never considered that which he had always known. Magic is of Love, not destruction.

*

The motionless figure, silhouetted against the sunset, might well have been mistaken for a statue, a cactus or even a tree, had trees grown in this barren land. Sun-bright eyes stared out from a burnished bronze face across the wastes. It could never have been said this was a patient man. Patience was never a consideration to him or his kind. He was waiting, watching, so that is what he did and with a total concentration others might have thought obsessional. He watched, and what he watched was nothing. Well, nothing yet.

Behind the watcher, where the dunes cast their shadows over the hollow, the folds of the Dathiir Tents hung still. The few tethered camels, lazing in the shelter of the stable awning, were still also. From somewhere beyond, a blast of sun hot wind lifted a mist of sand from the higher dunes. The guy-ropes pulled and groaned. Sand shifted from where it had settled to find another resting-place but there was no sound.

Over the whole scene hung an aura of unwanted expectancy, a pall of fear. They'd felt the cold grey touch of evil. They'd seen the creeping horror of the mists. They'd seen too the shadow warriors that lurked in its depths. They had felt the terrible, lonesome powerlessness of those faced with something beyond their comprehension. Perhaps they'd seen in their hearts the inevitability of their own doom.

From where he stood on the rippled sand of the dune crest, the man on watch knew only too well the same sense of doom, but it was not his nature to admit to such. He was on guard. He would wait and watch, and if something happened? Well? Then he'd face whatever it might be. For the thousandth time he resisted the temptation to feel the comfort in the hilts of the twin scimitars hanging on his back, sharp as the sand. He tasted the desert through the folds of his veil, scenting for change, expecting nothing, expecting anything. His eyes snapped wide.

For the first time in over an hour he moved, just a turn of the head as he scanned the horizon for whatever he'd sensed, first right then left. At one point he became still again, only now his stillness almost cried out. Following his gaze, the line would have tracked the final rays of the now dark red orb dipping behind him towards where their last light brightened the far-off purple mountains. First passing over the tent, where the blue curls of smoke had just begun to show, then up to the dunes beyond, rising into the darkening sky to the greater desert beyond and eventually to the distant hazed peeks. And in the space between? Well, in the space between came a speck of light. Something moved, something, someone.

Although he lifted the war-horn to his lips in readiness, he paused before making that blast of warning. Whoever this might be they came from the wrong direction, from the bitter sands where no man would willingly venture, **Hkamoot**.

Once again his eyes scanned the sands about him before returning to the figure. It was far, too far for even his hawk eyes to make out detail. Besides the image was troubled by mirage even though the time for such was passed. Still, the desert has its own mysteries and who was he to question what his eyes beheld? There was another matter also. This being, man, monster, Djinn or god touched the soul with the cool sweetness of the morning dew, for once slaking the endless burning thirst of the sand **Hkamoot**.

All at once he knew, though from where that knowledge came was a mystery. The image of the strange brown-clad youth rose in his mind and he had no doubt of its truth. 'Hey!' the excited cry flew over the sandsh 'Hey! Peelgreem. Eeees a yoo?'

The burst of distant laughter confirmed his excitement and acted as fire to his heart. For once he forgot his duty and blew a sharp, shrill blast upon the horn and blew and blew. His people fell from the shelter of their canvas shelters, clutching scimitars and spears to face whatever danger the warning seemed to declare. They stood bleary-eyed in the half-light of dusk, turned, looked and stopped open-mouthed to see their Khalif dancing on the dune's high rim. Only a few thought that he had gone insane from the sun. The rest couldn't really frame a thought at all. From his wild antics and even wilder gesticulation one after another turned and looked towards the East. One after another saw the figure appear over the dune rim, and one after another felt their faces lit by smiles.

Thus the desert man left his post and ran over the sands to meet the youth with a burst of breathless joy. 'Ah, Peelgreem, Yoos ees returnid ees no?' The desert man struggled as ever with the barbarities of the common tongue. 'Yoo ees findid yoos silf? Yesno?' He wiped away his awkwardness with a howl of laughter and slapped his hand on the man's shoulder, harder than was perhaps necessary.

The Wizard smiled as broadly as the other. 'Thank you, Khalif, my friend. I have indeed found myself.' He took both of the man's hands in his own and smiled his own warm greeting. 'I have found many things, my friend, many indeed.'

Were it possible the name Friend would have broadened that smile even more. As it was his face just glowed all the brighter. 'Come then, Peelgreem, I mus makid yoo welcoom.' He clamped his arm about the young man's shoulders and bustled him down towards the tents. The desert folk gathered about excitedly.

'Eesa my fren' Thee Peelgreem,' the desert man needlessly informed them. 'Eesa come back agin.'

They bowed their salaams and smiled their open greetings. Yet he saw the strange plainness of the encampment without understanding. He saw too the dour apparel of these normally colourful people but he left his questions for another time.

As might have been expected, the Khalif led him to the entrance of his own tent. Before entering though he stopped. 'Thee sands ees ot, thee desert dry... I 'as water...' Once again the desert people's ritual of hospitality was performed and the Wizard was ushered inside. As before, the desert people crowded in behind.

The heaps of cushions and the opulence of the former tent were absent here. This was sparse, no more than functional at best. The floor was for the most part but bare ground. 'Seeet Yoosilf eera,' the Khalif's voice boomed. He pointed a ring-encrusted finger towards one of the few mats.

'Yoos av a dreenk?' It was no question, for a glass of akhrak was thrust into his hand even before he had sat.

The first burning sip reminded him of the danger of the fiery liquid and, laughing at himself over the price for his lack of caution, he took up the glass of water they'd set beside him. He did, as he gazed into the crystal glass, just for a moment wonder how they might react but it didn't stop him, perhaps it spurred him to action.

For a moment he was still, stiller than the Mountains-of-the-Sun, stiller than the glaciers that caught the light of the skies in a thousand facets of crystal. He took the memory of that light also and formed a frozen jewel in the centre of the glass. There may have been an indrawn breath of shock when he picked the sliver of ice and dropped it into the spirit, but he wasn't listening.

The tent was silent.

'Aiyah! Yoo ees Peelgreem no mooore!' the Khalif decreed, his voice coloured by awe.

'No indeed,' he laughed, 'Khalif my friend. It is true. I am no longer the Pilgrim you once knew. I have walked that road to its ending and there I found the rainbow which I sought.' He paused, building the tension ever as competently as Shimmian the storyteller might have done. 'However, it was not in the rainbow that I found the answer,' he continued. 'Nor was it in the colour that I found my understanding, It was not in the journey either, nor in the lessons of those who helped or hindered me on my voyage of discovery. No,' he chuckled, 'It was in myself!' He picked up the glass. 'I am as you now see me,' and threw the water high into the air with a cry of pure excitement, ruby to amber, to gold, to emerald, to sapphire, indigo, violet.

'I am the *Wizard of Rainbows*.' And he laughed with the joy for the beauty that sang in his heart.

They gasped, fell to their knees before him touching their heads to the carpets in supplication.

'No! No, my friends,' he almost pleaded with them, shocked by the level of their fear. He bowed before the Khalif, took his hands and drew him back to his feet. 'No, please, do not fear me or my gift of light and joy. This is nothing of harm, just of beauty – come see.'

They stood as he directed and those brave enough, with many a startled, nervous laugh, complied and they took the jewels of his creation from where they hung in the air. They turned them over and over in their hands, passed them, one to another as they marvelled at the wonder of their making. Then he laughed once more and returned the beads to their true nature and the desert folk laughed with him as the water ran through their futile grasping fingers. Only they lowered their eyes when his own touched them and sat silent when he spoke.

Further words dried on his lips before they formed. The air of the tent became strained and awkward.

Outside, as darkness closed in, the fire pits flared and the smell of cooking drifted as a mystery through the tent flaps, wove about the poles and the hanging sand lanterns to call them back to normality. The desert people gathered together for their evening meal. Bread was brought and wine and salted lamb with rice. A strange, silent meal it was too. There are no words for such times. They sat awkwardly cross-legged upon their mats with their sabres resting on their laps. Men and women alike ate from the backs of their round shields as were they dinner plates, They were, as he already realised, dressed **Shabraht,** ready to fight, ready to die, clad, under their sand-coloured cloaks, in the black and red **Khatha** of the desert warrior. The shafts of their spears lined the walls.

The question lay heavy on his mind, driving away whatever enjoyment might have been possible from the meal and the company. Yet he had no idea how to frame his words or to find an answer to the thoughts troubling him.

'Where are the children?' Was his eventual query when the eating was done, his reticence betraying the tenor of his thoughts.

'Eees staydid behin in Dormon, Weezard.' There was a sadness in the Khalif's voice, a sadness tempered by his iron hard will. 'They ees safa theer. We ees no returndid to ours omes over thee sands **Hkamoot!** Ees sendid to thee sands by Thee Igh Sultaan. Ees bad thins ees comid. We ees protectid thee sands!'

The Wizard was on his feet also his face whitening with the impact of the words. 'Protect the sands? Protect from what? From whom?' he cried in horror. 'Who, who do you face?' Although in his heart he already knew what the answer must surely be.

The bonds are loosened.
The winds cry of it.
The earth trembles because of it.
The waters of earth are bound
in a whirlpool of awakening...
They tell of a wildness
Of powers reaching out to grasp that for which they lust,
Scheming, plotting, grovelling for that they desire.

'Who ees fightid, Weezard? Ees not know. Ees Djinn, an terrib bad. Eees thee Ghal, Thee Goblinks Horde. Ees seedid thee tereebil grey mist! Ees seedid thee grey warriors of the mist! Eees War ees comid! Thee Sultan-of-Dormon ee sendid us...'

The desert leader stood, drawing his scimitar and holding it over his head. 'EES **Jihad!** War!' With his words the others stood as one and holding their scimitars high clashed them, blade against shield. **'JIHAD!'** a single terrible cry. 'The ees tereebal bad, Ees Ivil. All thee peepul of thee sands ees ready to fight... **Jihad!**' That word again.

A thought trailed through the Khalif's mind. 'Ees you comedid weeth us Afendi? Eess thees why you comedid with yoo's magic from over thee sands? **Hkamoot!** To stand weeth us at thees terreeble time?'

The same thoughts coursed through the Wizard's own mind. *The waking of the whirlwind?* When he spoke his voice was cold, tinged with the horror of his understanding, 'Is this why I am here? I don't know. I have to find out what is going on.'

It seemed his words might have been a signal, turning once again the pages of Fate's endless scribing. For even as the last syllable passed his lips, there came a shout from the guard upon the high dune, a shout and a long, drawn out blast of a war horn. There was a scuffle, a rushed emptying of the tent. The desert people gathered together before the camp, peering up into the evening gloom at whatever caused the commotion. Soon they began shouting and gesticulating, their emotions raw over what was transpiring.

The Wizard followed, although his steps were slowed by a hesitancy unknown to the others. He could almost hear the scratching of Fate's eternal quill. He felt no surprise when the group of desert men came into view, struggling over the dunes. A scouting party no doubt; a patrol returning from their search of the sands. Nor, unfortunately, was it any surprise to see a writhing figure dragged between them.

'Agh! Fuck you! Shit gobblers.' The unmistakable guttural bark of goblin foulness cut through the night air. 'Fuckin bastard turds. Let me go!' The words were halted by a muffled curse as the being fell or was thrust face down into the sand.

'Wait!' His words were ignored. It was a pathetic creature, emaciated and dirty. They'd strapped its arms about a stave thrust over his shoulders. Two of the desert men forced it forwards. The Wizard wondered how long it had been captive. *Not long, No it would be long dead were that so.*

The Khalif barked a command and several of his men rushed out to meet the party while they were still descending the dune's shifting slope. They gathered about the goblin. Blows were struck. The yells grew louder as others arrived to torment the creature. There came a sudden sound of scuffling struggling movement. 'Agh! Fuck you all! Get your fuckin' 'ands off me!'

There was another shock in store for the Wizard. For as they dragged the goblin closer there came an awful recognition. *I know it!* It was the same creature he'd met when he journeyed with Hkainae on his way to Istar, the creature who had sat at their campfire that night.

It recognised him too. The eyes told it. Strangely there was no plea, nor even hope for help, just the memory. Perhaps even worse, despite the protest, despite the cries, despite the terrible fate that probably awaited, there was no real sign of fear, only the cold haunting grey eyes. It yelled out in pain once more, for some unseen reason, 'Agh! Fuck!' arching and spitting out at its tormentors. Then, horrendously, it looked up into the Wizard's face, and winked.

The Wizard almost screamed. He couldn't frame a thought, couldn't even ask a question. He simply watched, as the goblin was dragged cursing, spitting and struggling through the crowd.

Heedless of the creature's cries the tribesmen gathered about in a chanting, mindless throng. The goblin was pushed, pummelled, forced to kneel on the ground then the stave was roped to a post erected before the fire pit. The woe-begotten creature looked about itself. It had little doubt about what was to happen or that it would be terrible indeed. Yet still showed no real sign of fear.

Which was more than could be said for the Wizard. *Oh God NO! What are they going to do now?* Not that the question was needed. The Khalif's face shone with hatred and righteous anger. *What am I supposed to do about this? WHAT?*

The desert leader seemed almost calm with the knowledge his task. He walked slowly over to where the creature waited, drawing his curved knife with obvious intent.

With a feeling of terrible, inevitable doom the Wizard also went to stand beside the post. Hoping beyond hope he placed his hand on the Khalif's arm. 'What are you going to do?' he asked of the desert leader, not wanting to know the answer.

'Ees mine knife weel maka eem talkin.' The firelight glinted on the drawn blade. 'Ees maka eem answer thee questins Wee ees av.' The hatred and cruelty of his tone was worse even than the man's intention.

'No, my friend, there's no need for this. Let me talk to him? Let me find out what he knows and why he's here? Surely we don't need to harm him.'

'No HARM?' Shouted words of disbelief as the desert man turned to stare into the Wizard's face. 'Wassa meeenin' NO HARMIN' Eees Gha, ees goblink. Eees bad, Eees Eneemee. Eees not arm. Eeees KILL!' The Khalif's anger was burning like fire in his breast. He pointed the knife towards the goblin's breast. Clearly this man did not understand. 'Thees ees us eneemee. Thees ees wass wee ees fightid. Wee has **Jihad!**'

The others gathered closely around banging their shields with scimitar and spear. **'JIHAD!'** they cried again and again, **'JIHAD! JIHAD!'** driving all other sound away, all thought away. Slowly the din died and they could hear the Khalif once more.

'Eee ees our Eneemee! ee muss Die!' These were cold, final words that would bear no dissent.

'No, please.' The Wizard could feel Fate's cobweb lines drawing tight. 'There's no need to take its life. Let me speak with–'

A lifted hand stilled the words. The Khalif's eyes were hard as stone, as wild as the desert sand. What battle went on behind those bright fires was unknown. Eventually he made an offer. 'Thees ees my words. Yoo Eees not offa thee sands, **Hkamoot!** Yoo Ees nota **Shabraht!** You ees friend but ees not **Jihad!** As yoo ees saydid. Yoo ees speek weeth heem. Yoo ees askid yoos questidins. Yoo ees gettind yoos answers. Then he ees mine!' The tone of those words was no more than a sentence of death.

The words froze on his lips even before they formed. Yet now it was his turn to reply. He turned slowly, looked at the pathetic creature, meeting those cold grey eyes. There was no answer there. Almost wearily now he looked up into the faces of those about him. He knew now what he must do and what would then follow. There seemed no other option. *Fate has already made its choice.* He rested on his hawthorn staff, let his eyes travel over them, these hard people of the sands, friends? It was as an act of acceptance of Fate's hand that he pulled the hood of his cloak up to cover his head. 'As you said, Khalif, I am not of the sands, not of your people, not of your way.' He waited as the impact of his words began to spread through the waiting throng. 'I am the *Wizard of Rainbows!*' He heard their in-drawn breath of fear. 'It's not my way to take life, nor to stand by to watch as others would do so. He's as much a part of the world as you or I. You will not take his life!' The words were softly spoken yet all heard him. The Wizard's own anger was beginning to grow also, 'Who are you to take that which you cannot give?' He remembered Calin and the terrible cost she bore. 'What price will you pay?'

'We haff **Jihad!**' the Khalif replied, defiant. 'He shall DIE!'

The Wizard looked into the heart of the fire where he found a burning red that was as a memory of the setting sun. *Or is it the red of fresh spilled blood running wet on the stones?* He took that image, wove its vibrations through the flame until in the centre of the conflagration was a rose of pure energy. He lifted the rose and set it onto the hard earth before the goblin's now trembling form. Tendrils of fire, growing as a living flame climbed about the figure.

'Remember the rose, Khalif?' He waited, shivering inside with the horror of what he was doing. *Magic is of love NOT of power!* 'No one will touch this creature! This I command!' But the words screamed in his soul. Suddenly he knew the terribleness of what he had done and the reason for the fear on their faces; the awfulness of the doom laid upon him was worse than anything they might have done... *I can KILL with my magic.*

They looked at him, at the fire, at the rose and they could feel its heat burning worse than the desert sum. Fear whitened their faces, bright eyes that dared not look aside as they backed away from him, trembling with the terror that filled their hearts, leaving him alone with the goblin.

From within the folds of the tent, where they had fled his burning eyes, came the sound of their voices. He could hear them talking, arguing, anger and fear, even resignation.

He waited, unmoving, for their answer.

Eventually a decision was reached. The sounds of their discussions grew still. The door curtain of the tent drew aside and the desert people emerged once more.

The Khalif walked proudly at their fore, his head held erect. He was dressed for the desert, turbaned and cloaked. His water bag hung from his shoulder. His people followed him as one. If the desert warrior knew fear then he hid it from those who watched. He walked slowly, purposefully, although somehow the reluctance that he felt showed in his step. Nonetheless he came to stand before the Wizard.

For a moment he bowed his head in acknowledgement of own his powerlessness in the face of the Wizard's magic. 'Eees mighty Weezard, ees strong magic an we ees only peepul. We ees not know of Mageek. Only off thee sand. I ees Thee Khalif of Assad. Thees ees my words.' He was silent for a long time, though no one was counting.

However, when he did speak his words were strong and showed no sign of the fear that hid in his eyes. 'Yoos Mageek as saveed ees life!' Final words as the man bowed his head once more.

Then he straightened and looked the Wizard in the eye. If once friendliness had shone there, now there was none. This was a lord who spoke. His words were but a judgement. 'You know only off Mageek not off thee sand.' The accusation was sharper than a dagger. 'Thee sun ees hot.' He lifted his water bag and poured the contents onto the ground. 'I haf no wata!' He took a crust of bread from under his robe and dropped it to tread into the dust. 'My door ees close! I haf no food! My salt ees mine. I do as I wan wiv eet.' He held out a fistful of salt and then opened his hand slowly to let the grains fall to the earth. Then he turned on his heel, his back to the Wizard. His people turned too, as one. No words were spoken as the camp was struck even though night was upon them.

'Where are you going?' he called to their vanishing shadows, not really expecting an answer.

'*Jihad!*' Nothing else was said.

They were gone. All that remained was the Wizard, the goblin, still tied to the stake, and a golden bowl in which grew a beautiful red rose. Even as he looked the bloom withered and died.

*

The Wizard slumped down opposite the goblin who had watched in silence throughout. It had managed to work the spar loose from its stake and although still tied now sat leaning against the post. In the silver light of the newly risen moon the creature was revealed. It seemed an ungainly looking thing. Its ugliness born not just of grey flesh, flecked as it was with grime and the crust of vomit. Even its shape was unpleasant. At some time an injury had left a deformed shoulder, another, or perhaps the same, had clearly produced a shortened and twisted arm.

Cold eyes met the Wizard's softer gaze – relief? Fear? Who knows? Anyway it didn't try to turn aside as the Wizard stood and approached.

'What on earth are you doing here? What happened?' He tried to make his voice hard, demanding.

'Agh! They was goin' t' fuckin' kill me, fuckin' skin me alive most like, fuckin' sand-turds.' Those cold grey eyes looked up into the Wizard's face. There was no sign of gratitude, nothing but a tired resignation. 'You stopped them with y' fuckin' magic! That's what fuckin' happened. Agh!'

Now just why DID I do that? It seemed totally incongruous that this creature actually spoke clearer than the desert leader. The Wizard could almost feel the wall of the suspicion which had underlain the goblin's words. Then its foetid stench hit him and he found himself recoiling inwardly as the wave of revulsion washed through him. 'I mean how did they capture you? And why are you here?'

'They fuckin' drug me here! Agh!' It spat a phlegm-thick gob that hissed in the embers of the fire. The remnant dribbled from his chin. 'Do y' think I wanted t' fuckin' come?'

'But what were you doing out there, out in the desert?' He strove to ignore the drool.

'We was just tryin' t' fuckin' survive! Agh! It's fuckin' hot out there you know.'

'We? Were there others then?'

'When the fuckin' shit-bags came and…' The grey stare remained fixed on him. 'Agh! They ran away, First fuckin' sign of trouble! Agh! Left me to take all the crap! Agh! Shit-heads! Agh! Not one of them stayed to fight. Too fuckin' scared!'

'I still don't understand! What were you doing out in the desert?'

'What do you think we was fuckin' doin'?' It spat again. 'Agh! We got fuckin' lost.' Explaining nothing.

'So what now?' he tried.

'How the fuck should I know? Agh! Ain't you the fuckin' Wizard? Ain't you supposed to know?'

The Wizard stayed silent, tension mounting.

Suddenly the goblin began to chuckle, coldly, humourlessly. 'Agh! Are you gonna untie me?'

'What, so you can attack me?'

It actually laughed. 'Agh! Shit! You'd burn me to a fuckin' crisp and I know it. Agh! I saw that fuckin' magic stuff, I know when I'm outclassed. Agh! Anyway, You saved my fuckin' hide. It's yours now.' There was something sly about the creature's tone. 'Agh! You own me now. I'll do what you tell me.' His words sounded like capitulation, only. 'I'll serve you well, my Kla.'

'What do you mean I own you?' His feeling of discomfort was growing. 'I can't own you, I can't own anyone.' He remembered the goblin Icicle saying something similar.

'Agh! Well fuckin' tough!' The creature actually smirked. 'It's the fuckin' Law: a life for a life. You saved my life so it belongs to you now. I belong to you until I can save your life. Agh!' His laugh was like gravel. 'I can't see much hope of that. So I reckon that you're fuckin' stuck with me. Kla!' Somehow the word sounded like an insult.

'Look goblin, I'm NOT your Kla. I'm not anyone's Kla,' he tried. 'It might be your law but it isn't mine. I don't want to own you. I don't want to own anyone. I've got enough problems without that.'

'Agh!' The goblin spat onto the earth. 'Don't change nothing'. Agh! My life still belongs to you. You can kill me if you want. That's up to you, but unless you do you're stuck with me. Agh! It might be interesting f' me too.' It seemed somehow that the whole power structure here was turned back to front.

'I can always leave you tied up here!'

'Agh! True. Then I'd fuckin' die. That'd end it. Agh! It's all the same anyway. You decide.' The creature seemed to have won the discussion.

He could see no way out. 'Don't you even care if I kill you?' He asked as he cut through the ropes.

'Why care? Agh! I'd be dead that would be the end of it… We've all got to die sometime. What difference does it make when?' The goblin stretched and rubbed where the rope had scoured its wrists. He spat again and massaged the saliva into the grazes.

'Don't you want to live?'

'Live, die, what the fuck does it matter?'

The Wizard could find no answer.

After a while the goblin stirred and rose to its feet. 'Agh! I'm hungry. I want some food.' He walked over to the fire pit, grovelled on the sand rummaging for scraps. The Wizard watched with a mixture of relief and revulsion. It had come as no surprise to see it walk with an awkward, scuffling limp. The thought of sharing the trail with this disgusting creature was far from his liking.

It was close to midnight now and the moon shone high over the dunes. The night was still, waiting, watching, as if to see what might transpire. The goblin watched him also, somehow maintaining his guise of detachment. Its eyes following the Wizard's progress up the shifting sands of the dune until he finally stood at its summit, near to where earlier the guards had been posted.

The skies were spread about him here, more real than the sand. Somewhere, out in the distance, unseen from here, lay Istar. There perhaps Hkainae watched the same stars. It was not for that he had come though. He scanned the heavens until, far to the west showing as little more than a speck over the horizon, he found that which he sought. *Chelimbrelle*. His heart reached out to her, wherever she might be. *Do you watch also, my little elfling? Do you share this night? Will I see again your beauty, touch your wonder, and hear your laughter chiming on the woodland wind? Will you dance for me then, my wild woodland love?* But for once the image of her was hard to form and the memory of her laughter slipped as mist from his thoughts.

He didn't want to sleep that night. Not with the terrible thoughts, that circulated in his mind. *What am I that I can even kill with my magic? No one should be able to do that! Magic cannot be allowed to destroy! It would destroy everything. Magic should be constrained! Must be bound!*

The bindings are breaking!

No wonder they fear me. No wonder I fear myself. His discomfort over breaking with the desert people sat as bile in his stomach. As did the question of what he should do, where he should go? *Tabour? For there is power there, perhaps I might even find answers there. Tabour, for the Tower still calls me? What would await me there I wonder. Or would it be better to go to Dormon? The Sultan of Dormon might have answers, or Al-Sinnian and the Elves, or High-Caravail? What? WHAT MUST I DO?* Oh how he wished that his flame dancing love were here. She might have an answer. The remembrance of Fate's deft touch stayed with him too, darkening his thoughts. *Is this how it'll be, to travel my own lonely road forever?*

For a time it seemed that the night itself knew his pain, shrouding him with a cloak of sadness, but it was too much. Not even his own, lonesome, miserable thoughts knew the tenor of that emptiness or its terrible feeling of pointlessness. He knew then the touch of eyes, not goblin eyes, not even evil eyes, just orbs of awful, unexpected hunger, never peace, never rest, never time to know.

The form, when he finally discerned it far out over the barren land, was hard to identify. A figure dressed in moonlight, still as the sands, still as the night, She sat upon some kind of beast. He could not tell what. The distance, haze of approaching dawn, night mist, dew, whatever, denied him the truth. It might have been a horse although his heart told him it was another thing completely, a thing of horn and claw, of a sadness every part as full as Hers.

She waited there unmoving, and he knew Her eyes sought him, in knowing that he found no comfort and yet no fear. In the end he moved no more than She. *Who is She? What does She want? Why is She here?* He found no answer, not in the night, not in the silence that ruled the land, not in the mystery of Her being, not in himself or his own understandings. At one point he noted that She was gone. That was how it was. He did not question her going.

The goblin found him still there at dawn watching the sunrise over the desert. It had taken the stave that they'd used to tie his arms and now used it as a walking staff to help climb up the dune side. It sat on the sand nearby but did nothing to break the silence. The Wizard knew a kind of gratitude for that at least. The grief filling his heart over the loss of the friendship of the desert people was not to be denied nor cast lightly away. It was only when the man stirred and turned to look back down to the encampment that the creature spoke.

'Agh! What are you goin' t' do?' The guttural bark sounded almost like a demand.

'There was someone out there in the night,' he told the creature, not really caring if it understood or not. 'There was a mystery about Her, a strange loneliness, an emptiness deeper than the night... I don't know why, or what She wanted. She just waited there in the darkness.' He didn't notice the sudden whitening of the goblin's face. 'There are strange things happening. I've got to find out what's going on.' It seemed the right thing. 'I'm going to High-Caravail. Perhaps the King might have some answers.'

The goblin pulled itself back into its normal state of disinterest. It shrugged his hunched shoulders and stuck its staff into the sand. 'Agh! 's a fuckin' long way.'

'I've travelled further,' he replied. 'You can stay here if you want.'

'Agh! Don't matter. I'll come.'

'Why?'

'Why not?'

There seemed no point in continuing. There was no point in delaying further either. The Wizard descended back into the hollow and retrieved his possessions. Then, strapping them over his shoulders, he turned to face the north west. 'I don't suppose that you know where we are?'

The goblin spat. Said nothing.

'OK then Gob. We'll head out this way, see what we can find.'

Thus they started out, the Wizard leading the way up the dune slope and out into the desert. Behind him came the shuffling goblin. They walked in silence, awkward with each others' company. Long before noon the heat of the day had become almost unbearable. They stopped, rested in the shade of one of the tall cacti, which grew abundantly in this harsh land. Here they sat a while and drank from the Wizard's water bag.

'I can protect us from the worst of the heat,' he explained as he drew into being a cloak of soft blue light. It won't take but a moment.' The light began to grow, softening the harshness of the sun's heat.

'NO!' the goblin screamed in fear seeing the creation forming over them.

'It's OK, Gob,' he tried to reassure it, still building the shield. 'It can't harm us, you. It's only a thing of light, a shield to protect us from the sun.'

But the goblin grovelled on the ground moaning in terror, eventually lying face down on the sand not even daring to look. The Wizard took back the shield and the heat of the day bore down on them. *Why so afraid? It's hardly a danger to him.*

Before long the silence became an irritant. By midday it was just about unbearable. Respite came in the early afternoon in the form of a brackish desert pool. Several stunted palms provided a little shelter. Oasis? Well, that was one name for it. 'We'll camp here for the night,' he declared, stopping beside the larger of the trees. It seemed a good enough place.

'If we stay this close to water any others who come will find us here,' the goblin warned.

'It doesn't matter, goblin. I've no fear of others and they've no need to fear me.'

'Agh! Suit your fuckin' self then.' He jammed his staff into to the ground and began to urinate against another of the palms.

'Do you have to?' Annoyance growing once again. 'Do you have to do that here?'

'Agh! Course I do. You want me to piss in my bloody pants?'

'I mean here, where we're going to camp? Look, Gob, we're going to stay here tonight and I'm not fond of sleeping in a midden. Can't you go out into the desert a bit and do it there?'

'Sure, if you want me to. Agh!'

The Wizard thought the better of replying and set about making camp. The water, as he had feared, was bitter and barely drinkable. It would have to do. His brief exploration of the oasis brought a supply of dates and some of the yellow-fleshed cactus which had become his staple diet in the desert.

The goblin grunted something about hunting and wandered off into the wasteland. Time passed,

As evening drew in the Wizard began the task of building the fire for his meal. Gob sat itself at the pool edge and watched. As Icicle, in a time now long ago, so this goblin too was fascinated by the way the man tackled the task, with the order and the care that he took. The tinderbox flared and the first tendrils of smoke soon curled skywards. It wasn't long before the smaller twigs began to flame, followed soon after by the brighter crackling burst of the fire proper. The goblin looked on, for once silent.

He made a bowl of his usual unappetising cactus stew, gathered some dates from the trees. Still the goblin watched in silence.

Food for the goblin was another matter though. The creature had found a mixture of insects, grubs and three small rodents, which it now devoured raw with slobbering, belching, drooling delight. The Wizard forwent his own until his queasiness had subsided. The meal was done, night was approaching. They sat in the growing gloom. 'Agh! Do y' know what y' gonna fuckin' do then?' It belched and rolled sideways to scratch its rump. 'Y'know, what Y' gonna do when the fuckin' time comes?' Not one to beat about the bush was Gob.

'What do you mean?' The question was rhetorical. The thought had never left his mind.

'They'll all be fuckin' waitin' t' see what you'll do. Agh! An' you fuckin' know it.' It spat into the fire. 'She reckons that you'll listen to Her, understand. Agh! Drigla thinks you'll burn Her to a fuckin' crisp. He put ten fuckin' oaths on it, ten!' The goblin's voice ran thick with awe. 'Mind you, no one will take him up on that! Agh!'

'Drigla?'

'Agh! For a wizard you know fuck all! Drigla's only the Clan Lord of the Zatha Tribe. That's more than two fuckin' thousand goblins. His fuckin' Ghalg's over two hundred! And they're some of the biggest bastards you'll ever see.'

The earlier words coalesced into meaning, 'Look, Gob! I'm not about to burn anyone.' *Not ever!*

'Then She'll fuckin' freeze Y'!' A thought penetrated. 'Fuck!' It spat again into the fire. 'Agh! Gonna fuckin' freeze me too. Shit! That or you'll join Her. That'd be fuckin' worse!' It spat again. 'Agh! Worse for us, me, probably you too. You'll not find much to lust over between Her frozen legs! Agh! Bollix!'

'Who is She?' he whispered the question, not really expecting an answer. Even so the image of the figure out in the night rose in his thoughts, the sadness, the emptiness.

'Who fuckin' is She? WHO? You want t' know who this fuckin' Ice-Bitch is? Well I ain't fuckin' naming Her, not fuckin' me. Agh! Ain't my fuckin' place to do that an' you ain't got no right to fuckin' ask me. So I ain't.' The rings from where it spat into the pool spread outwards. 'The Ice Queen, that's what we fuckin' call Her, Dherlethae, but that ain't Her real fuckin' name. She leads the Tribes now. What She says they do! Agh!'

Dherlethae. The name meant nothing to him *Dherlethae? Dherlethae?* 'The Tribes?' Realisation. 'What – the Goblin Tribes?'

'Of course the Goblin Tribes.'

'But I saw Her, out in the desert. I saw Her there. She's no goblin!'

'Agh! I never fuckin' said that She was. She just leads them. An' they ain't all either. Agh! Not just goblins. There's the fuckin' Rock-breakers an' Howlers an', an' other things too.' Now, for the first time he actually sounded afraid. 'Agh! She's worse than all of them, burning with Her sadness. You'd eat your soul for her.'

Rock-breakers Howlers? What is he talking about? Reality and understanding began to slip into a mire of confused ideas. He clung to the things which he might understand.

'You say She leads them now? Leads them where, for what?'

"Cause She wants to! Agh! You don't go against her.'

'OK. What does She want with them?'

'How the fuck should I know? She's called the tribes together. Every fuckin' one. Agh! I reckon there's gonna be one hell of a fuckin' fight sometime. I can tell you that.' The goblin chuckled humourlessly.

It's happening again! The hand-of-Fate seemed heavy at that time. *And I still don't know what's going on!* 'She's out there somewhere.'

'Agh! She always fuckin' is! It's her nature.' He laughed again at some private joke, and then turned to settle down for the night.

The Wizard stood and walked out into the darkness. She was out there again. He knew it, knew the touch of her sadness. 'What do you want of me?' He whispered into the night. 'Why do you wait there with your terrible sadness? What answers do you seek?'

From behind in the dark of the oasis came the sound of a long drawn out snore and somewhere out in the wilderness a lone owl called, but there was no answer.

For the next few days they followed a rough stone trail leading them northwards again. It was an awkward road they travelled together now. They shared the journey, but could never have been called companions. Little was said. There seemed nothing worth saying. All the time the presence of the White-Queen travelled with them. They never actually saw Her, well no more than the vague, empty shadow left in the wake of Her passing.

The land began to change as they climbed the trail into the foothills of the Dormon Mountains. It was here, well not actually here for they travelled a different road, but in these same foothills that the Wizard had first met the goblin. He thought it a shame that he couldn't just leave him here on this trip too.

'I know where we are now, Gob,' he informed the disinterested goblin when they camped for the night in the shelter of a small copse. 'These are the Dormon Mountains, somewhere to the west of here the road from Tabour where we met before. I reckon that this trail must lead us through the hills to Dormon itself.' At least the goblin was listening now. 'I think we'll go there first, see what news I can find out.'

'Agh! What, y' gonna do with me when we get there?' the creature asked. 'They ain't gonna be too fuckin' happy t' see you bringin' a fuckin' goblin into their fuckin' city, are they?'

The vision of just how unhappy they might be flashed through his mind. *Oh no! I'd not thought of that.* 'I can't take you into the city. They'd not let me even if I wanted to... and I don't. They'd end up killing you, perhaps me too.'

'Not with your fuckin' magic they won't. You could fry the lot of them. Agh!'

His spirit almost screamed. 'Look, Gob, haven't you got it into your head yet. I'm not going to FRY anyone.'

'What's the fuckin' point in 'aving it then?' The creature lay back against one of the trees and stretched. 'Agh! I tell you. If I had power like that I'd do anything, have anything that I wanted, anything!'

'It's not like that!' Exasperation made his voice louder than usual. 'Magic isn't about power and getting your own way...' *But I can kill with it, destroy things, even life.*

'Agh! What is it a-fuckin'-bout then?'

His mind turned over a thousand possible answers, 'You'd not understand, Gob,' he replied in the end. 'It just isn't about power and destruction and killing.'

'You don't kill with it?'

'No.' *I hope that I never have to.*

'Not ever?'

'No not ever.' He committed himself to that path anew.

'Not even to save a life? Your own life?'

'No not even to save my own life.'

'Fuck!'

'What?' The sudden vehemence in the creature's voice set his nerves on edge. 'What's wrong?'

'Them!' Gob was looking, wide-eyed, into the night. Following his gaze the Wizard soon made out the shapes that had drawn up about them.

There came a harsh, guttural bark from the shadows. Gob returned the same, spitting on the ground once again. There followed an exchange, the content of which the Wizard could but guess.

'What what are you saying?' he asked of Gob. 'What do they want?'

The Goblin laughed, cold and cruel. 'Dinner!'

'We've hardly enough food for ourselves!'

'Ain't our food they wants for dinner. Agh! 's'fuckin' us!' Gob spat again. He was well named. 'I told them that you was a Wizard and that if they make any move that you'll fuckin do for them. I hope they fuckin believe me.'

For a moment the situation seemed hopeless indeed. *What is the point if I can't use it? No wait... She used magic... magic to fight them, used her dance of magical fury to protect me.* He stood, walked over to where the brushwood had been gathered for the night fire. What was the rainbow but vibrations of light? What was light but the energy of existence? He took the energy and bound it into a ball of glimmering light, a beautiful creation where the bonds of the universe were gathered in a web of glory which filled his soul with wonder. He set it at the heart of the wood, kindled the flame with the touch of his mind. The fire lit the clearing, the campsite, the goblin who crouched nearby and those gathered about the clearing.

'Shit!' Gob breathed into the night.

'Come,' he called to them, 'Come join us here. We mean you no harm.' They came too, reluctantly or willingly, curious or afraid. They came to sit in a circle about the fire.

There were eight of them, dirty, smelly, emaciated and worn. They carried a range of weapons, mostly clubs of one description or another. Two of the larger also carried shields, well bucklers made of wicker and hide. Six seemed to be goblin bucks, the other two females. These appeared no less repulsive than the others.

They sat in silence, waiting.

'Well, my friends,' he began. 'Do you understand my words?' One by one, as his eyes fell upon them, they nodded. 'That's something anyway.' He pointed to Gob. 'This is Gob,' he told them. He travels with me.' A sudden idea flashed through his mind and a broad smile crossed his face. 'He has up to now, anyway.'

The goblin was on his feet. 'Agh! What do you mean?'

'It's the law, Gob. You told me.'

'What's the fuckin' law?'

'Well, the way I see it is that by warning me that they were there, you just saved my life: a life for a life. Debt paid... I no longer own you!'

'Oh SHIT!' The Goblin saw the truth... 'You ain't saved yet,' he tried. 'It don't make no difference. I'm with you now. I follow you!'

'No, Gob, it isn't that simple,' he sounded almost sorry. 'You have your own responsibilities now.'

'What? Agh! What the fuck are you talking about?'

'These.' His eyes scanned over the small band that crouched about them. 'I guess that if you'd not warned them that they might have attacked and that indeed I might have been forced to use my magic against them. You've saved their lives too. It's the law. They're your charges now. They belong to you.'

Gob looked at him long and hard, his eyes travelled over the goblins too, lingering for a moment over the two females. 'Agh!' He spat again, started slightly as the spittle hissed in the fire. 'You've got a point, Wizard. I guess that I did.' There was something horrible about the sneer that stole over his expression. 'Did you hear?' he addressed his newfound charges. 'He says that I've saved your lives. You all belong to me now!'

'Prove it!' One of the larger males was standing clutching an axe and shield, ready to fight. 'How have you saved my life; GOB?' He spat the last word like a challenge. 'You better make it quick turd-eater, or he'll have to save yours all over again.'

'I stopped you attacking the Wizard, Shit-face! If you'd done it you'd be fuckin' dead now and that's sure. I stopped you. I saved your fuckin' hide! You owe me...' he paused for effect. 'A life for a life! So you fuckin' belong to me.'

The creature paused too, the effort of thinking contorting its face. 'Only if he can really kill with the magic!'

'Do you challenge me, Goblin?' The Wizard's voice was sharp as steel. *NO! Not that! I'll never use magic to kill.* Nonetheless he stood and faced the creature. 'Do you dare stand against me?'

The goblin took a step back but did not lower his stare. 'I've only his word that you're a fuckin' wizard, man. That and the trick with the fire! Agh! That don't make you no fuckin' wizard!' His defiance was growing.

'Don't you know me, goblin?' His voice was a hiss. 'Shall I name myself?'

There was a pause again as the goblin built his courage, 'Agh! Yes! Name yourself, before we skewer you and toast you over your own fuckin' fire. You an' him both!'

"Be still!" he commanded. The very air of the clearing began to shimmer with the lights of his rainbow. He wrenched a sheet of scarlet fire from its midst. The fire

already lit now exploded in a ball of incandescent fury. '*I am the Wizard of Rainbows!*' The colours of his naming were as ribbons of pure energy. He took them one by one and bound the creature before him. The screams filled the forest.

They lay on the ground, all of them even Gob, trembling with terror over what they beheld. 'No!' the challenger pleaded in fear. 'Stop! Please! My Kla. Don't destroy me. Please! Not like this!' And he crept on hands and knees to where Gob crouched. 'You are our Gha!' He touched his head to Gob's foot. 'We belong to you, Gob-Gha.'

Gob for all his fear knew what to do. He stood and looked at the Wizard. 'Please, Wizard, take away your magic before it burns us to nothing!' He fell to his knees once more.

The magic was gone. Now only the terror remained. 'GO!' he screamed at them, 'Go! Go! Go! Go.' They needed no second command. Their feet crashed through the woodland as they rushed to escape…

'Go!'

Go.

*

He was alone, totally. The woodland was silent now, silent as a grave. Only the crying in his soul continued. *What have I done? What am I? What have I become? I've turned all I loved to dust, all my truths into lies. Magic? What have I done with it? I've turned myself into a Magi! It's true, I'm no better than those of Varista. Rustle did right in giving me the Badge of that calling. I'm even worse than them. I knew what I was doing!*

He looked about into the dark. There was nothing, no one to see. Slowly, as if stricken by some awful injury he crumpled. His cry, echoing through the mountains was no less than Calin's Cry-of-Death. Oh yes. He knew a new truth now. The magic was his for good or ill, as was the price that must be paid.

Thus he hid himself, built a bower on the side of the mountain and sat there shrouded by his terrible fear, the fear of his own power.

A voice, faintly heard, wove through the maze of churning thought, penetrated the shield of his despair. 'Many indeed are the paths through time. It seems ours were destined to meet once again. I see this time you have prepared your own hiding place.'

'Go away.' His bitter reply was worse than his silence. 'Go and find another path to trouble! Leave me be.'

'Go away? Leave you be?' There was amusement in her voice. Surely no hint of the rejection he might have heard. 'May one not even look upon you?'

'Look upon me? LOOK UPON ME?' he shouted. 'Don't you fear lest the very sight of me drives you to madness? That the touch of my eyes burns your body to dust, your thoughts to mush, your heart to fear? How can you even bear to stand before me?'

'Who said I was standing?' The chime of her laughter rang in the morning air, sounding through his being, vibrating within the beauty that lay at its centre. The celestial chimes sang to him of forests and fountains, of the secret silent halls of the woodland, of the ringing springs of the wilderness, of the fireflies darting through the hidden mists of the Eshenmoor. For she did not stand. Rather, she spun her own dance of wonderful elven magic on the grass before him.

Come dance with me.
through the halls of your fears,
the rooms of your worries,
the chambers of your doubts.
Come dance with me.
into the future together?

He was on his feet his heart bursting, all the former self-loathing lost in the crystal fires of her eyes. His whole being now filled with the summer song of her presence. He took her in his arms, bound her to his breast, clung to her as the tears streamed down his cheeks. 'You've come?'

She returned his embrace with no less hunger, kissed his cheek, tasted the salt of his tears. 'You called to me, in your heart and in your soul, in your dreams and in your thoughts. Would I not come? Or…' she teased, 'shall I go again?'

'No,' he whispered into her mass of copper hair. 'Don't go. Don't ever go. Stay with me. Always.'

'Always?' Mystery touched her. 'Such a long, long time, my fear-filled love.'

'Wait!' He held her at arm's length, filled his whole being with the beauty of her. 'I…' But he could find no words. So he kissed her instead. A kiss that spoke volumes and the kiss that she returned to him said no less.

'And what do you see?' she asked as his eyes feasted on her, sated the hunger that had been his since their parting. 'What do you see when you look upon me with your bright, burning eyes?'

'I see one I feared I might never see again. My love has returned to me from beyond my dreams.' He ran his fingers through the long fiery tresses, kissed her eyelids, her forehead, her nose, her lips so sweet and tender. 'I see that I'm no longer alone, and that you're more beautiful than ever. And you, my sweet, secret, wonderful elfin queen, what do you see of me?'

She laughed, bright as morning. 'I see that my innocent, wandering Pilgrim has finished his journey. I see that the promise of your spring has awakened into its summertime of its glory.' She paused, head cocked as she looked back into his eyes. 'I see too that you have grown in our time of parting. The road has had its lessons, the desert its secrets. I see there are tales to be told over the campfires of our future. I see a pain.' Her eyes sad as the dew knew too well the nature of that pain. 'It seems you are beginning to know the price of your magic.'

He did not answer. For as was so often the case within the truths of her words, there was none to make.

Then she laughed again, dispelling the gloom ere it darkened his thoughts. 'Wait, I must bring something. Wait but just a moment,' she chimed. 'I have brought a gift for you.' She was gone but the fleetest of moments, returning with a large sack draped over her shoulder. She set the bag on the ground before him and giggling with her own secret jest she lifted a large round box. It was a wonderful thing crafted of tree bark. He looked on wondering.

'For you.' Laughing, she bent to open its lid and removed a splendid, wide-brimmed hat from within – grey, almost white, its crown rising to a point. She bowed low before him and, with a giggle of pure delight, placed it upon his head. 'See? Now in truth you look a wizard.' The peel of her happiness was like life itself.

'This is amazing. Wherever did you come by it?' he asked in incredulous wonder. 'It's the most splendid hat I've ever seen.' He lifted it in his hands and held it out for inspection.

'Some Pinexae lass asked me to bring it to you,' she answered simply.

The image of Pina's clear amethyst eyes brought a spark of light to his smile. 'Pina.' The Fire-Dancer turned her head in an unspoken question. She joined in his laughter though when he unwound the rainbow sash from his waist and tied this about the crown. It fitted to perfection; the tail left hanging down his back. 'There, I knew it was for a reason. How do I look?'

Laughing with happiness she curtsied to him. 'Ah, My Lord-Wizard can you not see for yourself?' she bubbled.

'But I cannot see myself,' he laughed with her.

'Of course you can,' she returned, eyes sparkling with happiness, excitement and the sheer mischief of her understandings.

Colour and light
my Wizard of sight,
seeing and being,
dull-day and bright-night.

'You can see whatever you wish.'

'Magic!' He spoke as were the word distasteful to his tongue. 'You'd have me use my magic in this?' He didn't believe her. 'Do you know what you ask? Don't you know the fear it causes? The desert men are brave and hardy, yet even they were cowed and cast trembling in fear. The goblins fled in terror! I made that happen!'

'I am not afraid. Besides, you are your magic.' She cocked a challenging eye. 'Or do you tell me that I too must be afraid of you?' Her interrupting words were soft and full of wisdom.

'But my magic is a terrible thing of power and energy.' He had to explain, to tell her.

But she insisted on laughing and spun a web of her own glorious dance about them both.

'No! Look!' He tried again as his thoughts began to clear. 'It isn't like that. Listen to me. My magic has the power to KILL!' There, he'd spoken the thought aloud.

She seemed not to hear him though. 'You had a sword once. You never killed with that. Why should magic change you?'

'It's true that I had a sword. I made it, made it of my own nature. It wouldn't kill, wouldn't let me kill.'

She laughed even brighter. 'Ah, but tell me in truth, my Wizard. Was it your nature or the sword which would not let you kill?'

'You don't understand!' He was almost crying. 'This magic is a terrible power. It has no such constraints, not any at all. It's more powerful than anything I could conceive. So powerful that, if I desired it so, I fear I could destroy everything.'

'Ah but I do so understand, my Wizard.' Her voice was soft as feather-down. 'Would not my dance rob men's minds of all reason should I so choose? Could I not bind their souls to me, to own, to command?' The day grew quiet and her voice was no more than the wind in the treetops.

'But you're good, and wise and beautiful and, and…' Words escaped him; thoughts tumbled, tangled and then drifted from his awareness. 'Your dance is the most beautiful thing I've ever seen. Just as you are the most beautiful being I've ever known.'

'Yes it is.' She spoke softly as to a child. 'As am I. I know who I am, what I am. I know the nature of my dance.' Her eyes held him. 'Do you not know yourself also?'

'Know myself?' He saw the image of himself caught in the happiness of her emerald gaze and he took the essence of the vision to build a mirror of light to see as she saw.

He was tall now, sun hardened and travel worn. The queue of his long, tied-back hair was dark. The hat, wonderfully proud and new with pointed crown was set at an angle to shade his bearded face. His long brown robe surprisingly showed little sign of wear. He laughed to see himself and stooped to retrieve his hawthorn staff from where he'd left it leaning against a tree. His mother's ruby glimmered on his breast. 'Well,' he admitted with a growing smile, 'I guess I do look a bit like a wizard now.'

She squealed in delight, turning as a firefly in the clearing. 'And so you should, for Wizard you are!' She stood back from him suddenly serious. 'So now, for me and for yourself the time has come.' The woodland grew silent, the day grew silent, the world itself grew silent and in the heart of that silence she spoke. 'So now I ask you true. Name yourself, Wizard!'

He understood her then. He understood her and the reason for her dew-spun dance upon the woodland sward when first he'd seen her. He knew the truth of her beauty and so showed her the wonder that was his. Thus he took the splendour of the rainbow from the centre of his being and coloured his thoughts with its truth. He filled their world with the mists of its glory until nature itself stood still to watch the full mystery of the moment. Every colour, every shade, every vibration, every name was his and he took of them and made then his own, not to possess, that was not his nature, but to love. 'I am the Wizard of Rainbows,' he called aloud to the world. 'I am the Wizard of Rainbows,' he told his elfling love. 'I am indeed the Wizard of Rainbows,' he told himself.

'Ah yes, so you are. The Wizard of Rainbows, Wizard-of-light.' A joy filled laughter that overflowed into his soul, spun him in a dance of happiness until her spirit awoke the wonder in the heart of his nature and he too leapt and spun in the clearing. His love flowed as sunlight through the halls of the greenwood and awoke the magic that was his to clothe her in the colours of his understanding and they were joined, perhaps as no others ever were.

I'll dance a slow waltz beginning our time.
I'll colour it red as the bright cherry wine
Of crimson and earth our hearts to entwine
So we'll dance in the light, incarnadine.

I'll spin a wild reel in the passion of youth
I'll bathe you in orange, my passionate truth
In the truth of our being our passion will grow
So we'll dance in the light, bright marigold glow.

I'll form a ballet with the power of my art
and turn to bright yellow the strength of my heart
For the power and wonder are ours to enfold
So we'll dance in the light of the sun's burning gold.

I'll dance to the love that is mine and is yours
As a fresh verdant gift that ever endures
A love that burns bright and shall so ever seem
So we'll dance in the light, love's emerald green.

Now hear my steps ring in a magic quadrille
Vibrations of love that declare how we feel
To resound in our hearts, forever true
So we'll dance in the light, our song sung in blue.

So now watch me step a new arabesque
As I show you my spell in deep amethyst
Let creation observe us and forever know
So we'll dance in the light, of pure indigo.

In silence and stillness I'll dance in your mind
In the deep hue of ever, Eternity's time.
In this strange dance of colours we ever shall be
So we'll dance in the light, Violet mystery.

I Shall dance you a dance in the colours of time
I'll colour each moment with a dance that is mine
Our dance of bright colour, the flames of desire
So we'll dance in the light of a Rainbow of fire.

They came to see them, the small creatures of the woodland glades, deer and vole, rabbit and badger. The birds too sang their greetings and spun their own ballet of flight through the sun-kissed bows of the woodland halls. Even the little-people came: the keepers of the forests, who danced in glee over the beauty of this time. Together they built a bower over where the lovers lay and set garlands of wild woodland flowers about their necks and crowned their heads with wreaths of magnolia blossom. Gifts were brought, the offerings from nature's larder to feed them. And, perhaps time stood still, for there was no haste, nor sense of urgency, nor anything to disturbed that meeting.

If they desired to linger forever there, then who could blame them? They strolled, hand-in-hand through this gentle countryside where others seldom trod. In the heart of these ancient mountains they found places to rest. Once, on the shores of a mountain lochan where the forest left a small clearing, they camped o'er looking the sparkling waters. The sun was warm and gentle during these days of late summer. The leaves had yet to see the need for other raiment though their fruits were ripe and plentiful. The lovers basked in the warmth or fished the water margins for trout. Here at last he learnt the technique of casting a fly to the rises.

It was not, as one might begin to think from the tale, a perfect place here, however much they too might have felt it to be. For in the glades they saw the signs of goblin passage, and knew as their spirits cried out against that cruel destructive truth. They saw where the burning of the creatures' fires had tortured the land and found there too the scattered bones of their greed. Nonetheless, the grey folk themselves remained unseen and, at least for now, undetected.

They were at peace.

In the evenings they'd sit in the darkness and he'd tell her of his passage through the land and of the people that he'd met on that journey of learning. Perhaps it was the contrast with the beauty that surrounded them here but he began with a description of Varista, the smell, the squalor, the hopelessness, the memory of the street urchin's thousand-year-old eyes still haunting his thoughts. He told her of the Magi there, their tricks and deceits and of the fear they spread before them. He showed her the brooch that Rustle had given him.

'You should wear it openly,' she reflected after he had explained about the ancient bookkeeper and the nature of the gift, 'as a sign for him.' And she took it from him and pinned it to the shoulder of his robe.

'I met with a story-teller,' he told her. 'Shimmian, they called him, although I'm still unsure if this was his true name. He'd been a fighter in his homeland, perhaps a Lord of his own kin. He was my friend, a companion of the road; well, that's how he put it. When I left Varista, heading towards the East, he came with me.'

'You must tell me everything and I will understand nothing,' she laughed. 'And as I know nothing anyway, I will understand it all,' she teased him.

He laughed again, knowing her jest and spoke of the road they had taken. 'Do you know Sanain?' he asked her, finding the answer in the question of her eyes. 'She is, was Calin. She too shared the road, Her and her Lady. There was something sad about her, sad and more terrible than anything I've ever known.'

Tears glistened on the elfling's cheeks. 'Did she kill?'

'She did.'

'Yes, I know Sanain.'

Later. 'There was a desert girl too. Hkainae, she too was my friend.'

She laughed, not ignoring his words but understanding. 'Ah, did you fill your travels with beautiful women all the way then?'

'I suppose I did,' he teased back. 'Only there's an image of a strange little elfling which robbed such beauties of any allure.'

When they finished kissing she sat looking into his eyes. 'And?'

'Right at the start, not long after we parted on the shore of that lake so far away.' He found the words hard. 'There was a goblin too.'

'A goblin!' She really was surprised.

'Yes, Her name was Icicle.'

'Icicle? A pretty name, for a goblin.' There was no rebuke, only…

'It was, is a pretty name, and she a pretty creature, in an odd sort of way. Although in truth I don't think I've ever heard anyone swear so badly.'

'Did you love her?' For once the little elf-maid seemed at a loss.

'NO! No that wasn't what it was about! I suppose in some way I pitied her although she needed no pity. At best she was my friend, and friend I called her. Only, I don't think she knew what friendship was. I promised to tell her the truth. If I can I'll keep that promise.'

They sat in silence, she, taking his hand in both of hers. 'I do not know how,' she tried at last, 'but she will be my friend too, should we ever meet.'

To that he leant over and kissed her brow. 'Fire and ice? No my dear Luminae. I doubt you ever shall.'

For some reason the Wizard found himself shivering. He noted too that elf beside him had drawn closer and pulled her cloak tighter about her shoulders. It wasn't cold. The day had been bright and sun blessed. Even the breeze was kind of breath. Their eyes touched, shared the question and together searched for an answer in the wilderness about them.

There, high upon a barren mountain slope their troubled eyes found Her, silhouetted against the sunset. They felt the touch of Her eyes returning their gaze too. Not the cold grey chill of goblin eyes, that they might have understood, but other, sadder eyes that burned their hearts with an echo of a loneliness they would never understand.

'Who is She?' He didn't expect an answer.

'They call Her Heledthera, the world's pain.' The elf's words were as an echo to that same loneliness, filled with sadness. 'She has turned Her face away from the living. All She seeks now is a final release from the pain that sets Her heart to stone. It was not always so.'

'I've seen Her before,' he informed the dancer. 'She followed me.' He spoke softly now, half afraid that the apparition might hear him. 'Firstly in the heart of the desert, and then again on the road to where you found me. She was there, watching as now. I only saw Her in the distance, never close enough to approach or to speak with and always so sad. I wish I knew what She wants.'

'She wants to see you. To know of you.'

'But why? What's She to me or I to Her?'

The elf turned to look into his eyes. He didn't understand the messages he saw there. 'She wonders what will happen when you meet.'

'When we meet?' He understood even less from her words. 'We'll meet? Where? When? Why?' What words of confusion.

But she answered him anyway. 'At Tabour when the time is come. Why? Because it is written.' There was something horribly final about those words.

'Don't we even have a choice in this?'

'You do. You have a choice in everything. You always have had that.'

It might seem strange that he wasn't angry or that he retained his trust of this little elfling who knew so much, but didn't tell. Only he did trust her, beyond belief, and he trusted that her nature would ever be true to him. 'Look I really don't understand any of this. What do you mean, "because it's written"? That doesn't tell me anything!' He was almost shouting now with the urgency of his need to know. Then suddenly aware of himself he calmed. Thoughts turned in his mind and turned, and turned. 'So we'll meet.' It wasn't a question. 'What then?'

'Ah, then, perhaps, we shall know what is the true meaning of The Vortex.' The word hung in the air like the knell of doom.

'The Vortex? Is that what it's all about?' She didn't answer him. So, 'Yes,' he answered himself, 'Yes, that's it precisely. You once told me that The Vortex is mine, and that it was therein where the hope lay. The goblins too, they look for answers at that time. So comes the vortex. What then?'

'No one knows, my love. No one knows, for then the writing stops.'

They lapsed into silence. The words and thoughts turned round and around in his mind, turning, churning, burning with their hidden messages. In the end he realised that once more he'd understood none of it at all.

And still She watched from the centre of Her loneliness. Perhaps the skies understood Her, for they bathed Her form in soft clouds, grey clouds, dark against the crimson sun. There could never be enough to warm Her; to comfort Her or to ease the pain of Her tortured existence. Not even when the sky turned black and wrapped Her in night's enfolding blanket.

And still She watched.

If there was anger in Her being, then it was no wonder, nor when the skies reflected that anger with fingers of fire. It was fire meant to light the mountain, to brighten the forest and to reveal Her once more. If it was She who cried out an answer into the black that followed then Her voice was of thunder and the winds rose up to reply with a bitter song of the tempest.

The night erupted in fury, a tremendous raging of the firmament. The heavens laughed at the earth with tongues of pure energy. Lightning crowned the mountaintops, leapt from peek to peek in jagged sheets of cloven fire. Then Thunder's terrible reply vibrated through the halls of eternity to rattle the foundations of the Earth and shake the very soul of existence.

They sat huddled together in the midst of Her fury and simply watched as the whole universe spun about them. They weren't afraid. Not even at the terrible climax when the peeks shattered and the higher trees burst in an explosion of fire. It was too much to awaken fear.

There was magic there too that night, a burning, furious magic raging throughout creation. He knew it, felt it too. Perhaps his nature even touched the wonder at its centre but it was not his. It was not his to touch or to understand, not his to love or hate, not his to question.

At its heart She stood. He could feel the depths of Her endless sorrow. There too, for the first time he saw the true beauty that lay at the centre of Her nature. *Heledthera!*

Waking was as a strange half-remembered dream. The Fire-Dancer lay enfolded in his arms, the sweet scent of her hair filling his being with calm. Yet on this morning something was wrong. He knew it even before he'd opened his eyes, before she'd opened hers. This was neither morning, nor night. Clouds, grey and chill, robbed the world of sense, turned the forest into a nightmare place of shadows and darkness. Colour itself seemed to have no meaning here.

The ancient yew tree, which had watched over their slumber had no answer and they, gazing about themselves in fear, had such a need for understanding. It didn't take long for them to realise the little people were gone, the forest creatures too. All was silent, still somehow empty. They were alone.

She took a hold of his hand, drawing his eyes towards her. He saw the tears wetting her cheeks and knew, in the tremble of her form, a match to his own fears.

'What?' He couldn't even frame the words.

'The Circles-of-the-World have ceased to turn.' She sounded matter of fact, accepting the unacceptable as a truth for which she'd awaited.

'Did you know?' She knew. 'It's written.' She nodded. Her unhappiness was more than he could stand and he took her in his arms, comforted her.

Later he lit a fire close by the water edge and then cooked their breakfast. They ate in silence. Neither could find any words to say. Eventually he asked the question that burned in his mind. 'Where is it written?'

'In Tabour.' The half whispered answer came as no surprise

'Then we'll go to Tabour and seek our answers there.' He gazed into her emerald eyes, held them. 'Will you come with me?'

She nodded her agreement. 'We shall be together.'

'That's just as well really. For I couldn't go alone,' he confided. 'Who else would I find to light my way?'

'Light your way?' But her eyes were already sparkling.

'Oh yes indeed, little firefly. Remember when we first met, didn't I name you "Luminae"? Will you shine for me? My own sweet Fire Dancer?'

Her laughter was a discordant burst of life, denying the gloom of the world on this endless grey dawn. The laughter of his own reply was no less, but they didn't care. Why should they?

'So we'll go together to face whatever Fate decrees. But I warn you also. This is a hard road for those who choose to travel with me, and I still don't know where this path will lead us,' he explained to her as he cut her a hazel wood staff, ready for the trail.

'Ah,' she still laughed. 'As you chose, then so shall I. Where you step, so I shall follow. Should you lead the way to doom, I shall still follow. Should the path lead to danger, then I shall trust that such is the need. If you lead me to the very Gates of Hell or the dread lair of the Beast, then you shall lead me back again? Will you not?'

'Oh yes, my fairy queen. From the Gates of Hell, from the clawed, grasping fingers of The Lord of Mists itself if that's the need.'

These words, a conscious echo of her own long before, reminded him of that first journey through the Galghathag and of the awesome greyness of the place. Looking about at this dour morning he was reminded also of the Galomist, a memory that turned his heart to stone.

'Is this of the Galghathag?' he asked, scarce daring to say the name.

'No, not that. This is still our world, our time, although…' The rest was left unsaid.

He sensed her dread of an unknown future. Sensed too that these very fears might be a possibility, dependent upon what he might do. It seemed an awful weight at that moment. Yet he hid his fear, his self-doubt, and laid his hand on her arm. 'This is indeed our time. No one, nothing shall take it from us.' He smiled to reassure her and picked up her staff again, held it out before him. 'Ah, but this is too plain a thing for your dainty hand.' Then with a laugh he caught a crystal memory of early morning sunlight sparkling on the water of the loch, formed it into a deep green gemstone, which he set at the staff's tip. Holding it before her, she saw herself reflected in its rainbow-shine.

Gathering together their few possessions they made ready for the journey ahead, remaining for most part as silent as the land about them. The greyness of the world lay heavy upon them, dampening their mood. Time seemed to have lost all meaning, no morning or evening, no day or night.

When the moment came they took a final look at the water, still now, still as silence. Taking each others' hand they turned and followed the path leading away from their camp.

Later, none might know when for time had lost its markings, yet whilst they still passed through the mountains, they found rest in a small forest glade and there cooked and ate a meagre meal and slept a while in each others' arms wrapped in his worsted cloak. When they awakened the mist had grown heavier, damp and cloying. There was no other choice. They carried on.

The path they followed was narrow here, and Luminae was in the lead. She stopped, suddenly, holding up her staff to stop him too. He could hear a noise, somewhere in the greyness ahead of them. He drew beside her. 'Can you see anything?'

Her eyes turned to him. 'Not really,' she confessed, 'But I hear voices.'

'Goblins?'

'No, I do not think so anyway.' She listened once again, straining, silence.

'We'll be careful,' he said needlessly as they moved forward once more. He led the way now. Only after several paces more he stopped again, peering into the mist as he tried to discern what lay ahead. There was a hint of smoke in the still air, wood smoke. From out of the gloom came the sound of a horse's harness, jingling, the shuffle of hooves on packed earth. 'I think it's people,' he whispered to her. 'A dwelling of some kind.'

The building, when they did finally reach it was as grey as the world. It was stone built, with slate roof and shuttered windows. The sounds of life were evident and the three horses that stood laconically chewing from a manger indicated there might be more than one inhabitant.

The stout wooden door was half ajar. From within came a beam of light. *Knock or enter?*

He entered. 'Hello.'

Seven faces turned towards him, hard faces, weather-worn, life-worn. Questioning eyes.

'We saw the door was open.' *It's some kind of inn.*

A woman, hard as the men, stepped through an arched doorway. 'Welcome!' Her tone half denied the word. 'This is no time to be abroad.' There was suspicion there too.

'We were in the mountains. I'm afraid we seem to have lost our way. Yours is the first habitation we've seen since…'

Her eyes spoke for her, inspecting, enquiring. She scratched the tip of her nose. 'You'd best take a seat.' Nodded to a table and two chairs. 'Will you want food?' Again the suspicion spoke in her eyes.

'That would be nice. I have money.'

She smiled, gap-toothed, at that. 'A drink too then?'

He nodded and pulled out one of the chairs for Luminae. 'Would you care for a drink?'

'Only water.' Her voice was sweet and gentle as ever. The tension in the room began to subside.

'And you sir?' the woman enquired. 'Ale or wine?'

'Just a glass of wine, thank you.' He picked a silver coin from his pouch, laid this upon the table.

'Wine and water it is then. That and food for two.' The woman was gone, the silver coin with her.

She was back shortly, and the drinks set upon the table before them. Surprisingly the glasses really were of glass, even crystal were he not mistaken. The wine too was of good vintage, subtle and light on the pallet. The Wizard found himself re-appraising their surroundings. 'Where are we?' he asked. 'We're, as you've probably gathered, strangers to this land. I've returned from the East and now travel to Tabour.'

The room grew suddenly silent again, dreadfully silent. The eyes turned upon them again.

'Why?' The speaker was a huge man, shaven head, a scar turning his face into a perpetual sneer.

The Wizard didn't turn aside from those eyes, nor did he blink. 'Who asks?' His voice remained gentle, no threat and no challenge.

'I am Fassael, once of Tabour.' He too did not flinch from the encounter. 'Who answers?'

He didn't know from where the answer came, only the rightness of its nature. 'I'm Prism. They call me Wizard.'

'And her?' Fassael still didn't flinch.

'I am Luminae, an Elf,' she declared needlessly.

'An Elf and a Wizard? Perhaps it is right,' Fassael considered, 'Perhaps you should go to Tabour.' The tension was easing.

An idea crossed through the Wizard's mind. He pulled a gold piece from his pouch, tossed it over to the woman. 'Here, drinks for any who wish. The road has been dry, for us and others.'

Fassael smiled. 'Been to the desert have you?' He signalled to the woman his acceptance.

'To the desert and beyond, my friend. Why else should I return?'

'Then I'll thank you for your drink and your friendship, Wizard. But that is enough. I'm not of the sands.'

'Who are you then, Fassael?'

The big man laughed. 'Me? I'm no one, well no one special.' The words were left hanging in the air.

'Who is he?' the Wizard addressed his question to the nearest of the others.

'He is Fassael Fire-born. The last to leave Tabour!'

It seemed a terrible answer and even worse that the Wizard didn't understand. *Again!* 'What do you mean, the last to leave?'

They looked at him in silence. Eyes flicked between Wizard and elf. Eventually Fassael answered for himself. 'The city of Tabour is no more.' He waited for the words to sink in. 'There was a fire, a terrible thing. The whole city burned, everything.'

'Everything save that bloody tower,' another interjected.

'What happened?' the Wizard asked the expected question.

'No one really knows,' Fassael explained. 'It seems that the fire started in the Lamp-lighters' quarters, right down near the Tower wall. It was a terrible thing, made worse by the oil that they use in their craft. But that was only the beginning. It is said that the Keepers-of-the-Tower took this as some sort of omen or sign.' He paused again as if for effect. 'They set fire to the Library! The whole lot was destroyed, everything, hundreds, thousands of years work, gone!'

'The fires began to spread, growing hotter and hotter until the whole city became a flaming inferno. Nothing is left now, nothing but a burnt-out ruin, that and the tower. It wasn't even scorched nor blackened by the smoke!'

Is this at my hand too? He couldn't speak.

'What of the people?' the elf maid asked for him.

'Some escaped. Some tried to fight the fires. Some ran away. Some did nothing. Some just died in the flames.'

'You were the last?' the Wizard found his words again. 'The last to leave?'

'I was.'

'What did you see?'

'It wasn't what I saw but what I felt. The Tower was happy, gloating over the City's demise. I don't think I'll ever return there. Not ever!'

What's happening? 'Why should you want to go back there?'

'You seem to know very little for a wizard, my friend,' Fassael laughed.

'It seems to me that I know even less than that,' the newly self-named Prism replied. 'But I want to know. As I live and breathe, I truly want to know.'

'The Kings are calling for us all to go. They say that there's a terrible time of war and chaos coming and that we should all go to Tabour to stand with the Forces-of-Man! But I still ain't going!'

So The White-Queen calls for the goblin tribes to rise. And now The-Kings-of-Men call for the armies to gather also. Perhaps they're right. 'I still intend go to Tabour,' he told them.

'To join with The Kings?'

'No. To go to the Tower. It has meanings, perhaps answers for me.'

The silence that followed those words was long and profound, but in the end it was broken by Fassael's strident laugh. 'Well, bugger me! Perhaps you're really a wizard after all!'

'Now that, Tabour Man, is something you can be truly sure of,' the voice was unexpected, and all turned to see the Sanain silhouetted in the doorway.

'Calin!' The Wizard was on his feet crossing the gap between them. 'Calin. Is it truly you?'

'You know her?' Fassael asked.

'Oh yes. We travelled a hard road together at one time.'

She bowed her head, but didn't smile. 'It's true indeed. We travelled together. Many other roads lie between that road and now though. Many things to change our paths…'

'Still I will not kill, Sanain.' The answer was simple. It was the answer that she needed. It was the truth.

Now she did smile, warmer that the fire in the hearth. 'I had to know.'

'And you?'

She half laughed, somehow delightfully self-mocking. 'Me? I'm still Sanain. Though I do my own bidding now.' She turned then to face the diminutive elf who had come to stand at his side. Any who watched close enough might have seen the glimmer of tears in the Sanain's eye as she knelt on the floor before her. 'He didn't lie,' she said simply.

'He never does, Calin-Sanain. He never does,' the elf replied. Her smile was like the welcome touch of spring. She took the Sanain's hands and lifted her to her feet. 'I know your name, Calin. It seems to me I would know your heart too.'

Then Calin began to laugh. 'Oh no surely not!' she giggled. 'Don't tell me, you've got a name just as strange and mysterious as his?' She wrapped her arms about the elf and held her to her breast. 'Never mind, I'll manage best I can.'

'He calls me Luminae,' the little elfling revealed. 'It makes my heart sing so I think that will do.'

'Luminae?'

'Ah yes,' the Wizard joined in. 'Luminae, The Fire-Dancer! And I, just for the fun of it, I now call myself Prism. I make the Rainbow.' He too took Calin's hands in his own and kissed her upon each cheek. 'So well met then, Calin-Sanain, come and join us. Take some food and drink. Tell us what brings you?'

'I came to find you, Prism. What else?' She settled into a chair. 'It seems that many seek to know the passing of the Wizard of Rainbows. They sent me forth to find you, the King of High-Caravail and The Queen of Asain, to bring you to Tabour where the armies gather.'

'And if I don't go?'

'Then I'll return alone to face The Kings and tell them the same,' she laughed. 'I'm not here to enforce their rule only to carry their message to you. And, I guess, if it's required, yours to them.'

He too knew the need for a time of silence. 'When you return you can carry my message back to them. I hope. It's a hard message though and may not be to their liking.'

'I expected no less, my friend. Don't forget I trod the mountain road with you.'

'That I never forget, Sanain.' *It echoes through my dreams on many a troubled night.* He offered her to drink from his own glass, she accepted. He drank too before continuing. 'Yes, I think I've a reply for them. You can tell them this; 'The Wizard of Rainbows goes where he pleases and is not at the beck and call of Lord, Queen or King.' Tell them also that I shall go to Tabour and will meet and talk to them there, should they still so desire. But they should know I'll not be there to do their bidding.'

She continued to smile. 'I look forward to seeing their faces when I impart that reply.' And she laughed again.

'You've changed, Calin,' he reflected, noting the amusement sparkling in her eyes. 'Have you seen anything of the others? Cog?'

She laughed for real now. 'Yes, my friend. I do see Cog. He's with The King's army on the Plain to the north of the ruin, Tabour.'

The name brought his thoughts back to the earlier conversation. 'You've been there?'

'Only to the edge of the devastation. There's nothing left.'

They were interrupted then, by the landlady bearing plates of piping hot food and a carafe of wine.

'Have you rooms that we might hire for the…' *There's no night now. No night, no day, only grey.* 'No, it's no matter. We'll leave once we've supped and rested a while.' He had another thought. 'But I'll purchase a bottle of this wine of yours if I may. I see a need.' He didn't explain further.

'You be careful where you go, Wizard.' Fassael was still near. 'There were shapes in that fire, shapes that I'd not want to face again.'

'Fassael,' the Wizard felt suddenly full of confidence, of the awareness of his own gift. He knew the rightness of the path he was now taking. 'I tell you; it's not the shapes I fear. Oh no. It's them who fear me. The only thing I fear right now is myself.'

Fassael laughed. 'Don't we all, Wizard? Don't we all?'

Calin left them long before they were ready to go. She stood and kissed their cheeks, Wizard and Elf and for some unexpected reason Fassael too. 'Do you need my protection, Prism?' she asked, fixing the Wizard with her gaze.

'No, Calin-Sanain. On this journey I need no protection. Or if I do it's none that you can provide.'

'And you, Luminae? Have you need for my sword?'

'Your heart, perhaps? That would warm me. Your sword? No. If I need someone to protect me then will not my Wizard?'

Calin smiled at them. 'It's probably just as well. I need to get back to my Cog. He'll only get into trouble without me.'

They laughed together and embraced each other briefly.

'I'll see you at Tabour,' was Calin's farewell.

'At Tabour, Calin.'

'At Tabour, Sanain.'

'Wizard,' it was Fassael who spoke as they too prepared to leave the inn, 'Can you truly cast magic?'

The Wizard looked at him long and hard. 'Magic isn't like that, Fassael. I don't cast magic, I AM magic.'

'Can I see?'

The Wizard remembered the fear of those who had seen before, the terror in their eyes, the horror. 'Why?'

'Someone once told me that true magic is beautiful, and I so need to see beauty.'

He was still for a long time, considering what he might do. In the midst of the fire an ember cracked, showing the chimney with darting specks of red. He reached into the fire and took such a speck, and in its heart he wrote the name 'Fassael' and then set the same into a stone. 'Give me your ring, Fassael.'

He did, taking it from his middle finger, holding it flat on his palm.

The ring hovered in the air, the stone too. The merging of the two was as the joining of hearts. 'Next time, Fassael, in the fire, you shall not burn.'

The man stood, tears streamed down his cheeks. There was no fear or horror here. 'I never do, Wizard; I was fire-born. Yet I thank you.' He took the ring and placed it back upon his finger. 'When it's dark and when I'm sad, or afraid, then I'll look upon the light in this wonder and then I'll remember the beauty of its making.'

In truth, it was the smile of the Wizard that the Tabour man remembered most though. He'd never seen such a happy face.

'You might not understand this, Fassael, but you've given me more this day than I've given you. The debt is mine.'

He was right, Fassael didn't understand.

*

Outside the mist seemed even thicker. This was no Galomist though, nor evil or in itself magical. It was a more natural thing born of the clouded skies and the saddened world. Nonetheless, it gave their journey a strange sense of the surreal as one might find when walking through the clouds.

They saw the shapes of other houses through the mist, indistinct outlines that spoke of a larger village. Yet they saw little more than shades as they passed by, and no sign at all of the people who dwelt there. Then hidden from view once again they followed the road away through the tree-lined mountains.

From out of the mist behind them came the sounds of movement. Something was approaching. 'Goblins?'

'No, not Goblins. Not here, not now,' she answered softly. 'I doubt that we shall see any of their kind this side of Tabour, my Wizard. It is an army, an army of men. I can hear the clashing of steel, the tread of feet. They march to war, my Wizard-of-Choices, To Tabour and war! All the armies shall march now.'

In an unspoken agreement not to be seen, they slipped off of the road to hide, several yards away, in the undergrowth beneath the trees. They waited there, not really able to see. On the road the soldiers marched on.

At one point the mist cleared enough to show them the ranks of the army as it passed by. They wore dark blue, carried round shields and long-bladed spears. A captain rode on a white horse, but he too quickly vanished into the mist. Eventually they had passed and before much longer even the sound of their marching feet was no more.

'So they all go to Tabour.' The Wizard knew again the dreadful touch of Fate brush over his soul. 'The goblin, Gob, said She'd called all the tribes to Tabour. Shall the whole world gather there for some terrible final battle?'

'No, that at least is in doubt.' She took his hand again and kissed his fingers. 'No one knows what will happen, my Wizard-of-the-Unknown, no one. It may be that it will be war, it maybe other. Those who seek to know though, they will be there.

Those too who seek victory at arms if there is to be war, they will be there and they will surely bring their forces to stand in the line. The Elves too, they march,' she told him as they walked back to the road. 'The Harp-Smiths, the Dancers and even the Crystal-Singers. The High-Dancer too, he shall come at their head.'

'The High-Dancer?' An instant of fear. 'Isn't he your master? Your Lord?'

'My Master?' she secretly replied. 'Why yes, for he is the master of all who tread the dance magic.' She took the Wizard's hand and lifted it to her lips. 'But that is nothing to be afraid of.' A gentle chuckle. 'Well perhaps you might feel a little fear. You see, my love, The High-Dancer is my father, I long to bring you to meet him.' She squeezed the Wizard's hand and gazed up into his eyes. 'He is my father but also he is a Lord of the Elves and a dancer of the High Magic. He comes also, to meet with you, and to see what transpires.'

'Your Father?' *She's daughter to The High-Dancer! No wonder her magic is so strong.* 'But what will he make of me coming out of the desert to steal his daughter?'

She laughed brightly, snuggling against him and slipping her arm about his waist. 'Steal? You cannot steal that which is freely given. He will make of you whatever you are.' Lifting her eyes she was suddenly still. 'But what will you make of him? He comes at the head of the Elven army. There are over two thousand bows in that host.'

'So many?' said the Wizard into the gloom as they turned back to the trail once again.

'Yes. So many.'

So, as always, the ever-moving quill of Fate's decree held sway. And, as it was written, so they came, each with their own reason, their own hopes or fears, drawn together for what ever might be. But what or who drew them?

They came from High-Caravail, their King clad in his golden armour and riding his six-drawn golden chariot. He came at the head of two thousand men at arms, shields and standards rich with the Royal-crown emblazoning. The Priests of Finestre, they came too, chanting as they trod their way. Four hundred of the Sevriet came, the horse people of Lodor. They came with anger in their eyes, for their grasslands were aflame and the herds would starve. From Santolin the King-of-The-West led a great army now joined with the levy of The Lake-land Cities. Together these numbered more than three thousand spearmen. The Legions of Bronden came too, all the fifteen hundred left of them. They already knew the taste of the cold, dark war that was upon the land, and had seen the fall of their oh so splendid city. They marched in silence for they knew the terror, which they believed lay ahead. Still more came, from Asain and Harithan, from Niss and the swamps of The Donaladin. They came from Dormon and the desert too and they came afoot, even their Sultan, for they would not lead their camels to the slaughter of war.

From the Elswood came the Elves, three thousand bows of the Greenwood. The Dancers came with them and The Harp-Smiths and the Crystal-Singers.

The sound of their marching was a terrible roar as of an ocean bound in the turmoil of a storm. Did they march to war? Some thought so and carried their terrible weapons of battle with them. Others though came unarmed save with the hope that led them on. On the plain, before the burnt ruin of Tabour, they made their camps, formed their ranks and set their pickets. The smoke from their fires darkened the skies still further.

But no army came from Rael, just a few blooded and beaten warriors. They had their own tale of horror written on their faces.

From the South and from the hidden lands of the West came other things, The Thirteen Tribes of the Goblin-Horde. Sheathed in mist were they, a mist of fear and cold despair. They came in silence, and they came not alone.

Standing on the final slopes of the mountains, looking out over the vast rolling plain, it seemed that the whole horizon was aflame with their campfires. The clouds were lit with the terrible red glow of the burning. Into the midst of this world gathering the Wizard and Fire-Dancer came alone. Their path led them out from the mountains onto the grassland. It was a plain flattened and churned to dust by the thousands of feet who had trod here. Hkainae's words of long before echoed in his mind. *'This too shall turn to desert one day.'*

The force of the gathering's anger, the weight of their concerns, their bright burning hopes and their oh so dark fears, bore down on the Wizard as a yoke of dread, slowing his steps. Yet he continued albeit with a dreadful reluctance dragging in his heart. He wanted no part of this, nor wished to mix or converse with those about them. He took the very essence of the mist into the centre of his being, cast a shield of its nothingness about them and hid from the eyes of any who might have watched. Thus they passed through the land, unseen.

There was one sight though that stilled his feet. It was long after they had ventured out onto the plain. The passage of time seemed elusive now, yet they were nearing Tabour. They moved through the ranks of the armies, passed by their encampments undetected. Then before them was a standard hanging limp from its spar, a flag of red and black, emblazoned with a golden palm tree and a silver star. *The desert people are here too, drawn into this Game-of-Fate along with the other armies.*

If there was calmness here it was to be expected. The Wizard knew the stillness of the sands. **Hkamoot!** The only real surprise was the vastness of the host. It was as if the desert itself had given up its entire people. In the centre of this vast camp was set a second great standard, that of The High-Sultan of the desert tribes baring the sign of Crown and star.

Is Hkainae here? he asked himself. *Is she too drawn into this web of fate?* 'These are the desert tribes,' he told his still bright elfin love. 'They are a hard people. Some might say cruel. They are Hkainae's kin though. I bare them no ill will.'

'Hkainae?' He had spoken of the desert girl before and she realised that he would want to seek her out. 'Shall we go unseen among them? To see if we can find her midst their tents?'

'No, Luminae, not that. If we go, then it'll be openly and not in deceit. I'll not hide myself from their eyes.' Thus he stripped away the illusion and they stood together before the Sultan's army. There was no doubt that they were seen. Even as the mists dispersed a cry arose from the nearest of the guards. A trumpet blast sounded over the camp. Then all grew still once again. Several figures moved out from among the tents and stood looking back at the pair. They could be seen muttering one to another in animated wonder.

The Wizard and Dancer waited.

After a time another appeared. It was he who eventually came alone towards them. He walked slowly, stately, wearing his pride as a cloak. There was no fear in his step. Eyes like coals peered at the couple who stood before him. If he felt surprise at the presence of the elf-maid there was no sign. He did not bow or dip his head. 'Welcome, travellers of the road. Your path leads you towards Tabour, as do all paths at this troubled time.' His voice had none of the awkwardness of the Khalif but rang clear with a soothing, baritone purr. 'Will you join with us? Share your road with ours, take rest within our tents?' He bowed his head slightly. 'The road is hot, I have water a plenty.'

The Wizard's raised hand stilled the words. 'Neither friend nor foe am I, Lord of the Sands, not to you or to any. It's sad, but I fear I can't share the road with you or your people. Nor can I accept your offer of hospitality although I know it's true and generously offered. I am but myself and I travel my own path.' He smiled at the Desert-Lord. 'I mean no discourtesy or ill will. Indeed I've trod the sands also **Hkamoot.** I know the value of such gifts. In keeping with that at least we might exchange tokens, if such be your wish. I would offer you salt, as it's the token of life and a sign of who I am. I choose life not death. I don't march to war.'

The man looked at him long and hard. He looked too at the diminutive elfling who stood at the Wizard's side. 'You choose life not death?' They were words spoken to fill the silence of his thoughts. 'I am Fahaeda, Sultan-of-Dormon, Vassiir of the Desert peoples. We come **Shabraht,** as desert kind. I have trod the wastes and slaked my thirst in the bitter pools of the desert **Hkamoot.**'

'I tell you this, Wizard. The grazing of our sheep has been put to the torch, the pools of the desert poisoned and desecrated. My land has been invaded, my people killed. I choose **Jihad**!'

The Wizard bowed his head in acknowledgement of the other's choice. 'That's your way, Sultan, not mine. I say again, I come in peace not war. I seek understanding not *Jihad.*' His eyes remained fixed upon the desert lord. 'That you know who I am I have no doubt, yet I don't name myself save as Prism, and that's little more than jest. Nonetheless, I chose to be known to you, to show myself first of all to your people for a reason. There's one I seek. I would know if you have with your people Guesta, Merchant-of-Istar, or rather Hkainae, daughter heir of Guesta? If so, I would wish to meet with them,' he explained.

'Guesta-the-Merchant I do know.' The coal fires still burned in that gaze. 'He does not travel with us, not he or his daughter.' There was meaning here although the Wizard knew better than to ask. 'Others of Istar are here though. They will be willing to take her place and to serve your needs.'

'I seek no one to serve me Sultan. Hkainae was but my friend of the road. I sought only to greet her for the sake of our friendship.' The Desert Lord bowed his head.

'Nonetheless, Sultan,' the Wizard continued. 'Will you accept my token of life?' He took from his satchel a small bag of rock salt. The world seemed to stand still.

Instead of replying the desert lord turned his eyes to The Fire-Dancer who stood silently at the Wizard's side. 'You tread a hard road, elf. Far now are the green woods of Elswood, distant now the sacred-tree. These are the lands of the East where the desert is Lord **Hkamoot.**' There was a menace here, unspoken but non-the-less real. 'Are you too of his mind?'

Her reply was a sudden, shocking, bubble of silk-bright laughter, which chimed as bird song over the plain, life amidst death, growth amongst decay. The Sultan's eyes opened wide in surprise as she spun on the earth before him, her whole being wondrously, gloriously aflame.

> *In the Halls of his mind,*
> *In the chambers of his heart,*
> *In the wonder of his being,*
> *In the glory of his love.*
> *And there shall I dance*
> *Forever.*

The Sultan smiled, his solemnity cracking as ice on a spring morning. His own laughter mingled with hers and with the wizard's. 'Lord, lass! Who are you?'

The Wizard clothed her in his rainbow glory and she spun a ballet of his colours. 'She is Luminae, The Fire-Dancer.'

Still smiling the Sultan bowed his head before them and reached into his robe to remove a small leather pouch, not unlike that of the Wizard. 'There's no harm in you, in either of you. Your way is not my way. But surely there is no wonder there, the forest and the desert shall ever be strangers.' He turned back to the Wizard, reached out his hand. 'I accept your token of life, Wizard. In this time of gloom you bring a light of hope, whatever that may portend.' He bowed again. Then taking a pinch of salt from the bag he placed it upon his tongue. 'Life,' he said. 'The gift of life indeed.' And then held out his own pouch.

The Wizard and Dancer both took of the Sultan's salt. 'The gift of life,' they said together.

'Will you not rethink? Will you not accept the friendship of the road and the hospitality of my tent?'

'Alas, it cannot be, Sultan,' came his sad reply. 'Were I to do so, then how could I contend with losing a gift as great as your friendship, should that be the need? It would break my heart.' Now he bowed low before the desert lord. As one, the Wizard and his elfling turned and walked away into the mist. The Sultan didn't move until they had gone, and not even then for some time.

They walked on, following the great road. About them now, as far as the eye could see through the gloom of mist and campfire smoke, lay the armies of men, rank upon rank, rows of tents and stockades of defensive stakes. The pickets of the cavalry and the rows of tethered steeds were just as countless. The standards hung limp. There was no wind. No breeze to clear away the stench. There were cattle here too, and swine and sheep and all the supplies and stores to feed such a vast throng.

'So many,' the Fire-dancer breathed. 'So many have come.' She took his hand once more, knowing that he would not reply and she drew it to her lips, brushed his palm with her kiss.

The ruin of Tabour, when it finally became visible through the gloom, seemed little more than the charred skeleton of man's endeavours. In the midst of the burnt remnant was the Tower. Even from the distance where the Wizard first spied it the tower seemed to spear the sky, a stark finger of bone pointing into the dark grey as if nothing less than Fate's grim warning.

The armies of men were drawn up North and East of what was once the city wall. They would not, could not enter the desolation. Their tents formed a great crescent reaching out across the plain. At the centre of the line, grander than any seen so far, were the tents of the Kings and Generals. Everywhere there was bustle, the constant hum of human life. The columns of smoke from the campfires seemed as pillars of a strange cathedral of grey. The clouds hung over all as a terrible vaulted ceiling. Everywhere the standards, simple and grand alike, hung limp.

However, it could be seen also that beyond the tower, beyond the ruined city was another army completely. On the great plain, beyond the stark white tower, the Grey Lady had gathered her host. The Goblin Horde had indeed arisen. The Tribes were ready for war.

They didn't stop again among the great encampment, nor did they let themselves be seen. He chose not to face the lords of this army as yet but led her beyond the rows of tented yeomanry, following the road down to where the city gate had once stood. It was a horrific thing to see. Even the stones, blasted by the heat, were now half crumbled to dust, a dust that billowed at the slightest breeze and now coated everything in its bitter grey. Beyond was worse. The dust was even thicker there. It rolled, dark and featureless to where the tower erupted skywards as a needle of white. He could understand easily enough why none would willingly enter that desolation.

'There are people here,' Luminae whispered.

There were. A small group waited, bunched together close to the ruin's edge. They stopped, still unseen. 'I know them,' he told her, perhaps with a touch of relief. 'They're friends. See there's Calin. I'll introduce you to the others. Though I wish this meeting were at a happier time.'

'My Lady.' He bowed before her, knelt on one knee for her blessing. 'It seemed fitting that we meet here where before we parted. I've returned. Though no longer a pilgrim.' He did not say his name.

She laughed and taking his hand drew him back to his feet. 'So you have, Traveller-of-the-road, so you have.'

'Greetings Harp-smith.' He smiled to Plie. 'It seems our paths were indeed destined to touch again.'

The elf's smile was no less warm than the druid's had been. 'It has been a hard road leading us to this dour time. My Lord Wiz–'

'Good grief NO! Plie.' He stopped the elf before the word was out. 'Just call me Prism.'

The Lady burst into laughter. 'Surely you jest?'

'Of course I do. Why shouldn't I?'

'Prism?' The Elf-smith tried again.

'Aye, Plie. I make the Rainbow.'

By this time Calin had finished smothering Luminae in her embrace. The Wizard introduced her. 'My friends, this is Ouray, Annquiie, Luminae, The Fire-Dancer. As another once said of his love, she is the heart song of my soul.'

The Lady smiled her welcome.

'Your father sends greetings,' Plie said. 'Yet he did not speak of your beauty, I shall berate him over that when next we meet.' The elf took her hands and kissed her brow. 'He waits to meet this Wizard of yours.'

Her peel of laughter as ever brought a swelling of happiness to the Wizard's heart. 'Soon enough he shall. For soon shall my Wizard name himself to those who wish to hear.'

'You came then?' Calin spoke solemnly. 'Not that I doubted that you would. Do you yet know what you're going to do?' The Wizard heard the in-drawn breath of surprise from the others. She'd asked what none other dared.

'It does worry me some,' the Wizard confessed with a lightness that denied his words. 'I think I'll just explain to him that I love her, and hope that he understands.' He intentionally misunderstood. Suddenly a tiny hand took hold of his.

'And I'll explain that this is he who I love also,' she answered brightly. 'Anyway he could never deny me.'

'That wasn't my question, Wizard.' There was no hostility in her voice or manner. Her smile assured him of that.

'I know, Calin. I just like having the excuse to tell people, that's all.' He lifted the Fire-Dancer's hand in a gesture of their closeness. 'Come then, Calin-Sanain. Perhaps it's time for you to lead us to those who wait. I would hear what they have to say.'

The Lady stepped before them. She looked once more into the Wizard's eyes. 'You've changed, my friend. It seems you now accept your lack of understanding rather than constantly trying to fight it.'

'I had to. It always wins.' He laughed again. 'We should go. It would be impolite to make them wait.'

Thus they followed Calin back towards the encampment and whatever awaited them amidst the ranks of men and elves. Now the green of the elves pointed tents could be seen, the sign of the 'Silver tree' also.

Now their movements were no longer hidden, people began to gather watching them walk over the grass. No one spoke but many were the questioning eyes that greeted them. Soon they passed through an easily parted crowd. None would face the cold-eyed stare of the Sanain at their head.

There was a circle of tents at the centre of the line, finer pavilions than those of the rank and file. At the heart of this circle was another, even greater marquee. It seemed this place had been prepared for their coming. A huge table was set there, ready for a banquet. Twenty or so chairs were placed around this. About the whole was a ring of even more chairs. *We've come to a meeting of Powers it seems.*

Calin directed him to the highchair at the end of the table. Here, having pulled out a seat for Luminae at his side, he sat as shown. There they waited; wine was brought, and fruit and bread and meats, but they didn't eat or drink. They didn't speak either, not even to each other. They simply waited, silent.

The first to come was a tall silver-haired Elf-Lord. He was dressed in green and gold, silk robes, a simple band of gold about his long hair and forehead. It seemed he floated rather than walked, every movement a thing of grace and wonder. The Wizard stood without thinking to do so.

'My Lord High-Dancer,' Luminae greeted him softly and proclaimed, 'This is he for whom you have waited.' She turned to the Wizard, 'This is my father, The High-Dancer of Al-Sinnian.'

Wizard and Elf both bowed. Neither spoke.

Another man strode into view, proud, head held high, his eyes shone with a certainty. He was clothed as a soldier, but no soldier was he. The gold of his sword hilt, the jewels that encrusted his shield told of that. Yet he too stood before the Wizard. Beside him came Cog.

The warrior smiled a greeting and pronounced. 'Elanthral Estobar, The High-King of High-Caravail!' Once more the Wizard bowed his head and retained his silence.

Next came a tall, slender man. His long golden hair was bound with a leather thong. His clothing was leather too. 'Cathiir, Horse-Lord of Pashad.'

Then, 'Sandor, King of The West.' *Santolin!*

'Heshmet, Lord of the Sevriet.'

'King Wenslow of Varista.' Tall, silver hair but somehow bloated, unfit in body.

'The Lord-High-Alchemist of Varista!'

'Starbinder!' The Wizard's hissed word caused Luminae to draw closer to him. She rested her hand upon his forearm comforting, calming.

'Fahaeda, Sultan of Dormon, High-Vassiir of the Desert people.' His smile was every bit as rich and warm as they remembered from their parting on the plain.

'Gessette of Niss, Queen-of-Asain.' She was dressed in armour and carried a sword at her side.

From the corner of his eye he caught the movement as Calin bowed her head slightly and saw her lips show the hint of a smile but she said nothing either.

'Aelfrett, Marshal of Rael.' The Wizard's head snapped round to see before him a young man, scarce more than a boy really. His clothing was tattered and blood-stained, the hilt of the sword at his side sweat stained with use. Eyes that spoke of both horror and pain. *What of Shimmian?*

More and still more came, lords and kings of men, lowly ones too, chieftains of mountain tribes and the smaller principalities. When the chairs at the table were full they sat on those about the area.

Then silence.

It was The High-Dancer who finally broke the silence. 'You are come.'

The Wizard still didn't answer. Rather he rose to his feet and, taking the bottle of wine from his satchel, walked about the table. At each position he stopped and poured the wine. When a servant stepped forward to help he lifted his hand and with a smile refused the aid. Having completed the task, still in silence, he returned to his seat. There, having drawn his own travel-worn goblet from his satchel, he poured his wine.

'Greetings, my Lords. Please share a glass with me.' He bowed to them. 'Who I am, you already know.' *Whatever that means.* 'I come as it's written. I mean no harm. I mean no good. I'm simply here.' He took hold of The Fire-Dancer's hand and drew it to his lips. 'I haven't come alone.'

Although her voice trembled slightly she spoke clear. 'I am Luminae, The Fire-Dancer.' She also bowed to the Lords before them.

She bowed again to The High Dancer. 'As is written, so it now is.' The Wizard felt her hand tighten upon his own. 'My Father, The-Lord-High-Dancer.'

'Greetings to you, my Lord-High-Dancer.' The Wizard stood and formally bowed his head. 'I have seen her Fire-Dance and set its glory in the centre of my heart.'

'Have you come to take her from me?' the elf-lord's voice was brittle.

'Good grief no!' he laughed aloud. 'I simply wish you to know that I love her. What could be more important than that?'

'As do we all, Wizard.' From down the table to the elf's right came the warming smile of The Sultan of Dormon. 'As do any who've seen her dance,' he added, his eyes mirroring the words. The High-Dancer's lips turned upward for a moment.

The Wizard continued, 'The Fire Dancer will do as she wishes and, whatever that might be, I shall accept and love her for it. I don't want to control her, to have her come and go at my wish or my beckoning. I don't want to take her from anyone.'

'Why are you here then? Why have you come?' the High Dancer asked. 'Do you seek to command us?'

'I command no one. I take no command.' *Is even he afraid of me?* He looked about at the assembled Kings and Lords. They waited in silence, expectant. *Do they want me to command them?* 'You asked me to come. Sent Calin-Sanain with your message. I assume that she returned with mine.' He caught the Sanain's nod. 'I came because of who I am.'

Looks were exchanged, confusion and doubts. 'And now you are here what do you intend to do?' The High Dancer continued to speak for all.

'I don't know.' Perhaps that shocked them more than anything. 'I was waiting to hear from you.'

'What do you mean?' the King of High-Caravail interrupted.

'I see all about the armies gathered for war. I see too the Kings of Men and Elves here in a union. I've seen, beyond the ruined city, that another army waits. I therefore assume there's to be a WAR!' He spat the final word.

'War?' the King of High-Caravail replied for all, 'Yes, there'll be war. The Goblin-Horde has marched forth from hiding. They come at Her,' he spat onto the ground, 'at Her bidding and they come armed and ready to fight. They shall not go unchecked.' The nods of agreement all about the table attested to the veracity of the comment. 'What will you do, Wizard?' The High King asked again.

His silence was long and the waiting even harder than they might have expected. 'I intend to be myself.'

'What does that mean?'

'He chooses life,' the Sultan answered.

'He always does,' the Lady Druid agreed.

There seemed no way to respond to that. They sat there in silence.

'Well I choose War,' it was the young Marshal of Rael. 'Or rather it was chosen for me, for my people.' He stood and began to pace before the table. 'It wasn't I who started this. They came from the mountains. Hard and grey were they, and the mists that succoured them were as cold as death. We stood against them. And they brushed us aside.' The words were horrid and the tone no less so.

'Shimmian?' the Wizard asked. *I've got to know.*

'My Lord Shimmian was first to stand against them… The first to die.' He stopped for he'd seen the pain of his words etched on this young Wizard's face and the glimmer of a tear in his eye. 'I'm sorry; I see you knew him. He was very brave but stood no chance. Then the mantle was passed to me. I am his nephew, his sister's son.'

'What happened?' *Do I really want to know?*

'They came out of the mountains over the Golgan. We didn't know their numbers, or their power for they came shrouded in mist. Shimmian our Lord went out alone and stood before them. Four came, grey things, not goblins or the like of anything I've known. They met him out before the City.'

'It was no fight! For although he was skilled in weaponry and fighting, they were full of power. The first seemed made of mist. Each time our lord struck his sword passed right through it without causing harm. The second smote the ground with a club as a drum. The earth shook as in an earthquake and the walls of the city began to crumble, the buildings to fall. The third cried out in a voice of hate and our Lord's sword shattered as glass. The fourth reached out to touch him. He died.' The young man was rent with sorrow. The Wizard's thoughts filled with the image of that creature on the plain.

'Then the goblins attacked. It was no battle. For they were as the blades of grass on the plain, and we but a few. We tried; we died. Some, barely two hundred of us, escaped. We have come here.' The young Lord of Rael drew out his battered sword with a flourish, pointing it towards the heavens. 'We DEMAND War!'

'*Jihad!*' The Khalif was on his feet too. 'They came to the sands. They have poisoned the pools, have turned the grazing lands to dust. The holy desert **Hkamoot!** has been invaded. I too demand WAR!'

'War is indeed come upon us,' now spake Wenslow King of Varista and the marches of Bronden. 'They came from the West. The mighty Lord Asheld, Guardian of Western Bronden met them in open battle. For three days they contended and on the third day Asheld and his army were no more! Even now Varista burns and its people perish. I MUST have revenge! I too demand WAR!'

'Heshmet! Once of the Sevriet!' the man announced himself again. 'The Plains of Lodor Burn! They have taken the Sevrie, the Horse Kings and used them as fodder for their tribes. I demand War!'

'The Donaladin is dying,' the Queen of Asain breathed. 'The mists of evil have touched the heart of the swamps and turned the glades to mire.'

'Santolin still stands,' Sandor said quietly. 'But we have the dwarves.' It seemed explanation enough. 'Santolin shall stand with the Kings of Men as they ever have.'

Others spoke too. One by one the tales of the goblin uprising grew. The Wizard sat frozen. The force of their hatred was a terrible thing, uncontrollable, unstoppable. He knew only too well what they would want of him.

The High Dancer was the last to speak. 'War is a terrible thing, my Lords. The slaughter, the loss of life, of beauty is an awful thing indeed to call into being. But the Circles-of-the-World have ceased to turn. The seasons have stilled. Winter shall not fall nor spring awaken. The Elswood shall die.' He let his terrible sadness fill the words, which drifted as ghosts over the kings, lords and the Wizard before him. 'We have no choice! There must be war. We must defeat Her. We must restore the world.' It was no surprise that his eyes were wet with tears.

At least it's not hatred that drives him. And then another thought. *Do Elves ever hate?* That seemed some strange enlightenment. He looked closer at the Elf Lord.

The High Dancer's eyes widened in an instant of fear as he sensed the touch of the Wizard's thoughts. He couldn't grasp the nature of that touch though, nor that which the Wizard sought in the rainbow of his being.

It's true. He has no hatred. None at all. It's as if his very nature is such that hatred is forbidden. How can that be? Surely everything has a portion of hate.

'Shall I tell you what I think?' It was the Lord of High-Caravail who spoke disrupting his thoughts. The hatred in his voice though was as a burst of flame. His tone was as iron, as would be his will.

'If you wish.' He didn't, wouldn't give an inch in this. He knew, only too well, the heat of men's hatred and the spark that would awaken that anger and turn it into blood.

'I do not speak lightly, Wizard, this you should know. I am one used to power and of the ordering of men. Yet we know of your power, the promise of your coming. We understand that your magic is greater than any who have gone before. Well that's what is written. If you go against them!' He spat the word. 'Then they would fall.'

'We are a great host, Wizard, and many are skilled in the arts of War, but we are of many different Kingdoms and who shall lead us? Well I think that you, with your magic, should be the one. You alone should lead the Armies. Go with us as our Lord. You are mighty. You are strong. You alone can lead us into the affray. Even She cannot contend against you in your power.'

'My power?' He lifted his head to show the Lord the tears that streamed down his cheeks. 'What power, Lord? The power to kill? The power to destroy? The power to turn order into chaos? You want me to use my Power to start a war?' He didn't believe what he was hearing. *Do they understand anything?* 'Do you really ask me to destroy the world?'

'Not the world, Wizard! Just them! They have no right to be here to defile all that is good.' The Wizard's eyes stopped him.

'I shan't be a tool for your hate.'

'There is another way.' It was the High-Dancer speaking once again. Only now he spoke softly, sadly. Once again the wizard felt that the Elf spoke against his true nature. 'You could go to face Her. You could make an ending of Her.' (*He can't even say the word!*) 'Your power is greater than Hers, Wizard! Can you not use that for good? Can you not force Her to turn the Circles-of-the-World once more? Even save her from that ice-cold sadness?'

'What of You, Elf-Lord? Couldn't you dance a dance to heal her pain? Can't you dance their minds to nothing? Their souls to dust?'

'My magic cannot kill, Wizard, cannot be used as a weapon in battle or to turn an other's mind. My magic is of Love.' He paused, knowing the truth of his own words. 'Only yours is as yet unbound!'

Only Mine.

It seemed such a reasonable request, an answer in itself. Not to kill or destroy, just to go and change what was. *Things are never that simple.* He looked up at the hate filled faces about him, saw the blood lust in their eyes and hung his head not wanting to look further. 'And then what?' He raised his face to the waiting kings again. His finger pointed to them although he spoke to the Elf Lord alone. 'Then, I suppose, they'll wave goodbye to the Horde and wish them well in their journey home?' His laugh was bitter indeed. 'Some fat chance! They'll use the moment to attack, to make their ending of their oh so terrible foe. No, my Lord, I'll not use my power for that!'

There came a sudden snort from the lower end of the table. 'Huh! I see no power. Just a man in a robe and a tall hat.'

An unexpected shiver of laughter turned the Wizard's frown to a smile. 'Oh Starbinder, I thank you for that at least. And indeed it is a very fine hat is it not?' *Where are The Pinexae?* The thought suddenly struck. *Aren't they come too?*

The Magi stood and walked, in a majestic swirl of white silk, to stand before the Wizard. 'Well?'

'You want me to show you my power?'

'What power?'

'You're not afraid?'

'No. I am the High-Alchemist of Varista. I am not afraid.'

Well you bloody well should be! He felt the gentle touch of the Fire-Dancer's hand on his arm. 'For your bravery at least.' He lifted his own goblet, 'Take a drink with me "Enlightened-One",' and offered the vessel to the magi.

Starbinder took the goblet and raised it to his lips with a smile of victory. The wine was fine, finer in fact than any he had ever tasted, refreshing and full with the essence of life. He drank deep, savouring the moment. When he placed the goblet back onto the table it remained full to the brim. The Magi's eyes widened in surprise. He looked up into the Wizard's face and saw at last what he had failed to realise. He had seen this man before. Just once before in his life had he seen *real* magic.

'It might have been fire, Starbinder,' he explained softly. The eyes turned wild with terror as the magus realised the truth. 'I don't harm anyone, Magi, not even you. Even Rustle knew that! Wasn't the wine good?' He laughed at the man's discomfort. 'Oh go away, Starbinder. You tire me.' The man shuffled back to his place, and sat head down.

'What happened?' the High King demanded of the Magus. 'What did he do to you?'

'I gave him a goblet of wine, sire,' the Wizard softly explained. 'He drank wisdom from its lip.'

'Do you play games with us, Wizard?' the High-Dancer's soft voice filled the silence left by the Wizard's words.

'Games?' His voice was like a sword. 'You ask if I play games? Well what would you have me do? I came to hear your words. I came to see if there were answers. Instead you want me to make war. Is that how you see me? No wonder that I see the fear in your eyes when you look at me. Is that really what you think I'll do? Destroy? Kill? Turn the plain into a place of carnage? Free the whirlwind?'

The Elf Lord looked about desperately trying to find a way. 'And if she asked you, Wizard?' He gestured towards the Fire-Dancer. 'You say you love her. Well, what if she asked you? What then?'

'If she asked me?' It seemed Fate was scribing the words in some terrible journal of inevitability. 'Then so would I do. I shall always do whatever she asks. Whatever!'

The Elf-Lord was still, weighing the words in his mind. Finally he turned to face his daughter. He held her gaze. 'Ask him. Ask him to go to Her, to contend with Her and if he cannot force Her to restart the Circles, then to kill Her. There is no other way.'

She looked at the Wizard, at the kings about them and at the Elf Lord, her father. Her eyes were wet with crying when she replied. Never had she defied him. 'I have done as you wished. Always, even when the words were not spoken I did my terrible duty. In forests of Naril I danced his path of learning. In the darkness of The Galghathag I danced a dance of burning anger. At the lake in Bronden I even danced a dance of farewell. But you should know too, at the Gate of The Galghathag I swore an oath that now you ask me to break. I swore I would never ask him to kill.' She stood and looked into her father's face. 'Is this truly what you ask of me?'

'It is.'

She turned slowly to face the Wizard. Took his hand and lent over to kiss his cheek. Using the same words as then she whispered, 'Fear not, my love, that I shall never ask of you, not ever.' The tears streamed down her cheeks as she slumped over the table.

'If you stand not with us, then you stand against us,' the strident voice of The Queen-of-Asain declared from further down the table. 'If you do not fight for us, then you may fight against us. Better to end matters now. Sanain!' Calin snapped alert to the sound of her command. 'Fulfil your oath! Kill him!'

She was still. Whatever battle went on behind her eyes unseen. 'No. He chose not to kill.' She turned away, soul torn by her broken faith.

He could see the world crumbling about him, the elf trembling at his side. Calin, oath-broken now stood alone. It was too much, far too much.

'So you HAVE come between us, Wizard.' The High-Dancer's accusation was more terrible than any. 'What now of our hopes, you who will not kill? Are you so much better than us then? Will you just stand and watch as the world falls apart? You choose to do nothing and by your inactivity destroy all those about you!' He spat the words as a curse. 'Then we shall do without your help, Wizard! We go to war!'

The Kings stood.

The Wizard stood too. 'NO!' he demanded as his magic began to flare. 'I am the Wizard of Rainbows. You will wait.'

He saw the Kings recoil in fear. Even The High-Dancer flinched in the face of the anger before him but the elf remained resolute. 'So you seek to command us after all?'

'No,' the Wizard whispered.

The Elf-Lord looked into his eyes and saw the pain that lay there. Perhaps it explains his answer. 'At most, Wizard, we shall give you one day. If we remain unchallenged you'll have twenty-four hours to find your answer. If not? War!'

Twenty-four hours? It's not enough! Then suddenly he knew what he must do.

'Luminae.' She raised her tearful face to his, for she had seen its coming also. He bowed and kissed her, oh so tenderly. 'This time it's I who must leave, although it breaks my heart to do so. I have no dance of farewell, no poem to soothe the moment. Yet still I must go. I travel a new and darker path now. One set for me alone.'

Even now, though her heart was breaking every part as much as his, she did not try to stop him. 'Shall we meet again? Beyond the dusts of this terrible time?'

'Oh I do hope so, my sweet Elfin Queen. Else I'll need to spend the rest of eternity seeking you.'

Then his magic flared as a swirling, spiralling light, revolving faster and faster, growing ever brighter, brighter than any had seen before. They backed away, unable to look beyond the brilliance, unable to face the impossibility of his beauty. Gradually the brightness faded and sight returned.

He was gone.

> On the sands that reach from the dream-time beach
> Where the sirens welcome the day,
> I heard you singing a dream-time song,
> A discordant fiddler's lay.
>
> (Part 1 of the Dreamtime)

Chapter Ten - The Book of Hours

So this is it then? Alone once more. Here, far beyond the picket lines and the row upon row of tented soldiery, in a place where the grass had not been crushed to dust, *at least that's something,* he stopped. And in this place of calm the Wizard gradually returned to his true form. Only now his cloak and demeanour were of darker hue and his rainbow was sharper than any sword.

What am I? What have I become? The awareness of what he'd just done was a burning fire in his mind. *I was no more than mist! No more than energy bound by thought. How can that be?* He looked at his hand, just a normal hand, looking no more and no less than it always had. But it was not a normal hand and he knew it. *How can anyone posses such a power? How can I? With magic like this it might be true, I could indeed destroy everything, perhaps even create everything too.* Oh the wonder of that moment, *I was the rainbow!* He could hardly keep from laughing aloud with the sheer love of that glorious splendour, but not for long.

In truth he already knew that deep within the light that burnt at his centre, showing itself as an echo of disharmony in the vibrations of his nature, was the touch of another. It was more with wonder than surprise he sought its nature and source and with a sudden shiver of disquiet that he realised such was hidden from him. He knew, had known even at the time, such power was never of himself. Yet, as he explored the wonder further he felt no touch of evil, only of power. *Where is it from?* He turned slowly and looked to where the tower still called to him across the grey ruin of the city. Perhaps it was there where lay the answer to the endless question. *Why?*

For a time he could do nothing. His mind spun with a thousand troublesome imaginings. *Do the powers play with me once again?* He'd never forgotten the mocking laughter of the Creature-of-the-Mists ringing out over that cruel battlefield on the Plains of Sarum, or the uncomfortable feeling of being little more than a pawn in some game of powers. *Fate's-plaything.* Emotions, raw and unbound tumbled though his awareness, transitory and elusive, fleeting as the will-o'-the-wisps of dusk.

Behind him the entire encampment was in furore. Voices, loud and discordant, the blaring of trumpets and all manner of horn split the dull greyness asunder. The army made ready for war! That terrible din served as a warning also. *Twenty-four hours. That's what the kings have given me. And I still don't know what it is that I'm supposed to do.* He laughed to himself in dry humour. *Well there's nothing new there. I never seem to know.* Yet over the whole terrible scene the White-Tower brooded.

A dreadful pressure bore down on the Wizard at this moment. It was no less than the weight of all the dreams of the past, the hopes of the future, the expectation of so many and the awesome responsibility, which was his own. The touch of Fate's unwelcome demands chilled his soul and filled him with the awful realisation, in some way he still didn't understand, his very actions were the fulcrum on which the balance of eternity rested. And still he didn't know what he was supposed to do.

There was something else too, something far easier to comprehend, however loath he might be to do so. In his mind, his every awareness he could feel it, the almost palpable aura of hatred and the sour, sick lust for death that hung over the plain. It tasted as bile on his tongue and clothed his heart in a blanket of dread. Once more his attention was drawn to the waiting armies.

So they hunger for war and, unless I can come up with an answer, it's war they'll have. Some terrible, final battle in which they'll end their sorry lives and spill their blood to eke the thirst of this cold, grey plain.

Is this what it's all about? That I'm supposed to stop the carnage? They live or die by my deeds? Is this my truth too? That in order to do so I must accept the power I'm offered?

NO! He rejected that idea. *Not that. I'm my own man and no plaything for the forces of Fate, or anything else for that matter! No! It shall be as I always say, 'I'll be myself!'* Nonetheless a cold hand of helplessness grasped at his heart.

But I'm powerless. I can save no one. I couldn't even save Shimmian. The well of sorrow was no less disconcerting than the pressure of expectation had been. He could see, in his mind's eye, the storyteller's smiling face. He could almost hear the echo of the man's raucous laughter. Instead there came a wind, dust-laden and smoke-stained driving all sound away on its ravenous breath. After there was silence.

Oh Shimmian. You've your own path now. There were tears for his friend but he was unaware of them. All he knew was the anger, the sense of loss, of hopelessness, even guilt. *Where was I when you faced a foe too terrible to conquer? Can't I, aren't I even permitted to save my friend? Must I simply destroy everything I touch, everything, everyone who touches me? For that's all I seem to do, even Calin. Now her oath is broken, what will become of her? And Luminae, my brave little dancer of the forest, even you I've forced into a path of disobedience.*

With the sadness, again came that overwhelming sense of loneliness He'd left her behind too, not that he'd had any real choice in the matter. He was alone once more. His words had been true. 'Who now shall light my way?' *I am alone!*

Shaking off the pall self-pity he turned to face the tower which stood brooding over everything. *And you, if in truth you seek to guide my way, do you have any answers?* he accused, *Do you know the secret that shall heal their wounds?* It didn't reply, just waited.

The dust, when his feet first took him into the ruin that once was Tabour, was an awful choking horror that billowed about him with every step. He was reminded, far too easily, of the Galghathag and the dust that arose from the destruction of the Darkling forest. *Is this to be the fate of the whole world if I don't prevail?* If any had the answer they kept it to themselves. He walked slowly, reluctantly on.

Eventually he stood where once he had stood before. The needle of white perfection seemed almost mocking as it reached up to pierce the clouds above. He did nothing. Said nothing, perhaps even felt nothing.

Ah you are come then, Wizard. Not a question.

'I am come.' Not an answer.

Show your magic then, Wizard.

'No.' *I'll not play this game. Magi I might have become, but I, at least have no need for trickery or show.*

Then how shall you enter the Tower?

'Why should I enter the Tower?'

It is written!

'Well I didn't write it.' The words stealing through his thoughts were beginning to irritate.

But You Must enter the tower!

'Then I suppose you'd better show me the way in,' the Wizard laughed, but it was a dry humourless thing.

When he walked forward through the portal he felt no happiness or sense of achievement, only the clawing grasp of Fate's unthinking hand. Thus he passed from darkness into light, into a brightness so intense that it denied sight and sent his senses recoiling in shock. There was no space and no direction, no beginning and no ending. The tower was light and he within became light also. But, what is light other than the vibration of existence? As was inevitable with one of his nature he found the essence of its rainbow within his own. He took of that light, examined each and every particle until he saw the truth of what was. Whether this understanding was reality or just a symbol matters little. He saw the tower as a lens, a thing to draw the light of the world. Where every image was taken and every ray held its own, individual meaning. He looked. He saw.

High in the mountains of Eribore a man fought alone with a thing of scale and claw. He was brave, this man, and a fighter of skill. Yet he weakened and no help would come.

On the fire blackened plain of Lodor, the horses were dying, starving. Even now their corpses littered the barren land. In the darkening skies cereban hover on even darker wings. At least they shall not starve

Over the mountains of Naril hung a pall of smoke.

On the sheep moors of Bronden a small homestead of three once thatched cottages lay as a burnt ruin.

In the smoking reek of Varista an urchin picked through the ruins scavenging for food.

On the plains of Rael there was a burning.

In the desert beyond Istar a small band of travellers camped beside an oasis. Hkainae and her father, Liam and others of their household. They seemed at peace. That was something. It gave his heart a measure of relief.

In and about Dormon the remnant of the Desert people awaited news.

In far off High-Caravail a woman, dressed in white damask with her golden hair bound with silken braid, stood upon a high balcony looking into the distance. Her face was wet with tears.

In Hereth... The Hall stood empty.

Perhaps that brought him back to reality for a time. *So they're gone too.* It came as no surprise.

Beyond the tower the armies were gathering in their formations. Calin, Coq at her side stood alone before all. She had drawn her sword and to all appearances now waited to die.

In the great pavilion The High-Dancer spoke to the other Kings. He spoke of the terribleness of war, the awfulness of slaughter.

The Lady and Plie made ready for war also. They rolled the bandages and prepared the dressings, and sealed their hearts for the terrors, which they knew they soon would face.

There was no sign of The Fire-Dancer.

He could look wherever he wished and see the images of passing time. The confusion that filled his mind was but the taste of his hunger to know. WHY? Gradually he became aware that these rays of existence drew together at the centre of the tower. He went with them, at this moment of no more substance than they. Here, at the centre, every aspect of the present was focused. Here every instant of time coalesced, was observed and finally was recorded.

He began to read.

The dust, when his feet first took him into the ruin that once was Tabour, was an awful choking horror that billowed about him with every step.

Eventually he stood where he had stood before. The needle of white reached up to pierce the clouds above. He did nothing.

Ah you are come then, Wizard.

I am come.

Show your magic then, Wizard.

No.

Then how shall you enter the Tower?

Why should I enter the Tower?

It is written!

'Well I didn't write it.'

'But You MUST enter the tower!'

'Then I suppose you'd better show me the way in,' the wizard laughed.

He walked forward through the portal, passing from darkness into light, a light that filled his senses, a brightness that denied sight. There was no space and no direction, no beginning and no ending. The tower is light and he within became light also. He took the light, each and every particle until he saw the truth of what is. He looked, perceived the visions of the world. Did he understand?

Gradually he began to realise the rays drew together at the centre of the tower. He went with them.

Every aspect of 'Now' was here, existing in this very place. It was as if each instant of time coalesced.

And herein was recorded.

He looks into the Book of Hours, and begins to read.

At the foot of the page he paused to think. Gradually the realisation came – *to turn the page would be to look into the future!* He returned to the open page and read the new words, which scrolled into view.

'At the bottom of the page he pauses. Perhaps he understands, perhaps not.'

The Wizard grew still turning things over in his mind. *I'm being tested. Should I accept the power and the gift of the magic that's offered and become what Fate would have me be?* It took little consideration; the choice was already made. *No I'll not turn the page. It's a trap. That's clear enough, although I'm not sure I really understand. This book is much more than it seems. Is it the very hand of Fate scribing the lives of Men? I can feel its power, its desire to control. It wants to be the mover of the Future, the Master of the Past. This thing is more powerful than me, more powerful than the beast. I think more powerful than Fate itself. It is the Past, the Present and the Future.*

'There are many choices available to you, Wizard.'

He spun around; shocked that he hadn't heard Her approach. He hadn't even sensed Her presence. Now She stood here before him as beautiful as silence, draped, shoulder to floor, in a gown of silver grey. Her long, pure white hair was bound with a filament of platinum and on Her brow a single diamond glistened. She was taller than he, older too, if age has any meaning to Her. The light that glistened in Her soft hazel eyes spoke of years untold, hard, sorrow-filled years the anguish of which resounded in his soul. A sadness, more brittle than ice, bore down on him and filled him with a reminder of his own sense of loss. She was a queen of stillness, an empress of sorrow.

'Who are you, Lady?'

'This is the Book-of-Hours,' she continued as if he hadn't spoken. 'Turning the pages backwards will enable you to see that which was, or you could look forwards, to know what shall be. The whole universe is there to know.'

'Who are you?' he asked again.

'Who am I?' She smiled without amusement. 'Can't you see me? Don't you know me?'

'I see you.'

'Then don't you also know me?'

'You were in the desert. I saw you there in the distance, in the mountains also. I felt your searching, your sadness, your emptiness. I knew you waited, watched in the night. I saw your storm in the darkness too, when you were Queen of the night. Gob, the goblin with whom I travelled, had a name for you. My sweet Fire-Dancer, she named you also. In the halls and the tents of men you were called by other names, ugly and beautiful alike, but none of them are truly yours. I shall not name you, not yet, at least not until I know truly. It was said that you would come to challenge me?'

'Challenge?' She even sounded surprised. 'Do I come to challenge? I had not thought so. I came to see, to know.'

So he sat cross-legged upon the floor. 'Sit with me Queen-of-Sorrow,' he bade Her with a gesture of his hand. 'This is a time for us to talk.'

'Yes,' she too lowered herself to sit before him, 'I shall talk with you, Wizard.'

He poured a goblet of wine, white it was, and crystal clear, for red would have been as blood and a mockery of Her sadness. She took the goblet and drank, and he too from the same lip. The tension in the air about them grew as the stillness preceding a storm.

'Why have you come, my Queen?' he asked when the goblet stood on the floor between them.

'I came to find answers and to give answers. I came to find understanding and to give understanding. I have come because you are the Wizard of Rainbows and because your time is near.'

'Yes, I am the Wizard of Rainbows.' He was, and it needed saying. 'Why should that draw you?'

She reached out and took up the cup once more. It seemed a gesture of defiance, as if to say *I'm not afraid*. 'Because it's the time.'

'The time?' There was no annoyance at the mystery of Her reply. 'Shall we speak in riddles or in truth?' he asked without rancour.

'Is there a difference, Wizard?' She passed back the goblet and he sipped the clear water within. 'I don't tease you in this matter. Nor do I seek to confuse. I'm unsure of the path to follow in this troubled place.'

'Start at the beginning, My Lady,' he suggested, returning the cup of wine to the ground.

'It isn't the beginning, for that would go back beyond things which even I know, but...' she held him with her eyes, 'I, we, we made a terrible mistake.'

'What was the mistake?'

'We thought to control the Chaos.'

'How can Chaos be controlled?' Perhaps he already knew the answer. 'If it were then it would be chaos no more.'

'Would that be such a bad thing?'

He didn't answer.

Again She reached out to take up the cup and sip from its lip. 'There seemed no choice, Wizard. They warred against each other and there were no limits to their power. It was either that or watch as they destroyed everything. They had to be stopped.' A tear shivered to ice in the corner of her eye. 'And now it is to be as you said, Wizard. "Chaos cannot be controlled," nor even contained. The bonds are breaking. It shall be free once again.'

'Would that be such a bad thing?' He mimicked Her question.

'You don't understand.'

'Tell me.'

She hung her head, hid her face behind the curtain of Her hair, and sat still and silent. He watched, but did not disturb Her. Eventually She looked up. In the crystal on Her brow a fire burned. 'In truth Wizard, I tell you there was no other choice open to us.' Such a terrible doom. 'We were so afraid everything would be destroyed. Now though even worse shall befall because of what we did. The only way now is to end everything.'

'Tell me,' he asked again.

'You carry his eyes, Wizard, perhaps I should have expected that.' Words that were out of context but She did not explain or wait for his question. 'We did what we thought was right, Wizard, and we were prepared to pay the cost. We had to stop them, to save the world ere all was lost. The raging chaos that ruled in that terrible War-of-Powers was too strong. We needed order.' Her laugh was bitter as aloe.

'Tell me.'

'Look to the people, Wizard,' she continued after a pause. Again speaking through the mists of Her sorrow. 'You've seen how, in the midst of winter, they light the Yule fires and pray for spring, spring when the land shall awaken and the sun return. You know the meanings of the spring feast and the harvest home held in token that the corn should grow. You've seen them dance to the sun in the midsummer's dawn, sit till midnight turns on mid-winter's night that the world shall turn. Yet they can no more stop the seasons than they can the winter snows. It's the Order-of-the-world, the First-Cycle. Spring follows winter, summer follows spring, autumn summer and winter fall and ever the spring has come.' There was something threatening about the silence that punctuated her words. 'How will the people fare when Order fails? Shall their hopes and prayers hold the Chaos at bay?

'They hated Order with their passions and power. Hated the constraints to their natures, the limitations to their extravagances. Then, then we had the power to contain their excesses. Then we were able to prevent their wildness from wrecking all. But no more.' Once again the clouds of Her sorrow spoke as much.

'You've seen the people give thanks when the corn grows golden or when the game move northwards to their summer pastures. For men then know that for now at least they shall live, that their children shall not hunger when the snows come. When they give thanks for the birth of their children their hearts grow warm for they see that the future has hope.' Her voice turned suddenly harsh. 'They know NOTHING!

'And, Nothing is what they'll have. For when Chaos awakens the world shall never be the same, shall never be as it should be. What then of their hopes, their prayers, their dreams and their fears? I'll answer that question. Their hopes shall be as dust, blowing in the wind, their prayers but screaming into the night. And their dreams? Their dreams will be nightmares from which there'll be no awakening. Their fears shall be forever.'

She laughed then as the wind that lifts the snows from the northern ice-flows. 'Not that it truly matters.' Words to freeze the soul. 'They think to cheat death with their festivals and prayers. I tell you death can never be cheated, not by them or any who live. Death always wins in the end. What's life anyway other than a short ray of light? Soon the darkness shall come.'

'Is this the cause of the sorrow that fills you?' He still couldn't grasp the fullness of Her words. 'For they say you bear the pain of the world.'

'Bear it?' Her eyes were chasms of emptiness. 'No I don't bear it, Wizard!' Her voice rang with an awesome self-loathing. 'It was I who created it. I thought my love would be enough.' Once more She laughed a laugh more bitter than any he had ever heard. 'And now, because of me, everything shall be destroyed anyway. That was our gift to the world. We've opened the Gates-of-the-Void and the endless path of Chaos. As before, the destruction and death of the Cataclysm shall follow. Once we had enough power to contend with such things, but no more. We threw it away in our pride.

'Well that I can't accept. I can't just watch as all that I valued, all I loved, all which I was charged to protect is torn apart before me. NO! I'll watch no more! I've put an end to it forever!'

'What have you done?' Even though he knew.

'I've stopped the Cycles-of-the-World, Wizard.' They were terrible words to hear, even though they were the truth. 'And without the Cycles...' The rest remained unsaid.

It was a long time before he could answer Her and even then he still didn't understand what She'd meant. 'The Kings said I should persuade you to return the seasons.' He looked into the sorrow of Her eyes. 'The Elf said I should kill you if you refuse.'

'What will you do, Wizard? For I shan't awaken that cycle of death anew. Rather I'd destroy it all myself than give them that victory!'

'I don't know what I'll do. It seems I never know. Tell me,' he asked for a final time.

'It's true, Wizard. You don't understand, not yet. I stopped the Cycles in order to put an end to the world! Bitter it is I know. It was my place to love the world. Now I destroy it.' Tears as icicles trickled over her frozen cheeks. 'But even so it's better than the chaos that would follow if I did otherwise. It was my only choice. The only way open to me.'

Is there hope here? 'Is there another way then?'

She stood, reached out, took his hand and helped him to his feet. 'There are two ways, Wizard! That of mine, and that of yours! Mine, as I have explained is to still the Cycles-of-the-World and to draw the armies to the final battle. My way is to end everything before it is too late, before they reach out to grasp the power, which they crave, the power to awaken chaos and open the gates of the Void forever. At least there shall be an end!'

'And mine?'

'You, and you alone, have the choice of another way through this maze of chaos and emptiness.'

'What is this way, Lady?'

'The Book!'

'What of the Book?' He turned and looked at the manuscript once again remembering that sense of terrible power and the threat bound therein.

'It's the Book-of-Hours, Wizard. The record of every instant, every act, every moment of time lies written therein.' She paused again letting the tension of her silence build. 'There's a possibility for you here also. You alone can write in the book; you alone can turn the page and create a new future. Even a new past.' She waited with a glimmer of hope lighting Her expression. When She continued it was as if every part of Her longing was placed in the words. 'You alone can change the words, Wizard. You can change the future, and the PAST!'

'I can change the words? Why me?' He struggled with the idea. 'If I can change them why can't you? You have the power to end the Cycles, Why not this also?'

'Because it's written, Wizard, written in his hand at the beginning... Now you alone can write in its pages.' She drew breath. 'Perhaps he knew the truth. Perhaps he foresaw the breaking of the bonds. Whatever, he gave the power to you and to you alone.' She pointed at the book with a trembling finger. 'There! It cost him everything, even his life. Don't you think we would have changed it if we could?'

He looked at Her, saw the fear in Her eyes. 'And what would you have me write, my Queen? What would you have me change?'

'No simple thing that's for sure. For I'm asking you to change your own fate, Wizard.' Her heart spoke the words. 'You could change what is to be. You have the power to bind the Vortex forever!' She was on her knees before him. 'Please, Wizard. With the Chaos controlled then there need be no more decay, no more suffering, no more war, no more carnage, even, no more death. Bind the Vortex, then they shall never prevail!'

Mine is the Vortex! The words turned around and around in his thoughts. 'They? Who are They?'

She grew still then. Her own thoughts turning in Her eyes, questions unasked, answers not spoken. 'They are the Lords-of-Chaos.' Whatever battle had taken place was resolved. 'Lords-of-Light and of Darkness. They warred against each other, lit the universe with the fury of their conflict. They even awoke the Cataclysm. They would have destroyed it all and for nothing but the hunger for that power.'

'We stopped them, the Well-Springs-of-the-Earth. The Lords-of-Creation and I.' She whispered the next words as if ashamed to speak them, 'We created the book.'

He turned the meanings over in his thoughts. His answer was long in coming for, as always he didn't understand. 'Wait. If you created it why can't you change it?'

'If only.' She laughed her self-derisive laugh once more. 'It's too powerful, Wizard, far too powerful. We saw that at the start when we began to consider its creation. Such a thing would be far too powerful, for thus it had to be to control the Maelstrom. It would be, it is, so powerful that if any were able to master its forces they could rule the world. That's its nature, the power we gave it. For we created it of ourselves, gave it our natures, Wizard, and we knew, once given, we could never contain such a thing. We had to make sure it couldn't happen. We made it so any who wrote in it would die.'

He struggled with the idea as much as with anything else She'd said. 'Are you saying that you want me to write in the book and then die?'

'Oh no, Wizard, not you. As I said, you alone can write therein. For he gave you that. He knew what he did and that he would perish. Yet did it anyway. It was he who named you "Wizard of Rainbows". He who made it possible for you to write in there. He made it so that you alone can change what is or what might be. Anything. Anything at all. You can even take death from the world.'

'I can do that?' *What am I?* 'You're telling me that I can even defeat death?'

'No, Not defeat. Simply take it away.'

'But...' *It can't be that simple!* 'If nothing dies, then the whole world would be...' He saw. 'To take away Death would be to take away life also. There could be no growth, no children, no spring and no harvest.'

'No illness, no decay!' she countered.

'No beauty.'

'What is beauty, Wizard? I'm beautiful. Am I not? Well at least as you see me now. Yet at my behest the Grey-People have risen up in arms to destroy the lands of men. Do you know why they follow me? It's because of beauty. Don't you see? Don't you understand? What's beauty to them? Is it a thing of value? No! What does it bring? Nothing except envy, hatred and greed. It gives them nothing but the knowledge of their own ugliness. I tell you, Wizard, beauty is only good when everything is beautiful. And when everything shall remain so.'

'Lady! Your words make no sense! If everything is beautiful then there is no beauty.'

'Ha! This you see at least! Beauty is but the beginning of decay. It can only exist if ugliness exists too. Life and death, health and sickness.'

'So you'd have me destroy the World also?'

'No. I wish only to take away the World's pain. To prevent the chaos that shall come when the Vortex is freed.'

'It amounts to the same.' Once more the terrible wave of Her sadness washed over him. 'Is there no other way?'

'You still don't understand, Wizard!'

'What don't I understand?'

'The Bonds are loosened, the constraints failing. Soon they'll hold no longer. And then? Then, when the magic runs free once more, they'll take it as a prize. No one could expect other. It was denied them for too long. For over three thousand years Order has held sway. Soon it will do so no more. Chaos shall rule and the Lords-of-The-Void awaken. If they're not prevented they'll destroy or enslave everything! Their rule will be eternal; the torment shall be endless. There's nothing else that can be done. Evil always wins, Wizard.'

She paused again, letting Her words sink in. 'There are no other choices now. Either we accept their rule, and the chaos that shall follow, or I still the cycles and draw the world into that final conflict, good and evil contending until there is nothing left anyway! It's either chaos or War. War and the Ending. Ending for ever the Cycles of Life and Death! Then there will be silence, forever. Then there might be rest.' Again the depth of Her sorrow was almost overwhelming.

She sank to the floor, kneeling before him in supplication. 'The only other way is for you to write in the book. Just one line, Wizard. Just one line to stop the carnage forever!'

'What would you have me write?'

'It's simple, truly. Where it is written '𝔄𝔫𝔡 𝔥𝔦𝔰 𝔦𝔰 𝔱𝔥𝔢 𝔙𝔬𝔯𝔱𝔢𝔵' just add the words '𝔞𝔫𝔡 𝔥𝔦𝔰 𝔴𝔦𝔩𝔩 𝔦𝔰 𝔱𝔥𝔞𝔱 𝔱𝔥𝔢 𝔙𝔬𝔯𝔱𝔢𝔵 𝔟𝔢 𝔟𝔬𝔲𝔫𝔡 𝔣𝔬𝔯𝔢𝔳𝔢𝔯.' That is all that is required.'

She stood again looking into his eyes, her hope shining as bright as the moon. 'You could do more, Wizard. You could do whatever you wish, anything. You can change the past, even return to life those who are dead. If you would end the rule of Death forever then simply write. '𝔄𝔫𝔡 𝔱𝔥𝔢𝔶 𝔩𝔦𝔳𝔢 𝔣𝔬𝔯𝔢𝔳𝔢𝔯, 𝔴𝔦𝔱𝔥𝔬𝔲𝔱 𝔡𝔢𝔞𝔱𝔥.' Will you not write the words?'

'It can't be that simple!'

'But it is!' She was bright as lightning now, full of power and wonder. 'It's just as simple as that.'

From where it came he didn't know, but suddenly he remembered the strange dream or vision that he had been shown. *Who broke the bridge, Man or Child? There never can be a safe way. Perhaps not even a right way.* 'Wait. I must have time to think.'

'You have all the time in the World, Wizard.' Her voice was that of the High-Dancer. 'Or, You have twenty-four hours.' Then in Her own voice: 'And time is passing. You must make your choice!'

There remained one final, unasked, question. 'Who was he?'

She whispered the answer, 'Gentil.'

Gentil? *The Wizard Lord of Maddon who served the Eloveen Kings during the Wars of The Stone.* 'Why me?'

'You are his heir, Wizard, the last of his line. He told us, begged us not to create the Book. We saw no other way.'

'You're telling me that he died in order to give me the power to write in THAT!' He spat the last word.

'He named you the *Wizard of Rainbows*. He wrote that "The Vortex is Yours." You can free it or bind it.' Just a slight pause, then She asked, 'What is your choice?'

To free it or bind it? I don't even know what the Vortex is! Order or Chaos, Life or death, Good or Ill? MY CHOICE! And there lay his answer. 'It's not my choice, my Lady. It never could be. I'm no Wizard-of-Order or of Chaos, no Wizard-of-Good or Evil either. Nor am I a Wizard of Past or Future. I'm the Wizard of Rainbows and my rainbows are of now! I'll not change the past or the future, they are not mine to change. What shall be shall be! It seems to me that binding the Vortex would make me the servant of that Book. I tell you I'll be neither servant nor slave to any. I am free!'

Her voice was of a soul in torment. 'So you carry his mind also! Why did he deny us? Why do you deny me this gift? It's only thus that I can contend with the evil that's my own nature, the evil which will waken in fury with the coming of chaos.'

'This is my understanding, My Lady. That were I to write in the book, were I to change the past, then the future would be controlled and if the future is controlled then it would be enslaved also. I'll never enslave another being! Let alone the whole World. I can't help you this way, My Lady.'

She heard his truth in that answer and knew that he, no less than Gentil, would not be changed. For a moment She slumped before him, beaten, broken. 'Then, please, I beg of you, turn the page and look into the future. Show me what will be. I must know the outcome of what I do!'

'I cannot! I will not. The future is for those who live in the now. It's theirs to know for themselves in their time.' He looked into her pain, matching her sorrow with his own. 'It could be so easy, My Lady, even for me. But it's not the way of life. We do as we do, not knowing the consequences of our actions. No you, as I, must face the Future without foreknowledge. If your choice is to bring War and carnage, death and destruction upon the land, then you alone shall make that choice. My way is of Life.'

She rose up before him, tall and filled with Her dreadful anger. Her eyes grew hard as the diamond on Her brow. 'So you hate the war? The death? The killing and yet do nothing? Well I'll tell you this, Wizard. I need to write no words in a book to create this future. Haven't you seen how they hunger for each other's lives? What will you do to bring an ending to that? I tell you, no pretty elfin ballet shall hold back their hands from the slaughter to come. None save you or I have that gift.'

She looked into his eyes once more seeing the surprise there. Her voice cracked with defiance. 'Did you not realise that it's I who constrains them? That it's I who has prevented the carnage until now? Well I only did it in hope of what lies in that book, of what you now deny me. Well, I'll hold them back no more!'

'And what of you then, Wizard? When will you dare to waken the promise of your power? Will you do as The Lord-of-Madness tells? Will you awaken your power so that even the Earth trembles at your coming and going? Are you ready to make yourself the most terrible thing in creation? The most terrible that is, but me!' The awful force of her self-loathing beat against his senses choking the words that formed. 'Don't you know it was me who created their natures, Man, goblin and Elf? Didn't I form the lives that they now so readily prepare to lose? Even the Grey-Ones, is not their hatred a creation of mine also, built from their jealousy of those who live, who love? Well then, I'll deny them no more! Then you'll see the truth? Oh yes, Wizard. You will come to me, come seeking an end of my creations. Will you continue to deny your own truth even then? So wait in your silence of time. There's no point! Ever I'll deny you and in the end it's you who'll destroy the world!'

She was gone.

*

He needed time to think, to get things into perspective, perhaps to try to understand something of what he'd heard. But there was no time and he couldn't think or even form the thoughts. The throbbing in his head drove all such away.

The sound of a drum, dark and bass, rolled out over the plain. Its beat, eighty to the minute, was as some giant heart tolling out the remaining life of the land. It caught the Wizard's attention, filled his mind with its pounding until he began to search for its source among the myriad images of the tower. He never found it, for his eyes were filled with other, more compelling visions.

The Goblin Horde had begun to advance, if that's the word. They came in silence, marching, step by step to the beat of that unseen drummer. First were the *Ghalg'd*, the War-bands of the Clan-Lords. Elite forces comprised of the largest, most ferocious and deadly of the goblins. They were dressed in black armour and bore huge rectangular shields that lesser creatures could not have carried. The *Ghalg'd* of the thirteen tribes came on in a single line, a line six files deep. Between each phalanx was a twenty-pace gap. It was as if thirteen solid blocks of iron moved over the land.

Behind the *Ghalg'd* were the *Groth*, thousand, upon thousand of the lesser goblins. Few of these were armoured or even shielded, although most carried weapons of one kind or another. These took up no formation, rather they were marshalled in a massive crowd by other goblins, brutes that drove them onwards with lash and goad.

Those of the Tribes proper, formed into shielded ranks, brought up the rear.

But this was not all. For with the horde came other things, creatures hard to identify or even distinguish. At the centre of the line were a group of great Trolls, terrible things, whose very existence seemed an insult to life. And, somewhere unseen, were the Warriors-of-the-Mist, The lords-of-The-Galomist. For that too came stealing through the ranks of the Horde, weaving in snake-like tendrils as they moved silently forwards, forwards towards their foe.

The other camp, in counterpoint to the horde's silent advance, erupted into a furore of activity. Horns blared, orders were shouted, drums and cymbals outdid each other in a chaotic storm of noise. Yet somehow the single drum was still the more insistent.

The ranks began to form, although under what direction was unclear. There was no overall plan or strategy. The impression of order was due to the fact that these were men trained well in the arts of battle. Sergeants barked out their orders. Captains and kings stood before their men, hoping to instil with words the bravery they too sought. In truth, each force, each part of this vast army was but a rule unto itself. And, as the battle neared each King, commander and general made his own preparation for the strife to come.

THEY WILL FAIL! There was little doubt. There was no way that this vast group of disparate, uncoordinated units could contend against that which bore down on them.

Nonetheless, the armies prepared. Nearest to the ruined city the Desert people formed in a five-deep shield-wall. Their left flank at least was protected for none, not even the grey ones, would willingly step within that desolation. Fahaeda, Sultan-of-Dormon, as was his people's way, stood at their centre and hoisted his own shield in the front rank, indistinguishable from the others save for the brightness of his burning eyes. Beside him Saihera, his favourite wife was no less the warrior.

To the right of the desert men's ordered ranks a mixed group of hill people had gathered, bowmen, axe-men and spearmen. They wore no armour and none but a few even carried shields, but these were hard men and they didn't flinch from what they soon would face.

Beyond these, on the trampled earth where the road cut through the plain, Wenslow had drawn up the one and a half legions of the Bronden march. Silent as the oncoming enemy were they, waiting, white-faced behind their round, hoplite shields, knowing only too well what was to come.

Behind and slightly to the right of Bronden's ordered ranks the horsemen of The Sevriet waited. Their long steel-tipped lances were as a forest of leafless saplings. With these were the riders of Pashad, mounted bowmen and a cadre of armoured swordsmen. These too carried no pennant or flag. They wanted not glory but revenge!

Sandor had formed a wide shield-wall some fifty paces beyond Bronden, allowing the horsemen the space to manoeuvre. On his right he'd placed the mounted knights of his bodyguard, to his left the knights-of-Eribore, thus sandwiching his army between the two cavalry units.

Gessette Queen-of-Asain gathered her force close to the King's horses too. As Sandor, she saw the strength to be gained from their protection of her flank. Her own legion was a block of shields. Before this though, stood her seven Sanain, the Sisters-of-the-Sword with Calin further forward than the others and at the centre. They stood still as death.

Beside Asain were the massed ranks of High-Caravail, Elanthral's golden chariot at the fore. Three thousand strong were they and their standards were near as many as their swords. These too were strangely quiet. Their white faces spoke of fear. Never in all the history of High-Caravail had its people taken up arms to march to war.

Beyond these, forming the right flank of the line were gathered many of the men of lesser kingdoms. Those of The northlands waited under the leadership of Joab, Prince of Ganesh. The Malshamics of B'vorne and Tsorlin stood under the command of Ysavre-ap-Dharath. Throughout the whole were other companies, contingents of every region of the land.

The Elves, for their part, did not form as a single group. Rather they were spread throughout the whole. Bowstrings were waxed. Arrow points were honed, sharp as needles. They had, each and every one, taken the seeds of their trees and planted these 'neath where they now stood. They would not flee, and if they died their blood would feed the growth of the tree's new beginning. If they lived? Well, then they would take up their seeds again for a more fitting time of passing.

Even these were not all. Before the tents, standing in silent prayer were the priests of Finestre and the many who had come not to fight but to witness what befell this day.

The drumbeat stopped.
The Horde stopped.
The Armies of men grew still also.
Over the plain, silence hovered on a raven's dark wing.
In that silence the mist grew thick as fog. It fed upon the fear that filled the air, on the smell of death that waited in the minds of those who knew. Thick was it and chill, and growing in power.

There came movement amidst the massed ranks of the still, silent Horde. A figure advanced, a terrible thing of greyness and decay. It came slowly, gloating on the dismay caused by its very presence. The mists that surrounded its form in mystery confused even its appearance. It stood tall, seven feet at least, and carried a great trident of darkness as a token of its power. It stood some fifty paces before the waiting army, a challenge, a threat, and many were the eyes that turned away not daring to look upon the thing.

Not all were cowed though. Even the Wizard, from where he watched, was moved to pride as from amongst the ranks of men the High-Dancer walked forward. He wore no armour, just his robe of the Greenwood. His longbow was left to the safety of others. He came unarmed and alone but he did not remain so for long. A second figure moved, walked forwards to join him, stood beside him to face the thing, *Calin!*

The nature of that meeting is unknown as were the words if any such were spoken. But when the mists coalesced about the two, forming into a weapon of grey ice, the Elf-Lord spun his web of magic and the mists recoiled in screaming steam. When the creature reared up in malice and reached out to touch the Elf-lord with a hand of death, Calin moved. If it was alive, it died. If it had other than life, then its existence came to an end.

This time the Sanain neither slumped nor cried out in pain. Rather she lifted her sword high above her head and called out into the now silent sky. 'I am Calin-Sanain,' she declared, her clear voice ringing out over the plain, over the waiting armies and all heard her. 'For Shimmian, Lord-of-Rael.' She pointed the sword at the grey horde. 'I slay any I choose, grey ones! Even those with no life to lose.' Then came her challenge, 'If that was not your greatest, then send them to me also. If it was your greatest then beware for I shall slay you also and with no more effort.'

From the massed armies came a cry of victory. They beat their swords and spears upon their shields. The blast of horns awoke the air and for a moment all felt nearly as brave as this warrior maid.

The reply of the Goblin-Horde came as a single drum beat. The cry of victory was stilled. Even so none came forth to meet her challenge.

After several lifetimes of waiting they turned about, Elf and Sanain together, and walked slowly back to their waiting armies. The High-Dancer returned to his elfin bowmen, Calin to stand once more at the fore of her Queen's legion. There came another movement. For Cog, and with him Aelfrett, Rael's young Marshal, walked forward to stand at Calin's side. Then they too grew still, waiting.

The drum beat recommenced and the Horde advanced once more. Thousands of sweat slick hands were wiped dry. Shields were lifted, spear points lowered. Here and there throats were cough cleared. Here and there a fear struck voice prayed for salvation.

Once again the drum stopped. The Horde stopped. The silence grew into a wall of strain. Seconds, minutes passed. Before the Horde, now but some forty paces from the waiting battle line, the mist grew thick. Its impenetrable moisture formed in a chilling shield to cover whatever transpired behind its grey veil. For those who watched, it seemed the mist was itself a terrible weapon of the enemy.

Then from that mist they came, the teaming masses of the *Groth*. They came running, faces contorted with hate and fear, hate of all who stood before them, fear of those who came behind. As some screaming, cursing, maddened mob they charged at the line of shields before them intent only on the blood-fest to come.

Elven bows strained. Eyes, more skilled in the hunt than the battlefield spotted their careering targets. Fingers, white with the strain of their grip held steady. *'TSa!'* Three thousand arrows took flight. Three thousand arrows soared through the grey skies. Three thousand arrows arched downwards. Three thousand goblins screamed in agony as the steel tips ripped their flesh apart. But three thousand was nothing in this throng. Over twenty thousand of the screaming creatures crashed against the battle line.

Bronden held, shields locked together as their spear points turned black with goblin blood. Santolin held also, although the crush of screaming bodies drove them backward against the ranks of horsemen at their rear. The line of High-Caravail buckled and turned into a melee of frantic struggling figures. At the fore of Asian, Calin, Cog, Aelfrett and the Sanain stood as a bastion against the headlong rush of death. Those that avoided them met only the wall of Asain shields and a fate no different. Calin and her Sanain-Sisters spun their dreadful ballet of death, her two companions doing little but protecting her flanks although that was a deed in itself. The bodies piled high about them. Was this a thing for song then the bards would have spun a ballad wondrous indeed, but it was not, and such a song was never sung. The bards too were a part of this terrible affray and their blood mingled with that of all who fell.

Slowly, inevitably the struggle turned to chaos. There was little chance of other. Heshmet of the Sevriet, watched as the great crescent began to give way. Seeing no other choice he raised his silver war-horn and sounded his challenge. The call rang clear over the carnage. They rose in their saddles and as one shouted out their battle cry, 'Revenge!' The horsemen charged, their lances spitting flesh, hooves crushing, teeth biting, swords slashing down. Blood flowed in a horrid sickly torrent as they cut a swathe through the packed goblin ranks, turning on their backs, crushing them between horse and shield. The Armies rallied, held fast. Even the chaotic, milling ranks of High-Caravail managed to regroup.

Despite all their ferocity, the goblins were no match for those who faced them. The horsemen wheeled through their midst. Arrows sped away their sorry lives. Sharp steel and hoplite shield were a wall they could not break. They fell. They died.

The Galomist too stole amongst them and wherever it touched they died, goblin and man alike. It mattered nothing. For the mist reached out towards those who waited, growing strong as it fed on the fear and the life-gift of the slain. Horses screamed in panic at its touch, spilling riders to the earth to be hacked, spitted or frozen.

The elfin dancers danced their own terrible struggle, life against death. Did they hold their own? Who can tell? For this mattered little either. It was but part of a wider plan, a stratagem of battle.

Then, in one instant, the tactic became clear, horribly so. Out of the mist came the real attack of the Horde. They came in five huge wedges, the great Trolls at the fore of each. These did not charge or hurry into the fray. They came on as before, marching to the beat of that unseen drummer. When they reached the backs of their own force they brushed them aside. Those who did not move were slaughtered without thought.

From his vantage point in the tower, the Wizard saw it all. White faced and fear frozen he screamed out with the full horror of what he was witnessing. Helpless, he watched as the first of the wedges slammed into the already disarrayed men of High-Caravail. He saw the King, his chariot turning round and round to the panic of his milk-white war-horses. The blade of his golden sword was black with blood. Grey hands caught at the harness, long thrusting spears locked the wheels, tipping the chariot onto its side, spilling its rider to the gore soaked earth. Horses reared, struck, terrified, dying even as the spears were raised over their master.

The Wizard turned away, unable to face the truth of that death.

What could he do? For surely he must do something. He turned to the book…

And these are they who are slain:–

Dromel of Astar	Fkalk Norb	Treltor, Sevriet
Palinmar, Sevriet	Brogg	Dormer of Bronden
Gormal of Asain	Tagh	ItalFLitt Pegla
Falkiir, Bronden	Tarrow, Freshhiem	
Lestre, Caravail	Cainal of Latal,	Ploigh
Haghal	Bruin, Sevriet	Staniir, Sevriet
Wrilgh Bruffal		

He screamed, heart-wrenched by the force of his impotency. For the list grew longer with every instant, the scribing faster than the eye could read:

Fiinael, Elf.	Strandil, Caravail.	Hanrad, Caravail.
Doost.	Jeltrow, Caravail.	Frewst, Elf.
Vors	Burvik	Brenil.
Porish	Fendre, Asain	Wrom
Seleem.	Dormon.	Cail Ashaeth,
Khour	Andar	Galmiir.
Tylmor, Pashad.	Elestre, Elf	Dormod, Dressan.
Forgel	Hartla, Sevriet.	Brehera, Dormon.
Lodgr	Kolm	Punghe.
Detal	Norlam, Varista.	Worlalse, Sevriet.
Khal	Vord	Damastig,
Caravail.	Stramfae, Asain.	Poogra
Jhita	Kylim, Dormon	Calfrel, Santolin.
Gorst, Tabour	Dietric, Elf	Ulg Haplag
Frodmil	Dormanal	Tadgaf, Caravail

Only Asain held against the might of that terrible assault. At the fore were the heirs of Alan Antol, the Sanain. They were as a light midst the darkness, but that light grew dimmer.

𝔅𝔯𝔬𝔤𝔞𝔱𝔥𝔞𝔤𝔞 𝔗𝔥𝔢 𝔗𝔯𝔬𝔩𝔩 𝔩𝔬𝔯𝔡 𝔯𝔞𝔦𝔰𝔢𝔡 𝔥𝔦𝔰 𝔰𝔭𝔢𝔞𝔯.
ℭ𝔬...

'NO!' The Wizard's scream of powerless fear filled the tower. He couldn't face it, not that! He caught at the book wanting to deny the reality of the words being scribed. In a gesture of futile anger he slammed it shut.

Silence!

Stillness!

A quiet more startling and profound than any war horn or drum. There is nothing, not a single sound. Even the images that fill the tower are still, frozen in a moment of time. Nothing moves. Realisation, when it cuts through his mind with a blade of fire, is even more shocking than the silence. *Time has stopped!* How can one contend with an idea like that? *It can't just stop, can it? Surely it can't? Time isn't like that. Is it?* There's no real question to challenge the idea though.

He knows the truth. The book lays closed before him. Inscribed on its cover:

𝔗𝔥𝔢-𝔅𝔬𝔬𝔨-𝔬𝔣-𝔥𝔬𝔲𝔯𝔰.

He reaches out in an almost unconscious move to open the pages once more. *NO! If I open it Time shall start again and they'll die!*

He can't do that. Can't do anything. He's powerless, trapped by his fear of the power that reaches out for him. He stands alone in the centre of the tower. How long? Who can tell? To him it seems an eternity.

Eventually, through a mixture of curiosity and boredom, his feet carry him out from the tower. His steps are soundless as he treads his way through the ruin. Even the carpet of dust lays untroubled by his passing.

The sight before him is a strangeness unheard of, undreamed of. In some unimaginable, nightmare tableaux, figures remain poised, statue-like, frozen in this single moment of time. Faces contorted in hate stare endlessly into other no less hateful eyes.

He flinches, recoiling from the sight of a desert fighter's sword thrust into a goblin warrior's throat. The splattered droplets of blood hang in the air as jewels of death. The expression of mindless hatred on the desert man's face is somehow worse than his deed though.

They fought well, these desert people. They died well too for the number of their corpses is high indeed. Yet their shield wall has broken and the remnant of the Sultan's army form into smaller units where they continue their struggle back-to-back in some hopeless attempt to fend off the foe. At their fore a great Troll, saliva dripping from its foul, fanged mouth as it screams a silent cry of berserk fury, hefts its great iron mace.

In the midst of the carnage he finds the desert leader, the Khalif-of-Assad who had befriended him on that journey through the desert sands **Hkamoot!** The man is frozen in time, his spear point spitting the goblin before him. The recognition of who the creature is might almost be expected. As in some horrid game, the act cries out the truth of Fate's inevitable victory. Gob! *So he got his goblin after all.* An awful sadness bears down on him. Tears wet his cheeks. *Maybe he was a loathsome creature but he didn't deserve that.* He turns his back and walks away, away from that, unable to think, or to face the horror before him.

There can be no escape however. The slaughter is everywhere, the blood and the gore, the shattered remnant of man and goblin alike.

Another sight grabs at his attention. A horse, one of the Sevriet, is frozen in time, spinning mid air to avoid the thrust of some great, grey Troll's trident. It is a sight of such unimaginable magnificence and beauty. Every sinew of the steed is a balance of perfect grace. On its unsaddled back, more of the horse than the land, its rider thrusts out its counter attack. He will not miss.

He walks down the line of motionless, struggling life. Images draw him; repel him. And the horrid fascination of it all leads him ever onwards. At last he reaches the Asain ranks and gazes upon the struggle at their fore. The shattered bodies of the slain are spread out in a grotesque circle from where the Sanain perform their task as butchers in some horrendous slaughterhouse. The passage of arms is little more than a trade in flesh. Blood lies in pools upon the trodden earth.

Here, in the midst of all is Calin. She is caught, mid-spin, even in this moment of frozen time the grace of her movement is a thing of stunning beauty. *How can such Killing be beautiful?* Unable to help himself, he reaches out to wipe away the tear tracing its line of wetness over her dusty cheek. All her attention is on the great Troll that looms beside her.

The creature's hand is empty, the moment captured as its arm reached the end of casting. The black pits of its eyes follow the hard flung spear that now hangs in the air barely inches from Cog's heart.

I've got to do something! I can't let him die! Grasping the spear's shaft he pulls downwards. It moves but slowly, resisting his attempt to turn the point away from Cog. With a final surge he forces it down into the gore blackened ground. *Well at least that's something.* The creature will not have time to recover, for Calin's Sanain sword is already on the path to rob the thing of life.

He looks up at her seeking reassurance that this will indeed be the case. However, when he turns back to Cog, his scream becomes the only sound in the universe. The spear point hangs once again before the warrior's breast. He snatches the weapon, stamps on it shattering the shaft. He stands there looking at the pieces on the ground, not daring to look aside. He blinks. The spear is gone, gone back to its deadly flight. *I'm powerless,* he realises. *There's nothing that I can do. When time starts again Cog will die.*

The flare of his magic builds within him, and clothes the weapon in a mysterious light. But nothing changes. *There must be something! There must!*

The answer reverberates in his thoughts. 'The-Book-of-Hours!' He wants to scream his own horror but the sound didn't come. *The challenge continues. It won't give up so easily, I should have known.*

Only the knowledge doesn't help. The spear point waits for Cog's life and can't be denied. *The book can change it. I can, just a few words, I can undo this, save Cog. Don't I owe him that? Don't I owe Calin that little happiness? Would it be such a terrible thing? Anyway, what's the point of the magic if I can't even save my friends?* Gob had been right. *If the book can offer that, is it so wrong?*

Gob too. *If I can save Cog then why not him?* His eyes see once more the death that surrounds him. *All of them, all who have died.* Her words too. He heard his own reply too. *I can do nothing.* Only doing nothing is no answer either and he knows it. *So Cog shall die, as Gob has died, as Shimmian too. What's the point? I can't even save my friends!*

Unable to bear it any longer, he turns away, stumbles, almost falls over the body of one of the Sanain. She lies here twisted in the throes of death. The blade that had stolen her life is still imbedded in her chest. Her face is smiling though, somehow calm as if peace has come to her at last. 'What in Hell's name is this?' he shouts into the silence. There's no answer. Not even from himself.

The tower is still standing as an insult to the sacrifice being made before it. In his heart he now hates that tower, even though it draws him. At least he knows now that he will never succumb to its offer of perfection and so he begins to retrace his steps. The future waits. He can delay it no more.

That book too waited, waited as solidly as the time it now denied, waited with the challenge mocking his failure with its silken promise of success. It was the hardest thing he had ever faced. *Should I have done as she asked? Should I have changed the words?* The thought was like a bolt of lightning illuminating again the choices available. *I still can! I could save Cog at least!* It was such a simple temptation. *But, it just isn't that easy. It never is. If I save Cog then why not Shimmian, or Gob, or all who have died. I could do it.* Such a compelling thought...

No I can't. That was the truth. No matter how sweet the bait, it was but a snare to trap him. *Once I accept that power and take it to myself, then I must accept everything which that power means. They'll become the slaves of my will. Once I change Fate I can never go back. By the very power of that act I'd become both Master of everything and a slave to That!*

He rested his hand upon its surface, half expecting to feel the pain bound within. *So it's by my hand that they're to die?* There was a truth there, although it was not in the opening of the book that they died nor in truth in his decision to leave Fate unchanged. *What kind of friend am I?* No they died just because it was the way things had turned out. That was all. They died because they fought in a terrible battle and in such battles many are those who die. Even so, he still didn't appreciate the reality of what he chose.

Seven times he tried to open those pages but could not. Finally he shut his eyes and reached out.

Cog of Rael.   Gwyll Brogathaga

Calin's anguished scream filled the universe, echoing over the chaotic melee of struggling figures. Perhaps for just an instant the masses paused from their slaughter, chilled by the awfulness of her loss.

It ripped through the Wizard's soul also, tore through his heart, his mind, his very being. It filled him with its own pain, its own anger, an anger so vivid that it awoke the rainbow at his centre, unbound his magic into a luminescent fury as terrible as any weapon of war.

His fires burst before him as he left the tower. There was no conscious intent to the move, no thought guiding his actions. At that moment he was the rainbow, the rainbow he, and his anger exploded upon the battlefield in a terrible, flaming whirlpool of unimaginable magic.

The crimson bands of his casting were worse than the blood-soaked ground, darker than the crusted blades they raised to defend themselves. The flickering tongues of orange fury sparked as bale-fire upon their weapons until they cast them aside. They would have hid from him then but there was no escape from his passion, nor the flaming of the fire that sent them sprawling into the filth and carnage, grovelling in the face of his power, Man, Elf and Goblin alike.

Something came at him from out of the carnage, a thing of grey coldness, of lifeless cruelty and madness. It rose up to reach out at him with fingers of caustic fire. He took it, bound it in bands of gold even brighter than the once brilliant sun and then cast it aside without even recognising that it had been there.

The Elven harpists stood in a group upon the plain, trying to calm his wrath with the beauty of their sounds. However his burning fury was not so easily stilled. He needed the anger, wanted the passion; only thus could he contend with the dread that filled his soul. He wrenched their golden instruments from them, even Plie, and shattered their echoing strings upon the beryl bright hardness of his wrath.

When the mist rose up to meet him he burst its chill heart to nothingness with a flare of azure light.

If the warriors and goblins, elves and trolls screamed in fear at his coming, if their minds recoiled in terror at the force beating upon their senses, what did it matter? Nothing was as terrible as the slaughter that had been meted out by their cruel hands.

'Is this what you wanted?' he shouted into the trembling skies on the wings of a roaring wind and in the fury of the whirling, turning maelstrom flickering through the heavens. 'Is this what you demanded of me? Well here I am. I will not be stopped now. This SLAUGHTER WILL END!'

Indeed the Battle was done, for nothing could stand against the force of his coming. They ran from him, fled in terror from the brightness of his magic. But where could they go? There was nowhere to hide, nowhere to flee, nowhere to run. He was everywhere. Seeing, in his lightning's desperate glare, the end of everything they had known they fell, sobbing in fear, crawled on hands and knees to escape the terribleness of his wrath, scattering each and every way. For this time at least they no longer fought, one against the other. At least now all were united in their need to escape.

He let them go, hastened their departures with indigo visions of freedom. Yet he watched them and when swords were lifted they turned to glass and shattered on the breath of his breezes. When they turned their faces of hatred towards those of another kind they saw his own wrath reflected and they turned screaming aside and he drove them onwards and away.

The Battleground lay still now, still and silent as night. Those who had gone left nothing but a field of the fallen. At its centre stood Calin, looking down upon the stricken Cog. Silent as frost was she, her Sanain-sword hanging limply from unfeeling fingers. She didn't cry, her grief was much too raw, too unthinkable for that. For all appearances, the spark of her life had fled. Only her spirit remained, clinging unwilling to an existence promising such pain.

This alone had withheld his hand. For this alone he hadn't killed. Nothing else could have restrained his power. He just couldn't contend with the awfulness of her sorrow.

There was within him an urge to approach her but even that was forbidden him. He couldn't face the emptiness of her eyes and he knew it. Thus it was from a distance that he watched as, with the help of the two remaining Sanain, Calin laid her lover's corpse upon a huge wooden shield. They bore him up, carried him in silence, a secret, sacred cortege stepping through the reeking heaps of the battlefield dead until the silence that surrounded them hid them with its own special cloak.

Among the desolation friends, just one or two, sought comfort from each other's strength. Arms, now too weak to hold a weapon, managed to hold those now too weak to stand. Together they struggled to find an escape from the horror, smoke and mist.

The druids were abroad, moving without fear where fear sought to rule. The helpless sadness of the scene filled them as they tried to find healing for the broken bodies that lay about them. He could see them kneeling in the midst of the carnage, even here seeking to mend the torn and savaged remnant of life. Even these he couldn't understand.

There was one, an ancient wise-woman, who sat sobbing beside the shattered body of a goblin maid. Her strength was not enough to prevent the life from slipping into the grey realms of death no matter how she tried. She tried nonetheless. He watched and at last found something calm in her selfless act.

There were elves here too, wandering about as mindlessly distraught as he. Where possible they served the druids, carrying the wounded to the healer's tents, seeking out the living amongst the dead. *Still they do not hate!*

When the time for night came, though there still was no night to fall, the field was empty and he stood alone on this now silent plain of the dead. *It's over.* With this realisation came the knowledge that there was nothing more he could do. The fact that he cried and called out in the grip of his horror meant nothing to him. It was nothing. What could have meaning in this place of death. His eyes, which could not bear to look, saw nothing else. Yet, for all that his mind strove to refuse acknowledgement of this truth, in this place, he was denied the solace of the madness, which had driven him after the battle of Sarum. Some 20,000 souls had perished here, though none ever counted their bodies, nor knew their names. Save for *that Book*, which he'd never read again. *Why have they died?* He had no answer. The only reality were the heaps of lifeless flesh, man, creature and elf alike, side-by-side now without prejudice or politic. They were all of the same nation now, denizens of the kingdom of the dead. There was no song, and no singer, no bard to speak of their bravery, nor any poet to mourn their loss. It was such a terrible waste, such a sad, pointless ending of so many.

He wept and, in his sorrow, his magic became still and he once more became just himself. His cloak was black, his wide brimmed hat also. The only colours to be seen on him were the rainbow sash tied about its crown, the blood red ruby hanging around his neck and eyes that shone like fire. 'I am the *Wizard of Rainbows*,' he called into the gloom and his rainbow was blacker than the void.

This time as he trod the path back through the ruin of Tabour even the dust seemed loath to trouble him. The tower also neither challenged nor welcomed his return.

'I have returned.'

The only reply was silence, the silence of fear.

*

> On the steps which splay from the dream-time way
> Which end in a rainbow of grey
> You danced in the way of the dream-time ballet
> When the footsteps start to decay
>
> (Part 2 of The dreamtime)

He sat, leaning back against the tower's smooth stone face. The idea of entering never occurred to him. The last thing that he wanted was to face that thing again or see what was being written there now. He pulled his cloak tighter against the growing chill, unsure if its source was within or without.

Images flicked through the halls of his mind compelling and repelling alike. He didn't want them or the memories so easily awakened. The wine didn't help. It tasted sour and reminded him of blood. The brooding, waiting silence made everything worse.

What now then? He tried to marshal his thoughts into some semblance of order. *I'm helpless. I can do nothing. For all my magic, all my power it's useless. I'm powerless. Filled with power yet powerless.* His effort failed. Thoughts tumbled through his mind as pebbles on the storm tide. As he tried to grasp at them they slipped away leaving little but half remembered snippets. *I did stop the Battle! The magic flared! But I was too late!* His mind overflowed with a thousand images of the carnage that had been. *Huh! I couldn't stop that! I couldn't stop the killing! I could have! I was too late! They all died.*

Another memory, *Gentil!* The name came unbidden. *He died too. For me? They all died, Shimmian and now Cog. Gentil died that I might have power. What use is that? I can't even use it to save my friends.*

A new image arose in his mind, the visions of his magic flaring behind his closed eyes. *No wonder they were afraid of me. I could have destroyed them all. I could have destroyed everything! It's a wonder I didn't. I could have so easily. It was only Calin's sadness that stopped me. God! Is that why he had to die? Just to prevent me from destroying everything?*

He answered himself. *No that's not the truth. I've always avoided killing. That's more like it. I avoid the killing because otherwise I might kill everything!* He laughed in dry self-derision. *So why's that so terrible? Why shouldn't I destroy everything? Why should I do or not do anything? Is my way any better than Hers? Is my inactivity any better than their hatred and thirst for blood? At least they know what they want even if it's just the death of their enemies. I don't even know that!*

This was getting him nowhere. He was achieving nothing and knew it. All the same he was reluctant to move. It was as if, in some dark corner of his soul he knew that once he started he might never rest again. *I might have stopped the Battle, but not the hatred!* he told himself. *The battle might be over but not the killing. That'll continue forever.* It was a truth that could never be denied.

I can't just stay here drowning in my own self-pity though. I've got to do something. Even the staff failed to provide its customary comfort when he pulled himself, reluctantly to his feet.

Beyond the ruin the smoke from the encampment hung as a dark pall. There was little sign of movement. It was still too early for the carrion crows although it wouldn't be long that was for sure.

There seemed to be little sign of the armies, either. One or two figures were moving among the fallen, but these were not the troops of the various armies. They'd probably abandoned everything in their haste to escape him. *No! I'm not going down that path again.* He checked himself. *I wonder where they all went?* But a disinterest, born of his feelings of helplessness left the question unanswered. *I've got to do something.* This time of rest was but a respite. The matter wasn't over yet that was for sure. *There must be something, some sort of way open to me!*

Eventually he left the tower and the cloying dust of the ruined city to make his way towards the tents. He chose to avoid the worst of that bloody battleground by following a wide loop to the south east of the camp. His earlier suspicion had been correct. The whole place seemed to have been abandoned. Many of the tents were torn and flattened, probably in their haste to escape. Others however were totally untouched, awaiting their owners' return. They'd have a long wait.

There were bodies here too. For the northern-most goblin phalanx had crushed to nothing the men of High-Caravail and rampaged through the encampment in a destructive frenzy. However the centre remained largely untouched.

The school of Druids and the Healing priests of Finestre had brought a semblance of order and assembled a hospital amidst the tents of Santolin. They did their best but it could never be enough.

In the great pavilion the table remained set, the meal left when the battle started. He wasn't in the mood to eat.

I wonder where they all went. This time he actually meant the question and unfortunately this time an answer came. It came as a cry rising to a scream, soul-wrenching in its terrible, timbre of fear and pain. It echoed over the plain, called through the lifeless land. It froze his heart worse than any deadly mist. He didn't want to go, didn't want to face the truth of whatever it might be. Regardless of his wants though, he turned and directed his footsteps out of the camp, away from the battle line and into the grasslands towards the source of that awful sound.

Tracks trailed through the tough brown grass leading him on. He could do little other than follow. It didn't take long, less than half-an-hour, to wish that he hadn't.

He didn't even recognise the body at first. It was a hump, like a boulder in the grass. He looked closer, wished he hadn't. The elfling was sprawled over a rock. An axe blow had shattered her face, severed her brow, eye and cheek with unbelievable brutality. They'd hacked at her body too, whoever they might have been, just an act of mindless savagery. *How could they have done such a thing? She's little more than a child.*

Why? He vomited both at the sight and smell. *Why?* As usual no one answered.

For some inner reason it felt right to bury her there. *I can't just walk away.* He dug the grave with his own knife and his bare hands. *I wonder who she was? What her name was? Who her family and friends might be?* He'd never know, in all probability no one ever would. Somewhere parents were missing their child. They'd wait forever, never knowing.

Eventually, although quaking with horror at the touch of her lifeless flesh, he picked her up and lay her in the pit, what was left of her. He'd found her seed clutched tight in her soft little hand. He placed it over her heart. *I hope she can be at peace now.* But he could find no words to say as he covered her with soil, or again as he turned to leave her alone in that sad, lonely grave.

There were other bodies too, corpses, shattered lives, limbs, more alone than ever. He didn't look, couldn't. There wasn't any answer to their death, well, none that he could recognise. Now all he sought was rest, escape from his own nightmare visions.

He moved southwards without really thinking, following a trail of bare, hard-pressed earth that cut through the trampled grass. By the time that trail had led him back to the road, he'd gone beyond the killing ground and was no longer confronted with the remains of the fallen. Even here though, he could still smell the rank stench of fear and slaughter in the grey, motionless air.

On reaching the road he turned eastwards. Then, where a narrow trail broke away to the right he took this lesser way, following that into the rougher grassland the south of Tabour. There wasn't any escape though, not even here. Through the whole he could feel that tower watching, waiting, wondering what he might do.

He was growing tired when he first smelt the smoke. A quick search of his surroundings revealed a dark and rose-lit column reaching skywards from where a fire was burning some way off to his right. Without really thinking he turned aside towards the glow.

There were eight of them at first glance, goblins, not that it mattered to the Wizard at that moment. Were they any worse than bloodthirsty men? They hadn't set a guard but sprawled about the fire in total unconcern. Two of them looked up as he walked slowly into the light of the fire. He felt their eyes on him, weighing him but without challenge and for a change with no real hostility.

The sound of groaning caught his attention, drew his gaze towards a ninth, previously unseen figure. He walked over. The goblin had been spitted by a long spear, one of the Pashad lances. Someone had broken the haft off but the wicked blade was still imbedded in its guts. It would die. There was no hope of other.

'He's dying.' The Wizard felt compelled to say something. More eyes turned to him.

'Agh! One of those bastards on a horse caught him out on the plain,' one of the creatures explained without any real interest. 'Agh! He'll die soon enough. Shouldn't cause us no bother.'

The words were undoubtedly true however callous they might seem. Even in the short space of time that the Wizard had been there the wounded goblin had slipped gratefully into an unconsciousness from which he'd never awaken.

After a moment the Wizard turned away from the wounded form and walked over to the fire. There he crouched before the flames warming his hands. It was cold. He hadn't realised just how cold before that moment. The lack of sun was beginning to tell.

'Agh! What do you want anyway?' One of the party had stood and now fingering the hilt of the scimitar at his side he was beginning to realise the strangeness of the situation.

'What do I want?' He'd not even thought of the matter. 'Nothing of you. I saw the fire. It was cold.'

The goblin seemed at a loss of what to say. After a while it sat down again and began to gnaw the meat from a bone. He didn't offer any to the Wizard. That wouldn't be the goblin way. Such an offer would have been refused anyway.

After a while the Wizard gathered some more firewood and built up the stack. Then he curled up in his cloak beside the fire. If he slept at all it was little more than a fitful doze. He gained no rest.

When he awoke fully they'd gone. The now cold corpse was all that remained, the broken spear still impaling. It seemed so sad, such a waste.

There were plenty of shrubs and small trees here. He collected together a large pile, even some larger pieces of wood that had fallen during some long past storm. There seemed little need for haste as he carefully built the pyre. Then having lain the body on this, he set the fire. It took some time for the wood was damp. He didn't want to use his magic, not now, not here. Eventually the job was done though and the fire began to steal upwards through the pyre.

'What are you doing?' He'd heard the approaching footsteps so the voice came as no surprise.

He didn't even turn around. 'He died whilst I slept. It seemed fitting.' Not that it was an explanation, nor that any was due.

'It's a goblin.' There was anger in the voice, an anger which stilled and froze to nothing when the Wizard turned his eyes towards the speaker. The newcomer was dressed in the green and mauve of the Ganesh Principality although the Wizard didn't recognise it as such. He was surprisingly young also, although the chill in his eyes spoke of more than years.

'Yes,' he replied at last. 'Well, it was a goblin. Now it's just a dead goblin. He was killed by some horseman's spear.' The fire flared, hissing and spluttering.

The soldier could find no reply. He looked back towards the trail where the other, sixteen spearmen were waiting. 'Was it alone?'

'I think they always are, even when they're in a group. Does it matter?'

'Of course it matters!' Exasperation. 'They're goblins. It's them that we're hunting.'

'Hunting?'

'They can't be allowed to stay here. Not in this land.'

'So you hunt them down to slay them? Treat them as no more than animals?'

He nodded. There was something about this being that made the soldier feel almost guilty. He drew himself up. 'Tell me. Were there others? Where did they go?'

The Wizard felt so weary as if he hadn't slept at all. 'They went their own way, soldier. It might be best if you went yours.'

The hand tightened, white knuckled on the spear shaft. 'My way is to follow and kill any of their kind! Will you help us?'

'Why all this killing?'

'Revenge.' Such a bitter reply. 'They've killed enough of us! Not just us though.' It was clear that he had a sudden need to explain himself. 'They are animals, anyway that's how they behave. There was a farmstead, about two hours' march from here.' He pointed back over the plain. 'Just a woman and her four kids. They killed them all, even the smallest. She was no more than three years, if that. There was no need. They had nothing the goblins could have used. They're just evil butchers.'

It was probably true. Not that it changed anything.

'Does that justify anything?'

'It can't go unpunished.'

'No I suppose not.'

The soldier turned and started to walk back where the others waited. 'Do you want to join us?' he called over his shoulder, almost as an after-thought.

The Wizard waved aside the offer and turned back to the pyre, not really interested if the man went or not.

When he finally left the camp little remained but a small pile of smoking ashes. He turned eastward walking out into the grassland rather than back to the road. It didn't matter. It seemed that nothing really mattered now.

Several hours of nothing passed by. Eventually though he chanced upon a river gully. The stream was just a narrow, half dried-up thing. What little water remained flowed in sluggish disinterest. It fitted his mood.

He followed as it meandered over the plain until he found himself in a small meadow cradled in the confluence between his stream and another. There were trees here, just a few, sheltering the water. Three of the wild auric were grazing on the far bank. It seemed strange that they didn't panic or flee with their usual timidity. But why should they? He was of no danger to them.

At first he thought to camp cold. It seemed too much effort to make a fire despite the chill in the air. Perhaps at this time he was even grateful to be alone and fearful least a fire draw others to disturb him.

His hunger though was another matter. He'd not eaten for some time now and there was no denying that. Rummaging through his pack provided little enough, just a half broken piece of way-bread. That was better than nothing. The water from the river was cold and ice fresh reminding him of his own chill.

Now, despite his earlier reluctance, he hunted for kindling over the meadow, found where some long passed storms had left a hedge of driftwood. The blaze of the fire seemed welcoming with its offering of heat.

What now? I can't just hide here pretending nothing's happening. The fighting isn't over. Their hatred won't go away just because of my bright colours. It's up to me to do something. I know it! I can't deny that truth.

Why? Always the same question. The answer that came unexpectedly into his mind was *'Gentil!' She said it was he who first named me and that I was Kin to him, his heir.* The difficulty was that even the name Gentil was but an echo running through his mother's stories.

Gentil, Lord of ancient Maddon. Eloveen-Friend, The first Wizard. The Watcher. Gentil the Wise.

They were but words. He sat back against the tree where he'd slept trying to remember. At first there were little than snippets of a tale. Gentil, alone of all men, was not afraid to face the Eloveen when first they came through the Ryngold. They, the Eloveen had named him friend and entrusted him with the gift of magic. At least that was what was said.

There was one Gentil who had also been the captain of the King's army when they stood against the dark Eloveen lord Elovsenal.

The stories told that another called Gentil had been in Lodor when Alan-of-Colon had first ridden out on his quest towards The Gwarle. Surely that couldn't have been the same one for the age of the Eloveen had lasted hundreds of years. In the tale of the Three, it was told that Gentil had set the quest into being. There had been a poem, something ancient as an epic. The Wizard couldn't remember the true words, just the outline of the tale.

Gentil was ever the mover of Fate! The hand of Fate! EVEN NOW? The thought screamed through his mind. *No! NOT AGAIN!* He felt once more the unwelcome chill of the knowledge that he was not his own master.

'WHAT AM I?' His cry rang in the air startling the Auric to send them fleeing back out onto the grassland. This time he had his answer. *I am the Wizard of Rainbows. He gave me that at least. Is being the toy of fate the price that I must pay?*

Nonetheless he knew that the magic was too much. There was something out of balance about this whole situation. *I'm not a God!*

Later he cut a willow wand and tried his hand at fishing the water. Perhaps it was too cold now or that there were no fish here. He did catch a small pheasant with an accurately thrown stone though and eased his hunger with that. Then he curled up, wrapped in his cloak, at the foot of the largest tree, not far from the fire. To him it seemed remarkable that he slept at all. In truth though it had been many hours indeed since last he'd rested and the wonder was that he had been able to continue at all.

*

Some four or so days had passed since the battle on the plain. Not all had been inactive. Keaval, Horse master of Lodor turned slowly in the saddle letting his eyes scan the dour landscape. He didn't mind the greyness; it suited the colourlessness of his own spirit. He'd seen the grass of his homeland burning, seen the great herds fleeing in panic before the smoke. There was nothing to live for now. That he was a captain of men meant nothing. That he still lived after the battle meant nothing either. His very life meant nothing, nothing but revenge.

He stood in his saddle gazing about himself. His twenty-three-strong band could not be seen. They lay hid in the gully, waiting. 'Now all we need is the prey.' Even though his men overheard him, he spoke to himself in a voice gruff and war hardened. He knew that he'd not have long to wait. They had planned this well. The goblin war party always came this way on their return to their lair in the hills. Well this time they'd discover that they'd done it one time too many.

Having dismounted, he tied the reins to a nearby tree. Leaves drifted earthward; dry as paper. The grass was turning brown too. The land was dying. Taking a fistful of the dry stems he rubbed them to dust between his fingers. The whole world was turning to dust. *Ah! What does it matter?* Soon the goblins would come and then he'd have one more taste of the revenge that he so hungered for.

It was not the goblins who came though, well not the first who came. Rather it was an old man. The stooped figure rested heavily upon his staff as his feet dragged him down the road towards the horseman.

Keaval waited; there was time enough. Eventually the man neared him.

'Greetings.'

The Wizard raised his eyes to gaze into the rider's face. He saw the shock reflected but probably didn't know its cause, if he even considered it. 'You greet me, Sevriet?' he asked, his tone as flat as his heart. 'This is no place for such welcomes.'

The horseman gathered his thoughts once his surprise over the man's youth had subsided. 'It's a grey time, and a grey road,' he addressed the stranger. 'To you at least I mean no harm.'

'Greeting? Harm?' He sounded bemused. 'Could you harm me, you or any of your companions?' He waved a disparaging hand towards their hiding places.

The Sevriet's eyes widened even more. 'You know of them?' He looked about seeking sign. He saw nothing.

'The goblins won't come, Sevriet.'

'They won't?'

'No, I told them of your trap.'

For some strange reason the answer didn't surprise him. 'Who are you?'

'It doesn't matter. None of it matters. The killing is just as pointless as everything else. I decided to stop it, this time.' He sounded sad, remorseful.

'But they burnt our grasslands, slew the Sevre.'

'So now you wait to kill them?' He didn't sound angry, just tired.

'They Kill. We Kill! It is war.'

'War? Is that what you call it? It seems that this is your only way with anything. To kill without even thinking about right or wrong!' the Wizard snapped back. 'So they hunt you and you hunt them. The slaughter goes on and on. There's no point. In the end all will be dead, all slain, all gone. What then?'

He couldn't find an answer to that sadness.

'Why hasten that which comes anyway?' In mimicry of the horseman's previous act the Wizard stooped and picked up a handful of the fallen leaves, crushed them in his fist the opened his hand and blew the dust away.

'I'd sooner die fighting than just crumple to nothing like that.' The horseman knew that well enough. 'There'll be no joy for anyone when the world dies.'

'Then it shan't die.'

The strength and surety of the Wizard's tone resounded through the horseman's being.

'I've decided,' though the decision only came with speaking the words, 'I'll go to Her and bring an ending to this waste!'

'What?' Despite the thrill running through him, the words meant nothing to the fighter.

'I'll go to Her as She said I would. She awaits me anyway.'

Keaval watched, unmoving and un-speaking, as the Wizard turned towards the East. He stayed there watching until the figure disappeared into mist of the distance.

*

He knew where to find Her. Had he thought to ask he'd probably known since She spoke her anger on the storm and set the mountains ablaze with Her sorrow.

She stood, quite still, half bathed in the mist, maybe half mist Herself. The silver of Her garments reflected on the water. Perhaps he saw Her before She saw him. It was of little consequence. She was waiting for him anyway. Of that there was scant doubt. She turned to face him. The smile that met him knew no warmth. Only the same terrible empty sadness as ever.

'So, you have come to find me, Wizard? Did I not say you would do so? I have felt your questing, your searching. Now you are here what would you do with me?' She smiled Her perfect, chilling smile and wet Her lips with the tip of Her lascivious tongue, though the moisture sparkled as frost on Her flesh. 'So what now? Shall you bind me with your lights? Enslave me with the terrible beauty of your colours? Compel me with the wonder of your rainbow? Kill me with brilliance of your magic?'

How can I win? How can I prevail against her? 'I am the Wizard of Rainbows, Lady.' He would not use the name Heledthera as the Elves called Her nor the Dherlethae of the Goblins, for these were not Hers and he knew that well enough. 'I don't kill! I won't take a life. Any more than you, who even so denies the truth of life to others!

'I've come to plead with you. Return the turning of the Earth circles, My Lady, let the World heal.' He struggled to think, to contend against what She was. His eyes were drawn to her, transfixed by her brittle beauty. She was tall, taller than he. Her skin was flawless, white, smooth, perfect as a porcelain marionette. Her silver gown clung tight, revealing as much as it hid. Her hair glimmered, as do cobwebs caught in the frosts of a winter's morning. She felt his eyes and smiled anew.

'What do you see, Wizard? What do you see with your burning eyes? Do you know? Can you see through the truths of my existence?' Her voice tinkled as crystal, cold, humourless, little more than a laugh of cruel self-mockery. 'Is that what you crave, to touch my emptiness with the fullness of your truth? To understand the depths of my mystery of ice?' Again She wet Her lips, spreading Her arms wide to reveal Herself to him. 'It was not always so.' The emptiness spoke through Her. 'Once I knew.' There was something compelling about Her as were She in truth an empty vessel that might be filled.

'What shall I do, Lady? Show you the mystery of your own nature? Show you the truth of your being in the colours of my world?'

'Why not, Young-Wizard? Is your world my world? Are your colours my colours? Is not my mystery my own to know or not to know? For I tell you, look at me all you wish. You shall only see what is me anyway.'

So he looked into Her mystery and spread the violet mist of his understanding over Her, bathed Her in its wonder. But She laughed her empty, mirthless laugh and accepted the gift of his strange mystery. She wrapped herself in its glory as if warming Herself upon its essence. Yet even as She did so the colour seemed to darken and She reached out greedily, drawing it to Her, breathed it, absorbed it until it was no more.

'So you like my mystery, desire the truth of my coldness?' she crooned as She began to stroke Her hands over Her own body, to play with the perfection of Her own form, swaying before him. Provocative? Yes and desirable.

'You shall see yourself as you are!' he tried again, even though as he did so he felt a tremor of doubt. The indigo bands surrounded Her, caressed, wound about Her body mimicking the movements of Her own fingers, suggestive fingers wandering over Her secret places, pressing, fondling, revealing her form.

'Ah is this how it is to be then, Wizard?' She smiled, though Her eyes were dull. 'Look all you wish. It is no trouble to me.' She reached for the clasp at Her throat drawing the gown open to expose Herself to his eyes. The rise and fall of Her breasts tore the thoughts from his mind. 'What no words, my Wizard? No words to give me?' She stepped closer.

'Oh yes I have my words, Lady. And I see your ways. Do you think to ensnare and enslave me as just another one of your sad minions?' The brilliant blue of his vibrations filled their existence. Like the fire of the northern lights, as the moonlight on the snow-capped peeks. She laughed Her laugh of emptiness and turned his light into playthings of ice, jewels that sparkled, earrings, a glistening necklace, droplets of crystal that dangled from Her upturned nipples. She laughed again, shaking Herself that the droplets fell as raindrops about Her feet. 'Ensnare? Enslave, what are these but words. I did not come to you but you to me. If I reject your visions, so what? I am as you see me, pure and cold and eternal. If I deny for this instant the call of death that follows, why not? I am here for the moment. I am here now. Is this too little? If I offer my present is that so wrong?'

'But where is the love? Where the happiness?' And the green that was his answer was mirrored in Her eyes. For one moment Her expression softened but just for a moment. She took his emerald gift and turned it to the green of envy, dull, tawdry.

'Love you say? Love? What is love but the justification of lust, the expression of hunger? I have rejected such and still reject its lies. So I'll meet your love with my own lust. Tell me, Wizard, can you not melt the coldness of my existence?' She stepped once more, even closer now.

'No, Lady, though I see your need, you'll not have my power,' he replied, shielding himself with a golden sphere of energy.

She stepped into the light. 'But you give it to me all the same, Wizard, although there was no need. I am here.' As were it liquid she bathed in its essence until it ran from Her, leaving Her naked before him.

His anger, even his fear is gone now. His only awareness is of Her and the lust that rises in his loins. The ray that he binds Her in is thick with the taste of his desire. She draws it from him, cups her hands to form a vessel from which She can drain the orange liqueur.

The touch of Her hand upon his own burns like fire and yet it freezes his senses as stone. Without asking, and without his resisting, She takes his crimson light and turns it blood red to spill upon the barren ground until it is gone.

She is close, so close that he is aware of nothing else but Her chilliness and his own desire to warm Her. 'NOW!' she calls out into the emptiness that surrounds them. 'Now!' she demands, pulling at his hands as She sinks to the hard dust-strewn ground.

He grasps Her, thrilling to the touch of Her icy flesh. He will warm Her, fill the emptiness of Her being with the heat of his passion. She laughs coldly as ever, taking his fires as nothing. She drains his warmth, his fire, his need until he is nothing but an empty vessel.

When there is no more to take She rises and stands before him cloaking Herself once again in Her colourless garments. Her eyes might have been almost sad when She looked down at him. 'What now, Wizard? Did I ask that you serve me? For what? I mean neither you nor any other harm. Only to know your magic can no longer awaken the fires of the world, no longer free the vortex that might enslave us all. I have done what I must, no more.'

She turned away head hung with Her shame to where the beast awaited Her. She was gone.

He knelt in the grey dust beside the lake. There was no sound in the whole world. It was as if eternity waited for his words. He spoke them. 'I have failed.'

*

> In the dark of the night you bathed in the light
> Of a sun of the dream-time lie.
> But when I heard the theme of your dream-time scream
> I covered my ears and cried.
>
> (Part 3 of the Dreamtime)

'Shit!' She'd fucked up big style this time and she knew it. 'Agh! Die, You fuckin' shit-grovellers.' Her insult, called out through the broken window was no more than bravado. They'd got her this time, *Fucking Bastards!*

Gorbal looked up from the floor where his blood was spreading in an almost perfect circle. He'd be no fucking use if it came to a fight, not with that bloody great spear skewering him to the boards.

There were about twenty, maybe thirty of them. *They're big bastards too, dressed in black and silver with sodding great round shields and those bloody belly-sticking spears.* She could hear them laughing as they waited.

'Icicle,' she told herself, 'I reckon that you're fucked proper this time. Agh! And there's no mistake about that.' Her laugh was no more than habit. She wasn't afraid to die. No one could have accused her of that. It was just a waste to have been got like this.

They'd escaped the plain all right. *Even the fuckin' horse shaggers hadn't spitted them with their fuckin' poles.* Then Gorbal had to get greedy, *Bastard!* She kicked him. His head lolled sideways. *Dead! Agh!* He didn't even feel it! It was all his fault too. He had to try to be big. *Agh! Arsehole.*

She wrenched at the spear. It didn't budge at first. Persevering though she pushed, pulled and shook it from side to side until the blade came free of the wood. It squelched, almost sloshed as she yanked it from his flesh. The dripping blood left a dark trail over the bare floorboards. It was a good spear though, long and heavy. The head, almost as long as her forearm, was leaf shaped, bladed on either side so that you could slash or stick with it. If she got the chance she'd get a taste of their blood before they got to her.

Outside they were laughing again. She hated that sound. It jarred on her nerves. *What are they fuckin' doing?* There was a lot of movement round the side of the next house. Anyway, she'd not have to wait long. Whatever they were about, it was pretty sure to involve her in something unpleasant.

Bollix! She took a long swig of the wine they'd found. It was gentle stuff. She'd have preferred vinegar or beer to that. It was all she had though, all they'd bloody found here, except them, the bloody spearmen. It had been a trap. Gorbal should have seen that at the start, the open door, the bottle on the table and he'd gone and fallen for it like a pillock. *Shit*

They'd got most of the band on the way out. They hadn't even had a chance to fight back and now their bodies were piled together in a heap where the soldiers had dragged them, even Norsch, poor little sod. Just a smog, not even old enough to try it on yet.

It wasn't that she felt any sorrow for them. What had they ever done for her? They'd had it easy really, just an arrow or the quick thrust of a spear and it was done. She doubted that it would be that easy for her.

'You coming out? Bitch!' the voice cracked, hard, cruel.

'Fuck off!' she yelled back at the unseen caller. 'Agh! That or come in here and let me spit you, you big fucking wanker!'

The others laughed. 'Suit yourself, Bitch!' There was ice in that voice. 'Makes no difference. Quick or slow, you die anyway.'

There was no way of denying that. *Agh! It's gotta 'appen sometime*, she told herself. She wasn't really sad for herself either. Well life had hardly been the greatest joy. Mostly fear, hunger and fighting. Looking backwards offered no real reason to go forward. There was nothing there. Well, only one thing, the image of the Pilgrim flicked through her memory. *My friend.* There was no irony to the thought. It was something she held of value, probably the only thing even though she didn't really understand what it meant. Most likely it was a power thing. Perhaps being a friend to him gave her something of his power. She breathed deeply at the thought. *Well it's something anyway. I wonder where he is now.*

She was trying to ignore what was happening outside. Her hope, that they might try to rush her and she'd at least get the chance to take one or two with her, seemed somewhat forlorn as she heard them piling the wood about the building.

'You fuckin' cowards,' she screamed in fury. 'Agh! Ain't even got the fuckin' guts t' take on a bitch!'

They laughed again. 'More fun to hear your screams as you burn, Goblin,' one proclaimed frankly. 'Don't worry; when you get done we'll sling the rest of your lot on the fire with you. So you can all go to hell together.'

She looked about, seeking some sort of answer, nothing! The wine looked suddenly inviting. She took a long swallow, and another. A figure showed silhouetted against the window. The bottle flew, crashed against his shoulder. She laughed at his cry of pain. Then lifted the spear. *Next time.*

It took them over an hour to pile up the kindling. They weren't taking chances. But eventually the work was done. She could see them gathering out on the road, far enough to be out of range of the spear. They built another smaller pile there. It was a crude thing, none of the skill her Pilgrim had possessed. Far too soon however the crackle of fire sounded and the first few whiffs of smoke drifted cloud-ward.

The spear was inviting now, not for them but to use on herself. Only that wasn't the goblin way. She'd be fucked if she'd let these bastards get the better of her. No she'd save it for her chance, if it ever came. She watched as they gathered about the now blazing pyre. They had torches, sticks with oil-soaked cloth. Soon they were flaming torches.

They always work together she noted, not for the first time. She envied them that. Goblins would have fought to see who would be the first. Mind you, they'd have rushed her anyway, not gone to all this fire stuff. *Why ruin good meat? Won't be long now.* She drew back her spear arm.

They spread out, avoiding the front of the hut, laughing loudly as they set about their task. She heard the rustling of the torches and the crackle of the wood catching through the wall.

She waited, unmoving.

The crackling grew louder, tendrils of smoke drifted before the window. Still she waited. Was it growing hotter? It would soon. She could taste the smoke now, acrid, reminiscent of campfires and full bellies. Small trickles of grey stole through the cracks in the woodwork, hazing the air.

The figure showed through the window, just for an instant, but it was enough. Her arm shot forwards, the spear hung in the air, slowing as time contracted. He didn't even scream. The blade took him just below the ear, caught on the back of his skull and angled upwards. The weight of the shaft was enough to pull the point up into his brain. She'd got her Kill! *Fuckin' last one though!*

Icicle heard the warning shout, *too bleedin' late,* and the curses that followed. She even laughed in her sense of achievement. Right then however the first flames scorched through the wooden wall, licked upwards with alarming speed to set the thatched roofing ablaze. The heat reddening her cheek with its own cruel warning of what was to come. She nearly screamed then. Bit on her lip until the blood flowed. But she made no sound. She'd not give them the satisfaction.

The floor was beginning to smoke too; she could feel the heat under her feet. Sat on the table, waiting. 'Agh! Shit!' She couldn't see beyond the window now. The smoke was growing thicker, hotter. She coughed, almost choked on inhalation. The fumes burnt in her throat, brought tears to her eyes. She began to wonder if there was any point in her trying for the door or going through the window. No, they'd have them covered.

The commotion outside didn't really intrude at first. She heard the raised voices, the shouting, and thought that it was them celebrating. But the voices were of anger, an argument. Steel clanged, just once.

'Stop? What do you mean Stop? It's too late! They're probably choked to death already.'

Other voices, shouts incoherent.

Another voice, louder, 'I say it!' *Say what?*

'Well! If you can get her out she's yours! I just don't see why.'

''Cause no one, nothing should die like that.'

It made no sense at all. Then the door opened and framed against the light was the biggest, ugliest looking bastard that she'd ever seen. Dressed in leather he was with a hairless head and a great scar turning his expression into a perpetual sneer.

She drew her knife, ready to fight. If he noticed he didn't show it. He just stood there in the middle of the flames and sort of smiled.

Her eyes widened. The knife was forgotten. *He ain't fuckin' burning!*

He moved towards her. 'Don't worry, kid, we're getting you out of here.'

The words made no sense. 'Agh!' She couldn't think of reply.

'Here,' he'd taken off a ring and handed it to her, 'Put it on your finger.'

She took it, weighed it in her hand. It might even be gold at worse brass, probably worth something anyway, and it was set with a bloody great, red stone. Perhaps fire burned in its heart, for it flickered with a life of its own. Nonetheless it felt almost cold in the palm of her hand. Then she slipped it onto her thumb. It would have fallen off any of her fingers. Suddenly she felt cold too, like the ring. Her eyes asked the question.

'I'll explain later,' he told her and reached out to take her hand. 'Come.' She didn't resist as he pulled her from the table and led her towards the door. The flames were like a roaring furnace. It didn't seem to matter. They just walked through.

Outside the soldiers waited, standing in a semi-circle watching. Their eyes reflected both the surprise and fear over what they beheld. They didn't try to hinder their passage and even stepped aside as the two approached. They said nothing, even though their eyes were touched with terror. This giant of a man led her through their midst, and beyond.

Still holding her hand as were she a mere smog, he led her into the cover of the woods surrounding the village. She still didn't try to resist. He seemed to know his way, following a rough trail deeper and deeper into the gloom. After a bit he let go of her hand. She followed on behind him, meekly. He didn't speak, nor she.

Once, when they were deep into forest, he paused, waited in silence listening intently for ten or fifteen minutes. There came no sound of pursuit so they moved onwards again.

Eventually the path led down into a steep sloped valley. There wasn't much there really – a few trees, the dried-up bed of a small stream, no rain. He stopped beside the opening of a small cave, not much more than a hollow in the slope, but deep enough for shelter. He'd carpeted the ground with straw and piled up a fair supply of firewood.

'It ain't much,' he told her. 'It's my camp when I'm out here hunting. I found it a few weeks ago.' He pulled out a sack from the back of the cave and produced a stone flagon and a couple of steel cups. When he settled cross-legged on the straw she did the same and watched as he poured the beer. 'Here, drink.' He held one out to her.

She took it, drank. It was better than the wine anyway. 'Agh! What do you want?'

'Who said I wanted anything?'

'Why then? Agh! Why'd y' fuckin' save me?'

'Didn't you want me to?'

She chuckled suddenly. *Well I'm still a-fuckin'-live.* 'Sure I did. But Agh! I still don't know why.'

'Because I could.' His eyes smiled, soft and brown, belying the cruelty of that scarred face.

'Ye'r. Agh! You fuckin' could.' She took another drink. Her attention turned to the ring he'd given her. She took it off and put it onto the ground before him. 'So what do we do now?'

'We?' He turned the ring over in his hand several times before sliding it back onto his finger.

'Ye'r. We! Agh! I belong to you now.'

He looked horrified. 'What do you mean? You belong to me?'

She laughed again. 'Agh! Well it seems to me that if you hadn't fuckin' come, I'd be roast goblin by now. So by my rights, you saved my life. Agh! I'll serve you well, my Kla.'

'Yes?' He didn't understand.

They're a bit thick these men. 'Agh! It's the law. You save a life, it belongs to you.'

'You belong to me? What does that mean?'

'Agh! It means that I'm yours now. I'll do whatever you want me to.'

'Oh.' He drained his drink and poured another. 'I don't want to own you. I don't want you to do anything.'

She was beginning to enjoy this, his discomfort. There was something innocent about him, a bit like The Pilgrim really. She remembered his unease about owning her. 'It don't matter, I'm still your property.' Then, 'Look, don't worry about it. I ain't gonna be no trouble. Agh! I'll do what you say.'

He was quiet for a long time. Then, 'Be free.'

'What?'

'You said that you'd do whatever I wanted.'

'Yes?'

'Well I want you to be free.'

She couldn't grasp that at first. 'Agh! I don't understand.' It was getting to be just like her meeting with the Pilgrim. She understood the words well enough but when she tried to make sense of them there didn't seem to be any. 'A life for a life. It's the law. I belong to you,' she repeated.

'You belong to me?'

'Yes.'

'Because I saved your life?'

'Yes.'

'Well what happens if you save mine then?'

What's he fuckin' on about now? 'Then we'd be quits. No debt.'

'OK then, Goblin. Kill me.'

'WHAT?' This was turning crazy.

'Kill me.' He spoke quietly but it was no joke.

'I can't just kill you.'

'Of course you can. You've still got your knife haven't you?'

She drew the weapon and looked at it, turned it over in her hand. *He wants me to kill him.* 'Agh! Why?'

'Because it's what I want. I'd sooner be dead than own another's life.'

She made her choice, tucked the blade back into her belt. 'No. I'm not going to kill you.'

'Good.' He sounded happy.

The confusion filling her head was unimaginable. 'You didn't want to die?'

'No. I wanted you NOT to kill me.'

'I don't understand.'

'Oh it's easy. I ordered you to kill me. If you'd followed my orders I'd be dead. You didn't. So you've just saved my life.' He laughed brightly. 'No debt.'

'Well I'll be fucked! Agh! No debt.' She joined in with his laughter. 'You're a strange bastard ain't you?'

'Probably the strangest you've ever met.'

She didn't want to disillusion him at that moment. So she just smiled.

After a bit he gathered a fire together from the wood store. *Well he knows how to make a fire anyway.*

However, when he put his hand into the pile and a tongue of fire began to flicker at its heart she nearly leapt out of her skin. 'Shite!'

He looked up and smiled at her. 'It's OK, Goblin, no need to worry. It's like the fire thing, just something I can do.' He brought a cooking pot from the back of the cave and set it over the flames. There was meat too, venison, hanging in the coolness. He made a stew, tending to the task with a shy, even awkward silence. Icicle began to feel that it would be her who had to take the lead.

'What happens now then?'

'What do you mean?'

'Well what do you want me to do?'

'I don't want anything. You're free. Do whatever you want.'

'Shall I go?' The words hung in the air.

After a little, he answered softly, 'If you wish.'

'Do you want me to go?'

Again she had to wait for his answer. 'I've travelled alone for too long, Goblin, and I've known far too many lonely campfires. So, to tell the truth, no I don't really want you to go. Well, not unless you want to. But I think you're alone like me. So why not, if you want that is, why not stay with me, share my trail and my camp?'

She looked at him, weighing up the choices. He would make a good companion. He'd not run away in a fight. He'd proved that already. He's strong and would make a good provider. He'd already saved her life yet not taken her as his slave. But it still made no sense. 'Agh! Why would you do this?' she asked. 'Why would you, a man, share the path with a Goblin?'

Now he laughed again. A bitter laugh of loneliness it was too. 'Haven't you seen already, Goblin? I'm not like an ordinary man. I'm fire-born. Not like the others and they know it. Besides, as I said, you're alone now, same as me. It might be good to share the trail.'

She laughed too. 'Agh! Then we'll make a good fuckin' pair won't we? 'Cause I ain't like the other Goblins either.' She tilted her face to look at him. 'I suppose you'll want to share more than the road, man?'

'I'll share what I have, and you can share as you wish. I'll not take anything that's not freely given. I tell you, Goblin, if we're to travel together I think it best if we can become friends.'

It was that word again, *Must be a man thing.* She smiled and confessed, 'I've got a friend.' He didn't react. 'He's The Pilgrim.' She wanted to impress. 'We met on a trail far away from here. He's my friend, and I am his.'

'Then if we meet I'll be his friend too. That is, if we are friends.' The words sounded true.

'Agh! Yes, We'll be friends. I'll be a friend to you.' Formal words. 'I'm called Icicle.'

'And I'm called Fassael. So we're named. Icicle and Fassael, Friends.'

'Friends,' she agreed.

They ate together. The cooked food wasn't too bad. *I reckon that I'll fuckin' 'ave t' get used to it 'cause if I'm with him it's what I'll get.*

Later, when Fassael lay out a blanket for sleep, Icicle came to sit on the ground beside him. When he opened his eyes to look on her she smiled. 'We're of the same band, Fassael,' she informed him, letting her hand rest upon his shoulder.

He said nothing.

'I want to share your sack.'

'Why would you do this?' He spoke quietly, his words little more than rasping breaths.

She smiled again, knowing his need. 'It's important, important to me.' She pulled aside his blanket and lay down beside him. 'We are together.'

Agh! She told herself later as she lay resting in his arms. *I reckon the Truce is binding now.* She smiled to herself. It seemed a great way to seal a Truce anyway.

The next day they hunted together, roaming through the mountains surrounding their camp. He even said that he was impressed by her ability to move silently in the forest and showed her the trick of setting a snare.

Even though he did manage to shoot a small buck it was becoming clear that game was growing scarce. It was as if winter was coming and the herds had migrated south. The few pools that remained were set with ice now. The ever-present mist formed frost on the branches.

'The land is dying, Icicle,' he told her when they once again sat before their campfire. 'If things don't change soon I think everything shall perish.'

Icicle heard his words, saw the concern in his eyes, but in truth she couldn't really see why it mattered. *Everything dies sometime. There ain't a lot of point in getting upset about it.* In deference to him though she held her tongue.

Eventually his restlessness became too much. 'Come,' he told her as he packed his bag, 'I've got to know what's happening.' He had packed one for her too. It was fashioned out of deer hide with padded straps and bronze buckles. It was bloody great. He'd given her a spear as well, long and with a sharp, flint-head. She liked that too. It made her feel that she could deal with whatever might come.

'I know of an inn that's not too far away. We'll go there first and see what we can find out. We can work out what to do when we know more.'

She followed on, wondering what he'd do. She'd never been in an inn. She'd only ever been in a house when it was empty or ruined. But she'd heard tell. 'Agh! I ain't sure that they'll want me in their fuckin' inn, Fassael.'

'You're with me.' It seemed enough. He rested his hand on her shoulder, a gesture of comfort. She didn't understand that either. It seemed that he liked to be gentle. She didn't mind though. *It's better than being beat up.* Once she even thought to take hold of his hand as they walked. That seemed to please him even more.

Now Fassael might have thought it wasn't far to the inn, he was a fast walker and knew his way, but Icicle saw things differently. Her legs tired easily and they'd had to stop to rest several times before finally coming out of the woods. In a clearing at the forest edge stood a small village shrouded by the ever-present mist.

Fassael seemed to know his way here. 'Come on. It'll be warmer inside.' She followed as he strode over the paved road and approached one of the buildings. Without even knocking, he pushed the door open and led her through into the inn. A bright fire burnt in a huge stone hearth warming the place as Fassael had promised. It was dim here for save the flickering fire there was no other light, but it wasn't at all gloomy. In fact it seemed quite snug,

There were several others here already: a group of four soldiers, leather armour. Their eyes widened on seeing the red-haired Goblin. Her grip upon the spear tightened. Two hunters, dressed like Fassael, looked up too. Their eyes paused, taking in the matter. Then they turned back to their ale. It was not their concern. A traveller of some sort sat close to the fire. He didn't look up. Last there was an old man sitting at a table behind a huge mound of food. This one was dressed in strange folds of bright silk. Even his head was wrapped in the stuff. His dark eyes sparkled and for an instant Icicle thought that he was going to speak, however his interest was short lived. His food was far too important a matter for interruption.

'What's she doing here?' the brusque barmaid demanded, her hostility a wall between them.

Icicle's free hand shot to the knife at her belt, but Fassael's fingers touched her wrist restraining her. 'She's with me,' he answered calmly.

'Oh.'

'We'll have some food and a flagon of Barley-ale, Josie.' He dropped several coins on the bar. A single penny rolled in a circle, spun almost mesmerising, before clattering to a halt. That seemed to break the spell. 'That's OK isn't it?'

'Sure.' She shrugged and drew the beer.

Fassael led Icicle to a table in a corner close by the fire. 'Sit here.' He pulled out a chair and she sat as directed. *What happens now?*

'You want a room?' Josie asked, placing the jug and two goblets before them.

'It depends.' He poured the beer as he spoke. 'What I really want is to find out what's going on.'

The barmaid looked at him long and hard but her only reply was, 'Food won't be long.' She wasn't about to offer any other answer.

'Fine. There's no hurry.' The woman turned away leaving them with their drink.

She looked back at the soldiers, *Fuckin pig-shaggers*, and met their returning gaze. She held their eyes, not turning away. In the end one of them took a step towards her. Only at that point Fassael turned to follow her stare. The soldier stopped. Whatever he saw in this huge man's eyes was enough to change his mind. He returned to the bar and his comrades.

The hunters were talking quietly to each other. They too felt her eyes and turned to look at her. There was no friendliness but no hostility either. One nodded his head; the other lifted a hand in greeting to Fassael.

The traveller by the fire still hadn't moved. She looked closer. The dark cloak was somehow familiar. It took several minutes before the truth dawned on her. *It ain't!* She stood, unthinking and crossed over to where he sat. *It fuckin' is!*

'Hello, Friend.'

The Wizard looked up with a start. He didn't speak, just looked at her. Those eyes were as empty as anything she'd ever seen. She stepped backwards involuntarily. 'What's happened?' She didn't know that she'd spoken.

Recognition came. 'Icicle?' Even the voice was as colourless as the mist.

'Agh! Of course it fuckin is!' She was shocked to the centre of her being. 'What are you doing here?'

'Where else? I have to be somewhere.'

By this time Fassael, seeing what was transpiring, had picked up the goblets and the flagon and crossed over to join them. He sat at the table without preamble and filled the Wizard's glass. Yet he too almost flinched at the cold emptiness in those eyes.

'You too, Fassael?'

'We're together.'

It took a moment for the words to sink in. 'Ah. Well it doesn't make any difference I guess. So welcome to the end of the world to you both.' His laugh was as brittle as the fallen leaves.

Icicle sat herself down beside Fassael. She didn't know what to say, what to do. 'Agh! You ain't the Pilgrim no more.'

'Pilgrim?' He seemed to turn the idea over in his mind. 'Pilgrim? No. That was a long time ago. Too long.'

They couldn't find a reply, and so sat there facing him. He lowered his head and returned to his hiding place behind that wall of silence.

Josie came with the food. Set it before them although none of them hungered at that time. 'He's been like this since he got here, four days ago. He don't say anyfink, just sits there. Maybe something's robbed 'im of his wits.'

It was too much, much too much. 'What about your fuckin' magic?' Icicle demanded. For some reason, she was beginning to feel angry.

'Magic?' As empty a reply as ever.

'Yes! YOUR FUCKIN' MAGIC,' she screamed at him, not even worrying that all the eyes in the place were drawn to her. 'Agh! You're supposed to be a Fuckin' Wizard now ain't you?' What did it matter if they all fucking stared at her?

'Oh, he's a wizard all right,' Fassael interjected, holding out the ring again. 'He made this for me.'

For some reason the stone reminded the Wizard of the ruby at his breast. His hand strayed to it, held it. 'You don't understand, Icicle.'

'Agh! What don't I understand?'

'It's useless.'

'What's fuckin' useless?'

'Everything.' He looked up into her eyes again. 'I am powerless.'

'Powerless? How can you be fuckin' powerless? You're a fuckin' Wizard ain't you?'

He laughed his terrible empty, self-mocking laugh. 'Sure I'm a wizard, the Wizard of Rainbows. That's what I am.'

'The Wizard of Rainbows.' Icicle repeated the words understanding nothing at all.

Fassael said nothing. He looked at the Wizard long and hard. His eyes burnt with their own inner fire. Eventually he spoke. His voice was hushed, calm, even friendly. 'What is the Rainbow?'

'The Rainbow is a lie, Fassael.'

'Tell me?'

'What's to tell?'

'Tell me about your rainbow, Wizard. Was it very beautiful?'

Tears began to well in the Wizard's eyes. 'Beautiful? You'd never understand.'

'Tell me.'

The Wizard seemed to think things over, finally he replied. 'I'll tell you a story.'

Once upon a time, in a land far away, there lived a boy. He was a sad and lonely child for his mother lived alone on the edge of a great forest where others seldom came. He had no friends and no toys and most of the time he was miserable indeed.

One day however, when he looked out of the window into the rain-filled sky, he saw to his amassment the most beautiful sight he had ever beheld. A bow of wonderful colour arched through the darkest part of the heavens. He gazed and gazed till his mind was filled with the wonder of its glory and he ran to his mother to tell her of what he had seen.

'Ah yes,' his mother replied, filled with joy that for this time at least he wore a smile on his face. 'This is the rainbow. It's a gift to show us that the rain shall end one day. What is more,' she explained, wanting to retain his happiness, 'What is more, they say at the end of the rainbow there lies a pot of gold.'

'Oh my,' he exclaimed and ran back to the window to look once more upon the glorious sight.

From this time whenever things were bad or when he felt unhappy or out of sorts he would recall the wonder of that rainbow and remember his mother's words. 'One day I shall find that pot of Gold,' he'd dream.

Now it came to pass, as it always must, that the boy grew older and became a man. Yet always he remembered the rainbow as a thing to lighten his darker moods.

Life was not easy for him. He passed from a childhood of unhappiness into a life of hardship and he never realised his dream of riches. At length he, filled with discontent over his lot, said to himself; 'I'll go out and follow the rainbow and find the pot of gold that lies at its end. Then everything shall be well for I'll be rich and happy.'

Without more ado he went to follow this path. Mile after mile he trod and many a road did he follow. Sometimes he caught a tantalising glimpse of the rainbow in the skies ahead but he never did reach its end. Even worse befell him though. There came a time when he could go on no longer. Exhausted beyond endurance he lay down at the side of the road.

And there he died.

'So that's the Rainbow. To the child it was a wonder and a dream to cherish. It brought both happiness and comfort. Yet to the man it was a peril beyond measure and the belief in its lie led him to his death.'

The Wizard grew still. For he'd heard his own words and knew, more than any, the truth lying therein. His next words were for himself alone.

'Illusions, for such is the nature of rainbows, are beautiful to behold but they're no guide for living. The real secret is to keep the beauty and to know the reality of the illusion. We are what we are. It's best to be ourselves and the paths we follow should be set by reality and not illusions.'

'Agh! Were you that boy?' Icicle struggled to find meaning.

'Oh no, Icicle. It's much worse than that. I was the rainbow that drove him to his death. Perhaps I'm the rainbow to lead everyone to their death.' But his emptiness had evaporated and a new light burnt in his eyes.

Fassael, who had stood in the flames and not burnt, knew his own truth also. 'So tell us again. Who are you, Wizard? What is your truth and what is your illusion?'

The Wizard laughed then. His laugh was as the tide washing upon the shores of Hereth, of the wind that freshens the treetops, of the chiming of his own nature. 'What a fool I've been.' There was no trace of his former self-loathing here, just the wonder of the moment. Colours began to swirl about him. His cloak too started changing from grey to violet to indigo to blue to green to gold to orange and red. Flickering bands of brightness danced upon his brow.

Icicle fell backwards, her chair clattering on the stone floor, her whole being filled with the fear of the chaos she beheld. *It can't be! It fuckin' can't! If this is true then nothing can be sure, nothing real. No! IT CAN'T BE!* Yet it was. The colours rippled through his being, through the air about him. It wove a splendour more beautiful than anything she'd seen before. It sang in her being, echoed in the caverns of her emptiness. Then, for just an instant, she knew the touch of happiness brush over her soul. It burnt worse than fire.

'I am indeed the *Wizard of Rainbows!*' And his laughter filled the universe once more.

When he returned to the table his cloak was the very colour of the rainbow, his hat too and his eyes burnt with all the wonder singing in his heart.

'Welcome, Icicle my friend.' He caught hold of her hands and drawing her to her feet he kissed her upon each cheek. 'It has indeed been a long and sometimes dark road.'

'Welcome too, Fassael my friend. Once again I'm indebted to you.'

Fassael laughed in reply. 'Well no mind. Perhaps the hope I see in your eyes shall repay me.'

'Perhaps. There is no surety in this.'

'Do you know what you're going to do then, Wizard?'

'I do, Fassael. I'll return to the Tower. Truth or illusion? That I must know. I'll do as must be done and then, having done it, I'll seek out my Dancer wherever she may be. Will you come with me?'

The man's face turned suddenly white. 'To Tabour?' His voice changed. 'You ask us to go with you to Tabour?'

'Yes, Fassael. Come with me to the Tower at Tabour,' the Wizard confirmed.

'I said I'd never go back.' Hard as stone. 'Why do you ask it?'

'Because it's a dark road now and I don't know where it'll end. Because I want to have friends with me and you, Fassael, I count as a friend. You too Icicle, you're my friend as well. Will you join me on this road?'

THUS THE LORDS OF CHANCE TOOK UP THE CHALLENGE OF FATE'S TWO-SIDED COIN. THEY TURNED IT OVER SLOWLY. IT WAS NOT MUCH OF A CHOICE BUT, EVEN SO, BETTER THAN NOTHING.

'For the ring I bear, that saved Icicle from the flames; for that I don't kill you for your request, Wizard.' The man was filled with power. Then returning to his seat he looked up with a boyish smile on his face. 'And for your words of friendship, Wizard, for them I'll join you.'

'And I,' Icicle coughed. 'Agh! I'm with him anyway.' She looked at them both and tried to smile. 'But not too much of that fuckin' magic stuff. It scared me so much I nearly shit myself.'

They turned to her in shock. Then burst into laughter. She joined in with them too, even though she didn't know the joke.

'So it's back to Tabour again?' the Wizard mused. 'It seems I'm ever called there. What will I find this time?'

They ate then, although the food had grown cold. They drank more of the beer also. And, while the Wizard told Fassael of what he'd seen since they last met, Icicle lay out on a bench and slept. Their journey had been long and she was tired. Besides she'd a lot to think about. Not the magic, she wasn't ready for that yet, but *What's this fuckin' kissing thing about?* She was only too aware of the Wizard's greeting. *Fassael likes it too. Don't matter. It don't hurt none...* She drifted off into whatever land of dreams goblins inhabit.

Before they left the inn the Wizard bought Icicle a thick woollen coat from the merchant. 'To keep out the chill,' he told her even though nothing could really do that any more. She was pleased to accept it, reckoned that this friendship thing was worth having. No one had ever taken care of her before. It gave her a feeling of security. It's true that she wondered what the price might be but it didn't matter. *There ain't no truce, so they can't fuckin' hold me to it anyway.*

They walked easily, three abreast for the most part, Icicle in the middle. She'd taken to using her spear like a walking staff, somehow copying the way that the Wizard held his.

The land continued to grow colder. It was dying. What little life remained in the trees slumbered, hidden until the spring should it ever come. No wind brought sway to the silent frost-bright branches nor came the snow to soften footsteps on the road. However, at least the coldness had driven the mist away.

You can get used to anything, the Wizard mused as they settled for a rest period. He stood watch, resting on a boulder a little way off from the fire. *It's strange how I don't even miss the night now.* Denying his own thoughts he looked up towards the dark grey sky. *Well, I do miss the stars*, he admitted.

Since leaving the inn he'd made it a practice to take himself away from the other two when they stopped, keeping watch whilst they made camp. It would have felt like an intrusion to stay close. Besides it gave him time to think. He needed time too for he still didn't know what he was to do. *Why should I? The more I plan the less I achieve. It's probably best just to let things run their course. It's about time I learnt to trust myself.* It was a good idea, but it didn't stop the wondering.

Fassael would call to him when food was ready. Then he'd join them again. They'd eat together beside their campfire finding what pleasure they might from each other's company. Then Icicle or Fassael would take the watch as the Wizard slept.

That watch was needed too. They'd found out on their second day on the trail. They were tracking their way down from the mountains now, planning to stop where the road overlooked the plain. It would have been close to where the Wizard and the Fire-Dancer had camped on their journey not long after the Cycles had stopped.

On this occasion the road was blocked. Someone had pulled several fallen trees to form a barricade. Ambush!

There was no need for warnings. Icicle had rolled sideways into the shelter of a wayside rock. Fassael took to the other side. His sword was drawn.

The Wizard stopped. The glow was almost imperceptible at first. It might have come from the Wizard. It might have been that the very ground on which he stood began to glow.

'Agh! Shite!' Icicle buried her face into the ground. She knew what the Wizard might do and did not want to face the fear his magic would awaken.

By the time the waiting men had thought to move, the whole scene was cast in rippling light.

'I mean you no harm.' Somehow there was no incongruity in his words. Those watching realised in growing fear that there was nothing they could do to harm him anyway. 'Go back to your homes.' He sounded kindly. 'There's no point in this.'

There was a burst of light.

Men screamed.

Icicle screamed.

Even Fassael gasped in shock.

The wood forming the barricade exploded.

'Agh! I wish you wouldn't fuckin do that,' she laughed. 'It scares the shit out of me.'

'Go back to your homes, to your families. There's nothing more you can do,' he called to them even as he reached down, took Icicle's hand and drew her to her feet. 'Come.' Fassael joined them and they continued down the roadway.

Those left behind looked at each other in confusion. After several minutes' silence the first began to pack his gear.

On several other occasions, before they reached their destination, marauding bands of goblins or men appeared to challenge them. On each the Wizard would approach them. They were of no danger to him. Their weapons could not harm him, not now.

'Go your way,' he'd tell them in his soft voice. 'There's nothing you can do here. Return to your homes, to your families.' Often they did so without demure. On other occasions they became angry and threatening. That is until his rainbow filled them with terror and they ran from him. He still hated the feeling of power he held but it was his truth. He would be what he was.

However, for the most part they travelled alone. It gave the Wizard a chance to observe his two friends also. He began to see the truth of what lay between Fassael and his red-haired goblin.

'It's a bit unusual to find a man who would willingly share the road with a goblin, Fassael.' Icicle was on guard and there was the chance to speak freely. 'Let alone call her friend.'

'Am I usual then, Wizard?'

He laughed his own soft reply, 'Are any of us? But in seeing you together I find a hope I really never expected.' He looked the man strait in the eyes. 'My heart tells me that you see her as more than friend though.'

Fassael felt the warmth of the Wizard's smile, a warmth that flushed red in his cheeks. 'Aye, more than friend, Wizard, much more. When I look upon her I feel my soul sing, When she's close I feel I'm alone no longer. Just the sight of that sunset hair makes my heart pound. Aye, Wizard, I brought her from the fire from pity. No one should know a death as that. But now it's pity no more.'

The Wizard's smile was an inward thing. In his heart a tiny Fire-dancer forever dwelt.

But when the goblin returned to the camp the Wizard saw something more. She joined them, sat next to Fassael, and even accepted his kiss and the touch of his hand on hers. She didn't object yet neither did she seem to desire the same. It was with a terrible sadness that the Wizard realised the man's feelings were not returned. He saw too the inevitability that Fassael would be harmed before all was done.

That stark white tower stood as always. Its flawless beauty seemed to shout an insult to the icy decay of the surrounding plain. From far out they saw its glistening spire looking more like a gravestone than ever. Fassael stopped, Icicle with him. 'I said I'd never come back.' He spoke more to himself than any one else. 'Yet here I am.'

'Agh! What is it?' Icicle felt the tremor of trepidation, perhaps the hand of Fate, touch her.

Drawing closer to her Fassael put his arm about her shoulder. 'It's called The Tower of Tabour, Little one. It's here our Wizard must seek his answers and where we too shall wait to see what part we have to play in this matter.'

If the Wizard felt fear he kept it to himself. 'My friends, you've come this far at my asking. I don't know what will happen here. I don't know what I'll do or what will be needed but I'll wait no more. I want to look Fate in the eye and see how it meets my challenge. Will you stay with me?'

'I'm here, Wizard,' Fassael answered. 'I need my own answers, my own truths too.'

'And I'm with him. Agh!' *For my truth.*

'There may be danger here.' He had to make sure they knew. 'We'll not be alone there. The Powers will gather for sure, if they've not already done so. It might be that I'll be unable to protect you. It's often been that way. It was with Shimmian, it was with Gob, and with Cog too. I couldn't save them. I might not be able to save you.'

They didn't know the names but perhaps they understood. 'I'm not afraid of danger, Wizard,' Fassael declared, slipping his arm about the goblin's shoulder in a gesture of support. 'And I'm here to protect my Sunset-Child, with my very life if the need so be.'

Sunset-Child! A name known of Fate, scribed in the Book of Hours, a name to turn Fate's coin of chance.

HEADS OR TAILS?
WHO SHALL WIN?
CHANCE OR FATE?
OR NOTHING?

FOR THE GAME WILL SOON BE IN PLAY!

'You may die.' These were hard words that the Wizard had to speak.
'Agh! What-the-fuck! We've all got to die some time.'

The Tower was forbidding indeed, reaching higher than they could see when they stood before its sheer face. About it the mist gathered as a fog so that now its whiteness seemed to float upon a cloud of grey.

For once Fassael shivered.

'Agh! Are you cold? Agh! I didn't think you felt the cold.'

'It's not cold he feels.' The Wizard too felt the familiar touch of that chill. 'We are awaited.'

They came from within the mist. Things of mist themselves maybe. They were colder than the mist could ever be however, a cold that stemmed from the very heart of the Void.

There were three at first. *Are these they who Shimmian met?* Then others came too. They were clad in an armour of mist and bore the weapons of war. *The Warriors-of-the-Mist.* He knew their nature. He'd seen them or their kind long before in that other dreadful tower. 'Why are you come?'

'**The game is afoot, Wizard. The ending approaches. We have come to see if you will free the magic. We want what is ours by right.**' Words that were spoken in the emptiness of nothing.

He felt his own heart chill in the face of the evil before him. 'But what if I don't free it?'

'**Then shall we wait until you do.**' There was patience in that whispering voice, the patience of death.

'And what if I never do?'

'**Never is an awful long time, Wizard.**'

'Do you challenge me, Dark One?'

'**It is not Our challenge, Sir Prism.**' The insult was as a stagnant, lifeless mire. '**And the game is not of our making. We but wait to see which way the coin shall fall. Then we shall take what is ours.**'

'Who are these?' Fassael demanded. 'Their touch is like the shadows who watched in the flames when the city burnt.'

Eyes turned upon the man. '**You are not alone.**'

'I am Fassael, Fire-Born.' He said his name with pride.

'And I'm Icicle, goblin.' She spoke clearly, not turning away from the gaze of these terrible grey creatures, but the tremor in her voice spoke only of her fear.

THE COIN TURNED FASTER IN CHANCE'S HAND.
HEADS? OR TAILS?

'**You!**' A pointed, grey finger was thrust towards her. '**You shall die here.**'
She had no answer.

Fassael stepped forwards, standing between the creature and his red-haired goblin. 'Not by your hand.' It was a challenge and a terrible, pointless challenge at that. For he could never even hope to prevail against one such as this.

'You would die for her?' There was disbelief in the question.
'I live for her. Yes, if that's the need I'll die for her too.'
'Why?'

Heads? or Tails?

'Yes why?' She turned to face the Wizard her fear lost in her confusion. 'Why would he do such a thing? Why would he give his life for me? He won't even own me.'

'Answer her, Wizard.' The creature's voice spelt out the words of fate. 'Why does he do this?' The time had come faster than any might have expected.

Heads? or Tails?

The Wizard saw the challenge and he saw too his own answer, He looked down into the endless pools of her granite eyes. When he spoke it was for her alone. 'Don't you see his eyes when he looks at you, little one? Don't you feel his breath quicken when you're near. Don't you know the meanings in his kindness? Don't you feel his love for you?'
'His love?'
'You know nothing of love?'
'No.' The saddest word he'd ever heard.
'Don't you feel the warmth in your heart when you think of him?'
'He's strong, a good provider, one to stand with in a fight. He reached into the fire and brought me to safety. He could own me, yet he set me free to do as I will. He calls me friend, I a goblin.' Her confusion was real. 'Yet I don't understand. You speak of a warmth in my heart. I know no warmth. The burning fire of passion when he lays with me, I do feel that. But that's not in my heart.'
'But surely…'
'Show me, Wizard. Show me what this "Love" is.'
He couldn't deny her, not this. So he drew forth a rainbow of purity, formed in its midst a beryl heart. 'Look and see.' He opened his own heart to her gaze. He showed her everything of the truths within. From her dance upon the green of their first meeting, to the sorrow of their first parting, he showed her the dance that forever sang in his breast, the comfort of never being alone. He showed her the torment of the desert and of the strength which that dance gave him. He showed the eternal rainbow and the wonder made pure by the knowledge of her love. He showed her of their meeting in the foothills of Dormon and of their dance of colour in the time of that meeting.

> *I shall dance you a dance in the colours of time.*
> *I'll colour each moment with a dance that is mine*
> *Our dance of bright colour, the flames of desire.*
> *So we'll dance to our love in a Rainbow of Fire.*

Heads? or Tails?

The tears streamed down her cheeks. 'How do I find it, Wizard? How do I find this thing to take the cold emptiness from me?'

'Tell him what you want.' The Wizard felt like he was speaking to a child. 'Tell him you know of his love and that you want to share it with him.'

Heads? or Tails?

She looked at him for a long time wondering.
The cold grey figures waited too.

Chance closed its hand about the coin, waited to throw.

'Fassael,' she called softly. 'Fassael, come here.'
He turned at the sound of her words and strode back to her. 'You called me?'
'I did.' She looked up into the face that towered over her. 'I want… The Wizard has spoken to me. He tells me of the love that you feel, of the warmth in your heart. Is this true?'
He knelt on the ground before her took her hand and kissed her palm. 'Oh yes, Icicle. It's true, truer than I can ever tell. Do you… Can you feel the same for me?' The words were hard to say in such a dour place as this.
'Of love I don't know, Fassael. I see your kindness and your strength. I see the tears that burn in your eyes. I hunger. I also want to know of this thing too. To feel the warmth in my heart. I too want to be able to love!'

Eternity stopped, awaiting the answer.

'Tails.'

Chance has chosen. The time had come
The coin flipped upwards, spinning through the Universe.

How shall it fall?

Heads or Tails?

'You cannot!' Shards of broken glass were no more cutting than that empty voice. They turned about, all of them. She stood before them once more, livid in Her terrible beauty. The beast, standing beside Her, filled the world with its emptiness.

Tails?

The Creatures-of-the-Mist backed away from Her sorrow. Better filled with hate than that.

Heads?

Fassael and Icicle knelt together, bowed their heads to the ground before Her.

Tails?

Only the Wizard stood.
'So you've returned. Is the ending so close? Now will you write in the book of hours?'

Heads?

'That's not why I'm here.'

Tails?

Her deep hazel eyes reflected the confusion his words brought. There was chaos there, an uncertainty of which She could not face. There must be meaning; there must be reason. Seeking an answer to Her own dilemma She looked about. First at the Wizard and saw again the horror of his colours and the chaos glowing in his eyes. She found no answer there.

Heads?

She turned to gaze at the others, The Creatures-of-the-Mist, the man and the goblin-maid that knelt before her. There was order here at least and she knew it. There was disorder too. 'This makes no sense! Man and goblin, you should kill each other. You are enemies eternal.'

Tails?

'I don't wish to kill her.' Fassael had only this answer. 'I'd die rather than that.'

Heads?

'And, I'll not kill him either,' Icicle replied.

Tails?

'Why Not?' she demanded of the trembling creature before her. 'Why will you deny the truth of what you are? What do you want here, Sunset-Child?' She named her as with a curse, Fate's name.

Heads?

'What do I want? Agh!' She paused, turning the words over in her thoughts. 'You call me Sunset-Child. If that's who I am, then I'll take the name as mine. And this, Agh! This shall be my beginning. I want only one thing.' Icicle stood strait. 'I want the answer which The Wizard promised me. I want to learn how to love.'

Tails?

The Creatures-of-the-Mist shrieked and jeered in their terrible derision. **'Love? You want to love? Goblins cannot love! Who are you to want such a thing? You are nothing! You shall have nothing!'**

Heads?

'Is this what he promised?' the Lady asked in a voice of frost. For Fate will not easily be denied of its prize.

Tails?

'No.' She hung her head. 'He promised to tell me the truth.'

Heads?

'And what truth do you want to hear?'

Tails?

Icicle turned slowly where she stood. She looked at the Tower high above, at the mist that clung to its face, to the Lady draped in her robe of silver silk, to the Creatures-of-the-Mist and the Grey-Warriors beside them. She looked also at Fassael who stood with her. But lastly she looked to the Wizard. She could see the fear in his eyes, knew also that he did not want her to ask. 'Who am I Wizard?' she whispered.

Heads?

'You're Icicle the Goblin.'

Tails?

'Who am I?' she asked again.

HEADS?
'She named you The Sunset-Child.'
TAILS?
'Who am I?'
HEADS?

His answer was long in coming. For in truth he didn't want to reply. 'You're Icicle and you're my friend.' The silence that followed was deeper than death.
TAILS?
'I'm Icicle, your friend. Will you do as you promised, my friend?'
HEADS?
The tears streamed over his cheeks. 'I shall.'
TAILS?
'Will you tell me the truth?'
HEADS?
'I shall.'
TAILS?
'Then tell me, Wizard of Rainbows, tell me, Icicle's-Friend. Can I love?' Her words hung in eternity.
HEADS?
'Be still.' He spoke softly as his rainbow sought the colours of her being. 'There's no need to fear.'

Her red is of anger and fire. It shines in her being and is the source of her hair.

Her orange is her desire for existence, of greed and of passion.

Her yellow gleams gold with the hunger for power.

Her blue is but the vibration of her cry in the night, echoing forever.

Her indigo a light that shines clear through her being.

Her violet is empty save for her name, Sunset-Child!

He sees no evil, other than what is natural to her kind. What he sees is worse, more terrible than anything he might have imagined.

She has no green!
TAILS?
Crouching on the ground before him she bowed her head in supplication. She knew the answer, but still had to ask. Raising her face she looked into his eyes, held him. 'The truth,' she whispered. Then louder, clearer: 'The truth Wizard, as you promised. Can I love?'
HEADS?
'It is not in you.' Such a terrible sentence to lay upon her. He had offered her the rainbow only to show her that it was a lie.
TAILS?
'Can I love?' she asked again.
HEADS?
'There's no green, Icicle.'
TAILS?
'Can I love?' For a terrible third time.
HEADS?
'No.'

Tails?

He saw her move, knew instinctively what she was going to do, even moved to stop her, to do something, anything. But at that moment she looked up. Eyes of emptiness held him. 'Without love, Wizard, what am I?'

Heads?

She looked at the Grey-Ones, no longer afraid. 'I'll never be as you!'

Tails?

Her eyes turned to Fassael. 'You saved me from the fire man. You gave me what none other would give. You gave what I cannot return.' The tears of her sadness shone on her cheeks. 'If I can't have that I'll have nothing. For without it I am nothing. This is my choice.'

Heads?

Time slowed, held by the awfulness of the moment, held as she pulled the glistening black-stone knife from her belt. 'It's of my making!' she proclaimed to the world, 'And of my ending.' Then plunged the terrible blade up through her tunic, through her breast and into the heart that beat beneath. It would beat no more.

The coin has reached its zenith now.
It was not for she it turned.
But, having turned, now begins its descent.
Heads or Tails?

She fell slowly forwards sprawling face down into the dust. Eternity stood still.

Tears marled his sight, distorting his view of her. 'Why?' Without even thinking he stooped to pick the knife from her already chilling fingers. 'Why?' he asked again. No one answered. He turned to The Lady, met only her gaze of stone. 'Why?' he screamed into the gloom. 'Why was she denied it?'

Heads?

'Because it was written.'

Tails?

'Written? Where's it written?' He didn't mean to ask. He didn't want to hear the answer. He already knew.

Heads?

She pointed with Her perfect, slender finger. 'There.' Was there a glimmer of satisfaction in her tone? 'And you, Wizard, you can change it, undo what has been done. She doesn't have to be dead. It doesn't have to be like this.'

Tails?

Without conscious thought he moved, entered the tower for one final cataclysmic time. She was with him. Perhaps She even led the way. They were alone here, alone save for the book. He could not resist looking at the words.

> Black is the blood of the Sunset Child,
> and Black the blade that steals it.
> A blade to destroy the Law of the Land
> or Black the Hand to heal it.

his hand is black now, black with the stain of her blood. His eyes flick back to the book. Time waits.

HEADS?

'See?' Once again she misunderstood his silence. 'You can. You really can un-write it!'

TAILS?

'Un-write it? Change it?' He was appalled. Besides, the knife was a burning fury in his hand. 'You really think, even now, that I would do such a thing?'

HEADS?

'There is no other way, no other choice.' She stood shrouded as ever in Her royal sorrow.

TAILS?

Anger ripped through him, burning as a fiery sword. It took his attention, focused as lightning upon the black-stone blade, on the still-wet blood spreading over his palm. 'No other way?' he screamed at her. 'You really believe by writing in that,' he used the knife as a pointer, 'I can make things right?'

HEADS?

'You must write in the book,' she commanded. 'It's the only way.'

TAILS?

The answer came with a startling clarity. He looked at the knife and saw that it was, as much as any other thing, but a part in this eternal game. His anger, now grey, focused on the weapon binding it to his own burning passion. His final words were whispered, 'No it isn't.'

HEADS?

'What?' Her eyes widened. Fear spread through Her every fibre. For She recognised the chaos burning in his eyes and knew here was something She could never control. 'What are you going to do?'

TAILS?

'The Fate-of-the-World writes in that book!' he yelled at Her, the knife held high over his head. Its whole form began to shimmer with impossible fire as the bindings of his rainbow took hold.

HEADS?

With blinding horror She saw.

TAILS?

'Well! It shall write no more!'

HEADS?

'NO!' But Her cry was nothing. The tower was nothing. Perhaps the whole world became nothing at that moment. Only the Book, the Knife and the Wizard existed. Then the knife stabbed down.

TAILS!

Did it scream? Something did. But he was beyond such hearing. The passion filling him was channelled through him, through the blade and into the page where it had struck. It came as a terrible flood of unimaginable power. Every particle of magic was centred upon this single point, the Wizard's magic, the knife's magic and the terrible magic of the Book. Lines of energy burst as lightning, becoming as fire, brighter and brighter until coalescing into a ball of unimaginable light. Within the sphere the magic wove its spell with filaments of brilliant, impossible colour until all that was left is a rainbow of Power. The knife and the book become brighter than even the light. Now only the rainbow remains. Soon this too is no more.

The Bindings tear asunder.
Order is lost.
The Heavens awaken,
Skies burning in a maelstrom of brilliance.
Winds arise, singing in the fullness of their fury.
The very earth shakes in its wakening.
The oceans rear up to meet the glory,
churning, burning, turning in a whirlpool of wonder

The Mirror Shatters,
the lens breaks.
Cracks, faster than time
Steal over that stark, white face of stone.
Spider fine lines, multiplying, spreading,
turning the Tower to grey,
grey as the dust.

Where now the Stones of Morning?

For the magic is free.

The world gasped.

Unexpectedly, in this terrible moment of destruction is also a moment of wonderful creation. At last The Wizard, standing at the centre of everything, understands. He looks at the Lady who kneels in the dust before him. There he sees the terror inscribed in the messages of her eyes.

'You have destroyed us all!' she sobs Her accusation.

'No!' he gently denies her. 'I've freed the Magic!'

Free! Constrained no more, it sings out its joy. It is Free of the bindings, free from the awful control exerted by that oh so hated book. Free from the powerless waiting. Free from the fear of those without faith enough to trust. FREE! It runs wild through the limitlessness of creation, a wonder, a beauty beyond compare.

The Empire-of-Order is done! And now? Now Chaos rules! Time becomes meaningless, space also. Form and substance are no more than a flame, bursting into a maelstrom of magic. In the centre of everything stands the Wizard, alone. He takes everything in existence, builds it into a column of power. He turns that power, circling, spiralling, destroying every bond that is, until there is nothing but the vortex of his magic.

It's MINE! The magic courses through every particle of his being. It fills him. *I am the Wizard of Rainbows! The-Wizard-of-Chaos. And why not? Am I not Chaos? Am I not power? What need have I for control? I am-the Wizard of Rainbows.*

Where now the Stones of Morning?

The stones of Morning? The Earth Stones? He sees them, as were he with them. He sees also the bindings of their being. *These too?* He can feel the hunger about him, the desire to be free of that constraint also. *Shall I?* There is temptation. He does have the power and he knows it. With one thought he could sever the binding forever.

But. I have known their nature within me from the very beginning. I have felt their passion and sipped from its cup. They gave me their power as a gift. I love them and what they are and they me also. I have heard their words in the vibrations of my being and seen their lights in the beauty of my soul. I know their truths and their mystery.

> *In the darkness was I,*
> *afraid and alone.*
> *I felt the ground under my feet, so I stood.*
> *In standing I saw the world*
> *My heart hungered.*
> *My body thirsted.*
> *and I desired to live.*
> *My desire became a fire in my breast.*
> *Burning, consuming,*
> *Until I flew from the flames on wings of air.*
> *Yet in the heavens was a beauty so rare*
> *that I could only soar on wings of love.*
> *I called to the heavens, spoke my love.*
> *I called to the world*
> *I called to myself.*
> *The Universe answered me.*
> *It came to me, showed me its being*
> *In the visions of life.*
> *It surrounded me,*
> *enfolded me,*
> *nurtured me*
> *and returned me to myself.*

He takes a single violet rose and set it at the centre of each circle. These are not mine to give or take. I'm the Wizard of Rainbows, not of Stones!

His laughter rings through the Halls-of-Creation, echoes on the Pillars-of-Existence, but it's not the laugh of happiness. For his hands are stained with the gift of Icicle's blood.

'I am alone!' His eternal cry. 'I am alone.'

But he's not alone. The bindings are broken and now they've come. Their brilliance is beauty incomparable, a wonder to shine in his soul. They are, in their natures, every part as magical as he. He could give them everything, everything that is his, but he sees only the stain of Icicle's terrible sacrifice. He is not of them and, unable to bear their light, he turns away from them.

Their cold, grey anger is worse than the call of death; their hate worse than the bitterness of evil. For he sees himself reflected in their need for vengeance. In his guilt, he sees himself the same as they reaching out with hungry, clawing, greedy hands to take everything they lust after, for everything which is his. But he is not as them either. For their grey hatred is of their nature and not of his. Unlike their cold existence he knows the warmth of a wonderful fire-dance pirouetting in the vibrations of his being. He knows the wrongness of his deeds as much as the rightness of his love and, in the truths of his recognition, he denies them the power they crave also.

'I am the Wizard of Rainbows!' Declaring to existence the fact of his uniqueness, his voice at last vibrating with the fullness of his nature.

The power which is still theirs lashes out at him rejecting both his imperfection and his beauty. They would slay him, or be slain by him. Yet he takes their magic and turns it into a rainbow of everything and returns it to them unharmed. He denies them even the satisfaction of failure.

'WAIT!' But they will not wait. They have waited for an age already and now they were free.

As a Wizard-of-Power, as a Wizard-of-Chaos, he might annihilate them all, consume them in the strength of his fires. Yet he is no destroyer of anything, save that Book! As the Wizard of Rainbows he sees more. He knows the emptiness of their perfection where nothing imperfect can exist, a love eternal with nothing deserving love. He knows also the torment of their greyness, the endless craving for what they cannot have. Can he not accept them? Whatever they might be?

The Queen-of-Sorrow had it right. Evil can only exist if Good exists also. Good if Evil. He sees the same within himself. He had looked into Icicle's empty soul and seen therein his own, good and evil.

Yes! This is what I am, A Rainbow-of-Life. Not good or evil, but a thousand hues of both. I don't kill, not for the love of life but because I don't hate what they are. For if I did then surely I would hate myself. There, he had spoken. *That's my truth and that's my reality. Shall I deny even that? No! I'll be myself, and no more than myself. If it's my way to accept them, well, can I not accept myself just as much? I'm not perfect and I'm not evil but I am beautiful. Yes even with my wonderful imperfections, I am still the Wizard of Rainbows.*

Now his laughter ran free, as free as the magic in the firmament, as free as The Vortex lighting infinity, as free as the fall of Chance's now unhindered dice. His Rainbows are of light and darkness. He cannot love these beings, light or dark, for he is not of their kind. He cannot hate them either, for that too is not his place, but he does accept them and the truth of what they are. In his acceptance he binds them in forms so beautiful they sob with joy. For his visions are his truth, and his truth reflects the wonder of their nature and they return the gift in their own truths.

One, a thing of darkness, comes forth from the shadows to confront him. 'I had my place, Wizard! I knew my nature and my truth however mean that may seem to you. But now you have taken it from me!'

'No,' he laughs, his happiness chiming through the firmament. 'I take nothing. I give nothing.'

'Then what would you have me be with your rainbows of acceptance?'

'Be yourself.'

'But you would destroy that which I am.'

A dreadful sadness fills him. 'To free the Vortex I did destroy. I did it in hate and for revenge, perhaps with love and sadness also.' But that was not the whole truth. 'I destroyed the Book in anger and so set the magic free. But I have chosen otherwise now. I wish to destroy nothing more. I am the Wizard of Rainbows, all rainbows, even the dark and bitter rainbows of hatred.'

Another comes, a being of light and beauty. 'Give me the power,' it pleads. 'Give me the power and I shall turn this creation into a thing of light and wonder beyond comparison, something pure and beautiful to last forever.'

From the memory of the White-Lady his answer comes, 'No. The power you seek is not yours. What would you be if all were light? The beauty you have is of yourself. Be what you are. It is what I say to all of you, light and dark, be yourselves.'

They bow to him for he is everything, light, dark and all the colours of life. But he laughs this aside also. 'I'm no more than you, no more than any and I want nothing but to be whatever I am.' He turns from them and in so doing he sets them free.

In the midst of Eternity he plays with his colours. Images so beautiful that the mind cannot perceive them. For thus is the truth of his magic, not to destroy or create, but to be. They are silent, those who watch, filled with awe at the splendour of his visions, mesmerised by the sheer beauty of that which he is. His rainbow is everything.

But he is alone.

They might see; they might marvel but they cannot understand. Only one ever truly did and this was because she saw with her heart and not her thoughts.

'Where are you?' His heart cries on the wings of the tempest, echoes through the halls of creation. 'Where are you?' But there comes no reply. For a moment his thoughts nearly froze. *No she lives. I can feel her heart beating in the centre of my being. But she is far, oh so very far away.*

There is a flash, a thunderous roar. He turns as their anger bursts. *So the battle continues even here?* For, darkness and light cannot exist together any more than they could exist alone. The war they fight is as old as time and shall go on forever. Yet now he stills their warring with rainbows of fire and of ice. 'Wait!' he demands, 'The struggle shall go on eternally, but for now I want a little peace.' And, for this time at least they comply.

In a space he created, formed of nothing but thought, he is alone. It is a place of possibilities, of choices reaching into the future and the past. Its substance has no more reality than the vibrations of his understanding. He knows though, and with a clarity borne from beyond understanding, if he so chooses at this moment he can create a new existence, even a new beginning. Within the fantasy of his imaginings he wonders just what within his glory he might wish to create. He laughs then, at himself and his fantasies, for he remembers the rose of his mother and the fire-dance of his love and both were better than anything he might dream. So he builds nothing new, changes nothing. Only the Book-of-Hours is no more.

The world does not belong to me. It's not my creation, nor even my charge. Should I wish, or make it so then I'd be worse than that accursed book, worse even than the Beast. The world is theirs, man, elf and dwarf, goblin and troll, horse and wolf and every other creature that walks upon its face.

There came a new thought: *In freeing the World I destroyed the Book-of-Hours. I've taken away their order, their certainty, their false safety. What shall I give in return?* He knew an answer to this also. *Nothing should be denied love. Nothing should be denied hate either. In that She was right. You can't have one without the other. It's their world. Let them at least have that. And as for me? I'm but the Wizard of Rainbows. The Rainbow alone is mine and that's more than enough.*

The rainbow he drew upon the heavens was of truth and beauty. However, when he withdrew his lights to face the reality of his own truth the world was grey once more.

He opened his eyes slowly and looked again at the scene before him. It hadn't changed, save that the Tower was now little more than a shell, a ruin of blasted rock. Icicle's lifeless form still lay stretched out where she had fallen. Fassael still stood looking down at her, unmoving, the tears of his loss glistening wet on his cheeks.

The Creatures of the mist had fallen back. They couldn't bide the power they'd seen. Even worse though, they had, for the very first, time seen the beauty that he was. This they could face no easier than they could his magic. He did nothing to hinder their going.

The Lady-of-Sadness remained. She had risen to her feet and now waited, head bowed for the fate that this Wizard-of-Chaos would lay upon her, which would be hers. The terrible form of her beast loomed over her shoulder.

Slowly, as if his own spirit was gone, Fassael sank to his knees beside the fallen goblin. 'She's dead.' There was no accusation. It was but a statement of truth, a truth that would probably haunt the man forever. 'I loved her. Now she's gone.'

There was movement. The white Lady stepped forwards to stand before him. 'So Wizard,' her voice was soft as sleep. 'So you did not destroy everything.'

'No. Only the book.'

'The Earth-Stones?' For a moment she could not believe. 'You have not touched them?'

'No, My Queen. It's not my way to destroy. The Earth-Stones aren't my responsibility. I see them as good. I think I probably trust them more than I trust myself but that's not the point.'

'But…' She looked down at Icicle's lifeless form. She saw too Fassael kneeling at her side. In seeing She knew the terrible fate her creations had decreed. Was Order ever worth such a cost? She had her own question and her own reply. There was but one possible. 'Kill me!' she pleaded, speaking to both wizard and man.

'Would your death bring her back?' There was still no trace of recrimination in Fassael's voice. Even the Wizard found that hard to understand.

'Please, I beg of you. End my existence!'

The Wizard was crying now. He cried for Her sadness, for the terrible lies that had driven Her to this place of despair, for the love he knew lay at the centre of Her heart. 'I can't destroy you, My Queen.' To do so would be to deny the truth of everything that had been.

'It's as I said, I'm only the Wizard of Rainbows. My Rainbows are of light, colour and shadow. Their nature is of beauty, not retribution or forgiving.' He looked at her again, still not really knowing. 'In my rainbows I seek to know the truth. In my visions my wish is to understand. Shall I know you? Will I see your truth within the shades of my reality?' He realised the answer even as he spoke. 'Soon your time will return and soon once more you'll free the Cycles-of-the-World. Soon indeed I'll name you.'

'But…' The words were hard to find. 'The Cycles: they were in your grasp. You could have done anything you wished. Why didn't you restart them?' He could have with but the turn of a thought.

'The Cycles were never my charge, my Queen, any more than were the Earth-Stones.' Again he wiped away the tears from his eyes. 'My words to The Powers were the truth. I seek only to be myself.'

She had no answer at all this time. Perhaps her steed had. It lowered its mighty head and stepped forwards. The great horn touched first at the Lady's breast, then the Wizard's.

He knew, with startling clarity, should it so wish that horn would part his flesh like water. *It might even be an honour, such a death.* The Wizard grew still as the earth. Time waited.

Slowly he lifted his gaze and looked into the abyss held within the creature's terrible eyes. There was a crystal, unexpected, as beautiful as sunlight on the high glaciers. It was like a sapphire of incomparable purity reflecting a truth no less pure. Within the centre of this truth She is there and, in the fullness of this truth, it knows her.

It has seen the empty look in her eyes, known all the truths by which she called herself 'Hag', one who has betrayed her children, a failure with a heart as cold as the winter snows. Nonetheless Her beast saw only she who had nurtured its life. Forever She has been as a mother to this being, cared for it, tended and protected it.

The creature knew too of her deeds; it has seen her despair and knows well that she casts herself as a 'Harlot' who has sold her passion for nothing and her truths for even less. What is her love but the cruel burning of the high summer sun, or the ice storms of winter? But it has known the tenderness of her touch and the loving comfort of her embrace. He has walked with her through the bright meadows and danced beneath the midnight moon.

It knows, in her pain, she sees herself as barren and cold as were she a seed never awoken to greet the new year. Still, it remembers her as a maiden too, full beautiful as the springtime blooming and still it thrills over the wonder seen in the fullness of her promise.

It saw she knew what she had become and knew also her belief that she shouldn't be allowed to live. Yet in its gem the image of her as a Child forever remained. For the creature remembered her coming as the greatest joy of its existence, dancing barefoot amongst the flowers of the new land.

The Wizard saw too the fullness of these truths and was filled with a wonder un-looked for even in his dreams. He took the Child by the hand and drew her to him where She clung, sobbing bitterly into his breast as tender and vulnerable as any child of the world.

Gradually her sobs grew less and she looked up at him with her wide childhood eyes. 'What shall I do?'

He ran his tender fingers through the gold of her soft shining hair. 'You will be yourself.'

'Myself?' She didn't understand his words or the feeling that lay beneath. Instead she shook her head in bewilderment, unable to grasp the reason for his gift. 'But you had it all, everything in creation. Who am I that you should trust me with such love?'

'You are as you are. At this time as a Child. Isn't a child a thing to love? Shall we not love you? Would that be so very terrible? I've looked into your creature's eyes and there I've seen your truth.'

The rainbow that he drew for her was as gentle as the spring rain and the beauty he showed her was no less than the full truth of her being.

'Life,' he explained his own understanding, 'Life is no more a thing to give or take than is death. Life is of freedom and change, of wonder and beauty. It can't be contained, or shaped into anyone's design, and Death? Death is but the passing of time, not a thing to fear or hate. It's as natural as the wind. The seasons must turn for that's the way of the world. Spring, summer, autumn and winter, these in truth are the ways of both life and death.

'Are the Oak-fires-of-autumn indeed without reason? Is the midwinter feast for naught but a salve for the fears of men? That's not the truth.' He showed her a new vision. 'No I tell you this. When they dance about the maypole or await the midsummer sunrise, when they cast the oak-branch to the fires of autumn or feast till the passing of midwinter's hour, it's not to cling to the strands of life, or to fend off the coming of death, but to acknowledge the gift of that turning forever.

'When they are stricken with illness, when age slows their movements and turns their blood to stone, when they come, as each and everyone must do, to that final doorway and pass from the path of life into the vale of death. It's but the end of their journey, not the end of the world. Besides, doesn't their end make room for another life whom all may learn to love?'

He saw the tears gleaming as stars and knew their healing touch. 'Let the seasons turn again? It is only right that they should do so.'

She moved away from him then, no more the Child than the Lady he'd once known. But she glowed as the sun and moon and her smile was a greater gift than any might know. 'And now, strange Wizard-of-Seeing?' she returned to his former words of naming, 'Perhaps now you'd find the words to name me?'

He bowed to her, knelt amidst the dust of this still loathsome place. He bared his head and spoke his answer. 'I name you The Child-of-Light, The Maiden-of-Promise, The Lover-of-Life, The Mother-of-Nature, The Keeper-of-the-world. Isn't that your name?' He rose to his feet, stood before her and looked up into her face. 'Yet in my heart I name you "Herethdale, Harvan".'

She bowed her head, kissed him lightly upon the brow and whispered, 'Thank you.' Though her words were spoken on the breath of a breeze.

'Come,' she spoke to her beast, not the Wizard. And now at last the creature tossed its head backwards and the flowing white mane rippled as silk in the air of its movement. A golden hoof stamped a whirlpool of dust beneath and it reared high over the Wizard revealing at last the true wonder of its truth. For thus it was, The Creature-of-Light which men, from the very beginnings of time, have called 'Unicorn'.

This time when the Wizard stood to face the Lady She was no longer The Child or The Maiden. Now at last She showed Herself in Her full wonder. She stood, resting Her gentle hand lightly upon the shoulder of the unicorn at Her side. In this, Her true form, She was no less beautiful than he.

Thus She mounted Her snow-bright steed and for the first time he heard the glory of Her laughter. For an instant the clouds parted and the first ray of dawn shone upon them. Her robe shimmered, blowing as the winds took Her hair in a fan of wonder.

She is gone.

In the emptiness that remained the first flake of winter's white gift drifted earthward.

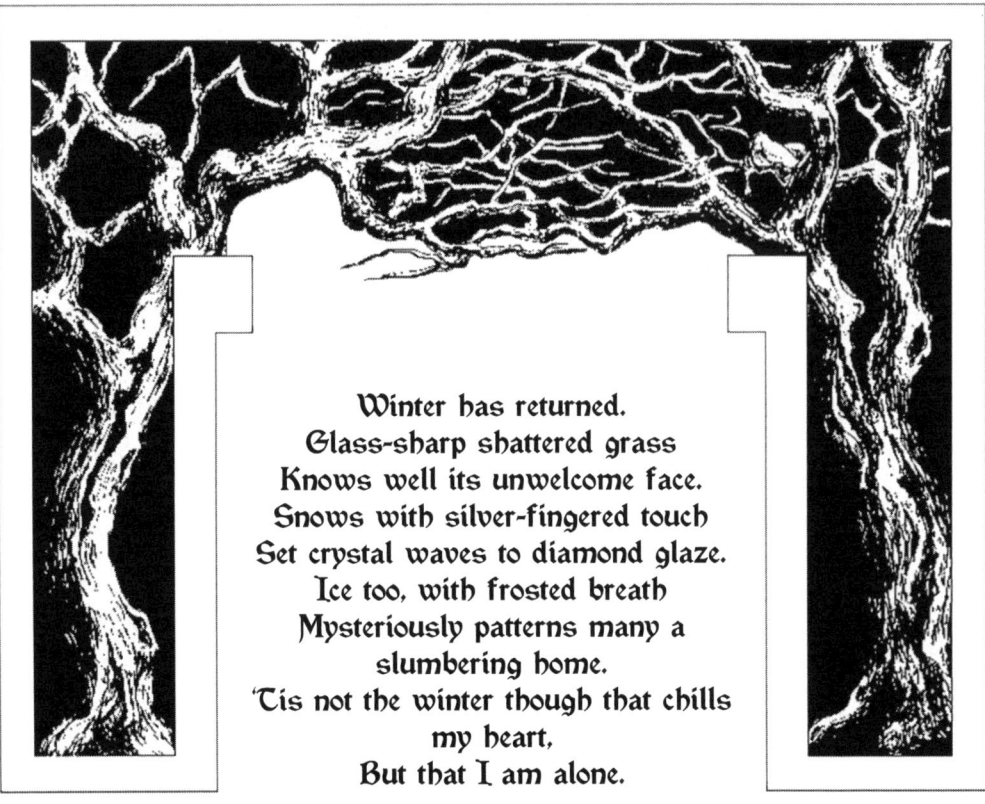

Winter has returned.
Glass-sharp shattered grass
Knows well its unwelcome face.
Snows with silver-fingered touch
Set crystal waves to diamond glaze.
Ice too, with frosted breath
Mysteriously patterns many a
slumbering home.
'Tis not the winter though that chills
my heart,
But that I am alone.

Chapter Eleven - A Silent Grave

THE CHANGE TO daylight was almost startling after the gloom of that awful grey world. However, it failed to improve things. Neither did it dispel the terrible reality of the scene before them. The Tower was broken, its once pristine face stained and shattered. The mysterious lenses were cracked and in many places had fallen away. The dust too looked sour and distasteful, as if contaminated by the events that had taken place. Smoke still trailed skywards from the camp, north of where they stood. In the thermals the vultures and carrion circled on patient wings. Death had come to Tabour.

Beside the fallen Icicle, Fassael knelt in silence. It is doubtful he even realised he was stroking her sunset hair. Somehow, for all his size, the giant Tabour man seemed almost child-like in his gentle sorrow. The Wizard looked on. He could find no words, not for the man or himself. *How would I feel if this were my Dancer? What if such a price were demanded of me?* He couldn't answer that either. He just stood there, helpless in his desire to help.

'I don't blame her.' He wouldn't either. Blame would be no answer. 'Even though she's left me.' He spoke to himself having forgotten, for the moment, the Wizard beside him. 'It was her choice. She made it plain enough. I won't blame them either.' He turned his words over in his mind. 'I don't think that I could blame her anyway, not for anything.' He still didn't move. 'I wish that I understood.'

'It was the book.'

'Book?'

'In the Tower; that's what it was all about, why it happened.' He stopped, realising that his words gave no answer. 'I can try to explain if you want me to.'

The man nodded.

'They, The Lady and the Powers-of-the-World, they formed a thing, a book to control the fate of the land. The-Book-of-Hours, they called it. They thought they could protect the world they loved from the ravages of chaos. They believed they could control Fate and so save the world from disaster. Instead they nearly destroyed it. They nearly destroyed everything. How can words be expected to do such a thing as bring Order to Chaos? They created the very thing that nearly destroyed us all. It was that book which brought it about.' He paused again. Fassael wasn't listening.

They stayed in silence instead.

'She doesn't look sad now,' Fassael eventually found words. 'Nor even angry, and she was usually angry about something or another. I think she's at peace now, if that's possible. Her torment is over.' He bit his lip but the pain couldn't take away his sorrow. 'I'll not leave her here though, not in this place, not with this dust and destruction. I want her to rest somewhere beautiful, somewhere special.'

The Wizard didn't reply. *He's right. We can't just leave her here, not in this desolate place.*

Fassael stood, looking about himself, seeing nothing. After a moment he crouched down beside Icicle and lifted her as were she a child, cradling her in his arms. 'I'll take her to the camp. We need to find a carriage for her. 'I'm not leaving her anywhere near here.' He didn't wait for the Wizard but turned and walked away. The Wizard wearily picked up his staff, slung his pack over his shoulder and followed on.

A semblance of order had settled over the camp now. The druids had built a tented hospital close to the road. It was where the desert-people had stood, fought and died. Their blood, with that of their foe, still stained the ground. Others had begun the task of repairing the devastation caused by the ravaging horde. One or two of the regiments had returned to the battleground, fewer men than there had been. They were quiet, quiet and sober, perhaps ashamed by the slaughter meted out by their hands. They'd started to bury the fallen, row on row, awful and stunning alike, so many graves, so many dead.

Several of the soldiers looked up as the pair approached. They wondered, stood watching but didn't speak. There was something in the demeanour of this huge man that forbade such. So they watched in confusion as he carried his burden to a table near to the hospital and laid her there with a gentleness almost unbelievable for one his size.

One of the druids approached, thinking he bore someone wounded or ill. The Wizard raised his hand and shook his head. They had no need of her healing.

'You stay with her,' the Wizard offered. 'I'll see what I can find. There must be a carriage of some sort here.' He had to do something. The memories of his last visit were too raw by far. Images sprang unbidden into his mind, the dead, the terrible carnage and the vision of the broken elf-maid he'd buried out on the plain. He could still hear her final cry echoing through his mind. It was all too terrible to bear. *What if my Dancer?* He couldn't contend with this thought either. So turning away from Fassael and his charge, he began to search through the camp.

They'd managed to repair much of the damage near the road but further to the north, where they'd yet to begin, he found what he sought. The carriage, half hidden in the shelter of one of the few remaining pavilions, had probably belonged to a lady and been left in the panic of battle. He recognised the fineness of the craftsmanship though. It was black with gold filigree and fittings with a black leather canopy too, folded for the moment. It might have been made for this task and would serve them well.

Finding a horse to pull the carriage was a different matter. He didn't know where to begin looking. Luckily one of the Sevriet troopers chanced by, a young horseman still shocked by the carnage of battle. A quick explanation and he left, returning shortly with a beast to match the carriage, black and suited to the task. They harnessed it together and the trooper went with him back to where Fassael waited. On the way they stopped several times and, whilst the soldier watched, the Wizard gathered together silks and brocades from the various tents.

The Sevriet continued to watch, perhaps unbelieving and for sure not understanding, as he fashioned a bed on the carriage. Fassael laid her there, gentle as a baby, and covered her with silk as were she something of immeasurable value. It came as a surprise to them, when they were done with their sad task, that the young horseman was still there.

'Why?' he asked his question.

'She's The Sunset-Child,' the Wizard replied softly. 'She died and through that death came the means to let the Circles turn again.' The eyes told him that his words had no meaning. *That might be best anyway.* 'He loved her, soldier. Now she's dead.' Perhaps this had more meaning, for the man turned his back and walked over to where his comrades waited. Every now and then he'd stop, turn and look back at the pair.

Once more the Wizard left Fassael with the carriage to find supplies for the road ahead. The young horseman joined him again, helped him gather what he could. It still took the better part of the remaining day to complete the task.

'Do you know where we should go? Where we might find a place for her?' Fassael asked. He seemed helpless, wanting the Wizard to take charge of things.

'The Elswood.' The idea came from nowhere. 'They say the forest glades hold some of the most beautiful places in the world. She's worth that at least.'

Fassael turned the idea over in his mind. 'Yes, The Elswood. That sounds right. Yes, we'll take her to the Elswood.'

'Do you want to start right away?' hoping he would, 'Or would you rather wait until morning?'

He'd not given it any thought. 'Morning? Yes I suppose there will be night now the circles turn again.' Thoughts turned behind the fires of his eyes. 'I think I'd sooner leave now, just to get away from here.'

Relieved to have the matter sorted, the Wizard finished the final packing. At the last the young Sevriet trooper returned to them. 'My captain asks if you'll need an escort, Lord Wizard?'

He turned to face the youth, startled for a moment by the awe that spoke in his tone. *Lord Wizard? Is that how they see me now?* He smiled gently. 'No it's all right. Thank him for the offer, but no. We'll be OK.' But the soldier still stood watching as Fassael led the carriage out onto the road. The Wizard waved a farewell hand and followed on behind.

Heading westward they took the trail away from the camp, glad to be rid of its sights and smells. The wind, no matter how cold, was a welcome change to the cloying stench of death that permeated everything back there. Some thirty minutes from the camp they turned northward at a fork in the road, walking into the face of the growing wind. Before long, night closed in about them. The sky drew its own veil of darkness over the plain and offered its gift of white. By midnight, unable to proceed due to the darkness, they stopped by the roadside and fashioned a lean-to-tent against the carriage side for shelter. Then, having fed the horse with oats brought from the camp, they unpacked and laid out their sleeping rolls to settle for the night. There seemed no point in setting guard. They chose to sleep.

Fassael was restless. He stirred many a time, rising from his bed to check on his charge. The Wizard could think of nothing to do or say that might help the matter. *Let it pass,* he told himself wondering; *would I be any different in his place?*

He let his mind drift, half in, half out of dreaming, seeking her presence through the gossamer strands of consciousness. He can sense her, her essence, somewhere, but she's oh so distant, little more than the faintest trembling touch on the vibrations of his being. He tries to reach out to her, calls her name, sends his love on the wings of his thoughts. Perhaps he is successful. Perhaps she knows. Perhaps...

...He flies as in a dream, a troubled dream of fruitless searching. She calls to him, alone and afraid but each time he nears her she is gone. 'She's in Danger!' A terrible fear grips him, tears at his heart with daggers of ice. 'What can I do?' But there's nothing. He runs through halls of cloying dust hunting for that which ever eludes him. There are thousands of doors leading from thousands of passages. She is here somewhere, near somewhere. She has to be. 'I'll find you!' He screams into this infinity of nothingness. 'I'll find you.'

But instead he awoke sweating, tossing and turning in his roll. *It was only a dream,* he told himself. *Just a dream.* But in his heart he wasn't quite so sure. *What if she truly is in danger? What then?* He slept again, dream-free this time, until morning.

Dawn shone bright, the night-time snows leaving the plain white with their passing. Their grey birth-clouds were gone now, gone to other places with their silent gift, leaving the heavens alight with a vivid, crystal blue. They waited, breath steaming, for the fire to burn and the ice in the water butt required breaking before tea could be made. However the chill only heightened the day's thrill of life. Over the snows small brown dunets called out their greetings. The Wizard even spied a hare, clad in winter's white fur, hurrying on its way. It should be good to be alive on a morning like this.

Perhaps it explained why Fassael seemed more at ease and somewhat less preoccupied than before, as he rustled up breakfast. The change lightened the Wizard's mood too when he set about clearing up the night's campsite.

Considering the inclement weather it was surprising how many others were abroad that morning. Bands of troopers still scoured the plain for signs of an enemy. A caravan headed westward. Probably the merchant hoped for a more favourable reception in Finestre now the warring seemed to be over. The auric hunters were out too. There were many mouths to feed on the plain at this time. Their trade was needed. On the distant road to the west a small army marched homeward. The black and silver of their standard told of Varista and the ocean far, far away. *What now will they find on their return?*

One of the patrols passed close enough to pause and pass the time of day, as the two were about to set out again. The soldiers, men of Pashad, were returning to the camp at Tabour now, they'd seen little sign to trouble them.

The two followed their trail as best they could. The snows weren't that heavy and the ruts of the road showed as a winding depression, easy enough to follow. They could have ridden on the carriage but chose not to. Besides, it was warmer walking.

Sometime shortly after midday they approached a place where a party of auric hunters had set up camp. They'd pulled their four great wooden wagons away from the road, where the wheels tended to stick now that the snow had begun to thaw, and drawn them to form an open-sided square. A fire was blazing in the centre and several of the leather-clad huntsmen could be seen moving between the camp and the picked line of some twenty horses a little way off. As the carriage neared, their presence was noted and three of the huntsmen walked out to wait at the roadside where they would pass. One raised a hand in greeting, his face lit with a crooked smile. 'You're still in time for dinner,' he called out when they were near enough. 'If you'd care to pause and join us that is.'

They looked at each other across the horse's back. Fassael nodded. These folks knew of the plains and what might lie ahead. 'Thank you,' the Wizard answered. 'Your fire won't go amiss either. It's a cold day.'

He'd not considered the stench that might linger about such a camp. Death is death and killing ever has its taste. They halted at that first touch. The Wizard set a line-post to tether the horse, placing a nosebag for its comfort and they left the creature munching happily enough to follow the men into their camp.

That roaring fire was indeed welcome. They stood before it, soon red-faced.

'I'm Rondall,' one of the men announced. They took him to be the leader. 'You're welcome to share a meal with us if it's to your liking. For our part we need to know what's happened since the battle, if you know anything, that is.' Rondall took out a knife and proceeded to pick at a piece of meat caught between his teeth.

'That's most kind, Rondall,' the Wizard replied, 'Indeed we'll be most willing to tell of what we know, little as that is. I'm named Prism and this is Fassael.'

'Anyfink is better than nought, Prism,' he laughed. 'We're about full to the top now and reckon there'll be buyers in Tabour now.'

'I'd think you've got the right of that. The camp there seems fit to become a small city. I'm sure they'll have need of all you can sell them. At a good price too I don't wonder.'

'All the better.' He smiled, turning to the others. 'Hear that, lads? He reckons the meat's needed in Tabour. Pickin's should be good eh?' His words were met with several sniggers and many a sly but hearty smile.

A table was brought, and long benches placed about the fire. They sat basking in the warmth as two women brought huge plates of meat to lay before them. It quickly became apparent that the general idea was to help yourself. Drawing his dagger, Fassael led the way. The Wizard found the meat a little tough. It wasn't unlike beef although stronger and with a slightly sickly aftertaste. Neither the huntsmen nor Wizard thought to interrupt the meal with conversation. They ate their fill, yet even so at the end plenty remained.

'Were you there, at the battle, I mean?' Rondall asked.

The Wizard looked up to meet his curiosity. 'No, well, not there to fight.' There was something about that smile that he didn't like. 'But that's where we're from now.'

'I was still away to the east,' Fassael offered. 'I'd no hunger to be a part of that slaughter.'

'I fought everyone was there.'

'No, not really,' the Wizard continued. 'There was more than enough though, more than enough to blacken the grass with their blood.'

'Don't like warring then?'

The Wizard laughed. 'I can think of better ways of spending my time.'

The huntsman joined in with his laugh. 'Too bleedin' right. I says to the boys, look there ain't no sense in us getting' killed. We'd do better keepin' to our own business and seein' what we can make out of what's left.'

'Well no one can blame you for that now can they?' the Wizard offered.

'Got our livin' to make.'

'Yes.'

'Wot line are you in then?'

'Pardon?' The Wizard didn't understand what he was being asked.

'Wot are you about? I mean what are you doin' out 'ere in this bleedin' wevver?'

'Oh. We've an errand to the Elswood. We were hoping you might be able to tell us something of the road ahead.'

'Must be important.' The huntsman's grin contorted to a sly leer.

'It is to us, Rondall, it is to us.' The Wizard was beginning to grow uneasy about the direction this interchange was taking.

'Got somefink in the wagon?'

They didn't answer. The Wizard's and Fassael's eyes touched. Both recognised just what was going on. *Oh no, Not again!*

'Must be somefink important. Stands to reason. You wouldn't be out in wevver like this if it weren't important.' He stood, still holding his knife. 'Anyfink of value? Ye'r, it's gotta be.' He turned towards the carriage. 'Mind if I takes a look?' He was determined to anyway.

'I'd not do that.' Fassael's warning was scarce more than a breath.

Rondall heard it though. He turned, slowly this time, to look down into Fassael's eyes. 'You wouldn't eh? Why not then?'

'Because I say so,' the Wizard's voice held no less steel.

He turned to this speaker, grateful for the chance to look away from the fire in the giant's eyes. This wasn't going quite as he'd expected. 'You say so? Who are you to say anyfink?'

The Wizard stood also now. He knew of the raised bows, as did Fassael. It didn't matter. All that did was the terrible certainty of what was going to happen. His voice sounded weary when he answered. 'This isn't necessary, huntsman. We mean no one harm and would sooner just be on our way. If there's cost in this I'm sure a silver coin will be more than enough.'

His smile broadened, cruel and hard now. 'Look, if you can give away silver like that, just what IS in that carriage? I fink I'm gonna take a look anyway.' He gestured to his men with a nod of his head. 'Watch 'em.'

'That isn't permitted,' the Wizard's voice was as a blade.

'Not permitted?' The words all seemed wrong. 'Why what 'ave you got in it?'

'The Sunset-Child, Rondall. She slumbers for all eternity. You're not permitted to disturb her rest.'

'The Sunset-Child? What's that?'

They didn't answer.

'Who don't permit it?' the Huntsman tried again.

'I don't.' There was more warning in that voice than any would have thought possible.

'And who are you?'

'You want me to name myself?' Somehow that was an even greater threat.

Rondall took an involuntary step backwards. 'Sure, name yourself. At least we'll know what to put on your grave.'

'You speak of graves, huntsman. Perhaps that's not wise.'

'GET THEM!' Rondall yelled out his command but he was far too late. The carriage had begun to glow, not slowly but in a flare of brilliant light, impossible in its intensity. Bands of pure energy reached out towards the man, bound him in furious magic until his screams of fear rang out over the plain.

'I'm named the *Wizard of Rainbows*, Rondall.' He spoke softly, which somehow only served to make matters worse. 'Now you know why.' He looked slowly about. Those of the hunters, who hadn't fled, crouched on the ground before them. Rondall, eyes wide with terror, could do nothing. Gradually the Wizard allowed the glow to die. The huntsman slumped to the ground.

Now, taking up his hawthorn staff, the Wizard held the man with his eyes once more. 'I did warn you. Some things are forbidden. You'd do well to listen to such warnings. Now we're going back to our journey. It's best you decide to leave us be I think. Who knows what might happen if you choose otherwise?'

Fassael stood and stepped back to stand beside the Wizard. 'We never wanted this,' he added. They turned together and walked over to the carriage. Fassael took off the horse's nosebag, un-hitched the reins and led the carriage onto the road once more.

None of the hunters said a word. None of them moved. Perhaps they'd learnt something of value. Probably not though.

By evening the clouds had gathered again and the snow was beginning to fall. They camped early, which was just as well, as by morning the skies were a sombre amber-grey and winds whipped up the snow into a blinding fury. They stayed in the camp finding a measure of shelter in the lee of a small thicket, not seeing anything better. Having turned the wagon to increase the shelter and brought the horse closer in there was little to do save keep the fire burning and while away the hours.

The morning passed, but brought neither sign of relief nor anything else to be welcomed. What did come was probably the last thing they wanted or expected. It began as a rumbling, a vibration felt through the ground long before anything became visible. The sound grew, rose to a roar like wind ripping through the tree tops, only there were no trees here. The pounding of hooves, thundering, deafening despite the snows, rushed towards them.

The two men stood, peering into the white to see what it was. 'Auric!' In sudden shocked realisation, Fassael caught the horse's reins and pulled it round the carriage. The Wizard jumped up onto the running board, his magic beginning to flare.

They came from out of the blizzard. Their wild maddened eyes flamed with fear; 5,000 crescent horned heads, 20,000 ground shattering hooves, a wall of crazed flesh and horn. There would be no stopping them.

His magic flamed out in a shield of terror, a horror even greater than whatever drove them onward and the wall of wildly careering auric parted, and flowed about them. The carriage became an island in a sea of terrified stampeding beasts. They were surrounded by sound, beaten by it, battered until their senses spun. Then they were gone. The roar of their passing diminished, disappearing into the snow. Silence returned. Well, the wind still blew.

They spent the remainder of the day there, sheltering from the storm. It was a time to think rather than talk. The silence allowing them to reflect over all that had happened. The Wizard's mind took him down many strange dark paths. At the end of each was the question. *Where is she?* There was never an answer though. *Perhaps she's in the Elswood.* But he didn't think so. His dreams spoke of a distance far greater. Perhaps here he knew again the burning spark of anger, which came with the knowledge that the Powers played with his life once more. *If I'm right then someone's going to answer for this.*

'When spring comes the melting snows will wash away all the terrible dust from the ruined city.' The Wizard was jolted from his reverie. 'It will be good to know the sun will look upon a Tabour with a cleaner face than Icicle ever saw. Is it because of her? I mean, is this because of her death?' Fassael asked, looking out to where the sun finally shone upon the winter's crystal landscape. 'Was her death the price that had to be paid so the world might live again?'

The Wizard looked up at him, his own thoughts broken by the question. He was even grateful for something to focus his attention on. 'I don't know, Fassael. In the heat of my anger over the senselessness of her death I destroyed the Book-of-Hours, thus freeing the Magical Vortex. So perhaps.' But hidden in his mind were the final words written in that hated book.

Black is the blood of the Sunset Child
And Black the blade that steals it,
A blade to destroy the Law of the Land
Or Black the Hand to heal it.

He looked at his hand. It seemed a wonder that it wasn't still stained black with her blood. 'This winter is hers.' The Wizard spoke as much to himself as Fassael. 'The spring which follows will belong to her also. It seems only right that we're taking her to where the world shall waken.' He thought for a moment. *What will we find there? What will we do when we get there too?* 'The goblins, if they bother at all, build a pyre for their dead, but I don't think that should be our way.'

'No,' Fassael agreed. 'I brought her through the flames at our first meeting. I shan't, even in death or at our parting, return her to them. No it's as you said. We'll take her to the Elswood and find a place for her to rest there.' There was a rightness in this. They were agreed.

'You know, I was thinking...' The words caused the Wizard to look up at Fassael's face. It came as little surprise to see the glimmer of tears. 'I wonder if we were ever meant to be together, Icicle and me. I mean, well, my nature is of fire. How could Ice stand against that. I hoped to melt her coldness with my flames, she, to cool my burning with her winter. The White-Lady, when we stood before the Tower, She said we were, or should be, enemies and that we should hate each other. I didn't hate her and she didn't hate me. But in a way the White-Lady was right. We never really had a chance.'

The Wizard could find no answer to that at all. 'But all the same, you did look good together. And, you were together for a time.' It was the best he could do. It's doubtful Fassael heard him anyway.

That night the moon lit a wondrous world of glistening white and in the darkness wolves serenaded a sea of diamond bright stars.

Come the morning when they rose and looked about there was nothing. Even the tracks of the stampeding Auric were lost beneath the all-covering snow. The sun glistened on a million facets of ice, on the pristine white of the land. Bright white it was, bright enough to hurt their eyes with its glare.

They looked at each other, the danger of travelling through such a land clear in their minds. Yet still they nodded in silent agreement and, having eaten, packed up their possessions, struck the tent, harnessed the horse and set out into the snows.

Once more they continued northward, hoping for the best, perhaps choosing not to think about the worse. They had a journey to make.

There was no difficulty in finding direction, for the sun was bright and the skies clear. Their passage through the drifting snows was another matter though. The road, the ground and whatever lay there was hidden and brought a caution to slow their steps.

Unlike before, they were completely alone now. Nothing else moved and even the wind had died. It seemed that sound itself deserted them, except for the soft crackling of hooves breaking through the crispness of the unblemished snow. Thus it came as a considerable shock to see a trail of prints cutting across their path. The nature of those prints came as a surprise also.

'They're fresh made, these,' Fassael commented. 'I'd have thought that we'd have seen the creature that left this trail.'

But the Wizard had noted more. In the centre of each print was a splash of colour. He stooped to look closer. A tiny plant was growing where the earth was bare, leaves of green and the minute buds of snowdrops peering up towards the sun. *It's* the Unicorn! It can't be anything else. 'Not this creature, Fassael,' he laughed brightly as his heart awoke. 'It seems we've friends in these parts.' He pointed. 'Look at the flowers where it's trod. The Unicorn leaves its own trail for us to follow.' He looked about, hopeful to catch a glimpse of the creature, but no. 'It'll lead us to safety, Fassael, we'd best follow the way.'

Thus they took the Unicorn's path and followed its far safer trail through this silent snow-white world. It was still a long and tiresome journey though, not that they really minded. Eventually, some thirty-four white and frost-crisp days later, they spied, as a dark line spreading across the horizon before them, what could only be the woodland paradise of the Elswood.

It still took them the greater part of the day to reach the tree line and here the Unicorn trail came to its end. They camped in the shelter of the first of the trees, and listened to the song of the forest as it soothed them to sleep.

She calls again and again. Not his name, for there are no longer words or even the memory of them but he knows it's her calling. He tries to follow, to reach out to her through the swirling mists of confusion. Still he can't find her. His own calling echoes in infinity and vanishes into the silence forever.

He awoke with a start. It was still dark and for a moment he couldn't grasp the reality of where he was or what had touched him. His heart beat fast, the sense of dread chilling his thoughts. He looked about. The moon was gone now leaving the night to the stars and they had little light to offer. Nonetheless, he knew something was out there. He could feel its cold malice in the vibrations of his thoughts and he knew that it was waiting beyond the trees, beyond the pure touch of the Elswood, lurking out on the plain. Peering out into the darkness he saw it, not far from the tree line.

There was something terrible about the discordant touch of that mind. It possessed nothing but a dread sense of evil that might well freeze the blood. From where he watched he could discern neither its form nor its nature yet he knew it was nothing he'd want to meet face-to-face. *It's been following our trail.* His understanding was clear about this much, as was the truth of it. *What is it?* He could feel its hatred; its chill despite and he knew without doubt that it was he the creature sought.

But there came a sighing as of the wind and a shining, silver light as pure as love. The Unicorn passed between the Wizard and the, the whatever-it-was. When the way was clear once more it had gone. Only the sense of danger-passed remained, that and the fearful cold lifelessness of its touch echoing in his thoughts

The trees were tall here, taller than any the Wizard or Fassael had ever seen. For the most part they were pine-trees, the famed 'Silver-Beam', which grew nowhere but the Elswood. There were other trees though and in the glades hazel and birch grew, elder and hawthorn. Small streams cut winding paths between the trunks and formed woodland pools where the creatures of the wild might slake their thirst.

A narrow path led the way, running beneath the trees; it was one they might follow, just wide enough for the carriage's passage. It seemed almost made for them. Perhaps it had been, for they followed its lead and ventured into the forest. Secret, unseen birds sang to them of seasons and nesting. Several times they caught sight of small red deer peering out at them from the undergrowth. The Woodland welcomed them and they knew it. Their spirits knew the breath of peace.

They trod that path for two days, wandering ever deeper into the Elswood. There were meadows here, only slightly snow specked, and avenues of oak to count the years.

As the shadows began to deepen towards evening they were led down into a small valley. It was a beautiful place, singing with gentleness to the music of a small stream spilling over a rocky outcrop to form a pool. In later months rushes and iris would grow at its edge, serenaded by the constant music of the fall. There were rose bushes too and, on the far slope, a bed of green which late spring would wake into sea of bluebell wonder. Beside the pool was a grave and beside the grave a figure.

That Calin should be here came as no surprise. It seemed, at this moment, the most natural of things. They walked down to near where she rested watching them, with sad, tired eyes. In her heart she welcomed their coming but she showed no sign. Again it didn't matter. They knew.

The Wizard looked down at the grave, at the sword lain upon its earthen mound. *Cog.* 'We've come a long way to find this place, Calin. There's none better. It's our wish to leave another grave here when we depart.' He reached out and pulled aside the silk to reveal the glorious spread of her scarlet hair over the cushion. 'She's called The Sunset-Child. She gave her life,' he told her, noting the widening of her eyes as the realisation that this was a goblin touched her. 'But we knew her as Icicle. She was my friend.'

Calin said nothing.

'She was my love.' Fassael's tears could not be denied. 'She died because she was denied her own love. She died because she couldn't return mine. She died rather than live without.' He knelt on the earth before Calin. 'Please, Calin-Sanain. I loved her.'

She didn't reply for a long time. Eventually though she nodded. 'In life they might have been enemies.' It was true. 'However, as it's both love and death which brought them to this place they may find peace here, together.'

Fassael crossed over the stream leading the carriage. Having unhitched the horse he tethered it to a nearby tree. Then by the pool, opposite to where Cog's grave lay, he began to dig. He worked in silence, slowly and carefully. He didn't want help, nor was any offered. This was a special, sacred thing and the Wizard knew it well. It was both his final gift and his goodbye. They stood and watched.

'When I first met Icicle it was far away from here indeed.' The Wizard needed words as he looked down to where she now rested in the cold earth. 'She tried to kill me then, with the knife which finally killed her, the same knife that freed the magic. She tried, though I don't think she really stood much chance. She shared my camp and my food though and she named herself my friend. It was at that first meeting when she asked, and I promised, to tell her the truth. It was that truth which killed her just as surely as her knife.' It seemed strange but there was no regret in his voice. 'It was a long journey indeed that brought her to Tabour although she never did explain why she'd come. I wonder, was it worth it?'

'When I rescued her,' Fassael replied from deep within his own thoughts. 'I brought her out of the flames from pity. Now I leave her here for love. For I will tell the world, I did, do, love her. Yes I do love the Goblin Icicle. You know, I didn't think a goblin could be so beautiful.'

'Yes,' Calin whispered, tears wet upon her cheeks. 'She was beautiful indeed.'

'And foul-mouthed.' They laughed softly together at the Wizard's words, for that too was Icicle.

Fassael knelt on the ground beside the grave. 'Farewell, Sunset-Child.' He kissed her cold, cold lips. 'Farewell, Icicle.' He kissed her a second time. 'Farewell, my love.' A third, final kiss before he covered her face with silk.

Thus they buried her, gentle with the falling soil, and placed a cairn of stones over her grave. At the last the Wizard formed a jewel as clear as ice that would remain forever. In its crystal heart he wrote her name.

Icicle, The Sunset-Child

Though winter ruled as much as anywhere, her frosted hand did nothing to diminish the woodland beauty. Here the wind knew its own song and the trees their tune. Through temple halls of silver-white pines the music of the Elswood flowed about them, bathing them in its secret magic. Did it heal? Who can tell? Yet they were at peace, if only for a time. Yes, there was that at least.

They spent the night there, slumbered to the music of the bubbling water and the wind in the trees. When they woke, in the clear cold light of morning, Fassael built a small fire and made tea. They sat together in silence, their sadness speaking for them.

'I'm going onward to Al-Sinnian,' the Wizard told them. Time was passing and he had to discover where she was. 'There are still things I have to do.'

They looked at him; perhaps they understood his need. Calin nodded. 'I'm not ready to leave yet,' she said simply.

Fassael seemed to nod in agreement with her and, when the Wizard stood and began to pack up his gear, they both remained seated. He would be going on alone. It didn't matter. All the same his movements were carried out in silence, his thoughts too heavy to speak, as he prepared for his journey.

When he was ready he stood before them. 'It's been a long and sad road that's brought us here. I hope the trails of the future bring you peace.' They didn't answer. But Fassael stood and held out his hand to pat the Wizard on the shoulder and Calin, with tear-glistening eyes, kissed his cheek.

There could be no farewells to those two lonesome graves, so none was made. He turned and without backward glance walked into the forest.

They stood together beside the water watching him go. It was only when all sign and sound of him was lost in the day that they took their seats by the fire once more.

*

It might have been cold here in the heart of the Elswood. The ice needles hanging from the branches told that it was but the Wizard didn't feel it so. Perhaps the wonder of the forest warmed him with its beauty or maybe his heart, at this time, was chillier than any winter snow. It might have been the case also that he missed the company of Fassael or even Calin but in truth he did not. They had their own needs and their own reasons and at this time he preferred to be alone.

The Elswood's beauty was rare and pure. It knew not the touch of taming hand but sang with a wildness all of its own. Those who tended the trees and the avenues knew better than to force nature to their design. They loved the land and for their love the greenwood returned a blessing of its own freedom.

Passage was easy through these forest glades, his footsteps light and silent on the bed of fallen leaves. Streams, chattering away to the trees, cut miniature gorges with their flow. In other seasons trout would rise to the may and hawthorn-fly though for now they hid in the deeper pools awaiting the warmth of spring. Red squirrels held council in the spreading arms of a sweet-chestnut grove, peering down to watch the brief disturbance to the forest's tranquillity.

Has she trod here, skipped her dancing way through these same avenues? Did she stop to wet her lips at this very pool? And in the truth of his heart, *Will she wait for me in the Halls of Al-Sinnian?* But he knew the answer to that as well. *No, she's in some other, far more distant place.* He knew it from her nightly calling. *Ever she calls me but I cannot come to her. I cannot reach far enough to find her.* The pain that filled him nearly overwhelmed him. *We are both alone.*

When darkness fell he found a clearing near to where one of the many streams ran. A place had been prepared, a fire lit, even a kettle of stew and stone-baked flat bread left for him. He didn't ask who. It didn't matter, nor that his journey was observed. Surely the keepers of this domain would know of his passage. Thus he set his sleeping roll in the open and lay to sleep staring up into the treetops.

She comes once again, her cry ringing through all the reaches of infinity. As always, no matter how he tries to touch her with his thoughts he knows the bitter taste of failure. He runs, soul torn, through the halls of his dreams. She is ever hid from him.

Nonetheless he awoke rested and the touch of morning sunlight brought a blush of calm to his troubled spirit. And thus, with the first rays still lighting the high branches and the first burst of gold stealing through the glades, he rose to commence his journey.

Even though there was no defined path nor any indication as to where to go, he had no doubt this was the right trail, such was the nature of the place. For sure the elves were here, though their signs were scarce indeed. It would seem a sacrilege to disturb this wonder. Once the Wizard heard the sound of their silver-tongued-singing winding through the trees, magical, mystical, fey. They, the elves, knew who passed through their land, if only by the sorrow which walked with him. For the moment they left the walker alone and passed word ahead to those who waited.

It was not long before the passage of time lost all meaning, day merging into day, each the same as the one before. It mattered little. Sometime the pathway broadened into a road to speed his feet. The touch of watchful elfin eyes was frequent now, though none approached. Often he heard the whispering of his name on the forest breeze. Was it understanding or caution that stilled them? Who knows? He was content it was so. There would be time enough for meetings.

That trail was long indeed, leading him deeper and deeper towards the heart of the Forest. The only trees now were the great White-Beam pines, as ever the sign of the Elswood. They towered hundreds of feet above the roadway, though their branches were not thick enough to cut out the sun. On many soft sounding wind chimes hung to give music to the hours. He travelled on.

A clearing opened before him, a wide swathe of meadow through which the road ran. Stopping at the tree line, he looked upwards to where, set shimmering upon the crest of a sunlit hill, stood the crystal city of Al-Sinnian. It was as no city of men this wonder but formed as if of crystal trees to mirror the forest it gazed down upon. From where he stood it seemed as a wall of glistening trunks reaching up to where the branches interlocked in a canopy of light. There was a sense of endless peace and beauty. Three of the seven sacred rivers could be seen coursing down the hillside. The symphony of their tumbling waters rang through the crisp air.

An elf appeared from the shelter of the trees beside him, somehow expected. He bowed low to the Wizard and, with a flamboyant wave of his hand, sang. 'Welcome to Al-Sinnian.' Somehow he managed to sound as much crystal as the city beyond. 'Your journey has been long and sad. May you find rest, peace and healing within our halls. We knew of your coming,' he continued. 'First there is time for a meeting and then for rest. A place is prepared.' Then he turned away, vanishing into the woodland.

Come then, the Wizard spoke softly to himself, *let's see what this fair city has to offer.* But his inner feeling was not easy or light. He knew in his heart what lay ahead. Thus, with this strange reluctance to awaken the future slowing his steps and the doom of the past pressing him forward, he stepped out into the open to follow the road upward. It didn't take long. Even so, by the time he'd reached the first archway several figures had emerged from the city to line the road. They bowed their heads at his passing but didn't speak. More elves appeared, continuing the silent welcome as he walked through into the crystal halls where even more waited to watch him stride down marbled thoroughfare. As the others, they waited in silence. In the background the strain of elfin-pipes brought a healing calmness to the moment.

The sunlight was caught and defused through the myriad facets of the crystal canopy to create rainbows of purity the brilliance of which awoke anew the magic that dwelt in the Wizard's heart. He felt his soul lightening and for once his loneliness diminished. The ringing chorus of the fountains' eternal song welcomed him every part as much as the city's people and he knew it also.

At length his feet brought him before a high archway through which a halo of emerald luminescence shone. It was here, at the centre of everything, where the Sacred Tree, which was the heart of The Elswood, grew. Standing before it, sheltered by the massiveness of its shimmering white bows was the High-Dancer. He was, as ever, dressed in his green gown and in his hand he held a staff set with an emerald gemstone, a staff well known to the Wizard. The elf-lord was not alone. The Lady druid stood at his side, Plie the harp-smith with her. There were others too, some he half recognised, but couldn't name.

At the Dancer's right hand though, robbing the Wizard of all coherent thought, stood another elf. Her hair was autumn, as was his dancer's. Her eyes even sparkled with his love's own joy. Without thinking he went to her, removing his hat as he came and then knelt on the ground at her feet, head bowed.

She reached out, touched a hand to his head as if blessing him. 'Stand Wizard,' she bade him in a voice that sang of her daughter. 'Be welcome among us.' He stood, looked down and near lost himself in the pools of her wonderful, smiling eyes. If any saw that his own shone no less it should hardly come as a surprise. 'Ah, I see the dance of my daughter alive in your heart, Young-Wizard.' Her smile brightening all the more 'When the talking is done perhaps we may walk through the greenwood and I shall learn if she spoke truly of you.' She giggled, bright as a sparrow. 'Will you colour me also with the light of your shining?'

'You, my Queen, I'll colour more brightly. I'll burnish your smile with the light of my love.' He smiled at the scream of delight that his reply awoke.

The High-Dancer stepped forward. 'We meet again, Wizard of Rainbows.' He spoke formally, though without coldness. 'At our last meeting I thought that we should probably never meet again, nor for that matter that any would. Perhaps also I feared too that one day we might. Our last parting was not easy.' His brow furrowed as memories crossed his mind. 'We are indebted to you, we and all who–'

'No,' the Wizard stilled the words with a shake of his head. 'There's no debt. What came to pass at Tabour was not of my choosing, nor wholly of my making. We paid our price for the breaking of that book, high and terrible was it indeed. What was needed to be done was done. Let that be enough.'

He paused again. Formality was required. 'You should know that I didn't come alone to the Elswood, Lord Elf. Calin-Sanain, whom you met before the battle, came first. Fassael-Fireborn came from Tabour with me. They each had their own sad reasons.'

The Elf bowed. 'They shall ever find welcome in the halls of the Crystal-City. Their names are known as is their sadness. May they find peace among the groves of the sacred forest.'

'It wasn't peace they sought, not they or I.'

The Elf-Lord's face whitened at the Wizard's stark reply, a shock mirrored on the faces of the others near enough to hear. 'Why then did you come?'

'Calin came to the Elswood to bury her love. He was named Cog of Rael, a fighter and a friend. He died in the battle at Tabour.' The next was harder. 'Fassael came to bury the pain in his heart. She was Icicle the goblin; some named her The Sunset-Child. It was her right.' He sounded defiant, waiting for them to challenge his words. No challenge came.

'And you, Wizard? Why have you come?'

'I came,' his eyes flicked back to the Elf-queen, 'I came seeking The Fire-Dancer.'

The High-Dancer recovered his composure. The words had not been too bad, no, not considering what might have been demanded. 'Nonetheless, I welcome you and wish you peace in these halls… She is not here.'

'That I know, my Lord. Too often I've heard her calling in the depths of my dreams. She's far from here, very far indeed. I came hoping to find word of her. I intend to find her, wherever she might be and I shan't stop until I–'

'ENOUGH!' the Lady-Druid's voice cracked like a whip. 'Say no more.'

The Wizard turned to her, as all there did. The question was as clear in his eyes as the danger that burnt in the air about him.

'There have been enough oaths.' She sounded as sad as anyone could. 'For now it's better to let the future to weave its own truths.'

He looked at her, seeking understanding. The others too sought answers with their eyes.

'Plie,' she turned to the harpist. 'You know of what I speak.'

The harp-smith nodded. Then moving slowly he lifted the golden harp from his shoulder. Save for one single note, he played no tune and the words were spoken rather than sung.

'Hear me you Powers of the World!
Hear me Weavers of the Webs of Fate!
Hear me You Governors of the Turns of Time!
Hear me Stones of The World-Spring.
For I shall make my oath unto you!

Know you The Beast
The Dark Fiend,
The Creature of Evil,
The Lord of Mists,
The Keeper of the Void
Then Know you my Enemy.

Thus do I swear,
By Sun
and by Moon
By Ocean and Sky
By Air and Earth
By water and by Fire
By the Powers of Day
and by the Forces of the Night

This do I swear.

I shall not rest.
Not for fear
Not for wealth
Not for sorrow,
Not for love,
Not for fate
Not even for death
Until I have faced my enemy.

Perhaps then, when all is done, I might find peace from the pain that so torments my soul.'

In these words was the path into the future set long ago. Such utterances spoken in the fell hours of night have their own consequences. One should well beware, for such oaths should not be rashly made. Many ears might hear such words and non may know or choose who might be the listener.' The Elf-Harpist's words hung in the air.

'They're your words, Wizard,' the Druid reminded him, though tears of sorrow glimmered in her eyes. '*Not for love*, You said it. *Not for fear, Not for wealth, Not for sorrow, Not for Love, Not for Fate, Not even for death.* Hard words, hard to say then and hard to follow now.'

'Yes,' he acknowledged. 'My words; I know them. I spoke them at the beginning of my journey on the Downs-at-Hereth. I'd forgotten for a time.' *Does it never end?* 'What must I do? Will you tell me?'

'No, Wizard. It's not for me to say "do this" or "don't do that". The words were yours, the oath yours, the hope yours also.'

He needed to think, to sift through the thousand snatches of thought that whirl-pooled through his mind. But thoughts would not form. Eventually he turned to look at the High-Dancer. 'We'll speak of her later.'

What more was said at that meeting the Wizard can't remember. His thoughts were full of the words of his oath and his quest. The memory of that terrible creature awoken in the castle of despair rose as a fury in his heart. At length the Elf-Queen took his hand to lead him through the shimmering chambers. She didn't speak, not even to ask him of her daughter. She knew much of peace did this quiet elfling. Finally she led him to a chamber where he might rest. A meal was served which, although not hungry, he ate. Then he lay on the bed and rested, perhaps slumbering through the night. It wasn't until late the following morning that she returned to tell him the High-Dancer had summonsed a meeting.

*

Days had passed but Calin hadn't counted. They'd stayed in the small clearing, tending to the graves, and seldom speaking. Neither had words for themselves let alone the other. They ate but sparingly and with little appetite or desire. When evening turned to dark they slept.

Calin woke during the deep dark hours of night. What had wakened her was unclear. Fassael lay curled in slumber close to the smouldering fire, so it wasn't him, but something had disturbed her. She rose to her feet, silent as always, and took up her sword without thought. There was something amiss. She needed to find out what. Fassael lay undisturbed. She might have woken him, to let him know but he looked at peace. A gentle smile turned up the corner of his mouth. She let him be.

Thus she went, moving into the forest, no more than a shadow amongst other shadows. There was no haste to her movements, nor was there undue caution. Every action was as it should be. She was Sanain.

It wasn't sound that directed her feet, nor even instinct. If the truth be known it was no more than a feeling and a feeling that both grew and troubled her. *There's something out here. Something that waits. It doesn't belong here.* It was the truth; she had no doubt of that. Despite stopping, several times, testing the night sounds for clues, she found none. The night was silent. *Silent as death.*

Passing time meant little to her. The first light came, silent as the darkness it replaced, lightening the woods to make her passage easier. What it didn't do was lessen her feeling of wrongness. At other times she might have felt a sense of contentment here, even protected, sheltered by the trees. Yet again she might have felt vulnerable. Who knows who or what might lie in wait amidst the trees? She felt neither. What she did feel was fear, a growing fear that belied the beauty of the land. It was an unknown feeling for her. She didn't even have a word to express the tightness in her chest, the breathlessness that followed every movement. She jumped at the slightest sound, as were she the rawest of recruits. You don't need words to know when something is wrong though. *Where are the birds? Where are the creatures of the wild?* There were signs of life everywhere. The trouble was that the signs were days old. There were none of now.

Not long before midday, in a thicket beyond the Elswood's shelter, she found the first indication of what was occurring. A winter-white rabbit hung from a branch where it had been spitted. Who, or whatever it was, had broken every bone in its body. The blood told the tale. The creature hadn't died until the very end when it's scull was crushed. Her thoughts recoiled from the sight, from the senseless barbarity. *Why?*

Next there was a raven, no different, then a fox, another rabbit, squirrels, stoats, even voles. Soon every tree or bush hung with lifeless corpses and she found herself walking through what was no less than some horrid, sick abattoir. All the time her own dread grew. She moved slowly, eyes alert for danger. By now anger had replaced that earlier fear but she wasn't so angry that her caution was lost.

The edge of the forest loomed, the grassland, still white with winter's gown. Who or whatever she sought left a trail of blood, blood and the remnants of its victims. She followed that.

The first hint of warning was the smoke; smoke tainted with the stench of burnt flesh. Soon, crossing over a small rise, she found the wagon. It was its leather covering which burnt. At first there seemed to be nothing more, save for the trail of blood. She found the bodies spread out on the snow several yards from the wagon. It wasn't a pleasant sight. Such things never could be. She guessed they'd been farmers of a sort. There were implements, shovels, a plough blade, thrown aside now with immoral carelessness. There were prints in the snow too, cattle and sheep. She knew nothing of farming, nothing of families either, for that matter.

She read the signs well enough to wish she couldn't. Whoever had done this had first contrived to incapacitate them. It had taken its time; time to dismember them piece-by-piece, making sure that they didn't die until the very end. They'd started with the youngest and worked their way up, so that they'd know what was coming, leaving the father until last. It didn't bear thinking about but the sight forbade any other. It was doubtful if any part left was larger than a hand. Who or whatever had done it had gathered the bits together and shaped them back into the form of the people they once had been. *WHY?* The question screamed through her mind. *What's the point in this?* She'd not find an answer for that either.

At first she thought to dig a grave for them but... the idea of touching those dismembered forms was too repugnant. It was easier, as well as somehow purer, to use fire. It might go some way to cleanse the place of the horror. It might, though it didn't, cleanse the images from her mind.

In the end she dragged the remnant of the wagon to where the bodies lay and built a pyre as best as she was able. The fire burnt bright that evening. It lit the land and shone on the snows that would soon obliterate all sign of what had been. She didn't linger there. No one would have done so.

*

They gathered in one of Al-Sinnian's great halls close to the noon hour, The High-Dancer and The Crystal-Singer, as the Queen was truly called. Plie was there also and the Druid. The Seventeen Elf-Lords were there too. Whatever came to pass this day must be known. Besides these came an ancient elf, bent and bowed as a tree beaten by the wind. He was called 'The Keeper' for he tended to the Sacred Tree. If any were Lord of this realm, it was he. Taking their places about a long table, they sipped cool white wine from clear crystal glasses until the moment for speech had come.

'Do you know what you will do?' The Druid spoke first, with all her customary directness.

'I do.' He'd thought the matter through during the long night.

'Will you tell us?'

'First I have questions.' He had, they burnt in his mind like slivers of heated iron.

'Ask your questions then, Wizard.' Her voice remained hard, as if she feared the answers she might be required to give.

He turned to the High-Dancer. 'Where is she?' It sounded like a demand.

'We do not know.' The truth of his sadness spoke. 'We had hoped that she was with you. Even though we knew that she was not. We hoped also that you would come seeking her.'

'What happened?' The Wizard's words remained hard but not his tone.

'At our last meeting on the plain at Tabour, after you had gone forth we were much distracted by what had taken place. We thought we had sent you to your death. Before we could do anything the Goblin Horde came and battle raged.' Tears wet his cheeks. *For the dead?* 'When the killing was done she was gone. We don't know when or where. We searched amongst the dead and fallen but she was not there. She had gone and there was no sign of her passing. We think she may have gone even before the carnage began. Her staff was left beside the table.' He swallowed, choking back his distress. 'I don't even know if it was me who drove her away.' The anguish in his voice was unbearable. 'Please, Wizard, go find her. Bring her back to me.'

'Yes, dear Wizard,' the Elf-Queen joined. 'Bring her back to us, from wherever she may be.'

'If that's what he intends to do then neither he nor you shall see her again.' The Lady-Druid's voice cracked as ice. She turned to the Wizard again. 'If you even try at this time, then all will be lost.' The terrible coldness of her words were the truth and he felt the reality of it seeping through his heart.

'I must fulfil my oath.' His words seemed no less awful than had hers.

'It's your oath, Wizard of Rainbows, and you alone can do so.'

He turned the matter over in his mind. Then another thought came to him. 'You know where she is.' It was not a question.

'Yes,' she whispered the reply that she'd sooner he'd never asked.

'Will you tell me?'

'No.' She stood waiting for his anger to burst upon her. Nothing happened. 'Were I to do so,' she started to explain, 'then you'd be unable to stop yourself from going to her, or even worse, calling to her to tell what you do.' Her voice cracked again. 'That would be fatal, both for you and for her.' She followed a hard path this druid. 'I ask you to trust me in this. When all is done, then you'll understand.'

'Is she safe?'

'No one is safe.'

'Will I see her again?'

'There are no longer any certainties in this. When that book was destroyed such ordering was gone forever.' For a moment her anger flared. 'And good riddance to it!'

He was quiet then. For the moment there seemed to be no more questions for him to ask.

'What will you do?' the Elf-Queen asked. She had listened to what had been spoken and realised its import to her daughter.

'I'll fulfil my oath, My Queen. I've no other choice.' Cold empty words. 'I'll go to the Galghathag to face my enemy in its lair.' They looked on in horror. 'Then I'll find her.' There was a terrible power in his voice that shook them all to the core. 'And heaven help any who try to prevent me!'

'So at last, Wizard, You go to war.' The Druid still seemed intent on confrontation.

'War?' *I hadn't thought so.* 'Why do you say that?'

'Because, in some measure, it's the truth.' She held his eyes. 'And because that's how you must look at the matter too. Your enemy has waited. I shan't name it. Did you think it would be easily done? It's plotted for countless years, knowing this time would surely come. It had hoped that you'd destroy the bindings when the Vortex was loosed, for then it would be free. But it knew better than to rely on that hope alone. It knows of your oath word for word, knows too, perhaps better than any, that you're coming to confront it. Were you not, then it would draw you there by other means.'

She drew breath; seeing the pale, which her words had brought, whiten his face. 'Aye, it waits for you, of course it does. It believes itself stronger than you and that it can overpower you, force you to do its will, force you to use your magic to break the bindings to set it free.' Again a pause to let the words sink in. 'If not? Then it will seek to kill you, to free the Vortex once again! It believes either way it'll be free of the bindings that enslave it, free at last to wreak its terrible revenge upon the lands of men. Then who'll undo the havoc that will rule?'

'Its legions are many, Wizard, yes even now, they're many and they're prepared. They've laid out their snares to find and trap you. Their master seeks every way to know of you and they are his eyes and ears. Do you think they'll simply let you be? I tell you, Wizard, and trust my words for they hold the truth of all my knowledge, I tell you from this time onward you should hide your movements so they never know of a certainty where you are or what you're doing.'

'Won't my magic hide me from their eyes? It did on the Plain before the battle.'

'Did it? Are you so sure? You must understand this: in their grey horror your magic flares as a beacon, a light shining in the darkness. Your enemy has watched your every move from the time of his awakening. He has gloated over every act, each moment of your journey. Your magic would just draw its creatures to you all the faster.'

'But…' He tried to grasp what she had said. All he could call to mind was the image of that creature which had followed them to the edge of the Elswood. *Aye, that thing followed me all right. Did I draw it to me? When I used my magic at the*

Hunter's camp and to ward off the Auric did I call to it? 'But if I can't use my magic what can I do?'

'Be yourself.'

Be myself. 'Yes.' He even smiled. At least he knew the truth of that answer. 'That's just what I must do, as must we all.'

She returned his smile, though it was but a gentle, secret thing. 'But Wizard,' she said, waiting until their eyes met. 'Don't forget your sword.'

Good grief, I had at that. I wonder if it still waits for me? And at that thought he smiled anew. *So even in this I follow a path predestined.* 'Yes, My Sword.' A new plan began to stir in his thoughts.

'This is what I think I must do,' he explained once the plan had formed. 'First, I'll take the road through the Lake-lands and cross over into Lodor. That's where the Sword awaits me. Then I'll go south, following my former route to Naril and enter the Gate there, as before.' He stopped at that. *Such a long road.* 'Then I'll make my way through the greyness to that dread castle. And then? What will be will be.'

They sat long in silence: a stillness that was eventually broken by the High-Dancer moving about the table to face the Lady Druid. He stood, hands on hips before her. She didn't flinch nor turn her gaze aside. 'She knows.' The Elf Lord's voice was cold, turned to ice by the truth he suddenly understood and now had to contend with. 'She knows where my daughter is.'

The Wizard looked at the Elf and back to the Lady Druid. 'Yes, she knows,' as he'd realised earlier. 'And so she told us.'

'But she told us nothing.' The condemnation was heavy in the Dancer's voice.

The Wizard didn't like the thought of that either. It didn't sit well with his feelings about the Druid. *She might at least say something.* But even that thought sounded discordant in his knowledge of her. *What if she does so? I'd not wait. Let alone go to Lodor for the sword. She knows of the Sword too.* 'She has her reasons.' *I'll trust her in this. She was always true.*

'What reason can excuse such hidden knowledge?'

'It's as she said, Lord Elf. If she did tell us, I'd turn aside from my path. I'd be unable to help myself and she knows it. What then? No, my friend,' he spoke gently, 'the ways of this Lady are not mine to question. Nor will I do so. When there was doubt she trusted me and the hope of what I might become. Now I'll trust her in return. I shan't condemn her. She is my friend.' *Who is She? Who is the Lady?* The question almost screamed in his mind.

'I'll do as I have decided. I'll go to meet my enemy. And, as I have already said, then, what will be will be!'

At the foot of the table, where he'd sat in silence throughout, the ancient Tree-Keeper stirred. He moved slowly, although without the awkwardness that age sometimes brings, and peace came with him. All eyes were on him as he walked about the table to stand beside the Wizard. 'So you are set upon this?' He looked down into the Wizard's eyes.

'I am, Lord. I can see no other way left to me.'

He reached out, took the Wizard's hand and held it between both of his. Held the Wizard's eyes in the timeless pools of his own. 'No other way? That seems the truth. For there is none we can see either. But that also is hardly any surprise. We relied on the writing in that cursed book for so long that now we can't even see the truth before us. Thus you are forced to face this terrible fate. At least know that with you goes the blessing of the Tree.' He rummaged in the pocket of his long gown and took out a small parcel. 'It is a seed of the Tree.' He told them all as he gave the package to the Wizard. 'Perhaps when all is done you could plant it where once only darkness was known.' He turned and walked from the chamber.

*

He falls but is unconcerned. Dreams are like that sometimes. He could fly, soar over the land, but chooses not to. There is something appealing about the green spread out below him. He likes mountains so he sees mountains, mountains and forests, rivers that fall from the heavens and lakes sparkling in the late afternoon sun. There is a meadow set between the trees, sun fresh and set with buttercups, as meadows ought to be. *I know I'm dreaming but dreams were never like this.* It doesn't matter either. He'll go with the flow, see where it takes him. Moving, walking or dream-shifting, he follows an avenue between tall sycamore trees. Dapple green shadows remind him of a thousand other forests but there's something familiar about this place.

Realisation. *It's like the Dormon where first we met.* It's still crystal clear in his memory. Some two miles to the north will lie the hamlet where he'd taken Icicle from the flames. To the south, down the road he treads, he'll find that small valley and the cave-camp. *But this is a dream.*

Even as he descends the trail he knows she's waiting. *Can I face her?* The thought is somehow remote, even impersonal. *Should I turn away?* It doesn't seem to matter. There's no real choice anyway.

As he already knows, she waits in the shadows where the cliff forms a sheltered wall. 'Icicle?'

She smiles almost shyly. 'Who else?'

He can't think of any reply, even more so when she steps out into the sunset-light. He's never seen her smile so brightly. 'Are, is…' stumbling over his thoughts, words. 'Is it you? I mean really you?'

She laughs, lighter, brighter than he'd known her. 'Am I me? Agh! Or are you yourself?' Then quieter than his sleep, suddenly sad, 'You do dream, Fassael. Agh! Although in this dream of yours I'm at least in some degree myself.' She walked over towards him, reached out and took his hands in hers. 'I'll always be here now.' Whispered words.

He can't grasp it. 'I don't understand. Are you a ghost? A wraith of some kind?'

'Ghost, wraith? Agh! Bleedin' hell no. I'm just here.'

'But…'

'I am dead, Fassael.' She makes no effort to deny it. 'The knife that took my life freed my spirit also. Agh! It freed me to be what I wanted, freed me to do as I wanted. Agh! I chose to be here.'

'But is this real or just a dream?'

'Agh! What does it matter? For now we're together, here. Ain't that enough?' She turns to stand beside him and leads him forwards down the trail. 'We walked in a place like this before,' she reminds him. 'That was a greyer world then though. Agh! Grey and cold.'

'Forgive me little one but I can't get my head around this. You say you chose?' She squeezes his hand in confirmation. 'If you're dead then how can you choose?'

'Why don't you burn, Fassael?'

Because I chose not to. 'Is it like that?'

She giggles in softly ringing joy. 'Sort of. Your choice was one of fear and pain. Agh! Mine was of freedom and...'

'And?'

'You know the truth of it, Fassael. I took my own life when I found I couldn't return your love,' she reminds him. 'It was all too empty and painful to do any thing else. However, it seems by doing that, I chose to be other than I was.'

'Other?'

She turns him about again. Tiptoes so that her eyes are almost level with his. 'They said that the choice of dying was in itself an act of love. So it seems I can love after all and so I chose to love you, Fassael of Tabour, you big fuckin' lummox. I chose to be with you. I chose not to die at that time but to live on in your soul.'

His tears are as fire and to Fassael fire was ever a cleansing thing. Dream or truth he'd not deny her. 'But why?' He kissed her brow. It still made no sense.

'For many reasons, Fassael. The first is because you loved me. The second is that having touched love I chose not to leave it despite all that death might offer.'

'And?'

The tone and passion of her answer shocks him to the core. 'The third, and apart from us, this is the most important, is for the Wizard.' So do her words.

'The Wizard?'

'He's in danger, Fassael, and he don't know it.'

'You know of this?'

'I know many things and nothing. I know he's in danger sure enough though.'

'Who, what danger, Icicle? I don't understand.'

'You don't have to understand. Agh! Just fuckin' go to him. He needs you, Fassael.' The strength of her conviction is beyond his control. 'You've got to go with him. Without you he'll be lost! Everything will be lost.'

He tries to think. *He went to the Elves. Is he in danger from them?*

'No of course not. Agh! They're just fuckin' elves.'

'You can hear my thoughts?'

She laughs again. 'Of course I can. Agh! I'm made of your thoughts.'

'Oh bloody hell, I can't cope with this!' he exclaims in exasperation.

'Well you'll just have to get used to it. Agh! 'Cause I ain't going anywhere.' Then back to the subject, 'He needs you, Fassael. Go to him.'

'Oh I'll go to him, Icicle. I think I know where he's gone.'

She looks at him long and hard. 'I'm with you now, Fassael my love. You're not alone any more, not even when you wake.'

'When I wake?'

'Agh! I'll still be here, still loving you.' She laid a hand on his arm. 'There'll be a time for us, my love,' she lingered over the word. 'Agh! For us there'll be forever. But for now time cannot wait.'

He kissed her, slowly, tenderly. 'You're with me?'

'Always…
  Always…
    Always…'

He sat up, rubbing his eyes. Dawn was just lightening the trees. *Was it real?* **Fuck off!** *The shimmer of her laugh denied his doubt. I didn't know.* **Well you do now.** He felt her laughter run through his thoughts and found himself laughing with her. *If anyone sees me like this, they'll think I've gone mad.* **Who said you weren't already?** She had a point.

The need for haste was on him as he packed ready for the road. He could have done with a saddle for the horse. *Tough!* He made do, using a blanket from out of the wagon and a rope to hang his few possessions about its neck. He'd ridden bareback before.

It did trouble him that Calin wasn't there but it couldn't be helped. As Icicle said, 'Time cannot wait.' He doused the fire, taking time to remove all trace, and mounted the horse. *She'll be able to read the signs if ever she returns.*

He paused by the grave. *That's where I buried you.* She was silent for a long time. **Thank you. It's nice here.** *I ain't sure that I'll ever get used to this.* They laughed together as he rode from the clearing.

*

Another day had passed and Calin was drawing ever nearer to the source of that evil. She knew it was a trap too by now, probably one set for her alone. The trail was too clear, too obvious. It, whatever it might be, was drawing her down a path of its own choosing, a trail leading her ever onwards through the still deep snow.

Now a small coppice rose out of the white. It was here it waited. She felt its darkness reach out to envelope her as she stepped beneath the trees. It came as a shiver, a trembling, a renewal of the dread she'd felt at the wagon.

As then, the signs of death were everywhere, hanging from branches, splattered over the ground, the sickening stench scenting the air with its own foul taint. She halted, drawing her sword and looking over the scene before her. That she didn't gag was surprising but her anger was growing, replacing any other feeling even that of dread. She was Sanain. Her anger was deadly.

There came a scream from nearby, a scream of utter terror and life-numbing pain. It had found others abroad and had brought them to this, its lair. It had them staked out on the ground and even now crouched over one, the last, intent on its unholy work.

The reality of that sight shook her to the core. She knew it or if not it then the creatures of its ilk. She'd known this touch of evil on the plain when she'd travelled with the Lady. Forever would she remember the darkness of its oh so empty soul. She'd known it before Tabour too. Maybe that gave her hope.

'Stop!' She shouted her demand, even as it raised a taloned hand over the face of its final terrified victim. By then she was ready, if you could ever be ready in such a situation.

It turned slowly, the gaping maw, welling with the blood of those it had killed. She felt its eyes on her, felt its thoughts tearing at her, drawing at her. It was like sleep, only a sleep of nightmares and horror. She raised her sword, held it before her and, more by instinct than design, called to mind the light of the Druid that had saved her before and felt its compulsions die.

It screamed in hideous exaltation, '**So you have come then Champion?**'

Whatever fear she had felt was gone now. She could see her enemy. What more does a warrior need? The sword sang in her hand. 'Yes. I have indeed come. I intend to put an end to your work.' She spoke her challenge.

'**You are come, Champion, because I summonsed you.**'

Champion? 'I came because I chose to.' She also chose to deny its words.

It crouched slightly. The dribble of blood formed a dark ruby pearl, which dropped, soundless to the earth. '**What do you intend?**' There was no fear in the voice, just a strange curiosity.

'I am Calin-Sanain.' Well it was some kind of answer. 'Who, or should I say what, are you?'

'**I am Death.**' It might well have been.

'No.' She even managed to smile. 'I've seen death too many times. I know its face and its hand. You're not death.'

'**I am fear.**'

'Perhaps,' she smiled again. 'I can't claim to know fear.'

'**You'll know me well before this day is done!**' The threat sounded real enough.

'Fine, I don't mind learning, if the teacher is good enough. Though I doubt you are.' She felt it coiling, knew that it would soon strike. She even knew that she stood no hope against it. It wasn't to be a fight of weapons and skill but of power and will. She wasn't even afraid, just sad that this would be her end. She shook the thought away. Then, continuing to circle the thing, laughed. 'You'll have to do better than that.'

It replied with its own sick, derisive snigger. '**You are strong, Champion. Good. The greater shall be the cost of the knowledge you bear and better the reward for its gaining.**' It began to circle her, with every step she felt the power of its will bear down on her. '**You can not kill me.**' Its breath was little more than the hiss of a serpent. '**Not even with your pretty shining sword.**'

'If that's so I'll just have to find other means.' Still she was not daunted. In truth she should have been. She was hardly a match for a Creature-of-the-Void such as this. She backed away, still holding her sword before her. It circled slowly with her. She could even feel its confidence growing.

'**There is no haste**,' it sighed, all the time continuing to sidle around her. '**Where is he?**'

The question took her by surprise. 'Where is he? Where's who?'

It laughed again for the game was to its liking. '**Where, Champion, as if you didn't know. Where is the Wizard of Rainbows?**' Still it circled.

She tried to think. *It asks of the Wizard. Why? What does it want?* 'Do you imagine for one minute that I'd tell you that?' She knew then she'd probably not win in this fight. She even thought of lowering her guard to get it over with and felt the thing sense that very idea. It turned back towards her. All she could see was the gaping hole of its blooded maw, the hollow pits that were its eyes.

'**Oh yes. You will tell me, Champion, or I shall keep you alive in total torment until your screams bring him to me.**'

At that moment its last victim moaned in agony causing her anger to flare again. *How dare this thing exist?* The world became crystal clear. It came, rushed towards her, its evil rasping a sigh of death rising into a discordant scream of victory. Too bad. The sword sang as it sliced through the air. It sang of life, as she willed it would, the life the Dwarven craftsmen had set in its steel. This thing, regardless of how evil, regardless of how powerful, regardless of how much it hated, could never contend with that power. It ceased to be.

The scream filling her world at that instant was not born in the taint of evil coursing through her spirit. It was not from the sudden dark fire of the life-lust burning in every particle of its nature. It was not even for the knowledge of the immensity of the crimes against life that had fed its hunger. No. What filled her scream was a single image found in the depths of the thing's final, sick memory.

The Elfling writhes in fear as they wrap her in bands of dark power, as they freeze the magic that is her life and as they drag her into the gaping pit of some terrible black castle. The howling glee of the watching creatures fills the void.

NO! The word screamed through her. 'NO!' she screamed aloud into the growing night. But the truth would not be denied. *They have her. They have His elfling, Luminae, The Fire-Dancer. They have her.* And the horror of that idea was worse than anything she'd ever known.

Her mind slammed shut, anger flaring through her. A cold anger that even the creatures of darkness could never face. 'I'm going to find her, her and the Wizard. This should not have been done!'

There came a sound, from somewhere behind her and she spun, her blue flickering blade sensing for danger, as does a snake's tongue. It wasn't danger she met. It was in all probability worse than that. The young soldier tried once more to move, to lift its head at least.

She went to him, knelt down beside him. There was no hope. It had started at his feet and hands, working slowly, breaking, rending, tearing at his flesh. It had even used the man's own sword to slice open his belly.

No, there's no hope. She knew too much of death to think otherwise. 'Who are you?' It was important that she knew that at least.

'Taiir, Sevriet,' he gasped the words. Shock had gratefully dulled the pain. 'You?'

'Calin-Sanain.'

'You killed it?'

'Yes.'

'Good.' He gasped again, body shaking.

'Lay still, Taiir Sevriet.' She wanted to ease his passage. 'I shall mark your grave.'

He nodded, even smiled his gratitude. Then, surprisingly, he whistled, sharp and shrill though the effort cost him much in the blood-beat currency of life. In but moments there came the sound of hoof beats approaching fast. The stallion was blacker than night. It stood over them, as still as death.

'I call him Sabin...' the Sevriet told her, following her eyes. 'The Night-Hawk... He'll be your steed now... I have to go... on another journey.'

She'd not deny him. 'Sabin,' she repeated the name.

'He's a good horse. More than I ever deserved.'

'I'll take care of him.'

'If you…' But he said no more. Life drifted away with a gentle sigh.

Calin buried him beyond the tree line as she'd promised. She gathered the other remains and set them on a pyre. That the coppice itself would catch fire and burn to nothing was probably a blessing.

With the first flames licking through the wood she turned to her new horse, Sabin, and walked to where it stood. It saw her coming, fixed her with its coal-black eyes when she stopped but an arm's length away and held its gaze with her own. 'We shall be friends, Sabin-Sevre.' She bowed to the beast. 'We are well suited.' Sabin declined to answer. It tossed its head to show off the fineness of its long midnight mane. Perhaps that was its reply.

As the sun broke free of night's dark shroud she mounted the coal-black steed and, without even a final backward look, turned away from the place. She had things to do and time was passing.

*

The Wizard left the Crystal-City in the early morning hours ere the sun had begun to light the treetops. The Lady and the Harpist Plie went with him. At the Lady's suggestion they left quietly so even the elves, save those who had been at the meeting, knew nothing of their departure. The intention was to journey southwards at first, deceiving any eyes who chanced to watch. This way of suspicion did not sit well with the Wizard though he understood the need. Had the Lady and Plie not gone with him, he would probably have ignored the risk. For now though he did as she asked.

One day out from the city they turned westwards, following a new trail through the woods. There was nothing arduous about this journey. They'd brought a pony laden with provisions and were able to travel at their own speed. Each night they would camp beneath the trees and sleep away the hours of darkness at peace. Well, peace for most. Throughout his dreams her calling grew more frantic, more alone and he too felt the panic of her fear as a constant drain on his heart. He didn't speak of these dread things though. They were not for others to know.

Some fourteen days after leaving Al-Sinnian they reached the forest edge once again and looked out from under the eves upon Esthill, a land of hill and mountain, mountains indeed that climbed to disappear in the thick blanket of snow-cloud. The long grass was white with snow also and the puddles formed in the ruts of the road shone with ice. It seemed that winter had waited for him.

'It's time to bid you farewell, Wizard of Rainbows.' The Lady had tears in her eyes. 'It's a long, dark and perilous road you now follow and I can't in truth foretell where it'll lead you. There are no words now to tell us of things we might fear, nor of good or ill. Perhaps that's best.' She waited a moment, reached out and held his hand with an almost desperate intensity. 'I fear these are our final words also, Wizard of Rainbows, and doubt now the mists of the future will ever part for another meeting. I give you my blessing, for what it's worth, and I wish you safety and happiness when all is done.'

For his part, he could find no words at all. He'd thought she'd always be there, waiting. He remembered the creature out on the plain on his outward journey and the goodness that she had brought into being to save Calin from its terrible curse of decay.

He remembered also that she'd trusted his magic when even he'd doubted its truth. He bowed to her and knelt on one knee before her. 'You trusted me, Lady, before my magic had awoken and before I'd even called myself by my own name. Will you trust me again? I neither know the future nor even wish to, but I'm still who I've always been. No matter where my path leads me, nor how dark it becomes I'll be none other than that.'

He stood again and kissed her on the brow. 'This is a time of parting that neither of us can delay. You're my friend, my Lady, and, together or apart and whether we meet again or not, such you'll always be to me.'

'I hope so, Wizard, but friendship and trust are such a strange things to know.'

Plie stayed in the shadows of the trees but they could hear his gentle harping.

Fare-thee-well, my friend
Many are the paths through time
And who shall know where ours now lead?
Perchance we shall meet again
Who knows?

Until that IF,
Fare-thee-well
though we do not part
In the Halls of our minds
In the silence of our moments,
In the stillness of our being
There we shall dwell.

Words, which he might carry, wherever his path might lead him.

*

The morning sunlight was clear as eternity. The day, the third since leaving the shelter of the Elwood's lofty trees, still cold with winter's crystal touch, promised to be fine. Even the snow, still lingering in the shadows and hollows, refused to dampen that hope.

Now the wooden halls of the Elswood had fallen behind the Wizard was alone once more and, if the truth be known, he was glad of it too. The road he followed, as Plie had explained, wound through the foothills of the Divide. Two days after leaving the trees he reached its junction with the greater, western trail that carried over the mountains into the Lake-lands beyond.

This new trail snaked through the rolling land as a grey ribbon. Carts and carriages had recently passed that way and if the signs were true there would be others on the road also. Perhaps his solitude would be short lived after all.

As if to confirm the fact the sound of bells came ringing through the morning. Bright bells, clear as the day, light and lively, tingling a greeting before he'd even seen the wagons which now appeared over the brow of the nearest hill. *Pinexae!*

There were two of them. *I've not seen the Pinexae since returning from the East. What bodes here I wonder?* He knew too much to think it a thing of chance.

The brilliant sky-blue cloak of the Elf who leapt from the leading wagon was of little surprise also. *I might have known it.* 'Niivalsta!' The tone of welcome in the Wizard's voice was no lie. Neither was the smile that met his words.

'Hello, my friend,' the Elf laughed, 'No longer a pilgrim are you being.' He turned to hold out his hand to the lass who skipped down the path to join him.

'Pina!'

She smiled like mystery and as always his questions turned to nothing, his thoughts to calm in the depths of her eyes. 'Ah, 'tis the Wizard of Rainbows no less. So we meet anew now that both our former questings are complete.' Her voice was no less mesmerising than her eyes. For a moment he was so enchanted that he'd quite forgot that she'd never spoken before. Her laughter peeled about them. 'Words are so much easier than thoughts Wizard, though thoughts never lie. But it is good to hear your words and good for you to hear mine.' Then she smiled again and lent over to kiss his cheek.

'Wizard.'

'Yes, Niivalsta?'

'This meeting is not of chance.'

'I didn't think it was.'

'We should a camp make, so that talk awhile we can.'

He didn't demure though the day was but new and he had hardly begun his journey. 'If you say so.'

The wagon had drawn close to them now and the elf caught the bridle and led the horse onto the small meadow by the roadside. The other wagon followed. The occupants of this joined those in the centre.

'These are Tsiera and Cloure.' Both were Pinexae. Tsiera was clad in gypsy style, as was Pina. Cloure was dressed like a rover, black leather shirt and trews with a wide red sash. Their amethyst eyes held the Wizard a while and then they both bowed and warmed the campsite with their smiles.

'They are as was I,' Pina explained. 'Their words are silent.'

Without suggestion the Pinexae Cloure gathered together a fire that was quickly ablaze. Whilst he was doing this, Niivalsta formed a small circle of benches. The Wizard, as seemed to be his role these days, poured wine and Pina served a platter of dried meats and bread.

'We are know of your journey,' Niivalsta began as they settled to eat. 'It is seeming to us that, perhaps, joining with us is a way you might choose.'

'You know that I cross over to the Lake-lands?'

'This we know and where beyond.' The elf smiled. His secrets would be safe. 'This no journey as our last, is. Then walked you into knowledge. Now walk you into war.'

War! 'That's what the Lady said also. War, although I do not kill.'

'Can you take life from that which has none?' Pina offered mysteriously. 'Besides, it may be you'll find you have no real choice in this.'

No choice? 'I've already made my choice, Pina.'

'Have you?' She laughed and he began to doubt his own resolve. 'But that's as may-be. Others have yet to make theirs.'

'Still. I will not use my magic to kill.' He was defiant in this at least.

'Good, It would not serve you so to do.' She handed the platter about the group again. The Wizard replenished their drinks at the same time. It gave him a moment to think.

'You're telling me that I am in danger?'

The Elf answered, 'No, Wizard, we are telling you that YOU are danger. That to escape such danger you cannot, for you cannot escape yourself.'

'You carry the danger with you, Wizard,' Pina explained. 'We but confirm what you and others already know. You were followed to the Elswood by something dark and ill. They know where you went. They know too that you will soon leave the haven of the trees. Their eyes are busy, as busy as their minds.'

'And?'

'And, we would be of help in this. It seems to us that those who watch might not see you as one amongst the Pinexae. We too travel to the Lake-Lands.' She smiled again.

'What of the goblins?' He had to know.

Her expression was somehow strange, maybe even guilty. 'We bear them no ill, neither any good. They are not our concern, Wizard.'

'What are your concerns then, Pina?' *And where in the midst of them do I fit?* 'You must know that I'll no more do your bidding than I would the kings of men or elf.'

She paused, looked closely at him. 'Threefold, Wizard. Firstly, we ask of ourselves, Why are we here? The powers rise, and are we not a part of these things? Were not the Neleven-Fey brought here for such? When the power of the void is gone from this sphere, why then should we remain?' She laughed again at the confusion on his face and added, 'Save for the beauty of the land, and the friends we have about us. Yet for all that, there must be an ending.'

He didn't understand. *I seldom do.* 'And second?'

'Secondly, because you know our name, Wizard. Our name and our nature, as we know yours, your nature and your power.'

'And third?'

'And thirdly because you carry his eyes and he alone, in all this world of colour, never turned against us. Yes, ever did he call us friend.' But there was sadness in her expression that failed to match her words.

Gentil the Wizard. He didn't reply.

'Shall your joining with us be?' Niivalsta asked, against the crackling of the fire.

'I'll be pleased to go your way,' he accepted. 'But,' an afterthought, 'but my journey, my quest comes first to me. I don't intend to make another oath till the last one's done with.'

'I hear your words, Wizard, and I know of your oath,' Pina spoke solemnly 'Now hear mine. We the Pinexae, Neleven-Fey, we too are sworn. We, The Pinexae will not fight in the battles of men or of the grey ones, save to protect our people. We so swore when the paths of men and ours were sundered. On this journey we'll listen to your words and do as you bid us, if it seems right, even fight at your side if the need be to do so, to protect ourselves. But we don't join in your war. We have futures of our own.' She looked to the elf beside her. 'Niivalsta shall do as he thinks right.'

'The wood in my bow is strong and of the Elswood, my arrows are true,' the elf intoned. 'But my mind and my heart are with the Pinexae. I shall be as a friend.'

'Won't my joining you place you and your kin in danger?'

'All are in danger anyway, Wizard. The more so should you fail. But if the eyes which seek you should look this way, well then they'll see no more than a Pinexae caravan and even their eyes can't penetrate that brightness. Perhaps thus you can cross over into the Lake-lands unseen.'

Is that a lie? I'd not wish it so. Perhaps not. It is a strategy. They'll see what is. If they mistake the truth, is that a lie? It is. Yes it would be a lie for the intent is to deceive.

'This seems to be as a lie, Pina.'

Her eyes drooped. 'It is so,' she confirmed. 'Or at least a deception to lead astray those who would hinder your path otherwise.'

'How shall we travel?' Back to business.

'You, Niivalsta and I will share the first wagon. Tsiera and Cloure will take the rear.'

The disquiet over the secrecy of the matter sat ill with the Wizard as it had in the Elswood. However it was more as an omen of unease than a disagreement between companions.

However, now the time had come for them to go. As Niivalsta led their wagon back onto the road, Pina and the Wizard climbed aboard. Then, as planned, Cloure and Tsiera followed on behind.

Riding on the wagon seemed strange, and at first uncomfortable. The vehicle was sprung and the road in good repair, but the seat felt hard. Pina just laughed at him and said he'd get used to it in time anyway.

To pass the hours away Pina asked him about his travels, after they'd parted in Finestre on that other journey. He told her of Hkainae and of the desert. He spoke too of the land beyond the desert and of the mountain.

'My people don't travel that road,' she'd told him. 'None have since before the Cataclysm. There are too many sad and painful memories beyond the sands.'

'Hkamoot.'

Her eyes, maybe for the first time since that long-gone-day when they'd met on the road from Varista, actually showed surprise. 'You know words of that tongue?'

'It's what the Desert people say when they speak of the Sands,' he told her.

'Yes, that would be so.' She waited before continuing. 'It's the name they gave to the Time-of-Fire **Hkamoot A Shevrili Na Gwarrlha** Fire and Ice then Darkness.' She didn't explain.

'There seems to be much about the Pinexae that I don't know, Pina.'

She laughed again, just a soft chuckle. 'And it seems to me, by understanding that much, you already know more than most.'

His impression at that moment was that she was playing some strange game with him, with everyone. *Does it really matter?*

*

You know I've never looked at things in this way before. He knew her surprise when first she touched his thrill of wonder over the beauty about them. Beauty seemed such a strange concept in the normal cold pragmatism of a goblin mind. *Perhaps when things are quieter and when the time comes to rest, perhaps then we'll walk here again*, he told her. *Yes I think I'd like that*, she confided. ***There are many things to know.***

They were moving deep in the heart of the Elswood now, Fassael leading the horse for a time, walking through the wonder of late afternoon. *It is beautiful here, Icicle. I wish...* **Agh! There's no point in wishing. We're more together now than we ever were, anyway.** There was that, however strange it might seem. *They say Al-Sinnian is the most beautiful of all.* **Who says?** Laughter filled his mind again. **Anyway, I thought you said I was.** He smiled and continued on his way.

As with The Wizard, time and the passing of days had little meaning here in the green wood. Were it not for Icicle's chill warnings of the need for haste, Fassael might have been tempted to linger amongst the gentle groves. However the warnings were there and he travelled as far as he might through the hours of daylight. And at night? At night he learnt to live again.

The Elves knew of his coming and prepared to meet him in their groves. They even saw him moving through the avenues but didn't approach. They didn't understand. How could they? To their minds he should have been borne down by his sorrow. Instead, his laughter often rang through the forest and the call of his happiness seemed to awaken the first glistenings of spring.

Thus the word of his coming went ahead of him and, when he climbed the hill towards the shimmering crystal city, they came forth to meet and welcome him. **Elves! I've never really met an elf before. I saw some. Several, but they were either dead or captive. These are beautiful too.** One came to lead the horse away. It would be groomed and tended well. Fassael had no doubt of that.

With his senses reeling from the sheer beauty of the place and the constant thrill of Icicle's wonderment in his heart Fassael found himself led towards the meeting place. There, in the shade of the Tree as had the Wizard before, he was welcomed by the High-Dancer.

'Fassael of Tabour, your name comes before you. Be welcome and be at peace. May you find rest and comfort in the crystal Halls.' The Elf-Lord bowed low. 'I am the High-Dancer.' He bowed again and gestured to the elf at his side. 'My Queen, the Crystal-Singer.'

Fassael bowed in return. However Icicle and his own haste-led bluntness ruled the moment. 'I seek the Wizard of Rainbows.'

A human-lady, in a sweep of green, stepped forwards. 'Of course you do, Fassael Fire-Born. We shall speak of...' Her words drifted to a halt as her eyes widened.

She sees me! Icicle's startled exclamation filled his mind.

She did too, in a way that Fassael couldn't begin to grasp. For a moment her brow furrowed as she sought to understand what she saw. Then a smile of pure wonder lit her face. 'How...?' She sank to her knees bowed her head to the ground at Fassael's feet.

You paid a high price, Sunset-Child.
Agh! It was worth it.

When she stood to face Fassael again it seemed the Lady's heart had lightened. 'There's a mystery here that's like to wake the universe.' And she leant forward and kissed the giant man on each cheek.

The elves stood aghast. They'd never seen the like of this strange meeting.

'I'm known as The Lady, a Druid-of-the-High-calling,' she told him, ignoring the others' reactions. 'I know of the Wizard of Rainbows and call him friend as do you. We'll speak of him and other matters later. Now you shall meet these other friends.'

Introductions were made – Plie the Harpist, The Keeper of the Tree and others. Their names passed him by.

The moment of recognition almost froze him when he looked at the Elf Queen. 'You're her mother.' Fassael took and kissed the Crystal-Singer's hand. 'I met her one time in the Land of Dormon,' he explained. 'She travelled with the Wizard on his journey to Tabour.' But his thoughts were in turmoil, driven so by the sudden shocked silence in his mind. *What?*

The Elf-Queen smiled, near as bright as the Lady. 'And you should know also that the High-Dancer is her father,' she informed him. 'You shall tell us of this and of all you know of her and the Wizard.' Then, her mood changing, flying as a fleeting wind or a cloud passing before the sun, she continued. 'She is not here. She is lost, gone. We do not know how to find her.'

Fassael felt the sadness of her words like a blow. 'Isn't she with the Wizard?'

There was no answer.

'Has he gone to find her?' he all but demanded.

But again the words were met in silence, a silence that echoed all the more in the space of Icicle's withdrawal.

Without warning, the growing tension was smashed to smithereens as hooves thundered hard and loud on the paving. The black war-horse reared and iron shoes sparked bright on the marble where hooves had never trod. Heads turned, shocked by the sacrilege though the rider paid them no heed. Calin had more on her mind than custom or propriety as she careered through the shining hall to the doorway of the Crystal chamber. Dismounting in a single leap and leaving the reins to dangle free, she strode through the arch. Her boot heels beat a sharp tattoo needlessly announcing her entrance.

Taking in at a glance the scene before her she chose the Lady. 'It called me Champion. Why?' She didn't even try to explain.

The Lady's face whitened. 'Because that's who you are, Calin-Sanain.'

'Where's the Wizard?' she asked, her voice hard and demanding.

'He's not here.'

'Has he gone after her?'

If anything, the Druid's face whitened even more. But she didn't answer.

'You know.' It was no question.

Still she did not reply, but turned on her heel and walked into the shade of the Tree.

'I asked the same,' Fassael informed her. He saw no need for greetings. 'They say they don't know where the Dancer is. They've yet to answer about the Wizard.'

Calin crossed the few paces to stand before the High-Dancer. She gave no greeting but simply spoke her words. 'I know.' She saw his eyes widen in surprise. 'Is that where the Wizard's gone? To find and rescue her?' No response. 'Do you know what's happening?' She turned to the Tabour man. 'Fassael? Do you know where he is?'

He paused but a moment, waiting on Icicle's words. None came, although he could feel the tension of her anger building. 'No. I only know that he's going into danger.'

'Peace,' the High-Dancer's voice sang soothingly over the assemblage. 'Be you welcome in the Crystal Halls, Calin-Sanain. It seems there are many words to be told. This is not the place.' He turned to one of the elf guards, 'Take her horse. It must be groomed, fed and rested.'

'It must be ready to ride by first light!' Calin snapped.

'Mine too,' Fassael added. 'We'll go on together.'

'Have a saddle made ready for Fassael's steed,' the Elf-Lord added. He knew the rightness of their words though, as yet, not the meanings.

Fassael nodded his thanks.

'I shall have refreshments brought,' the Elf-Lord explained. 'We will meet in Council in one quarter-hour. Come, Calin-Sanain and Fassael-of-Tabour,' he held his hands out beckoning them follow. Take a moment to rest and wash the dust from your faces.'

It wasn't far. As he'd promised he led them to a small chamber already prepared for their coming.

What the Hell is going on? The thought rang through Fassael's mind. **Agh! Hell is the right word.** *What do you mean?* **I saw her.** *Who? What? Who did you see Icicle?* **Her. That Elf-Queen's child. I saw her in the wastes beyond the Stone City. They had her!** *Who? Who had her?* **The Greylon.** The word meant nothing. But the tone of her thought drove the blood from his cheeks in horror. **She was being taken back to their Lair, back to the darkness.** *When? When did you see it?* **Before the battle, but not long before.** He felt the touch of her sorrow fill him…

…Then **Oh fuckin' hell no!** She saw the truth in Fassael's troubled thoughts… **His LOVE!** She screamed.

They met, as the High Dancer had decreed, some fifteen minutes later in the grand council chamber. There, as they sat about a long table, a feast was set before them; crystal classes glistened with water-clear wine.

'Welcome again,' the Dancer began, 'though I am unsure if welcome this be. It seems that once again things arise to trouble us. First let there be introductions. I am The Lord High-Dancer, Dancer of the High-Dance. This is my Queen, The Crystal-Singer. Beside her sits Plie the Harp-Smith and, by him, Lorrelii Song-Master. Next is The Tree-Lord.' The ancient elf, sitting at the end of the table, bowed to the newcomers. 'Fassael-of-Tabour.' He stopped as the Lady, sitting to his right, touched his arm.

'Fassael-Fire-Born,' she corrected, perhaps she wanted to say more.

'Fassael-Fire-Born and Calin-Sanain.'

Again she interrupted him, 'Calin-Sanain-Champion.'

'Champion. Beside you is Giiral Bow-master, keeper of the Greenwood and then Tremalsha The Fountain-Lord. Lastly is The Druidess who dwells with us at this time.' He paused for a moment. 'We have gathered together to speak of what we know and of what we just fear or surmise. It is a time to speak freely. Who shall begin?'

There followed an inevitable awkward pause whilst they waited.

'You said you know where she is?' It was the Crystal-Singer asking about her daughter. It was her right.

'Not exactly where, but I know something. However what I know is evil indeed,' Calin tried to speak gently, though her words could never be harmless. 'If all are willing, I'll start by telling what I know.'

The Queen nodded, the High-Dancer too. Others about the table had no disagreement.

'There was a thing out on the plain, at the edge of the forest,' she began. 'It was as nothing I've met before, unless one includes that creature I slew before the battle at Tabour. Its intent was evil and its actions even worse. It feasted on the lives of its victims, on their fear and their pain.'

'What happened?'

'It drew me to it, thinking to ensnare me in its evil. When I came it asked me of the Wizard, threatened to steal my soul unless I told where he was.' She heard them gasp.

'And?'

'And I destroyed it.' But her tone was of horror relived rather than victory gained.

'What happened then?' the Lady asked again. She, at least, knew of the price Calin paid for her calling.

'Its evil washed over me, filled me with the horror of its nature. Its thoughts were filled with visions of evil. But worse, far worse was the image it showed me in its last instant.'

'Image?' the Lady continued.

'It was of her.' She turned towards the Queen, tears blurring her sight of the Elf. 'They had her, bound her in darkness. She was helpless, not even a spark of her fires still burning. She's in their hands.'

'Whose hands?' the Elf-Lord had to hear the truth.

'Creatures-of-darkness, things like the one I slew. They've taken her back to their lair.' How do you answer a thing like that? How could any. 'It's where I intend to go. If I can I'll find the Wizard first. If not, then I'll still go, alone if need be.'

It's as I saw! Icicle's confirmation was tinged with relief. 'You won't be alone.'

'How can this be so?' the Dancer's voice shook, mirroring Calin's horror. 'How can they have taken her?'

She was betrayed, handed over to them. Icicle's thought was a blade ripping through Fassael's mind. *Who?* But she gave no answer. 'Is that where he's gone?' He had to ask. 'What he's going to do? Has he gone to rescue her?'

'No,' the Lady quietly replied. 'He doesn't know where she is. I didn't tell him. Although I can say this, the path he takes shall lead him there all the same.'

Their eyes were on her, all of them.

'The Galghathag?' the Dancer spat the word.

Neither Calin nor Fassael knew the name. 'The lair of the Lord-of-Mists,' Plie answered their ignorance. 'She has been taken there?'

The Lady nodded.

'Why? You knew but said nothing. Why?' the Elf-Lord demanded.

'What good would words be?' She was strong, this druid. 'Had I spoken, then what?'

'It was the truth,' the Queen replied for them all. 'Should the truth not be spoken?'

'Truth? Is that so? Do you hear your own words, Queen of the Elswood? Tell me. What truths could ever come from the Lord-of-Lies? What truths would you believe? What truths would you act upon?' She stood and began to pace about the table. 'The-Lord-of-Mists' deceits are many and subtle beyond understanding. What would you do that was not a part of his scheming? Is this as you think I should have done, spoken this truth and sent him into the beast's snare alone?'

'No. Not alone,' Fassael spoke, Icicle might even have stood beside him.

'No, not alone. Where is he? Where does the Wizard go?' Calin asked the Lady.

'He travels to Lodor.' Her answer was gentle, still. 'He's gone there to retrieve his sword.'

'His sword?' Calin vaguely remembered him talking of such. *Once I made my own Sword, Calin.* 'How does he travel? And how best can we overtake him?'

'How? He travels with the Pinexae, with Pina and Niivalsta.'

'That is good anyway,' the Queen sighed. 'The Pinexae are good and pure and are ever the friend of the Elves and the land.'

'Don't be so sure.' Was it Fassael or Icicle who spoke? Her mistrust was as a burning brand in his thoughts. 'Are any truly a friend to the Wizard?'

The Lady gasped in shock and turned to look at the man. 'What do you know, Fassael?'

'That there are many truths and many lies. I've seen both and been touched by both. I prefer to choose my own path. I'll tell you this much though. I trust the Wizard for his rainbows of wonder. Calin I trust for her sorrow and for the sharing of graves. Myself I trust for the fires of my choosing... But I'll trust none other.' It was his time to stand.

'Don't you trust the Elves?' the Lady asked, aware of their eyes turned towards him. Was it wise to talk of mistrust in their own halls?

'I know nothing of Elves,' he replied. 'Nor do I know of you, Lady. By what token should I trust any?'

'You shouldn't.' Her words were stark and bare as stone. 'It's better to mistrust everyone at this time. Perhaps thus you might hear the truth if it's spoken. You were right to question the friendship of the Pinexae. Their truths are not the same as yours, their needs are not your needs.'

The High Dancer tried to understand. 'What threat would they be to one such as he?'

Fassael had no answer either, only Icicle's warning cascading through his thoughts. **There is something very wrong here, Fassael.** *What? What do you know?*

The Lady looked slowly about the chamber but did not reply.

Fassael did, or rather Icicle did speaking through him. He wished she hadn't, wished that her words were untrue, wished that... 'It's them what handed her into the Greylon's grasp. Agh! They've sent her helpless into the Dark-Lord's Lair.' It was the truth. They were standing, all of them, faces shocked by the horror in Fassael's voice. 'They handed her over, before the battle started. They came under a cloak of mist, brought her to the Greylon. Agh! And they took her away…'

'It's what the creature knew,' Calin's words were like death. 'Though I didn't see the Pinexae, I knew she'd been betrayed. That's the vision I saw in the creature's death-thoughts.'

'But why?' The Crystal Singer's voice shook and tears streamed over her alabaster cheeks. 'They are our friends. Why would they…'

'Ever have the Pinexae stood with us,' agreed the Bow-Master. He didn't want to believe. None of them did.

Their eyes turned towards the Druid, all of them. It was the Dancer who spoke. 'You know, Lady. You told the Wizard that you knew, even though you didn't tell him what you knew.' The words were an accusation.

She met the Elf-Lord's eyes in stillness. 'Yes.'

'Why?' Calin asked the question this time. 'Why was she taken?'

'To draw him, the Wizard of Rainbows, into its Lair. When he knows where she is nothing will prevent him from going to her.' She let the words sink in.

'It makes no sense,' the Dancer continued. 'Why would the Pinexae want him destroyed? They are Neleven-Fey, Lords-of-Light. Why would they give him over to the Forces-of-the-Void, over to their eternal enemy?'

But one there understood. 'Oh yes, it makes sense all right.' Calin was horribly sure of that. She felt their eyes on her looking for her answer. The question wasn't needed. 'The Wizard is very powerful indeed. We all saw that at Tabour. He'll be hard to better, if anything can. And, he might even be victorious. Even if he's not, the Lord-of-Mists and his creatures will be weakened by the struggle to overcome him.' She turned to The Lady, 'Is that not right?'

'You see clearly, Calin-Sanain-Champion.'

'That is why she was taken.'

'Why?' The Crystal-Singer still didn't understand. She had to know.

The Lady answered although Calin might have done so also. 'The reason is two-fold. First of light, She'll draw him there; force him to fight against those who hold her. There's no way, once he knows where; he'll not go. Secondly, for the Lord-of-Mists; by her being there the Wizard's hand will be weakened, his focus confused by the choices to be made.'

'I still don't understand,' Fassael spoke for most there. He looked to the Lady. 'Tell us.'

She turned slowly, looking at those who stood before her. There was sadness in her eyes. 'For him, and for the trust he gave to me, for her and the beauty of her dance, for you also, Calin, and for you, Fassael, for the wonder I see in your eyes, for these things I'll tell you this much.'

There was something in her manner that denied any response as she walked slowly about the table. 'Sit,' she bade them, each in turn, 'Sit,' as she passed them by. 'Sit.' All did so without demure

'It's known by some, although not many, that the Pinexae are in truth those once called Neleven-Fey. Consider what that means. They are as has been rightly said "Lords-of-Light".'

'But…' The Crystal Singer struggled to grasp meaning from the words.

'But the Darkness rises.' It was a cold realisation that filled Calin. It froze her heart to stone.

'Yes, Calin. The Darkness rises and they know it. And, in the truths of their understanding, they know their role is to contend with it when it does. It's why they came through the Ryngold at the beginning of time. When Elovsenal fell their task was not complete. The Evil was cast down but not defeated. Long indeed have they waited for the time to come again. As Calin said, The Darkness rises.'

Calin finished, 'So the War is not yet done.' She didn't need confirmation. 'The Wizard and his Love are but pieces in some eternal game of Powers. How can he face them, both Light and Dark? How can he stand alone against them?'

Fassael perhaps had an answer. 'Because he's not of light or of dark, Calin. He's the Wizard of Rainbows, all the Rainbows of the World.'

'Yes, Fassael.' The Lady smiled and nodded to his reply. 'He stands, as always, amidst a War of Powers, truths and lies, but how will he know the difference? I'll tell you. There was one choice made early, ere the vibrations of now began to sound. He once made his own sword. Without which he will be doomed.' There, the words were said.

'Not with me beside him,' Calin was diamond hard, shining with the sharpness of her anger. 'I'm going with him.'

'And I,' the Tabour man was no softer than she.

'And we shall come too,' the Elf-Lord confirmed.

'No, My Lord, not yet,' the Lady countered his offer. 'In this there will, as always, be but three – The Wizard, The Champion and The Free-Man.'

'Why?' Calin asked again.

'It's ever three. More would not help.'

'Why us?'

'Would you choose another, Calin-Sanain? You are the Champion. It is your place. Fassael goes because it is his choice so to do. The Wizard goes because he so swore. Thus it is.'

'I still don't understand.'

'What don't you understand, Fassael?'

'That in knowing these things you didn't even think to warn him about the Pinexae. Didn't even warn him to shun them.'

'He's in no danger from them.'

'But...'

'It's in their interest to see that he passes safely through the land. With them he'll be safe. Don't forget the things that hunt him. The things of the kind which Calin slew.'

'But with his magic they could be no match to him,' Fassael protested.

'True, but if he uses his magic he'll reveal himself.' She sat. The matter was done and her words also. 'The one thing that he does need, and that beyond all others, is his sword. It bears his nature.' And no one knew what she meant by that.

*

So the Pinexae wagons climbed up and down the slopes of this meandering road. As Shimmian had said, long, long ago, on that other trail through these mountains, the journey over this pass should take about two weeks. In truth it took nearer to three but that was due to the weather more than the pass, and even this wasn't so bad. The snows seemed to wait until evening to do their worst and the high winds did as much as anything else to keep the road clear. Besides, the road-builders had provided shelter along the way and in one small valley they even found the welcoming light of an inn.

They stayed there overnight, taking comfort in the warmth and shelter offered. Though for the Wizard there was no respite to his nightly calling and he feared his heart might break with the loneliness of her echoing cry.

That evening, as they sat together warming themselves before the inn's great hearth, the landlord came to them. 'Excuse me for bothering you.'

Pina looked up. 'Yes?' She wasn't hostile.

'Well, see, I was wondering about your journey and I was thinking to myself that it might not be safe in the mountains at this troubled time.'

'Not safe?' the Wizard asked.

'No sir, you see there are these goblin things all over the place these days, since that battle that is. They're only too ready to attack any small party that they see. Wouldn't it be best to wait until some troopers come, so that you can travel under their protection?'

'Thank you for your concern but we're in no danger, Landlord,' Pina spoke quietly. 'Especially from the grey folk.'

Niivalsta, the Wizard noted was looking uncomfortable, his eyes seemed restless, flicking between the man and Pina. *There are more secrets here.*

'But… Are you telling me that they won't harm you?' the man couldn't grasp the idea.

'What I say is true,' Pina confirmed. 'There is no enmity between us. We, We the Pinexae, that is, we bear them no ill will…' She hesitated.

'That might be true, and I'd not say otherwise,' the Landlord continued. 'But I ain't so sure they see things in the same way.'

'I've no worry,' she seemed reluctant to voice her words, perhaps frightened by the reaction they might awaken.

'You seem very sure?' the Wizard's tone held the question.

She looked at him, 'The Pinexae have Truce with the Grey-Ones,' words punctuated by silence.

Truce? Time, Terms and Gain. It was hard to respond to that. No one did. It was even hard to try to consider the matter. The very concept seemed impossible. *The Pinexae are in Truce with the Goblins? How can that be?* He asked his question very slowly. 'What is this Truce, Pina?' *What are the terms and what is the gain?* His voice was cold, the question tasting bitter with the contradictions of his thoughts. There were lies here, lies of omission at the least. *Whatever could the Pinexae want that the goblins hold? And, Why has she not spoken of this?*

'Between the Pinexae and the Goblin-Peoples, Wizard. Although we are unlike we have no enmity. We are not at war.' And in answer to his doubts: 'I said this before when you asked of me. We, The Pinexae, will not fight in the battles between men and the Grey-Ones save to protect our own people. We so swore when the paths of men and ours were sundered.' There was more that might have been said. She held her tongue.

The Wizard heard her silence. The wall that grew was of sadness.

'I'm not your enemy, Wizard.'

'No. But I thought you were my friend,' was all he could reply.

'Your friend?' Her eyes widened a fraction. 'Yes I believed you thought that also.'

'So, who protects who?' he asked quietly. It was probably the best question.

'Whilst you're with us, no harm shall befall you.'

'Would it, were I not with you?'

'They are goblins.'

'I've no hatred of goblins, Pina.' They were the only words left to him.

'But you go to war, Wizard. And your war is against those who rule the goblin peoples.'

'So you tell me.'

'So I tell you,' she paused. 'Friend?'

He turned the matter over in his thoughts. 'Yes, Pina, even with your secrets, still I call you friend.'

She looked down into the crackling fire. 'Some secrets are hard, Wizard.'

'Yes, some are hard.'

Three uneventful days later they began to pass other dwellings and soon even more. At last the road started to descend into the huge vale that was the Lake-Lands. From high in the pass they could see the sunlight glimmering on the blue waters of Lake Lavine far below. On those shores rested the greater of the Lake-Cities, Latal.

The Wizard found something almost familiar about this country. The criss-crossing of hedges, neat red-roofed cottages, the sense of practical, countryside order spoke to him of home. The snow was lighter here, for the circling mountains provided shelter from the worse ravages of winter. It was still chill enough for the Latal folk to wrap up warm though and the chimneys of the farmhouses trailed smoke into the crisp air.

Although only the first of the great lakes could be seen from here, there were actually five in total, Lakes Lavine and Belmar, which were the headwaters of the system. These both led into Lake Ord, the smallest of the five. From Ord a vast river, The Causewater, ran southwards before widening to become Lake Connel. Lake Connel narrowed to a tight channel known as The Drommin and then flowed into Lake Strell and on to the Water-gate where the waters of Lake Strell flowed out from the Lake-lands, through the Circling-Mountains on their journey to the far away sea at Varista, the River Cri.

There were four major cities. Latal, on shore of the high waters of Lavine, was seen as the greater. It was there the Council-of-Cities met. Then there was Duin, which lay close to the confluence of Lakes Lavine and Belmar, and Hithin-in-the-Lake on Lake Connel. The Last, Castle-Strell, stood guard over the Water Gate

The lands about Latal were, although well tended, a little wilder than those found further south. Forests clung to the mountainsides where deer and the wild pig, bourin, might be hunted. Still, the folk were plentiful and welcoming.

The Pinexae seemed to become strangely animated in this land. They laughed and sang in an image of happiness. Cloure sat on the wagon seat and played wild fandangos on his guitar as the two wagons descended. Soon the children of the villages knew of their coming and raced to join them in a merry, screaming throng as they passed along the road. Niivalsta brought out his flute too setting the children to skip and dance alongside the wagons.

The Pinexae's amusement awoke even more to the children's merriment. They danced among them and platted their hair with silken ribbons, allowed the smaller children to ride upon the wagons and fed them sugar tit-bits from a seemingly endless supply.

The Villagers too, with many a beaming face would wave their greetings from farmhouse door or pasture gate.

The Wizard too warmed to the moment, wishing that he might lighten their eyes further with the wonder of his colours. But no, he thought the better of it and stayed on the wagon with his hat pulled low over his face. Soon enough the children learnt that there was little to be gained from troubling him and so let him be. But his heart was heavy.

It was nearly nightfall when the wagons wound down the rolling road towards the high walls of Latal. Lights were already shining on the battlements and the smoke of evening fires hung over the rooftops. They didn't enter the city though. It seems such Pinexae trains were part of normal Lake-Land life. A ground was prepared, outside the city close by the lake, with picket lines and hearthstone paving for their fires. It was to here that Pina led the party.

It soon became clear theirs were not the only wagons spending the night here. Four others awaited them. The seven Pinexae, who had already set their camp, had seen the newcomers' arrival and now waited before their wagons in a line to greet them.

Thus the Wizard, still perched upon the wagon seat, first witnessed the strangeness of the Pinexae meeting. Pina dismounted and, followed by Tsiera and Cloure, walked over to where the others stood. She moved from one to the next. To each, she stopped, bowed slightly with eyes locked on theirs. Then she placed her hand upon their forehead. When she was done, Tsiera and Cloure did the same. Then the others also. This continued until all had met.

The waiting group now turned towards the wagon where the Wizard waited. They bowed low even Pina and he climbed to the ground to do the same. It seemed a greeting of sorts.

Then it was time to set up camp, though the Wizard kept watch upon the Pinexae activity also. He was quite fascinated by the silence, which emanated from their presence.

Another thing, which came as a surprise, was to find that Pina continued to cook for all the Pinexae. Now he knew that she liked to prepare their food but… In truth it seemed that her doing so was more than just an act of kindness. The others of the Pinexae deferred to her and seemed to do her bidding as were she some kind of leader among them. *Strange*, he thought, *but no matter.* He left his consideration regarding these observations for another time.

They bathed in the ice-cold waters of the lake that evening and lit their fires on the shores where the city lights were broken into a million sparkling shards by the rippling waves.

Then, in the growing darkness, the Pinexae began a new dance. They started by forming a circle, standing still, waiting. Then as one they began to move. It was strange, almost mesmerising to watch. Their movements were identical, each step, each turn of the head, each gesture. They turned slowly at first, without beat or tune, then faster and faster. The sound of their footfalls became its own music, a wild drumming. Still they went faster. Now their movements were a blur and the sound of their dance was as the roar of a waterfall. Then as instantly as they had started, they stopped.

Once again the mood changed. Guitars were brought and Niivalsta, who had sat aside during that first dance, took up his flute and began to play his wild elven reels. Pina danced for them all now, wild and alive and filled with beauty. The city folk, hearing the music came out from the shelter of their walls and gathered about the campsite to watch with wonder the revelling of these strange beings.

Yet in the shelter of his wagon the Wizard found it hard to share their jollity. It seemed incongruous somehow: his quest, his fear for the Fire-Dancer, the weight of the future such a terrible burden, resting on his actions. Yet they danced and laughed, as had they not a care in the world. Perhaps they didn't. Perhaps it was only the Wizard who was troubled by such doubts.

Later that night came the sound of more jingling horse-bells and another four wagons pulled into the encampment.

*

The two riders came through the dour drifting rain hunched over their saddle-bows. At least the wind was light. The weather had changed on their second day out from the Elswood. Now the last vestige of winter white was gone from this rolling land, although the mountains towering above them gave no such guarantee. It would be a hard journey at this time of year. They had no illusions about that.

They rode for the most part in silence. Perhaps time would bring a companionship between them but they were in truth still strangers. Fassael had yet to see her sword-prowess and Calin had yet to understand the meaning of 'Fire-Born'.

The day had turned well past noon when they reached the junction with the Western-Trail. Being still too early for camp they turned westward towards the mountains. Neither relished the prospect of that journey.

'We'll carry on until dark,' Calin announced. 'We should reach the climb before nightfall tomorrow.'

Fassael didn't answer. **Who the fuck does she think she is?** Icicle's sudden bite of indignation flashed across his mind. *She knows what she does. I see no need to object. It's bleedin' clear that you ain't no goblin.* True enough. He'd even learnt to laugh in his thoughts. Icicle responded in like.

Calin had noticed where the fire had burnt close to the junction even though they'd taken pains to remove any sign. There were others who used this trail. Perhaps they might meet some who knew of the Pinexae wagons or who had seen the Wizard. It was something to hope for anyway.

Night found them several miles further down the road. In the sloping sides of a valley, where the road-makers had cut a passage, they found an overhang to provide a measure of shelter from the rain. As Calin unpacked their supplies Fassael sought firewood amongst the trees that lined the riverbank.

'It's not going to be easy lighting that,' Calin commented seeing him build the fire. He didn't answer. She'd find out soon enough. *How's she gonna cope with that then?* Oh she'll be OK. She's made of iron is that one.

Calin turned to watch him when he knelt before the stack. He felt her shock of surprise as he took the fire of his being and set its embers amidst the wood. The moisture hissed, driven to steam in an instant, then the flame took hold and the rock-face was lit by its sudden brightness.

Calin even laughed. 'So that's what they meant by Fire-born. I wouldn't mind knowing how to do that.'

Fassael turned to her with a rueful smile. 'Sorry not to warn you.'

'You wanted to see how I'd react?' She turned the idea over in her mind. 'Yes, I'd have done the same.' Then she continued, 'Now we've got the fire, are you any good at cooking. It's not something I've ever really managed to learn.' She'd unstrung the hunting bow from her saddle and was suddenly gone. There wasn't a sound. Nor was there any when, some fifteen or twenty minutes later, she returned with a small buck slung over her shoulder.

OK, So she's got her skills too, Icicle conceded.

Fassael butchered the meat with skilful ease. He made a stew, cooked slowly in a pot hung over the flames. 'It's better cooked slowly,' he told her. 'Gives time for the juices to thicken and pick up the flavour.' He made flatbread too, griddled on a heated rock. When the time came they lent back against the embankment, their clothes steaming from the fire's drying warmth and took of the food.

'Now this is really great,' Calin declared. 'If we get the time you're going to have to teach me…' She'd said the same to Cog, long ago on that journey to High-Caravail. The memory closed as a blanket of sadness over her. 'Well, anyway…'

He knew her sorrow. He'd felt the same, lived the same. *She grieves for her loss.* **Agh! It cost much did that Book.** Fassael didn't ask her to explain. 'Should we mount a watch?' They hadn't up to now.

'No, Sabin's Sevre. He'll wake us if there's a need.' Perhaps the horse understood. It scraped its iron-shod hoof on the ground before returning to its careful hunt for spring's first tender shoots at the road-verge.

Darkness and the night closed in about them. The rain turned to drizzle and then to mist. The fire, having served its need was left to diminish.

*

It took a further two weeks for the Pinexae caravan to pass from Latal to Castle-Strell. They were easy weeks too. The road running down the lakeside was paved and kept in good repair. At the Heel of Lake Devine they crossed over the rushing Causewater on the spanning bridge to the western shore before continuing southwards. Thus they passed into a gentler land, neat and cultivated. The towns they passed were ordered and the atmosphere of prosperity ruled over all.

There were more of the Pinexae too. It seemed no day could pass without their meeting more of the bright-painted wagons and each night the silent dance grew. By the time they'd passed Lake Ord and looked out over Connel to see the 'Floating-

City', there were more than forty of the corvettes snaking down the road and in the evening half-light some eighty-three joined in the dance.

'We've our own lives to live and our own paths to follow, Wizard,' she'd answered, in response to his questions regarding such a large gathering. 'The Rising-time is near. Long indeed is it since the Pinexae were fully together. Soon we'll know the joy of the Full-Dance once more. Besides, won't our numbers make it even easier for you to hide? No one shall know of your passing through this land. Don't trouble yourself about the comings and goings of my kindred. Their fate is not your concern.'

If there was truth here then there were questions also and questions which needed answers. However such questions were not voiced and such answers were not provided.

The Wizard was not the only one to be concerned though. As their numbers grew so too did the wariness of the Lake-Land folk. A troop of cavalry awaited them several miles north from Castle Strell. Pina approached them, the Wizard remaining hidden, and she spoke for a long time. Eventually she beckoned the train onwards though the troopers kept post at their flanks.

That night, as on every other night, they danced their strange music-less dance. Where before it had seemed mysterious and exotic now the Wizard began to feel truly troubled by its intensity. It seemed that for the Pinexae there was nothing else in the universe but their joining-dance. There were meanings here touching more than they. Oh yes indeed, there was no doubt in his mind, these too have a part to play in, as the Lady would say, 'the Turning-of-the-World'.

Thus the train wound out through the Water Gate and set out down the road towards Varista. The days were once again colder here. The shelter of the mountains lost and the snows rolled down from the north with frosted breath.

*

The first hint of blue-grey smoke drifted over the snow-fresh roadway, its welcoming taste following quickly after. They'd seen scant sign any others were abroad for the past three days and now the hope of news hastened them onwards.

The inn, The Eagle's Roost, lay close to the mountainside. There was a lean-to stable and clearly enough rooms to serve their simple needs. To one side a paddock would, later in the year, provide pasture and grazing for the mounts of any who travelled that trail. For now though the shelter of the stable was more welcome.

At the sound of their hooves upon the stone paving, the door to the inn opened and a man stepped out. 'Two for the night? Five coppers all in.' He called after a moment's appraisal. Then in response to their nods of acceptance, 'Stable your horses, the lad's sorting out the straw. He'll lend a hand. Beer?'

'Aye. Beer will be fine,' Fassael responded. They hastily bedded down their horses and, with the lad's help, laid out straw and fodder before seeking their own comfort beside the roaring fire of the barroom. The glasses of beer awaited them as promised, a fine dark ale made with all the brewer's art. It wasn't too much longer before they were engrossed in the piping hot soup and fine white bread that the landlord provided to warm their insides, welcome indeed after the camp-fare of the road.

The man's young wife came briefly to offer her welcome before scurrying back to her stove and the landlord lent against the bar waiting on them. To his eye they seemed a strange pair these two travellers: the giant Easterner who seemed almost gentle and the slender warrior-woman with eyes of stone. The silence that sat with them seemed almost threatening. They spoke seldom and if there was any friendship between them neither gave any sign of it. He kept his distance and waited to see what they would do.

Over the past three weeks, Fassael had learnt to respect Calin's silence. He knew her loneliness, its cause and the pain that filled her. He'd even tried, several times, to raise the matter of Icicle but somehow the time had never been quite right. *It don't fuckin' matter.* Icicle commented on his failure. **She hurts and her anger gives her strength.** *Still, I think that she should know.* How else could he explain the change in his mood? Did she think his grief a shallow thing? He hoped not.

For her part, Calin had long learnt the futility of trying to judge the actions of anyone. If there was judging to be done it should be of her. She'd seen the change in Fassael and, although she didn't understand was, in her way, pleased to see his pain eased. That wasn't for her though. Her sorrow was to be cherished as something special, something to drive her, something to feed her anger. It wasn't revenge she sought, that wasn't her way either. She'd a task to do and the will to do it. The anger gave her an edge. Beside, she might meet more of those *Greylon* things before all was done. It was a thing to look forwards to.

'We should try to get some news,' Fassael suggested when they'd finished their supper. He took her lack of reply as assent and continued, 'Hey Landlord.' calling him over, 'Come share a glass with us and tell us what news.'

The man did so willingly enough. He was young for his profession but able enough and with the requisite share of humour the job demanded. 'There's not much to tell really.' He managed a smile, nonetheless. 'Since the snows came there hasn't been too much trade save for the returning troopers. Still once the thaw sets in things are like to improve.'

Calin continued to stare into the flames. 'We were hoping for news of any Pinexae caravans that might have passed by,' Fassael tried. 'We're trying to catch up with a friend who travels with one of them.'

'Pinexae? Well there's a thing.' He seemed bemused by the question. 'You know they seldom come this way, even at the best of times. I reckon that since I came here, and that's nigh eight years now, since then I don't reckon more than four of their wagons have passed through. Then this winter alone there's been more than seven trains of them. I reckon that there's got to have been more than twenty wagons in all I'd say at a guess. The last was but two and a half weeks ago.'

'That many...' Fassael wondered which one, if any, the Wizard had been with. 'Were they alone or did any others travel with them?' It seemed a way to proceed.

'Well, I always understood they usually travel with the gypsy-folk, that's what my dad always said, but no, not at this time. There was one lot though, not the last ones, but about two or three days before them. There was an elf with them though.'

'An elf? That will be Niivalsta,' Calin spoke, her tension perhaps lessening a little. 'Dressed in blue was he?'

'Yes. That's right, you know him? It was bright blue leggings and jerkin. There was him, three of the Pinexae and another man, a strange, quiet fellow with a big hat. He didn't say much. They stayed overnight and went off again the next morning. Said they were travelling down into the Lake-lands.'

'That's them. The one in the hat is the friend we seek.' Then, realising that Fassael had never actually met Niivalsta, she added, 'The Lady said that he would be with the Pinexae Pina. Niivalsta and she are together. I imagine the other two travel with them.' Well, at least they knew they followed the right trail.

The calculation was easily made. 'So we're still two or three weeks behind. I'd hoped we might have made up more ground than that.' They didn't seem to be gaining much. According to the Lady they'd been about four weeks behind when they left Al-Sinnian.

'The snow's slowed us,' Calin agreed. 'Once we're over the mountains we should make up some of the distance.'

'You come far?' the innkeeper was hesitant to ask. It was not his way to pry into the affairs of others. It didn't encourage their return. 'Not that it's any of my business.'

'Oh, I guess we've been all over,' Fassael was friendly enough. 'But on this journey we're up from the Plains via the Elswood. I reckon this journey's only just begun though. We're a fair way behind them.'

'Three weeks is a fair way indeed,' the Landlord commented. 'That will see them, let me think, yes they'll be the best part through the Lake-lands by now. That's if they've carried right on through.'

They looked at each other. Time was indeed passing. For a moment Calin thought to leave now, to travel overnight. But no, the horses needed rest. They'd just have to make up time as best they could.

'There's no point in fretting about it.' Fassael apparently had the same thought. 'It's an early night and an early start for us though. We need to be on the trail by first light.'

'If you like I'll call you about an hour before dawn.'

'There's no need. I'll be awake.' There was something about this woman's voice that forbade any response.

'You're young to be running an inn like this.' Fassael knew the cause of the landlord's sudden stillness and thought to distract him.

The man turned to look at him, smiled at the friendliness he found in the giant's eyes. 'It was my dad's place.' The smile was replaced by a frown of sorrow. 'He went with the Army, went down to Tabour, to the battle. He never came back...'

'Many never did,' Calin replied softly. 'Many never did.'

*

'The time of our parting nears, Wizard.' It was two days from The Water Gate, out on the rolling plain that now reached as far as the eye could see, into the west beyond sight, even to where the distant sea continued its endless turning. The Pinexae had already formed their great encampment and danced their nightly dance when Pina came to him, unexpected, out of the night.

She sat on the wagon step beside him. 'Soon our gathering will be complete and council must be held.' She paused but he asked for no explanation. 'It's a thing between us and not for other eyes. Even Niivalsta cannot stay with me at that time.

He'll await me in Varista for when the calling is done.' *Calling?* 'I'll take him as far as the village of Grassington on the Varista road and then return to my people. If you come with us you could follow the wilderness-road beyond the village. That will take you almost all the way to… to… To where you have to go.'

'When do you and Niivalsta intend to part from the train?' It seemed that his own problem was solved. He'd been troubled for some time about just how he could leave the caravan without betraying his plans. Why he should wish to hide them was something else but he knew in his heart that it were better they didn't know. *We all have our secrets.*

'Tomorrow, my friend. Then the Gathering will swing westwards before heading north to the meeting place. We'll take the road south. Grassington is about four days' journey.'

There seemed little more to say about the matter. They ate their supper and took to their sleeping rolls.

Not long after first-light the wagons began to move. The three, The Wizard, Pina and Niivalsta stood by Pina's wagon as they passed by. As they did so each in turn bowed to both Pina and the Wizard from the wagon seat. Then the world grew silent, silent and empty. The wind picked up the final dusting of snow and reminded them of winter not yet quite passed. Pina flicked the reins and the wagon moved. Their journey continued.

Lodor where the wild horses run. He'd never thought to see these lands again. It wasn't the same though. Fires had ravaged the grasslands, blackened the earth with soot. The snow still hid much of the devastation and in truth the spring would bring its new awakening to the land. For now though, the Wizard well understood the Sevriet's anger at such senseless destruction.

The snowfalls had been heavier here, heavier than beyond the mountains by far, and their camp that night was cold. Despite their fire the wizard huddled, wrapped in his cloak to carry out his watch. It was near midnight that Pina relieved him and he stole into his bedroll.

She screams and screams. Not in pain but in silence. She's alone, totally, endlessly. He can't reach her, can't find passage through the confusion of powers that surround, divide them. As before he awoke with tears streaming down his face. *Luminae!* But she couldn't hear him.

'You cried out in your sleep.' Pina's words came as no surprise, nor that she sat beside him.

'Her calling is strong tonight, Pina. I must go to her. I must find her and comfort her.'

'So you shall, Wizard. When the time is come, so you shall.'

More mysteries. *Always others know what I don't. Even the Pinexae.* 'When the time is come? What does that mean? What time? When?'

'You march to war, Wizard of Rainbows.'

'So you say! With whom am I at war?'

'With your enemy. Who else?'

'My enemy?'

'It was you who named him so.'

Yes, I named him. 'What do you know of this?'

She stood, walked over to the woodpile and placed a few more logs upon the fire. A thousand fire-sprites danced on the midnight wind. She crouched before the flame warming her hands. 'I know many things, maybe too many.'

'Tell me, Pina. Tell me what you know.'

She stood again, her back still towards him. 'And can you know as I know? Can you see as I see?' She began to walk away from the fire.

'Wait!' He rolled from his bedding and stood to follow her retreating figure. 'I have to know. I have to understand.'

Pina stopped, turned slowly and lifted her eyes to meet his own. Once his thoughts might have turned to nothing in the depths of those orbs but now he refused to look aside. What was there to fear in their amethyst pools? 'What will you see, Wizard? What will you find to answer the aching emptiness of your ignorance?'

'What will I see, find?' Even now he'd not really considered the matter fully. 'Will you tell me?'

She laughed, but the laugh was a challenge. 'If you gaze at the sun will your eyes not burn? How then will you know the light when you see it?'

For a moment he thought that he understood her. 'You are Neleven-Fey.'

'We are. I am.'

He waited, turning the matter over in his mind. 'Still I want to know.' He decided. 'It's the way I chose for myself. I have to know. And… yes, I have looked at the sun. At its heart lies a stone of the deepest violet. Yes, I do want to know what you are.'

'Even Gentil never asked that.'

Gentil? What's he to do with… 'You knew him?'

'He was a friend to the Neleven-Fey. Wouldn't we know our friend?'

Her answer trickled over in his mind. 'I remember what you said when first I heard you speak. Words indeed can mislead, even when they tell the truth. You've not answered me, Pina, Pinexae, Neleven-Fey. I asked, did YOU know him?'

She nodded. That was better than words. He understood then, at least in part. In her eyes was the full answer, in the centre of all that she was. He did look and was not blinded by the light that shone there. In the rainbows of his understanding he saw her. He almost cried with sadness. *Is this any better than with Icicle?* In her soul there was no shadow. 'You do not die.' It was no question.

The wave of sorrow that was her reply almost overwhelmed him. 'It doesn't matter.' But it did. It mattered so much that for her, and for all of her kind, life had lost all meaning. 'Some are killed. Many, in the wars of men, many were slain.' She sounded defensive. 'We can die.'

Perhaps it was then he reached some kind of understanding about the intensity of the Pinexae's strange dance. 'It is a long journey indeed which has no end, Pina.'

She, who could have faced anything but his pity, stood and walked away into the darkness, leaving the Wizard alone with his thoughts.

The touch of sunlight on his face awoke him. He stretched, yawned, took a gasp at the crispness of the air and sat up. Of the Pinexae wagon there was no sign. *They are gone*. It came as no surprise. The words spoken in the night had been too much for her to bear.

He crouched before the fire, rekindling the flame with frosted breath and rummaging in his satchel for tea. *It's a quick breakfast and then I'll be on my way, firstly to Lodor. Lodor where the wild horses run. What will I find there this time I wonder? There and on the waiting downs.*

*

Perhaps the day was warmer; for sure the Wizard hoped so. He'd had enough of snow. The first signs of spring had begun to show, though in truth there was still little to see. Most of the snow had melted and the first green blush of new-growth gave the earth the appearance of verdegris. In a few weeks, hopefully, the land would awaken fully.

He didn't know how far he'd come since leaving the road. It didn't really matter that much. From the maps in Al-Sinnian he knew by heading due West from the Water gate the trail would lead him to the Downs. That was enough.

He'd things to think about as he walked on, things a plenty and the Pinexae were not the least of them. They were movers in this game of Powers, of that there was little doubt in his mind. But what was their part? He felt disquiet whenever he tried to think about it. Why had they hidden their nature from men? *Truce with the Goblins?* That still made no sense. For some strange reason he felt used and that seemed ill indeed. *Ah, but who uses who? They came, as the tale goes, unto Ancient Maddon to help men in their fight against Elovsenal. It was men who rejected them, turned against them. Perhaps they have need for secrets...*

But now *they come together... Why?* He knew too much to think it a thing of coincidence. *They come together as I go to meet my enemy... Have they a part in this? They are Neleven-Fey... They came to fight the Darkness... And the Darkness has awakened...*

The sun was nearing its zenith when he saw the riders. There were about ten, perhaps twelve, of them, *Sevriet most likely in this land*. They must have seen him also for their horses turned at the same instant. He walked on a little, then waited. They would be with him soon enough.

He was right. They were riders of the Sevriet. He'd seen enough of their kind at Tabour to recognise them. As to be expected they rode their large Sevre steeds, armed and clad in leather armour, ready for trouble. The troop split about 200 yards away, and then four approached him.

'Welcome,' he called out before they had the chance. 'I'm heading for the High-Downs.'

The four dismounted and as one took the horses' reins the remaining three strode forward. 'Greetings.' Their probable leader spoke. 'This is a long way from any of the cities, and few anyway would wish to venture out into Lodor at this time, let alone as far as far as the High-Downs.' There were, not unexpectedly, questions in his voice.

The Wizard leant on his staff with an air of casual ease. 'My feet agree with you, Sevriet. Indeed it's been a long and cold journey from the Water Gate. Though, in truth, I've travelled much further than that.'

'Might one ask to whom we speak?' the horseman continued.

'Of course.' He'd not lie to them. They'd been at Tabour. They'd fought bravely, died bravely too. They'd earned that respect at least. 'Some call me Prism. I'm also known as the Wizard of Rainbows.' He watched their faces blanch. 'Don't be concerned, my friends. I bear none any ill will. I'm going, as I said, to the High Down and the Circle there. There's something I need there.'

By this time the rider had gathered his composure. 'Welcome to The Lodor, Lord Wizard.' He bowed his head. 'Your name and fame are well known to us. May we be of some service to you?'

He smiled, hoping to disarm them. 'It's OK; I seek no service. I'm no Lord either, just one who walks abroad in the land. My needs are little, friends and company, a warm fire on cold nights, news of what transpires in the world and fair weather to speed my passage.'

The Man smiled in reply. It was the sort of answer a Sevriet might give. 'I am named Khornar, son of Heshmet. As I said, be welcome amongst us.' Then in explanation: 'We are on patrol. Things have been abroad in the grassland, dark and unwanted things. It might be best if we accompany you for a time. Thus at least we could offer the friendship and warm fire part.'

The Wizard considered the matter. 'I have need for haste, Khornar'

'Then all the better. We'll provide a mount of the Sevre to speed your journey.' He laughed. 'There, I knew we'd find a way to serve.'

The Wizard responded to his humour with a smile. 'I'm no horseman, Khornar, but I'll take your offer. As I said, my need is for haste.'

The matter seemed settled. It's a wonder that one of the Sevre didn't appear out of thin air, but no. Khornar turned to one of his riders with instructions and watched the man leap onto his horse and pound off towards the second group.

'Will you halt for lunch?' Khornar offered. The second party now wheeled towards them. 'It will take Dunlain an hour or so to bring a horse from the Yurt-Hall.' Then, in explanation, 'Our main camp is some miles North-West of here.'

Nodding his acceptance the Wizard looked about for a suitable spot. There was little to choose. Anyway, two of Khornar's men were already laying out matting whilst another staked out a picket line for the horses.

'You said you were looking for something?' he asked of the Sevriet leader.

The sudden frown crossing his face did not bode well. 'Aye, and nothing to our liking. There are things abroad that should not be, dark and evil things.' He seemed to need to explain, now he'd started. 'We don't know what it, they are. In truth as far as I know, no one has even seen them, well not seen them and lived. Some time ago, not long after the fires had ceased to burn, they started to make themselves known. They came up from the south.' He spat with distaste. 'Nothing good ever comes from there. We started to find their victims.' Suddenly he stopped.

'Victims?'

'Yes, well what was left of them.' His voice was cold now, cold with fear. 'It, they don't just kill them. It strips their flesh, drains their blood, tears them apart.'

For some unknown reason the image of the creature he'd seen at the edge of the Elswood rose stark in the Wizard's mind.

'They come from Naril, we're sure of that. A troop was sent there. They sent word that the whole land was lifeless and that they were going to investigate further. They never came back.'

The Wizard was almost grateful when one of the others brought some dried meat and bread over. 'Thanks.' *For the food or the interruption?*

'There wasn't much we could do at first, with the army gone east to Tabour, but now that my father has returned we're going to try to find out what's going on.'

'Your father? Heshmet. I remember him. We met at Tabour before the battle.' The image of the tall Sevriet Lord returned. 'We spoke but little though.'

Nonetheless his words brought a smile to the man's face. 'Yes he said he'd seen you there.' There was a pause. 'He said that you stopped the battle.'

'Yes, There was too much killing, too much horror. It had to end.' The very thought filled him with pain. He turned away from the horseman. 'I never want to see such things again.'

If Khornar had intended to press the matter, the tone of the Wizard's voice stopped him. 'It's still a good ten days' ride from here to the Down.' He tried after a time of reflection. 'If we hurry we might make it in eight.'

'I am in haste, Khornar.'

'We'll make it eight then.' He laughed the words, then went to tend to his horse, leaving the Wizard alone with his thoughts.

It was almost an hour before the riders returned with the horse. It was a grey that could have been the twin of that he rode when first he left the halls of Hereth. *Hereth? How do things fare there now?* Unlike those of the Sevriet, this one was saddled. *Just as well*, he thought, *I doubt I could manage without.*

'We name her, Mirrowmist,' Khornar informed him as he handed over the reins to the Wizard. 'You'll find her suited to your needs. She's gentle and moves swift and silently when of such mind.'

The Wizard patted the neck of his new steed. 'Greetings, Mirrowmist, may the road go kind with us.' The horse looked down at him, its deep almost black eyes holding his with an unexpected intelligence. He laughed a little awkwardly. 'I hope you don't mind bearing one not of the Sevriet.'

It still held his eye so he lifted his palm to its muzzle that it might know him. After what seemed a very long time the Horse-Queen turned her gaze away. What she understood was anyone's guess but when the Wizard walked over to his pack the Mirrowmist walked beside him.

It took but a moment for him to hang his belongings over the saddle and to tuck the staff behind the saddle roll. The Sevriet were already mounting their steeds.

No words were spoken but at the same moment four of the party wheeled aside and rode away to scout the path. The Wizard, now also mounted, rode beside Khornar and the journey was begun.

Indeed they did travel fast, faster than the Wizard, who was at best only a competent horseman, was comfortable with but at least this way the miles passed quickly.

They didn't stop until nightfall. The camp was set quickly and the fire soon blazed to brighten the darkness. The Wizard ate but sparingly of that offered and sank with grateful, exhausted eagerness into his roll. Sleep came instantly.

The endless echo of her lonely fear fills him, calls in wordless, meaningless horror. I'll come, he answers, knowing that she cannot hear him. I will come.

Morning came seemingly before he'd known more but a moment's sleep. They breakfasted in dawn's half-light and were in the saddle even before the sun had risen

*

It took a full week's travel for Calin and Fassael to pass across the Lakeland valley, climb up through the Circling-Mountains and down their western face into the Forest of the Dressan. The passage was growing easier with the first breath of spring's awaking. On the lower slopes the trees were beginning to bud and in the sheltered places crocuses showed their bright yellow and purple faces towards the sun.

It's true that they might have turned southward at the Latal, taken the gentler road southwards following the Pinexae down through the Lake-Lands. That would have taken more time though and, from information gathered from the Lake-lands folk, they seemed to be gaining but a little on the wagons.

'There's another way we could try,' Calin had suggested. 'Instead of following the road on down through the Lake-Lands, we could take the pass through the Circling Mountains, cut down through the Dressan forest and head straight out into the plain from there. If he is, as the lady said, going to the Lodor Downs then we'll cut his journey by a third.'

'I don't know these lands Calin,' he confided. 'But I trust your judgement.'

'Well I reckon if we continue to follow his trail and if he's gone directly to the gate then we'll probably never catch up even with the horses. This way, if he turns east once through the gate to head for the Downs, we should cross his path in the grassland or even meet him there. There are passes enough through the mountains and the snow should cause us little problem. See? It's only the highest peaks that retain their covering of white.'

They took the higher path.

Unlike the Elswood the Dressan, when they reached it, truly was a wild place. What few paths ran through the trees were game trails and ill suited to their needs. Nonetheless, once they'd passed into the deeper forest, where the denser foliage discouraged the undergrowth, they made good time. It came as a surprise therefore, when one mid-morning they stumbled upon the track. There'd been no signs of men or others since entering the forest, yet clearly this way was much travelled. The ruts where wagons had passed ran deep and the ground was cleared of any growth by hoof-falls.

So they turned aside from their trail, following the direction of the Wagons. Calin had already begun to suspect who would be found at the trail's end. She had words for them to hear.

Sure enough, it wasn't long before the pair rode out from the shelter of the trees into a great forest meadow. The brightly painted wagons were there, drawn up in one large circle. 'Wait here Fassael,' Calin suggested. 'I'm going to speak to them.'

That the camp was silent didn't matter to Calin. She rode from the trees, through the line and into the centre. Despite her request Fassael came with her, slightly behind.

For a moment she wondered if they'd known she was coming. *Probably so.* But that was unimportant too. They were gathered in a ring within that of their wagons. Though at first seated, they stood as one when the two rode to the central clearing. Calin brought Sabin to a halt and dismounted. Fassael though remained in the saddle and, although he hooked his leg casually over the saddle-bow, his hand rested upon the hilt of his sword.

Pina came slowly forward. The questions were alive in her amethyst eyes. She stopped, but some five paces before the Sanain, bowed her head and smiled. 'Welcome my friend, Calin.' She even sounded unsure. 'What a nice surprise. We didn't expect to see you...'

Her words of welcome were silenced by Calin's hardness. The Sanain held her with her eyes, there was no life, no light there, only danger and the threat of sudden death. Even worse was the Sanain's stillness. She didn't blink or smile or... Then she moved and that was worse than her stillness. The tip of her sword rested on Pina's breast. Just a flick of the wrist and the Pinexae would have died. Everyone there knew it. 'I've not come to be pleasing. I've not come in friendship.' She turned slowly, first to the right then the left. Her eyes touched each one of the Pinexae. They found nothing but ice in that look. All the time the blade remained still.

Sabin stirred, stamped a hoof, loud as a cracking whip. As one the Pinexae started. A trickle of blood beaded where Pina had pressed against the blade.

'Where is he?' There was no doubt of whom Calin spoke.

Pina swallowed nervously. 'He has gone on his journey into the Darkness.'

Not to Lodor? 'Did you tell him, tell him where she is?'

'No.'

She doesn't know where he goes. Good. She held the Pinexae's eyes, eyes that once would have calmed her to silence with their beauty but was neither calmed nor mesmerised by their depth. The tension grew. 'Why shouldn't I kill you, Pinexae?' She spoke at last.

'Why should you?' Pina's voice spoke of her fear.

'You called him *friend* yet you did that to him!'

Pina's face blanched. She had no answer.

'Why?'

'We had to be sure he'd go.'

'That's what the Lady said.'

'It was the only way we could be sure. The Bindings grow weak. Soon they will break. They MUST be broken.'

'Had you asked he would have gone anyway,' Calin sounded sad. 'Wasn't he your friend?'

From the saddle Fassael had his own words, his and Icicle's. 'Couldn't you even find the heart to trust him? No! You had to send her there! Had to ensnare him in your devices. Have you got any idea of what it's like there? Have you any inkling of how the Death that rules that land will affect her? Why was this matter so very necessary? What was so needed that you'd actually even think, let alone conspire, to send someone into that place?' He ran out of words. 'What's so important that you'd risk that?'

She answered in a whisper. 'The war rises again, Man-of-Fire. This time there must be an ending.'

It wasn't a good enough answer, none could have been. Calin continued, 'Is this why you gather? That you prepare to march, to play your part in this war?'

'It is.'

The sword was returned to its scabbard. Calin almost felt their sigh of relief. 'Don't be deceived.' She spoke loud enough for all to hear. 'If I so desire she'll die before you can even move.' There was no softening, not in her voice or the diamond cut of her eyes.

Again time passed before anyone spoke.

'As you've plotted, I now assume that the Wizard of Rainbows has gone to rescue her and so to face the Lord-of-Mists.'

Pina nodded. 'He left us when we passed out onto the Plain. He went on alone. He doesn't know she was taken there, where she is held. We, I didn't tell him.'

'Well we shall. We're going to find and tell him all that we know. We intend to join him and if possible even help him,' Calin said starkly.

Fassael added, 'He'll not be alone.'

'Who are you?' Calin asked Pina directly.

'I am **Pina Altheka Pinexae**.' She spoke softly still.

Calin listened to the words, turned them over in her thoughts. 'Are you Their Queen?'

'We are one, Calin-Sanain. I speak for all.'

'Do you answer for all?'

'I do.'

'You sent him to contend with the Lord-of-Mists, to awaken the Darkness.' She did not ask. 'You are The Neleven-Fey, Lords-of-Light. Do you mean to contend with that darkness when it comes forth?'

'Yes.' It was better that she spoke simply. 'It is why we are here.'

'Then, Pina Altheka Pinexae, we'll meet again.'

'Will you be there?'

'We shall, both I and Fassael. We'll stand beside the Wizard.' She saw the shock on their faces once again.

'You're not needed,' Pina tried to protest. 'This war is not–'

'No,' Calin stopped her again. 'It's not for you to say whether I, we, are needed or not. This is My world, Neleven-Fey!' The name was spoken as an insult. 'Not yours.' She let the words sink in. 'And, I'll stand against any who threaten it, Light or Dark. Make sure that you don't become my enemy.'

'When we come again from The Darkness he might wish other and I'll obey his command. Until then I stay my hand. We'll meet again when the Darkness breaks, Neleven-Fey. That or I'll come seeking you.' She turned, mounted Sabin and they rode from the camp.

The Pinexae didn't move.

*

The days passed quickly during that ride over the grassland. It seemed that each day the green of spring's awakening brought more growth and soon the creatures of Lodor's high-grass would be returning. There should have been peace at such a time but there could be no calming of the fears that filled the Wizard's breast.

By the second day he'd begun to grow used to Mirrowmist's easy gait. His confidence was growing too, though he knew he'd never be able to match the horse-skill of those about him.

Although it was the Sevriet way to ride in open order, spread out over the grassland, Khornar chose to stay close to the Wizard. They didn't talk much; there seemed little to say. Even at night, when they camped under the stars, the riders found their charge surrounded by his own stillness and let him be.

One of the party, Georliss, had been at Tabour and seen the wonderful terror of the Rainbow-magic. He knew within his heart the almost intoxicating fear that the Wizard might be driven to use his power again. He chose to set his bedding near to Khornar and the Wizard. Once he even found the courage to speak.

'I was at Tabour.'

The Wizard turned to look at him, smiled gently and nodded. 'Many were there. Many died. Too many, far too many.'

The Sevriet hadn't expected to find such gentle sadness in the Wizard's face. He was moved. 'It seems to me that it could have been much worse.'

But no reply came to that. The Wizard sat hunched before the fire, his wide brimmed hat pulled down to shadow his face. He didn't even look up when the Sevriet returned to his place.

Will they want to come with me when I go south? Will they follow me into the Land of Shadows? he wondered. *I couldn't bear the idea of leading more of them to their death.* The awareness of the thing that roamed the land troubled him too. He'd not forgotten Khornar's words on the matter. Nor had he forgotten the image the words had awoken. *They wait for me. It's just as The Lady said.* 'They've laid out their snares to find and trap you. Their master seeks every way to know of you and they are his eyes and ears. Do you think they'll simply let you be?'

It was not self-aggrandisement that led him to such thoughts; just the awful knowledge of what was real. He remembered the creature that Calin had slain at the start of the Battle of Tabour, and the thing at the edge of the Elswood. *No, these people, no matter how proud, could never stand against things like that.* His eyes drifted over the camp. For a moment he wondered if he should leave, go on alone, lest they insist on joining him. There seemed little point at this time. *When the time comes I'll go alone.* Instead he pulled his cloak tighter and looked back into the heat of the fire.

Five days later, days of flatness and nothing, the first sight of the Downs showed on the horizon. They camped that night with the knowledge that they'd reach their goal tomorrow.

'By midday,' Khornar informed him, 'we'll reach the lower slope. Do you want any of us to accompany you when you climb to the Circle?'

'No, it's OK, Khornar.' He spoke softly. 'What awaits is for my eyes alone.' He wasn't even sure that the horseman didn't look relieved at his answer. 'Your help has been welcome indeed and my journey speeded greatly. Perhaps though it's time that you return to your duties.'

'Yes...' He didn't sound convinced. 'But...'

He never got to voice his doubt. For at that moment one of the scouts rode into the camp and, leaping from his horse: 'Riders are coming!' he exclaimed. 'Two of them. They're not Sevriet.'

In an instant the camp came alive. All there knew their role. Horses were led away into the growing darkness. All but three of the riders vanished too. They were ready for whatever transpired. At least they thought that they were.

'Ho!' A voice called from some distance. 'Bring in your men. We mean no harm.'

The Wizard was on his feet. 'Calin!' It was a shout of pure joy.

From out of the darkness came a laugh. 'We've found you then.'

'And Fassael. What?' But the question didn't matter. The two rode out of the darkness to dismount before the Wizard. Without planning to do so the three joined hands and looked at each other.

'There are tales here.' The Wizard was the first to speak.

'Yes.' Calin was as hard as ever. 'We followed you from Al-Sinnian on the Lady's advice. There seemed a need.' It was clear she would say no more in the hearing of others.

'Khornar,' he called to the Sevriet captain. 'These are friends. Calin-Sanain and Fassael-of-Tabour.'

The man stepped forwards and bowed his head. 'Be welcome to Lodor, friends. You'll share our camp this night?' He could hardly tear his eyes from the giant man who stood before them.

'Thank you, Khornar,' Fassael replied. 'We've come far today. Your offer is most gratefully received.'

By this time the others of the Sevriet were returning to the camp. A second fire was lit and the bustle of such moments returned.

'Do you know who she is?' It was Georliss, talking to Khornar.

'Who she is?'

'She was at Tabour. You know the tale. She went with the Elf-King and slew the creature of darkness before the battle started.'

All eyes suddenly turned towards Calin, eyes of wonder and awe. 'Is it…'

'Yes. It was me.' There was no hint of pride in her voice. 'I am Sanain.'

'Is that how you ride one of the Sevre?' Georliss asked. None had failed to recognise the nature of Calin's steed. None would. Seldom are others permitted to ride one of the Horse-Lords.

'No.' Her voice was suddenly softer. 'This is Sabin. He was the gift of Taiir-Sevriet.' She paused. 'Of this I shall tell later.'

Tell him. Agh! Go on, tell him about me. Wait Icicle, the time is not right yet. **Oh bollix, Agh! Still, I suppose you're right. Soon though, soon.** Ok, soon as I can. It would have to do. Fassael turned to find the Wizard looking at him. An unspoken question seemed to hang on his expression. 'Later, my friend. There are many things to speak of. Many.'

On cue, food and drink was brought and Khornar led the proceedings ensuring their guests were well catered for. They ate, as is the way of those wise of the trail, in silence. It was when all were finished that the time for talk came.

Calin turned to Khornar. 'We thank you again, Sevriet. There are things to say and now's as good a time as any. I spoke of Taiir-Sevriet.'

'Taiir, I know,' Khornar answered with the hesitation of expected bad news.

'And I,' Georliss added. 'We rode together at Tabour.'

'He'll not return.'

They had already surmised as much. 'Were you there?'

'Only at the end and that was too late.'

'Can you tell us what happened?'

'Some. There were eight of them, Sevriet. My guess is that they were on patrol. They were met by a thing of darkness, a thing far beyond their power to resist. When I came upon the place only Taiir remained living and he but barely. It wasn't an easy death though he died bravely. The thing had fed upon its victims' pain and fear. It will feed so no more.'

'You killed it?'

'I'm not even sure it lived, well not in any way we might recognise but yes. I slew the thing.'

'Good, you gave them that anyway.'

'Taiir still lived at that time. He told me his name and he gave Sabin as my steed. I had great need for one such as he. I buried Taiir Sevriet in the earth of the Great Plain and I marked his grave with his name as I'd promised. The others? I set a funeral pyre. I had little time.' She sounded sorry she'd not done more.

'We thank you, Calin-Sanain. You honour his memory and have avenged his death.' He stood then, took a handful of earth, which he threw high into the air. 'Taiir-Sevriet. May he ride the high-winds forever.'

He turned back to Calin, 'I'll go to his family and tell of your words. You've done both they and all the people of the Sevriet a service that shan't be forgotten.'

Calin knew better than to deny fate. She bowed her head in acknowledgement of his words.

After a suitable pause she turned to the Wizard. 'We've come to join you in your quest, Wizard of Rainbows. We've knowledge that you need and words for your hearing. Tomorrow we'll join with you to go and get what you seek. After, you'll hear our words and we'll make plans.'

The Wizard looked from the warrior-maid to the giant man. There were messages in their eyes, questions and answers and mysteries. His thoughts turned but his lips were still. He nodded his head. *Yes, they're right, not here.*

'The thing you slew,' Khornar had been turning the matter over in his mind, 'What manner of thing was it? There's something abroad in this land also. We don't know what.'

'It's nature was of pure evil, Khornar, but I have no name for it.'

'Greylon.' Icicle, through Fassael, had the answer. 'They are creatures of the Beast.' *What do you know?* **Too bloody much!** They all turned to him. 'It is a name the goblins give them.' That explained nothing.

'Goblins?' Khornar sounded shocked.

But Fassael smiled to himself for a moment, then. 'The goblins hate them as much as you.'

'It seems, Fassael-Fire-born, there are things we have to discuss indeed.' It was the Wizard who broke the growing tension. He'd noted the change in Fassael's mood and perhaps even recognised, without understanding, the touch of goblin eyes in the man's smile.

'Tomorrow my friend,' Fassael laughed, 'Tomorrow you're in for many surprises.'

'So it seems. So it seems.'

They rose with the sun and as promised by noon they stood at the foot of the downs staring up to where the slope reached for the heavens. They dismounted, all, and lunched.

'What should we do?' Khornar asked.

'You've been a great help to me, Khornar, but now I and my friends have another path, one you cannot follow. As I said, I have to climb the Down and I doubt that I'll return this way.' He took the Sevriet's hand. 'It's probably best you return to your search.' Then came another thought. 'No. Send a rider to Heshmet. He must be told what you have seen and heard. If he'd be of further service then a rider might be sent to The Elswood to tell those of Al-Sinnian of the same.'

'Of some they know,' Calin interrupted. She too turned to the Horseman. 'The Horse-Lord must be told that The Pinexae shall come to Lodor. He should neither help nor hinder them. Let them make camp as they wish. But no more.'

'The Pinexae? They seldom come into this land.'

'Nonetheless…'

'I'll carry your messages.'

'What of the horses?' Fassael returned to the matter at hand. 'We can't take them up that slope.'

'Leave them to run free,' Khornar answered. 'If you need them they'll know. Sabin and Mirrowmist are Sevre. It's their way.'

There was little more to say. The Sevriet watched the three start their climb. Then, at Khornar's command, they mounted and wheeled away. They too had a long journey ahead.

The three horses watched the proceedings with a total disinterest. After a time they too wandered off southwards. Silence descended over the plain.

*

The dwarf, sitting on the circle's centre-stone, hadn't actually moved for two days. This didn't trouble him. Time is of little consequence for the dwarven people. He was waiting and this task would come to an end soon enough. He preferred to enjoy each moment rather than to fret away the passing of hours.

He'd watched the sun rise sometime earlier and the memory of its brilliance stayed with him. It was a wonder, that sun. It reminded him of a great furnace. *But what strange metal would be smelted in a forge such as that?* The dwarven tales had it that Banmaldruun, the great smith of the Over-world, hammered out the strands of time there and cooled them in the moon's silver pools. But these were children's stories and no one could ever mistake this dwarf for being a child.

They called him 'Master-Smith' although he did have another name were we able to pronounce it. It was the sound of '*The second hammer-fall on the primary blue-red blush of cooling steel that proves its worth*'. But it was a name within him rather than on him. Such is the way with dwarves. Why should we expect to understand?

Why was he there? The answer to that is simple. He was waiting for the Wizard of Rainbows and he knew that soon the Wizard would come.

High indeed was Lodor's Down, far higher than the Wizard remembered that's for sure. Although the three climbers made light of the matter and even competed to climb the fastest, it was more than four hours before they neared the top. Yet once there the Wizard stopped, awed to silence by the circle that waited. Once again he felt the familiar touch of the stones' power and sensed the wind-song of their timeless waiting.

He wasn't surprised to see Fassael actually kneel on the grass before the megaliths or Calin bow her head to them. What did surprise him was the figure sitting upon the altar-stone at the circle's centre.

'Welcome back, Wizard of Rainbows.' The deep baritone of the Master-smith's voice brought back a thousand images of his time Before-the-Flame. He grasped for meaning in vain. 'I have waited long for your coming,' the Dwarf continued. He stood, walked towards the Wizard and with a smile of welcome burning in his eyes he took the Wizard's hands in his own. 'You have grown since our last meeting. You have done well.'

'Well?' *Have I?* 'I'm not so sure Master-Smith-of-the-Carrow. I've done as I had to. Not all was good.'

'And not all steel is crafted to weapons of war, Wizard of Rainbows. You are as you should be. That is well.'

'I am.' Here at least was a truth he could grasp. 'It's been a long road from the Carrow.'

'All roads are, Wizard of Rainbows, all roads are.' The Dwarf turned to face Calin. 'Ah, Calin-Sanain-of-Asain.' He bowed. 'When last we parted, I had not thought that we might meet again, let alone at such a time as this.' He chuckled at some private joke. 'Such are the paths through time. Do you fare well?'

'I live, Master-Smith-of-the-Carrow. I live.'

The Dwarf almost flinched at the coldness of her tone. 'To what end, warrior?'

'I travel my road. I do my deeds. I fight my battles. At this time I follow the Wizard.'

'Is the Wizard of Rainbows your Master?'

'I own no Master, nor any Lady, Master-Smith-of-the-Carrow. Neither have I he whom I loved, whom I couldn't save. I have my sword, Sanain. It's all I need.'

'I shall think on your words, Calin-Sanain-of-Asain, they sound heavy to my soul.' She bowed her head to him but said no more.

'Of you I know, though we have not met before, Fassael-Fireborn-of-Tabour. I am The-Master-Smith-of-The-Carrow. I offer you my greeting.'

Fassael stood towering over the dwarf-lord yet, as the Wizard knew only too well, he felt small and childlike despite the disparity of size. ***Bleedin' hell!*** 'Your greeting I return Master-Smith-of-the-Carrow.' He nodded his head. ''Tis a strange meeting in this place. You knew we were coming?'

'The Wizard of Rainbows marches to war. It was to be expected that he would come to retrieve his sword?'

'You're not the first to say this.'

'True enough, but I am the first who is prepared to tell you why.' The Dwarf's voice was hard. 'The Druid would have done so were it her choice. It was not.'

'Will you share your knowledge?' Fassael wanted to know. 'The whole truth of the matter?'

'It is one of the reasons I am come.'

'One of the reasons?' There was suspicion in the man's tone.

But the Dwarf laughed, a deep booming chuckle. 'Your caution does you proud, Fassael-Fireborn-of-Tabour. Here it is not needed. I stand before you as a friend.'

Fassael seemed to suddenly relax. A smile warmed his scarred and weatherworn face. 'Then friends we'll be, Master-Smith-of-the-Carrow. Have you a camp? My feet ache and my belly rumbles for food.'

'I had need for none until now. But come, I did prepare a place.' He led them out of the circle to a shallow bowl some twenty or thirty yards from the nearest stone. He'd set a pyre there, and stacked enough wood for several days' burning. There were other things too. Several bundles of cloth, bedding too, laid out near the fire under a canopy of canvass tenting.

'Is it safe to have a fire here?' Calin queried. 'We'd be seen from miles away, up here.'

'If they wish to see, then let them.' The Dwarf truly didn't seem concerned. 'Perhaps it might be right if they do.' He crouched before the pyre and with a spark of tinder, set the first flame into being. 'Are there any whom you would rather not?'

'There are goblins on the Plain,' Fassael informed.

Again the Dwarf chuckled to himself. 'Should that bother you, Fassael-Fireborn?'

Fassael's eyes widened in surprise. 'Is there nothing you don't know?'

Returning to his laughter, the Dwarf-smith picked up a large pitcher. 'I know enough to understand that you will thirst after that climb. Come sit yourselves, drink some ale with me?' He poured four large stone tankards full to the brim from a wooden cask and as he did so the three travellers complied with his suggestion, seating themselves about the fire.

They sipped the beer and eased their bodies for a moment. 'Is there a need for haste?' the Wizard felt he had to know. Everyone else seemed to think there was. Then he smiled to himself. 'Sorry, I'd forgotten for a moment that Dwarves never have need for haste.'

'There is need for care,' the Master-Smith's tone was now serious. 'Just as there always is. If each hammer fall is to serve its need then steady must be the hand that wields it. How much more so when we try to forge the future?' He began to unpack one of the parcels. It contained food, meats and cheeses and large slabs of bread. 'We shall eat as Fassael-Fireborn-of-Tabour requested. Then I shall tell my tale.' He didn't wait for their agreement but commenced to carve and hand round the food.

They ate in a silence broken only by the crackling of the now brightly burning fire. The sun was lowering its head and the plain below was already cast in night. They had more ale and second portions of cheese and bread.

'Is now the time to speak, Master-Smith-of-the-Carrow?' Calin rested her cup at her feet.

'It is, Calin-Sanain-of-Asain, now is the time.' His eyes turned back to the Wizard. 'Let me pour some more ale and I shall begin.' They waited as he did so. 'I said that I came to inform you of what is, Wizard of Rainbows. It is a long tale. I believe some of this you already know. Yet, to be sure, all must be told. There is great danger here, and great hope.'

'Are we in danger then?' Fassael asked. He sounded more alive than the Wizard had ever heard him.

The Dwarf smiled and stroked his long beard. 'Danger, Fassael-Fireborn-of-Tabour? No, not here. Though, as you know, danger is with you and that should be understood.' He drained the remainder of his ale, set the tankard to the ground.

'It has been said, my friends, that you march to war. I can tell you though; this shall not be as any war you have known. It is a war of powers, Powers before which you might see yourselves as small and insignificant. Be not deceived,' he paused, musing perhaps over his words. 'Ever it is three. Three Kings, Three heroes, three Ages. And now three powers.' The last words sounded harsh.

'Three Powers?' the Wizard asked.

'Aye, as always. The Forces-of-Light, Those-of-The-Void, and, this time, those of neither.'

'Me?'

'Yes, Wizard of Rainbows, you.'

'But I want nothing of this.'

'Nonetheless.'

Resigned to what must be the Wizard agreed, 'Nonetheless.'

The Dwarf stood and began pacing slowly about the fire, his hands clasped behind his back. 'To the beginning then, for that is where understanding lies. Aye.' His voice changed, growing stronger, deeper, formal.

And from the time of that beginning there was ever war between the Lords-of-Light and the Powers-of-the-Void. They could not abide each other nor would their natures permit the other to exist. Yet it was their nature also to ever be at balance and this they could not tolerate either.

Thinking then that surely one or the other must prevail they made a pact. It was a terrible thing indeed and should not have been. They chose to take their struggle to the Lands-of-Men. Within the Lands of Maddon they would wage their final war and thus was eternity to be decided. Whoever proved victorious would rule forever.

'How do you know this?' It was Calin who asked. She sounded angry, her eyes lit with fires. Indeed she was angry. What had she to do with Powers and their plans?

'I that is we, the Dwarven-peoples, were brought into being as a part of this struggle. When the Cataclysm came.'

'The Cataclysm?' Calin again.

'There are many things here, I go too fast.' He smiled to himself. 'Who said that dwarves are never hasty? Well back to the start again. Of what I tell, some you may know, some not. Even I, a servant of The Well-Springs-of-the-Earth, know not all. What I know I shall tell.'

'As I said, the War-of-Powers has ever raged and has ever remained in balance. When the challenge was made and accepted, then was this begun.

The stories tell that in that beginning, The Lords-of-the-Void sent forth a Stone-of-Power, an evil thing designed to enslave the people of Ancient-Maddon that they, The Dark-Lords, might rule and thus prevail. It is said this was the first act of the War-of-Powers in the Lands-of-Men. It was not!

No the first act was of the Lords-of-Light. They sent a spy into Maddon. One who would see what transpired and would so inform the Lords-of-Light. Thus it came to pass. This was not an evil thing, for the Lords-of-Light are pure and strive to do good.

Yet it should not have been and through this first act it became possible for the 'Stone' to enter the Land.

Maddon was a land of balance and the balance had to be maintained. Thus came the Stone and the sway of Evil took hold. This too needed to be righted.

The Tale of The Eloveen is known. They came through the Ryngold to challenge the power of the Stone. However, Elovsenal, the greater of the Eloveen-Kings, found the Stone-of-the-Void. He recognised its great power and sought to use it for his own ends. Thus he was turned evil by its nature. Then came the first struggle, called by men the-War-of-kings, in which the Eloveen strove against each other. Ever were the forces of Evil the stronger.

Then from the Ryngold came the Neleven-Fey. They came dressed for war and they came in might and bore down on the forces of Elovsenal. There was no way he could stand against them and thus he fled back into his own lands.

He was still mighty and, with the dark magic of the stone, a sorcerer of great power. Thus when they confronted him was he able to wreak such a terrible fate on the world. For although he was vanquished, he set into being the Darkness-of-the-Gwarle. In that time the Lands of western Maddon were cast into darkness, without day or night and thus were divided from the Lands of the East.

Yet the struggle was not done!

The years passed, Evil arose many times within the darkness and many times did it come forth to make war upon the lands of men and ever did the sons of men, with the Neleven-Fey at their sides, prove the stronger.

However there were other, more subtle forces still at play. There arose a terrible enmity between men and the Neleven-Fey. Although it seems a thing of great sorrow and though the Neleven-Fey were in no way to blame, men turned against those who seemed to have what was ever denied them. Eventually the Neleven-Fey left the Lands-of-Men and hid in the south by the shores of the sundering sea.

The Story continues that Once again the Evil arose in the darkness of the Gwarle and this time Elen-the-last-of-the-Eloveen went to war against the Forces-of-The-Void. He was named Elot, for he stood for the Lords-of-Light and he bore the weapons of light that were the Elmest.

At that time however other moves were made. Alan-of-Colon, Antol, known also as the Warrior-of-Man, went out from his home and entered the darkness of the Gwarle and set into being a new vibration in the fabric of reality.

There came also one other. This was one who was not a part of that eternal battle, who perhaps should not have come at all. However she loved the world for its many colours and came of her own free will and bound herself to the Land for ever. She was Harvan, named Herethdale, Queen-of-the-World.

These three, Antol, Elot and Harvan went unto the lair of Elovsenal and they broke asunder the stone of Power thus ending the Years of Darkness.

One might think that this was a good thing, that the Powers of Goodness had prevailed over those of Evil, and thus, for a time it seemed. For the Neleven-Fey realised the pendulum of fate had swung in their favour. They took the chance to come forth from their secret Isle and dwelt anew in the lands of men and great indeed was that time of wonder and many the gift they brought to the land.

But the balance had to be restored.

All was not well. For thus came the Cataclysm.

'You said it before,' Calin interjected.

'It's not easy to explain this. Neither I, nor any with whom I have spoken clearly understand. Perhaps the Wizard here might know more, perhaps. Anyway...

A dissonance had been formed, a discord in the song of creation, a vibration through the halls of existence, which tore asunder the bindings of the World.

At first the deeds of the Powers were for good and many were the things that came into being for the benefit of the land at that time. The Neleven-Fey were good teachers, and Maddon became a place of beauty and wonder.

However, such power cannot exist alone. The Darkness was not gone, but hid in its own place. Those with a mind to do so gathered together shards of the dark Stone-of-Gwarle. Although these had little of the Stone's former power they still had its hunger. These beings too sought out the power that was free and they gathered to themselves a terrible, hungering strength. Once again war was brought into being, a war of Magic and Power and there were no limits to that which they, Lords of Light or Void, were willing to do in order to win.

In the midst of all this magic a terrible thing was created. It had no name, nor for that matter any form. What it was in essence was a magnet for Power. Not only did it draw power though. It took that power, magnified it. In the end that power became so great that it could be contained no more. Thus for the first time the Vortex was loosened.

This, Wizard of Rainbows was the nature of the Cataclysm.

The fabric of reality was torn asunder, the skies burnt with fire, the land itself flowed as molten rock. Man and beast were but as ants trod under the heel by the energies that flowed.

Then woke the Well-Springs-of-the-Earth and the Forces-of-Creation, then too came Harvan, who had hidden from the face of men through her years. Having looked upon the devastation being done they were moved to anger. They took their own powers, powers of nature and life and of binding and they formed a new order to the Land, of men and elf and goblin. In the Secret places of the Earth the Dwarven-People were brought into being. Servants-of-The-Well-Springs-of-the-Earth are we. It was our forefathers who set these Circles and brought into being that which we call "The Galghathag". Not for itself but as a boundary, a binding to constrain both the horror of their ice-cold greed, and the terrible brilliance of that endless drive for perfection. The Tower, too, we fashioned, to witness the order. Thus was the Land made anew and in a far different light than was Ancient-Maddon. For the binding separated the forces of the Void from those of Light so man could grow as he might.

But they feared the return of Chaos, the Well-Springs-of-the-Earth and the Queen of the World; they thought to constrain it forever and created The Book-of-Hours. They never meant to bring harm, never to prevent man from growing, but that is just what they did. Balance must be.

'Man?' Fassael asked.

'Yes, Fassael, man. For Elf, and Man and, for that matter Goblin too, are but forms of the same.'

'And the Dwarves?'

The Master-Smith laughed. 'We are not as man.'

'What are you also Lords-of-Light?'

'Good grief no. We are of the Earth and to the earth we go.'

'You don't live forever then?'

'No, nor would we want to. Our span of years is tiresome enough. No, my friend Fassael-Fire-Born-of-Tabour. We need our years to learn to wield the power required to do the Well-Springs-of-the-Earth's work. It is enough.'

'And now?' the Wizard, who had sat quietly listening, asked. 'Your words are not yet done.'

'True, Wizard of Rainbows, not yet done.' His eyes grew sad, shoulders stooped with the weight, which rested upon him. 'We come to the next forging. This time it is you, Wizard of Rainbows, and yours seems the hardest part.' He hesitated, almost as if afraid to continue.

'You'll tell him everything?' Fassael asked. The meanings and the truth behind his words were heavy indeed.

'It is why I am here.' Then to the Wizard again: 'It has been said, Wizard of Rainbows. You go to war even though it is not your war, nonetheless you go.'

The Wizard grew still, turning over in his mind all that had been said. He knew the truth of it far too well. He knew it and the power of which the dwarf had spoken. It had touched him too often with its deft hand. 'It seems I've always been driven by others' hands. Even at the beginning, when that thing came in my father's place it was but a part in this... This...'

The Dwarf reached out and laid a hand on his shoulder. 'Do you know what you must do?'

'What I must do? I'll tell you what I intend to do, if that's the same. I intend to go into the Galghathag and face my enemy.'

'Why?' His tone was brittle, almost confrontational.

That stopped him. 'Because I swore it.'

'So?' He continued to challenge.

'Are you saying I shouldn't go?'

'No, Wizard of Rainbows. What I am saying is that you should know why you go. You should know also for whom.'

'In the beginning, they went to war against me.'

'No,' the Dwarf interrupted him. 'You are of no more consequence to them than any other tool they might use. No more to their foe either.'

He didn't understand, even now. 'Will you explain Master-Smith?'

'It is why I am here.'

Calin turned, lifted the jug of ale and refilled their tankards. Both she and Fassael dreaded to hear spoken what both they and the Dwarf knew to be true.

'I sense that your words are hard and that you'd rather not speak them.'

'No, Wizard of Rainbows,' the Dwarf corrected him, 'I would rather have it that they were untrue and need not be spoken at all.'

'Speak then. Nothing can be worse than not knowing.'

'In the heart of the Galghathag you will use your magic and shatter the bindings that constrain the Creatures-of-the-Void.'

Not so terrible. 'Must I use my magic there? Surely I have a choice here. Perhaps I could contain myself.'

The Dwarf remained silent for several minutes. No one thought to break the moment. 'You have always had a choice, Wizard of Rainbows. And that is a part of the problem. For there are many hands, other than yours, that would take a part in this thing and not just those of the Lord-of-Mists.'

A sudden thought crossed the Wizard's mind. 'The Pinexae, Neleven-Fey, are in truce with the goblins.'

'No, I fear that too was part of the great deceit. Their truce is not with the goblins. The grey-folk are but servants to others. It is with these the truce was made. But what was the price for such a truce as that?'

'I don't understand.'

'Both Light and Dark seek this war, Wizard of Rainbows, and both have spun their webs for its making. Perhaps those of The Creature-of-Mists are less hid.'

He didn't like the sound of that. *Are these the words that the Dwarf fears?* 'What has been done?' He sealed his heart.

'As I said before, Wizard of Rainbows, you have a choice in all things. That was always the truth of your nature. Despite your oath, you might still have chosen not to go into the Galghathag.'

'And?'

'They had to be sure you would. They had to be sure you would both enter the Galghathag and break the bindings to free them to continue their struggle.'

He was on his feet; the scream of his thoughts tore through his soul. 'Say it!' He demanded. 'Tell me the truth.'

'I would never lie to you, Wizard of Rainbows, nor even try to hide the truth from you, not even this truth. It was they who took her, Wizard of Rainbows, The Pinexae, Neleven-Fey.' He spat the word as were it an obscenity. 'They gave her over to the Creatures-of-the-Mists, sent her into the greyness, into its lair. They know that you will come for her.'

'Yes,' Calin felt compelled to speak. 'I slew a thing… It knew also. They intend to draw you to them. They know you'll go to her, that nothing will stop you.'

'And so you shall, Wizard of Rainbows, just not as they expect.' The Dwarf didn't sound sad now.

The Wizard looked up at him, saw the smile that warmed his face. 'You've hope in this?'

'Hope or folly,' he replied. 'They think you will come alone, with your magic flaring as a beacon.'

'He is not alone.'

'No, Calin-Sanain-Champion and no Fassael-Fireborn-of-Tabour, he is not alone. And, they do not know of the sword either, not even the Neleven-Fey. They think, Wizard of Rainbows, you will fight their battle and destroy the Dark-Lord. He, The Dark-Lord thinks, once the binding is removed, he will either slay you or turn you to fight for him. They do not know you.'

'They don't know me?'

'Who are you, Wizard?'

'I am The Wizard of Rainbows.' Then, suddenly, he did understand. 'Not of light or of darkness nor of good or evil. I am of this world as is my magic. It is on me that the Balance rests.'

'Yet they have conspired against me and now I know.' The lights of his terrible magic began to sparkle behind his eyes as the anger flared. 'Indeed I now go to war, Dwarf. Who comes with me?'

'I do,' Calin began.

'And I,' Fassael followed.

'What must we do?' the Wizard asked, knowing that he would get no reply. 'Have you council in this too?'

'All I counsel is that you do not use your magic until there is no other choice.'

'That's what the Lady advised also.' He heard his words and realised their truth.

'She knew,' Calin's voice was cold, hardened by the truth she still had to contend with.

'The Lady? Yes she knew.' He'd realised earlier that others might have difficulty with this. 'She told me so in Al-Sinnian.'

'But she said nothing.' The condemnation was heavy in her voice. 'She knew but said nothing.'

'She had her reasons.' *She knew of the Dwarf-sword too and of my need to come here.*

'What reason could excuse that?'

'Had she done so I'd not have come here first. What then? No, Calin my friend, the ways of the Lady are not mine to question. Nor will I do so. When there was doubt, she trusted me and the hope of what I might become. Now I'll trust her. I'll not condemn her. She is my friend.'

'Even in this? I don't know that I can forget...' However her voice was softer now.

Who is She? Who is the Lady? he asked himself, not for the first time.

He felt the Dwarf's eyes on him. 'Do I do wrong in trusting her? Master-Smith?'

The Dwarf smiled, an inward thing, but he did not reply.

There came another thought, terrible in its reality. 'She's been there since Tabour?' He spoke his thought. It made matters worse. 'That's well over three months. What have they done to her?' Once again the light of his magic began to flame in his eyes. 'She's been there so long yet I've done nothing!' Even the Dwarf took an involuntary step back.

'No, my friend Wizard of Rainbows.' His voice was gentle. 'I think you still do not understand the nature of The Galghathag.'

Again it seemed meanings were slipping away from him. 'You'd better explain this too.'

'You went there before. How long did you stay?'

It still made no sense. 'Three days. Why?'

'And how long passed whilst you were there?'

'How long?' But the memory of the shepherds returned, the shepherds and their words, telling him that five years had passed since the battle at Sarum. He had a sudden image of Douglas Staffbinder who seemed to have aged far beyond his years. 'I think I see,' he tried.

The Dwarf laughed. 'Perhaps, let us make sure. This is how it is. Within the barrier the Flow-of-Time is deflected, thus for every day which passes in that grey domain, one whole year passes here. Think, Wizard of Rainbows. Once you reach the gate it will take time for you to reach the creature's lair and even longer to find what you seek. But it is hours not days. In her mind she is but recently arrived.'

The Wizard sat again and picked up his drink. He had to think things through, to get things into perspective. Others knew of this, yet… 'Why have you told me this? I was going to the Galghathag anyway. There was no need to tell me this just to make sure.'

'I told you, Wizard of Rainbows. I will not lie to you nor keep things hidden. If I trust you it is because of who you are, not because of my deceits. No Wizard of Rainbows I trust you to be yourself.'

'I do prefer the truth.' It was his way of saying 'thank you'.

Is now the time? Yes Icicle, now. 'There are other truths here also, my friends.' Fassael broke his silence.

'Other truths?' Calin was surprised by the lightness of his tone.

'Truths of which you will speak, Fassael-Fireborn-of-Tabour?' the Dwarf asked. He too knew the touch of the unknown.

'It seems the right time to do so.'

'Yes, this is a time for the telling of truths and you too shall have your say,' the Dwarf continued. Yet before you begin,' he opened one of the parcels. 'I have brought things that you shall need.' There came the jingling of steel rings. 'Fassael-Fireborn-of-Tabour,' he said quietly, 'Stand.'

Fassael did so.

'Your name is known in the Halls-of-the-Carrow and throughout the kingdoms of the Dwarves. They know of your actions in the Fires-of-Tabour. They tell of another fire and one pulled from the flames, and they tell of your loss. Though they know the need for her death, they know too the sadness borne by you.'

Fassael took a sudden, deep breath.

'Forgive me, I meant no hurt.' The Dwarf bowed low before the man. 'Your deed was one of great kindness. For it, I and all of the Dwarven Peoples hold your name as true. We honour you, Fassael-Fireborn-of-Tabour and we call you Friend. Ever will you find rest in the Halls-of-the-Carrow. My people have sent this to you as a token.' He lifted a coat of glistening chainmail. It was not silver, nor even bronze, rather it shone as red as had Icicle's wondrous hair.

The tears on Fassael's cheeks mirrored that shine as he took the coat and lifted it over his head. Icicle was silent with wonder. She'd never seen such a thing.

The Dwarf now wound a studded belt about his waist and lifted a round-shied for him to take. Emblazoned on its face was the sign of a single red flame.

Fassael smiled, nodded and took up the shield also. 'We thank you, for your gift and your words. You should know though, I bear no hurt.' That took them all by surprise. All three looked up at him. He laughed but gently. 'I don't even know how to begin.'

The Wizard looked hard at the man whose words had drawn him back from his inner battles. *This is no longer the same Fassael I left in the Elswood's silent grove.* Of that he was sure. Somehow, the growing darkness made that difference all the more startling. 'You've changed, Fassael my friend. I thought so when we met at the horsemen's camp. Now I'm sure. There's something different about you. Something very different indeed.'

Fassael laughed brightly. 'Agh! Of course there bloody well is. I didn't think that we could hide it from you.'

'We?' He turned Fassael's words over in his mind. *Icicle? How can that...* 'I'm not sure I understand this at all, Fassael. What's happened?' Even then he was reaching out with his thoughts. Their rainbows filled the universe; bright and more alive than any he'd seen. He knew her luminescence, every hue, and regardless of its impossibility and he knew enough not to deny such a truth. For the names of Fassael and Icicle were bound in a helix of wonder. Why should he expect to understand?

'She chose not to die.' The words seemed so inadequate. 'Instead, she chose to be bound to me by love.' There came a subtle change in his voice. 'Agh! Bollix! Did you think I'd let him go as easy as that?'

'Icicle?' It was hard to believe even though he already knew the truth.

'Sure it's me, my friend Wizard. I chose not to take the oblivion that knife offered. Agh! They said that my act was of love, that I could love after all, despite everything. Agh! I chose to love then.'

'I haven't the faintest idea what you're talking about. Who said?'

She laughed through Fassael's joy. 'Agh! You never fuckin' did.' Then, 'oops. Sorry.'

They joined together in a moment's bemusement.

How strange can things get? The Wizard wondered as he sat staring out into the dark. He'd still not managed to grasp the full reality of what he'd seen in Fassael's heart. *Is this too another part of Fate's strange game?* But he didn't think so. *No, I think this is something that nobody even considered. I wonder what it really means?* He'd probably never understand. *Nothing unusual there then.*

Calin interrupted his thoughts. 'What are you talking about?'

'She's inside me, Calin, inside my mind, my soul, if you like. Icicle, my goblin, that is.' He saw the doubt in her face. 'It's true, Calin, really. I mean she's really there, not just that I think about her. At first it was very strange,' Fassael confessed, 'But gradually we seem to be growing together. To tell the truth I'm not always sure whose thoughts are whose.' *Mine are the rude ones.* Her laughter filled him. 'She said, "Mine are the rude ones".' Knowing Icicle, that was probably the truth of the matter.

'You know what?' Calin spoke from the darkness, not that she'd really understood any of the matter. 'I reckon that he's even stranger than you, Wizard.'

The Dwarf-lord bowed low once again and turned to Calin. 'And you, Calin-Sanain-of-Asain, are you not also just as strange?'

'Me?'

'Yes, Calin-Sanain-of-Asain, you.' He laughed at the surprise on her face.

'Me? What's so strange about me?'

'You have come a long way since you stood on the shores of Donaladin, Calin-Sanain-of-Asain. In you there lies another hope.'

'In me?'

'Yes of course in you. Who else but Calin-Sanain-of-Asain, Alan's heir could be Champion-of-the-World?' He laughed his deep burnished laughter.

'I don't understand.'

'You do not?' Now it was the Dwarf's turn for surprise. 'But it is at the very centre of your own nature. It is who you are.' He sounded horrified that she didn't know.

'Do you know?' There was a hunger in her voice. 'What do you know? What do you know of me?'

He replied with a sadness that reflected his surprise. 'Indeed this is a night for tales. This one I had not expected. Yes, Calin, I know. Now it seems another story must be told.' He refilled their goblets. Then, standing with his back to the fire he began again.

'This tale is but part of the greater tale of the Years-of-Men. It knows its beginning long, long ago in the mists of time. It begins also with the Tale of The-Eloveen and the Stone-of-Power, of The Three Heroes and the End of the Ever-night that was the Gwarle.' He took a long draught of ale.

In that time it is told, Alan-of-Colon and Avondale his Queen came out from the mists of the Elexan on the back of Clodev-the-Eagle. They returned to the field of Droven-Gate in the Land of Ancient-Maddon. They came in great sadness also, for Elen, Elot, Last of the Eloveen-Kings had been slain in the desperate struggle to destroy the Stone-of-Power.

Now it came to be that The Lords-of-Men, of Delward and Droven, of Rolam and Elscri, of Hanthor and Colon and even the remnant of the army of Lodor, had gathered at the Gate of The Delward at Gentil's command. Thus they were met and made much of. Gentil-the-Wizard had told all which had befallen and, at his behest, the Lords of Men set Alan as King over all the Lands of Maddon.

Thus Alan took up the silver-crown of Maddon and ruled the land from Saril in the heart of the Delward, where once stood the Talosind. He took Avondale for queen and together they reigned over a land at peace.

In time Avondale gave birth to a daughter whom they named Sanin, for her hair was black as satin-night, but they had no son. Thus it was Sanin took up arms and learnt of war and of weapons from her father's hand. She grew proud and as noble in spirit as any man and she took to the sword and the bearing of arms as were it her birthright.

The years turned and Alan grew weak in body with the passage of time. The leaders of those who had dwelt in the darkness of the Gwarle had by this time become lords of their own estates and built their own cities. They saw his weakness and began to contend with each other for the power, which was his.

Thus it was Sanin stood as champion of Alan and fought as were she a man. Mighty was she too so none could stand against her. But time fights its own battles and Alan her father passed from his life in this plain of existence.

At his pyre the Kings came to Sanin to ask her to be queen in the stead of her father. However, to their, and many there's surprise she refused them, saying 'I am a warrior. My hands are stained with the blood of my enemies. I shall be Champion of the Land and of its King for as long as I am able, but I shall not be its Ruler.'

Thus it was that Adam, Lord of Delward was crowned King and Sanin, as she had promised, became his champion.

In time Sanin married, although the name of her spouse has passed from beyond memory, and she too had daughters but no sons. Of her daughters there were two Drelst and Cathiir yet they were also called Sanin, for they followed in the way of their mother and bore arms as champions of the King. Thus the name Sanin came to mean Champion and Servant. For ever did the Sanin serve the needs of men but never sought for power.

There followed an age, known as the Slumber-Years. In this, for hundreds of years, peace lay upon the face of Maddon and the people prospered and grew in wisdom and knowledge.

He paused, drawing a breath before continuing. His next words came hard.

However, as I have already told, it did not last. Those who craved for power became too greedy and thus was the Cataclysm born and the Land was torn asunder and put to flame and torment.' His voice grew quieter now. *'Men and creatures and much of what lived perished in that time. The skies burnt with flame and the very earth flowed as molten rock and Maddon was no more. There came a time of darkness too when the sun, unable to face the anguish of the land, hid its face and darkness ruled once again. In that darkness the Ice fields formed and crept over the land and of those who still survived even more perished in the frozen waste, which the land had become.*

At this time The Well-Springs-of-The-Earth and the Forces of Creation awakened and put out their power. Harvan too came forth in anger and Gentil-the-Wise walked abroad wrapped in his cloak of power.

Eventually the fires and the ice were subdued and the Sundering was brought to the World. He sounded angry.

Of the Sanain, for thus were the daughters of Sanin now known, it is said they had led their people through the darkness and had stood ever against whatever would harm them. The peoples were divided at this time. Men went each to their own cities and lived as they would. Ever though, the tales spoke of The Sanain and ever were they Servants of the World.

The Dwarf grew silent. He turned, stooped to pick up one of the packages. From this he first removed a small earth-stone broach, silver and jet, which he pinned to her scaled tunic.

'Just a sign that you serve the Land, Calin-Sanain-Champion,' he told her quietly. 'It is the very one which Sanin wore at the beginning.' Then he uncovered a shield. It was black also, black save for the sign of the Earth-Stones emblazoned in silver on its face, 'Here, Calin-Sanain-Champion, it was made and brought for you to bear, to protect you from more than arrows.'

She took the shield from his hands. 'I thank you for your words, Dwarf-Smith. They are a greater gift than any I even hoped to gain.' She fingered the broach. 'As for the shield? This I'll carry with pride. I see its need too. I go as you wish with the Wizard to the Galghathag.'

'You do as you think best, Calin-Sanain-Champion. It is not for the likes of me to tell you otherwise. Do you not realise yet? In this you, all three of you, are free to be, or do as you will. There are no constraints, no bindings, no oaths and no obligations. You are free. Free to be yourselves.'

They sat long into the night, even ate two more meals, for dwarves have a fondness for fine food or, come to think of it, food of any other kind. 'Once more then, Master-Smith-of-the-Carrow,' the Wizard suggested, 'Let's discuss what we're going to do. It's best if we have some sort of plan.'

'It is no plan, Wizard of Rainbows, at best you might call it a hope. Tomorrow the three of you shall continue on your journey. I would think it should take three or four weeks to reach the Gate. Long indeed is it since I've passed that way. Then shall you, Wizard of Rainbows, Fassael-Fireborn and Calin-Sanain-Champion do as you must.' He grew stiller than the stones. 'And then? Well? What shall be shall be.'

Nothing was said when, as the first rays of morning began to kiss the megaliths, sparkling on the mica to turn the circle into shimmering light, the Wizard stood and walked slowly into its glorious halo. Nor did they speak when he returned holding the sword, still in its scabbard, in his hand.

The Dwarf-Lord was waiting for him. In the darkness he'd garbed himself in his travelling-leathers and hung his axe upon the belt about his waist. Now he bowed to them, bowed so low that his beard touched the grass. 'We shall meet again, Wizard, Champion and Friend, if the future so decrees.' He didn't wait for their reply but turned on his heel and walked away northward. They watched his back until he disappeared from sight over the side of the down.

'Well?' the Wizard was lost for words.

Fassael and Calin smiled together.

The sun, still winter-white, smiled at them too. A raven resting on the highest of the stones cawed out its greeting, or farewell. They picked up their few possessions. The Wizard strapped his sword over his shoulder whilst Calin and Fassael hung their shields upon their backs.

'And now we go to war,' the Wizard called aloud that any might hear. The raven heard, although it didn't understand. They're not that bright are ravens.

> Now drink a toast in Burgundy
> Seeking meanings in that mystery.
> Within the wine-mirror of the crystal glass
> Dazed by the rings of my trembling fingers' grasp
> An apparition forms.
>
> (From: The Song of the Sunset Sands)

Chapter Twelve – To the Gates of Hell

HIGH ON THE downs' grassy slopes the three companions looked over the land where they would soon travel. Although the season was changing, it was still a pale sun that lit their forms and a winter clear sky that surrounded them. Nonetheless it seemed a time for posing. The Dwarf-Smith had named them, good names, names to be proud of. They suited these names well.

The Wizard, as ever, shone with the rainbows of his nature. His sword haft protruded above his right shoulder. It felt comfortable, right. His hat, still splendid as on the day he first wore it, shadowed his face in mystery. His cloak billowed in the wind. He needed no magic at that time. He was magic, as magical as life, as love, as anger! 'I am the *Wizard of Rainbows*,' he called to the wind. 'Who dares shine against me?'

Fassael, standing beside him, was bathed in glory also. It was a glory as red as the sunset shining in his heart, red as the memory of the goblin's love in the centre of his being, red as the fire, which didn't burn him, red as the flame of his nature. He was unlike others, nor had he any wish to be so. 'I am Fassael-Icicle, Fire-Born and Knife-Torn. I have chosen my own destiny. None can deny me that.'

Calin too, still dressed in black as was her choice, stood as proudly as any might dream. She bore the Earth-Stone-Shield with pride, her tunic with the Earth-Sign upon it also. All her life she had hungered for one she might serve. Now she served the World. 'I am Calin-Sanain, Alan's Heir.' Her tears were of joy. For now at last she knew who she was.

They looked at each other, laughed and, as was only right, their faces reddened. *Still, We do look very fine.*

They didn't linger any longer than had the Dwarf-Lord. Time seemed pressing and powers, dark as storm clouds, were looming. On the climb down the slope Fassael posed the question of calling the horses back. But no, as the Wizard said; 'We journey to places where they can't go and will face things they can't face. Better to let them taste the freedom of spring and the newness of the grasslands.' *At least while they have the chance to do so. If I should fail...* But that wasn't a matter to be considered.

By midday they were far beyond the slopes of the downs. It seemed perverse but the fires, which had burnt away the long grass that might have hindered their passage, now lent speed to their feet. They knew enough to take care though, walking in each other's footfalls, leaving but a single trail through fresh-grown grass shoots. Fassael came last, his huge feet obliterating all trace of the others. They saw no sign that anything else was abroad. By nightfall the downs were little more than a blue shadow far behind them.

So the passage of days turned. The land was little more than a vast, featureless, rolling expanse of green, without even trees to break the monotony. To his disappointment the Wizard could find nothing recognisable to waken memories of his first journey. In fact there seemed nothing to see at all. Save the endless carpet of new-grown grass. There were no signs of birds or, for that matter, of any other living thing. No trails cut through the grass but their own. They walked in a silence broken only by the sound of their muffled footfalls and the song of the wind. Still, the season was turning and the chill northerner had given way to a gentler southern wind. Perhaps this would bring the geese and other fowl and see again the return of life.

There might not be life here but there was death. Corpses, burnt and sad, cathedrals halls of time-bleached bones, the remains of the Sevre, the horse-lords of Lodor littered the plain. Now the chill of winter's breath no longer ruled the land their rotten stench tainted the wind. The Wizard fought the temptation to look away. They deserved better than that, once so proud and free, the true keepers of the grassland. *Are any of the wild herds left south of the Downs now?* He wondered. *Is anything left?* The fires had been terrible indeed. *What happened to the Auric?* The unbidden image of the beautiful creature he'd met among the grasses so long ago brought its own aching sorrow for so many things now passed. *Perhaps it's better like this*, referring to the silent emptiness. *Perhaps the land mourns for them.*

In the night *he moves again through the secret passages of his dreams. Still she calls out her endless, lonesome plea. He doesn't answer or even try to any more. Now at least he knows why he can't reach her and why the distance seems so far. 'I come,' he tells himself. 'Each step brings me closer.' His mind is sharper than his sword, his rainbows more deadly.* 'Someone will answer for this!'

They trudged on with little but their determination to drive them. For the most part walking in silence, filled with the sadness of their own thoughts. The clouds had gathered with the threat of rain or perhaps more snow and the grim greyness of the skies matched their mood. The Wizard pulled his cloak tight about his shoulders though even that failed to keep out the chill wind. *Wind? What wind? There is no wind!* The awareness of that fact stole over him. *If not wind then what?* He scanned the horizon, both with his eyes and mind, but found nothing. Nothing at all save the silent call of the land's emptiness. For now, he said nothing.

Then, for a second time, came the secret thought of another mind brushing over the edges of his consciousness, troubling his soul with an unwelcome hint of contamination. Again he sought its source. He found nothing but he knew too much to deny its truth. *It seeks for life.* He could tell that much. *Does it search for me? Or does it lie in wait for any who walk abroad?* He had no answer to that or the cold dread its nature had left on his spirit. He would keep vigil. Nothing further touched him but still he was wise enough to mistrust that silence. The Lady's words turned in his mind. *They've laid their plans and they seek to snare you.* Was that what he had felt? *Is that thing a trap set for me?* She said that I was followed to the Elswood, that thing I saw when the Unicorn came. Has it followed me here? For that touch had been evil indeed.

'Calin, Fassael.' They lifted their eyes to him. 'There's something out there.' He nodded towards the still distant mountains. 'It lies hidden, waiting, watching. As yet it's far away but it knows we're coming. We must take care.'

'I always do.' Calin meant no rebuke. 'Do you know where it is?'

'No, not yet. All I felt was the barest touch of its coldness upon my soul and that was bad enough. I'm not sure I want to face a thing of such terrible emptiness.'

'What was it?'

'I don't know, Fassael. I almost hope that I never find out. Only, I doubt we shall be so fortunate.' As if to confirm his fears there came again that lifeless touch. He found himself shivering, revolted by the feeling of contamination that followed in its wake. He tried to follow the thought but lost it somewhere in the emptiness.

But Calin had her own answer and her smile of expectation was every part as terrible as was the watcher's tainted thought. 'It's of the kind I slew before the battle and again on the Great Plain near to the Elswood.' Her anger brought a sudden glint to her eye.

'The Greylon,' Icicle whispered on Fassael's breath.

The Wizard considered Calin's words. 'Yes I think so. There's a terror that walks abroad in the land. There can be no doubt of that. The Sevriet spoke of it,' he told them, his voice as cold as the words. 'I've never known its like. I fear it is, as the dwarf said. The Barrier already weakens.' *This is the beginning of which they speak. The Bindings begin to fail. What horrors shall we face when it finally breaks?*

Fassael, seeing the Wizard's face grow pale, let his shield slide down to his arm and he loosened his sword in its scabbard. Calin, at the same time, moved sideways making room for her swordplay should such be required. The need for a hidden trail was of little importance. Their presence was known.

However, there came no more than the hint of danger and the breath of evil on the air. They continued onwards.

More days passed, cold and cloud-grey days which seemed to suggest that spring might yet be denied. Their feet grew tired, as much for the doom laid on the land as on the toil of the journey. They were drawing closer to those forbidding mountains and found themselves cowed by the dark jagged peeks. At least there was cover here, thickets and small trees. Before too long they entered the wooded slopes of the foothills where at least they were sheltered from prying eyes. Caution slowed their steps, for such shelter might hide other things, if any lurked in the shadows, and often Calin went ahead to scout their path. There were signs of others here, goblins most like, but their trails were old and this woodland seemed as lifeless as the plain had been.

The silent emptiness began to grate on their nerves. So too did the lack of game. It felt unnatural, somehow wrong. Soon even the slightest sound had them starting with shock.

To make matters worse the Wizard was touched by another cause for disquiet. No matter how he looked he still didn't recognise anything. He'd hoped to see again the glade where he'd first met the Fire-Dancer or perhaps the vale where he'd watched her climb over the rocks to fish for trout. His hope was left unfulfilled.

The trouble was that this unfamiliarity only added to the burden of his concerns. He had enough worries of what lay ahead to contend with. Other things troubled him too. Doubts, vague regrets and even vaguer fears crept through his thoughts. Cold, unwanted haunted musings stealing through his mind. At first he wasn't even aware of them when they pried into the darker places of his memory. Then he felt their cobweb tendrils and slammed his mind shut.

Eyes, colourless and cold eyes, haunted that land. Eyes that waited, knowing he would come. Once again he felt their fleeting touch as a shadow passing over his thoughts.

'Something watches,' he told them. He reached over his shoulder and toyed with the hilt of his sword, freeing the blade a little lest it caught at the moment of need. 'Something cold and dark. It's waited, watched since it first felt us out on the plain. It knows we're here.'

Calin slipped her shield from off her shoulder, held her sword staff in her left hand behind the shield, keeping her right free. Then she turned slowly examining every part of the darkening land about them. There was nothing to see, or if there was she didn't see it.

But the trees loomed menacing and brooding, casting shadows over their thoughts. It seemed a land made for trouble. They didn't question the Wizard's perception of their danger.

'It'll wait till dark,' Calin surmised. She sounded calm, confident, perhaps even excited by the thought of battle. 'If it means us harm.' Not that there was really any doubt in her mind. Her anger had begun to grow. *Ever they seek to trouble the peace of the Land. Ever they would rob us of those we love.*

'Oh it means us harm alright,' the Wizard informed them with chilling certainty. 'There's a foul taste of cold malice in its heart and little more.' He looked to Calin. 'What do we do?'

'We build for a fire and wait,' Fassael offered. 'Then we'll see what comes.'

I'm not that sure that I want to see. He shivered with revulsion over the feel of the thing and kept his mind sealed against any more of that sick probing.

'The rise, over there,' Calin pointed to a small hill. It was free of trees or scrub. 'It seems as good a place as any.'

They cleared a circle on the hill's crown, placed fire-stones in a ring and set about gathering whatever kindling they could find. There were a few soap-wood bushes, at least they always burn well, and beneath the trees, at the edge of the clearing, found enough wind falls for their need. They built their pyre and, as Fassael had suggested, waited.

The light breeze rattled the thinner branches where the first spring buds were beginning to form. They looked about anxiously, expecting an attack at any minute. Nothing came.

'Are you ready to fight, Wizard?' Calin had to know. To her it mattered little if the answer was yes or no. She was ready for battle and needed to know where the steps of her dance must take her.

'My magic is forbidden me. I've no other choice.' His tone was hard, determined. 'I'll not be stopped. Not now. Yes, Calin, I'm ready to fight.' *But to Kill?*

'When the time comes to light the fire you'll be ready?'

'I am ready,' Fassael replied sternly. 'Don't let it touch you,' Icicle warned, 'Its touch is death.' Calin and the Wizard turned to look at him. There was no answer to such words.

They grew silent, waiting. Nothing moved save the treetops, the slowly sinking sun and the eternal dance of stars. There was no moon to light their camp this night. They weren't sure if this was an advantage or not.

It waits, watches.

Calin moved. She spoke in a whisper but to their jangled nerves the words were loud as a scream. 'Keep watch, Wizard. You'll probably feel their coming before we see them.' She opened her satchel to take out a strip of the dwarf's dried meat and began to slice off small pieces for the others.

There was an endless patience in the chill that touched the Wizard's now open mind, the patience of death. 'Oh I can feel them alright. They're waiting, biding their time.'

'Should we go to them?' Fassael asked as Calin handed him the food. 'Take the fight to them? We might take them by surprise.'

'No I don't think so. Not yet anyway. Eat. There'll be time enough.'

Fassael ate, the Wizard also, though hunger eluded him. Then they sat on their packs and waited.

It grows colder. That was the first sign. *Cold as the grave, colder.* He said nothing, but reached out and touched Calin's arm. She nearly jumped, not quite though. Fassael looked at him. He nodded.

An unwholesome stench tainted the breeze now. It came creeping on unwelcome wings, whispering of death and corruption but there was still no sign of movement, or none they could discern. But it was dark now and though the stars were bright they gave little light to the land. The hiss as Fassael drew his blade seemed loud in the stillness. The Wizard copied him though Calin remained motionless.

There was comfort in the feel of the weapon. He held it, point down, his hand resting upon the cross-guard. *Soon they'll come.* He wasn't afraid, not of those who were coming. Any fear was of what he might do, or not do, of how he might act. He sealed his magic, determined in that at least. *I'll keep it hidden unless there's no other choice.*

The cold began to seep into their hearts. *Galomist? No, it isn't that. Something else.* He let his thoughts become as cold as the touch, followed it back to its owner. The brightness of the life that was his recoiled in shock at the blank emptiness of the creature's being, an emptiness that filled his every sense with the essence of evil. *It's not alive!* The thought screamed through him. *What the hell is it?* He felt the mind behind that touch recoil also, as if his life had burnt it.

Its screaming cry ripped through the shields of their bravery, echoed, death-hollow over the trees. 'They come!' the Wizard needlessly shouted the warning, leaping to his feet to meet whatever came.

Behind him the fire exploded into life, lighting the scene in a brilliant flare. A circle of creatures surrounded them, horrid things of grey, decaying flesh, hair-less, clothes-less and stinking with corruption. They'd crept forward in the darkness and even the Wizard hadn't sensed their closeness. Once they might have been men or goblins, these things, but now they were something else completely. Skin hung as torn fabric from their flesh. In places even the white of bone showed through. Eyes, white as their emptiness, shone dull as stones. Mouths gaped, white-toothed grins of thoughtless hatred. What made things even worse was the way they hissed through those teeth, a terrible, unnatural sound, as if death had found its voice.

Again that soul-wrenching scream shattered the night's silence. They charged, rushing forward in an awkward, loping run. Arms, seeming longer than arms should be, bore sticks and rocks but few, if any, real weapons.

Calin twisted sideways as the first neared. Her Sanain sword sang its battle song but the sound of it striking came as no more than the crumbling of dry-leaves. She gasped, stepped away in shock as the thing collapsed at her feet. 'No blood, No life.' The horror in her voice said all there was to say but it didn't slow her steps nor the singing of her blade.

Fassael was fighting too, cursing under his breath at their obscenity. A stone crashed against his shield. And then a second of the things, sword-struck, crumpled to a grey heap at his feet.

Two of them rushed towards the Wizard. He too struck out. He did it without thinking, instinctively and full of need over the horror of what they were. The first he nearly missed. It stumbled right at his feet that his cut passed over its head. He slammed the blade down, piercing through its shoulder, breaking the bond of whatever held power over it. He met the second of his attackers on the upswing. Then turned to face a third as it reached out with grasping claws towards his face. The blade severed its neck and it joined the growing heap. He felt no shame in the act, only the revulsion over those he struck.

He could hear Fassael panting as he fought at his back and knew Calin was moving too in her battle-dance. For every one that he or Fassael broke, the Sanain took another five. But there seemed to be no end to their numbers. A rock struck his left arm numbing his fingers so he almost dropped his staff. Again and again his sword bit their lifeless flesh. Still more of them came; more of them fell. In truth it was no contest.

As suddenly as it began it was over. There were no more left to fight. The three companions stood gasping over their exertions. The piles of the things lay in a grotesque circle of rotting flesh all about them. 'What the hell are they?' Calin asked as she kicked one aside.

'I don't know Calin.' His memory turned. 'But hell seems to be the right word. The Lady said the name "Gnolls". They might be those.'

'The goblins call them Grawl. They're the Greylon's slaves,' Icicle, or Fassael answered. 'Do you think there's any more?' he asked. 'I'd as soon not stay here if we don't have to.'

The Wizard let his mind reach out. Almost instantly he felt the well of hatred strike back again, a blinding burst of darkness. But his mind was strong and filled with anger now, anger and an overwhelming sense of revulsion over the evil will of the thing. *It's not one of these things. It's something else. The Greylon?* It had some sort of consciousness, something corrupt and filled with hunger, a hunger for life, life that it could destroy, that it could consume.

'There's something else out there. Something bad, very, very bad.' His voice shook with both the reality of what he had felt and the anger which flared in his mind. He laid his staff next to the fire and stooped to pick up a flaming log. 'I'm going to find it, face it.' The firelight flickered on his face, stark, sharp with determination. But his eyes burnt brighter than the flame.

They went together, lit by the flames of his torch. The search was slow because the firebrand gave barely enough brightness to light the small area about them. Shapes, distorted by their fears loomed ominously about them. Bone fingered branches pulled at their clothing. The only sound was their breathing.

The Wizard knew when they found the spot. The cold emptiness of its presence lingered in its wake. It was little more than a small hollow sheltered by an overhanging rock, trampled now, but no sign of whence it had departed. They discovered where the gnolls, if that's what they were, had lain in wait also. The earth was bare there. If anything had lived there it had recoiled at the touch of those beings.

'We must keep our guard, Wizard.' Calin knew. 'We're awaited, trailed. Now they know we're here they'll not leave us be, not now.'

Having returned to the hill to gather up their gear, they walked away from the place. There was no way they could have stayed anyway. They walked long and far that night. Despite the darkness and risk of foes hiding amidst the trees it seemed best to keep moving. They didn't even speak of what had happened. It wasn't the time. They'd wait for the sun for that.

By unspoken agreement they stopped at daybreak. Fassael built a small fire and they boiled a pot of tea. He cooked up a stew also which they ate sitting before the fire warming their hands on the flames.

'What do you make of it?' Fassael began. 'Although Icicle has a name for them, I've never seen anything like them before. Agh! It's why I left the fuckin' Grey-Lands. They're new. Came with the Greylon. I took one fuckin' look and I was off.'

Calin looked up sharply. She'd never get her head around this thing about Icicle. 'No, nor have I. We'd best consider the matter. I don't believe that I've even heard of the likes of them.' She turned to the Wizard. 'You say that they were gnolls?' She wasn't ignoring Fassael but just couldn't handle the matter yet.'

'A guess, Calin. That thing out on the plain, which tried to steal your life, the Lady said that was, or might be a gnoll. *That or one of the Shape-changers.* I don't know if I'm right though.' He paused for a moment. 'I'll tell you one thing though. There was no good in them, no life either. I think the other one, the thing that fled when we approached; I think they did its work. And, and that thing was nothing but pure Evil.'

'Evil?'

'Aye, I could feel its nature.' He didn't even like saying the words. 'It feeds on souls, Calin, takes its life from those it slays. Perhaps that's what they were. Creatures of whom it had taken their souls.'

Calin shivered. 'Then it's the same as the thing I fought on the plain. It fed on the lives of its prey. It tortured them so they died in total torment. It fed on their fear and pain also. I guess, if that's what it wanted of them then, it's what it wants of us now.'

There was no acceptable answer to that. *Just what was it? There was that thing which had followed us to the Elswood. The thing that the Unicorn sent fleeing. It had had the same feel about it. Was that what Calin had met?* Dread settled in his heart. He had begun to see with an awful surety just what horrors might lie on the road ahead.

They rested there till mid-morning, each in turn managing to catch an hour's or so sleep. Then it was time to move on. No further sign of the things showed. In the light of that early sun they set out once more. Their eyes were alert, their bodies tense for what might occur. Nothing.

That night they did light a fire. It was probably as much for comfort and the hope that it might deter any approach than for any other need. They were grateful for its light and for the warm food it allowed. However when they stood guard they moved far away from the light and hid in the shadows of the trees.

For a time Calin sat staring out into the night, her mind filled with a mixture of vigilance and thought, both intrigued and shocked by the events of the last few days. She sat in the darkness polishing her blade. She looked at her new shield too. *Made for me. It even has a clip for my sword.* It did too, beside the handgrip. You only had to slap it there and it would hold. *This Fassael, he too has his shield.* There was a question there but it wouldn't form. *What strange things have come to pass?* she mused. *I sleep in the same camp as a Wizard and a man with a goblin living in his soul. Man and goblin who at other times might have killed each other. I wonder if I'm right to think of the Goblins as enemies... Cog did... But... Who knows?* The thought of Cog took her down other paths. Strange paths of mist and the unknown...

...Cog waits for her wrapped in the swirling mists of silence. 'It can't be.' But he waits all the same 'Cog, is it truly you?' He doesn't answer but smiles and opens his arms to welcome her. She steps forward. 'But...' She can't find the words, can't understand what's happening. He's so close that she can feel his breathing. His breath is her breath. Her breath is his. His arms are open wide, waiting to hold her. She steps into their embrace. His eyes are as pools... dark pools of forgetfulness, where she can sink forever. Forever... Forever...

'Agh! Get off her!' Icicle's scream ruptured the silence of the night.

Calin moved from sleep to wakefulness in an instant. There was a shape looming over her, dark, evil, stinking of corruption. Its great maw yawed open, drawling with lust over the life it craved, with hate over what it could never have. And... And the Sanain-sword was in her hand, in its breast. The creature fell away, its final endless cry echoed into a silent scream as it crumpled to nothing. She hadn't even had a chance to see what it looked like. Its final thought was of her, her and the life that filled her, the life it believed it would soon possess. No scream of horror filled her this time; just anger over the obscenity of its nature and her sense of relief. It would trouble the land no more.

Fassael stood still, his face even whiter than usual. 'What the…?' The question wouldn't form. Even his mind had been lulled to silence.

The Wizard crouched close to the fire. He too had grabbed up his sword. Sleep fled into the sea of fear. *I didn't even sense it!* That thought was near as frightening as the thing itself.

Calin was on her feet now, the night suddenly threatening. But nothing came to disturb them. Gradually all three began to relax.

'The Greylon,' Icicle informed them through the still shocked Fassael. 'It froze your fuckin' thoughts.' Then she laughed, 'Agh! Didn't fuckin' know about me though.'

'It didn't know about you?' Calin echoed in a half crazed bemusement. *Well there's no denying that.* She gathered her thoughts 'Thanks, Icicle. I reckon you've just saved our lives.' *How in Hell are you supposed to talk to someone you don't…?*

'That makes us quits.' She didn't explain.

Dawn chose the moment to break the covering of cloud and the sun, bright as freedom, sent its first spears of awakening into the heavens.

They looked at each other, at the ground where the thing had fallen. No more than a stain of corruption remained. There seemed nothing more to say so they packed up the camp and were soon on their way again.

Did you see the speed that she moved? Icicle still moved to wonder by the Sanain's reaction was alone in not wanting to leave the matter lie. *I don't even think that the Greylon saw its end coming. No one could match that. Agh! Shit! Is that why they call her Champion? …She's Sanain Icicle. Her whole life, every moment had been spent in training for battle … Still.*

Three further days passed without mishap. They began to relax, if Calin ever relaxed. Perhaps there were no more of the things. Maybe they'd be left alone but it was doubtful.

The first signs of spring were beginning to show here, buds on the branches would before long become catkins. A few snowdrops gathered in the shelter of the trees to bid farewell to winter. There should have been a wakening of joy here, of winter past and for the return of light. Instead there was silence. Perhaps, now that the thing was gone, life would return.

They paused mid morning in a small meadow between the trees. Its gentleness brought a sense of ease to the Wizard's breast. There was something familiar about the place. In a moment of recognition he suddenly knew where he stood. He felt his heart swell and turned eagerly to his companions.

'It's here I first saw her.' He smiled, the first time in days. 'We must have come Westward of my first path. I hid over there.' He pointed to the very thicket. 'She came out of the morning, danced her magic over this meadow, as free as life itself. She was so mysterious at that time.' His thoughts wound away on the journey of his remembrance. *Under that tree … her first kiss…* 'She led me from here, showed me the way I had to go. I didn't understand her or anything she said at first… She's always been like that… But her love remains within my heart forever now…'

In the Halls of my mind.
Aye, but in what halls dwell you now?

He had the answer also. It wasn't an answer he wanted or needed. *I'm coming. I'm coming.* When he turned back to the others his face was white and his tone dark. 'It took two days to reach the gate from here.' Reality had its own sobering breath. 'If we make good time we could be there before tomorrow night.'

They looked at him, moved by the sudden change in his mood. Fassael shifted his pack. Calin chose to examine their surroundings. Neither wished to waken the devils stirred into being by his thoughts. They knew them only too well. *Have they harmed her? What do they do to her? Will she live? Will she be waiting for him? And, if so, what then will she be?*

Thus they followed that trail up into the mountains as he and the Fire-Dancer had done before. The land was even more shattered than then. Trees were burnt and ring-stripped, hacked from the ground and left to rot. There was a reckless, thoughtless hatred in the desecration of so much beauty. It might even have been with relief that the Wizard stepped into the clearing before the rock wall, were it not for what he knew lay beyond.

The same stone waited. It was where the Fire-Dancer had sat before leading him. Now he too chose to sit there. 'That fissure is the way we must take.' He told them, pointing to the crack in the rock. The burden of what he knew lay beyond was heavy on his mind, 'The Gate lies in there.'

'We're not afraid,' Calin reassured him.

'I am, Calin. I am.' He was too, frightened of what awaited him there, of what he would find, of what he had to do and whether he would be able to do it. He was afraid also, terribly afraid, that he might be too late to save her. *What foul thing holds her there? What are they doing to her? What if they've turned her into one of those things?* But he had an answer for that at least. *Then truly I'd loose the Vortex and destroy them all.* And this thought was more terrifying than anything. It was the truth.

'We're with you Wizard.' Calin's strong hand rested on his shoulder. He was shivering.

'Aye, we're with you until the end.' Fassael also felt the need to lay a hand upon his arm. *Me too, although I know the reasons for his fear.* She didn't.

'We're together, the three of us.' He accepted their offering and their friendship. It was more than any who existed beyond that barrier could claim. But still he hesitated. *The time's not right.* The knowledge was instinctive. *The hours have to match.*

It was past midnight when he finally stood. Calin slipped her shield to her arm and drew her blade. Fassael picked up a fallen branch. Its light was not much but just enough to see by. They turned towards the cliff.

That narrow crevice was just as he remembered it. Feeling its touch of despair grasp at his heart, as drawing the Dwarf-Sword, the Wizard moved slowly forwards. The greyness bathed them in its cloying touch. It would have been so easy to lash out a shield of wondrous brightness to dispel the horror of the place. It was harder not to. The magic of his being was revolted by the feel of the cold hatred surrounding them. It wanted to be free, wanted to chase away such sadness, to colour the world with its brilliance. He contained it, controlled his own wildly beating heart and stepped forwards another tentative step.

The figures on that arch, lit by the flickering light, were every part as foul as he recalled. He wanted to look away; embarrassed that Calin should have to look on such. However, as had the Dancer long before, his eyes scanned the shadows least anything waited. Calin too was tight-sprung, cat-like, and lethal in her readiness. Their eyes met. They nodded and stepped forwards.

Fassael's torch chose that moment to die plunging them into the darkness, a darkness far worse than he remembered, worse than he'd feared too. It cloaked them in horror, a horror of what might lie here, of what might lurk unseen nearby, waiting for their souls. He felt Calin close beside him, near his right hand. Her breathing was shallow, fast. Fassael-Icicle walked a few paces ahead, footsteps silent. The touch of the damp mist made their flesh crawl.

There came a cry, soul wrenching and bitter as bile, echoing against the wall of rock, to set their hearts and minds afire with thoughts of what kind of creature might make such a sound. The knowledge of the thing that had stalked the Naril gave truth to their fears. Even worse might lie here. They waited, crouching close together, with swords drawn, eyes wide, ready for whatever might come. Nothing did.

'We can't continue this way. We can't even see where we're going,' Calin whispered. The words drained away into the blackness, lost themselves somewhere beyond hearing. If they returned, on secret, silent, whispering wings, it was but a cruel jest in mimicry of their fears.

'What do you suggest?' the Wizard asked. *Suggest?* The blackness breathed back.

'I don't know what to suggest,' she sounded almost afraid, were that possible. 'I've never been here before. How can you do anything in this?' *Do anything... anything... any thing... thing.*

'It wasn't as dark as this then, well only when night fell.' His thoughts churned. He had to make sense of this. 'There are times of dark and light here. Not that you'd ever call it day. But I think you're right. We can't just stumble about in this. We'll have to wait until it gets lighter.'

'If,' Fassael-Icicle added. *If.* The night agreed.

'Have we anything to give us a little light?' Calin asked, ignoring Fassael's doubts. 'Though on second thoughts, in this place that probably isn't such a good idea. Who knows what might be drawn to it?'

The Wizard stooped, felt about on the rock-strewn ground. 'I think we'll be able to clear an area here where we might wait,' he offered. *Well it's an idea.*

Both Fassael and Calin followed his suggestion, scraping about until they had enough stone-free ground to set their camp. They didn't unroll their bedding. Rather, they sat, huddled in their cloaks, eyes peering into the nothingness that surrounded them. None of them thought to sheath or set their swords aside. There was something of comfort in their hardness. They didn't sleep. Well you wouldn't would you?

It's dark because it's the start of the year. Realisation came in the night. *One day one year. As the day grows lighter the Year will turn. Can I afford to wait?* Not that there was any choice.

He reached out with his thoughts, following the echoing sense of her being. The image was clearer here, although the touch of her life was feather light, the cries and pleading gone. *Her light grows dim. I can't wait long.*

There were things which moved unseen in the darkness, cold things, cruel things, creeping things, things of hate and despair but they didn't approach those who listened to the slithering of their passing. Many times cries echoed in the darkness but if there was meaning in the sound it was hidden, save for the terror left in its wake.

More time dragged by but there was no measure of its passing. *Perhaps it'll never grow light again. Could it be that, now the forces of Darkness grow strong they shun the light and deny its place in their foul domain. But no, it's not their domain. It's their prison. No wonder it holds such sadness.*

Seemingly, even the darkness could not contain all the torment this dour land held. There came a rumbling, a vibration as of distant thunder. There were lights in the skies, red lights and burning as of some terrible smelting. They crouched staring out into the shattered darkness wishing that it had stayed dark. Flares, sparking and reeking of terrible deeds and worse creations. Jets of searing red and purple flame spat their obscenities into the darkness only to be followed soon by the shuddering roar of their moment. *What forges are these and what blades beaten on them?* They huddled close together, cowed by the night rather than their own vulnerability. There was nothing they could or would do. Thus the hours passed them by.

When the light did eventually steal furtively back the change was almost imperceptible. At first the Wizard thought it might be an illusion born of staring too long at nothing. But gradually, over about half an hour, shapes became visible. Now the rock-face beside them could be distinguished, grey and cold as the light. Then other boulders lying nearby came into view. The ever-present mist hid further sights, but they gained the impression of some kind of growth fifty or so yards ahead from where they sat.

'This is just about as light as it gets.' Fassael-Icicle stood, perhaps heartened now that he could see a little. He stretched, easing the aches from his limbs. 'What's that?' He pointed to the rise where the growth was nearest. 'I'll see what lies there.' He walked into the mist, sword in hand, never quite out of sight, and then returned. 'It's a forest of ferns,' he told them. 'Horrible bloody things that glisten with some sort of slime. I wasn't about to touch any of them, they're probably caustic or poisoned.' He was getting the feel of the place. 'Beyond that I could just make out a field of Mgusk.'

'What?'

'Mgusk, fungus. They're the only edible thing here. Taste like crap though.'

'Before, when she brought me through this realm,' the Wizard told them, changing the subjectt 'there was something like a true forest here. She called it "The Darkling Forest". The trees had no life. The Galomist...' the Wizard remembered that all right, '...it crumpled to dust.' He shivered.

Fassael crouched down again. He opened his pack and took out some of the dried meat. 'Look,' he handed round the food. 'We can't just sit here.'

'It's OK, Fassael,' the Wizard spoke through the meat. 'I'm looking for a sign to see what way to go. Last time there was a road, well a trail anyway, that led us through.'

'Is that what we're doing? Passing through?'

There was truth in the question, a truth of fear and a reluctance to stay. 'No not this time.' The truth had to be denied. Even as he spoke the mist cleared a little. No one said anymore. For, through the lingering fog, at the very edge of their vision they saw it. The great, grey castle towered over that vast dust plain, hanging as it were upon a cloud of smog. It brooded there, dark and cold, waiting. Nonetheless there was something horribly compelling about the sight. It seemed to be the only substantial thing in the whole place.

'The Castle-of-Mists,' the Wizard hardly dared breath the words.

'There?' Fassael's voice actually shook. 'You're going there?'

'There,' he acknowledged. 'I've no choice.'

'Bollix!'

'How far do you think it is, Calin?' She had an eye for such things.

'It's hard to tell with this mist but I'd think no more than twenty miles, probably more like fifteen.' She turned and looked at the Wizard. 'Are you sure that's where you want to go?'

'Sure? I don't know that. And as for wanting? It's the last thing I'd wish for. But it's why I'm here and it seems the only choice left for me at the moment.' He looked again at the Towering fortress, felt his heart quail at the very idea of entering those shadowed halls. 'It's where I have to go, even if I go alone.'

'You'll not be alone, my friend. I at least will go with you,' Fassael assured him. 'That too is my choice.'

Before Calin could speak there came the rattle of falling stones. 'Look out!' Fassael yelled, although Calin's sword was already singing its anthem of battle. The stench of rotting flesh washed over them followed almost instantly by a stumbling rush of the grotesque Gnoll things. They bore weapons this time, swords and cleavers, dark with rust it's true but deadly all the same. Did they know what they did? It was hard to tell although something seemed to drive them. Perhaps it was simply their terrible jealous hatred of the life now forever denied them, for they were intent on the destruction of any they recognised. They fought, as in Naril, to the hissing sound of their horrid, lifeless breath, a breath that burst at the touch of Sanain steal. That sword did its work well and soon there were some twenty lifeless heaps littering the grey earth about them.

The three crouched close together ready for further attacks. None came, only the rolling mists. 'Were they sent against us?' Fassael's voice shook as the thought of the 'Soul-Stealer' gripped his heart with ice. And the dread that filled Icicle's thoughts of the 'Greylon' seemed even worse. 'Does one of those other things wait here?' Not that he really wanted to know.

The Wizard tasted the gloom with the echoing vibrations of his thoughts. All he found was a cold, empty lifelessness and an aura of hate, hate and terror. However, the hatred was unfocussed and he found no trace of thought or will, good or ill directed towards them. 'No,' he advised the man. 'I can't sense anything like that anywhere near. I think these things roam alone here doing as their emptiness bids them. They're just the guards of this Kingdom of the Damned.' But the terribleness of that idea was even worse than their torn and shattered bodies. 'Perhaps our swords do bring them peace.' It was a thought to cling to.

However, at that very moment, as if giving lie to his words, a spasm stirred one of the fallen forms.

'What!' Calin's voice rose an octave as she watched the creature begin to rise. 'It can't!' She wanted to deny it but such denial was not allowed. A hand clawed for its cleaver and a second of them began to struggle to its feet. Her sword broke the bond again. Even so several more were beginning their own obscene wakening.

Fassael swore a sharp, meaningless curse, as he too began to hack at the slowly rising bodies. One of them grasped at his sword as if to wrestle it from him. The fingers were left hanging to the blade until, with a second blow, he thrust it into the thing's chest. He didn't scream, but it was close.

Wounds gaped with horrid, bloodless corruption. Eyes, as cold and empty as their existence, sought out the living and found only the touch of steel to silence their hissing breath.

One of them stumbled towards the where the Wizard waited with his sword drawn. However he felt a terrible reluctance to strike as if doing so would contaminate the blade. It loomed before him, swung its rust-red cleaver in an arc towards his head. Despite his revulsion, he rammed the blade upwards, spitting the thing through its breast. For a moment it was still, completely motionless as if it were made of stone. He wrenched the blade out. The thing remained standing, only now it seemed that a fire burnt within. From the wound the fire spread, blackening the flesh, even bone. Finally the remaining shell crumpled to dust. 'Shit!' It was all he could think to say. By then another of the things was attacking and his attention was filled with the need to fight. This one too knew that strange ending of fire.

For a time all were down again. The three stood panting from their exertions. 'I'm not sure they're even trying to kill us,' the Wizard declared. 'They just want to end this existence. They want us to kill them.'

'How?' she demanded, her anger mounting as once again a body stirred back into movement.

'Watch!' Stepping about her, he let his sword do its work. Maybe the thing found peace in the flames that consumed it. He hoped so.

'What happened?'

'It's my sword, Calin. It knows the truth and the lies of their being. It can't kill what's not living so it denies the lies of the life they mimic.' From the depths of his memory came Pina's words. *'Can you take life from that which has none?'* So she knew *of these things too.*

Calin didn't understand him but it didn't matter. 'Fine. Let it deny some more life so we can get on our way.' However her Sanain-Sword still had its own work to do.

Before long all the gnolls were fallen and then once again they began to rise. The Dwarf-Sword struck and the light flared. However when he tried to end those who were fallen the same did not happen. *They have to be active for it to work.* As if to prove the point, the one he had just struck began to rise again. This would be its last time though.

'Is this what we'll have to face on the road ahead?' Calin asked. 'I mean, are these things the troops of the Dark-Lord?'

'These? Yes I suppose so.' The terrible vision born of that reality filled his thoughts. 'Oh god, just imagine what would be if these ever pass beyond the veil.' Before he continued his sword bit again. 'Imagine a battle, Calin, a battle where the enemy cannot be slain, where even the dead of your own side rise up and turn against you. Imagine that, Calin, friends and brothers, comrades in arms, who you'd have to slay again and again forever.'

She did, it was easy to do with these corpses strewn about them, and her face whitened with the horror of the idea. 'Is that what will be? I mean, is that the future if we fail?'

'The Dwarf said my magic will break the binding, the barrier that keeps these things away from our land. When that's gone, then yes, the Dark-Lord will indeed lead his army to war.' He watched the truth alight on her thoughts. He continued softly, 'There's worse than these though, Calin. These things are but the simplest of the enemy's creatures. Don't forget what creates them.'

'But in Naril they didn't wake to fight again,' Fassael protested, as he too struck out at another of the things.

'Look this is new to me too,' he protested. 'I'm just trying to work it out as I go!' He felt defensive as if he should have known. 'I don't understand any of it at all.' *I never do.* 'But I think they can do this because of the evil of this place. I think it's what sustains them. Beyond the gate the darkness barely leaks, as yet. However when the binding breaks that evil too will be free. Then Heaven help us all.'

Another gnoll rose up before Calin. 'This one's yours.' She stepped backwards allowing the Wizard room to move and watched the creature flare and crumple to dust. 'Besides,' she continued with a wry smile of death, 'In this kind of fight your sword seems to serve us better than mine.' She sheathed her blade and began picking up her possessions.

Another of the creatures began to stir. The Dwarf-Sword did its work. 'Let's get away from here,' he told them. 'I've no liking for this spot. There are things to do.' The edge to his voice was deadly.

They faced the castle together. It still hung there on its cloud of mist, watching over this tortured land and couldn't be denied. Fassael slipped his pack over his shoulder. He kept his sword drawn, his shield on his arm. 'I'm ready.' He didn't sound it. 'Well, as ready as I'm going to be.'

The Wizard sheathed his own sword though and grasped the hawthorn staff tightly. *I've been on other journeys,* he told himself, *but none were as loathsome or dire as this.*

Calin said nothing. Her sword was in her hand, her shield on her arm but her eyes were sharper than any blade.

There was no path for them to follow or if there was it was hidden beneath the moss or the dust. The land sloped downwards from where they'd fought in the lee of the cliff, but there was little to hinder their progress. Nonetheless they took care. Soon the sight of the tower was hidden again behind the wall of mist.

For the last hour or so the mist seemed to have been growing thicker. It clung to the ground now, hid even their feet. It had a taste too, burnt, like that of heated stone. The trouble was that there was no heat. It was cold instead, cold and damp and dirty. Where the moisture ran over their faces it left trails of soot, hollowing their eyes with grime. There was nothing amusing about their clown-like faces though.

'Damn this place.' Fassael spat to clear the muck from his mouth. 'Even the air is foul.'

'It's the forges.' *The Master-Smith would curse here too. Fire should be clean. How else to prove the steel?* 'They're preparing for war, the war they think I'll awaken.' He recalled the flaring of the night, the thunder of the hammers. 'And they've had long enough to do it.'

As if to confirm his words there came the sound of thunder from somewhere hidden far away. 'What mischief do they forge now though, I wonder?' There was no answer to that. They walked on.

Although there was little to hinder their progress they still did not travel fast. For the most part the tower was hid in the smog and on the few occasions when their view cleared they found that they'd veered from their path considerably.

Icicle was of little help here. Her childhood had been spent far away, near to where the forest had once been. 'What we could use is a guide,' Fassael declared when once again they realised that their feet had strayed from the way.

'Agh! Guide eh?'

They spun, all three, Calin faster than sight. Fassael's sword was still in his hand. The Wizard crouched between them ready to meet the danger. He'd not drawn the dwarf-sword though, not yet.

From the rocks, piled up to the right of where they stood, came a laugh. 'Agh! That made y' fuckin' jump.' Another burst of laughter followed.

'Wait, Calin,' the Wizard warned. 'Let it say its piece.'

'Didn't shit y'selves did y'?' There was a scrambling, a scuffle of rocks and pebbles, and then a shape appeared from where they looked. That it was a goblin came as no surprise.

The Wizard straightened. He too managed a laugh. 'You got us there alright. Didn't hear a thing.'

'Agh! What the fuck are y' doin' here? Don't y' know what's goin' on?' He walked across to them. He was larger than many of the goblins that the Wizard had seen before; broad shouldered with stocky frame and well muscled arms. Even so he seemed to present no threat. He stopped before Calin, eye to eye. Nothing was said but eventually it was he who turned aside.

'Bloody hell!' He looked up at Fassael. 'Agh! You're a big bastard ain't you?'

Fassael too laughed. 'Bigger than you, goblin, bigger than you.'

'What are y' doin' here then? Agh!'

The Wizard answered. He spoke quietly, deadly, 'I'm about to start a war, goblin.'

'Agh! Fuck me!' He was taken aback. 'Just you three?'

'No, well, just me really I suppose, but I'm only going to start it.'

The goblin walked about them looking at each in turn once again. 'Agh! Now if it was 'im who'd said that, I'd not have been surprised. Agh! But you?' All the time though his real attention was on Calin. His life hung in the balance and he realised it.

'You'll have to wait and see, goblin. You'll just have to wait and see.'

He chuckled, still not sure. 'Agh! Right.'

'And you?' Fassael asked. 'What are you doing here?'

It was the wrong question. If it were possible the goblin would have turned paler. His eyes widened with fear and he began to look about nervously. 'Don't ask! Agh!'

They exchanged glances. 'Why not?' Fassael asked slowly.

"Cause you don't want t' know.'

By now the Wizard did. He drew his sword, not threatening, and held it for the goblin to see. 'See this, it's Dwarven, this blade can destroy them.' The goblin's eyes widened even more. 'We fought them nearer the gate, so I know.'

The goblin looked at him. *What does he know?* But it said nothing.

'We mean you no harm, goblin,' the Wizard tried. 'It seems to me that you're ready to live.'

'Live? Am I ready to live?' It laughed without humour. 'Live? I ain't sure that any can...' There was more meaning that just the words. 'Agh! NO!'

They spun following the goblin's startled eyes. It staggered out of the mist, grotesque as ever. Half its face had been ripped away, and its left arm was bare to the bone. Yet again they heard the hiss of its unnatural breath and nearly gagged on its rotten stench.

Calin put up her sword. 'Yours I think.' She stepped aside for him to pass.

Thus, with the overwhelming sense of the goblin's fear driving him onward, the Wizard stepped forward to meet it. The whole matter was over in seconds. He parried the clumsy swing of its axe and the sword bit and, as before, the creature burnt with that inner cleansing light and collapsed. It wouldn't rise again. *God! I'm even getting used to the things.* The thought drove away any sense of victory.

He heard movement. Turned to find the goblin kneeling on the earth before him.

'Look there's no need for that.'

'Agh!' The horror in his voice made it sound somehow shrill. 'It was Drawsel. Once it was anyway. Agh! He was a stupid bastard and fuck-all use when it came to fighting but...' He looked up at the Wizard. There might have been a glimmer of hope in his elongated eyes. 'If they get me. Agh! Do that to me.'

'They won't get you, goblin.' Trying to sound confident.

'Agh! But if.'

'OK then. If.' A thought, 'Are you coming with us then?'

'Agh! Too fuckin' right I am.' He clambered back to his feet. 'I've fuckin' killed him five times now. Just one blow and that was it. I ain't seen anyone else who could do that.'

'OK, we'd better share names then. This is Fassael.' The man nodded his head.

'I'm Calin-Sanain.' Her eyes were still.

'Agh! What do you do?'

'I fight, goblin.'

'Fight?' There was an edge of disbelief in his voice. It didn't last long though. The Sanain moved, faster than thought, surer too and the shimmering dance of her blade proved more than words ever could. 'Shite!'

'They call me Wizard, though for now my magic stays silent. And you?'

'Me?' He seemed surprised that they wanted to know. 'Agh! My tribe name is Horge.' He looked at the two as if questioning their reaction. 'What's the truce then?'

The Wizard continued to direct things. 'There isn't any truce, Horge. We have a need. If we stay together we can protect each other. That's enough isn't it?'

Horge looked uncomfortable with the idea. But he nodded nonetheless. 'How come you'd let a goblin join up with you?'

'How come you'd want to?' Fassael added. *He's alright, this one,* she told him.

'Fair comment! Agh! So where are y' goin'?'

The Wizard turned slowly. The Tower was barely visible through the smog. 'There.'

Again the goblin almost shrank. 'What for?'

'He said it before, Horge,' Calin laughed. 'We're going to start a war.'

'Fuck Me! Agh!' There was little else that he could say.

'Have you got any gear?' Fassael asked. It was time to be moving on.

'Agh! Na.' He stooped to pick up the fallen Drawsel's axe. 'I got this now.'

They turned and headed off again.

Horge stopped after about ten paces. 'Agh! Look.' He tried after a moment or so. 'Agh! If you want to get there then you don't want t' go this way. It'll take fuckin' days an' lead you right into the worse of it.'

'How then?'

'Agh! It would be best t' swing up through the old Gharganol, and then down through The Dog-Pit. There's a half decent road there. For the weapon trains,' he added.

The Wizard stopped again. 'You know your way about this place then?'

'Course I do. Agh! I been here all me fuckin' life.' He paused. 'That's what's so fuckin' wrong with it. Agh! They've changed everything. Bastards!'

This didn't seem to make any sense. Which was nothing new. 'Hang on.' He struggled to get his thoughts in order. 'We don't actually know what's going on here, Horge. Perhaps you'd tell us?'

'Agh! Sure.' He turned to his left and climbed up the short slope. They followed on behind. It was incredible just how easily he could cover the ground.

'It's only been about six, eight years or so.' He spat. 'Agh! Before that it was mostly OK. Some of the Ghal could get a bit mean and if any took a fancy t' y' hide it could get a bit hairy, but I was big enough that most didn't even try.' He smiled. 'Agh! I 'ad my own bitch then, an' a band of sixteen. We was OK. Lived up near the Skorld, at the edge of the forest.'

'What happened?' Calin too was becoming interested.

'Agh! Like I said, about two years ago things started t' change. The Greylon came, they and their fuckin' mists. They said that we was needed t' do their Lord's work. What fuckin' Lord I ask y'? Turns out that "The-Time-of-Change" as they called it, was comin'. We had t' work in the Dog-Pits, mining, an' on the forges. There were weapons t' be made. We'd either work or…' It was clear he didn't want to explain.

'Well, that's what we did. It wasn't too bad really. Not at first. We got fed lots and even knew a bit of safety. They'd stopped the warring then. Said there would be enough later when the 'Way' was open.' He stopped and turned to look at them. His face was filled with as much horror as anything they'd ever seen. 'Agh! We didn't know.'

They left the question unasked and Horge continued: 'They made us, my lot, part of a raidin' party. We had t' go out into the other place and bring back prisoners. There weren't ever enough. Usually we took them up t' the Castle. The guards would come and take them inside. We never saw them again after that.' His tone was hollow with horror.

'The forges was burning all the time now. Agh! Horrible things they were, took your breath away if you got even close. I don't know how many fuckin' weapons they wanted, but there were never enough. Then the killin' started. We didn't know at first. It was only when the Tribes marched that it became plain. We never saw them again. We didn't know who'd gone and who 'adn't. There was more work now. They came with whips and... and...' He couldn't say the words.

'Then we began to see the... them things, Grawl we called 'em. They was fuckin' everywhere. Agh! They didn't need no rest, or no bleedin' food. Bodross, who was supposed t' be the Gha of First Line, went to the Greylon. He only asked what was goin' on. I saw it! I did truly.' He was shivering yet somehow having started he couldn't stop himself now. 'That thing put its hand on his head and his eyes caught fire. He died right then but he didn't lie down. When he turned t' walk back down to us I just ran. I ain't no scaredy, but I wasn't goin' t' face that. I hid up in the rocks. Then I saw it too. He killed them then, that thing, all of them. Then these fuckin' horrible things crept out of the dust, they crawled into their mouths or up their noses and then they started to get up again. Only it wasn't them any more, not them at all. There was a fight, down near the Sheds. They never stood a fuckin' chance. Now they're all like them!' He stopped again and turned to the Wizard. 'You won't let that happen to me?

'Next thing was something terrible happened up in the Castle. I never did know what. Then the forest turned t' dust. Just like that; one moment it was there then puff, it was gone. I've never been so scared in all my fuckin' life.

'I've hid since then, up in the rocks near where I found you. I run out of food and couldn't stomach any more of the Mgusk. I was goin' t' try the Dogs. Then I reckoned t' get the fuck away from here. I don't know what's in that other land but it can't be worse than this.'

He was silent then, for really quite a long time. 'That's where you're from ain't it?'

'Yes.' He didn't feel like saying any more. The story seemed only too real. The memory of that last visit also. *I never even considered what it must have been like for them when the forest was destroyed.*

'When you go back. Take me with you?'

'That I shall, Horge. If it's at all possible,' Fassael answered. He'd barely understood half of what the goblin had said, but it was enough to know the creature needed his protection. 'You can be sure of that.'

True to his word Horge did seem to know his way here. It took them about half-an-hour from when they'd met to cross over the rock-strewn land and reach the road of which he'd spoken. It was a good choice for this was indeed a far more passable way, the surface packed hard by thousands of marching boots. Horge stopped at the side of the road and pointed away from the castle. 'That's where they went, the Tribes that is, marching to war. I reckon I'd have done best to have gone with them.' He might well have been right.

'We'd have met earlier then,' Calin replied. 'I met your tribes.'

'Met them?'

'There was a battle, Horge.'

He thought that over for a bit. 'A battle and you're still living. Are you saying that they're all dead?'

The Wizard interrupted, 'No. I stopped the battle.'

'You stopped it?'

'Yes. It was all wrong.'

This needed thinking over too. 'Agh! You're telling me that you stopped that one there, but you're gonna start another one here? Agh! Don't make no sense.'

'No, it doesn't does it?' the Wizard laughed.

Thus they turned their backs to the goblin tribes' road-to-war and headed off into the gloom. The way passed through a bare, rough-rock landscape of shattered stone now. Gradually the sides became higher, steeper, hinting that it would soon lead them down into an even darker place.

Horge led the way. 'Agh! This is the first cut of the Slide,' he explained. 'It goes down in t' Gharganol and then right on in t' the Dog-Pit proper.'

'The Slide?' Fassael asked.

'Agh! You'll see.'

Sure enough they soon did. The roadway became like a gorge bordered with cliffs. Had there been sunlight then none would have shone here.

Calin was on edge. The place seemed made for an ambush. She bade Horge and Fassael shadow the Wizard. The goblin went to the right, Fassael to the left, whilst she moved on ahead. Still, nothing disturbed them, as yet.

After a while they began to notice caves opening into the rock-face. At first there were just one or two but before long they could see hundreds of them. It was like a rock town with steps and balconies to afford access.

'The Gharganol?' asked Fassael, not that there was any doubt. 'Agh! I always wondered what it would be like. They never let me near.'

Horge lifted a bemused eye at the huge man. *They're all fuckin' odd, this lot.* 'Agh! There used t' be more than ten-thousand goblins livin' here.' At that moment he might even have had a sense of pride. It was quickly dispelled. 'That was then. They're nearly all gone now. Most went to the wars and of those left there ain't many.' He stooped to pick up a rock, threw it high against the rock. It fell. Clattering down the face and landed near to where he stood.

The emptiness of the place began to weigh on the travellers too. Their voices seemed louder than they'd wish in these narrow confines. The feeling of vulnerability told as well, of being overlooked as they moved through the murk. They would be glad to be gone from the place.

But in truth it was not that empty. Eyes watched them, fearful, grey, goblin eyes, eyes that had seen too much. They waited, watched, wondered with half fearful expectation to see what would happen. What is more, those being watched wondered just the same.

They came to a place where the road opened out into a wide space. It was like an amphitheatre, serried slopes reaching high over them. There were beings up there, looking down at those who had entered their prison. Their eyes were still.

Calin stopped. 'Wait.' This time was for her and she knew it to her core as she walked forwards. There was a remoteness to her actions as were her mind somehow separated from what was happening. It was often like this in the midst of battle. She considered the matter. She might have felt discomfort under the cold grey gaze of the watching goblins. She might have even felt fear, for their expressions were hardly welcoming. She felt neither. *They seem lost.* The thought echoed in her being was the truth. *They're alone as I am.* Their eyes were as cold as ever; empty. It was almost painful to see them.

She stopped, sheathed her sword and turned slowly about. 'I am Calin-Sanain.' Her voice was clear and sounded unnaturally loud in the bowl of the arena. 'I have met your kind before. Often have I fought with them and often I have killed. The last time was at Tabour on the Plain-of-Blood in the Lands of Men.'

She let her eyes drift over their ranks. There was little order here. They sat or stood up the terraced slopes on every side. 'They fought well. I have no complaint.' Her words might have been goblin. They held a hardness the goblins would understand and brought a stirring through the gathering but nothing more.

Some there bore arms. Others were even dressed in partial armour. Most were dishevelled though and none appeared to be any threat.

'Agh! Why are you here?' A voice boomed from above, no softer than hers had been.

She let her eyes seek out the speaker, found him high on the terrace. 'We have come to start a war. I thought you should know.'

'Who do you fight?'

'That depends, goblin. Any who stand in my way. But our enemy isn't of this land, not even of this world. It doesn't belong here.'

The goblin stood and crossed over to one of the stairways. 'You think you can win? Agh! Do you think that you can kill those things?' He spoke as he walked but there was no challenge. He wanted to know the answer.

'I already have, goblin. At the start of the battle at Tabour I did. A second died at my hand on the Great Plain near the Land of the Elves. Beyond the Gate, in Naril, I slew another and that was but twelve days ago.'

'If you really can kill them, maybe your words will be worth hearing.' There was no concession, just the acknowledgement that he might consider what she had to say. He began to descend. Tension grew thick. Perhaps the strain of the moment and of its significance was beginning to break through the indifference of the horde.

The sound of a single drumbeat thrummed through the smoke-thick air. In an instant the goblins were standing, all of them. Their faces were lit with shock, perhaps even fear. It seemed the sound had frozen their blood. The huge goblin who had been approaching down the steps appeared to freeze too. His face became mask-like, eyes wide. He didn't stop moving, just walking, and toppled slowly forwards, maintaining his rigidity throughout, until crashing face down on the lowest step. His body shattered as glass. The whole arena was silent, frozen in time.

Pulling the shield from her back, she sought the source of the drum. It came again, vibrating through the ground. She could feel the waves reaching out to her, wanting to shatter her too but her shield denied its power. *It was made and brought for you to bear*, the Master-smith had said. *To protect you from more than arrows.* It couldn't touch her and she knew it. Without thinking she started to climb the steps close to where the goblin had fallen. She hadn't even realised she'd drawn the sword, but felt its comforting weight in her hand. If she'd ever known a friend it was this blade.

Once more the booming din assailed her, beat on her with a wall of noise. It meant nothing. For now she saw the Drummer. It looked up from where it waited, clad in black-scaled armour, armour as was her own and the shock of that was greater than any attack might have been. It too was Sanain! *It can't be!* But it was. Her move to battle readiness was instant and instinctive. 'Who?' The question was unfinished. It turned its face towards her and she looked upon her own face, her face, her form, her hair and her armour. She stopped again, struggling to comprehend.

Suddenly, seeing the truth, she laughed, mocking its nature. 'Is that the best you can do?' She stepped nearer. Her sword was a needle of energy.

When it lifted the drumstick again she spoke. Her words came slowly, measured and full of her power. 'If you even think to touch that thing again I'll ram it over your bloody head.' She'd not missed seeing the gore that dripped from its sides, nor did she miss the truth regarding the nature of the skin. *Is that where its power comes from?*

It stood, stepped away from the instrument and from the illusion it had wrought. What it was she didn't know. It was similar enough to the other thing she'd encountered on the plain to set her mind ablaze with anger.

'**You don't belong here!**' it screamed at her.

'Yes I do,' she whispered in reply and turned slowly away, She could feel their eyes on her as she stooped to wipe the contamination from her blade on the tough ferns that grew between the stones.

'It's one of the reasons we've come,' she told them. 'It had no right to be here.' So she picked up the drum, though half afraid it might burn her hands with its evil, and she cast it down onto the road far below. It hardly made a sound when it smashed against the packed stones. Now she descended once again. They continued to watch, Horge, Fassael and the Wizard too.

'Those with the will, come down,' she demanded. Many moved to comply with her order. 'Bring wood.' Others hurried to obey. They probably needed the order to calm their fear.

It didn't take long, two, perhaps three minutes. She built the pyre herself and, though the touch of the blood revolted her, she even placed the drum in the midst of the wood. For an instant the thought of Fassael crossed her mind. She beckoned him forwards. His fire exploded, raw and rapid, ripped upwards through the wood consuming the drum with its energy.

Another truth became manifest then. As the flames took the drum a figure crumpled, fell lifeless to the earth revealing that not all here were alive. The obscenity of the whole thing flamed in her heart. 'Throw them onto the fire also,' she directed. They complied, perhaps in the hope that these at least might know peace as their souls were freed by the flames. The fire would last for several hours, perhaps longer, for they'd begun to add more wood to keep it alive. Perhaps the light kept their fears at bay.

It was time to move on now but it seemed that fate was determined to interrupt them. Their way was blocked by eight goblins. These were larger than many of their type, nearly as big as Horge. They looked capable too.

For a moment Calin thought they were going to fight. She readied herself. However, there came no attack for instead they fell on their knees before her.

'Agh! Kla, Master. Let us follow you?'

'Oh get up,' she sounded exasperated. 'I am Sanain.' She nodded towards the Wizard. 'It is he, the Wizard of Rainbows, who chooses our path.'

'Agh! Master.' They turned to him. 'Let us follow you, my Kla? We will serve you well.'

He was probably just as exasperated as Calin. This was the last thing he wanted. Exasperated, relieved and still half numbed with shock. He'd been expecting more horrors, not these pitiful things. 'I am no one's Kla and no one's master! If you want you can join with us but I'll have no followers.'

They clearly didn't understand. 'Agh! Horge,' one of them recognised their goblin companion. 'What's he mean?'

'Agh! He means he don't want you hanging about 'is arse all the time, Scorl. If you want to come with us its OK but it's your own fuckin' choice. Agh! Do what you fuckin' want.'

'Agh! Look, shit-head, I ain't no arse-licker. I saw how she took on that fuckin' thing. I reckon, if she follows him, 'e must be worth following. Anyway, Agh! It'll be safer with them than hangin' about here.'

The Wizard laughed. 'So you want to join with us?'

'Sure. Agh! We'll make truce.'

'No truce, goblin.' The Wizard was becoming tired of this. 'If you want to come then come. If you want to go, then go. I won't hold you to anything.'

'Where are you goin'?' another of them asked.

'To war.'

'That's OK with me,' came the reply. 'I reckon that you'd make some fuckin' good warring.'

'You don't know the half of it,' Fassael added to the matter. He didn't explain and they didn't ask.

'Agh! Got any weapons?' Horge asked with a practicality they'd not seen in him before.

'More than you could ever want,' Scorl replied. 'The caves a' fuckin' stuffed full of them. Come and see.' There followed a time of more scrambling goblins. They returned bristling with weapons. Horge had found a helmet and shield. Most of the others had some kind of armour too.

My very own army. The Wizard smiled a humourless smile to himself. *Twelve of us. Well it's a start.* 'If you're ready I'd like to be on our way again.'

'Where we goin'?'

'There.' He pointed to the looming tower. It said quite a lot that not one of them questioned his reply.

Some five minutes later many more, those of the goblins with the heart to think, began to follow on behind. It seemed the right thing to do, to see what would happen.

Nearly an hour had passed since the others had joined them. They were now twelve, all armed and dangerous. It was probably more like eleven and one other in truth, for the grey folk hardly dared to even look at Calin. They saw the death living in her eyes and gave her a wide birth.

Of the goblins, it might be said Horge was their leader and they treated him as some kind of go-between, being half afraid to address either Fassael or the Wizard.

It didn't matter. The Wizard hardly felt like talking anyway. The damp ugliness of the whole place was taking its toll on both his confidence and his sense of purpose. It wasn't enough to slow him or to lessen his resolve. It just made the whole situation more difficult.

Horge had sent one of them ahead, not too far, they could see him all the time, but enough to give warning should he spy anything. He hadn't. Another was left trailing behind, though it seemed that Horge had to spend an inordinate amount of time telling him to move back further.

The road closed in again and they continued to descend. Now the caves were more like caverns, gaping holes in the rock-side. There was mining equipment here, picks and shovels, buckets too. Piles of smelted but un-forged iron and pig-iron had been left to rust in heaps at the road-side. It all seemed such a senseless waste of good metal. The stench of burnt iron stung the Wizard's nose and throat. His discomfort was as much with the anger over such careless use of the metal as with the brimstone tainted air. Several times one or another of them noted movement in the shadows, gnolls again but they seemed condemned to other fates than attacking the party.

They entered a place that might indeed have been Hell, where several of the furnaces were set. Their gaping mouths still belching out the foul, sulphurous smoke, thickened the air with their stench. Despite the desire to be gone from here as quickly as they might, their steps were heavy. The heated atmosphere made breathing difficult so that even their best effort was little more than a slow walk. Ever the smog thickened.

*

The wheat-fields, reaching even to the lower slopes of the Dollin, were transformed to gold in the morning sunlight. The blackberries were ripened too and soon the orchards of Santolin would be ready for the harvest. The World seemed good at this time. On the walls of Sarum the Guard's captain knew the signs well. Soon the flights of gander and red-duck would be seen over the mountains. Not long after the recently harvested fields would begin to glisten with autumn rains. It always rains in autumn. Still there could be worse things.

It was probably luck that led his eyes to rest on the gap where the road ran down from the heights. Thus he was the first to see them, a flash of sunlight caught on metal. Next came, as a shadow where the sun still shone, a wave of darkness stealing over the brow. It didn't move fast and before long the captain recognised the order in what he watched.

'Shield-man!' his voice cracked. 'Ask Sir Terall to attend here.'

The man was quickly gone leaving the captain to continue to watch. By now he realised that this was an army of some kind. *Coming out of the North? There are no kingdoms there.* He beckoned another of his guard. 'Go to Blue watch. Tell Sergeant Duffen to raise the guard.' The urgency in his voice brought an instant quickening of the guardsman's step.

Still watching that on-coming ribbon of darkness, he moved over to the Northgate postern. 'Prepare to close the gate!' His voice rang loud in the confines of the gatehouse. Feet pounded on the cobblestones. He was calculating. *One hour to come down to the tree line then three from there to the plain. Then one further hour before, at the earliest they'd arrive. That's plenty of time.* 'No!' he countermanded his order, 'Hold on that!' He felt their eyes on him. 'There's a force coming over the Dollin. But we've time enough to prepare.' Several anxious eyes turned northwards.

In truth they came faster than he'd reckoned. By the time Sir Terrill had donned his armour and climbed the steps to the guard-walk, about fifteen or twenty minutes, they were already approaching the tree line. 'They're coming fast, Sir,' he addressed his commander. There was no need to explain to whom he referred. 'I guess if they carry on at this rate they'll be here in about four hours. That's some going.' He was almost impressed. 'Last time I was up that way it took me over six hours to reach here from up there.' However, what was more concerning was all were not yet in sight. Every moment still more crossed over the Dollin to join the others.

'Who are they?' The question was rhetorical.

'Should I go to find out, Sir?'

'Yes I think so.' The Commander was beginning to gather his thoughts. 'Yes. Take a patrol, ten troopers. Go and see who they are. Don't confront them and if they try to attack you, then run hell-for-leather back here. I'll raise the Full watch and inform the King.'

'Sir!' the captain barked, 'I've summoned Blue-watch.'

'Good. Be on your way then, Fanchett. And good luck.'

'Thank you, Sir.' He was already turning towards the steps.

In less than eight minutes Fanchett and his troopers rode from the gate. Though the need was for haste, all knew better than to race the horses too much. It was wiser to leave them rested for the time, should it come, when they had need to flee. Still it didn't take more than half an hour before they'd reached the end of the grassland and taken to the road through the trees. About half a mile further on they met with the first scouts.

'Hold!' The gruff command brought them to a sudden standstill. *Dwarves?*

'Are you Captain-of-the-Guard?' There was no preamble. Just a rustling of bushes and the speaker strode out onto the road. There was no question. He was dressed for war!

'Captain Fanchett, of The Santolin Watch,' he informed the dwarf.

'Good, Captain-Fanchett-of-the-Santolin-Watch. Go tell your King we are coming. Your horses travel faster than our feet.'

'What do you want?' He caught himself. The dwarves are the honoured friends of the Santolin Kings. 'Sir,' he re-addressed the dwarf in softer tone. 'Is there any message I should give?'

The dwarf smiled. 'Aye, Captain-Fanchett-of-the-Santolin-Watch. Tell him that The Iron-Army marches!' Then in reply to the captain's look of shock. 'Do not worry, Captain-Fanchett-of-the-Santolin-Watch, our destination lies far from Santolin. We are but passing through on our way south. The Master-Smith-of-the-Carrow shall attend on Your King before nightfall.'

'If it's acceptable I'll send three riders back. The rest shall remain with you.'

'Yes, Captain-Fanchett-of-the-Santolin-Watch, that is acceptable.'

The three riders wheeled away and galloped into the distance. And with their departure another five dwarves stepped out of the woodland. 'Genlesfallowardingly!' the first dwarf addressed one of the others. 'Inform the Master-Smith-of-The-Carrow that Captain-Fanchett-of-the-Santolin-Watch has come and that he has sent riders to the King-of-the-Stone-warding to tell of our coming.'

The dwarf bowed, turned and began trotting back up the path.

'Can you tell me what's happening?' the captain asked, dismounting to stand beside the dwarf. He still towered over him.

The dwarf looked at him and for a moment he felt childlike in the face of such age. 'We march to the Realm-of-the-grasslands-which-men-name-Lodor,' he began. 'This is the rising of the Iron-Army. We march in defence of the Land.'

'But whom do you fight?'

'We fight any who come forth from the Darkness, Captain-Fanchett-of-The-Santolin-Watch. It is told that soon the bindings shall break and, when so, that terrible things, the Golnorgaloshinden, shall enter the land.'

He heard the dwarf's words in silence.

'The time of endings that was decreed at the beginning of the warding is near. Thus does the Iron-Army come forth. It is not without good cause our forges grow cold.' There was a strength and anger in his voice that made the captain almost fearful. 'We serve the Well-Springs-of-the-Earth.'

His words meant nothing to the captain or his men, but they knew enough to question no further. *The dwarves march to War!*

*

Each, at the same step, came to an abrupt stop. No one had spoken. It seemed they'd walked into a solid wall of hatred. In the back of his thoughts the Wizard heard Horge gasp and curse under his breath. He lifted his eyes to see what waited ahead.

Whatever it was stood in the road before them – tall, taller than Fassael. At first the Wizard thought it a troll of some kind, but no. He could see no face. Even its form was wrong, somehow human in shape but not even that. He almost screamed at the first touch of its thoughts upon his mind. It was like being invaded by a swarm, a million writhing thoughts of death and desecration. It wasn't lust but worse. Its whole attention seemed fixed upon the single driving jealous hatred of all who possessed the life it was denied.

It spoke; only the voice was as the whisperings of a thousand different tongues. 'You should not be here!' The words crackled, hissed.

'Nonetheless we are,' Calin answered, her sword already in her hand. 'And we aim to pass by too.'

Beside her the Wizard grasped the hilt of the dwarf-sword. There was something about this creature that made his skin crawl, a revulsion far greater than any he'd ever known.

It stepped closer. '𝕻ass? 𝔇o you think we can be challenged? 𝔄sk that!' It pointed at Horge. '𝔄sk that what happens to those we touch. 𝔇o you so hunger to become one of us?'

She lunged, sword spinning in a shining arc, slicing right through its abdomen. Nothing happened. It was as if the sword stroke had never been. Its grasping reach was too slow to catch her as she leapt backwards with a cry of horror.

'See!' the voice continued. '𝔜ou cannot harm us. We are invincible.'

The anger filling the Wizard was as nothing he had known before. *This thing can't be allowed to exist!* He wanted to use his magic, wanted to blast it into nothingness. For an instant he almost did and probably would have but for the Lady's words echoing in the depth of his soul. He stepped forwards before either Calin or Fassael could stop him, drawing his sword as he moved. Horge grunted, but the Wizard's attention was wholly focussed upon the Creature before him. 'You lie.' He spat the accusation.

'𝔏ie? We shall see who lies...' Its writhing hand reached out towards him. It would probably have said more but he interrupted with a shout.

'Yes lie! Everything about you is a lie. Even the life you mimic.' His words, driven as much by his panic as his anger, were every part as sharp as the sword. But that blade knew enough of truth and lies to tell the difference, enough to part the fabric of the lies that bound it. For a moment the sword hung in the breast where he'd thrust it.

'𝔑o...' The cry was never finished. It broke into a thousand different cries, denials, freeing the blade that had undone its bindings. Now the buzzing, chittering, writhing mass dissolved into individual murmurings as the creatures that had made up its form lost the cohesion of the evil. They crawled away into the dust.

The others backed away also, even Calin, though there was no danger now. They wouldn't have borne the touch of a single one of the insects not even to crush it under foot.

'What in Hell's name was it?' Fassael gasped.

'Hell's name is right.' The Wizard's anger still burnt in his voice. 'It was a terrible lie. It thought to make its own life. It was simply evil, a mimicry of life. I think it had taken all the insects it could find and bound them together with its power to make that form.'

'Shite!' Horge exploded beside them. 'Now I believe you, Wizard!' He turned to Fassael. 'Agh! Is that why you follow him?'

Fassael even managed to smile. It was one of the hardest things he'd ever done. 'I don't follow him, Horge. We're together, that's all.'

'Shite!'

It had begun to grow dark again, though they all knew night would bring no peace. They were nearer to their goal now, much nearer. As Horge put it; 'Agh! If we get any fuckin' closer they'll be able t' piss on us from the walls.' Even that wouldn't have mattered too much. They stank as bad already.

The Wizard said nothing. He looked up at those grey stone curtains, as were they a symbol of death. His heart could have been no less troubled if they had been. They'd moved away from the furnaces over four hours ago yet still the stench lingered on his clothing.

Through the fog of his thoughts came the awareness of the others watching him and he suddenly realised he'd stopped. He knew then he wouldn't go any further, nearer until either he was ready or morning came. 'We'll camp here through the darkness,' he told them. 'Let's get off of the road and find a hollow or something.'

Scorl knew where to look. This was his domain. He led them to a clay pit on the very slope of the Castle mound. It would provide shelter from the prying eyes of any who looked down from the walls. There was even a rudimentary cave, shelter for those who slept. It would serve their needs well. They settled quickly, eyes ever watchful, and made camp.

For a time Calin vanished into the dark. They never heard her go. They never heard her return. 'About half an hour behind us there's a band of nearly a hundred and fifty goblins,' she told the Wizard. 'They've followed us from the fire. I told them to camp where they were.'

Do I lead a goblin army now? The idea seemed somehow ridiculous. He almost laughed.

There was no question of fire and food had to be taken cold also. Calin, Fassael and the Wizard ate the last of the supplies the dwarf had given them. From now on they'd hunger. What the goblins had they didn't want to know. 'We'll need a guard all night,' Calin directed. 'Do it in pairs and wake me the instant anything happens.' She told them as she un-slung her sleeping roll and began to settle down.

The Wizard, close beside her did the same. Fassael stayed sat, peering out into the darkness. *What will morning bring? What will the future hold for any of us?* There could be no answers at this time and the Wizard knew it. Therefore resting his hat over his face and closing his eyes, he sought the pathways of sleep. *Soon*, he told his thoughts, *Soon I'll come to her... Soon...*

Sleep did come, a strange sleep of images and omens, of hope and fear. However throughout the dreams slipped by without his knowing, only their tainted haunting remained.

Something startled him into wakefulness. The scream lingered, hanging in the air as a reminder of where they were. He could see the silhouette of the two goblins on watch. They were close to each other, eyes shifting jumpily at any sight or sense of light. Calin lifted her head slightly and their eyes touched, shining red in the glow where furnaces still lit the skies... From somewhere, far, far away there came a rumbling. Somewhere else a plume of gas ignited. Another grumbling roar followed. Then all was quiet again.

He could hear one of the goblins snoring in his sleep. There was something almost comforting about the normality of the sound. He let it drift over him...

It was dark again. The great furnaces had grown dim. The night too was quiet. It might even have been the silence that woke him. He sat up, striving for silence too. His heart was pounding, his thoughts churning. *I can't reach her anymore! SHE'S GONE!* The truth screamed in his soul. *Where is she? What's happened?* He reached out again and again striving to trace the trail of her being, to feel the touch. *NO!* Although the darkness was full, there was still enough of that foul red light left from the burning. He could see their eyes, all of them, even Fassael and Calin.

'You cried out in your sleep,' the giant told him. 'What's wrong?'

'Everything!' His soul still screamed, resounding in the emptiness it found. 'I can't feel her!'

'What?'

'The Dancer, my heart, my... I can't feel her.'

He didn't understand. Who could? 'You can't feel her?'

The Wizard was standing now. Staring up at the castle wall. 'She has drawn me, called to me through the pain of her loneliness...' He couldn't seem to frame the words. 'I can't hear her any more.'

They were still, all of them. What words could they say? Finally it was Horge who tried. 'Agh! Have they... Is she dead?'

DEAD? Dead... Once again the thought was denied. *No! Not dead.* That silence was not of death. 'No...' He was hesitant, unsure. 'I don't think so anyway. I'd know that. No it's more like she's been hidden from me.' There was a truth in those words that he could grasp. The anger began to build again. 'If they've done anything to her, harmed her, hurt her I'll destroy the bloody universe.' There was no lie in his words either. The others flinched away from him. The light in his eyes spoke of madness, madness and a power they could never comprehend.

'What shall we do?' Calin asked. Even she knew the touch of fear at that moment.

The Wizard turned to face the gate. He pointed at it with his staff. It seemed a wonder that it didn't explode with the intensity of that look. 'I've waited long enough. Now I'm going in there to get her.'

'What about us? Agh!' Scorl cried out in fear. 'What about...'

Fassael laid a hand on his shoulder. 'This is our time goblin. It's why we've come. We're going in there.' He heard their gasps of horror. 'You can come with us, or wait here,' trying to keep his voice level as not to frighten them any more.

'Calin, Fassael,' the Wizard too had not forgotten how to speak with kindness. 'I'll need you with me when we pass through the gate and into the courtyard beyond.' This he knew at least. 'I fear we'll have a terrible duty there.'

'I'm with you, Wizard.' Fassael had drawn his sword. Now he rose and stood beside the Wizard. 'We'll do as we must.'

Calin didn't need to answer. She knew.

'Agh! Us too. We can't just wait here for one of them things to come for us. I'd sooner die fighting than that!' Other swords were drawn too and other oaths spoken.

'Oh I think we'll be fighting alright, Horge. If not here and now, then soon.' Fassael even laughed. He could feel his own madness begin to grow, for there comes a time when fear will no longer serve. 'Agh! What the fuck!' Icicle spoke through him. 'Who wants to live forever?' He lifted his shield then and turned to the Wizard.

'Agh! Shit! We've all got to die some fuckin' time,' someone else agreed.

'I'm ready,' Calin spoke with the quietness of death.

'Ready?' He'd not even been listening to what they were saying but he turned now and looked at them, Calin, Fassael and the goblins. Their expressions were hard, determined. *Yet some of them will die before this is done.* 'Yes,' he nodded. 'It's time enough.' He drew the dwarf-sword, watched its blade sparkle in the growing light of the strange false-dawn.

'Got any plan?' Fassael asked. It didn't matter to him then. The question was just in case.

'No plan, Fassael,' Calin answered, as was her right. 'We go in through the gate and do what we have to do.'

'Fair enough.' The man turned to look at his force. *They'll do.*

It took no more than five minutes to climb up to the road and not much more before they stood before the gate. They'd managed it in silence too, which was something. Then they just stood there dwarfed by the massiveness of the entrance. The gate looming over them was over thirty feet high and studded with great iron rivets. Glances were exchanged, worried frowns speaking of their fears. Hands, some already sweating, clenched tighter on weapons.

When the Wizard sheathed his sword and walked the final few paces to the gate Calin went with him. They found it unbarred, not even fully closed, although the gap wasn't quite wide enough to pass through though. He placed his shoulder against the iron and began to push. At first nothing happened, then the hinges squealed and he felt the door move. Fassael joined them, and several of the goblins too. The doorway gaped wide.

He knew just how the scene would be even before he'd looked. It was a thing of his dreams, bad dreams, the troubled dreams which tormented him on many a tortured night. It remained unchanged from those dreams too, the cloisters dark and the stone flagged courtyard, the perpetual parade of the damned and even the cold grey keepers waiting in the shadows. The same cold grey warriors who now turned their gazes upon those who dared enter their domain. He heard Fassael's horrified gasp and knew the goblins had entered behind him and were even now spreading out. But what he knew most was the cold hatred of the eyes that speared him.

He resisted the temptation to draw his sword and stepped further into the yard. Tension grew drawn taught on bands of indecision. *Soon.* The others followed.

The hopeless parade of the damned drew to a confused, uneasy halt. They looked about in bewildered fear now the force that drove them was diverted. He even felt their questioning eyes touch him. However his thoughts were focussed elsewhere. He recognised the bowl and, even though he couldn't see it in the gloom, knew of the pit that lay in its shadow. *I'll destroy this obscenity before I go on*, he promised himself. *This at least will stop.*

'What in hell's name is this place?' He heard Fassael's voice and remembered his own reactions from before. He didn't answer the man though. His mind was on other things. They'd stepped out from the cloister's shade, fifteen perhaps twenty of the grey warriors, filled with their own hatred. They bore weapons, swords and pole-arms and moved with a horrid, reptilian silence. There was no doubt regarding their intention. The Wizard didn't move, though Calin, Fassael and the goblins did, fanning out in an arc on either side of him in readiness for the struggle that would ensue. The Wizard however had seen something other than these grey warriors-of-the-mist to trouble him. He felt the cloying touch of its cold emptiness and he knew there lay the true danger.

Then with a scream of fury the grey-ones charged. They came in a rush, weapons raised ready for battle. And battle they found. They found it in the form of Calin, silver and black, whose every motion was a ballet of violence. They found it in Fassael too, he and his goblin band and they found it harder than they'd expected.

In an instant the courtyard was filled with the sounds of strife. It swirled about the motionless Wizard but didn't touch him. Even the screams of a goblin pierced by a black-iron blade's burning fire couldn't distract him. He had his own battle of wills to fight.

These grey warriors-of-the-mist were fighters few ever encounter, well practised in their art of killing were they and intent on the destruction of their foe. Yet Calin fought as Sanain fight and her sword knew well its task. Nearer to the gate Fassael and Horge fought back to back. They were well matched and none of the grey warriors could come near to them without feeling the bite of their swords. Soon of the enemy but two remained. Of the nine goblins, four had fallen, Scorl amongst them. A *high price. I'll not forget them*. He didn't watch as Calin put paid to the remaining warriors.

'**Wizard**,' the thing called, echoing with the emptiness of its nature. '**Wizard**, **Wizard**...' Now all the attention was on him, on him and on what he might do. Even the damned ones turned to face him. He knew their pain, their hopelessness, their fear and the fate this thing of evil had decreed for them. *It shall not be*. The magic of his nature might well have burnt bright here, might have cleansed the corruption of the place in the beauty of its flare. But no, still he held it in check. This was not the time for such. He drew the dwarf-sword, held it before him.

He let his gaze fall upon those about him. One, the nearest to where he stood was a young woman, more of a girl really. *What on earth is she doing here?* She could be no more than seventeen summers, if that. Yet here she was and her sad eyes knew only too well the dullness of her life of sorrow.

'Go,' he offered with a smile, his voice soft and gentle. 'Go over to the Gate. We'll protect you. At least for now there's no need for you to fear.' She looked at him, nodded and did as he had suggested.

He approached another, a goblin this time, twisted by the crippling touch of the slave driver's lash. 'Go, You don't have to stay here.' There was even an elf here, its body showing every cut and scar of the torture that had robbed it of beauty. 'Go. We'll protect you.' One by one, 'Go.' And they turned and did as he had bid them.

He was close to that pit now, closer than he'd ever wanted to be, the pit and that blood-filled bowl. The stench was overwhelming, its evil worse than the aura of death hanging in the air, worse than the cruelty, perhaps even worse than the thing now moving towards him. 'Hold!' His voice was firm. He would not be denied.

'**Wizard**.' It called without words, simply echoes of death. '**Wizard**.' He didn't flinch from the darkness cloaking it as a robe or from its eyeless gaze. It was as he'd known it would be. '**You are not wanted here**,' it called.

He stood before it untroubled by its formlessness. Whatever shape it took would be a lie anyway. 'You're wrong there. I'm wanted very much. The Lord-of-Mists has taken great pains to get me here.'

'**No. It is only your magic that we want. You are nothing.**'

'Nothing?' Even though it was now within the range of his sword he didn't strike. There would be little point at this time. He knew it too. Instead of attacking he did just three things. First he brought out the ruby from where it hung about his neck and held it for all to see, glowing in the gloom. Secondly he laughed, neither mockingly nor cruel, just the laugh of life over a death it doesn't fear. His third act was to reach out with the sword and tap its blade lightly against the side of the cauldron.

The chime from that touch was more unexpected than anything imaginable. The sacrificial-bowl shattered into a thousand shards of blackened iron. Its contents becoming a dark, evil dust swirled and fell, almost mist-like, into the maw of the terrible pit.

'**Wizard**,' it loomed over him, terrible in its hate. '**Will you use your magic against me? Do you dare – No pretty sword will do.**'

The Wizard laughed again, lightly as at the first kiss of morning upon the dew-wet meadows of Hereth. 'Not yet, the time for such acts isn't here. It's true I've come as it was known I would. However I choose my own path. I choose my own deeds too.' He held out the jewel as if offering it as a gift. His voice was gentle 'If you tire of this empty existence reach out, take this. You'll feel no pain.'

It screamed in fury then and, for a moment, almost lashed out at him. Then the stillness of the void returned as a cloak to hide its anger. Slowly now its attention fell upon Calin. She met that gaze in silence and it found no weakness in her, no fear, no point where its hatred might gain a hold. Thus to Fassael and to those who crouched trembling at his side. '**These ones are mine. They shall not go.**' Again he began to reach towards them with a hand of death.

'If you think to touch us beware.' Fassael's voice burnt bright as his eyes. He held up own his hand and revealed the fire burning in the centre of his palm. 'I'm not like him. I saw your like at Tabour, in the flames and at the Tower. I don't promise such a painless end.'

It hissed as if the fire had set to steam the mists of its gaze and then turned about three full turns observing all there was to see. '**What do you want?**'

'I'm going into the Castle! It holds what I seek.' There was no mistaking the determination in his words.

'**To do that, Wizard, you must first pass by me.**'

'Fine.' The sword moved like lightning parting the fabric of space, of truth, of lies and of that thing of darkness. It didn't make a sound. The cloth of its covering fell slowly earthward. 'It didn't belong here,' he proclaimed as lifting the cloth with the tip of his sword he let it slip into the darkness of the pit.

They were silent. Calin, Fassael, the goblins and those victims of the evil he had just released. They'd seen things they should never have known and known terrible things by which they should never have been touched. What was worse though was that they had heard the sound of beauty in this realm of ugliness and had felt the gift of hope awaken in their hearts.

Calin turned slowly, her eyes as a hawk's. 'We are alone.' The Wizard wasn't sure if she was pleased or not by the fact.

'What killed it?' Fassael had to know.

'Nothing. It was dead already.'

'What sent it away then?'

'Nothing really. We just weren't afraid of it anymore. It fed on fear.'

Horge had been inspecting the fallen warriors. He'd swapped his sword for one of theirs. He wasn't one to miss a chance was Horge. 'There are more of these things out there.' He pointed towards the gate. 'They'll come soon. Agh! The fight will be harder next time.'

Fassael turned to look at him. He wanted to stay with them, to protect them. He looked back towards the Wizard, to Calin, back to the goblins.

The Wizard saw too and knew the battle raging in the giant's mind. He, however, saw an answer. 'You must guard the gate, Fassael. Calin and I will go on. You must guard it until our return.'

Once more Fassael looked between the Wizard and Calin. 'Guard the Gate?'

'When we return the way must be clear.'

Fassael was silent. Perhaps he felt that they were offering him an escape. Perhaps the guard was needed. Perhaps... He asked the forbidden question. 'And what if you don't return? What then?'

'It changes little, Fassael. You're needed here. Besides, you've new charges now. If, as you ask, we don't return then take them to safety. Take them to where the sun still shines.' As if to punctuate his words the sky brightened and for but an instant he was even bathed in the morning's golden light. It was but an instant though. 'You could go no further here, Fassael. That thing was not the worse.'

'What will you do?' Fassael-Icicle had to know.

'We'll do as we always intended to do,' Calin again answered. 'We'll enter the enemy's lair.'

'And then?'

The Wizard reached out and stilled Calin's reply with a gentle touch of his hand. 'And then, Fassael-Fireborn, I'll do as I must.' The last words were bitter and hard as stone, a stone which glowed with a spectrum of wonder in its brittle hardness. 'After all, I am the Wizard of Rainbows.'

At that Fassael even managed a smile. 'Yes you are.' There could be no other reply.

Resting upon the stone step before the iron door, which led into the Tower, *The way will be down not up*, the Wizard and Calin watched Fassael distribute the few weapons they could find amongst his now growing group. 'We're not done yet,' he told them. 'But, if we can survive, I do know the way to safety.'

They gathered close to him as sheep about a shepherd. He would protect them.

'What about...' It was the young woman who spoke. The first he'd freed. Her eyes were on the Wizard and her look of concern brought a frown to her face.

He stood again and walked over to her, took her hand and raised it to his lips. 'My child,' for so she seemed to him, 'If you can ask such a question in a place like this then it matters not about me. But for you I'll answer. I've come seeking my love. She lies, as a prisoner, somewhere in this dark place. I'll not leave her here.' He wiped away the tear that formed in the corner of her eye. 'Don't fear for me. I know where I am and I know the dangers before me just as I know my own nature. I'm not afraid.'

'Take care of them, Fassael. They're a gift of life.' He walked up the steps to stand before the door. 'Come, Calin.' He turned, not awaiting her reply and pushed open the door.

When the white-gull cries for freedom,
or blooms the last rose, out of season,
When the call of caring wakes me,
when the fear of feeling, takes me,
When the pain of parting rakes me,
When the Shattered-Rainbow breaks me.
I shall find peace,
Alone.
Upon the Sunset-Sands.

(From: The Song of the Sunset Sands)

Chapter Thirteen - The Passages of Doom

It should have creaked. After all it was that kind of door, made of solid oak, with iron hinges, studs and a great dragonhead ring handle. Instead it opened with silent, deceptive ease and closed the same behind them. It was dark beyond, as he'd known it would be but not dark enough so they couldn't see even with the door shut.

Calin stood guard with her Sanain-sword drawn while the Wizard conducted a brief search in the gloom. He found a torch nestling in a bracket beside the door. A tinderbox sparked and soon the room was lit in the flame's yellow glow. He looked about once more.

They were in a hallway, dusty and dour as was only to be expected. Stairs reached upward, a great winding span of black marble, once shining but no more. However, he'd already chosen against that way and so turned to face the darker choice regarding which of the four doors, two on either side of the stairs, they should take. *One of these then?* He walked over and opened the nearest. It led to a simple chamber, empty save for a dust-laden table, even darker than the entrance-hall. The next opened into a long passageway, the third to another small room. The last was locked. *This way?* He paused. *No, the passage is best. Passages lead somewhere.* 'We'll go this way,' he informed the Sanain.

She nodded. 'I go first.' That was her place. She dropped her round-shield to her arm and clipped the sword's scabbard into place. She'd not sheath the blade again until the matter was over. She too looked about and sensed the nature of her surroundings. Then, as she'd said, she walked over and opened the door.

The air was stale here, stale with the dampness of the Darkling-Forest's migrated grey-moss. The floor was slick with moisture too. *No matter.*

They walked cautiously forward into the gloom. It took some fifty time-pained paces to reach the next door. He'd counted every one of them, an exercise to calm his beating heart. Everything else was silent.

This door opened easily too and they entered the chamber beyond. It was vast, so much so the light of the torch barely reached the arching ceiling. There were windows too, the glass cracked and dirty. Not that there was any real light anyway, but enough to see. The once fine tapestries covering the wood-panelled walls were rotten now. Their ripped and frayed remnants hung thick with cobwebs. The sense of ages past ruled and recalled a time when decay had yet to blight all which was beautiful. That was long ago now though, too long for more than an echo of what had been to remain.

He went to the table. Its dark stained surface was hacked and split, as were the sixteen chairs set about it. The thick, dour-grey dust covered everything. Sometime someone had laid it out for a banquet, one never held. This too was shrouded in a dust-grey gown of web. It seemed sad such an effort would go to waste.

Calin stopped, crouching but slightly, her sword held as a shining needle before her. She was ready to fight and the Wizard knew it. He'd known too the touch of cold grey eyes from the moment he entered the hall but he'd chosen to ignore them until ready. When he did look up he met the stare of the goblin slouched upon a huge carved throne at the far end of the hall. Cold grey eyes were they, eyes that didn't blink even when the Wizard's gaze touched them.

It was big, perhaps nearly as big as Fassael, and both its plate armour and the great sword, resting across its knees, looked to be free of rust. They waited, all three, unmoving as the tension about them grew. One of the great moths fluttered about the torch. There came a hissing of burnt wings. Nothing else moved.

'Agh!' It spat with casual dismissal. 'You got past the Gyslah then.'

The thing in the courtyard? 'It didn't belong here. I sent it away.'

The goblin's eyes widened for an instant. 'Agh! Good. It was a horrid fuckin' thing. They all are. Still, not many could have done it. Agh! Who are you?'

'Me? I'm called the Wizard of Rainbows. And you?'

'I've been waiting for you.' The tension grew again.

'You have?' He wasn't surprised.

'They said you'd come. I thought I'd hang about to see if they was right. Agh! I've never met a Wizard before. Never killed one either.' The words came as no surprise.

'I take it that you're about to try.' Calin breathed her challenge.

The grey eyes shifted to her. 'Agh! I've got to go through you first?'

'You do if that's what you intend.'

The goblin shrugged.

The Wizard spoke again. 'Why?' It seemed worth asking.

'Why What?'

'Why the fighting. Why the killing?'

'Agh! Because I'm a goblin an' goblins is the enemy of men. I'm bound to The Lord-of-Mists too, Wizard. Agh! And you're his enemy. Shouldn't I kill you? It's what I do. Agh! I kill my enemies before they kill me. And, besides, if I don't, Agh! You'll probably destroy everything.' It stood, on second thoughts it was even larger than Fassael, and hefted the sword over its shoulder.

Calin moved, circled about the table to stand between them.

The Wizard stepped backwards cautiously. 'It doesn't have to...' But seeing the inevitable about to begin his voice quickly rose. 'Don't! Don't kill him!'

The goblin struck. It was fast for all its size but nowhere near as fleet as the Sanain warrior. The Great-sword cut nothing but a swath of air and clanged loud and sparking on the hall's stone flooring. The first trickle of blood oozed from a diagonal line down its cheek.

Calin crouched, circling to meet its next attack.

It came on in a rush, the great-sword once again cutting an arc through the air. The Sanain moved and the goblin's severed shoulder plate fell away. 'Fuck! You're fast.' Perhaps he even admired her for that. He even grinned as he continued to circle.

'Faster than that, goblin.' The sword became a blur surrounding her with a wall of steel. It became clear then she'd no need of her black shield. The second shoulder plate followed the first to the ground.

'Shit!' The goblin backed away. There seemed no point in trying anything. He knew he'd never even reach her.

She didn't try to follow up. 'You don't have to die, goblin.' Her words were spoken softly, not as a challenge. Then nodding towards the Wizard she added, 'He doesn't want your death, nor do I.'

The creature looked at her, saw, despite her words, the certainty of its death in her eyes. Then slowly it turned its gaze back to the Wizard. The slightly innocent smile found there was just about the last thing he'd expected.

'Why do we fight, goblin?' the Wizard tried again.

'Agh! What do y' fuckin' mean?' He wasn't afraid even though he saw his own death in the flickering of the warrior-maiden's glistening blade. 'We fight. Agh! I kill you or you kill me. Agh! That's how it is.'

The Wizard sighed. 'It doesn't have to be. I mean it doesn't have to be like this. Look it's true. I really don't want to see you killed.'

'You don't want?' It was clear he couldn't understand what was happening. 'But...' The effrontery took over. 'Agh! What way of fighting is that?'

'It's my way. I bring life not death.'

'But, you've come here to destroy us. What's the fuckin difference?'

The Wizard even managed a laugh. 'No I haven't!' *But it's what they all think.* 'I've come for many things but not that. As I already said, my path's not one of destruction. It is probably true; I'll have to face my enemy before all's done but that's the Lord-of-Mists and not you. Besides, it's not my main concern at this time. What I've really come for is to find someone who's been brought and imprisoned here. I've come to set her free. I think it's likely that I'll set everything free in doing so.' *That's what The Master-Smith said anyway.* 'She was brought here to draw me. I came. That's why I'm here. Will you stand in my way?'

The Great goblin looked between him and Calin. Neither moved. It took him a long time, weighing up the possibilities. It could die here, or live. For once it chose life. 'Agh! Go where y' want. It's your bloody life. I'll not try to stop you.'

Calin's eyes remained harder than steel. 'You couldn't if you wanted to, goblin.'

The goblin snorted. The challenge remained.

'Enough! Let it end.' He spoke to both of them. 'We might never be friends but if we're not going to kill each other we might at least try to be civil. I say once again, for any who might hear me, this my path and I'll not be prevented from following it, even if it does mean our killing everyone or everything we meet.' His voice grew softer, 'But in all truth, goblin, I really don't want it to be that way.'

'Agh! I thought you'd bleedin' say something like that.' He even managed a rueful grin.

'Will you tell me where she is, The Elf-Dancer? It's her I seek. Do you know?'

'Agh! The Elf? Yes. You've come for her then? They said y' would, that you had no choice anyway. Yes I do know. They took her to the Temple.'

'Temple?'

'You'll know when y' get there, if you ever do. Agh! I ain't the only one in the place.'

'We never thought you were.' Calin also managed to smile.

'Which way?'

The goblin nodded towards the other door, the one behind the throne. 'You go down.' A thought crossed its mind. 'Agh! You know they'll be waiting for you, Wizard, don't you? They'll try to stop you and they ain't like me.'

'I expected nothing else. It changes nothing.'

It thought this matter over too. 'Good luck then. You'll fuckin' need it. Agh!'

'We may meet again, goblin.' He could read the question in its eyes. 'When I return, perhaps then.'

The goblin didn't reply. It turned and walked down the passage towards the castle-door.

'Wait,' Calin called.

It turned to look back.

'Outside, in the courtyard, a friend of ours waits,' she informed him. 'He's a man called Fassael-Fireborn. Help him if you're of a mind. He fights those who come against us.'

'What?' He couldn't believe what he heard. 'I thought y' said y' didn't want killing.'

'Trust us, goblin,' the Wizard tried. 'Some of those who fight with him are goblins. Those he fights against are not. I'm not even sure that they're living.'

It spat, knowing, only too well of what the Wizard spoke. 'Agh! I'll see.' That was enough. The door closed behind him.

They looked about the chamber once again. 'It must have been the Great Hall of the Castle,' the Wizard surmised. 'Although I think it's been a long time since anyone feasted here.' He wiped a layer of dust off of the tabletop. The cutlery was tarnished and dull, the silver platters too. 'Maybe one day...' It all seamed so sad and wasteful.

Calin had been silent for some time, watching the Wizard walk about the room. *Sure I let it live, why not? Do we always have to hate them? Fassael doesn't. He even loved a goblin, Icicle. But she died... As did Cog... As did Hadiira and Herlra-Sanain too...* Her sadness returned as a damp, dark shroud. *Do all we love have to die?* And then that terrible, unspoken thought tripped through her mind once again. *Will she? Oh God No! Not her too? Not the Wizard's love. Surely he won't have to pay that price. Could anything be worth that?* She had an answer for that too. *The Land. Will that be the price he has to pay to free the Land? God I hope not.*

'I'm glad I didn't kill him,' she confessed aloud as she put up her sword. Then, 'It's a strange journey this is. Who'd ever have thought I'd be reluctant to kill a goblin, especially one like that?' She laughed at herself, shrugging off her sadness. 'Oh well, never mind.' With the Wizard following, she crossed before the throne heading towards that other, darker doorway.

The tension grew almost palpable as Calin pulled the door wide and peered into the darkness beyond. The former passage seemed to continue onwards, reaching out into the gloom. There were noises somewhere ahead, shuffling sounds, sobbed breathing, half smothered cries of anguish, alone and sad. She could see nothing but felt the touch of dread as the darkness closed in about them. The hairs on her neck lifted. *Danger! Well it's only to be expected.* The flickering light of the Wizard's torch revealed nothing but her shining blade and the cobwebs that spluttered in the flame. They moved onwards.

*

In the castle courtyard Fassael had been busy. Once the Wizard and Sanain were inside and the door closed he knew he'd not have to wait long before trouble came. He knew too that he'd better be ready when it did. *Ready for what? ... To fuckin fight, Pillock!* She laughed humourlessly through his consciousness.

'Horge,' he called the goblin over with a beckoning hand. 'Set someone to watch the road and mount a guard on the gate. I don't want any surprises. I reckon what we already know is coming will be bad enough.'

The goblin grunted and turned away to begin organising what troops they had. Of the twenty-three there only seven, not counting the man and himself, would be any use if it came to a fight. Some of them had acted together. They'd already pulled the corpses under shelter of the cloister and covered them with cloth. *Probably better out of sight,* he told himself. *It won't stop them stinking in a bit though.* 'Agh! Who wants to stand watch?' There didn't seem much to choose between them.

'My eyes are still good,' the Elf whispered beside him. 'I'll man the watchtower.' No matter how broken his body might be, there was strength in his heart and the renewal of hope had set his spirit afire.

It seemed a good idea and Horge nodded his agreement. 'You got a name, Elf?'

'A name? It seems so long since... Yes I suppose that I have. I am Mirarriir.'

'Miirr...' His tongue tripped on the word.

'It is OK.' The elf smiled. 'Just call me Elf. That will be fine.'

With that settled the Elf limped off towards the stairway to the guard tower.

Horge sent two of the first band to shut and bar the gate. Then went himself to examine the defences.

Meantime, Fassael had two of the others search for wood. He wanted a fire. It wasn't really cold but the atmosphere of the place chilled his spirit. Icicle had never actually been here before but she knew enough of its reputation and this knowledge did nothing to ease his concerns.

The girl, she who had spoken to the Wizard, found a broom and, drawing water from the wellhead, had begun to scrub at the blood-stained paving. It seemed such a pointless act only there was a rightness to it that prevented Fassael from asking her to desist. Some of the others joined her. Maybe at this time gestures were better than nothing.

'Hey!' the Elf called from his new vantage point. 'There are more goblins coming up the road.'

'How many?' Horge asked.

'About eighty or ninety,' came the reply. 'They approach up the trail. I think they are armed.'

'I'll go.' Fassael wanted to see, to understand what was happening. They unbarred and pulled the gate open as he approached and he passed out onto the causeway. There was indeed a large band of goblins approaching and indeed they were armed and looked ready for a fight.

'Stop,' he called as they started up the incline. They came to an untidy halt. He could hear uneasy mutterings from their midst. 'Tell me,' he tried again, 'What do you want?' *Well, you've got to ask something.*

'Agh! Where's the one who killed the Greylon, the Drummer?' *Calin.*

'Why do you ask?'

'Agh! We'd rather be on her side than against her.' You could understand that. 'We reckon they (*spit*) ain't gonna let the matter rest.'

'So?'

'So we're for her. They don't mean fuck all to us. We couldn't stand up to them. Agh! If we even thought of it they'd come and fuckin' kill us. We've come to give oath to her.'

'Her name is Calin, Calin-Sanain, Alan's-Heir.' He saw their eyes widen, *Goblins don't give names, Fassael... Tough, because I ain't no goblin... I am.* Her chuckle filled him and brought a smile to his crooked mouth. 'How many have you got with you?' He'd already been counting.

'Eighty-six, and there's some twenty-odd smogs.'

Smogs?... Children... Oh. He'd not really thought about that possibility. 'OK, get them inside, just the courtyard, and then we'll try to work out what to do.' He shouted out to those inside. 'They want to join us. Open the gate.'

The way was opened once again. They marched, ordered and disciplined, past Fassael and passed inside. One remained, he who had been their spokesman.

'I'm Fassael-Fireborn,' he introduced himself. 'They, Calin-Sanain and the Wizard, have gone into the castle. I'm charged with keeping the way clear. I give the orders here.'

Their eyes locked but only for a moment. The goblin nodded his head. 'Fair enough. Agh! I'm Clan-named Drewsel. There are three Gha here. I'll name them.'

He takes your command, Fassael, Icicle informed. *The giving of names gives you power over them. His power too.*

'What of the smogs?'

'Bring them in also. I'd not want anyone living left out there.'

Drewsel shrugged as if to say, 'What the hell do smogs matter?' and, turning back towards the land, gave a shrill whistle. A group of scrambling goblin kids appeared over the roadside. They ranged from about five to twelve years of age. All were dirty and dishevelled, Fassael noted as he watched them pass by.

'Come.' He led the way and soon the gate slammed shut behind them.

The courtyard was packed now. *Well, I guess we've got our own flipping army now,* Fassael told himself. *I'd better do something to take control of the situation.* 'Right,' he called aloud, 'No one goes beyond that door,' pointing to where the Wizard had gone. 'Everywhere else needs searching. We need to know if there are any more of the Greylon here.'

He turned to the girl, still sweeping. 'Look, lass, it's a bit of a cheek, but, will you look after the goblin children? Find them somewhere to rest and if possible something to eat.'

She looked up at the huge man and smiled. 'Children? Here?'

'It seems so, although they're just the goblin kids. Will you take care of them? I don't want them falling into any harm.'

'Of course I will. Children are children after all.' She turned towards where the group had gathered. 'Come with me.' They followed her like lambs into the shelter of one of the watch-towers. She'd settle them into a room there.

Then back to Drewsel. 'Get some of your lot up onto the walls. And send some others to see if there's anything to eat about here. I reckon we're going to need some food.'

'Fassael,' Horge had approached unnoticed, 'Do you have any fire? None of us brought any flint.'

Just wait to see what they make of this then. He felt Icicle laughing with expectation. 'Don't fret, Horge. I'll sort it.' He walked over to where they'd gathered the pyre. There was an expectation building, a tension in the air. He could feel their eyes on him. The tension grew even greater as he stooped and thrust his hand into the centre and let the flame free once again. The whole world was silent save for the crackling of the now burning wood. Every eye was on him.

Drewsel walked over to stand before him. The goblin first bowed his head and then knelt on the ground actually touching his forehead to the stones. 'We'll serve you well, My Kla.' *What? ... He gives himself to you, himself and all those here. When they call you Kla it means that you own them. Don't you remember when we first...?* He smiled at the memory.

'Stand, Drewsel.' The goblin did so, even managing to retain an air of dignity. 'I am, as I said, Fassael-Fireborn. I'm no Kla, nor am I your master or you my slave. We're together here in troubled times with an enemy to fight. We'll be comrades in arms. That's enough for now.'

There came a laugh from the doorway. All eyes turned to see the great goblin framed in the opening. 'Agh! You're just as fuckin' strange as those bastards inside.' He walked over to where Fassael and Drewsel stood. 'You'll be Fassael then? She said you'd be here. Even told me your name.'

'You've got me there then. Yes I'm Fassael. Well actually, Fassael-Icicle. Are you going to tell me yours?'

'Agh! Why not?' Even though such a thing had never been before. 'I'm Drigla Clan-lord of the Zatha Tribe.'

Bugger me! Her awe filled his being. 'Your name is known, Drigla.'

The goblin laughed. 'Fuck all good it does me though. Agh! The Wizard said, if I wanted, I could fight alongside you.'

'And do you?'

Another laugh. 'Yes, Agh! It might be interesting.' A thought crossed his mind. 'You want my oath?'

'No, Drigla, I need no oath. You'll fight or not fight. It's all up to you. The Wizard and Sanain have let you live. That's good enough for me.'

'Who else have you got?' Drigla was looking about at the others. If he expected an army of seasoned warriors then he was disappointed. He probably didn't think much of those he did see either.

'I'm Drewsel, N'gha, Lord Drigla. Agh! My Gha are Korbah,' a tall but almost skinny goblin stepped from the crowd. 'Fawl,' a second, far stockier warrior, 'and Mordekt.' Fassael was surprised to see this was a female. Her eyes were no less hard than the others and as those she bowed her head to Drigla.

'Can they fight?'

Fassael, or perhaps Icicle, intervened. 'They can die.'

The Goblin snorted a laugh. 'Fair enough. We can all do that.'

The matter was interrupted again. 'Something moves.' The elf watcher called from the wall. 'I cannot quite make out what it is though.'

'Bloody hell!' The surprise in Drigla's voice was no lie. 'You've even got a bloody elf with you,' he declared as he followed Fassael towards the steps.

'We've got all sorts here, Drigla. I'll take any who want to be here.'

'Bugger me! Agh! Things are getting more interesting by the moment. I ain't ever met an elf I never wanted to kill before.'

It didn't take long before they stood looking out over the grey land. 'It's a mist of some kind,' the Elf explained. 'I thought at first it was the dust of something moving but now I'm not so sure.'

'Agh! Bollix! It's fuckin' Shevrii.'

That's an Elf word, Fassael thought. It wasn't. The look on the elf's face told that. 'What's that?'

'The Ice-mist.' There was a hint of fear in his voice. 'It's as the Greylon have been saying. The Lord-of-Mists is set to arise.'

'Does that change anything?'

'No. Agh! I want nothing more to do with them. I'll stand with you still.'

'Over there,' the Elf pointed again, 'Look.' There were shapes moving now, grey, unholy shapes, bathed in the mists that spawned them. Weapons glinted in the strange half-light.

The army of the Damned. From where the thought came, Fassael had no idea. 'I guess we'll not have to wait too long to find out.' He drew his sword and checked its fine honed edge. 'I reckon they're coming our way.' Again the madness was growing in his breast. 'Should we stay here or go out and meet them?'

'Agh! Don't reckon it fuckin' matters,' was Drigla's reply. He was right, it probably didn't.

*

It was colder here than the Wizard had expected. The awful dampness robbed the air of any warmth. His torch spluttered and half-died then flared again. Not for the first time, he reached over his shoulder to stroke the hilt of the dwarf-sword but still he left it in its scabbard. *For now anyway.*

They'd met no one, nothing, during this journey through the passages of the Castle, although the Wizard was sure they were being watched. From the darkness surrounding them the sounds of torment continued and these might well have been worse than anything chanced upon, sapping the will and lying heavy on their hearts.

Following another flight of stone steps they went on downward. It was the third since leaving the Great Hall. Calin continued to lead, stepping with caution least her feet slip on the slime.

At one point the Wizard held out his hand for support on the wall, a mistake he'd not repeat. The unwholesome liquor still cloyed to his palm despite his best efforts to wipe it away. The darkness seemed to be growing too, the loathsome humour of the place drawing life from the flame.

Down they went, down into the depths of the castle, down into the depths of the earth, below light, below life, below knowledge, below thought. All was darkness, all save that spluttering yellow flame.

Several times they'd been forced to halt, to clear away the thick strands of web blocking their way. Both hated the task, half fearing the spinners of the stuff would return to challenge them. They'd seen their eyes shining red at the edge of the flame and heard their scuttling movement in the darkness ahead.

Eventually though, they did reach the bottom of the stairwell and there entered a wider chamber, a hallway of sorts, where the opening of several passages offered a way onward. It was cleaner here, perhaps the need for the decay gone. 'This is about as far down as it goes,' the Wizard informed Calin. He didn't know how but he was sure that he was right about it.

'Which way?' Calin's voice was cold. She hated spiders, she always had. They'd know that in Niss, during her training, known it and used it to try her mettle and strengthen her spirit. She might not be afraid of them any more, she might not be afraid of anything, but still she loathed them. It's hard to focus your anger on something so inhuman. *Give me an enemy I can fight.* It's easier, cleaner that way.

He looked about hoping to find a clue, found nothing. There was sign others had been here. That was something at least but the footprints left in what remained of the dust gave no hint of where he should go. He listened. Far away something, someone screamed. From somewhere else came the sound of metal scraped on stone. A door clanged shut. A drawn out sob of pain whispered its echo down the stone walled passages.

'Wait.' He didn't know. 'Let me think. There must be a clue, some way of knowing.' Calin's eyes were on him, questioning. He tried to feel that lonesome thought, to trace her through the gloom. The taste of her lingered here as in his dreams but... *Where is she? Which way?* A wave of despair washed over him. *I've got to find her! I've got to...* There seemed so many choices, so many ways, yet only one of them would take them to her. *I've got to do something.*

To make matters worse the torch spluttered its last, died and plunged them into total darkness. 'Damn!' Calin cursed under her breath. 'That's all we bloody well needed. How are we supposed to go on if we can't even see? This is hopeless.'

From whence the thought came he didn't know. *Hopeless? No, there's always hope*, and then… *A light for when even hope fails.* At that moment it felt almost like his mother was with them. Perhaps her gift had been for a time like this. His hand fastened upon the ruby. There was comfort there at least and memories of times long passed, of home, of happiness, of peace and of love. The jewel warmed and offered its own pale gift. He smiled. *There's ever an answer in love, for me and for you, my Fairy-Dancer. I'm coming.*

He turned to Calin. 'Nothing is hopeless, Calin. See?'

She returned his smile but didn't answer him.

There came another thought too, drifting through the passages of time on secret wings. It was of Ra, the Medicine-woman's daughter back in Hereth, Ra of whom he'd not thought of for an age. *Any path that leads to where we must go will suffice*, she'd said, although he didn't understand what she meant at the time. Now though, he laughed softly to himself. 'This is my path, Calin,' he told her. 'Where my feet fall, there are my steps. It doesn't really matter which way we take. Come.'

He held up the jewel to light the gloom and took the passage before them. She followed this time. The expression on her face was of pure wonder, even though she hadn't understood a word he'd said.

The way was lined with doors here. Each set with a grilled window. The rooms inside were cold and dark, no more than cells, empty now though. But, who had they held?

Ahead a light called out to them, vague at first but brighter as they drew closer and, after several minutes more, the passage opened into some sort of anti-room, perhaps a guard-post. This place wasn't empty.

Again Calin's sword blade glistened in the light. *Is it now time for the battle to begin?*

The Wizard's hand touched her arm. 'Wait.'

Seated on a stone bench was a man. He was dressed in grey, cowl-hooded, priest-like and filled with his own nameless power. At his feet a young woman sat slumped in a dejected heap. She too was dressed in grey, the tired grey of despair and hopelessness. However, about her neck on a slender chain hung a small, bright, butterfly-pendant that caught the ruby glow of the Wizard's gem and seemed to fly free in the flickering light caused by his movements.

As the Wizard stepped forward into the halo of the Priest's torch eyes touched him, a mind of power also, cold and heartless power. It wasn't evil, as one might have expected it to be. Rather this Priest seemed to possess no feeling at all, as if emotions were too trivial for his lofty concerns. The Butterfly-girl felt empty, as if her spirit, too afraid to exist in such a place, had fled and now lay hidden in some dark recess of her being.

Very slowly the Priest stood. No word was spoken as he walked forwards, nor when he stopped before the Wizard, just beyond arm's reach. They looked at each other; not in challenge but nonetheless they assessed each other's power. The Priest's gaze followed the Wizard's, noting with disinterest when this newcomer's eyes touched upon his pathetic charge. 'She is of no account.' Words no less hard than the voice that spoke them.

'Who is she?' It seemed a place to begin. There were truths and lies here, games of power to trap the unwary.

'She has faced the Void that is the Lord-of-Mists. In doing so she lost the truth of her own nature in the vastness of his being.'

'And you?'

'I am the Silent-Singer.' It was a strange and unknown name. 'I serve in the Temple-of-Emptiness. I am the Priest-of-Emptiness.' He probably was, for so it felt. *The Temple of Emptiness? Of the Void? The Temple of The Lord-of-Mists?* 'It's to the Temple I go, we go.' *He's a Priest of Emptiness. Does he also serve the Lord-of-Mists?*

'So I understand.' His disinterest still ruled.

'It's said I'll find who I seek, the Elfin-Dancer, within that Temple. It's also said that she was taken there to draw me.'

'Yes, so it is said.'

'Are you here to help or hinder us?' He had to ask.

'Neither. I but serve in the Temple and sing my songs of silence.'

'And her?' he asked again of the Butterfly girl. 'What of her?' *She's as empty as his heart.*

'As I said, she is of no account.'

If she's of no account, why is she here? 'Will you let her go? Will you let her return to the land of her kind?' The wrongness of this situation was beginning to sit as bile in the Wizard's breast.

'Let her go?' The idea seemed meaningless. 'Whatever for? She is nothing.'

'Nonetheless,' he continued. 'Will you?'

The cold eyes fixed on the Wizard, held him in their grasp. 'Do you come to challenge me?' the Priest asked at last. This time there might even have been a spark of interest in his voice.

He'd wondered the same. *Shall I free her with the fires of my Rainbows?* But, 'No, I mean no challenge. I, as I assume you realise, am the Wizard of Rainbows. My magic is not for battles and destruction and that's what I believe such a challenge would bring.' *Does he want such a battle?* 'No. It's just that I see a great sadness here, an echo of what should not be.' He turned fully to face the girl. She seemed so lost, so hopeless. 'And I'd like to seek a way to find what she's lost, so she might be set free. Thus I ask, set her free. Let her go. Let's see if she can escape her own doom.'

'She cannot.' It sounded so final.

'Then you've nothing to lose.'

'True,' he considered the matter. 'Neither have I anything to gain.'

In the passage opening behind the Wizard, Calin was beginning to grow uneasy. There were things close by now. She'd heard the sound of a carefully placed foot, the rustle of cloth. Her eyes glistened with expectation and her anger began to rise. *They'll wait until the Priest has had his say*, she realised, then turned her attention back to what was transpiring in the room.

Why now? There was no real answer to that. Perhaps it was simply the meaning of the Wizard's own words, that and the reality of his own nature. *Because my magic isn't of battle but of life, of life and creation and of growth. Perhaps that, in part at least, is the answer. That I've come not in a blaze of wild magic but with the gentleness of spring. Long ago I chose not to kill. And this remains my way. Yes this, I am sure, is the truth of my rainbow.*

This time he didn't resist the pull of power as his magic began to grow. It was, as he intended, a gentle thing this waking of power, a thing of light and beauty, nothing of the terrible energies that were so often bound within his rainbows. From the memory of all that was lovely in the lands of men, of the gentle light of the Elswood, the golden gift of the desert, the vast openness of the great grasslands, even the awe inspiring majesty of the Mountains-of-the-Divide, he took a simple crystal and bound his vision into the form of a single glistening jewel.

The Priest's eyes were on him. Now at last there came a touch of true interest. 'If she fails, Priest. If she fails then this will belong to you.'

'And if she succeeds?'

'It'll belong to her.'

'Will you aid her?' It was acceptance.

'If I can. It's through the jewel that I'll try.'

The Priest slowly nodded. Maybe the light of the jewel still flickered in his eye. Maybe it even shone in his heart.

The Wizard moved slowly, walking over to kneel on the floor before where she sat. She didn't move nor even flinch when he placed his hand under her chin and lifted her face to see her eyes, such distant, empty eyes, clear as the blue of cornflower blossom. She remained just as still when he lifted the jewel before her face and let its sparkling rainbows pass over those eyes.

From wherever she hid, the light of his magic called to her. When she heard that call and looked into the light of the sparkling gem she saw the mirror he'd set in its heart, a whirling point of wonder. There wasn't, could never be, such a thing in this place. She knew only too well. She'd seen the emptiness reaching forever, lost herself in the barrenness of unending nothingness. Now she had seen it though and she was drawn as a moth to a flame and her spirit flew on gossamer wings towards the light. She knew she'd never let go of this beauty again, no not now. Her eyes followed the light, even when he moved the jewel and placed it in her hand. She saw her own being reflected in the gem's beauty and thus knew, in its honesty, she was no less lovely. How could that be?

She lifted her eyes to those of the Wizard who knelt before her and saw that same beauty reflected there. She swallowed. A tear trickled over her cheek. 'It's beautiful.'

He said nothing but took her hand and helped her to stand.

She even managed to look about herself then, seeing the cold grey ugliness that surrounded her, the Priest, the Wizard and the black-clad warrior-maid who stood at the entrance to the chamber. It was no wonder that confusion filled her moment. 'What? Who?' But the light still turned in her mind and she looked once again at the jewel in her hand. 'What should I do?' It was unclear to whom she was speaking.

'Whatever you choose,' the Wizard replied softly. 'The jewel is yours, yours to cherish.'

'Yes.' Even the Priest accepted that now.

For a time she was still. She turned her head slowly looking about the chamber. Perhaps something of her memory returned, something of the horror and despair that ruled this place. 'I've been here too long. I don't belong here.' There was no longer any doubt of that. 'No. I shan't stay.' Once more she looked at the jewel in her hand. 'Yes, I'm going.'

Surprisingly the Priest walked over and held out his hand to her. 'I'll show you the way to the door.' He spoke quietly too. 'Perhaps I've been here too long also.'

Their eyes met and, after a moment, she smiled and took that offered hand. 'You did me no harm. You did me no good. You were here though, so at least you know. Yes, I think it's time we both left this place and found again what of life remains.' And to the Wizard: 'Thank you.'

Calin stood aside as they walked past.

The Priest stopped, turned. 'I truly hope that we never meet in combat Wizard.' He didn't wait for a response but turned back and led her away.

Calin walked forwards now. 'You used your magic.'

'It's what it's for, Calin.'

'But they'll know you're here now.'

He laughed aloud and drew the Dwarf-Sword. 'So they will. So they do.' It didn't seem to matter at that moment.

The attack was instant, three grey warriors, each from a different side passage, moved to surround them. However both Calin and the Wizard were ready. The Sanain-sword sang of War. The Dwarf-sword sang of Truth. The first died silent, unaware it even faced death in the black clad figure before it. The second's own weapon shattered to the Wizard's cathedral chime and its wielder fell back in surprise before fleeing. The third met Calin's with a skill to match hers, yet it too fell in the fury of her anger.

Others came but seconds after. They moved like snakes, silent and deadly. They died like snakes too, silent and permanently. Calin smiled again as she stepped over their bodies. 'There, they know I'm here too now.' That smile was terrible indeed.

There were more cells here, cold loathsome cells. Their doors hung open as a sign. *No doors are needed here now. But where are they all gone?* He knew with a terrible sense of horror. *The Pit. The Awakening.*

Cobwebs once again hung as lifeless shrouds. It was as a mausoleum, still, dank, dark. They moved on together, for the way was not narrow and the Wizard's ruby lit the way.

There were other attacks, things coming from the darkness. Some were terrible things of fire and madness. Others were colder than death. She met them with her own replies and, with the Wizard, carried on. These were frantic, deadly affairs but none ever came near to threatening. In his heart though the Wizard knew without his Sanain guard he would have never made it through. *For this I thank the Lady,* and *did she even know of this dread path?* It was a thought to muse upon.

They came to stop before a huge door, the ring of its great iron handle as big as many a man's shield. On closer inspection he discovered the whole thing was made of iron, forged in some unimaginable foundry. It felt cold to the touch, ice cold, death cold, so cold that the Wizard jerked his hand away in horror. *I can't stop here,* he told himself, *I've come too far for that now. She's near I can sense her.* But, despite that thought and despite the hope driving him, he still hesitated. His spirit all but recoiled from the prospect of reaching for that handle a second time. Drawing the dwarf sword he rang it against the iron. The purity of its chime was dulled, lost in the loneliness of the place yet surrendered no secrets. The door was no more than it seemed and that was terrible enough.

There came a rushing of footfalls behind them, more of the cold grey warriors. Calin was fighting again; bodies were falling. 'Quick!' she gasped, 'Get it open. More of them are coming. If they've got bows we'll be done for.' As if to punctuate her words an arrow skittered across the floor-slabs. A second thudded and hung quivering on the face of her shield for a moment before she snapped it off.

He half wondered if his fingers would freeze on the iron when he took hold of that ring. Then, if he would even have the strength to turn a catch that big. *Is this a thing for my magic?* It wasn't. At first the ring wouldn't turn. He twisted with all his strength without success. Then, using his hawthorn staff as a lever, he tried again. Even so it took all of his strength to move the lock. Metal squealed, rust-raw and angry to be disturbed. He pushed, 'It's open!' and threw himself inside. Calin was with him, helping him to slam the door shut again. CLICK! They lent against it, panting.

Things crashed against the door, swords or stones or… That was a matter for Calin though. She crouched beside the door still breathing heavily from her exertions. Her eyes were wide but the sword in her hand didn't waver. 'I'll hold the door.' Her words were punctuated by the clamour outside. 'Do as you must!'

He heard her words but didn't respond, for he had other things on his mind. Now he must turn to see just where it was they'd entered. The darkness beyond that cold iron door was not of light or its absence. The dark was of Evil. It bit at the soul, sent screaming even the thought of bravery.

However, it was not bravery that drove the Wizard forward but a single burning awareness. *She's near.* He knew it louder than the horror, louder than his fear even louder than the emptiness, which dragged at his every movement.

At first he could see nothing. Nothing save the faintest glow from the ruby at his neck. *In the darkest places shall this bring light.* The words were like a mantra and the memory of her love filled the jewel again. The place seemed to be a temple of sorts, perhaps a shrine or chapel to evil. *The Temple-of-Emptiness? of the Lord-of-Mists?* Its vast vaulted ceiling reached high over him, stone arches, barely visible, though their shadows almost shouted of hidden dangers. There was a torch, unlit, left lying on the stone floor. He went to it and picked it up. The tinderbox wouldn't strike here. Frustrated by his failure at even this simple task he turned away.

Perhaps daylight, far beyond the grey-stone walls, sent a gift. Maybe it was some other thing, good or ill, for it seemed as if the light grew brighter. It wasn't much, not much at all, but enough to see the sickly blooded floor. His eyes tracked the dark stain, touched upon the even darker stone of the altar set at the centre of the chamber.

He lifted his eyes, following the shadows of blackness. *What is it?* The fear in his heart cried out in shards of broken ice. His whole body seemed ready to deny the truth of what he now saw.

There's something on the Altar!

He moved reluctantly forward but he couldn't, dare not, dare not know what it was, who it was but his feet carried him all the same. Tears were streaming over his cheeks as he looked down at her stricken form. They'd lain her there to wait for him. *So still, so pale.* Blood now matted her glorious copper hair, crusted in obscene globules upon her brow and her cheeks. He'd known in his heart they'd never let him come to her, never let him take her from their grasp. For a moment the magic swelled inside him. *NO! I'll not give them that. Not like this.* He bowed over her, kissed her cheek with tender...

She's warm!

And that was even more shocking than his fear. Slowly, scared his first thought might be false, he reached out and touched her hand. It was cold, that was true, but not the chill of death. *It's true. She's still alive!* He lent close enough to feel the feather-light touch of her breath on his cheek.

'Calin,' his voice seemed lost in the space between them. 'I've found her. She lives.' But Calin's attention was no longer on him or his words. In the darkness beyond they beat at the door, pushed at it in their eagerness to fight.

'Luminae,' he spoke her name, his secret name. 'Luminae, it's me. I'm here. I've come.' There was no response, not even the flickering of an eye. 'Wake up.' He tried but she didn't stir. He looked again at her blood-caked face. *Is she wounded?* Closer inspection showed no sign of any. The dread in his heart began to grow as he realised there was meaning in the form of the blood. *What have they done?* There were words and signs, meaningless to his eye and all the more terrible for it. *The blood's not hers.* It was a sigil of sorts, some kind of enchantment.

'Where are you?' he whispered, to her and to himself, stroking her hair. 'Where have they sent you?' *Where indeed?*

There came a jarring clang, stealing his attention for an instant. At the door Calin was struggling. Forms, grey and vague tried to force their way through. They didn't make it. Not this time.

He was at a loss as to what he might do. There was nothing for him to fight here, not even if his magic woke. There was nothing here save the Silent-dancer, himself and Calin. The Sanain, he knew, could do nothing more than defend them. Surely that was task enough.

He sat on the edge of the black stone and tried to think. It didn't come easy, especially with the struggle taking place so near. However, far more compelling than even that was the dreadful hunger of the stone that filled his every awareness with its endless craving for power. It was, as Icicle's black dagger had been, a thing of power itself, dark and fell. He knew that power, saw through its terrible history that this also was part of the endless struggle and in this he even felt a measure of familiarity. Yes, he understood this much of its nature at least. And he denied it its desire. Things of the present were more pressing than the hunger of its ten-thousand-year-old greed.

He reached out to take hold of her tiny hand, held it gently as he tried to think. It helped. *Where is she? Where have they taken her? Where am I for that matter?* He looked about again. There was nothing more to see. 'We're in the Castle of the Lord-of-Mists,' he spoke aloud hoping, maybe, that would help. Maybe it would shut out the din of Calin's struggle. 'The Lord-of-Madness, the Lord-of-lies. What more should I expect? I was here before so I ought to have known... Well no, it wasn't here exactly. It was a dream then. Now it's true.' *True? Is anything ever true?* He almost laughed at that thought. *Not here anyway. Nothing is true in this place. It's all lies and... and... we were asleep then. Asleep, yet we came. Is that where she is?* The recognition of this truth became real to him. *That's it! That's exactly where she is.* And the dreadful knowledge too... *It's where the Lord-of-the-Void waits also, where he waits for me to come!* And now, at last, he knew the way he must follow.

Nonetheless, before taking this path, he paused, brought out his water flask from the satchel and bathed her face. *I'll not leave her with that blood on her. Not that.* He combed her hair with his fingers; lay it, fanned out in a halo of glory, over the black stone's surface. She was here, near enough to touch, to stroke, yet not here at all. He leant over her and kissed her lips.

'You'd better do something soon, Wizard. I don't know how much longer I can hold them,' Calin called from the door. Words punctuated by the sound of hammering beyond.

She was right. It was up to him. He was alone, as he'd always known he would be when the time came.

'Calin,' he explained. 'I'm going to her, going down a path where you can't follow. Protect me. Protect her. He sat on the alter beside her, then lay beside her, his head by her head, his arm by her arm, his hand by her hand. He took that hand realising that he was not quite so alone as he'd thought. He could feel her life now, weak, afraid, barely hanging on to its own nature. That thread of life was as a trail to follow. He closed his eyes and sought the way…

*

He stands in the same room, can even see himself lying beside her still, silent body. Calin is there too, watching the doorway, sword drawn. She shines pure as crystal, a million facets of shimmering life, so beautiful he almost reaches out to touch her. But that's not why he's here.

He looks down at the Dancer once again. She's no less lovely than Calin. From her heart he can see the thread of her life, fragile as time. *I'll follow this.* And he takes up the image of his staff. *This is no strange thing,* he tells himself. *I dream. Shouldn't I choose those things which make me who I am?* So he turns from the altar, following the tenuous strand of her thought, following wherever it might lead him.

He walks as were he and the Castle about him real. The dream-door opens with but a thought and he passes into the darkness beyond. The grey things that wait, crushed up against the door, are no more real than he. The horror of their vile nature repels him all the same. There is fear in his heart and caution in his step. He knows only too well that this dream is not of his making but a part of another's dark plan. *What snares are set here to trap me?*

There are steps, downward, for him to follow *ever down* and, as in the Castle when they came, they are dark and un-trodden, web hung too but by what strange thing? The ruby at his breast glows bright here though, bright enough to see. *A light for when other lights might fail.* Several times he halts, forcing himself to clear a path through the cobwebs. He hates the task, fearing lest the spinners come to challenge him. He can see them scuttling away from his light, huge things, black and shiny, back to where their mistress waits midst her webs of evil. Their eyes shine, with the sour green of her envy, in the darkness.

At the foot of these stairs stands a circle of cold black stones; not Earth-Stones nor of their ilk, but horrendous guardians of the way. And through that circle his feet take him into the places beyond. Places where tormented souls scream out for peace, where cruel and heartless creatures deny them even the silence of death.

He takes a path of fire, dark fire that blazes with midnight and pain. If it burns him he has no awareness of it. If it shows him visions of torment he does not see them.

He follows a passage cutting through vast cliffs where screaming banshees shriek out their endless, echoing cries. He denies their warnings and their curses. He has other things on his mind.

He walks through a forest of dust, where the trees reach out to grab at his life with rotten wooded fingers. Even these he passes by, though saddened by their decay.

In the midst of a vast plain the grey tower stands alone. *Yes, I guess that's how I should've expected it to be.* That it reminds him of the Tower of Tabour is but an insult to all that has passed before. The gate is open, the courtyard empty, for now. The passages lie silent. He knows the way…

He comes, at last, to another door. *One of the mind?* A door through which none may return. He turns aside. *This isn't my way, not the way to her.*

Then a second door blocks his path. *Those who pass this way seldom return.* He turns aside once again.

Then a third, and perhaps this is the most terrible door of all. It's the one he knows he must take, the one through which she has gone.

He knows this door. *I've passed through this before.* Its cold iron handle is no less daunting this time, though it opens with little but the touch of his mind. Once again he moves into that Temple, the same temple, and sees the same terrible altar of stone.

She's here, as he'd known she'd be, sitting cross-legged upon the black stone staring at nothing with empty, sightless eyes.

But this isn't the same Temple at all. It never could be, for he has entered into the domain of the Lord-of-Mists, the realm of the Creatures-of-the-Void. There is nothing here at all, nothing to see, nothing to feel. There is no hot nor cold, no light nor darkness, no substance and no time, no time and no change. There's nothing, nothing but he, the cold black altar and she.

He approaches. 'I have come.' But she doesn't respond.

'**Why have you come?**'

He starts to turn as the words wash over him, oh so slowly. It's here just as he'd known it would be. It's massive, greater than anything in the universe it fills, and all of it is empty. He feels its power now, its power and its anger, its greed and its terrible impotence. He can't look. To do so would be to lose everything and he knows the truth of this only to well.

He turns his back to it and gazes at his love instead. 'I've come for her.' Even the words are hard to form and lost in the silence as they are spoken.

'**Yes! You have come for her.**' Is it mocking him?

'She shouldn't be here.'

'**Nonetheless, here she is.**'

'I intend to take her from here.'

'**As you already know, Wizard, that was always the intention.**'

He thought over the words. *Truths and lies.* 'This I do know. Your intentions were many as were your plans. It's also true that I have come as you planned it. Yet

I'm not here to do your bidding. I've come as I said. I've come for her. Will you try to stop me?'

The Lord-of-Mists laughs, bitter and cruel. '**You have grown, Wizard. Both in power and in knowledge. So I too shall ask my question. Will you try to prevent me from leaving this place?**'

'And if I do?'

'**Then I shall slay her. This is my domain, my Kingdom.**'

'And then I'll destroy you.' It's no idle threat. They both know it.

'**Will you try to stop me from leaving? Will you seek to destroy me with your power?**'

'I don't wish to use my magic.'

'**Then you cannot save her.**' Words that sound so final.

'We'll see.' He looks down at darkness of the stone altar. 'You know who I am as I know you and your true nature. You are strong and evil and filled with the very essence of the Void. Yet I can tell you this. If you try to hinder me, to prevent me from leaving with her, then indeed I'll awaken the power of my magic. The power I hold at the centre of my being now. That truth you know also.'

'Shall I loosen the full beauty of my rainbows? Shall I fill your emptiness with may rainbows of infinity? Do you think you could stand against that? Do you think your Void, your emptiness, your nothingness could exist in the light of my Vortex?'

There is no weakening to the power of the thing. '**Why should I want to prevent you from leaving with her? Is that not my plan?**' Then, gloating over every word, it explains. '**This is, as you well know, a dream Wizard, a dream that traps us all. For her it is a dream in which she shall dwell forever unless you can awaken her, unless you break the bond of that dream. Dare you? For, until that dream is broken, nothing can leave this prison of emptiness, not even you. And, only your magic can free the way, Wizard of Rainbows. Shall you use your Magic and free us all?**'

'So, that's the price that must be paid.' He understands well enough. 'It's as the Dwarf said. Through my magic the barrier shall be broken?'

'**That bond and many another. As she saved you with her dance-of-fire, so you can now save her with your limitless rainbows.**' It is triumphant. '**Shall you?**'

He pulls on her hand, draws her towards him until she slides from the altar and stands, barefoot on the floor beside him. 'It's what I intend.'

'**The other problem is, Wizard,**' its hideous laughter fills the void, echoing, '**that even if you do awaken her, you must first find your way back!**' It's gone and only the empty, eternal threat remains.

They are alone, totally alone, stranded in emptiness. He reaches out to her, takes her hands in his own and looks into the fathomless pools of her eyes. He kisses her brow. 'I'm here, my love. I'm here.'

'There is nothing... nothing... nothing.'

Her sadness is more awful than even the emptiness of the Lord-of-Mists' evil. It burns in his breast as if he had wounded her with his being. 'I'm here, my gentle Luminae. Can't you see me?'

'I can see nothing. There is nothing to see... nothing...'

'Listen,' he tries, 'Listen. It's me. Can't you hear me?'

'I can hear nothing... There is nothing to hear... nothing...'

He leans forward to place a kiss on her oh so cold lips. 'Can't you feel me?'
'I can feel nothing… There is nothing to feel…'
'But what of love? Can't you even feel my love?' He answers his own question in the waking of his magical flower. Again it's not a thing of power, nor a thing of energy but of beauty, beauty and love…
'What of Love?'

> *Love's a red which begins as the sun on the sand.*
> *And which grows in the world as the gift of the Land.*
> *It's an orange that feels with much more than the hand*
> *The gift of desire and the gift of the Land*
> *It's a yellow so bright to enfold where you stand*
> *To fill you with life and the gift of the land.*
> *It's a green that you'll know. It is yours to command*
> *From the whole of my heart and the gift of the land.*
> *It's a blue which resounds through creation grand*
> *To sing of your beauty, the gift of the land*
> *In indigo light you shall see as I planned.*
> *As a light in your soul and the gift of the land.*

Thus he spins his first rainbow. It is for her and her alone. If you wonder about the violet, don't be troubled. It's there also, bound in the mystery of his understanding and in the rose he sets in her glorious copper hair.

However, such beauty cannot, when all is said and done, exist in the Void. It cannot be and yet it is. And the very paradox of its beauty opens the way back to him. She follows that way, follows that light, just as bright and shining as his rainbows of everything.

Her eyes open, she looks at him, sees him, knows him. 'The gift of the Land?'
'The gift of life, the gift of love.'
She looks about. Eyes, seeing nothing, grow wide with fear. Her scream of terror echoes through the emptiness that surrounds them. 'There is no life… There is nothing at all.'
'Come,' he tells her softly, knowing she hears him.
Yet in her eyes there is a fear beyond his imagination. It is as if she stands alone and terrified in the centre of Hades. 'But there is nothing here, nowhere to go. I'll be lost forever…'
He reaches out to her.
'Take my hand,' he whispers.
'I am afraid.'
'Take my hand. I'll not harm you.'
'It is not safe.'
'Take my hand,' he asks again. 'Trust me.'
'How can I trust you?'
'Ah but how can you not? Will you not trust me? For I am the Wizard of Rainbows, your Wizard of Rainbows.' And those that he cast were Rainbows in which the nature of his love for her ever sang. 'And you are Luminae, my own sweet Fire-Dancer. Wouldn't I come to be with you? And where shall we be? Where shall we dwell? Where shall we dance to the morning?'

In the Halls of my mind
In the chambers of my heart
In the wonder of my being
In the glory of my love
There shall you dance forever.

Slowly tentatively she reaches out to take his offered hand and he leads her back through the paths of their dreaming.

Beyond the Tower the plain is endless. There is nothing here, least of all the knowledge of where to go. Even the thread of their lives seams lost in this vast emptiness. Where shall he go?

Suddenly they are alone no more. There are beings here, things of the Void, grey and formless and filled with their endless emptiness. They come at the pair lashing out with weapons of hate and death. But they are nothing. His magic erupts as a burning star, a bright shield of living against their eternal anger. For a third time the tendrils of reality, ever fragile, are ripped asunder, not by the power of his magic but by its gentleness. Even these things of decay know it and are stilled.

Yet, perhaps this stillness is worse than their violence, their wonder more terrible than their hate. For in the silence of their withdrawal the Wizard and his love are alone, totally, endlessly and the blanket of grey lifelessness that surrounds them is a blanket of sorrow that smothers their last vestige of hope.

There is nothing to see, nothing to feel, nowhere to go. They stand looking about themselves for an answer... There is none. Things such as answers, or even questions have no meanings. Nothing has any meaning... They are lost...

Now, unexpectedly, in the depths of his soul comes a chiming as of his own nature and he knows that vibration only too well from the every hammer fall of its crafting. He knows too, in the echoes of his spirit, where its chiming lies. Back he goes, following the trails of his own life. She clings to his hand as were he the only thing in existence. At that moment he probably is. Back they go, back through the conflagrations of time and space...

In the lifeless avenues of the forest the trees sigh, with memories of lost springs and endless autumns, in the wind of their passing.

In the grey passage through the vast cliffs the banshees, having seen the glories of his wonder, shriek no more. They hide, ashamed of their pointless haunting.

The paths of fire are nothing now for his touch cools them in the beauty of his midnight, heals them with the breath of his rainbow of life.

Even the Halls of Hades grow still, so not to trouble their passing.

They come to the guarding-circle. Its stones reflect the beauty of his rainbows on every facet. They too shine with that same wonder, no longer menacing nor defiant. In their shadow there grows a tiny forget-me-not, startlingly blue in the darkness.

Not even the Web-mistress, or her spinning disciples, can delay them. For he matches her spite with a beryl purity that even their cobwebs shy away from his coming.

*

The Wizard was not the only one to fight his battle during this dark time. Calin had known the instant he left her. The loneliness was like a bolt of pain, a pain which ever burnt over her loss of Cog. And it was a pain that flamed her anger and fuelled her fight.

She fought well indeed did Calin-Sanain-Alan's-Heir, fought as only Sanain might. Although her enemies were many and dour indeed she stood against them. However, inch-by-inch, they managed to force the great door ajar and propped it open with their corpses. Yet still she fought on and their bodies piled high in the doorway.

They had no fear, these grey things of horror, no fear and no doubt and they met the biting blade of her sword with a carelessness beyond imagination, at least six of them in the first struggle.

Others would come and she knew it. She'd be unable to prevent them from entering now with the door wedged open. *No matter.* The shield sat easily on her arm. The Sanain sword was light and sharper than thought and her anger was a fury greater than any fear they might hope to create.

But only just. A lone figure stepped over the fallen and entered through into the chamber. She knew the face of this one, and the lies that drove it towards her. 'Cog,' she whispered the name, for thus it seemed to be. Cog death-struck yet living, his mouth gaping with the lies of their deceits. Her spinning sword-dance spared neither him nor her and her anger was as a crucible of fury when she thrust her blade where the troll's spear had struck before. It's true tears glistened wet on her cheeks, but still she did as she had to do.

Shimmian came next, laughing with his horrid, lifeless insanity. And fell next also.

More came as in some horrid parody of those she had known. Her sister Sanain, as if returned from their graves amongst the grasses of Tabour, came now to trouble her with the cold pointlessness of their deaths. Though she cried out in the grip of an almost overwhelming sorrow she fought on and stayed not her sword, not even from the Sevriet Taiir who came, broken limbed, into the fray. Then came those she had slain in the course of her life. They came with their accusations and their hunger for vengeance. Some who came were skilled in fighting, others not. It probably didn't matter. They fell the same…

And they rose again the same also… She screamed as she fought now. You could expect nothing else. It was the true waking of her nightmare. Backing away, her sword still spinning its web of steel about her, she tried to contend with what was. They came with her also, circled her, surrounded her, the altar with her charges also. One lifted a great cleaver over the Elf-maid. The creature fell before it could strike but it would not be the last to try.

Panic filled her thoughts at that moment. She couldn't fail! *I need something to give me an edge, something to stop them. The Wizard's sword! It slays them!*

She didn't pause in her fight but her shield was sent flying into their midst and suddenly she faced them with two glittering swords. Instinctively she knew the worth of the Wizard's blade even before she brought it down in that long blinding arc. No one could have expected the shock of the contact though, least alone the Sanain-fighter. The grey warrior's weapon shattered into blackened shards but that was the least of it. Every weapon in the chamber rang to that chiming, resounding with the truth bound in the sword's dwarven blade. They crumpled, each one who had before risen to fight again. They would rise no more. Those remaining fell back in the face of a new terror.

Yet even this was not all. The temple had begun to grow light, light and bright as day, even brighter. She turned to look at the figures asleep on the altar. They were afire, shining with the full wonder of the eternal rainbow, which lay at the heart of the Wizard's being.

That the Warriors-of-the-Mist fled didn't matter now any more than the tears Calin shed for the wonder before her. For the Wizard had opened his eyes.

Slowly he sat up, turned sideways and, slipping from the altar, rose to his feet. He took in the scene at a glance and knew the truth. Calin's wait had been no easy thing. He thanked her with a smile, as much of sorrow as of gratitude.

Now he turned to look down at the Fire-Dancer. She still lay upon the altar. Her eyes were wet with tears. 'I was so afraid.' He took her in his arms, held her as if there was nothing else in creation. She too clung to him. 'My magic, my dance,' she sobbed. 'They have stolen it, taken it from me into their emptiness.'

He knew how to answer her. It was the same gentle answer she'd brought to him. 'Do you remember the first dream?' he asked her through the tenderness of his understanding. 'Do you remember the river and the bridge? We chose the water. When I started to drown you saved me and again when I thought I was doomed, even a third time. Yet in the end I too reached down and bought you to safety. Will I not do so again?' Her eyes glistened with the tears of the memory.

'We should leave this place.' He lifted her down from the stone. 'Can you walk?'

'I don't know.'

'Try then. Just one step at a time.'

'Just one step,' she echoed him as he drew her off the black stone.

'And two?'

'And two.'

'And if two, then why not three? Three or more, steps on the floor, Beginning again. Beginning once more.' Such was the web of his love-spell as was the colour of his dance.

Her eyes turned to him, not understanding but trusting, knowing the truth of his love for her.

'Beginning?'

'Aye, back to the beginning, our beginning.'

> *Will you dance with me?*
> *Through the halls of the Future,*
> *Through the realms of our lives,*
> *Through the fires of our dance,*
> *Forever.*

Then she answered at last. 'Aye, I'll dance.'

> *I'll dance you a dance in the colours of time*
> *and colour each moment with a dance that is mine,*
> *Our dance of bright colour, the flames of desire,*
> *So we'll dance to the light in a Rainbow of Fire.*

She didn't laugh. Now wasn't the time for laughter, but her smile was enough.

'Can you dance, my little fire-fly?'

'Aye, my love, through all the mists of ever.'

But she'd begun to see, to look about the chamber. The gory sights of Calin's battleground were not pleasant, nor the lingering sense of death and evil. As the awareness grew in her mind she turned to look where Calin stood watching. Her emerald eyes widened in growing surprise. 'Calin. You are here too?'

The Warrior-maid smiled. 'I had to come. Nothing would stop me. Fassael too. He waits beyond to defend our escape. We couldn't let your Wizard come alone. We came into the darkness together.' And so saying she held out the Dwarf-Sword and the Wizard took it from her to re-sheath over his shoulder.

'Where are we? The Galghathag?'

'I don't know,' he answered the Dancer truthfully. 'Things have changed. For all I can tell they're still changing. I think it's probable I've just destroyed the binding of the Galghathag forever. We've come to the Castle of Mists, though and the mists remain.'

She didn't understand at all. She probably didn't need to. The newness of each moment in contrast to the emptiness that had filled her was almost overwhelming. 'Is that good?'

'Good or bad, my love, it's what had to be. It was the price I had to pay.'

'I knew you would come,' she whispered as they embraced again. 'They tried to deny it, said that you were too full of your magic now, that you would forget me, that I was nothing in comparison to the wonder of the Vortex. But in my heart I knew.'

'Did they harm you?' Had her answer been yes, he still might well have destroyed the universe.

'Not really harm. At first when I came seeking you, I thought, I mean, the Pinexae said, this was where you had to go.' When his hand tightened upon hers she lifted her eyes to his. She spoke her truth. 'They sent me here to draw you, to trap you. Did you know?'

'I'm not sure it's quite that simple, but yes in the end I learnt of it. However, I didn't come alone and I wasn't trapped by their snares, good or bad.'

She pondered long over the idea. 'I thought they were good, the Pinexae, the Neleven-Fey.'

'Good? Probably they are, in their way. They're lords of light. They don't belong here any more than do the things of the Void. At least the Pinexae know it.'

She returned to her tale. 'When I was surrounded I tried to dance my freedom but they bound me in ice and froze my fire with death's sour breath. They filled my mind with lies, my heart with fear... But I knew in my soul you would come.'

Should you lead me to the very Gates of Hell
then you will lead me back again.
Oh yes, my Fairy-Queen, From the Gates of Hell
From the clawed, grasping fingers of The Lord of Mists.
Should that be the need.

'That was the need.'

'You came.'

'We came.'

He kissed her and she him. Then they stood together. There were things to do. The future would not wait even for these two.

'Where now, my Sweet-Wizard?'

He took her hand once again. 'Come we should go to see what's happened.' Even though at this moment he really didn't care. He was with his love. He would never part from her again by choice.

Calin was watching them. Her tears left trails through the battle grime of her cheeks. She'd fought alone, fought a battle none had known, that none could see, and she'd won. It was this victory which finally calmed the anger in her soul. Now she stepped towards the iron door took that great handle without fear and pulled. The darkness of the passage beyond came as a surprise. She'd thought somehow everything would be different now.

'I've had enough of darkness,' he told them both and his magic shone. Even the shadows fled. 'There, that's better.'

The Fire-Dancer snuggled into his side and, as they walked on in Calin's wake, her arm crept about his waist.

You're safe now. I'll never let you go again. He lifted his arm about her shoulders, kissed the top of her head and then they walked back through the halls.

If there were things still lurking in the darkness they didn't see them. Either they hid or were gone. It was just as well. He would have stood no darkness at this time of their rejoining.

The journey, through these dark passages and up those even darker stairs, took the best part of two hours. Yet they came to stand at last before that second door. When they entered the grand hall the sunlight came streaming through the cracked and grimed glass forming patterns of bright and shadow on the stone floor. Cobwebs fanned out from the candelabra, from the grand-table and from the legs of the chairs. The stench of decay remained but it was stale reminder now, as damp when the rain has gone.

'The sun shines.' The awe in her elfin voice sang as bright as the dawn chorus over the trees of Eshenmoor. 'It shines where it has not shone for so many years.' The tears sparkling in her eyes were of pure happiness. 'You?' Laughing to see his cheeks redden. 'It was you. You who did it, It's you who have made this so.' She turned about him, dancing lightly with her joy. 'And just think, you once said you needed me to light your way through the darkness.'

'And so I did.' He caught her up, kissed her. 'And so I still do.'

'But look,' she sighed. 'The darkness has gone.'

Gone? The cooling of his mood was like the sun passing behind a cloud. 'No. Not gone.'

She grew still too. 'What?'

'Many things have happened since last we met, many dark and sad. And all is not yet done,' he told her. Leading her towards the other door. 'It will take time to tell it all.'

At Calin's touch, the door swung silently wide and they emerged into bright sunlight.

The brightness was a lie. The chill of the day told it, spoke of a wrongness, for the sun was bright and the skies free of clouds. It should have been warm. Yet this was no matter of weather, oh no. This was the cold grasp of the Void and it caught at their hearts and stilled the words of wonder they might have voiced, just as it robbed the sun of its power and the day of its welcome. They felt the threat hanging heavily in the air and sought a meaning.

Perhaps they found something of an answer in the figures waiting high on the battlements. The Wizard recognised Fassael's giant form, though the Tabour man's eyes weren't turned their way. They were looking outward and what they saw they watched with an intensity that spoke of nothing but terror.

'Come,' he spoke to softly to Calin and, taking up Luminae's hand again, they climbed the stair to where Fassael waited. *As I said, it's not over yet!*

At the sound of their arrival the giant turned to face them. 'You're back.' He grew still as he looked them over but his smile of welcome, no matter how sincere, was coloured by other thoughts, other fears.

The Dancer reached out and touched his hand. 'We meet again, Man-of-Fire, and for the first time Child-of-Ice.' The Wizard had told the tale on their journey through the castle. 'I said once that if we met we shall be friends.'

'She doesn't know what to say.' His smile broadened. 'And, aye and it seems, as always, we meet in troubled times.'

Calin walked over to the Wall and gazed to where the others watched. The sea of dust remained, reaching out towards the far away mountains. The plain was still though, wreathed in tendrils of grey mist. There were armies marching in that cold grey land. Yet no mortal armies were these. She recognised the nature of those colourless warriors, knew the dreadfulness of their hate. *And they are here. Bathed in the mists of their master.* Even now, in the light of day, the eye refused to acknowledge the truth of their forms.

She knew too the others who waited upon that plain. *So the Neleven-Fey came.* Shining white were they, white and bright as starlight. The Neleven-Fey, Lords-of-Light. There were not many, not many at all but those that were marched onwards to war. The white and silver of their banners caught the light of the new sun and spoke of a purity never known in this place. Still she felt a degree of surprise.

'It started about an hour before the sun broke through.' Fassael spoke, unsure if they were listening or even if they wanted to know. 'The grey army began to gather out where it now stands. We thought they would come against us. It was still grey-dark then and their mists were as ice. I don't think we could have held out against them.' It was a truth showing in every face of his small force. 'They didn't attack us though. I think we're below their interest. They just waited, much as you see them now. I think they must have been waiting for those.' He pointed towards the Army-of-Light.

'Is this the battle of which the Dwarf-Lord spoke?' Calin mused over the sizes of the armies. 'The battle for which all time has waited? It seems such a mean thing for so great a cause.'

'No.' The Wizard hardly knew he spoken at all. The futility of it all clouded his thoughts. 'Such a battle never can be. Light cannot exist without dark, nor good without evil. I learnt that long ago.' He looked again at the gathering armies. 'There may be a battle and all here might well perish. But, in the scheme of things, it will amount to nothing. There can be no ending, save the ending of everything.'

And still they watched as the armies marched on.

As Calin had noted there weren't that many, of the Neleven-Fey no more than eight hundred spears, of that darker grey force scarce more than that.

Is this what we do then, just stand here in the sunlight and watch? There was a reminder of Tabour, a sense of helpless, hopeless, powerless impotence. Now, as they watched, the armies formed their lines. *Soon.*

The Wizard fairly jumped with shock when Calin placed her hand on his arm. He looked down into her tear stained face. 'Don't let it be,' she whispered. 'I know that they're the Neleven-Fey and what they did to you, but not this.'

She was right. This should never be.

'Come then.' He already hurried down the steps, the Fire-Dancer, Calin, Fassael and even the goblin Drigla close behind. 'Come!' he shouted to the goblins that surrounded them, his voice now trembling with power. 'I tell you my friends, this shall be a war like no other!' The first blast of his magic threw wide the castle's gate and they passed, as a great throng, out onto the causeway.

Now there were not two but three forces abroad under the new sun's rays. And, what is more, even these were not all. For through the dust of this dour land others came hurrying, unexpected and all more the welcome for it.

They saw it, Calin and the Wizard, Fassael-Icicle and Drigla, Horge too and he wondered as much as any. At the edge of their vision, from the East came marching the armies of men and of elves. It was the elves who led, the High-Dancer at their fore, and the elves in their silver armour shone scarce less than the army of light. Beside the elves came men dressed in the black and silver of Varista and on their flank those of The Lake-Lands. And from the West, dark and filled with power were the solid ranks of the Iron-army and with them the men of Santolin and Lodor. *The land has risen up also.*

'*Wait!*' he commanded. His voice, louder now than echo of creation, filled the plain and every eye fell upon him. Their voices were stilled by his silence, their eyes filled with the flare of his rainbow. He felt her hand sneak into his own and he knew that both Calin and Fassael walked with him as he moved forwards into the very centre of everything.

'Why?' he asked his eternal question; the question of which everyone, everything had an individual answer. 'Why are you all here?'

From far ahead he heard the Dwarf-Lord's answer. 'We have come to see what transpires.'

Close at hand he heard the goblin's barked laugh of agreement. 'Perhaps we've come to fight in the last battle.'

The High-Dancer's voice was no less clear. 'We have come for answers.'

'Aye,' spoke Santolin, 'We've come to know.'

'We have come to die,' Pina whispered from the heart of her army. Yet, still he heard her.

But the things of emptiness had no answer. The truth was that they should not have been there, any more than should the Neleven-Fey.

It may seem strange, but there was no fear at that moment, not with any there. It could be that war and carnage would rule. It could be that the very world might come to an end. It could be that this moment was the end itself. It didn't seem to matter. There was, however, a burning need for a resolution.

Is this my time? Is this why I'm here? He turned and walked slowly towards the white and silver army, not needing to see where Pina stood. The tears stinging his eyes were over the pointlessness of what had been, of what might yet be.

He held her eyes with a gentleness that none could have expected. His words were soft also, without recrimination. 'Had you asked, I would have gone,' he told her. 'Had you asked, I would have faced it in its lair alone.'

She knelt on the ground before him, her head almost touching his boots. 'I'm sorry.' It was true. She was but, as yet, she didn't know just how much.

He took her hand, pulled her back to her feet and gazed, once more into her amethyst eyes. 'Should I grant your wish? Should I help you die?' *Is this what I'm supposed to do? Am I here to mete out death with the hand of revenge? Am I here to destroy everything with the flame of my anger?*

She looked him full in the face, marvelling at what she saw. Her eyes still shone with fear and the certainty of her ending. She spoke the truth. 'We want to live; we want to die. We have lived too long. Yet now the time has come we are afraid. Perhaps that is why we sent her to them.' She looked at the Dancer. 'I'm sorry.' She found no reply in the Elf's face. To the Wizard again, 'We wanted you so angry you would not withhold your magic from destroying us if we're victorious.'

'If we're victorious? If we ARE victorious? You're going to go on with this obscenity?' He couldn't even grasp the idea. He turned again and looked over the grey army so near, so cold. *The last Battle? Never!* 'Do you really think that I'm going to permit this path of destruction to continue?'

'But...' Pina was no less shocked than he. 'But the battle has to be, the struggle has to end! It's the whole point. It's the whole point of everything.'

'No it isn't!' he screamed at her. 'That isn't what it's about at all. It never was. You never understood.' His tears flowed freely, unstoppable. 'Never!' he called into the air. And his magic blazed as once again he woke the Vortex of his nature. A nature the like of which none could even imagine. For, despite all their fears, it was not a thing of power and destruction but of wonder and purity. 'You don't even see that. It's what he gave me. Why he died. Didn't you know he loved you that much? He made me what I am. Gentil did. He gave me everything. Do you think it's just so I could destroy with it. Never!' Once again the Wizard whispered his truth. 'Don't you yet see? I'm the Wizard of Rainbows, of the colours-of-life of sounds-of-creation, of the shades-of-truth and of the eternity-of-love. That was the purpose; that was the reason. Love not hate.'

Then, unbelievably, he knelt on the ground before Her. With tears rolling down his cheeks he asked. 'If he loved you won't I also? If I love you, won't you love me in return? Won't you know my truth, my friends? Won't you see my colours? Won't you hear my sounds? Won't you breath my love? Can you burn in my power? Will you feel my desire? Will you have my beginning? Will you share my Rainbow?' And his rainbows flamed, growing brighter and brighter so none might look upon them. 'Will you take my love?' He asked in colours of everything. 'Will you take my love?' He asked a second time whispering his words on the winds of the tempest. 'Will you take my love?' The third time and now his words were in silence. Thus he coloured these beings of light with the full wonder of his spectrum and awaited their reply.

And as he asked so they answered and as they chose so the gift was given.

Thus, when the beauty of his lights diminished so they might be seen again, the Lords-of-Light, Neleven-Fey, were gone. Only the Pinexae remained. 'Still you loved us? Despite all we did, despite all we desired, despite… Still you loved us?' Pina had no other words. She felt the shadows of her new nature and the hunger of the little life she had left to live. And then, finally, she saw the true enormity of her crime and the wonderful beauty of his sentence.

The Wizard stood and looked about. The grey army was gone too. They could no more face the truth of the beauty they had witnessed than they could the truth of their own emptiness. Had they asked it of him he would have granted them no less than he had the Neleven-Fey but they couldn't ask. Instead they'd gone back, back to the coldness of their empty existence, back to hide there, forever.

Is this it then? Is this the end?

He turned again, looked to the Dancer standing close to his side. And now he saw, for the first time, the terror held in her eyes. He too, slowly and reluctantly followed her gaze. Now he too knew that same touch of fear, as did everyone, everything there.

For the mists had become as a boiling sea of horror, blotting out the sun, blotting out the sky. A great shadow passed over the land, a shadow of fear and terror. They clung to each other, soul struck by the dread of its passing.

'What?' she asked, unknowingly, although she already knew the answer. 'Has it truly awoken?' And then the truth: 'The Lord-of-Mists has come.' And every word she spoke cried out of her fear.

He didn't reply. But, his sword was in his hand and his eyes burnt with an anger the like of which she'd never seen.

At the heart of the mist a form had begun to grow. Beyond all imagination, beyond all nightmare, beyond all the visions of madness, this thing became real.

They screamed then, grovelled in the dust to escape the horrendous reek of its coming. Yet there was no escape. For right then, in the swirling dust before the Castle gates, the Lord-of-Mists descended. It flapped its ragged wings sending whirlpools of dust to obliterate everything, breathed its decay into the skies so even the sun recoiled.

'Kneel before me lest I destroy you all. I am Your Master and your Lord,' the Dragon demanded. Its terrible voice filling eternity. They did every one of them, for there was no denying the awesomeness of its presence, goblin and man, dwarf and elf even those who once were the Neleven-fey, falling to the ground, grovelling in the dust before its might.

That is most did. However there was at least one who did not, one who now walked slowly forwards and stood looking up at the great beast before him.

'Bow before me. Fall on your knees.'

He didn't shout, nor even tremble as he spoke. 'I'll bow to no one let alone one such as you.' Those with enough wit remaining heard the voice and looked up to where the Dragon stood. He was tiny against it, seeming as nothing but a crimson speck in the shadow of its awesome power. If they'd thought to see the Wizard, they were mistaken. This was no wizard.

The Dragon reared, looming over him, ready to kill. '**Why are you here?**'

Everyone there asked themselves the same question. *Why is he there?*

He ought to have trembled with fear in the face of such power, to have quaked with terror at the horror before him but the man's voice remained steady. If he felt fear then there was no sign of it. 'I'm here because I choose to be. I'm here because this is the world in which I live. I came with my friends and with those who found hope in the promise of what might be. So, go away,' he told it. 'You don't belong here.'

For a moment there was even a whisper of hope. The calm of this man spread out over the field. But it was not so for long. The Dragon roared and once more they hid their faces and clung, trembling, to the ground. Flames of darkness and hate enveloped the man. They didn't even hear his death-scream, just the terrible wave of heat and sound washing over them. If any glimmer of hope remained, then it perished with him in the conflagration. Only, as the flames died and when the mists of their burning cleared, he still stood there.

'**Why are you not afraid?**'

Why isn't he? They all asked themselves, all too aware of their own terror.

'I'm not afraid because I choose not to be. I've faced many dangers and seen many horrors. It may well be that you're the worst, or even the greatest, but then, why should that bother me?'

A second time the Dragon's flames surrounded him. *He cannot survive this time!* Nonetheless their hope had regained its spark of life and their eyes sought for him as the fog cleared. They were not disappointed. He stood there, unscathed.

'**Why do you not burn?**'

It was their question once again.

'Because I choose not to. Long ago, as a child, I was given to the fire. When the flames wanted to claim me I chose not to die. I chose not to burn but to live with the fires within me. You are nothing, no one, to deny me that choice.'

For a third time the flames roared, lesser now, for those watching had seen what had transpired and their own fear was beginning to dispel.

'**Who are you?**'

And everyone there wanted to know.

His voice was gentle. 'I am Fassael-Icicle, Fire-Born and knife torn. I am as I choose to be.'

'And I,' said he who now stood at Fassael's side, 'I am the *Wizard of Rainbows*.'

The silence of that moment filled eternity. They watched not knowing what to expect, not knowing what they should do. The stench of the dragon was overwhelming but somehow it just didn't seem to matter any more. One or two even regained their feet.

'**Why are you come?**'

'Because I also chose to come.' The magic, which was the centre of the Wizard's nature, flared bright as morning. 'It seems to me this is the time for such choices, for choices and choosing, for beginnings and endings, Dragon.'

'**Who are you to demand such things as endings? Can you not see? There will be no endings. I am invincible. I shall rule forever.**'

It would. Nothing, no one could prevent it from doing so.

'No,' the Wizard spoke quietly as he turned slowly about looking at the scene before the castle. He saw them all, man and elf, goblin and dwarf and the Pinexae standing beside them, now as much a part of the world as any. 'This world is not for you to rule. It doesn't belong to you and you don't belong here.'

'*Do you challenge me, Wizard? Are you come to kill me with your oh so terrible magic?*' The sour taste of ridicule filled its every word.

They knew. *Even his magic will be nothing against such power.*

'I do not kill, Dragon. Not even one such as you.'

'*Then how shall you gain power over me?*' Its exultation was everything and they all saw the inevitability of his failure.

However the Wizard still spoke as a whisper, 'I don't want to gain power over you. I just want you to go away, to return to your empty domain and let us be.'

'*And who are you to demand anything of me?*'

'I am, as I said, the *Wizard of Rainbows*.' And he surrounded himself with a halo of brilliance. 'I am a Wizard-of-the-Land. I have faced the Vortex and won.'

The Dragon laughed and the hatred vibrating in the heart of that laugh was more than enough to still the rainbow in its forming. '*Wizard of Rainbows?*' Its voice dripped with the bitterest of scorn. '*Wizard of Rainbows or Wizard of Illusions? What rainbows? What illusions? They are nothing but the playthings of children.*'

'Playthings? Yes, surely they are and playthings of wonder and beauty also. But you also know that it's these same playthings which freed you from your prison.' Once again he drew out the wonder of his magic forming a rose of purity for all to see.

It reared higher; the mockery of its words was as a deadly blade, sharp and poisoned. '*Is that so, my Wizard? You seem to have mistaken the truth here. Have I not led you every step of the way. From the very beginning did you not know the touch of my planning? What? The Wizard of Rainbows? Chasing after dreams like some demented half-wit, serving no man and no purpose, a waster of time and of reason. What foolishness was that then?*' Awakening in his breast the very fears of his childhood.

'*Am I wrong? For me you turned against your magic. For me you went to war. For me you stole through the path of dreams to my awakening and for me you fled screaming from the same? For me you thought even to challenge The Lady-of-Cycles. And, though you realise it or not, Her madness was of my words and my making? And, don't forget, She even stilled the Cycles at my command. And for me you now stand here.*'

'My choices were all my own.' He still spoke softly and freely although his words now denied the truth that lay in the Dragon's words. 'The Lady also freed the Cycles again. And the magic of the Vortex is mine alone.' However, as he spoke the words, one of the rose's thorns pierced his thumb. The bloom fell slowly to the ground and every eye there watched it fall.

'Vortex?' Again the cruel laughter boomed. '*You fool! The Vortex was yet another tool of my making. Nothing else could break the barrier between the universes. Do you not yet see? It is you who has brought me here. You pathetic fool. You thought to free the world. Now look at what you've done.*' The laughter smote against him in a wall of iron hatred. '*All you've managed is to bring about its very ruin.*'

It turned its eyes to those who watched. '*For I tell you all, it is ruin I bring, ruin and silence and nothingness. And now you see. Here he is, the Wizard of Rainbows who shall defend you all and now you know also, He's nothing but my servant, who comes and goes at my beckoning. All on his own he has brought about the downfall of everything!*'

The foetid stench of its breath washed over him. He felt it looming. Soon it would strike. *Servant? Is that what I've been?* He knew this was no time for denials, even of all the things from which he wanted to hide. He knew this truth far too well. Had he not learnt that lesson on the eternal Mountain? Faced that truth Before the Rainbow? *Did I do it alone? No! I've never really been alone.* His grip tightened upon her tiny hand. *I'm not alone now and I never was. You knew me. You believed in me. You saw my future through the wonder of your being.* Thus he grew in strength once again. *So many touched me, called to me, believed in whatever promise they saw in me... What of them?*

Accept the truth.
Accept its reality.
Be at peace.

Yes my friends. I'll accept the reality. Whatever it may be. I'll face this truth too. Its words have truth and those I'll hear. And the first rainbow that he cast was within his own being and he coloured it black, the black of the Void.

'He came for me.' The words were whispered and wavering, but still they were spoken. And the Wizard turned to see her standing beside him. 'He came for me as I did for him. Was our love also a part of your making?' Even the Dragon seemed shocked.

Fassael-Icicle returned to his side. 'He told the truth although he knew it would cost him everything. It was his truth that set me free, free to be what I am. Was this too a part of your making?'

Calin also came. She looked up into the Dragon's terrible face. 'He did not condemn me,' she spoke her words. 'Was his acceptance a thing of your creation?'

'He chose to love us, though we betrayed him. He gave us the gift of life and of death. Was his gift of your making?' Pina asked.

Then came Drigla. 'He even killed the Greylon who gave you power.'

'No Drigla,' the Wizard too spoke quietly, for his understanding was growing. 'I didn't kill it. I simply sent it away. It didn't belong here.'

He turned once more to face the Dragon. 'I am, as I said, the Wizard of Rainbows. I don't kill with my magic, not even those who are nothing but evil.' His next words were even more shocking. 'And you, I'm beginning to see now, are not wholly evil.' He took a deep breath. Now the moment for truth had really come. 'There is truth in your words, Dragon, be you the Lord-of-Mists, of-Lies, of-Madness or of the-Void. And yes it is true, you did indeed draw me here. I agree, you've plotted through the ages of ever to have me set you free. And as you have planed so I've done. These things are all true

'But, am I your servant? I think not. And for sure, even you can see that I'm not alone. Perhaps, as you say, I am a part of your creation but it's not a part as you planned it. This I see clearly now. You see; your way is one of ruin and hate, whereas mine is of beauty not destruction.'

He looked up unflinching into that terrible face and saw nothing there but rejection. It was the rejection of everything, even of existence itself. Yet the Wizard knew enough of rejection. He knew of it only too well, too much even to bear. For he carried it, in the words of his father's spite, at the very centre of his soul forever. He'd not put such a dreadful curse on another. 'I'll not reject your words, Dragon. They contain much that is true and the truth is at least something I can try to understand. For indeed, at the very beginning it was you and your planning that helped form what I now am.' He took the scarlet of all beginnings and coloured his acceptance with the same. 'For this alone I do not reject you or what you are.'

He looked at the Dragon again, and saw the awful strength of its decaying, gnarled skin. He could see, without doubt, no sword, even his dwarfish blade, would penetrate such scales. *For what, of what, from what, does this Dragon require such protection? Is its existence really so fragile? Perhaps the cause of its fear is the knowledge of the reality of its own pointless nature.* It needed consideration. *Don't I know this fear too? Isn't it the same fear that drove me ever onwards until my rainbows were rejoined? And didn't this very fear come from the tortured coils of its planning?* Thus he took his hurt and bound it unto this creature's overwhelming lust for the life it could never possess, and he coloured it orange. It was an orange no less than a gift of his own sparkling magic.

Now it loomed once more over him, its great body threatening to crush the whole world with its might. *Why such power? Why the need for so much strength? This is a thing of the void. Surely it should be of emptiness and silence.* He realised then, its form was simply an expression of the desire for the power, which it endlessly craved. Its craving was, in truth, no less than proof of its lack. *But what of my power?* He smiled at the thought. *It brings me beauty. It has the gift of that.* Thus did he bathe it in the golden light of his own secret power and yes, perhaps it knew the taste of that beauty also.

Yet even the enormity of its size was nothing compared to the hatred emanating from its very essence, its every action, its every thought, its every utterance. He recoiled from that hatred as were it a poison to his soul but even then he knew truth of his answer. *This hate has formed me in part. This thing, Lord or Dragon has, through its hatred, even given me the wonder of the Vortex, not for power as it wished, nor for destruction as it hoped but for the beauty of its creation.* Thus he coloured the Dragon with the emerald light that was the expression of his love. *Shouldn't I love the giver of such a gift?*

It saw his magic flare, perhaps it knew fear, perhaps it even knew wonder, for its roar filled the universe. In the midst of that tumult he held his Dwarf-sword before him until the fabric of its steel vibrated to the terribleness of the sound. But his own vibrations were purer, gentler and sweeter. Soon the blade knew again the song of its nature and chimed once more to the cathedral-song of the Wizard's soul. And the azure glow, which shone from both the weapon and Wizard, was reflected for all to hear.

Now at last, through all the hues of the rainbow of his spirit, the Wizard saw the truth once more. *Light and dark, good and evil, thus is the Dragon. It has formed itself as a thing of the void where in truth the void has no shape and no form.* He looked anew at the Beast and saw its full wonder at last. Not in its power, not in its form, not even in the impossibility of its nature but in the simplicity of every tone and texture, of every shade of understanding. It too, in its own unique way, was beautiful. The softness of the indigo haze with which he bathed its glory was a vision beyond all comparison.

And now at last, to the horror of all there, he knelt in the dust before the Dragon. As he did so he drew, from the rainbow at his centre, a mirror of pure violet and he held it before the Beast for all to see. 'Yes,' he called, his voice louder than any silence could hide. 'Yes, now at last I kneel to you, and yes, I'll even do as you ask, if you ask it. Yet I do this not because you command it but because I desire to do so. Now I ask this of you, Lord-of-Mists, look and see what I see, look and know what I know and fill your emptiness with the truth of my understanding.'

The Dragon was stiller than death and as silent as stone.

'You've come forth from the Void, from nothingness and pointlessness. None here would blame you for this. Wouldn't any wish to be free of such horrors? However, it's here to our world you've come. I don't know if you realised it or not but this is a world of Colours, Lord-of-Mists,' he gently explained, 'Not of emptiness. You say you'll be the ruin of the World. What so you can turn this land of colour, beauty and change into nothing more than a replica of the very place from which you've managed to escape?' This too was a truth. 'What would be the point in that?

'No, Lord, if you truly wish to escape the emptiness then you've come to this world not to destroy it but to be a part of it. You've come to wonder and to know the glory of its nature.'

He stood again and, as he did so, held his image of the Dragon at the heart of the mirror. Finally he held it out so the creature might see itself through his eyes.

'And you, Lord Dragon, in such a world as this, should you not also bear the colours of your nature? I, as I have said to many, am the *Wizard of Rainbows*, a Wizard of lights and a Wizard of colours and these will be my gift to you, should you choose to remain.'

Once again the world grew still. The Dragon turned its head looking over those who assembled there. **'Shall I stay? Shall I still rule this world?'** it asked them all and not one there trembled at the touch of its gaze.

With the simplest of answers, the Wizard spoke for all there, 'Only if we're permitted to love you.' He took his violet rose from the heart of the mirror.

'Love?'

'Yes love,' he confirmed. 'For your strength we'll offer our weakness. For your lust we'll offer our desire. For your power we'll offer our acceptance. For your hatred we'll offer our love. For your terrible roaring we'll offer our songs of harmony. For your endless emptiness we'll offer our visions of beauty. And, Lord-of-Mists, Dragon-of-the-Void, for your mystery I offer this rose.' He walked slowly towards the Beast.

He might have died, then and there, in the heat of its fires. He would have done nothing to prevent such an end and it knew. The creature saw the tears streaming from the Wizard's eyes and so did nothing. Even when he reached out to set the flower upon the Dragon's scaled brow it remained still.

'This is what you might be.' He spoke to himself as much as the Beast. 'Rainbows are of every shade, every colour, every hue. You can be whatever you wish to be. The one trouble is, in the end, it's you who has to choose to make it so.'

The Dragon was totally motionless. The world was motionless, even eternity. But slowly, oh so very slowly, its horror began to fade. The mists grew as a haze, hiding its form and its nature and gradually they too faded to nothing. All that was left was the small violet bloom. It lay in the dust, placed gently, at the Wizard's feet.

It was the Dancer who, still standing at his side, reached out to take his hand. 'You have won,' she tried, for he had indeed done so.

'No,' he sounded heart-broken, 'I lost.' For that was the truth also.

'Is it over now?' Calin asked.

'It's probably never over,' Fassael-Icicle answered.

Drigla walked slowly forward. He stopped beside the Wizard. Then, with a delicacy his size might have denied, he stooped to pick up the rose. 'Will it grow?' he asked.

A tear trickled from the Wizard's eye, slid unfelt over his cheek. 'No. I'm afraid not. It was made in the image of the Dragon. He chose not to be.'

In Drigla's hand, the rose also turned to mist and was blown away on the breeze. 'That's a shame.'

From the Elves, only one came forward to stand with the Wizard. She stopped before the Dancer, and looked at her with a mother's eyes. 'He found you?'

'I always knew he would.'

The Crystal-Singer turned, stood on tiptoe and kissed away the tear from his cheek. No words were needed.

'What now then?' Calin sounded lost. No answer came to comfort her.

'Agh! Bollix!' Icicle called. 'Ain't any one got any fuckin' food. I'm bleedin' starving.'

The sheer surprise of the words shocked them back to reality. The Wizard laughed. And his laughter was like the coming of spring.

'For that, Gentle-one, you'll have to wait until nightfall,' the Master-smith answered quietly.

Gentle one?

They looked at him, even the Wizard. Had he taken leave of his senses?

But the Dwarf just smiled and soon his smile turned into a laugh of sheer joy. 'Well, as always, it seems that the Dwarves must keep to the order of things,' he boomed. 'Look I don't know if you realised it my friends but it happens that the Barrier fell at the midday hour.' He continued to laugh at their bemused faces. 'Day to year,' he explained, though only one there actually understood.

Then with a gentler tone: 'What I am saying, my friends, is the year has turned and indeed tonight is midsummer's eve. Tomorrow? Tomorrow shall be midsummer's day; the first to be known in this place. A time to begin again.'

So indeed, perhaps finally, the circle has turned back to its beginning.

They gathered at twilight on the plain before the castle where the Dragon had stood. There they'd built the Mid-year bonfire. It seemed a pity that the only wood to be found was from the furniture from the grey castle, but on this night of all nights the fire was essential. The great tables and chairs from the hall had to serve and were brought and piece by piece broken and stacked to form the pyre. Even the goblins helped, although they didn't understand what was happening.

The Dwarves had brought provisions. This was ever their way and they'd been prepared from the start as had the Pinexae, which should have been expected also. The feast was laid out upon trestles beside the road in readiness.

Thus they came together without rancour or hostility. They'd seen the Dragon and through this were united. Finally, when the sun had truly hid its face, Fassael-Icicle, as was his right, set the pyre ablaze. They sat about its bright flames in a large circle and shared the night.

Some knew the songs and some didn't. Some knew the meanings, some not. But they came together in friendship this night, elf and man, goblin and dwarf and even the Pinexae, for this was the first time ever, and they broke their fast with corn and mead and they shared all they had as is rightly done.

After they had eaten, in the dark of night as they waited before the fire, Plie the Harpist took up his golden harp and to its mellow calling the Crystal Singer sang.

> Everything is a Circle.
> Every day and night and dawn.
> Every moment has its beginning.
> Every death is but one who was born.
> And tonight, for just one instant
> All who sit and watch are as one.
> We hold hands, and wait out the darkness
> And sing to awaken the sun.

In the light of this dawn, as the sun awoke to their singing for the first time over the land once called the Galghathag, they looked about themselves and thus they found the Wizard and his elfling love were gone. None there were surprised. Who would have been?

However, when they looked at the ground where the Dragon had stood there, in the last embers of the now cold fire, they found a small shoot growing.

'It's the seed of THE tree,' The High-Dancer explained, remembering the Wizard's visit to Al-Sinnian. 'It was the Tree-Keeper's request of the Wizard.'

'I shall tend it,' Fassael-Icicle offered. 'It was born in the ashes of the fire.'

It is true also; this was a time of beginnings. However, these new paths are for other tales and for others to tell them.

> Once I walked on blue crystal mountains
> And greeted the dawn with its vista of fire.
> Now I'm alone, content with your dancing
> Untroubled.

Epilogue

FOUR YEARS HAD passed. The late spring sunlight danced sparkling on the singing Dingle-water as the Wizard and his Dancing-love walked hand-in-hand along the winding, riverside path. They were silent for the most part. There is little need for words when togetherness is enough. Swallows made their swooping flights but inches from the surface to catch the evening mayfly rise. The flickering of kingfisher blue was no less instant when the minnows showed in the pools. On a long hazel branch a lone heron watched in superior indifference. Peace, if anything, ruled the hour and everything was as it should be.

However, the figure who waited for them that evening was completely unexpected. Few came this way now the Wizard and the Fire-Dancer had returned to Hereth. Yet here he sat, cross-legged upon one of the flat boulders where the river flowed down towards one of the deeper pools. His saffron robe was travel faded, his sandals worn and his face knew only too well the kiss of the sun.

The Wizard smiled and, remembering another such as he high on the slopes of a mountain in the land beyond the desert sands, he bowed his head in greeting.

'Ah,' the mystic began, 'It is indeed the Wizard of Rainbows is it not?'

Again he bowed his head acknowledging the truth.

'And, Wizard of Rainbows, now that you have found your Rainbow, and now you have taken your journey and now you have faced the truths of your nature, and now you have returned to whence you began, can you now answer the riddle?'

'Tell me once again,' he replied, his smile all the brighter for his understanding. 'Tell me, what is the riddle.'

'The Wizard of Rainbows and The Fire-Dancer are walking a riverside path through a wood when they meet a mystic sitting upon a rock.'

'What is the riddle?'
'Who is the dreamer?'
'I am.' It was the truth.
'Ah!' The mystic was smiling also now, 'But who am I?'
With that the Fire-Dancer squealed with delight and spun a pirouette of glory about them so that a thousand birds rose to fill the evening sky. 'That's no question,' she laughed. 'For that's the answer, the answer to everything.'

It is too.